MR 9 '95	DATE DUE		
MR 10 '95	AG 01 '95		
MR 22 '95	AG 17 '95		
AP 5 '95	SE 09 '95		
AP 21 '95	SE 25 '95		
AP 27 '95	SE 30 '95		
May 18	OC 21 '95		
JE 6 '95	NO 06 '95		
JE 13 '95	NO 22 '95		
30 '95	NO 28 '95		
JY 07 '95	FE 07 '96		
JY 22 '95	JE 17 '96		

WHERE THE WILLOWS WEEP

WHERE THE WILLOWS WEEP

Patricia Shaw

St. Martin's Press
New York

Library of Congress Cataloging-in-Publication Data

Shaw, Patricia.
Where the willows weep / Patricia Shaw.
p.   cm.
ISBN 0-312-11914-3
1. Australia—History—1788–1900—Fiction.   I. Title.
PR9619.3.S4815W48   1995
823—dc20   94-34235   CIP

First published in Great Britain by Headline Book Publishing PLC

First U.S. Edition: January 1995
10 9 8 7 6 5 4 3 2 1

We live in deeds not years
In thoughts not breaths
In feelings not in figures on a dial.
We should count time by heart-throbs.
He most lives
Who thinks most – feels the noblest
Acts the best.

Philip James Bailey

Remember the rain . . .

Remember the rain blowing in from the hills? Still, we waited, watching the gentle diversion from our content until the flat drops spatted the glass, laughing teasing happy to be part of our joy. Then, as if aware of an audience, anxious to please, to entertain, bard at our court, rain coloured our world with all the dark exciting hues of sharp discord, and we felt a loving hand in ours. Slowly, too soon, it lowered the heavy curtain, certain of applause, of speechless wonder, wrapped us in warm grey sound that stayed sentinel strong and permanent.

And it was then we knew we were secure.

Prologue

Two girls rode listlessly along a bridle track towards the main road leading away from Rockhampton. Both rode side-saddle and both wore the dress of the day, white blouses and long dark skirts, but while Laura had on a plain felt hat, Amelia preferred a fashionable straw boater with a blaze of ribbons that now hung limply in the humid air.

They were the best of friends, these girls, thanks to the endeavours of their fathers – few families in this small, country community could afford horses for their daughters, let alone the smart Thoroughbreds that now carried their riders so splendidly through the rough scrub. Amelia's parent was a wealthy man but Laura's father had an added claim to fame, he was a Member of the State Parliament.

As Amelia often said, and insisted upon, she and Laura were the leaders of the young social set of Rockhampton. It irritated her when Laura laughed at her pretensions: 'Don't be ridiculous! There's no social set here, only people.' They argued about their status long and hard because there wasn't much else to argue about and it always came down to the same thing – Amelia Roberts cared about such matters while Laura Maskey couldn't care less.

'What did we have to take this stupid track for?' Amelia complained.

'It's a short cut,' Laura told her. 'And it's cooler this way, and much more interesting.'

'Who says so? The flies are appalling.'

'Well put on your net.'

'I will not wear that ugly thing on my good hat. Let's go up to my place, I'm hot and bored.'

'What will we do there?'

'I don't know about you, but I'm going to sit in a cold bath. It must be a hundred degrees already.'

Laura sighed. 'I wish we were near the coast. I'd love to go for a swim in the sea, it's the most wonderful feeling to bathe in salt water.'

'Yes, and ruin your skin in the sun.'

'Oh, bosh.'

The horses took them out of the bush on to the open road and Amelia breathed a sigh of relief. 'At least there's some air out here.'

'And dust. We need rain.'

1

'Are you coming home with me?'

'I might as well,' Laura agreed, riding alongside Amelia now. 'If I go home, Mother will think of things for me to do. She's expecting quite a few ladies for tea.'

Amelia nodded, understanding. Her father was a widower so there was no mother in her home to keep a watchful eye on this pair of young ladies.

At a curve in the road Laura noticed another track. 'Where does that go?' she asked Amelia.

'Down to Murray Lagoon.'

Laura stared at it as they passed by. 'That really annoys me,' she said. 'I mean, why should the lake be out of bounds to women?'

'Because that's where gentlemen swim. Hardly the place for ladies.'

'Exactly. Why aren't we allowed to swim there? Why do we have to put up with this heat while they cool off in the lagoon. It's not fair.'

'There's always the river if you can dodge the crocodiles,' Amelia grinned.

'Oh very funny! I heard they've got a diving raft and all at the lagoon.'

Amelia pulled her horse to a halt and turned to Laura. 'I wonder what they wear?'

'Who?'

'The men, silly. While they're swimming.'

'How would I know?' Laura waited while Amelia adjusted a stirrup, and then took off her hat to shake out her damp curls.

'Won't your brother tell you?' Amelia asked.

'Leon wouldn't tell me the time of day.' She laughed. 'They probably wear long-johns. Carter Franklin, our bank manager, goes out there. He's so fat, he must look a trick in his underduds.'

'Oh, you are awful,' Amelia giggled. 'Maybe they don't wear anything. I'd love to know.'

'So would I,' Laura grinned.

'Then I dare you to take a look.'

Laura stared at her. 'Don't be mad. I can't just ride up to them. I'd get shot at dawn.'

'You don't have to. Stick to the bush so they can't see you.'

'You want me to spy on them?'

'Why not? It'd be a shriek! And we'd be the only two women who know.'

'Then why don't you go?'

'Because I dared you first. Go on Laura Maskey. I double-dare you.'

Laura wasn't one to procrastinate. She was more inclined to act first and think later. Amelia was right, she decided. It would be funny to spy on the men. Serve them right for being so selfish. 'Where will you be?' she asked Amelia.

'It's too hot to stop here. I'll go on home and have cook make us a slap-up afternoon tea.'

'With hot scones and blackberry jam,' Laura demanded, in payment for the dare.

'Done,' Amelia laughed.

Laura wheeled her horse about and cantered down the road, turning into the track to make for the lagoon. Her horse trotted easily down the well-worn trail but when he smelled water he became more eager, so Laura kept a tight rein on him. She took off her hat, stuffed it under the saddle and guided him into the shelter of the tangled scrub, forcing him to step slowly as she shoved foliage out of the way and ducked to avoid heavier branches.

Ahead of her she could hear them shouting and laughing, enjoying themselves and that made her all the more determined to keep going. The horse seemed to understand now that they were on a furtive venture and he trod softly through the lank green undergrowth until Laura slid a hand down to stroke his face. 'Ssh now,' she whispered. 'Be still. This will do.'

Carefully she moved a leafy branch aside to get her bearings and almost jumped in surprise to find she was directly opposite a small jetty. 'Spot on!' she murmured, congratulating herself, because she had a grand view of the swimmers only about fifty yards away.

It was an effort not to laugh. She wished she'd insisted Amelia had come too. There they were, more than a dozen gentlemen cavorting in the lagoon, by the jetty and on a clever pontoon, anchored in deeper water to allow them to dive.

Perspiration streamed down Laura's face, and insects buzzed about her as she watched them enviously from the humid hide. The wide lake looked so cool and inviting she almost forgot the object of this exercise but peering more closely at the swimmers she was quite startled for a minute. Then she began to laugh, almost choking in an effort to keep quiet. None of them was wearing a stitch. They were all cavorting in their birthday suits! Gentlemen of all shapes and sizes dashed along the jetty and jumped off among the swimmers while others climbed up on to the pontoon to stand there shouting happily to their fellows like a bevy of Adams in Eden.

'How rude!' she giggled, wiping her face with her handkerchief. At twenty, Miss Maskey had never seen a naked man before and they intrigued her.

Suddenly, something rustled in the undergrowth. Born in the bush, Laura had the same reaction as the horse – a snake? But the horse was faster. Spooked, he reared up and crashed forward. The soft branches, hiding them, gave way and Laura hung on as the chestnut shot forward into the open, into forbidden territory! She managed to control him before he'd gone very far along the sandy shore but she could hear the men shouting angrily at her as she spun the horse about. Ignoring them, Laura gave the chestnut his head and she

3

galloped away, laughing, her dark hair flying. She'd won the dare! Let them shout their heads off. What could they do to her? It was too late, she'd seen them in all their glory.

For these two girls, this was just another prank, but one thing leads to another and for the daughter of Fowler Maskey, Member of Parliament representing this electorate, this escapade was to have far-reaching and tragic consequences. Country towns are conservative and hot for gossip, especially this little river-town, a mere ten years old, that was struggling for recognition. Townspeople, eager to shake off the tag of being just a rough mining town, were sensitive about their image – as Amelia would say, 'their social status'. They yearned for respectability; they were fierce neighbour-watchers and church-goers with curious behaviour and familial failings kept behind closed shutters; and no one was more aware of the atmosphere than Laura's father, their representative, who relied on their goodwill to hold his seat, for Fowler Maskey was an ambitious man.

Chapter One

The sun rose molten gold from the sea over Moreton Island to add lustre to the pristine waters of the bay, where singing whales luxuriated after their long journey from the south, unaware of the cruel harpoons that lay in wait for them. Light and retreating tides lifted glistening mangroves from the steamy darkness, and battalions of birds rose, bickering, to begin their day's work along the banks and shoals of their bounteous river. Undisturbed, they flew over the small ships that plied the thirty miles from coast to township, to feast on nectar from red and white bottlebrush that lined the shores, and to swoop from stately eucalypts on any likely prey.

This was the age of the great canals, and the wide Brisbane River had taken its place as an important watercourse serving the capital of the huge new state of Queensland. Residents of the blossoming city preferred not to recall that their home on a bend of the river had begun life as a harsh penal settlement for doubly convicted transportees. And as they strolled their streets they had already forgotten that men in chains had toiled under the whip to forge roads and erect sturdy government buildings in a subtropical wilderness. Men and women of their own kin, from the British Isles, had suffered fevers, malnutrition, and torture at the hands of regimental warders, and had died unlamented, never realising that their labours were not in vain. They had laid the foundations of a city and through their bitter struggles had set the pace for the hard, tough men needed to pioneer this great land, many of whom were offspring of these same convicts.

But wait. Maybe the ghosts of these convicts were grinning now, along with survivors of the prison days, as together they roamed the streets, free at last.

Only thirty years had elapsed since the Moreton Bay penal settlement had been closed down in response to public outrage and the boundaries of the town of Brisbane thrown open to settlers. Lacking the fare home, which transported convicts were expected to pay when their terms of servitude ended, many were forced to stay in Australia. Others remained by choice to grow old in caustic observance of their former keepers. They lived to see the new state, still ruled by the first premier, Sir Robert Herbert, struck a body blow which came from, of all places, the motherland.

★ ★ ★

Governor Sir George Ferguson Bowen, who shared with Herbert the privilege of a first in the raw colony, left his tranquil home overlooking the river and stepped into his carriage accompanied by his aide, Captain Leslie Soames. He could have walked to his destination in a matter of minutes but Her Majesty's representative could not be seen marching up the muddy road like any commoner.

This was a rare occasion. Usually the parliamentarians were summoned to his residence but this time he did not wish to alert the gentlemen of the press. A summons to Government House carried with it a sniff of political or social news, and either way, the members involved, for their own aggrandisement, made certain that word was abroad before they stepped to his door.

He was dressed, for him, in plain attire, to avert any suspicion of formality, although his lady, the Countess Diamentina, had seen to it that he was the epitome of elegance. Even in the steamy climate he disdained the shantung and cotton suits that had become the fashion, deeming them ugly and inappropriate for his exalted position. On this day he was turned out in a black jacket with a high braided collar, breeches and gleaming boots. His silk shirt was overtaken by a fine wool waistcoat and a silk cravat which was held in place by a pearl pin.

As he passed through the portals of Parliament House, a smile on his handsome face, he removed his grey topper and gloves in the nonchalant manner affected by locals, no matter their aspirations. Crowds in the lobby stared, bowed, bobbed and backed away as he passed by, and only one, the brash reporter from the *Brisbane Courier*, dared call to him. 'What are you doing here, Governor?'

Bowen inclined his head magnanimously, demonstrating his good humour and lack of concern. 'Why! Mr Kemp! Surely you must know the races have been cancelled due to this morning's sudden torrent.'

He was rewarded by a titter from the audience. Everyone knew that Tyler Kemp was a dedicated punter.

'Is the Premier expecting you?' he persisted.

'I daresay he will be by this.' Bowen's smile was still genial. There had been no time for appointments, the matter was urgent.

'And what is the business of the day?' Kemp asked.

'Purely a social call. I have never believed, as you know, in the ivory tower, and what more interesting place on a dull day than our Parliament?'

But Kemp would not give up so easily. 'The House is sitting, sir. Will you require admission?'

Bowen consulted his gold fob watch and returned it to his waistcoat pocket. 'I believe the House is just now rising.'

As expected, the Premier had been informed of his presence and Bowen was relieved to see he'd wasted no time in coming to greet him.

'Your Excellency! Good afternoon. Do come through. Perhaps you'll join me in my office?'

'A pleasure, sir.' The Premier, he knew, must be astonished at his

6

sudden appearance, but the man wasn't short of brains. He hadn't given so much as a blink of surprise. A consummate politician, he had often been heard to remark, referring to nearby company, 'Not in front of the children.' And today was no exception to his rule.

Bowen was tall, known as a fine figure of a man, but Herbert was taller and much heftier. As he escorted the Governor down to his office, Tyler Kemp dropped back. Not even he would muscle in on these two imposing personages with an aide at heel.

'Tea or coffee?' the Premier asked.

'Coffee, thank you. Soames takes coffee also.'

With viceregal permission, Herbert took his place behind the large mahogany desk and engaged the Governor in small talk, recognising that the real purpose of the visit would emerge in due time. Bowen was grateful for the respite, since he was the bearer of bad news and would prefer to discuss the matter without interruption.

Herbert called to his secretary, who hurried away. In a very short time the young gentleman returned, wheeling an autotray with a silver coffee service on the top ledge and an assortment of biscuits on the lower level. 'Shall I pour, sir?' he asked.

Herbert nodded. 'Your Excellency, might I introduce my new secretary, Joe Barrett?'

The china cups rattled dangerously as the Governor rose. Barrett was caught between the pouring and the handshake in a fit of nervousness.

Herbert laughed. 'He makes a better secretary than a waitress. Give him a hand, will you, Soames?'

The captain's eyebrows shot up and his thin nose twitched at the impudence of such a request, but he had to obey, whisking coffee to his governor with drawing-room ease and retreating from the demeaning task as soon as possible.

'Graduate in law, Sydney University, is our Joe,' the Premier said proudly. 'Got honours, too, didn't you, son?'

'Yes, sir. Will that be all, sir?'

'For us, yes thanks. But I want you to take a look at that bill the Minister for Lands is threatening to push through. It's got more holes than a pair of old socks.'

'Right away, sir.' Barrett, as yet unused to such noble company, fled.

'They're getting away with murder up north,' Herbert told the Governor amiably, 'squatting on lands far past the limits. I'm from up that way myself, so I don't begrudge them the size of their properties, just our loss of revenue while they dodge leasehold fees.' He drank his coffee in a few gulps. 'We've got to engage more surveyors, a lot more, to handle all this work.'

'I wouldn't do that just now,' the Governor said mildly. He rose and walked over to study some pen sketches of Brisbane town, straightening one of the frames. 'These are excellent. Who did them?'

'You'll never believe it.' Herbert grinned. 'Our mate Mr Kemp.'

'Good God! Quite a talent there. Pity he doesn't stick to his artistic endeavours.' The sketches seemed to have caused him to reminisce. 'I remember when I first came here and was handed the Treasury report.'

'Ah yes.' Herbert smiled. 'That must have been a shock. What did we have? About five bob in the coffers to inaugurate a state. Not the most auspicious start.' He heaved a sigh. 'But we're over those lean days. Unless your suggestion that we don't employ any more surveyors rings a warning bell.'

'Quite.'

'Oh well, give me the worst. Spoil my Christmas.'

'There's a rumour, just a rumour at this point, mind you, that the Agra and Masterman Bank in London has problems.'

'God Almighty! Don't even breathe such a thing. My budget will be in ruins. We're into them for a million pounds for railway construction, among other things. If the credit dries up . . . I hate to think!' He took out a large handkerchief and mopped perspiration from his face.

'That's why I thought it might be advisable to hold back on any extra expense at this stage.'

'Thank you, I appreciate the tip. I've got a party meeting this evening, the last for the year. I'll start tightening the reins immediately. And start praying.'

By early February, Fowler Maskey, Esquire, the State Member for Rockhampton, was aware of dissension in Herbert's cabinet and was pleased by it. Now in his fifties, Fowler was an influential man thanks to the wealth inherited from his father, one of the élite New South Wales squattocracy. Before his death, John Dunning Maskey had purchased land in the Rockhampton area, predicting great opportunities in the new state, and Fowler had taken his word for it.

He had moved his family north, built a house to complement his ambitions and settled in as one of the new town's elders, despite the fact that his wife found the heat unbearable in the summer, and his son, Leon, now twenty-two, loathed the rough-and-ready river settlement. As far as Fowler was concerned, however, Leon's complaints fell on deaf ears. Leon was not a scholar, nor could he be trusted to manage any of the Maskey properties since he had no interest in sheep or cattle. He was a good-looking chap, though of slender build, with fair hair and his mother's blue eyes. 'Horses for courses,' Fowler allowed. It suited him to have his son with him. He socialised well, was a fair cricketer, and managed a respectable game of cards. He was also much loved by hostesses, an asset at parties. For Fowler he was a bee, buzzing about to keep his father informed of the latest news, moods and developments.

Fowler's wife Hilda felt her son should be given more responsibility. 'What's to become of him if he's permitted to fritter away his time like this?' Fowler didn't care. He wasn't interested in dynasties. He only cared about himself and his endeavours. What would become of his family after he kicked the bucket was the least of his problems. Leon, he guessed, would have a whale of a time with his inheritance for a couple of years and end up dead broke. The prospect amused his father.

When Leon had declared he preferred to live in Brisbane, Fowler had agreed. 'By all means. Live where you like as long as you support yourself.'

'That's not fair,' Leon had argued. 'I've nothing to do in Rockhampton but be your runner.'

'You're contributing to your father's career, my lad,' Fowler had replied amiably, 'and if you go anywhere else without my say-so, you won't get a bean from me.'

So Leon stayed. Most afternoons he could be found cooling off at Murray Lagoon where a gentlemen's bathing pool had been established. His evenings were spent at the Criterion Hotel or the Gentlemen's Club on Quay Street, within walking distance of the family home.

It had surprised Fowler that his daughter, Laura, actually liked the town. She enjoyed their imposing two-storeyed house with its wrought-iron balustrades on the front veranda and the long balcony upstairs. The house was right on Quay Street, which, Hilda Maskey complained, afforded them no privacy, but it suited Laura to be right in the centre of things. Unlike her brother, she was not above sitting out on the veranda chatting to passers-by, whether friends or strangers.

She was a headstrong girl, tall and healthy, with the same silky blonde hair as her brother, but bolder than Leon. Too damned bold for her own good at times, but she'd be married and off Fowler's hands soon enough. Lately she'd been nagging him to take her out to see the goldfields outside Rockhampton, but that would have to wait, he was too busy. Gold. He smiled. Rockhampton had become a town overnight, thanks to the gold rush at nearby Canoona. More strikes had quickly followed. It was a marvellous thing to have gold fields springing up in one's electorate, adding to the already growing cattle industry.

Old John Maskey had certainly chosen wisely. There was a big future for a parliamentarian in Rockhampton if he played his cards right, and Fowler intended to do just that. And as he'd told Hilda, 'I expect my family to support me to the fullest. While I'm here you arrange to entertain as many locals as possible, and while I'm away in Brisbane do some charity work. That always makes a good impression.'

'What charity work?'

'How do I know? That's a woman's job. And get Laura at it too.'

'Laura?' Hilda had bristled. 'She won't do anything I tell her! She's

9

only interested in the horses, always off riding somewhere. And that's your fault. You let her run wild.'

'Then find her a husband, that will settle her down.'

Fowler allowed his thoughts to idle in this manner to keep his head clear for his next move. Stationed by the wide window at the end of the corridor, apparently taking a breath of air, Fowler had placed himself so that the door to the Cabinet Room was between him and his office. As soon as the honourable gentlemen emerged, he, a lowly backbencher, would be right among them, simply making his way to his own room. Premier Herbert was a stickler for cabinet solidarity but an early bird could easily catch a worm, in the form of a minister off guard, ears still tingling from being boxed by the leader. Fowler was certain that Premier Herbert had lost his grip and that it wouldn't take much to edge him out of the saddle. A few burrs in the right place could shift him now.

There they were, being bundled out, faces aghast, trouble brewing. He pressed forward, moving among them, listening eagerly to the gush of in-house complaints. He collared a big fish, the Colonial Treasurer. 'We're in full support of Raff's petition to upgrade the Brisbane wharves, sir. I hope you won't let us down.'

'All in good time,' the Treasurer snapped, pushing past him.

Fowler moved into step with the Postmaster-General. 'Steamy old day, isn't it?' But when the minister merely nodded in reply, Fowler pressed on. 'I have to tell you I'm getting bagfuls of complaints about the mail up my way.'

'You got the telegraph, didn't you?' the Postmaster-General snarled, and Fowler hid a smirk. Of course they'd got it, against this fellow's advice, but it was marvellous what a few quid towards members' campaign expenses could do to pull an appropriation vote out of the hat. 'We did and we're grateful to you, believe me, but the diggers can't afford to telegraph every time they want to contact their loved ones. They're pretty savage, they say fortnightly mail is just not good enough.'

'Then you'd better tell that to the Premier,' the minister said as they rounded the staircase. And then, over his shoulder as they parted ways, 'Or Macalister.'

'Who?' Fowler asked, surprised, but the minister's door slammed shut.

Arthur Macalister, Member for Ipswich and Secretary for Lands and Works. Why ask him? He was a nobody, a grim tub-thumper. No one asked his opinion. But Fowler would, and right now, with the utmost speed. He rummaged around his office for two bottles of good whisky, stuffed them in a carryall and strode off to pay his respects to Arthur.

'My dear fellow,' he said, noticing an air of excitement in Macalister's office. 'Forgive the intrusion, but I have been remiss. Several of my constituents asked me to drop these little gifts in to you at

Christmas but I missed you. Dredging of the Fitzroy River is under way now, thanks to your good offices.'

'Good man,' Macalister said, stowing the whisky among maps in an overstuffed cupboard without offering Fowler a drop. 'Sit you down, Maskey, I wanted a word with you.'

Fowler caught sight of his own florid face in a brass jardinière on a pedestal behind his host, and the distortion reflected a wide grin under a drying clutch of gum tips. Or rather he hoped it was the distortion. If there were trouble, he must not appear to welcome it. He pursed his thick lips to counteract the effect.

Arthur, representative of an unruly mob of coal miners, was fairly jumping with excitement, and a tic developed near his right eye, above his bushy beard. 'There's going to be a spill,' he hissed.

A spill! Jesus! Fowler's mind raced. He wondered, as every other politician in the building would now be doing, if he should throw his hat in the ring. Who could he count on? He could call in a few favours. To be Premier of Queensland, the most powerful man in the state! Immaterial that he had inaugurated a move for a separate state in the north with its capital in Rockhampton and himself, of course, as premier. The separationists could go jump! This was a much bigger prize. He almost laughed. If he won the day the state would stay intact, he wouldn't let them cut loose.

'Did you hear me, man?'

'Yes. I could have predicted it – Herbert's none too popular – but it's still a surprise.' Obviously he had Macalister's support and the Scot could bring him a handful of southern votes.

'None too popular? That's an understatement. The man's gone mad. If we listen to him, all of us will lose our seats. He's hellbent on cutting back on public works everywhere and raising taxes and charges across the board.'

'You don't say?' Everyone knew Herbert's penny-pinching was causing rumblings, but this was past a joke.

'I say,' Macalister continued, 'that we have to block him. Are you for us?'

'I would have to be,' Fowler said. 'The future of the state is more important than one man. He has no financial judgement at all. I've always said that. We need a leader who understands that the economy of Queensland depends on a balance of wise investment and expansion. If he pulls back now we'll die on the vine.'

'Exactly my sentiments. If I'm elected I'll do just that.'

'What?' Fowler jerked up in his seat. 'You're standing?'

'I am and I'd appreciate your support. I believe Herbert made a mistake in passing you over for the ministry, considering that a few of my colleagues are rolled-gold deadheads. You can be assured that I won't make the same mistake.'

And pigs will fly, Fowler thought. That was the oldest trick in the book, a carrot for donkeys. Macalister as Premier? Preposterous!

11

'Herbert sucks up to the viceregal set, that's his problem,' Macalister continued. 'Never a chance of that with me, they'll no' be impressing me with their fancy ways.' He fixed his eyes on Maskey, the tic beating a warning. 'Can I count on you, then?'

'Of course,' Fowler said. His dreams of leadership might be fading, but the separation movement was suddenly reinstated in his plans.

The two men shook hands and Fowler hurried away to investigate his own chances. Finding himself among the also-rans, he gave his solemn support to two other gentlemen lobbying for high office.

'None of them will beat Bob Herbert anyway,' he told Leon, who was always happy to accompany him to Brisbane. 'You get out there and nose about. If I have to vote for Herbert I want something for my money.'

He lit his pipe and began preparing a statement for the Rockhampton press declaring Herbert a traitor to the north, a leader who reserved all his energies, and the public money, for the south-east corner of the state, ignoring the needs of the good citizens of the north. His essay was rising to a torrent of vitriol against the Premier when Leon came dashing back. 'Herbert's resigned!'

'What?' Fowler almost knocked the inkwell over.

'He's resigned, I tell you! Just now. He said he'd give his reasons later.'

'To hell with his reasons – when you're dead, you're dead. So who's in the lead now?'

'I don't know.'

'Well find out, you bloody fool. Get down to the bar. Shout a few drinks, expensive ones, that draws the flies.' He crumpled the press release and flung it into the wastepaper basket.

Two days later, the new premier, Arthur Macalister, announced his ministry, but Maskey's name was not on the list. Fowler immediately went to work on a new press release, praising Herbert, claiming he had been driven out by a bunch of ratbags who wouldn't know how to run a chook-pen. And who had elected a dour penny-pinching Scot as their leader, a man who knew nothing and cared less about conditions in the north? He called for a public rally in Rockhampton to demand secession from the southern stranglehold and the formation of a new state with the Tropic of Capricorn as its southern boundary. Rockhampton, he didn't need to remind them, set on Capricorn would be the capital.

He found Leon taking tea on the long veranda with two young ladies and beckoned him over. 'Get back to the hotel and pack your things. You're going home.'

'Why? What have I done?'

'It's not what you've done, it's what you're going to do. You can catch the mailboat this afternoon. It sails at four. I want you to deliver a statement to the local newspaper and set up some meetings for me.

I've written out your instructions, you can study them on the way home.'

'But I promised to take Miss Lynton to the theatre this evening.'

'She'll just have to find someone else to take her. This is more important than watching a lot of pansies leap about a stage. Now get going. I might be able to find passage home next week, otherwise I'll follow you in a fortnight. Just see that you do exactly as I say. I want them properly stirred up by the time I get home, and a substantial welcoming committee waiting for me when I step ashore at Quay Street.'

'How will I know which ship to meet?'

'I'll telegraph you, won't I?' Fowler sighed.

With Leon well away on his legitimate business, Fowler left the House early to visit a certain Mrs Betsy Perry in Spring Hill.

'Why Fowler, my dear, what a naughty boy you've been. I thought you'd forsaken me.'

'You know I wouldn't do that.' He smiled, stepping inside with a proprietorial air. After all, he owned the house. 'We've been busy finding a new premier but now that's settled I'm entitled to relax, wouldn't you say?' He dipped a mischievous finger into the soft cleavage of her full bosom and she giggled.

'Now, now, business first. I've got your rent and the list of customers. We've been so busy I had to put an extra girl on over Christmas.'

As the riverboat chugged upstream Leon stayed, sweltering, in his cabin – up top was like a furnace. He couldn't conceive why anyone would choose to live in Rockhampton, miles from the coast and its cooling breezes. It was set in the river valley between two ranges, which turned it into an oven in the tropical summer, and was made worse by the infernal wet season. Brisbane was hot enough in summer but this place, more than three hundred miles north and so closer to the equator, was infinitely worse. He didn't believe a climate could be any hotter right on the equator.

Although he'd never been there, Leon dreamed of London, its chilly weather and the grand life a person could have there. All the right people went to England – they even called it 'home' – and he would one day, damned if he wouldn't! He daydreamed about escaping from his father to the good life in faraway England, of telling his father off before he left, or perhaps just leaving a farewell note. If only he had the money.

He hadn't bothered to telegraph his mother to tell her he was on his way, because if he'd done so she'd be there on the quay waiting for him, and he wanted to savour his freedom. Fowler's messages could wait.

Eager prospectors shouldered him aside in their rush to get ashore and Leon stood back disdainfully. Everyone knew that to travel more than ten miles out of Rockhampton was to take your life in your hands, what with the natives fighting for every inch of their land. That pleased Leon – he was quite sympathetic to their cause and he didn't care who they killed. It would suit him if the blacks won and they had to shut down this miserable apology for a town. Not that he would dare express those views, he'd be strung up. Most of the residents regarded the blacks as animals, vermin even, to be cleaned out of the district. Smiling, he wondered which of these ruffians were headed for a very nasty death.

As he strode down Quay Street he nodded to a few squatters whom he knew, cattlemen with their big stations in the Fitzroy River valley and out beyond the hills. They didn't let the blacks bother them, they just kept on fighting and eventually, of course, they'd win. At a price. Most of them, and their stockmen, carried spear scars which they valued like war wounds. In the bar at the Criterion, encouraged by their mates, men were always dropping their trousers or removing their shirts to show off the scars, a practice which Leon found disgusting, along with their boasts of how many niggers they'd killed. Even women and children. They were the most appalling lot! Leon had tried to tell people in Brisbane what was really going on in the north, the murders and massacres of hundreds of blacks, but they didn't want to listen, or they retaliated by asking how many white people had been murdered by the blacks. He wasn't much good at debating, and even less successful at trying to explain that the country belonged to the blacks, so he was usually shouted down. Only Tyler Kemp had listened to him and had written a story, but his paper wouldn't publish it. And then – wouldn't you know? – Fowler had got wind of it.

'What the hell do you think you're doing?' he'd roared 'Giving a reporter that pack of lies.'

'It's not lies.'

'Of course it's bloody lies. If the blacks look for trouble they get it. That's all. And you keep your bloody mouth shut from now on. Do you hear me?'

'Yes.'

'A wet-behind-the-ears bloody know-all, that's what you are! I ought to shunt you out to a station for a while to see how you like it. See how bloody smart you'd be if the blacks started chucking spears at you! Those station people are the salt of the earth, their cattle herds are going to be the making of Queensland. As it is, we are maintaining the south – the north is where most of the primary producers are, working against the odds to support the layabouts in Brisbane.'

Leon was relieved that his father had gone off course and begun speechifying on his favourite subject: 'North Queensland versus the South'. One day Fowler Maskey hoped to be premier of a cutaway state called Capricornia. And he'd probably succeed, Leon thought.

He walked into the sudden gloom of the Criterion Hotel and bought

14

a pint of beer for his thirst and a short rum for his spirits, propping himself moodily at the end of the bar until he realised that there was more than the usual commotion in the crowded room.

'What's up, bartender?' he asked.

'The blacks attacked Aberfeld Station. Ken McCraig got hisself killed in the fight and one of his stockmen, Tommy Pike, was wounded something terrible trying to save his boss and died of the wounds the next day.'

'Good Lord! And how is Mrs McCraig? She's a friend of my mother's.'

'Ah, the poor woman, she's holding up, and her two little girls, they're safe, she had them hid under the bed.'

'I suppose they'll be quitting the station now,' Leon said, but the bartender shook his head.

'No bloody fear. She aims to stay put. Her brother's coming up from Sydney to take over.'

That would be right, Leon mused. Once those grazier families got their hands on land, nothing could make them let go. His grandfather had been the same, opening a string of sheep stations and then cattle stations from Bathurst right through to Queensland. And with managers running them, Fowler and Uncle William were reaping the rewards. He wondered how much his father was worth. Must be around a million. And yet he chose to live in this stinkhole. Power, of course. After money came power, and trailing money came the sycophants, who hoped some of it would rub off.

Captain Cope, known as Bobby, had spied Leon and was heading for his corner. Leon had mixed feelings about Bobby. He was well educated and was excellent company, but his occupation was a worry. The man had charge of a troop of Native Mounted Police, recruited from the south, and they had a nasty reputation. Led by white officers, they were issued with uniforms, rifles and plenty of ammunition. Their job was to 'clean out' tribal blacks, and they showed no mercy to their fellow Aborigines. Leon had seen them riding through Rockhampton looking more like a pack of thugs than soldiers. Even some of the cattlemen had reservations about the use of native police, but Bobby had no such qualms. 'They have a job to do,' he told Leon, 'and they do it. Unfortunate but necessary.'

'But I hear they kill whole families,' Leon had objected.

'Only on rare occasions. Besides, if you're cleaning out marauding dingoes, you have to get rid of the pups as well or they breed and the problem remains.'

'I find it rather disgusting,' Leon had ventured.

'And you're right, old chap. But it's not your concern, is it?'

He now descended on Leon with enthusiasm. 'Glad to see you back. What about a game of billiards before lunch?'

'Suits me,' Leon said, 'but I thought you'd be out on the hunt.'

'No, I don't go off half-cocked. There are posses charging about everywhere. I'll have my force properly equipped by morning and

15

we'll ride out there and deal with the murderers.'

Or anyone with black skin, Leon guessed. He wished there were someone who could go on ahead and warn the blacks of these newly introduced troops. At least that would give them a fair chance. As fair as it could be with spears against guns. It would be amusing to see Cope ride into a trap.

He delivered Fowler's statement to the proprietor of the local newspaper and decided that was enough for one day. Tomorrow he'd set about rousing the separationists, after they'd had time to digest Fowler's tirade against Macalister and the southern-based Parliament.

As he walked into the house he could hear his mother's distress. She was shouting and weeping at the same time. When Hilda Maskey decides to put on a turn, he sighed, she makes certain the world and his dog knows about it. Pity she didn't engage in these hysterics when Fowler was home, but she wouldn't dare. He husband claimed he liked peace and quiet in his house, and Hilda had long since learned to obey or face one of his rages, which far outdid hers.

Leon's arrival startled her and she swung around in surprise. 'When did you get home?'

'Just now,' he said, tossing his hat on to the credenza. 'But I heard what happened. I'm sorry, Mother.'

'You're sorry?' she cried, clutching at the dining-room table for support. 'What good will that do? She's gone too far this time. God knows what your father will say. And he'll blame me as usual.'

'Who has gone too far?' he asked her, bewildered.

'No one.' It was Laura, sitting easily in a leather armchair behind the door. 'Mother is overreacting.'

'Is that what you call it?' Hilda wept, mopping her face with an already damp handkerchief. 'What else should I do when my daughter has disgraced the family? Leon has just arrived and he already knows about it. The whole town's talking.'

Leon discarded his jacket with relief and undid his collar. 'The whole town is talking about Ken McCraig's death, Mother, but I should be interested to know what you are on about.'

'Oh yes, poor Ken. I've written to Mrs McCraig inviting her to come and stay with us for a while, but I'm glad she isn't here now.'

'Why?' He looked to Laura, who shrugged, lifting her thick fair hair away from her neck and fluffing it for coolness. The room was hot so he opened the windows.

'Don't do that,' his mother complained. 'You'll let the heat in.'

'I'm letting it out,' he snapped. 'Look at that wall, it's already starting to mould. In this climate you have to leave the windows open or the house smells musty. Now what's gone wrong?'

'Then you haven't heard! That's a mercy, better you hear it from me. That sister of yours, the hussy, rode out to Murray Lagoon today.'

'You did what?' he cried. 'To the bathing reserve?'

16

'Yes,' Laura said defiantly. 'Why shouldn't I? It's only four miles out of town, it wasn't as if I was in any danger.'

Leon was as appalled as his mother. 'Are you quite mad? That is an area reserved for gentlemen.'

'Then I think they should have an area for ladies. I should greatly enjoy a swim. I think it is quite unfair that we have to swelter while men cool off in that lovely lake.'

'You see?' Hilda almost shrieked. 'She has no shame. You shouldn't even discuss an idea like that in front of your brother.'

'I hope there were no gentlemen present.' Leon sniffed.

'Oh but there were, Leon. They were having a wonderful time flopping in and out of the water like big fat frogs.'

'Oh my God! Mother's right, you're shameless.'

'No I'm not. I think men leaping around in the nude are a bit shameless, if anyone is. And to think they forbid women to swim, when' – she laughed – 'we've got less to hide than them.'

'You were spying!' he cried. 'I hope no one saw you.'

'Obviously they did,' she said, 'or Mother wouldn't have heard about it.'

'Mrs Mortimer told me,' Hilda whispered. 'Her husband told her and she felt I ought to know.'

'She couldn't get around here fast enough,' Laura said sagely. 'She must have broken a world walking-record.'

Leon was flabbergasted. 'What if someone mentions it to me? I'll be in an appalling position.'

'You can always say I'm not your sister, I'm only the maid,' she offered.

Leon was far from amused: 'God knows how Father will take this.'

'That's what I've been telling her,' Hilda wailed. 'Fowler will have a perfect fit.'

Laura wasn't worried about Fowler's fits. Like his speeches he was all rattle. She wondered if people really did believe all that tripe he dished up to them, as if, like a hell-and-damnation preacher, he was the only one who could save them. In this morning's paper she found the statement that Leon had delivered yesterday. He'd called it a 'press release' but Cosmo Newgate, the proprietor, had published it as a letter. She couldn't wait for Leon to come down to breakfast so that she could show him. It would be his turn to have a fit, he was such a sook. Laura could never understand why Leon and their mother could not stand up to Fowler. Hilda especially. If she made an effort she could make life damned unpleasant for her husband and bring him to heel, but instead she moaned and sighed, content in her perpetual discontent, accepting his bullying as a wife's lot.

Hilda had been happy enough, Laura mused, when they'd lived on the head station in Bathurst, where she'd proved herself to be an efficient hostess locked into the social whirl of wealth and prestige.

But Fowler's ambitions had dragged her away from her friends and family to the outlandish Queensland town where, in no time, she'd found herself wife of the local Member of Parliament, who spent more time at the State House in Brisbane than at home. Mercifully, Laura thought, but her mother complained about that too.

To Laura, growing up on the station had been fun. She'd always been a busy child with a great love of horses and a large collection of pets, and she'd been very happy until they'd sent her to boarding school in Sydney. She still thought of that time with rage. While Leon had enjoyed boarding school, she had hated it. The mistresses had been appalled by her language, learned from the men in the stock-yards and shearing sheds; they had punished her severely for being lackadaisical in her work, for being rude and defiant, a tomboy, not to be countenanced in young ladies. And finally, when she'd run away to take refuge at her uncle's house in Sydney, they had expelled her. She'd been expelled from the next school too, for constantly taking unchaperoned walks along the beach nearby. They did not understand that the school gates represented not only prison gates to a girl like Laura, but a challenge. Egged on by other girls, who delighted in the presence of this rebel, she had even gone sea-bathing in the wild waves at Coogee Beach. That had been a joy she would never forget – the tingling crystal freshness of the surf, and the power of it had been the most marvellous sensation . . . even though a policeman had arrested her as she emerged.

But that was the end of her schooldays. Laura had been permitted to stay with Uncle William and his mad wife in their Bondi mansion while her father began to rearrange his affairs. From afar, he promised to give her the whipping of her life, but eighteen months later, when the family sailed for Rockhampton, he had forgotten all about it. Laura always yearned to go back to the country and she vowed that eventually she would. As she told her friends, she would marry a squatter and live happily ever after with her own stable of horses. Or maybe she'd buy her own station. Uncle William was very fond of her and had promised to remember her in his will. And so he should, Laura thought. Her exile in Bondi had been very convenient for the Maskey family. William's wife, Aunt Freda, was prone to nasty 'turns', as they called them. In fact she became violent and would attack staff with a carving knife, so William had dreadful trouble keeping his servants. None of them would live in, so Laura became his housekeeper and the only person who could calm his wife.

'She's frightened,' Laura would explain to them. 'That's all. She thinks she's protecting herself. She hears voices from somewhere telling her people are going to kill her and she has to defend herself.'

In the end, though, poor Freda was consigned to a lunatic asylum and William no longer needed Laura's services. Eventually, Freda died there and William left to reside in London. After those ordeals, Rockhampton wasn't so bad at all. She loved to ride along the banks of the deep-flowing Fitzroy River or sit in the shade of the weeping willows feeling as languid as their drifting greenery. Sometimes she brought her sketchbook to try to capture the picture-postcard scenery but she never considered her efforts did the great river justice.

The maid brought in a telegram addressed to Leon, which her mother opened. 'Your father will be coming home on the next mailboat,' she announced.

Laura frowned. 'You're always on at me for my manners. I believe it is extremely rude to open other people's mail.'

'A telegram isn't mail,' Hilda retorted. 'Besides, it's only from your father.'

'What's that got to do with it? You didn't know that until you opened it.'

'I'll thank you to mind your own business. If I were you I'd be more concerned with your own behaviour. Don't think your father won't hear of your latest escapade.'

'Oh I'm sure he will,' Laura remarked sarcastically. She sliced deftly into a juicy mango, turned a quarter open and sucked the sweet flesh from the skin. She could hardly tell them that Amelia, daughter of Boyd Roberts, one of the leading lights of the town, had dared her to go.

She grinned. Everyone said Amelia was such a nice girl! She was always dressed so prettily in pinks and blues and fussy bonnets, with her dark hair pin-curled around her face, but behind the façade Amelia was an absolute villain. She was up to more tricks than a monkey on a stick but was never caught. Her ways were underhand, and at times, Laura felt, a little mean. She eavesdropped on everyone who came to their large, airy house up there on the range, repeating all the gossip to Laura. When the two girls sat primly at afternoon tea with her father and his friends, Laura would suddenly find her coffee laced with alcohol, usually cognac, and she would have to drink it, under Amelia's bland stare, knowing that her friend too was swallowing alcohol.

Mr Roberts was a tall, handsome fellow, aged about forty-nine, Laura guessed, with dark hair greying at the temples and a small clipped moustache. He had resigned from his regiment and travelled north to find his fortune – and he had found it in quite a spectacular way. People said that Boyd Roberts had been one of the first prospectors to strike it rich at Canoona, riding back into Rockhampton with his saddlebags bulging with gold. He now had two mines, and was said, as his wealth increased, to have the Midas touch. But his good fortune had not extended to his wife, who had died of pneumonia several years ago.

He built a grand house on the range overlooking the town, staffed it with servants so that his daughter would always be well cared for, and spared no expense for his little Amelia. She could have anything she wanted. It surprised Laura that Amelia's needs were so trivial. She had no wish to travel, to know anything about the outside world; she was interested only in her wardrobe and the beautiful jewellery her father bought her, because they were part of her plan to attract the right husband. At eighteen, she had her life all worked out. She would marry, and she and her husband would live here, with her father, happily ever after in the house that she loved.

Every so often, eligible young ladies would be brought to the house, which Amelia had christened Beauview, to meet Mr Roberts, but Amelia saw these young women as a threat. Ridiculous things would happen to them: their gloves would go missing, they'd find themselves balancing on a cane chair which had suddenly become rickety, or mice would scamper about their skirts. But more subtle was Amelia's way of complimenting them. She harped on about their clothes, their hairstyles, their jewellery, forcing flustered women to talk only about themselves and their apparel, knowing that her father was becoming bored with the conversation. Truly a visit to Beauview could be a disconcerting experience for ambitious widows or nervous single ladies, but it was a stage set designed by Amelia, and the odd thing was, Laura mused, her father, the suave and charming Boyd Roberts, never seemed to notice what his daughter was up to.

Leon came in to breakfast, immaculate in a white ruffled shirt and beige breeches, and immediately noticed the telegram on the table. 'Is that from Father?'

'Yes, dear,' Hilda said. 'He'll be home on the next mailboat.'

Leon nodded without enthusiasm. 'I have to arrange a welcoming reception for him, and you two will have to attend.'

'Of course.' Hilda smiled.

'Father's letter to the paper has been published,' Laura remarked innocently.

'What letter?' Leon snapped, grabbing the paper. He soon found it and sat down depressed. 'Oh my God! I'll get blamed for this.'

'Why, dear?' Hilda asked. 'What does it matter as long as he is able to put forward his view?'

'It matters a great deal. Any ratbag can write a letter to the paper. If Cosmo had published his statement, the reportage would appear as news and not be relegated to the back. It would also give his argument more support.'

'So you don't think Cosmo wants a new state in the north?' Laura asked.

'Oh, he won't give an opinion yet. But it's clear he doesn't want Father as the premier.'

'Who would he want?' Hilda asked. 'Your father as the sitting member has the experience. No one else can hold a candle to him.'

'Except Mr Roberts,' Laura said.

'Roberts?' Leon was startled. 'He's not interested in state politics.'

'Oh yes he is.' Laura smiled. 'Amelia told me.'

Hilda clanked down her teacup. 'Glory be to God! Isn't it enough

20

that we have to suffer a dangerous fellow like that in our town, without having him aspire to the Parliament?'

'Mother!' Laura snapped. 'I don't know where you get these tales. Mr Roberts isn't a dangerous man, he's very nice.'

'Fat lot you know,' Leon said. 'That man has a bad reputation out on the diggings. They say he jumped those first claims at Canoona, that the Starlight mine belonged to an old Scot who mysteriously disappeared.'

'Then why didn't they have the law on him?' Laura retorted.

'Because no one was prepared to take on Roberts and his henchmen. They still won't.'

'I don't believe you. And he employs miners, not henchmen.'

'You'd better not go to that house any more,' Hilda told Laura. 'Your father won't like it. Besides, I hear he entertains his ladyloves there in quite an indecent manner.'

'He does not! With Amelia standing guard, any ladyloves, as you call them, would be lucky to last ten minutes.'

'Really?' Leon said, interested, but Laura wouldn't enlarge on the subject, it would be disloyal to her friend to do so.

Summer torrents had the town awash when Fowler arrived home, so only Leon was there to meet him at the quay, a poor start to his campaign. He grabbed the proffered umbrella angrily. 'Where's your mother?'

'She's waiting at the Criterion with Laura. I have arranged a reception for you at the hotel but not too many people have turned up.'

'Fools! Afraid of a drop of rain!'

'It's not that. They're celebrating at the pub down the road. There's been another gold strike, a big one, they say, at Crocodile Creek.'

Even though Fowler lodged this information in his mind as yet another nail in the coffin of southern representation – the riches of the north outstripping their contribution to the state's coffers – he was still annoyed. He strode into the commercial dining room where refreshments were laid out on gleaming white tables, buffet food down one side and drinks on the other, with no more than a dozen people standing almost guiltily betwixt.

His wife came over and kissed him. 'Welcome home, dear. How was Brisbane?'

Ignoring her, Fowler hissed at Leon, 'Is this all?' He was accustomed to at least one hundred people at his meetings. Gold or not, Leon should have done better than this. 'There's enough food here to feed an army,' he said, pulling Leon aside. 'You'll make me a laughing stock. Get out there and find more starters.'

'Where?'

'I don't bloody care where. From the bar! In the street! See who is staying in the hotel. Just get them!'

21

His professional smile back in place, he made the rounds of the few loyal supporters. 'All the more for us,' he joked, helping himself to a whisky. 'Come on now, enjoy yourselves. Our plates runneth over! I tell you, folks, it's good to be home.' He shook hands, complimented two ladies for braving the elements, and tried not to watch the door as an odd collection of strangers filtered into the room.

His daughter was standing by him. 'Looks like you'll have to offer more incentive next time,' she said.

'What are you talking about? What sort of incentive?'

'I don't know. But if you've got competition it'll take more than a free feed to get them to your meetings. No one's exactly starving here.'

There was a glimmer of truth in what she said about incentive, and he tucked that morsel away too, but competition? 'What competition?'

'Mr Roberts is opposing you at the next elections.'

The news shook Fowler but he was a good poker player. 'So what?' he said. 'I'm the Member for Rockhampton, I won't have any trouble holding the seat for Queensland, or for Capricornia.'

'Is that what they're going to call the new state?'

'It's obvious, isn't it? Rockhampton sits on the Tropic of Capricorn.' He had only been making conversation with his daughter to fill in time; now there was a small crowd at the door, so he plunged over to greet them.

Laura drank a glass of ginger beer, helped herself to a plate of wine trifle and retired to the sidelines as Leon placed a box covered in red plush between the top tables.

Seats were found for the ladies when Fowler stepped up to address the gathering, and Laura made sure she was placed where she could view the room without turning her back on the speaker. Fowler's speeches bored her, she preferred to study the reactions of the audience – it was something to do. Laura knew the talkers, the dozers, the wrigglers and the ardent listeners, and most of all she looked for hecklers. They made the events interesting. Unfortunately there weren't any today and as Fowler went on and on, she almost dozed off herself. That would bring the wrath of God down on her! She straightened up and saw a tall fellow over by the opposite table sneak a chicken leg, and then another, munching cheerfully as he listened to the momentous affairs of state. Laura grinned, and, noticing, he winked at her.

When the speech concluded, Carter Franklin, manager of the Commercial Bank, and, of course, Fowler's banker, made a short welcome-home speech, as prearranged. He then announced, to a cheer, that Australian sovereigns had been approved as legal tender in Great Britain.

With that Fowler stepped up again. 'To mark this momentous occasion I will be presenting newly minted sovereigns, as souvenirs to

22

some lucky guests at my home next Sunday. It will be open house from two p.m., and you're all invited.'

Quick! Laura thought. And quite brazen! He had picked up on her incentive hint. The campaign should be quite fun if it were to be a race between her father and Amelia's. Money against money. She doubted that anyone else could match the pace.

Leon was standing nervously beside her. 'It wasn't a bad show after all, was it?'

She felt sorry for him. 'No. Not really. At least he got to talk to a few new faces instead of the same old mob. Who's that chap over there, hoeing into the apple pies?'

'MacNamara. I caught him just as he was checking into the hotel. He owns Oberon cattle station, east of the Berserker Range. Not short of a quid, that family. They've got a string of stations from the Hunter Valley right through to Townsville.'

Laura nudged him. 'Father wants you.'

Leon looked back to see Fowler beckoning him and rushed away, so Laura wandered over to the stranger. 'Did you enjoy your lunch, Mr MacNamara?'

'I certainly did, Miss Maskey.' He grinned. 'I was starving. I just got into town in time!'

She was intrigued that they had both gone to the trouble to establish identities, and flattered. He was very tall and she thought he had the most beautiful face, if that could be said of a man. Soft brown eyes under dark curly hair, smooth features and a lovely smile. A friendly smile. She didn't want him to go. 'Can I get you a drink?' she asked.

'I'd rather have a cup of tea.'

'Then you shall have it,' she said gaily.

She sat with him while he had his tea, answering his questions about the meeting. Gladly.

'Your father's quite a talker,' he said. 'But I wish he'd stick to the one job.'

'Which is?'

'The one he has. Representing this district in State Parliament. I'm against separation. It's too soon. Queensland needs all her resources, it would be disastrous to split at this early stage. Divide and conquer is old but true.'

'But who would conquer us?'

'Finance. Huge debts would only inflict poverty on the people. The state is struggling as it is – two treasuries fighting over the one purse would be ludicrous.'

'But in the north we have our gold and our cattle, we're practically supporting Brisbane and those southern districts.'

'You don't really believe that?' He was obviously astonished.

At that moment Leon approached. 'Excuse me, Mr MacNamara. We have to go. Mother says to come along, Laura. I'll get Father's luggage.'

MacNamara's eyes twinkled. 'You've been listening to too many of your father's speeches. I hope you'll forgive me for enjoying his hospitality under false pretences, but a hungry man could hardly refuse.'

'That's quite all right,' she said magnanimously. 'I find your opinions quite interesting. I hope you enjoyed your lunch. Actually, I have an engagement to lunch here again tomorrow. Perhaps we could continue the conversation then?' It was a most outlandish lie but she'd have to get here somehow. Amelia would have to accompany her.

'I don't think so,' he replied. 'I've got a lot to do tomorrow.'

'Very well.' Laura retreated, but extended her hand. 'It's been nice meeting you.'

Laura knew it was a schoolgirlish thought, but had he held her hand just a little longer than necessary, as if he didn't really want her to leave? Probably not. But she was warmed by his touch, and a tingle of excitement went through her as she left with her parents. MacNamara! He was just divine. She couldn't wait to tell Amelia. And she had seen his hesitation. He just might find the time to be in for lunch – after all, he was staying in the hotel.

For the second time that week Laura put aside her comfortable country clothes and dressed for 'town', such as it was. She chose carefully, knowing that she had been rather forward with Mr MacNamara the previous day, afraid that she might have frightened him off. Some men were quite offended when ladies took the lead, as if it were their God-given right, like dancing. But then, she smiled, she doubted Mr MacNamara was that stuffy.

She laced up her corset easily – not even for him would she choke herself into tight stays – and slipped on a long lawn petticoat and over it her favourite dress of blue shot silk. The bodice was low cut, nice and cool for these hot days, and the neckline was edged in a fine-pleated ruffle of georgette, just enough to finish it off. The dressmaker had wanted to busy up the neckline with layers of lace but Laura had refused – she hated frills. She had insisted on a slightly dropped waist with plenty of material in the skirt so that it hung freely, accentuating the lovely colours made by light and shade in the folds. After some argument she had allowed the dressmaker to add extra pleats at the back, with a large, flat bow, almost a bustle, at the waist. She had to admit, as she studied the effect in a mirror, that in all the dress had turned out to be very stylish. She added a leghorn straw hat, flipping the band of elastic under her hair to keep it in place, and began searching in a drawer for matching gloves.

'Where are you going?' Her mother was at the door.

'To lunch with Amelia.'

'I told you not to go out to the Roberts' house any more.'

'Father hasn't said I can't go.'

'He will. I expected you to stay home and help me with arrange-

24

ments for this party he's sprung on me,' she complained. 'He doesn't bother to consult me, just tells the world to come along. Open house on Sunday afternoon, he says! Which means I haven't the faintest idea how many people will turn up, or what sort of people I will have to entertain. It's really too bad of him. Am I expected to cater for all the louts and floosies in the town?'

'Mother, I have to go.' Laura interrupted the litany of laments. 'I'll give you a hand tomorrow.'

'And how will you get out there?' Hilda asked. 'You can't ride in that dress.'

'Amelia is calling for me in her carriage.'

Hilda gave a cluck of disapproval. 'It's scandalous the way that girl's father spoils her. I never heard of a young girl having her own carriage and driver.'

'It's only a small carriage,' Laura said, trying not to antagonise her mother, who had taken it for granted she was going out to Beauview and not just down the street to the hotel. 'Mr Roberts had it built to scale and it is so comfortable. In the wet season it is just marvellous. You ought to have a carriage here, Mother, you really need one.'

No one else in the town had a carriage of any sort. When it didn't suit them to ride, the women rode in gigs or pony traps. Amelia's special conveyance caused a lot of gossip and envy in Rockhampton, which delighted her.

Hilda followed Laura downstairs, still grumbling. 'It's just as well Amelia is such a nice little girl, so well mannered, or her father would have her completely ruined.'

'Yes, of course,' Laura agreed, stifling a laugh. 'Here she is now.'

'Good morning, Mrs Maskey,' Amelia called from the window as her carriage drew up. 'I hope you are well.'

'Yes thank you, Miss Roberts,' Hilda replied stiffly as Laura climbed in. Given this first chance to examine the carriage at close quarters, her eyes roved over it, taking in the liveried driver who closed the door and stepped up to his seat. She made no comment, though, except to call to Laura: 'Don't be late, we have guests coming to dinner.'

'Who're the guests?' Amelia asked.

'It's only Mr and Mrs Franklin,' Laura told her. Then she ducked her head. 'Quick! Look down. Captain Cope is coming down the road.'

'Bobby Cope? Don't put on such a face, I think he's very dashing.'

'Well I don't, he's a lecher.'

'He's not a lecher, he just flirts a little and I don't mind that at all, he's fun.' Then, 'Your mother seemed quite calm. I'm surprised she allowed you to go to the hotel unescorted.'

'She didn't, she thinks we're going to your place.' Laura grinned. 'What did your father say?'

'He didn't ask. He wouldn't be so dreary.'

25

Laura sat up. 'Tell the driver to stop! We're passing the hotel.'

'Don't panic. It's quite all right. I told him we'd take a turn through the town first. Give them something to talk about.' She adjusted her tall bonnet which was lined with pink-and-white check to match her gingham dress and tied under her chin with a pink satin bow. 'Lean back now,' she said as the carriage spun along Fitzroy Street and then turned left into East Street. 'Look straight ahead, Laura,' she instructed. 'You'll spoil everything if you start waving to people.'

'I'm not going to wave to people!' Laura said indignantly.

'Maybe we ought to stop here and do a little shopping,' Amelia suggested.

'No! Definitely not! We'll be late for lunch.'

'Oh, very well. You're so keen to get there I think you are really gone on this fellow MacNamara. I'm dying to see him. Are you sure he'll turn up?'

'I don't know. I told him we'd be there.'

'But he likes you?'

'I'm sure he does. He has black hair and the loveliest smile, so handsome, except for a small scar on his cheek, but that seems to add to his looks. Sort of manly . . .'

'Oh my,' Amelia said. 'You'd better watch out, I may take a liking to this dreamboat yourself.'

'Don't you dare,' Laura warned.

The two young ladies stepped grandly from the carriage and swept inside to the lobby of the Criterion Hotel. As their eyes adjusted to the sudden change from the outside glare, they ignored the stares from men in the bar on their right and moved forward towards the dining room.

Gunnar Thomas, the publican, emerged from the bar and eyed them curiously. 'What can I do for you, ladies?'

It was unheard of for young single girls to dine alone but Amelia had her answer ready. 'We shall be lunching here with my father,' she announced. 'And it would be ever so sweet of you, Mr Thomas, to place us by the door so that we can watch for him.'

'Of course, my dear, of course,' he replied, and Amelia nudged Laura triumphantly as he bustled ahead to place them.

'What a lark!' Amelia whispered as they sat sedately, coolly surveying the room and the other guests.

Knowing that stares were being directed at them from behind potted palms, Laura studied the red velour drapes at the windows with their gold-tasselled accessories, the grandfather clock, and the paintings of hunting dogs that hung on the walls, for as long as she could so that Amelia wouldn't think she was too anxious. Her eyes went involuntarily to the door, but there was no sign of Mr MacNamara yet.

'Would you ladies like to order, or would you rather take some light refreshment until the gentleman arrives?' a waiter asked them.

'We won't wait,' Amelia said loftily. 'He could be a time yet. I'll have oysters, please. And roast chicken. What about you, Laura?'

'The same,' Laura said, hardly interested in the food.

Amelia, though, had a healthy appetite: 'We'll also have plum pudding and plenty of whipped cream.' She passed the hand-written menu card back to the waiter. 'And we'll have some fresh bread and butter while we're waiting.'

When the waiter withdrew, she turned to Laura. 'Let's order a bottle of wine.'

'I don't want any wine,' Laura said. 'And neither do you. Don't be ridiculous.'

'I'm not being ridiculous. You're a spoilsport. And where's your friend anyway? Why don't you go and ask if he's in?'

'No. I wouldn't dream of it.'

'I would,' Amelia giggled. 'If he's as nice as you say I'd go looking for him.'

The waiter brought them a cob of beer bread and a chilled bowl of butter curls, and then returned with a platter of large fresh oysters in their shells.

Amelia gazed about the room, a sweet smile on her face, causing disapproving starers to whisk their eyes back to their own affairs, then turned her attention to the oysters. 'I'm dying to see this beau of yours,' she said, as she demolished them one by one.

'He's not my beau,' Laura said.

'Not yet.' Amelia grinned, then glanced at the door. 'Oh, look who's here!'

Laura's heart leapt for an instant but then plunged in disappointment as Bobby Cope approached.

'I can't believe my eyes,' he gushed. 'Two lovely ladies sitting here fending for themselves.'

'We're waiting for Mr Roberts,' Laura told him coldly.

'I haven't seen him,' Cope said. 'Might I join you in the interim?'

'There's no need,' Laura replied, but Amelia's response was simultaneous. 'That would be very kind of you.' Laura glared at her as she continued, 'It's rather awkward to be left here on our own.'

There was no stopping him. He settled at the table and at Amelia's invitation decided to join them for luncheon. 'Have some oysters,' she said. 'They're absolutely delicious.'

'I don't know,' he said. 'I don't quite take to them. You don't seem to be enjoying yours, Laura.'

She blushed. She had been eating them as slowly as possible to delay the meal, to give Mr MacNamara time to appear. 'Yes I am,' she mumbled.

'Well, I must say you are looking simply stunning today. That dress suits you beautifully, doesn't it, Amelia?'

'Yes, quite.' Amelia pouted. 'Did you make it yourself, Laura?'

27

Realising that she was about to become the butt of one of Amelia's contrived conversations, Laura turned the tables. Amelia hated people to talk politics. 'What do you think of the new premier, Macalister, Captain Cope?'

'He's a dolt,' Cope said. 'I was discussing him with your father last night. By the way, he invited me to your home next Sunday. I believe it will be an entertaining afternoon. Perhaps you'll allow me to be your escort?'

'Bobby, I don't need an escort in my own house.'

'A party? Next Sunday?' Amelia interrupted. 'Am I invited?'

'Of course,' Laura said absently, one eye on the door.

'Marvellous.' She smiled. 'Now I shall have to choose a new outfit for the occasion. And why don't I have a tea party at home one Sunday too? Would you like to come, Captain?'

'I should be honoured,' Bobby said. His heavy features displayed little enthusiasm, but Amelia seemed delighted.

Laura couldn't imagine what she saw in Bobby Cope. Admittedly he looked well in uniform, but his clipped hair and wide military moustache did little to improve his plump features and thick, loose lips. And even though he had a debonair manner, his hooded eyes belied gentility; to her they were cold. Mean. Not that Amelia agreed – she found his eyes exciting and mysterious, everything about him appealed to her. 'You only like him because he's chasing me,' Laura had said. 'You're just being contrary. He's not a nice man at all.'

Now Amelia was in her element, even persuading Bobby to order a bottle of wine. But as the meal dragged on, Laura despaired. It became obvious that Mr MacNamara had not changed his mind. Maybe he really did have a lot to do today, she told herself. But if he found her interesting, surely he could have made an effort.

Luncheon over, Amelia sent Bobby off for her carriage. 'So your friend didn't turn up. What a nuisance. But he could be in the bar, or in his room. Why don't you ask?'

'I couldn't do that.'

'Oh nonsense! I could.' She called the waiter over. 'Please enquire if Mr MacNamara is in the hotel.'

While Laura sat nervously, awaiting the verdict like a prisoner at the bar, Amelia was bubbling with excitement. For her, the outing had been a huge success.

'No, miss,' the waiter said on his return. 'Mr MacNamara went out early this morning and he ain't come back yet.'

'Oh dash,' Amelia said to Laura. 'I'm even more curious now. But I know what to do. When you get home, filch some of your father's stationery and send him a written invitation for Sunday.'

Laura's eyes lit up. 'Yes, I could do that. It wouldn't require a signature. But he might have left town by then.'

'It's worth a try. You can't hang about here all day.'

Bobby Cope was back at the table before they realised it. 'What are you two little rascals plotting?' he laughed.

Amelia fluttered her eyelashes at him. 'Oh my, what a thing to say! I was just suggesting we all go back to my place, we could have a game of cards.'

'Righto,' Bobby said. 'It's just as well I came along. Mr Roberts must have been delayed somewhere.'

'He forgets things,' Amelia said airily. 'Come along now.'

'No, I'll have to go home,' Laura told them.

Amelia smiled mischievously. 'Of course. Laura can't come, she has a letter to write. You'll just have to play me, Bobby, and no cheating.'

Laura was depressed, and irritated. She had made a perfect fool of herself going to all that trouble to meet a man who didn't even bother to look in on them. She wondered why he had affected her so much. After all, they'd only talked for a few minutes. But she kept seeing the merriment in his eyes. What colour? Brown, they were brown, bushman's eyes, with almost a squint from the sun, but so tender. Caring. And his voice. Soft, with just a trace of an Irish accent. He had talked to her as if they were the only people in the room. She tried to push him from her mind, bewildered that a stranger could upset her so much. She was relieved when she could escape from Amelia and Bobby, glad to be home. Forget MacNamara, she told herself, you're playing silly games just like Amelia does. You ought to have more sense.

'Your father wants to see you in his study,' the maid told her.

Laura flipped her hat on to the hallstand, loosened her hair, and tapped gently at the study door.

As soon as she saw them she knew there was trouble. He was at his desk, his face beetroot red, and her mother was standing beside him, hands clasped together in her martyr's stance.

'About time!' he shouted. 'What have you got to say for yourself?'

'I told you not to go out to the Roberts' house,' Hilda added.

'Oh that.' Laura smiled. 'I thought better of it. We had a very proper luncheon with Captain Cope at the Criterion.'

'You've got a cheek!' Fowler roared, standing up to tower over her. 'You ought to be ashamed to show your face in town. You have no regard for my position, no thought for this crucial time in my affairs. You are behaving like a hussy! I can't afford scandal now or at any other time, and you deliberately scandalised the whole town.'

'She won't listen to me,' Hilda said. 'You're the one who spoils her. I might as well be talking to the wall as talk to her.'

'How old are you?' Fowler glared at Laura. 'Twenty?'

'She'll be twenty-one soon,' Hilda added primly.

'Twenty-one!' Fowler echoed. 'Most girls of your age are married by this.' He turned on his wife. 'It's no wonder she can't find a husband with the reputation she's getting.'

'What reputation?' Laura said. 'People hardly know I exist.'

'Is that so?' Fowler hissed. 'Is that so? Then tell me why the

29

Sergeant of Police felt it his duty to take me aside and ask me to keep my daughter away from Murray Lagoon? My daughter! Out there! The whole town talking and I'm the last to hear of it.' He paced across the room. 'I blame you for this,' he accused Hilda. 'You had a duty to tell me. Not leave me to be a laughing stock, with a daughter who is nothing but an embarrassment to the Maskey name. Well,' he continued, 'there's an answer to the problem. I'll have no more of this. I want her name changed, do you hear me?'

'Her name changed?' Hilda stammered. 'How . . .?'

'Oh, for Christ's sake, don't play daft on me. Find her a husband. Marry her off. You women know how to arrange these things, now get to it.'

'Don't I have any say in this matter?' Laura asked. She realised now that going out to the lagoon was a stupid thing to have done, but her father was overreacting.

'No, you don't have any say. There are plenty of young fellows who could be persuaded to marry you, given a decent dowry. Captain Cope for one, I've seen him eyeing you.'

'I will not marry Bobby Cope, and you can't make me.'

'Then you find someone else. I want to see you married as soon as possible. Your days of running wild are over; you will marry and settle down and get out of my hair.'

Laura didn't mean to but she couldn't help looking at his balding head. Her glance infuriated her father even more. 'You think you're so bloody smart,' he said, 'but you listen to me. You do as you're told or I'll disown you. You're no different from Leon. Now get out of here, the both of you. I've got work to do.'

Chapter Two

Four years prior to these events, the MacNamara twins, John and Paul, had come to the parting of the ways.

Ever since the tragic death of their father, the lads had worked on the family cattle station, Kooramin, out on the Liverpool plains in New South Wales. It had settled into a steady, flourishing property, one that Pace would have been proud of had he lived. Pace and their mother, Dolour, had pioneered the cattle run, and their three sons – the twins and the younger son, nicknamed Duke – were born on the station. In those days it had seemed to be the back of beyond, but now other properties were operating for hundreds of miles into the west, roads and towns had opened up, and Kooramin was a valuable asset.

The twins were barely into their teens when Pace had died and the loss had been an emotional crisis in their lives. They'd believed their Irish father to be indestructible and were looking forward to welcoming him home from his explorations in the north, when his partner, an Argentinian cattleman, Juan Rivadavia, had returned with the shocking news that Pace had been killed by tribal blacks.

Months of turmoil followed. It hadn't been easy to pick up the reins dropped by the stubborn Irishman, who had dreamed of owning the best cattle runs in the land. Only their loyalty to their father's dream had saved the family from a serious split. They loved Kooramin and that took priority over family moods and administrative arguments.

At first the two lads had been pathetically eager to help their widowed mother and they vied with each other to please her. A strong, passionate woman, she understood their intentions but disapproved of the competition. 'It's not a race we have here. I'll not have you break your necks for the joy of it.'

As the boys grew and became more confident, the novelty of pleasing Mother began to wear off. They had their own ideas on herd management, ideas they'd picked up from other cattlemen, but Dolour wouldn't listen. And it was the devil's own job to make her hand over the cash they needed to buy better strains of breeders, even to buy better equipment.

John was the first one to break: 'Mother, this just isn't working. I can't stand by and watch Kooramin deteriorate just because you're too mean to spend a quid.'

'Don't speak to me like that,' she'd said crossly. 'You don't know what it's like to be poor. I do and I'll never let it happen again. I have the three of you to worry about.'

'But we're not poor. The drought has broken, we're getting good prices for the cattle and top rent for the leases on the other stations.'

Dolour smiled at him, seeming to capitulate. She pushed back her thick red hair which now was tinged with grey. 'Oh, very well then, if we need money we'll sell the land in the far north.'

'No you don't,' Paul intervened. 'That belongs to Duke, and it stays in his name until he comes of age and he can decide what to do about it.'

'I hate the place,' she cried. 'Your father died there. I don't want Duke going anywhere near it.'

'Mother,' Paul said patiently, 'we've been over this before. And I hate to keep saying it, but Dad wanted that land up there, it's prize cattle country. He went after it and he got it. It was his wish that Duke should have it because he knew that region wouldn't be habitable until Duke was older. I'm sorry if it upsets you, but it is not for sale.'

His mother glared at him, tossed her head and strode from the room.

'Thanks a lot. She'll be in a temper for days now,' John said.

'And what would you expect me to say?'

'Nothing. I wouldn't be surprised, though, to find she uses the Valley of Lagoons to change the subject. We didn't get any more money out of her, and I want to hire some fencing contractors. Otherwise we do it ourselves.'

Of the two, John was the quieter, the more emotional, at least on the surface. Paul buried his feelings in humour.

'I often think of Father,' John said. 'He still seems close, watching over what we do.'

'Oh go on!' Paul scoffed. 'You've been listening to Dolour's prayers. Pace was never interested in the day-to-day nuts and bolts of the station, not really. He was too busy with the big spread. He and Rivadavia bought the big run in the Brisbane Valley and then they went after more land. If he was alive today he'd be out chasing more and more and we'd still be here with Dolour running the head station.'

'That's a bit unfair,' John objected.

'No, it's not. This isn't a criticism. I admired him. I'd love to be able to do that, to open up a station of my own, but imagine asking Dolour to back me. She'd throw an Irish version of the vapours.'

'Well do me a favour,' John said. 'Don't mention it right now. We need to prise some cash from her for immediate use. I might ask Mr Rivadavia to speak to her. He'll understand.'

'Why bring him into it?' Paul objected. 'This is family business.'

John shrugged. He was fond of his father's former partner but Paul had reservations about him, and was inclined to be moody when Rivadavia visited them. Although Paul denied it, John felt that his brother blamed Rivadavia for their father's death. Or maybe he just couldn't come to terms with the fact that the blacks had killed Pace and allowed Rivadavia to go free.

Juan Rivadavia had been so distraught at Pace's death that he had not laid claim to a yard of the big cattle run that he and Pace had pegged in the Far North. He had just said that Pace wanted Duke to have it, and he had registered the run in Duke's name.

'It was very generous of him,' John had remarked to his brother.

Paul had frowned. 'Generosity or guilt.'

'That's cruel, he was bloody upset.'

'I know, I know. I don't want to talk about it.'

Since then, it appeared to John that his brother had never been able to make up his mind about Rivadavia. After he had done all he could to help the MacNamara family, Juan Rivadavia had left his Hunter Valley property in the hands of a manager and gone home to Argentina with his daughter, who had married someone over there. Gossip had it that Juan had kept her away from local fellows he considered ineligible. He was quite a snob where Rosa was concerned, John thought ruefully, remembering that he'd been madly in love with the gorgeous Rosa himself, though she'd never given him a second glance. Then again, the Argentinian was very wealthy and John supposed a gentleman like that had to take care.

He did often think about Pace; he was very proud of his father, and Paul's caustic attitude would have been more hurtful had he not understood that it was just Paul's way. The friendship between the Irishman who had come to Australia penniless, and the already rich young immigrant Rivadavia had always intrigued John. The two men had seemed to have little in common. Pace was a blunt, plain-spoken battler, while Rivadavia was a cultured, sophisticated person who moved in Sydney's viceregal circles. Like most country men, though, they shared a great love of horses, as well as that other thing, the obsession with owning great tracts of land. That had been the meeting point; both men had taken up the challenge to ride a thousand miles into the north, into dangerous country inhabited by hostile blacks, to claim virgin land in territory made famous by the German explorer, Leichhardt. They had actually met Leichhardt, an experience which John envied. To have known the 'Prince of Explorers' and have seen his maps! What an amazing experience! It was Leichhardt who had inspired that mad thousand-mile ride the two men had undertaken.

But all this was history. When Juan returned from Argentina he became a frequent visitor to Kooramin. Eventually, he and Dolour were married, and they took Duke to live with them in the Hunter Valley. Dolour handed Kooramin to the twins, who, at last able to run the station their way, were fired with a new enthusiasm. At first there were arguments between them but they gradually settled into a routine and worked together successfully.

The double wedding seemed a natural progression in their lives.

John married Eileen Doherty, a Bathurst girl, and Paul married Jeannie L'Estrange from Moonee Downs, another cattle station to the north-west of Kooramin.

At first the new era was exciting. Four young people working together and enjoying each other's company brought zest to the small community, and the station hands responded eagerly. After six months, though, rifts began to appear in the MacNamara household. Paul was surprised and embarrassed by his wife's attitude to Aborigines. She was hard on the station blacks, especially the young girls who worked in and around the homestead, which brought her into conflict with Eileen.

Finally his sister-in-law came to Paul demanding that he speak to Jeannie. 'This has to stop,' she said. 'While you're out during the day she gives the girls hell.'

'What can I do? I've asked her to ease up on them but she has an ingrained dislike of blacks. I was hoping that she'd learn to understand them a little better in time. We have to be patient with her.'

'I have been patient, but I'm seeing her true colours now and I'm not prepared to put up with it. She stalks the place like a martinet, picking on the girls all the time, switching at them with her riding whip. And this morning was the last straw – she gave young Bessie a beating for breaking a plate. If she beats any of them again I'll take the whip and try it on her. See how she likes it.'

'Oh God! Don't do that. I'll talk to her.'

'Don't just talk to her, tell her!' Eileen said and stormed away.

Paul tried: 'I want you to be nicer to the gins working here, Jeannie. They do their best.'

'Their best?' Jeannie laughed. 'I'd hate to see their worst. Lazy good-for-nothings, the lot of them. I don't know why we can't get rid of them and employ clean white maids.'

'Because this is their home, Jeannie, and it's up to us to look after them. If we give them jobs it helps them to assimilate into our lifestyle . . .'

'Why do we want them to assimilate? They're a filthy lot, and the sooner they are all wiped out the better.'

He was appalled. 'What are you saying, woman? You're talking about human beings!'

'They're not human beings. Just because you've got a few tame ones around the place doesn't make them like us. My father says they're no better than animals. Worse, in fact. He says they're an infestation up our way.'

'I see,' he said quietly. Then, ominously, 'I've heard tell that your father organises blackfellow shoots. Would that be true now?'

'Why not?' she replied defensively. 'It's the only way to clean them out. The buggers kill our cattle just for the hell of it.'

'I'm not surprised if you treat them like that.'

She faced him defiantly, hands on hips. 'Your own father was murdered by blacks and yet you're on their side. Strikes me you haven't got the guts he had.'

'You leave my father out of this. He died in a fair fight over land. It doesn't take guts to kill innocent men and their families in cold blood. And it doesn't take guts to belt into little black gins who are too frightened to defend themselves. You use that riding whip in my house ever again and I'll . . .'

'So that's it. Eileen has been pimping, has she? She thinks she's so high and mighty. She's always criticising me, in fact she's a real pain in the neck. When we were first married you said we'd have our own station but I can't see any sign of it. How long do I have to go on sharing a house with her? And when she has her baby I suppose I'll be expected to run the place while she puts her feet up.'

'We're not talking about Eileen.'

'Yes we are. Why don't you ask them when they're leaving?'

'John and Eileen aren't leaving. We are.'

He turned on his heel and strode away. He had already discussed a new station with John and he knew now it was time to make the move. Since Eileen was due to have her child in a few months, it would be better for her to stay on at Kooramin.

John had laughed. 'You're all heart, mate. I suppose that hankering you have for new pastures has nothing to do with it? With your volunteering to move on?'

'Of course not.' Paul grinned, but then became serious. 'I always wanted to be like Pace, to be able to get up and go, and see new places. That's why I thought I'd take a look at Queensland.'

'It's a big state. You don't want to get too far off the beaten track. You need to find the market first and then look for land.'

'That's why I had in mind some country around Rockhampton. They say the gold strikes created an instant town and this one is forging ahead because it's a good river port.'

'But is it good cattle country?'

'I've heard it is but I'd have to check it out.'

'If you wait a while I'll come with you.'

'Righto, but don't forget I'm the buyer. You're staying put at Kooramin.'

Two months after Eileen gave birth to John Pace MacNamara, known to all as Jack, the brothers set out for Rockhampton. They rode through northern New South Wales, on over the Darling Downs to Brisbane, recalling that this was the route their father had followed several times. They then followed the picturesque coastal trails north. Since they'd been brought up on Kooramin, an inland station, the two men were fascinated by the sea and they made a holiday of this coastal leg of their journey. They swam and fished off bay beaches, camped on stunning headlands admiring the views, and stayed over in isolated taverns. Bushies at heart, they were still wary of attacks by bushwhackers or marauding blacks and so they were heavily armed and always alert.

They rode over an eerie place known as Ironstone Mountain that was littered with huge boulders, and were confronted by several tribal Aborigines who emerged from a cave. For a few minutes Paul thought there could be a problem, but they were permitted to pass, and when he looked back he saw that the blacks' cold, hard stares had changed to grins.

'I wonder what that was about?' he said.

John shook his head. 'God knows.' He removed his hat and wiped sweat from his forehead. 'I'll be glad when we're over this bloody mountain. The heat coming off those shiny boulders is terrible. You could cook a steak on them. They're the weirdest-looking rocks I've ever seen. I wonder what they are.'

'Some sort of dark mottled granite by the looks of things.'

They toiled on, their horses picking their way around the boulders. The trail seemed to have disappeared, so they dismounted and led the animals to the edge of an escarpment to get their bearings.

'Good God!' John cried. 'Will you look at this!'

Spread out before them was a magnificent valley bordering a wide river.

Paul stared. 'That'd be the Fitzroy River,' he said lamely, unable to take in the beauty of the landscape before him. He'd been told there was good pastureland up here but this valley surpassed all his expectations. Deep-green mountains reared up far to the east, forming a natural backdrop to this verdant scene which held the brothers spellbound.

It was John who decided it was time to move on. He peered down the steep escarpment. 'Now we know what the joke was,' he commented.

Paul laughed. 'Yes, the cunning buggers. They knew we'd run out of road up here. But it was worth it to get a bird's-eye view of this place. It's journey's end, mate. This'll do me.'

There was no sign of the blacks as they retraced their steps and found another route down the mountain.

Paul was excited, already talking about overlanding cattle and speculating as to who might be spared from Kooramin to help him set up the new run.

'I hope you're not too late,' John worried. 'I shouldn't think there'd be too much of that land going begging.'

As they had expected, Rockhampton was a busy little village, set on the south bank of the river just below a barrier of rocks that jutted out into the swirling waters, preventing river boats from travelling any further upstream. They soon learned that these rocks had given the town its name, a simple solution to an oft-argued question in these frontier areas.

There was plenty of activity on the wharf and surveyors were busy marking out the streets. They rode through the town in a matter of minutes, nodding appreciatively. They'd already seen fine healthy cattle grazing along the trail and they watched another mob being herded into a paddock.

'Hereford,' Paul remarked gleefully. 'They're in good nick.'

'My bloody oath they are,' his brother replied. 'I'm glad these herds are a long way from our territory. They'd be some competition, I tell you.'

'It's all so green,' Paul laughed. 'I can't get over it. I bet they don't even have droughts here.'

'You're getting carried away,' John cautioned. 'They'll have their dry spells just like everyone else. We've just come in on the end of their summer rains, remember?'

'Yes,' Paul said, though he was not entirely convinced. After the open plains of their home territory with its fierce, dry summer, this was another Eden. And it was only about forty miles from the coast. A wonderful place to raise a family. That thought caused him to frown. Jeannie was distressed, and a mite jealous of Eileen into the bargain, because she had not yet conceived.

He had laughed. 'What's the hurry? We've plenty of time.'

But, apparently, that was the wrong thing to say. She had accused him of not caring about her feelings, of not caring about her at all, when, in fact, he did. He loved her, she was his wife. He sighed. The sooner they moved on, the better, so she would not feel she had to compete with her sister-in-law all the time. They'd be much happier in their own home.

Disappointment struck as a week passed and the brothers were unable to locate unclaimed land. They talked to the surveyors who were based at the York Hotel in Fitzroy Street, since their maps of the locality were the most up to date, but their replies were not promising.

'Most of the pastureland around here has been taken up,' Charles Conway, the chief surveyor, told them. 'Well out to at least three hundred miles.'

'I knew we'd be too late,' John groaned. 'Pastoralists have had nearly ten years to dig in.'

'It doesn't take long,' Charles said. 'The Archer brothers were first and they took up prime land, then came Ross and Birkbeck, and others, like the Carlisles out of Camelot. Then there are a few smaller stations like Airdrie and Oberon and Deeside. Your best bet is to head west, follow the Fitzroy until it meets up with the Isaac River.'

Paul was depressed. What a fool he was to think time would stand still for them. And how Pace would have laughed. Pace, who had ridden into virgin country time and again, and staked his claims well ahead of other land-seekers.

For the third time they called on William Wexford, the Lands Commissioner.

'It's a waste of time,' John complained. 'We'll just have to head out west. It'll be easier to buy a station out that way, since we seem to have been left at the post.'

'No,' Paul said.

'All right. Then there's no alternative. If you want a station we'll have to keep going north until we find unclaimed land. We'll peg out a run ourselves.'

'No. I want land here.'

'You're so bloody stubborn, Paul. No one is going to stand aside for you. We either move on or go home.'

Wexford was pleased to see them. 'I've got some news for you lads. Oberon Station is on the market.'

Paul was delighted. 'Oberon? Where's that?'

'About fifty miles north of the river. It cradles into the ranges. A fine property, too. Not a big spread – it's about forty square miles, so it's easily managed, and it's well run.'

'We'll go out there tomorrow,' Paul told him.

John was more cautious.

'Who owns it?'

'Angus Scott. He hails from Armidale, down your way.'

'Why does he want to sell?' John persisted.

'Ah well, that's what I have to tell you. His wife was never happy there. Her brother was killed in that massacre at Cullin-La Ringo out near Springsure. You would recall that terrible affair – nineteen whites were murdered by blacks.'

'Yes, I remember,' Paul said. 'But that's a long way from here.'

'Only a few hundred miles,' John murmured.

'The point is,' Wexford continued, 'that his wife got the willies after that. She was scared stiff of the blacks. And, as I am sure you are aware by this, there is no shortage of blacks in this neck of the woods. The Darambal tribes can get rather nasty at times. Anyway, Louisa couldn't stand the worry. She took the kids and upped and left. Angus has been hoping she'd come back, but not her. She has been insisting he sell up and he's finally agreed.'

'Is it really dangerous?' John asked.

'Depends what you call dangerous. The blacks are a problem from Capricorn on, but people learn to cope.'

'If you treat them right there shouldn't be any trouble,' John said.

Wexford shook his head. 'No tribes will allow the peaceful occupation of their country.'

The brothers were silent, avoiding each other's eyes, reminded once more of their father, who had believed in peace, and had died fighting.

On the way back to their hotel John warned Paul, 'If you do decide to buy Oberon you'd better not mention the blacks to Jeannie. She hates them.'

But Paul had made up his mind. 'We'll have a good look at the property and if the price is right I'll take out an option on it. Then I'll

38

talk to Jeannie and let her know exactly what we're getting into. I couldn't bring her up here without giving her the full story. It has to be her decision as well as mine.'

Jeannie was so excited about Oberon Station, and being mistress of her own homestead, that she threw her arms around Paul. 'I knew you'd find a place. And a going concern too! It's wonderful. I was worried that you'd end up marking out a new run at the back of nowhere and I'd have to wait until a house was built. But Oberon! It sounds too good to be true.'

'Maybe it is,' Paul warned. 'Come and sit down, I haven't given you the full story yet. So far I've only taken out an option on the property.'

'What? Oh you fool! Why didn't you grab it? What if someone else offers him more money?'

'Just hear me out,' he said. He explained that the blacks in the area were a serious problem, that the Darambal tribes were not prepared to give up their land without a fight.

'Their land? What a joke. They don't have land. Blacks are an itinerant lot, they never settle anywhere.'

'Their territory, then.' He brushed a strand of hair from her face. 'Jeannie, the Aborigines up there can be dangerous, you have to understand this.'

'John said there are other stations established around Rockhampton and families are in residence. Why is Oberon so different?'

'It's not. Angus said he's had a few visits from some wild blacks waving spears and making a bit of a ruckus, but nothing serious.'

'Then what's the problem?'

'Stations have been attacked. Lone riders have been killed. A lot of people have died on both sides, black and white, and no one can say when the trouble will end.'

She frowned. 'I can't make you out. You want this station and now you're trying to talk me out of coming with you.'

'Oh, for Christ's sake, I'm not doing that. I won't buy the place unless you are sure you want to live there. Angus Scott's wife was too frightened to stay . . .'

'And you think I'm a coward like her? Well, let me tell you, plenty of women live in the north. I wouldn't let a bunch of dirty blacks scare me off. They come anywhere near me, they'll get a dose of lead. They won't come back in a hurry.'

'I hope that won't be necessary. I intend to make peace with them if I can. Giving them food is a much better way to stop the fighting than provoking them.'

Jeannie relented. 'I suppose you're right.' But later she smiled to herself. It was better to agree with him than have him turn down the station. John had said it was a superb property and the town of Rockhampton was shaping up to be a very pretty riverside town. And Oberon, strangely enough, was more accessible than Kooramin. It was a long, hard ride over the mountains to Sydney from this station, but Oberon was only a couple of days from Rockhampton. From there they could take a coastal steamer to Brisbane or Sydney. Jeannie had a sister in Brisbane, she could come to visit with less trouble than it took to get right out here to Kooramin.

She hugged herself. She was just dying to see her new home. At last she would be able to furnish a place the way she wanted it, not live surrounded by someone else's trappings. Her house would be beautiful. She would have the best of everything. Paul could afford it, the MacNamaras were a wealthy family. Their widowed mother, Dolour, had remarried after the death of her husband, this time to a super-rich grazier based in the Hunter Valley. When the old folks passed on, each one of the three MacNamara sons would be worth a mint.

As for Paul and his worries about the blacks, best to humour him for the time being. Jeannie had no intention of encouraging blacks, tame or not, around her house. Paul lived in a dream world. Jeannie knew her father was right; the only good Abo was a dead one. She was a crack shot, she could defend herself the same as any other woman on an outback station, so they wouldn't want to be bothering her. Besides, Paul and his stockmen were always armed, they'd see that the blacks kept their distance.

She hurried out to make sure that Paul wrote to Angus Scott right away to take up that option. If he missed out on Oberon she'd never forgive him.

Chapter Three

Had the two girls known of Paul MacNamara's movements that day they'd have turned the smart little coach about and gone right back to Beauview, because that was where he was headed.

Not that he hadn't considered returning to the hotel for lunch after visiting his old friend William Wexford. And then he corrected himself. Not for lunch. He could get a bite to eat anywhere. He just wanted to see that girl again, the one with the merry smile and flirty eyes. Miss Maskey. Even now he was tempted to turn back. There was something about her, as if he'd known her for years. Or maybe he'd found her so darned attractive that he imagined that. Whatever it was, he knew it would be a mistake to go back. He'd been thinking of her ever since they'd met, unable to dismiss her, wanting to see her again. To talk to her.

As a single man he'd have been there on the dot, waiting for her. But he was not single and that was the end of it.

Resolutely he turned the horse up the hill towards Beauview. It was important that he had a few straight words with Boyd Roberts.

He rode up the long, curved drive, appreciating that the landscaper had shown the sense to reject a straight path up the hill so as not to tire the horses hauling vehicles. The grounds, he had to admit, were superb. Wide stretches of lawns were shaded by palms, and tropical blooms glowed on exotic trees. The house was much bigger than he expected, a high-set timber building, painted white to reflect the heat, with pretty juliet verandas jutting out over the lawns. White lattice-work gave them privacy and a cool, gentle air. The place irritated him. How could a bastard like Roberts have built such a lovely house? It seemed a contradiction.

A maid took him through the lobby, across polished cedar floors to a cool, dim parlour and as his eyes became accustomed to the gloom he took in the opulence of the fellow's house – the deep armchairs of soft leather, brocade drapes sewn with gold thread, side tables inlaid with mother-of-pearl. Imported rugs were soft underfoot and lamps twinkled crystal. He was tempted to ping one with a fingernail but decided against it just in time.

Boyd Roberts strode in, looking very suave in fine wool trousers and an expensive white shirt open at the neck. 'Mr MacNamara?' he asked, extending his hand, and Paul shook it, feeling that it would be churlish to refuse. 'Would you care for a drink? I'm having a whisky.'

'No, thank you.'

Roberts poured a whisky from a decanter and held up a crystal glass. 'Water, then?'

'No, thank you. I came here to talk to you about your men.'

Roberts seemed not to hear him. 'Have a seat, it's just as easy to talk sitting down.' He ushered Paul into one of the armchairs which wheezed luxuriously as he sank into it. The leather was cold, relaxing. Then he pulled over an occasional chair and draped himself on it, one arm hooked lazily over the high back. Standing, Paul was taller than Roberts but now his host looked down on him. He felt like a small boy being towered over by an elder.

'Now what about my men?' Roberts lit a cigar.

'I'm the owner of Oberon Station,' Paul began.

Roberts interrupted him. 'I'm aware of that. A pretty little property it is too.'

'And I'm aware of that,' Paul retaliated. 'So I don't need those louts of yours trespassing on my land.'

'I presume you mean prospectors acting on my behalf.'

'If they were decent people I wouldn't mind, but they're not. They're thugs and you know it. They've beaten up other prospectors, caused fights with my men, killed my cattle, and now I hear they're antagonising the blacks.'

Roberts all but yawned. 'What a tale of woe! And who are your men? Prospectors too, I don't doubt. No wonder they clash.'

'They are not prospectors, they're stockmen. And at least you admit there are clashes on my land.'

'I'll admit no such thing. I am giving you the courtesy of accepting what you say as truth, though no doubt exaggerated. The miners in my employ are simply going about their legal business. You can't expect them to have drawing-room manners.'

Paul pushed himself up out of the armchair. 'I expect them to obey the law. I expect you to instruct them to do just that or fire them. And it isn't just my property, they're causing trouble on other stations in the locality, too.'

'Is that so? Strange that I haven't had any other complaints.'

'You haven't had any other complaints? What about Jock McCann? He complained to you, and a few weeks later he was bashed up by your men. We've got all their names, Roberts, and we'll be watching them from now on. They'd better not try anything like that with me or I'll use my legal rights and put a bullet in anyone who tries to stand over me.'

Roberts stubbed out his cigar and strode over to pour himself another drink, waving the decanter at Paul. 'Sure you won't change your mind?'

Paul's mouth was dry, and he would have loved a drink, but he had to refuse. It was obvious now that asking Roberts to control his men was a waste of time.

'I don't know anything about McCann,' Roberts said, eyeing Paul slyly, 'except that he suffered an accident on his property, broke his leg . . .'

'They broke his leg,' Paul corrected.

'He broke his leg,' Roberts continued calmly. 'And he's having a devil of a time with it. Won't seem to mend, Doctor Forbes tells me. Chalky bones. Some people have chalky bones, you know, disastrous if there's a break.' He walked over to the window to peer out. 'The grounds look magnificent after the rains. I employed a Sydney fellow to landscape them for me. Best in the country, they say.'

'You're lying,' Paul said flatly. 'McCann told me he came here. All I'm asking of you is common decency. If you will not order your men to behave, then I can't draw any other conclusion than that they are following orders.'

'I would have thought you had better manners than to walk into a man's house and call him a liar.'

'What else can I think? We have enough problems out there without this. For the life of me I can't understand why you can't or won't control those bastards.'

'That's your word, MacNamara.' His eyes glittered from his silhouette against the sharp light outside, and Paul was reminded of a snake in his gloomy nest. 'From my point of view they're simply hard-working souls trying to do their best.'

'Bloody rubbish,' Paul retorted. He picked up his hat. 'All right. If you won't talk sense, then I'm banning your blokes from Oberon. You don't need to worry, I'll tell them myself at the point of a gun. And I have a good legal reason to do so. Jock McCann will back me up.'

Roberts walked with him to the front door, not at all put out by Paul's threat. 'I doubt you can call on Mr McCann for help. Didn't you know he has sold out?'

Paul stared. 'He has what?'

'Yes, the leg, you see. He couldn't carry on. I made him an excellent offer and he accepted.'

'You bought his property?' Paul was thunderstruck.

'Yes. Poor fellow was greatly relieved.'

'But why? What do you want with a cattle station?' Unable to stop himself, Paul looked about at the house, the proof of Roberts' wealth.

'Assets, sir. When the gold runs out I'll need to be prepared. Don't trust the banks, land's the answer. And I've become quite fond of the Rockhampton surrounds since I decided it was time we got rid of old Maskey. I intend to be the next Member of Parliament for this district. One establishes one's credentials by displaying confidence in the area, so I am investing here to quite a large extent.'

Paul jammed his hat on his head. 'Good luck to you, then,' he snapped. 'But don't expect my vote.'

43

'I don't. I should like to buy Oberon Station. You name your price, take the money and go. Your troubles will all be over.'

'Is that a threat?'

Roberts feigned surprise. 'Of course not. I'm simply bidding for your property.'

'It'll be a cold day in hell,' Paul shouted at him as he marched down the wide front steps.

To placate her parents, Laura wore the dress her mother had bought for her in Sydney. It was a fussy yellow voile with a wide satin sash, and it belied its cool appearance. The bodice fastened right through to the neckline and on to a stiffened choker collar. To make matters worse it was lined with heavy yellow satin, even the sleeves, and all that material required a starched calico petticoat to make the skirt stand out. As she buttoned the tight cuffs Laura felt hot already. And dreary, as if robbed of her self. The colour did not suit her and she knew it, not with her fair hair and suntanned face. It was the sort of dress that Amelia, her opposite in colouring and style, would love.

'Today, though,' she told the mirror, 'we play the dutiful daughter and I'll look as wishy-washy as all the rest in their Sunday best.'

She was at the door with her parents as the first guests arrived, and soon there was such a crush in the house that Leon set up a refreshment table for gentlemen in the side garden. Elderly people preferred the veranda and the parlour was awash with pale shades as giggling girls gathered to gossip and eye the door, watching gentlemen pass by. Their mothers sat in state at the far end of the room, fans beating incessantly like trapped birds. Laura took her time stopping to address each one, willing herself not to be among the doorwatchers but hoping that Mr MacNamara would appear.

Determined not to give the gossips any more cause to criticise her, Laura mingled quietly until Amelia arrived. Breaking with tradition, as usual, Amelia stood out in a glossy green taffeta, cut low in the front. Her dark hair was swept up and pinned under a perky little green hat. She extended a gloved hand to Laura: 'My dear! What a roll-up! Half the town's here!'

'Your father didn't mind you coming?'

'I told you. He doesn't mind what I do. He was highly amused at your father giving away sovereigns.'

'That was my idea,' Laura replied defensively.

'Oh really? Well, it certainly worked. Now tell me – did you invite Mr MacNamara?'

Laura shot her a glance of caution. 'Yes.'

'Is he here?'

'I don't think so.'

'Not again! You'll have to forget about him. Obviously he doesn't reciprocate.'

'There's nothing to reciprocate.'

'Not much. I've never seen you so captivated by anyone before.'

'I am not.'

'Whatever you say. It's hot in here with all these hens – let's go outside.'

Laura saw her mother beckoning. 'I can't, not now. You go out to the veranda, I'll see you later.'

'Your father wants you,' Hilda said. 'He's in the study. And on your way tell Cook we need more scones in the drawing room. And tea.' She mopped her face with her handkerchief. 'I'll never forgive your father for inflicting this on me. It's impossible to cater in this crush.'

Fowler greeted her with an unusual display of affection. 'Ah, my dear. Come on in.'

Bobby Cope, drink in hand, was standing by her father's desk, grinning owlishly. Laura thought he looked tipsy already, but maybe not.

She listened mute, stunned, as her father told her that Captain Cope had asked for her hand in marriage, and had received his approval. 'You're a very fortunate girl,' Fowler enthused. 'I foresee a long and happy life together for you young people.'

'I'm the fortunate one,' Cope said. 'I'm extremely fond of Laura, have been from the first day I saw her.' He moved over to Laura's side. 'I was almost tempted to ask you yesterday, at lunch,' he said to her. 'You looked so wonderful . . .'

'What lunch?' Fowler asked suspiciously.

'At the Criterion,' Bobby told him, anxious to please. 'Just as well I came along, Boyd Roberts didn't arrive . . .'

'You were meeting Boyd Roberts?' Fowler asked her angrily.

'I was with Amelia,' she replied flatly.

'Don't put on that bored voice with me, my girl. I won't have you associating with Roberts.' He turned to Cope. 'And I expect you to see to it.'

'Of course,' Cope said, accepting his role.

Laura just stood there, unable to grasp this ridiculous situation, as Fowler dismissed them. 'Now run along, the pair of you. We'll announce the engagement at an official function. I'll have to check my diary. Right now I have important guests waiting for me in the drawing room. You go and help your mother, Laura.'

She laughed as Fowler rushed away.

'What's so funny?' Bobby asked.

'You've just found out we're not important.'

'I hardly think so. He didn't mean it that way. I admire your father, really I do.'

'Then you'll have to learn not to take any notice of him. I'm the one you have to listen to. I am flattered by your proposal, Bobby, but I can't accept.'

It was his turn to be taken aback, but he soon recovered. 'Don't be silly. Of course you can. Give it time, you'll get used to the idea. Your father has given his blessing, Laura, I almost felt that it was his idea.'

'And it probably was.' She saw him glance at himself in a wall mirror, smoothing the ends of his thick moustache, congratulating himself, and that annoyed her even more, but she tried to be patient. 'Bobby, just forget the whole thing.'

'You don't seem to understand that I love you. I want you to be my wife, and you will be, you'll see.'

Laura fled to the kitchen where she bailed up her mother. 'Do you know what Father has done?'

The harried servants looked up, interested by her tone of voice.

'Yes, and you should be very happy,' Mrs Maskey said, arranging thin sandwiches on a platter.

'I am not happy. I am furious! Who does he think he is? Ordering my life around!'

'Not now, dear,' Hilda said. She called to one of the maids. 'This tray goes into the drawing room and the other one to the parlour. And bring back the empty cups.'

Rather than face anyone outside, Laura remained in the kitchen helping the staff, refusing to accept that she could be forced into marriage with Bobby Cope. 'They can't make me,' she said.

Cook looked at her. 'Make you do what, Laura?'

'Nothing,' she said. 'It's nothing.'

All roads, it seemed, led to Fowler Maskey's house this sultry afternoon. The hotel was closed, as usual on a Sunday, until teatime, but it might as well have shut down, Paul mused, since there had been a general exodus after the noon meal, staff and guests alike scooting off along Quay Street.

He stood and stared moodily at the gate, looking out over the river, cross with himself for wasting this day. He should have gone fishing, as he had previously intended to do, but he'd procrastinated, the invitation to Maskey's afternoon bash sitting idly on the dresser in his room. It was unlike him not to be able to make decisions and that had him in a state of mild confusion. Even though he disapproved of Maskey's call for a new state, Paul believed he should support the present incumbent rather than help to clear the way for that bastard Roberts to become Member for Rockhampton.

His meeting with Roberts still rankled. The man was an out-and-out crook. A standover merchant! There was no chance of Roberts getting his hands on Oberon – that didn't really bother Paul – but discovering that Boyd Roberts was very popular in the town had been a shock. Last night in the bar he'd almost got into a fight with staunch supporters of Roberts who resented his criticisms of the man. No one would believe that such an affable gentleman would engage in such tactics.

Paul smiled grimly. And that, of course, he realised now, was why Roberts had been so candid with him. Townspeople were simply not concerned with events out on the stations unless they were of the spectacular kind, like attacks by blacks. Miners appreciated Roberts' success, they saw his career as the pinnacle of their own hopes and dreams. And, as with Fowler Maskey, they hung on his coat-tails, awed by the wealth of these men.

A butcher bird sang from a far tree, clear notes heralding finer weather, hopefully the end of the wet season, and as the three rich notes, tone-perfect, rang out again Paul walked back up the path to the hotel. It's not just politics, he admitted to himself, it's that girl, Maskey's daughter. She had him glued to this lonely spot, unable to make up his mind what to do with the afternoon. He couldn't go to Maskey's house because he didn't want to meet her again. Wrong. He did want to see her again, there was an ache in him for her, so there was a damn good reason to stay away.

The veranda was deserted. He ambled disconsolately past a row of deckchairs and on towards the two large cane chairs that held pride of place at the far end. Everything was so quiet, except for a clump of bamboos nearby that shifted nervously, their mild clatter like familiar voices.

He stared at the chairs and grinned. The ladies who sat out here had a strict pecking order, and Grace Carlisle, matriarch of the big Camelot Station, occupied the lead position of late.

Bored with his own company, he raised his hat mischievously to the empty chair. 'Good afternoon, Mrs Carlisle. How are you today?'

As he turned to walk back, a voice from one of the open French windows replied, 'I'm very well, thank you.'

Paul stiffened, embarrassed. He knew the voice. Why the hell had he done that?

'Do you usually talk to chairs?' she asked him as she stepped out on to the veranda. 'Or have you had one too many?'

'Neither,' he laughed. 'Just making polite conversation.'

'With my ghost, I presume.' She was wearing a loose silk kimono over a sturdy black dress, and her thick white hair was caught up in a pink net.

'I'm sorry,' he said. 'Did I disturb you?'

'No, it's time I got myself moving. You're young MacNamara, aren't you?

'Yes, ma'am. Paul MacNamara.'

'Ah yes. Oberon Station. How are you doing there?'

'Pretty good. It's great country.'

'Yes, but don't let all this green fool you. We can still get nasty droughts up this way.'

'I'm building some dams against the possibility. I saw enough of droughts in New South Wales. But you can't do much when the pastures turn to dust.'

47

'That's a fact,' she replied. 'Let's hope we have good years ahead. Where's your wife?'

'She's visiting her sister in Brisbane. Due back in a couple of days. I'm waiting to take her home.'

Mrs Carlisle nodded. 'Have you had any trouble with the blacks out there?'

'None to speak of. The mob on our property seem quiet enough. They keep their distance – hang about on the northern boundary. And I've had a few visits from strangers from time to time, but they seem content to back off with a sugarbag of tucker.'

This wasn't quite true. His wife preferred to chase them off with rifle shots. A bone of contention between them. Jeannie claimed that feeding them only made them cheekier, refusing to accept that quite a few of the poor fellows looked half-starved.

Grace Carlisle slipped the net from her hair as she contemplated the subject. 'It's damned hard to know what to do for the best. Feed them or fight them.'

'I prefer to feed them.'

'Good for you. But like the land itself, you never know when they'll turn on you. We've tried every which way and we still get trouble.'

'If our blokes would stop hunting them we'd have less trouble.'

'Probably, but it's hard to restrain our men when families are killed in raids by the blacks.' She sighed. 'The hatred on both sides is too strong to contain.'

'I disagree. We, as civilised people, should set the example.'

'Turn the other cheek? My dear, I hope you're never put to the test.'

He wanted to say to her that the MacNamaras had already been put to the test. None of them had considered revenge when Pace had been killed by northern tribesmen, even when some of their neighbours were clamouring for troopers to be sent up there. He remembered his mother's words. 'An eye for an eye? I'll have none of it. We left that behind in Ireland. Pace knew the risks.' But these were thoughts he couldn't put into words now without sounding like a preacher.

Mrs Carlisle, however, seemed to have lost interest in their conversation. She was watching people strolling past the hotel back towards the town. 'Looks like Fowler Maskey's guests are retreating from the fray. Why aren't you up there?'

He shrugged as if he hadn't given it a thought.

'It might be interesting to take a look now.' She smiled. 'I always like to know what Fowler is up to. The man is an absolute rogue, of course, but not in the same class of villainy as that other contender for the seat.'

'I'll go along with you on that,' he growled.

'Then perhaps you would care to escort me, Mr MacNamara?'

'By all means,' he replied, with a calm that he did not feel.

As he waited for her to 'tidy up', as she put it, he smiled wryly at his

48

own weakness. 'You didn't need to be pushed – you jumped,' he accused himself. 'Handed this convenient excuse, you can't get there fast enough. What a fake you are.'

He wondered if he'd have a chance to talk to her again. To Miss Maskey, this girl who had made such an impact on him that he was in danger of forgetting his wife. What strange creatures we are, he thought, realising that his attraction to Miss Maskey was so strong that he was nervous now, like a star-struck kid.

When Mrs Carlisle emerged, still in the black dress but wearing a very large black hat decorated with silk flowers, he felt more at ease, having convinced himself that Miss Maskey would probably have forgotten him by this. After all, the girl had just been polite, nothing else. He noticed that Mrs Carlisle had added a glittering diamond brooch to her costume and was pulling gloves over some spectacular rings. War paint, he thought in an odd aside, civilised or savage we all have to put on war paint of some sort.

Fowler Maskey didn't recognise him, nor did Leon; they were too busy fussing over Grace Carlisle. And overdoing it, Paul thought as he picked up the cynical glint in her eyes.

They were ushered through departing crowds at the front door, past the noisy parlour and on into a large drawing room where personages and special friends were assembled. There the door was closed firmly behind them to shut out nonentities.

A flushed Hilda Maskey was summoned, her face red from heat and exertion, to pay her respects to Grace Carlisle, and she in turn called on the maids to bring cold water, hot tea and fresh cakes.

Settled comfortably in a firm wing chair, with Paul standing respectfully behind her, Mrs Carlisle addressed her host: 'I hope you have kept one of those souvenir sovereigns for me, Fowler.'

Paul smothered a laugh, knowing that this formidable old woman was the last person who would want a free sovereign, but Fowler, in his serious world of self, was unable to discern any humour.

'My dear, need you ask?' he replied magnanimously. 'Leon, get a souvenir for Mrs Carlisle.'

'I'm sorry, Father, they're all gone,' he replied.

'Then find one,' Fowler muttered through clenched teeth, and Leon hurried away.

'And how are things at Camelot?' he asked her as he pulled over a chair and gave her his full attention, wasting none on her companion.

Paul helped himself to tea, polished off some buttered date scones and returned to Mrs Carlisle's side as several people drifted over to speak to her. She was obviously accustomed to holding court.

The room was stuffy, made worse by the smell of camphor emanating from men's suits and ladies' voluminous dresses recently released from camphor chests. He was relieved when Grace Carlisle tugged at his sleeve. 'You don't have to stand there like a guardsman,' she whispered when he bent over her. 'You'll find that the gentlemen usually take refreshments out in the side garden under the jacaranda tree.'

Not needing a second bidding, Paul slipped quietly away and made for the front door, where he bumped into Miss Maskey herself.

She looked flustered but made an attempt to be cheerful. 'Why! Mr MacNamara! I didn't know you were here.'

'I came with Mrs Carlisle,' he said, then peered at her. 'Are you all right?'

'Yes. Thank you. Excuse me, I really have to go.'

He stood back to allow her to pass, but she stopped abruptly and turned on her heel to face him. 'I usually go for a walk along the river bank at five o'clock. Why don't you join me?'

Her voice was strained and defiant. He didn't know what to make of her strange request but he managed to stammer, 'If you like,' before she rushed away.

'Good God!' he said, to no one in particular as he wandered around to the side garden. He was also aware that his reply had been about as gauche as possible, and he worried about a more polite response, but she'd caught him by surprise. For that matter he found the Maskey household strange too, with the guests divided into pens according to their worth, like sheep at a sale.

The tree was a rich green canopy shading a trestle table bar, and about thirty male guests were taking full advantage of the free liquor. The long damask tablecloths looked war-weary, stained by red wine like fresh blood and scattered with empty bottles. Several young men were lurching boisterously around the lawn, shouting inanities at each other, and another youth, propped up against a lawn-roller, was snoring fitfully.

Paul recognised Bobby Cope at the centre of a group who appeared to be celebrating rather than enjoying an afternoon drink, but he stayed clear. He had no time for Captain Cope and his mates. Instead, he poured himself a rum to which he added some ginger beer.

Leon Maskey came out of a side door, took in the scene and with a shrug walked over to Paul. 'Mind if I join you? I hate these shows.'

'Be my guest,' Paul laughed, and watched as Leon, disgusted, righted half-empty bottles and poured himself a whisky.

'Where's the barman got to?' he asked Paul.

'I've no idea. But your guests seem to be making the best of it.'

'Drunken sods!' He looked moodily about and then turned to Paul. 'I'm afraid I've forgotten your name.'

'MacNamara. Paul MacNamara.'

'Oh yes. You're with Mrs Carlisle. Last I heard she was giving Father a dressing-down for backing separation.'

'She's right,' Paul said. 'And did you manage to find her a sovereign?'

50

'Oh, that. Yes. I had to buy one from a fellow, had to pay him double its worth, the crook.'

Paul made a mental note to tell Grace Carlisle. She'd appreciate the joke. 'What's going on over there?' he asked. 'What's Cope looking so pleased about? Has he executed another daring raid on unarmed blacks?'

Leon flashed a curious glance at him and for a second he reminded Paul of Laura, but then his face became expressionless again, as if he were trained not to have an opinion. He gulped his whisky. 'In answer to your question,' he said in a bored tone, 'our Captain has been up to something far more daring. He asked for my sister's hand in marriage, was granted the honour by grateful parents and was promised that a substantial dowry would be forthcoming.'

'Which sister?'

'I've only got one.'

'He's going to marry *Laura*?'

'Correct.'

'I see,' Paul said quietly. 'I met her a little while ago and wondered why she looked so happy.'

Leon missed the irony in his voice. 'Laura looked happy? Well I'll be damned! I've been expecting the roof to fall in all afternoon.'

Laura worked. She swept through the ground floor rooms, cleaning and tidying with a vigour that surprised the servants, who'd never before seen her show any inclination towards domesticity. She felt she had to keep moving to ward off the panic that was threatening to engulf her.

Bobby Cope was among the last to leave, and she allowed him to give her a peck on the cheek rather than make a scene in front of the remaining guests. That left her feeling even more humiliated. She had always seen herself as a free spirit, able to do as she pleased within her own rules of propriety, but now she realised all that was fanciful. The pipe dreams of an adolescent. Now faced head-on with Fowler's implacable decision, her self-confidence eroded, she was afraid. This was the girl who had scoffed at her mother's weakness in dealing with Fowler, at Leon's subservience. Would she have the strength to defy him, and if so, what was to become of her?

As if he'd overheard her thoughts, Fowler tapped her on the shoulder. 'Captain Cope told me on the quiet that you don't seem to be too enthusiastic about this marriage. But I told him that's poppycock, your usual contrary carrying-on.'

'It isn't. I don't wish to marry him.'

'What you want and what you'll do are two different matters, my girl.' His bulk towered over her and she set her shoulders so as not to appear to wilt before him.

'This is my household,' he said, lowering his voice so that the maids couldn't hear, 'and while you are here you will obey me. You will live in the lap of luxury and when you marry Cope you will continue to do so, I'll see to that. No daughter could ask for more. But if you defy me you're out on your ear. Is that clear?'

'You're going to cut me off without the proverbial penny?' she flashed back at him in an attempt at confrontation.

He merely laughed at her. 'I couldn't have put it better myself. Just so long as you know where you stand.'

Working without an apron, she'd spilled tea slops on the dreary yellow dress and that gave her a small pleasure. She threw it on the floor as if discarding authority, took a cool bath and changed into a plain white blouse and navy skirt, buckling on a soft kid belt.

The house was quiet. Leon was nowhere to be seen, her mother was lying down and her father had retreated with Carter Franklin and a bottle of whisky to the cool of the fernery at the rear of the house. Laura hurried to get out of the place, away from them. The afternoon had been turmoil but she did remember that mad impulse to invite Mr MacNamara to walk with her. And she was pleased now that she had. Whether he came or not didn't really matter, she told herself, it just made her feel better that he might. That she had given herself a chance to defy her parents.

'There's hope for you yet,' she said to herself as she crossed the road. 'If you keep on defying them they could give in.'

She sat on a bench for a long while, feeling quieter now as she watched the tranquil river moving out to sea, and a family of black swans riding peacefully at the water's edge.

Lost in her reveries, she was started when he did appear.

'So there you are,' she said. 'I'd just about given up on you.' She was so distracted, she forgot that this man was a virtual stranger. For hadn't he lodged in her thoughts all week? A constant companion. He seemed like an old friend, and right now she needed a friend.

'I wasn't sure you meant it,' he replied. He had discarded his jacket and was wearing an open-necked shirt with the sleeves rolled up, revealing strong, sinewy arms.

A real bushie, she thought, long and lean and not as good-looking as I remembered him, but he still has those big brown eyes . . .

'Do you want to walk?' he asked her, bringing her back to earth, and she jumped up, glancing nervously over her shoulder.

'Yes,' she said. 'I have to get away from here for a while.'

'Right. Then we'd better go this way . . . away from town.' He didn't offer to take her arm as they followed the uneven track along the river bank, nor did he intrude by making conversation, and she was grateful because suddenly she could feel tears stinging her eyes and she was afraid they might spill over.

He pulled aside the wiry branches of casuarina trees to allow her to pass and she felt comfortable with this genial person, comfortable enough now to be able to make an effort to talk; she had, after all, issued the invitation. 'I'm sorry, Mr MacNamara. I'm not much company, am I?'

He turned to smile at her. 'I wouldn't say that. I'm enjoying the walk. Have a look there. Someone has put some crab pots in the water. If I weren't on my best behaviour I might be tempted to grab a fat mud crab on the way back. It'd go well with a couple of beers.'

Still finding it difficult to cheer up, she picked up on his words. 'So you're on your best behaviour today?'

'My dear Miss Maskey, I sure am.'

'Call me Laura.'

'Only if I'm Paul.'

'Righto. Paul. Why are you on your best behaviour?'

He handed her down the bank to a sandy stretch. 'Because if any-one spots us, that hive of gossip back there will have a right royal time.'

'Why? Is it a crime for two people to go for a walk now?'

'Depends which two.' He took a stick and began dislodging oyster shells from a rock.

She sat on a low grassy knoll to watch. 'Any luck?' she asked.

He shook his head. 'No, they're too old. Looks like the Abos cleaned this spot out ages ago.'

'So what's wrong with these two taking the air?' she persisted.

He dropped the stick and came over to sit beside her. 'Well . . . for a start, as of today, I hear you are betrothed.'

'Oh. You know about that?'

'Yes. Added to which, an engaged lady strolling out with a married man is the sort of thing guaranteed to give Rockhampton a seizure.'

He was married!

Laura froze. This time she'd really done it. She'd made an absolute ass of herself. Since the ground wouldn't swallow her, she tried bravado. 'I don't care.'

'You should,' he said gently.

'Then why didn't you tell me you were married?'

'I didn't have a chance. Maybe I thought you knew. Anyway I'm telling you now.'

'Well, where's your wife?' she asked angrily.

'She has been down south. I'm expecting her back on the next boat.'

There was silence. They both stared at the river as if they'd never seen it before until Paul spoke. 'Truth time. I'm sorry to have given you the wrong impression. But I wanted to come anyway.'

'Why?' she asked, feeling dull now and even more depressed.

He considered this, and finally replied, 'Let's say I can give you half an answer. You looked so upset earlier on I thought maybe I could help somehow, and then I thought it was none of my business. And then I figured you might be expecting me . . .' He stopped and grinned at her. 'And have you noticed I'm not making any sense at all?'

'It doesn't matter. I'm glad you came.'

'And what about your engagement? Aren't girls supposed to be starry-eyed at this time?'

'I believe so,' she said, her voice tight, her expression as bleak as cold stone. 'But most girls have some choice. I haven't been given a choice. I was just informed that I am to marry Bobby Cope. Orders, you see.'

'And you don't want to marry him?'

'I can't stand him!'

'That's good to hear. I haven't got a lot of time for him either. Why don't you just explain that to your father? Maybe he doesn't realise what sort of a character Cope is.'

'He likes Captain Cope. He thinks he's doing a great job.'

Paul sighed. 'I think you're making a mountain out of a molehill here. If you don't want to marry Cope, then don't. They can't make you.'

Laura burst into tears. 'You don't know my father.'

He put an arm around her. 'Come on now. It's not as bad as all that. You just have to stick to your guns and keep saying no. Even Cope can't be that thick.'

'Don't you believe it. He's got a hide like a rhinoceros.'

He seemed to realise, all of a sudden, that he had overstepped the bounds of propriety in his sympathy for her. 'Sorry,' he said, withdrawing his arm. 'I shouldn't have done that.'

'Oh, why not?' she replied crankily. 'At least you're agreeing with me, even if you are married.'

He laughed, a deep, infectious laugh. 'That's the sort of Irish logic my mother uses. You remind me of her.'

Laura dabbed at her face with a handkerchief, the bout of tears receding. 'Do I look like her?'

'No. Dolour's a fiery redhead. And she invents the rules as she goes along. I think you do too.'

'Is that wrong?' Laura's question was almost a plea. She desperately needed some approval to restore her confidence.

'No, don't change. You're just right the way you are.'

The sun was glowering pink as it descended through a high bank of clouds. 'We're seeing the last of the wet season,' he remarked.

'About time,' she said wearily. 'I suppose I ought to be getting back.'

'What about your mother?' he asked. 'Wouldn't she put a stop to this?'

'Mother? Not likely. If he says "Jump" ' she asks "How high?" ' '

'I see.'

'No, you don't. Men can do what they like. Women get handed

around like dinner plates. But they're not going to do it to me.'

'So what happens next?'

She stood up and confronted him. 'What do you care? Is this just an interesting conversation you can relate to your wife when she comes home. Guess what? I met Fowler Maskey's daughter, you know, the MP, and she's a real misery . . .'

He took her by the shoulders and shook her. 'Stop it! I'm on your side. Remember?'

'I'm sorry,' she relented. 'I think I'm a bit hysterical.'

He was still holding her and he looked into her eyes with an intensity that seemed to storm right through her. 'We keep saying we're sorry to each other, so let's start again. I'm not sorry we're here. I wanted to see you again, just one more time. And now that I'm here, what would you say if I kissed you?'

'I'd say, "Mind your manners, you're a married man." '

'So it'll be worth it,' he smiled, 'just this once.' He took her face in his hands and kissed her softly.

'Maybe twice,' he whispered and Laura felt herself melting to him as he kissed her again and her arms crept around him.

Together with him, in his arms, sheltered by the overhang of trees, Laura experienced the first passion of her life. She exulted in the sweetness of his mouth, the smoothness of his skin and she knew she'd been right the first time she'd met him. This was the man for her. The knowledge only lent a bittersweet aura to those wonderful moments and she responded eagerly until he drew away.

'It's getting late. I'd better take you home.'

She could have gone on kissing him forever. That house in Quay Street had lost its importance, but he was walking back with her now, holding her hand. Reality was about to replace romance.

Finally, within sight of the town he stopped. 'I think this is where we have to say goodbye.'

'Goodbye?' she echoed.

'It has to be, Laura.'

'Didn't that mean anything to you?'

He kissed her again, on the forehead, and for the last time on the lips. 'It meant everything to me. Everything. From the first time I saw you.'

'Then why didn't you come to lunch with me the next day. Why have you wasted all this time?'

He shook his head. 'Because I had a feeling this would happen, and I knew I shouldn't let it.'

She thrust him away. 'So why now, for God's sake? Why the hell now? At the last minute! I care for you! What do you think of that? And I don't even mind saying so, because in a few minutes you'll be gone out of my life. And then I'll have to forget you. In time I probably won't even remember your name.'

'My God,' he said. 'You're just as prickly as my mother, too. But listen to me. If it's any consolation, I feel the same as you do. But it's all wrong.'

'Then go,' she said miserably, even though his words had excited her. Just my bad luck as usual, she thought, to find him and then find him married.

He began to walk away, then turned back. 'Oh cripes,' he said. 'It's not all that easy. What are you doing tomorrow?'

'I ride in the mornings.'

'What time?'

'About seven o'clock. Before it gets too hot.'

'Then ride out past the sawmill. There's a track turns off to the south, I'll meet you at the corner.'

'Which way is south? Left or right?'

'Do you know the shepherd's hut on the hill?'

'Yes.'

'Well stay on that side.' He hesitated. 'And if you change your mind, don't worry. I'll understand.'

He caught up with her past the sawmill. She looked a picture in a plum-coloured outfit and she was riding side-saddle with the lovely grace that women seemed to be forgetting these days. A lot of country women now rode astride, including Jeannie, who claimed side-saddle was for cissies.

'You looking for anyone, miss?' he called as he cantered up beside her.

'Yes,' she said, looking coolly at him. 'I had to meet someone out by the old shepherd's hut, but you can ride along with me if you wish.'

'Good of you,' he laughed and they continued on together.

'I'm glad you found me,' she said at length. 'I lied. I haven't the faintest idea where your shepherd's hut is.'

'Then I'll show you.'

They dismounted at a row of eucalypts and he took her hand. 'Up there, see, on the side of the hill. That old stone building with the shingle roof.'

'I see.' She hitched her horse to a tree. 'What did they want shepherd's huts for anyway?'

'Someone tried to run sheep here, someone who had no idea what he was doing. But it was too wet for sheep and he couldn't find anyone mad enough to sit in a hut and watch sheep all day. It's never been lived in but there's a good view from up there. Do you want to go up?'

'We might as well.'

'Ah! We don't sound very enthusiastic this fine morning. Is it too steep a climb?'

'No.' She set off across the slippery slope, digging her polished boots into hardy tufts of grass for support, and he grinned as he followed her.

'Don't worry about me. I'll bring up the rear and catch you when you come tumbling down.'

Tumbling down, she echoed to herself as she climbed on, testing each foothold carefully. Everything seems to be tumbling down around me, and I don't know what I'm doing here anyway. I must be out of my mind. As if I'm not in enough trouble without encouraging a married man.

A tuft of grass came away from the damp ground and she slipped, but he caught her about the waist and heaved her on. 'How are things on the home front, Laura?'

'About as bad as they are here,' she retorted, angry with them both.

His reply was ambiguous. 'Never mind. We'll get there.' He skirted ahead of her and reached down, taking her hand. 'Come on, once we get to that rocky section it's easier. I should have realised with all the rain we've had that this hill would be like a slippery slide, and I can't have you breaking your leg on me.' He hauled her towards the crest of the hill and they made their way across a small plateau scattered with rocks.

'There now,' he said. 'It's a splendid view. Worth the effort.'

Laura nodded as they looked out over the town, feeling better now, as if she had managed to remove herself from that worrisome scene.

'Have you ever been up on Ironstone Mountain?' he asked.

'No.'

'I'll take you one day. My brother and I first saw the valley from there and it was a knockout. That was the day I made up my mind I wanted to live here.'

Laura stared at him. 'You're incredible! You'll take me up to Ironstone Mountain! When will this happen? Or will you bring your wife too?'

'Why not?' he laughed. 'And we'll bring Captain Cope as well.'

She turned on him. 'Why do you have to make a joke of everything?'

Paul walked a few steps to the edge of the plateau and looked down. 'Because I don't know what else to do,' he said quietly. 'I can't tell you my marriage is a misery. It's not. I can't say to you I intend to leave my wife, because I wouldn't do that. It's selfish of me, but I've only got this one day left in Rockhampton and I hoped we could enjoy a few hours together.'

'Have you got any children?' she asked, to avoid admitting her own part in this encounter.

'Not yet,' he replied. 'Do you want to go back?'

Laura looked up at him. 'No. I just want to stay here with you and forget that the rest of the world exists.'

They watched as a curtain of rain blotted out the far hills and moved swiftly across the valley towards them. 'We'd better shelter in the hut,' he said.

'Can we get in?'

'I think so. The door's missing.'

She was laughing as they ran for cover. Once inside, they stood at the window to observe the elements. Laura took out a handkerchief to clean the grimy glass as thunder rolled over them and flashes of lightning lit the gathering gloom. 'I love the rain,' she said. 'I love it when it really pelts down.'

'So do I,' he said, and kissed her.

While the storm swept over them and steaming mists clouded the open doorway Paul drew her to him, and in the safety of his arms Laura felt all of her worries melt away. He was kissing her, caressing her, but as their desire mounted he wavered and moved away, gently releasing her.

'What's wrong?' she asked, dismayed. 'Don't you care . . .'

But his smile reassured her. 'There's the trouble. We've too much caring here for our own good.'

Laura slipped her arms about his neck, nestling into him, her lips soft on his cheek, and whispered, 'You don't believe that.'

This time when her mouth met his it was with renewed fervour. They made love gently at first and then with a passion that enthralled her. She had never felt so cherished, and fearing that she would never experience such joy again, she clung to him as the rain eased and the skies began to clear.

'The storm's over,' he said and her eyes filled with tears. We are over, she thought, I have to say goodbye to him now. And back home the storm is only just beginning.

He assisted her down the muddy hill and they rode back towards the town. 'Will I see you again?' she asked him, and as he looked at her his soft brown eyes seemed to embrace her, to take such pleasure in just seeing her with him that Laura glowed, knowing she had broken through his resolve.

'I don't know . . . I hope so. I'll try to see you next time I come to town.'

'When will that be?'

'I can't honestly say. There'll be so much work on the station after the wet, but I'll be back.'

'Don't worry, I'll wait for you.'

He reached out and took her hand. 'You mustn't do that. You have to get on with your life.'

'Let me be the judge of that.'

'Neither of us can be accused of good judgement right now, my girl.' He reached for her horse and reined it towards him so that he could give her a peck on the cheek. 'You're so lovely . . .'

He seemed at a loss now, not knowing what to say to her, so Laura stirred her horse. 'I'd better go.'

Further down the road she turned to wave to him, and her heart sank. He already seemed a distant figure – a lone horseman back there in the shimmering heat like a mirage, unreal.

The next morning, Bobby Cope came to call, to tell her that he would be taking his men out on patrol for a few days. This good news was tempered when he produced a neat, single-stone diamond engagement ring.

'I'm sorry,' Laura told him, 'but I can't accept this, Bobby. I don't want to hurt your feelings but I did not agree to this engagement and I simply can't marry you.'

'Oh Laura, don't be foolish. Why not? We've always been friends. Your parents are happy, you'll be happy.'

She put the ring back in its box and snapped it shut. 'I don't love you, isn't that enough?'

'No, it's not. Your father shouldn't have sprung this on you like that. He said you can be contrary with him. I wish he'd let me speak to you myself.'

'I think you should have asked me first, not him.'

'It doesn't matter now.' He put the box on the table. 'I'll leave this with you. You need time to get used to the idea. I love you, I'm mad about you . . .' He reached out for her but she pulled away.

'Don't! If you're so keen to get married why don't you ask Amelia? She's keen on you.'

He was offended. 'I don't want Amelia, I'm in love with you. And I think deep down you really do care for me.'

She saw him glance at himself in the mirror again, and it occurred to her that he was more in love with himself than with her. That was why he could not accept this rejection – he did not believe her.

Just then her mother came into the room and smiled as Bobby put a strong arm around Laura, holding her to him. 'I was just leaving, Mrs Maskey. I have a busy time ahead of me.'

Angrily Laura released herself from his grip. He pretended not to notice, so she deliberately stood back and allowed her mother to escort him to the door.

'Goodbye, my dear,' he called to Laura, and left without waiting for a reply.

Hilda picked up the ring. 'Isn't it sweet? I like single settings.'

'Since when?' Laura asked. Every one of her mother's rings were very large and ornate.

'They're quite suitable for young girls. You ought to put it on.'

Laura was surprised at how calm she was now. 'I'm not putting it on and I'm not marrying Bobby Cope.'

'You told him that?'

'Yes.'

'Didn't look like it to me.' She sniffed. 'He seemed very happy. You'll settle down, the prospect of marriage takes a bit of getting used to, that's all. We'll make the formal announcement when the Captain returns.'

Laura shrugged. 'No one's listening to me. If you all want to make fools of yourselves, go ahead.'

★ ★ ★

Fowler Maskey was a politician whose overriding concern was for his seat, by which he meant his personal position in society. No one else in the Maskey family had even aspired to such heights, and so, wealthy though they might be, and rather snobbish to boot, Fowler was regarded with awe. He had brought the family name into prominence.

Losing his seat would be a disaster that he couldn't bear to contemplate, a frightful humiliation. There were times when he hated his constituents, one and all, because he was perpetually at their mercy. He didn't give a damn about their trivial complaints nor, for that matter, he mused, about this bloody town – whether it sank or swam. Except in the context of his electorate, his seat. It was of paramount importance to Fowler that it stayed afloat, that it didn't revert to a ghost town after the gold rush.

This morning, though, as he sat in his study checking his mail, his thoughts were on the State House in Brisbane. Trouble emanating from there could affect his faraway electorate, although he was not sure to what extent.

Fowler didn't understand monetary systems, or even how banks operated, except to honour his cheques which were drawn on the substantial Maskey accounts, structured and enriched under his brother William's management. The trouble was that Fowler, like so many of his colleagues in the parliamentary arena, thought he knew. He was convinced that he understood finance, and so, uninhibited by doubts, he often climbed ponderously to his feet and delivered orations on appropriation bills and amendments.

It had come as a shock to him to read in the *Brisbane Courier* that his speeches were all bluster and balderdash, with no content, and he had demanded that the reporter, Tyler Kemp, retract his lies. But Kemp had laughed at him. 'Don't come the bully with me, Maskey, I'm not one of your lackeys. If you had any idea what is really happening to the economy of this state you'd shut your big mouth for a change.'

One day, Fowler breathed to himself, recalling the humiliation of that moment, Kemp would pay for his insults, he'd see to it. Mild though the criticism was, in parliamentary terms, he still smarted at the assault on his dignity.

He was just as much in the dark now, faced with a telegram from Premier Macalister recalling Parliament. Admittedly, news had just come through that the British bank, Agra and Masterman, had failed, but why would that cause such a commotion? Fowler was aware that Queensland had borrowed from Agra and Masterman but there was no need to worry. They should simply turn to another bank. After all, he grinned to himself, our Treasury is only a borrower, not an investor.

His wife interrupted him. 'Fowler, I must talk to you about Laura.'

'What about her?' he replied crankily, not looking up from his desk.

'I don't think we should rush this marriage. It might look as if it's a shotgun affair.'

'Give it a couple of months then. I have to go down to Brisbane. Damned inconvenient, I had a number of important meetings arranged.'

'I suppose they'll have to be postponed,' she murmured. 'But Fowler, I'm worried about Laura.'

'What now?'

'She says she won't marry him.'

'She'll do as she's told. You can start organising the engagement party. It has to be the biggest and best ever seen in Rockhampton. I'll be in Brisbane for a while, but when I come back I want to know that plans are in hand. And I want everyone important invited. Especially all the station people. I need their support for a new state.'

'Where should we hold it? Here at home?'

'No. At the Golden Nugget Hotel. They've got room to put up marquees for extra space. And I want no expense spared, do you hear me?'

'Yes, dear. But perhaps you'd better speak to Laura yourself. Fortunately Captain Cope is away at the minute so he can't hear her complaints.'

'Cope is very popular in this district. He's doing what the white regiments should have done long ago, making this constituency safe for settlers. I don't want to hear her bleatings. You see to it that she behaves herself. Now, I've got work to do, kindly allow me to get on with it.'

'The boat's in,' Leon told him. 'It won't be sailing until four o'clock this afternoon so we've got plenty of time.'

'We? You will stay here and keep an eye on things. It's bad enough that Macalister is dragging me down there on the pretext of this trumped-up crisis. The bloody fool just likes wielding the whip.'

'I suppose he needs advice,' Leon said. 'The Government is in terrible trouble.'

'Tommyrot! It's not our fault if some English bank collapses.'

'Father, the State Treasury is going down the drain with it. I thought something was wrong when Premier Herbert started tightening the purse strings. The budget depended on the million-pound loan from the A and M Bank, and now that money doesn't exist.'

Fowler was silent for a while, trying to digest this. How could money not exist?

'I'm well aware of the situation,' he snapped, saving face. 'But I don't see what it has to do with me. It's Macalister's problem.'

'It will be everyone's problem, I fear,' Leon told him. 'If the Treasury is broke, then public works will come to a standstill, and a lot of workers will lose their jobs, from civil servants to labourers. It is quite possible that works like our new post office, for instance, will be closed down.'

'What?' Construction of an official post office had just begun in East Street and the residents were delighted. Fowler had claimed that he had been responsible for having the monies allocated for the building. If work ceased on it he'd look a fool.

'I have to hurry,' he said.

Jeannie MacNamara stepped from the boat tired and irritable. 'That damn captain ought to be horsewhipped,' she told her husband. 'There were three gins on board and he let them use our privy.'

'They could hardly sit over the rail,' he laughed.

'It's no laughing matter. He had no right to let them on board. I want you to report him. Look, there they are now!'

The way she spoke Paul expected to see three black whores stepping from the landing barge but instead the girls were dressed in neat cotton shifts and wore bright bandannas to hold their wiry hair in place. They stood barefoot on the wharf, eyes downcast, looking shy and nervous, obviously waiting to be claimed.

'God, Jeannie, they're servant girls, don't make such a fuss.'

'I might have known you'd say that . . .' she began.

He stopped her with a kiss on the cheek. 'Whoa! What happened to ' "Good morning, dear. I'm pleased to see you" '?

'Oh, well, I am. But these things upset me.'

'Where's Clara? Did you leave her behind?'

'No. I forgot my umbrella. She went back for it.' Clara Carmody was Jeannie's maid. True to her word, Jeannie had refused to employ Aborigine women in her household and had soon found Clara, a local girl, daughter of a miner, as live-in help. She was a quiet country girl of nineteen, a good cook and housemaid, and Paul had to admit that Jeannie was right. It was easier with a white servant who knew what she was doing, and more importantly Clara was company for Jeannie. The two of them got along very well.

'And how is your sister? And her family?'

'They're all well. Dave bought another furniture store – he runs that one and Kath runs the one in Charlotte Street. She's really smart, she knows that business backwards. And wait till you see what I've bought! A beautiful mahogany sideboard.'

'Oh no! Where are you going to put it?'

'In the parlour.'

'The parlour's got so much furniture in it now you almost need a plough to get a clear run through it.'

'I'll shift out the old sideboard, put it in the dining room.'

'We've already got one in the dining room.'

'That old thing. It can go in the shed until you build that new wing you've been promising me.'

Sometimes it seemed to Paul that they might be Kath Jackson's only customers. Everything in the house came from the Jackson store and he could see no end in sight to the cumbersome purchases that were shipped to Rockhampton and brought on by bullock team to Oberon. The old sideboard that Jeannie referred to had only been resident in their house for about a year. He groaned but made no further comment. He looked back down Quay Street with a quiver of guilt. This was not the time to be criticising his wife.

He brought the buggy around, packed in the women's luggage and helped them on board. 'I nearly forgot,' he told Jeannie. 'We won't have to stay at Cooper's Inn tonight. We've been invited to overnight at Camelot.'

'Really?' Jeannie was thrilled. 'How did this happen?'

'I met Grace Carlisle here in town. She invited us.'

'How marvellous! I wish I'd known, I'd have worn something better than this.'

'You look just fine.' And she did, he thought sadly. Jeannie was tall for a woman, and rather bony because she expended so much energy all the time, but she was strong and healthy. The holiday, though, had added some weight to her figure and she looked well for it.

He went back for his horse and caught up with them on the sandy road out of town.

'Where's my rifle?' she called to him.

'Here you are. Ammo's under the seat.'

She gave the reins to Clara, took the rifle, examined it carefully to make certain he'd kept it clean and then placed it in the leather sling attached to the buggy rail, at her right hand.

They crossed the river on the ferry barge and the women stood back as the ferrymen helped the horse and buggy up the slippery far bank. Then they headed north, Jeannie at ease driving the buggy and Paul riding ahead, well armed and constantly alert, his eyes searching the thick scrub for any signs of trouble.

It was a hard, hot day in Brisbane, the sky a sharp blue, and eucalypt trees cringed as they faced the sun without the respite of rain.

Fowler Maskey was perspiring freely in his white tropical suit, rivers of moisture gathering at his wide girth and soaking through the starched cotton. He strode along the wharf, waving his stick angrily at a departing horse-cab. There were no others to be seen. He took off his pith helmet and mopped his head, cursing the heat. Brisbane, like Rockhampton, was lodged in a river valley, and on days like this, he knew there was as much hope of catching a breeze as there would be in a bat-filled cave.

Other passengers stepping ashore from the coastal steamer were also looking about for transport, standing, bewildered, among mounds of luggage. But the wharves were strangely quiet. Even though several ships were lined up at this river port, the warehouses were closed, no labourers were toiling noisily with cargoes, there were no sailors staggering about, and no Chinese porters diving forward to earn their pennies. The usual hustle and bustle of the wharves had been transformed into an ominous tableau of inactivity.

Was it Sunday? he wondered, consulting his memory. No. It was well and truly Wednesday. So where were the workmen? The wharf labourers? Fowler was appalled at this dereliction of duty. He would certainly speak to the Premier about this state of affairs. People coming ashore from ships shouldn't find themselves stranded on deserted wharves. It was simply not good enough.

He noticed some ladies, with luggage piled around their skirts, looking hopefully towards him. Surely they could not expect a Member of Parliament to act as their porter? To escape their unspoken request he picked up his suitcase and marched busily along the quay until he was able to disappear into a lane beside the Customs House and make his way into William Street.

Here at least he found a form of normalcy. Shops were open and some vehicles passed by, but there were still no cabs. He made for Queen Street and his home away from home, the Royal Exchange Hotel. Ahead of him, at the corner, he saw a crowd gathering and he hailed a horseman returning from that direction. 'Hoi there, sir! What's going on up ahead?'

The fellow looked at him curiously, then dismounted from his horse and hitched it to a post. 'You're Maskey, aren't you? The politician?'

'That I am,' Fowler said, pleased to be recognised.

The stranger spat on the dusty ground. 'Then if you don't know what's happening, you don't deserve to have your bloody job neither!'

'I don't understand,' Fowler said, affronted.

'That'd be right,' the man sneered and ambled away.

'Well I never!' Fowler said. 'What a damned cheek!'

He continued on his way, his suitcase heavier at every step, aware that his clothes were becoming damp and dishevelled thanks to this unaccustomed effort. He was determined to make his own way, though, and to make no further impulsive enquiries. He would find out what was going on through the proper channels.

Until he moved in among them, Fowler had underestimated the size and the mood of this crowd, and he tried to hurry through, to get to the other side and on to his hotel. But they were moving with him. Or rather he found himself surrounded and being swept along by the herd that seemed to dissipate and converge at intervals. Voices growled and shouted all about him, and no one seemed to notice him until he decided to give up and make for the shelter of some shops. 'Excuse me,' he was saying, using his case as a buffer. 'Excuse me. Let me pass, please.'

'Yes, let the gent pass,' an angry voice roared, and Fowler's hat was flicked from his head. There were bursts of laughter as he tried to retrieve it and it was flung into the air and then tossed from hand to hand. Giddily, he gave up the chase and bent to pick up his case, to find it had disappeared.

'My luggage!' he yelled, his voice lost as the anger of the crowd increased.

No one cared. Placards were hoisted. 'Jobs!' they shouted as one. 'Give us back our jobs!'

Behind him a woman screeched, 'Our kids are starving while the likes of this fat fart live in luxury!' She shoved Fowler in the back and he went sprawling. Only the proximity of so many bodies saved him from going down. He grabbed coats and managed to steady himself as the sound of shattering glass took the attention of the mob. Terrified, Fowler realised he was in the centre of a full-scale riot as the crowd lurched on, hurling stones, smashing windows and screaming abuse. He saw men and women looting shops and gravitated with them to the footpath, where he was able to escape, unnoticed, down an alley. He staggered against a wall and then reeled drunkenly on, to collapse on to a low flight of steps, his heart pounding.

Another man came running down the alley. Expecting an attack, Fowler tried to rouse himself. The man stopped suddenly. 'By God, it's Mr Maskey!'

Fowler looked up and sighed. This was the last straw! To have Tyler Kemp see him like this, hiding in an alleyway like a derelict.

'Come on, I'll give you a hand,' Kemp said, helping him to his feet. 'Looks like you got run over by the mob, sir. A nasty experience. They're out for blood today. Are you hurt?'

'Not really,' Fowler said, making an effort to recover his breath and his dignity. 'Just a bit battered. But what in God's name is going on?'

'You don't know?' Kemp said.

'I shouldn't ask if I knew,' Fowler said testily. 'I've just got off the damned boat. Lost my bloody luggage to those louts too! Where are the police?'

'They're standing by down in George Street, so the mob took a different turn. It's my guess they'll disperse with the spoils before the police get over here. The situation is quite simple. The Government's out of cash so they've shut down public works and every second man is out of work. No work, no pay, no food for their families – and this is the upshot. Food riots. Parliament has been recalled. But you'd know that.'

'I didn't know it was this bad,' Fowler said. 'I'd better get on to my hotel.'

He was still unsteady, so Kemp assisted him through to Adelaide Street and along to the back entrance of the hotel. Although he couldn't bring himself to say so, Fowler was glad of the company; he would have looked too conspicuous on his own in this bedraggled state. When Kemp took him through a rear door and sat him in a back room while he went for the manager, Fowler forced himself to acknowledge the assistance. 'Very courteous of you indeed,' he managed to admit.

'No trouble,' Kemp said. 'I'm sure you'd do the same for me,' he added with a grin.

Safe in his hotel room with a tray of buttered bread and cold chicken, and a bottle of French brandy, Fowler had no intention of appearing at the House until his wardrobe had been replenished and he had studied the backlog of Brisbane newspapers delivered to him by a hotel servant.

Fowler had always been of the opinion that men who wore store-bought suits were not gentlemen, and here he was now, decked out in a black twill, looking like an undertaker and regretting his decision to leave his son at home. He was feeling quite poorly after a morning of domestic incidents. His suit had been returned from the Chinese laundry in good time and sufficiently starched, but, and his ears turned deep red as he recalled, a patch had been added to mend a large tear in the seat of the trousers. To think he had walked along a main street in Brisbane, after that fracas, with a hole in his pants! Fowler wondered nervously if Kemp had seen it. Or the hotel manager. It was too embarrassing to contemplate.

So he'd had to summon his tailor again, after giving him instructions to supply him with several new suits and all the necessary accoutrements to replace his lost luggage. This time he'd sent the fellow off to purchase a presentable outfit off the peg, since Fowler could hardly emerge in patched trousers. And this was the result, this apology for decent apparel.

He wasted no time among his companions in the House, apologising for his appearance and describing how he'd been set upon by the rioters, gradually finding himself quite the hero, since none of the other parliamentarians had actually seen the violence. And, to his delight, in reading Kemp's account of the eruptions, he came across lines pertaining to his misfortunes. 'Mr Maskey, Member for Rockhampton, present at the fray, was manhandled and was fortunate to escape serious injury.' The way Kemp had written the article it almost sounded as if Fowler had been there by choice, and on this occasion Fowler had no complaints about a slight distortion of the truth.

The Speaker, having read the article, requested Fowler's presence at a committee meeting, where doom-laden faces about the table warned him well before the discussions began that the situation was even worse than he had imagined.

The Speaker, James Mitchell, reiterated that not enough money was available to pay all of the public servants, and in the ensuing noisy reactions, Fowler managed to lodge the question uppermost in his mind.

'But surely this will not affect country electorates where public works are essential?'

Mitchell cast a withering glance at him. 'All such works are essential. They simply have to be curtailed for the time being.'

'And how long is the time being?'

'Difficult to say,' the Speaker replied carefully. 'The Treasurer has to reassess the financial situation . . .'

'That won't be bloody hard,' Jock Campbell, from the Darling Downs, snapped. 'It doesn't take much assessing to look in a purse and find it bare.'

'That has already been established,' Mitchell continued patiently, 'and the object of this meeting is to discuss methods of refinancing our loans.'

'Why wasn't this done months ago?' another member asked.

'Because we weren't to know that the A and M Bank would collapse,' Mitchell said.

'I reckon Herbert knew, else why did he pull the belt so tight.'

As Fowler listened to the chorus of shouts and recriminations he recognised panic and steeled himself not to become infected. He knew as well as they did that all of their seats were in danger. This fledgling Parliament had not yet gravitated to cut-and-dried parties as at Westminster. Here it was every man for himself, with the wrath of a suffering populace directed squarely at their politicians. It was quite unfair, he told himself, that they should be pilloried like this, but Jack Public was never known for his fairness, and blame was now rolling mercilessly at them like a tidal wave. Meanwhile these fools were at one another's throats, searching for a scapegoat.

'I don't believe,' he said, in his most statesmanlike voice, 'that we should be casting about for blame. I was under the impression that this committee was convened to find a way out of this morass.'

'Hear, hear!' Mitchell said, relieved.

Many and varied were the suggestions. 'Bring back Herbert! Get rid of Macalister!'

'No, we should listen to Macalister. He has the answer.'

'Raise taxes. Let the rich pay.'

'Try other banks.'

'We are doing that,' Mitchell told them, 'but so far without success.'

'Borrow from Victoria, they're rolling in gold.'

'Triple the bounties to any man finding new goldfields in this state, more like it.'

In the end three men with sheets of financial statements dominated the meeting. Their brows furrowed, they talked of forward projections, interest rates, viability, short-term loans, guarantees and the responses from British banks. They went on for so long that Fowler became bored and was almost asleep by the time the meeting broke up.

Once outside he went in search of the Premier. One thing he had gleaned from the meeting was that Macalister claimed to have the answer to this state-wide problem, and Fowler needed to know what that answer was. Even though he was still cross with Macalister for passing him over in making prestigious appointments, if he could clean up this mess then all power to him.

Macalister received him civilly. 'How did the meeting go?'

'We have several options open to us,' Fowler told him grandly, 'and a report is presently being prepared. But as you know, due to being caught up in that riot and losing my belongings, I'm rather a latecomer to discussions. It was mentioned at the meeting, however, that you have put forward a proposal.'

'Ha! So they're going to have to listen to me after all, are they?' Macalister crowed.

'Quite possible,' Fowler replied without a blink. 'But I'm behind the times and I didn't want to slow down discussion by requiring an explanation of your proposal. Besides, I would prefer to hear it from you. Some gentlemen seem to garble these weighty matters beyond recognition.'

'They do, they do,' Macalister said. 'Sit down, Maskey. There is a simple solution but it's too easy for those fools, they like to complicate matters. You saw for yourself how serious the situation is. The workers and their families are starving and I'm always for the working man. I'm from the working class myself and I won't stand for it. Ipswich is in uproar, I've had food riots up my way too. We have to help the workers and help them now.' He thumped the desk to illustrate his point and Fowler wished he would cut the speeches and get on with it.

Eventually he came to his theory and Fowler was impressed. Macalister was right. Away with all this floundering and running cap-in-hand to the British banks. The best way to overcome this crisis was to print their own money.

Or that was how Fowler saw it. 'Inconvertible government notes,' Macalister said. 'I've already worked out the design with my people back home. Greenbacks we're calling them until we come up with a more prestigious name. Don't you see, with our natural resources of wool, mutton, beef and the gold that we will locate in time, we can't miss. We have to have faith, man, faith in ourselves, that's what's missing here. We'll have enough in our coffers eventually to back our own notes and to hell with the banks.'

Fowler found all this hugely interesting. When the time came for separation the new state could do the same thing. Why, he'd even have the opportunity to see how it was done.

'What do you say then?' Macalister asked him, his beetling brows signalling that a negative response would not be appreciated. The warning was not necessary.

'I'm for it,' Fowler replied. 'When can we get this under way?'

'That's the problem. I have to talk these dithering fools around. So far I've only got a few starters, but you mark my words, this crisis can't be resolved any other way. Let them all go back to their electorates and face the music for a few months, that'll bring them to heel.'

Fowler shuddered. He too would have to face his voters with a full-scale depression on his hands like blood.

'Is there no other way?'

'No. In the meantime I'll go quietly along with the arrangements – the technicalities will all be sorted out by the winter session of Parliament. By then our nervous nellies will be pleading with me to lead them to a safe shore.'

'And the workers?' Fowler asked their champion.

'Unfortunately, their situation will deteriorate substantially and I can't help that. I can't be held to blame because I won't allow Queensland to be beholden to banks ever again. We'll all just have to ride out the storm until my proposal is accepted.'

Tyler Kemp wandered into the saloon bar of the Royal Exchange Hotel to find old Fowler holding court. It had been a busy week at the paper, covering the riots that were becoming almost a daily occurrence, but while there was plenty of copy from that angle he was frustrated at the seeming inability of Parliament to agree on a solution. They'd rise at the end of the week still procrastinating, appointing still more committees, fiddling while Rome burned.

Tyler was the son of hard-working Scottish immigrants. His father was a timber-getter who laboured in the dense mountain forests of northern New South Wales, hauling the great logs behind bullock teams down to the Clarence River. The eleven-year-old lad who'd come with his parents from the mighty city of Glasgow to an isolated log cabin had been entranced. He was Robin Hood with a real bow and arrows; he was a crusader with his own blackamoor, an amused blackfellow of the Bundjalung tribe that inhabited the area.

Their Aborigine neighbours were an amiable and crafty lot, fascinated by the white family. The women liked to watch Tyler at his lessons with his mother out under the trees. They brought their children and stood nearby in polite and sombre silence as Tyler scratched on his slate or read from his books. They understood that these sessions were important to Connie Kemp, even more so than to her son, and afforded her their respect, though not understanding the ritual.

They loved to trade, but you had to watch them. Young Jugalag was a real villain. He sold Connie the same wild honey – which they called sugarbag as they became conversant with English – twice in the one day, stealing it from the muslin safe at the back to bring it round to the front. And when she discovered the trick there was delighted mayhem as she chased him through the woods with her broom.

When Tyler's sister was born, the black women were the midwives. When Dadda Kemp was pinned under a slide of logs by the river, it

69

was the black men who came to his aid, lifting off the great logs and carrying him home. Fortunately, pushed deep into the mud, he suffered no more than two broken ribs.

Tyler had none of the complaints of his contemporaries about their miserable childhoods. He loved life in those green and misty woods, and as he moved into his teens his father taught him the trade; he was as good an axeman as any and he could push, coerce and tease their beloved bullocks into massive work on those heaving slopes. His father also taught him to shoot game, and then for a hobby set up targets, proud that his son had become a crack shot in his teens. While Connie attended to his education, Dadda was a great believer in physical fitness. On Sundays, with his treasure, a small gold fob watch, Dadda would send Tyler off on cross-country runs, with Aborigine observers placed at strategic intervals to make sure he didn't cheat. They would yell with uninhibited excitement as Tyler came puffing up the steep slopes, barefoot, trying to beat his own time.

Soon the blacks joined in. They wanted to race too. So Dadda chose their best and pitted them against his son. Try as he might, Tyler could never beat them, but it was much more fun because at the end of the day Connie would invite the participants to join them in a supper of roasted wild fowl and charcoaled potatoes.

They were content, his parents. A genial pair whose one extravagance was their Saturday-night whisky bought from river traders. And he was content, too – until they announced they were sending him away.

He could still recall his shock. Their explanations. Their revelation that they had been putting money away for his education, which he'd understood was complete. They wanted better for their son, they told him, but he couldn't imagine what might be better. Connie had won him a cadetship with the *Moreton Bay Courier*. She had handed several of his compositions to travellers going north, requesting that they be posted or delivered to the boss of that newspaper. With each one she included a candid report on her son's attributes. 'He's upright and true. Needs a push at times to keep his mind on the job. Spelling comes easy to the lad but not sums, and he has a good ear for words. Therefore his father would be honoured if you could teach him to be a writer, and would be willing to pay the fees by instalments.' It did not occur to Connie Kemp to write the usual motherly letter, glowing with praise, and she never doubted that the travellers would fulfil their promises.

Her faith was rewarded. The letters reached their mark and the editor was intrigued. When the third composition arrived, he saw that this lad did have some merit as a writer, and in a rare magnanimous mood he replied, offering Tyler Kemp that cadetship and informing the woman that no fees were necessary. The lad would be paid five shillings a week, and more, perhaps, depending on his ability.

People from all over the scattered community converged on the Kemps for Tyler's send-off, and a great party it was too, with entertainment by local Aborigines, who staged a special corroboree for the occasion.

Looking back, years later, Tyler realised that there must have been hard times, sad times, in that tough environment, but they had receded from his memory, which retained only the liveliness of his resourceful parents, the beauty and intrigue of the bush, and most of all his sudden descent into civilisation.

It took him a long while to adjust to town life, to overcome his shyness, to learn to fend for himself in cheap lodgings, and he was only happy in the newspaper office. A willing worker, Tyler was at everyone's beck and call, and proud of it, and when he finally won a desk to himself he was on his way. Because Tyler was an excellent and reliable reporter.

Only one matter caused him great misgivings. The townspeople, he found, had no time for Aborigines. In fact, many hated them, and to hear his dear friends referred to in such a vile manner was a shock. He loved to read the prestigious newspapers from other cities whenever he could find copies, but he recoiled in horror to find that they too, like his own paper, which was now entitled the *Brisbane Courier*, were prejudiced against blacks. Whenever he tried to speak up on their behalf he was howled down and ridiculed, and only a few lone souls shared his opinions.

As his prestige grew, Tyler Kemp became accustomed to respect for his political assessments, but he nursed a grudge all the while against those with anti-black sentiments – which was practically everyone he knew. He realised it was a hopeless cause and that knowledge soured him. The source of his resentment faded but the sourness became habit. Eventually he didn't mind being known around Brisbane as a stubborn, irascible character. It made people nervous and gave him an edge.

So this was the make of the man who strolled over to Fowler Maskey in the Royal Exchange Hotel, seeking more information on the financial crisis.

'Feeling better, sir?'

Maskey beamed on the sandy-haired reporter. 'Indeed I am, much better, thank you. God knows what might have happened to me at the hands of those ruffians if you hadn't come along.'

Tyler grinned. When he'd found Maskey there wasn't a ruffian in sight, but if the old bloke wanted to play it that way then let him. Tyler's mind was on more important matters. 'I believe the Committee on Finance is about to present a report to the Premier. Can you give me an inkling of how they intend to proceed?'

The Member for Rockhampton, delighted to be quizzed by Kemp in front of his fellow pastoralists at their favourite watering hole, drew himself up and placed his glass firmly on the counter. 'I certainly can.

I was invited to attend that meeting and I can say, here and now, without equivocation, that I have never come across such a sorry bunch of bunglers.'

'Is that right?' Tyler said, interested.

'It is indeed. To my knowledge the report will contain nothing specific, they couldn't agree on anything and it boiled down to hot air. I made a suggestion that wasn't acted upon, of course. These Brisbanites are not interested in the opinions of country folk . . .'

'And that's a fact,' a bearded squatter agreed.

'However,' Fowler continued, 'in subsequent discussions with the Premier I found we are in agreement, and a solution to our predicament is in sight. Queensland will be back on course in the next few months, once my colleagues in the House understand the proposal.'

'And this is a proposal the Premier intends to run with?' Tyler asked.

'He is all in favour.'

'And are you in a position to reveal this plan?' Tyler asked slyly. It was a challenge he often used to bait politicians, who never liked to admit to a position of weakness.

Fowler hesitated for a few seconds. Macalister's idea was sound, but he would need as much publicity as possible to swing the members behind him, and public pressure would do that. 'The public,' he said, 'is demanding action, and we intend to take action to stop this slide into outright poverty. A government can't just sit back and wring its hands. We have to have faith in ourselves and in our own considerable resources, by which I mean we can and will underwrite our own achievements. We intend to issue inconvertible government notes!'

He stuck his thumbs in his waistcoat and nodded sagely as his audience digested this.

'Will it work?' Bert Dayton asked.

'It could,' someone else said.

'A bit dicey,' was another comment, and as they mulled it over among themselves Tyler put his money on the counter and ordered a double whisky. He noted the reactions as the revelation infiltrated other groups along the bar, and he didn't like what he saw.

'A sound proposition, eh, Kemp?' Fowler asked him, and heads turned.

'It's bloody madness!' he snorted.

Fowler affected a benign smile, even though he was surprised by Kemp's remark. After all, the fellow was known to be a cranky type. 'Now, now, young fellow, you have to give this some thought,' he said. 'No point going off half-cocked.'

'I'm not going anywhere,' Tyler retorted. 'I haven't finished my drink.'

He seemed to consider the subject not worth discussing, and that suited Maskey. With the reporter present it would be better to switch to safer ground. 'That's good,' he said, 'because you must join me in a celebration while you're here. I was just about to order champagne to toast my daughter's betrothal.' He turned to his friends. 'Advance notice, gents. Warn the families to prepare for a journey north. I'll be sending out invitations to Laura's engagement party.' He beckoned to the bartender. 'Champagne for all, my good man. The finest you have.'

He was at his jovial best as corks popped and the company swooped on the glasses. 'I believe in supporting my home town,' he announced, 'and there'll be a celebration in the city of Rockhampton as grand as any down here.'

'The city of Rockhampton?' a stranger sneered. 'I heard it's a one-horse town without the horse!'

Fowler laughed. 'That's what they said about Brisbane. And Rockhampton hasn't got to live down the smell of a prison settlement. Rockhampton will be a great city one day, right smack in the heart of the best cattle country in the world. I ask you, sir, to drink to Rockhampton.'

The next toast was to Maskey's daughter, Laura, and to her intended.

'Who is this lucky fellow?' Dayton remembered to ask as the glasses were refilled.

'Captain Robert Cope,' Fowler announced. 'Formerly of the New South Wales Regiment, now with our Native Mounted Police, based in Rockhampton.'

Not averse to free champagne, Tyler Kemp had downed two glasses and was preparing to leave, wondering if this outrageous story of Maskey's about government notes was worth only a few lines or a full-scale blast. The mention of Cope's name stopped him in his tracks.

'Who?' he asked. 'The fiancé?'

'Captain Cope,' Fowler said proudly. 'Highly thought of in our community.'

'Is he now?'

Sensing more publicity on a less controversial issue, Fowler was expansive. 'You're included in the invitations, Kemp. Have you visited Rockhampton yet?'

'Can't say I have.'

'Then you will be most welcome. I hope you'll be able to attend our gathering.'

'I won't miss it for the world,' Tyler said, and left the bar.

Outside he breathed in the sickly smell of frangipani blooms and sewage, and wished himself back in the clean air of the mountains. His parents, ageless, were still there. The log cabin had grown into a cottage with a fence and a garden. His father owned a sawmill now, but the genial Scot was still the best axeman in the district and he still had his bullock team. Nothing much had changed, except that the Aborigines were gradually drifting away or had fallen foul of white men's sicknesses. Some of the old families remained but instead of being masters of their forests, they clung to the Kemps and other settlers for sustenance and advice.

'Captain Cope!' Tyler spat the words into the dirt. 'That murdering bastard!' He'd read the reports on Cope's activities with hollow rage. The hero, cleaning out districts for settlers, terrorising Aborigine communities with the force of the law behind him. A law that gave him *carte blanche* to kill and kill and kill!

Tyler felt sick. Sick at his inability to do anything about this but wring his hands like Fowler's colleagues on that other matter. Powerless to stand up for those innocents. To speak out for their rights, because they had none.

Cope was small-time – there were other Copes about the land – but a combination of Cope and Maskey was terrifying. A man didn't have to be too bright to realise that if Maskey even considered Cope as a son-in-law then he approved of Cope's assignments. And if Cope was backed by the state's representative up there, he would inherit far too much power. White people who might object to Cope's murderous exploits would have no voice to speak for them. Maskey was their representative in the only place where it mattered, and Maskey would not denigrate his son-in-law.

Tyler called into a dingy tavern, bought another whisky and retired to a corner to think this through. His aim now was to bring down Fowler Maskey. First he'd write an article exposing the government notes as the act of desperate, irresponsible men. Then he had to search out any dirt he could get on Maskey. And then he would go to Rockhampton. There had to be someone up there prepared to stand against Maskey, and whoever it was would get his full and consider-able support. He would pull this moneyed fool off his perch. There were too many rich squatters in power anyway. Tyler resented inherited wealth.

He held his glass up to a smoky lantern. 'You're on your way out, Fowler.'

This particular tavern was the haunt of a local gent known as Ferret, whom Tyler often used to do some legwork for him. Ferret was, in appearance, the opposite of his name, a short, rotund fellow with a pink and smiling face. His clothes were drab but neat, and his round steel spectacles gave him an owlish look. Not a person who would stand out in a crowd. But that was his stock in trade. Ferret was a great one for digging out information and saw himself as an unofficial private investigator, although others found that title a bit grand for him; Ferret had in the past done a couple of stretches for forgery.

When Ferret appeared, Tyler beckoned to him and the little man eased himself into the booth. 'You have a job for me, Mr Kemp?'

'Yes. Do you know Fowler Maskey? The Member of Parliament.'

'Not personally, no, but I could recognise him.'

Tyler slipped ten shillings across the table. 'What do you know about him?'

'Very little, I'm afraid.'

Tyler knew information wouldn't come that easy. No matter what Ferret had to disclose he would spin it out for a few days to build up expenses. 'He's over at the Royal Exchange now. I want you to nose about, dog him for a few days. Find out anything you can. Who are his chums? Is he as well off as he pretends? Has he got any enemies? I just need to know the score on him.'

'Not a problem.' Ferret smiled. 'I'll look him over.'

Tyler Kemp's article on the proposed government notes made the front page, but curiously did not create the furore that he had anticipated. In some areas, quite the reverse. Macalister berated the editor for not giving him a chance to develop the idea. Letters for and against the plan poured into the *Courier*, and those in favour far outweighed those against, although Tyler had a suspicion that quite a few of these letters were instigated by Macalister himself. Arguments raged in the pubs, and a woman berated Tyler in the street for trying to sabotage the efforts of a good 'puir mon' like the Premier.

When he wrote a more subjective piece warning of the pitfalls, it was relegated to a back page. 'Stop worrying about it,' his editor told him. 'They'll never get this balloon off the ground. I think you got sucked into believing they were serious about such a measure. It's just a furphy to take the pressure off for a while.'

'Fowler Maskey didn't seem to think so.'

The editor laughed. 'Well, there you are! You yourself said Fowler's a blowhard. I can't believe you fell for it.'

Still smarting from that conversation, Tyler went in search of Ferret. Regardless of what Fowler had to say, Macalister was the one to watch, and he was busy drumming up support. What if he did manage to get the backing? What then?

He was so incensed by the financial quagmire that could lie ahead that he turned back and confronted his editor with this scenario, but once again he failed to impress the seriousness of the situation upon him.

Disgusted, he announced that he was thinking of taking a holiday, and was not impressed when the editor cheered up no end. 'Good idea. You deserve a break. Going down to see the folks, are you?'

'No. I thought I might take a look around up north.'

'Excellent. It's good to keep in touch with country people. You get out and have a bit of fun, clear out the cobwebs.'

Ferret didn't have much to say. 'Clean as a whistle, Mr Kemp.'

'I was afraid of that.' Tyler scowled. 'Bloody squatters!'

'Yes, it's as you say. Good family. Bank accounts you couldn't jump over with a horse. Got a wife and son and daughter up there in

Rockhampton. Don't know much about that end of the world, but his mates down here are all well-to-do bushies, as you would expect. He's a big punter but the bookies love him, pays on the knocker. Likes his booze but he can hold it, hollow legs they reckon. Plays cards and can get nasty if he loses, I hear, but that ain't no crime.'

'Bad temper?' Tyler echoed, clutching at straws.

'Ah yes. I met a bloke who knew him out on the family station. Said Fowler can get real mean – flogged a cook himself for selling off station rations, but it was all hushed up.'

'I knew it,' Tyler said. 'That hail-fellow-well-met attitude is too good to be true. Those piggy eyes of his can be like flint. Still, that's not much to go on. How much do I owe you?'

'Another ten will see it out,' Ferret said, pocketing the shillings that Tyler handed over.

'There was one other thing,' Ferret said, eyeing Tyler's wallet, and the reporter sighed, knowing he'd paid up too soon.

'Worth a pound, I'd say,' Ferret added.

'The last lot wasn't worth a pound. I could have found all that out for myself.'

'Then you should have, Mr Kemp. I wouldn't mind another drink.'

Ferret had his own ritual. He sat stolidly, unblinking, as two more whiskies were delivered. 'Your good health, Mr Kemp,' he said, his voice mild, his face expressionless.

'Ten bob,' Tyler said.

'Ten and ten,' Ferret countered. 'The information is in two parts, so to speak.'

'We'll see.'

Ferret took that as a bargain struck. 'Our friend frequents a certain house in Spring Hill run by a Mrs Betsy Perry.'

'A whorehouse?' Tyler said. 'Which one?'

'Number five Chelsea Lane.'

'It's a new one on me.'

'Not so new, just high-priced and Betsy don't let anyone in she don't know. Like a club it is. A mate of mine delivers goods there, round the back, of course. But he says she buys nothin' but the best food and grog. And they got girls there all colours.'

'Any boys?'

'Cripes no. Betsy won't have none of that.'

'You're ripping me off,' Tyler said. 'If I wrote a story on Maskey visiting a whorehouse I'd get run out of town. I reckon Brisbane's got more brothels than Bombay on payday. Their customers would have my hide.'

'I said the information has two levels,' Ferret said indignantly. 'This one is different. Mr Maskey owns it, he owns the building and the business. Betsy just runs it for him.'

'What?' Tyler was delighted. He'd struck gold. 'You're sure?'

'No sweat, Mr Kemp. It's his all right.'

'Good man.' Tyler slapped down the pound and Ferret left. The journalist considered his options. He hadn't managed to damage Maskey on the government notes, but this would topple the church-going hypocrite from his pedestal. He wouldn't release the information just yet; the place to drop the bomb would be right in Rockhampton, in the heart of his electorate. He had yet to find someone up there to oppose Maskey in the forthcoming elections. If he gave that candidate this information to release in the local newspapers, Maskey would be history. Country people were notoriously pious, on the surface anyway.

He did a little jig of glee as he headed for the shipping office. He'd take the next boat to Rockhampton.

But Tyler was about to be thwarted again. His campaign to oppose the government notes had fallen flat, and his plan to expose Fowler was about to collapse because other individuals, with their own sly plots, were at work.

Betsy Perry had long been trying to buy this lucrative business from Fowler, but his price was too high. She had considered moving premises and starting out on her own, but she knew she'd lose Maskey's well-heeled mates. Fowler would simply appoint someone else in her place. Now, though, she had him.

The delivery man, Charlie Tuck, had given her the tip, for a price, that Ferret had been nosing about number five Chelsea Lane, and everyone knew that Ferret did nothing for nothing, and never on his own behalf.

So, in her turn, Betsy put someone on Ferret's tail, and he came up with the goods.

'We have to talk,' she told Fowler, late that night when he was in a relaxed and receptive mood, sampling the excellent brandy she had just purchased.

'What about, my dear?'

Betsy perched on the wide piano stool, smoothing the folds of her gold satin dress. It was now or never. This was the opportunity she had been waiting for. She watched as he lit his pipe, taking his time about it. Sometimes she wondered why a man as rich as he was bothered with the business. One of her customers, though, had once said to her: 'The more money you have, the more you need. The poor don't try, because everything is inevitably out of their reach. Rich men see things on an escalating grand scale and there becomes no limit to their needs.'

Of course he hadn't been referring to Fowler, just talking generally, but now Betsy realised that she too had joined the march for money. She had a good life here but she wanted more.

'We've got a problem,' she said, by which she meant that he did.

'Nothing that you can't solve, I'm sure,' he replied, lounging back in the velvet armchair.

'It has come to my ears,' she told him, 'that a certain agent has been enquiring into who owns this place.'

He sat bolt upright.

'A bloke known as Ferret. He's an informer.'

'Never heard of him! An informer for what?'

'Newspapers,' she whispered.

'Christ Almighty! You didn't talk to him?'

'Never. He wouldn't dare front me. But he's good. I hear he's been up to the titles office. Your name is on the property, Fowler. They could cause you terrible trouble.' Some time earlier, Betsy had considered inventing a tale like this, but she hadn't had the courage to act on it. Now it was real it was easier to lean on him. She saw he was anxious and sweating, so she twisted the knife. 'They say he's working for Tyler Kemp, the reporter who wrote that awful story about you the other day on the front page of the paper.'

'Kemp! That blackguard! A man talks to him in good faith and what does he do? Tries to make a laughing stock of me. Well, he'll laugh on the other side of his face when Macalister puts this bill through the House.'

'He sounds an out-and-out rat,' Betsy agreed, 'but if he's after you, and he writes us up, we won't see any more customers for dust. They'll all run a mile.'

Fowler knew she was right, but it hurt him to let go of a cash business like this, cash of his own that came in without any effort on his part and was outside William's jurisdiction Even though his income from the stations was substantial, it annoyed him that William knew to the penny what he had. Or thought he knew.

'We ought to close down,' Betsy was saying, 'to protect your reputation, before Kemp gets his claws into you. I'll take the girls and leave. You could rent the house to a nice little family for about twelve shillings a week and Kemp won't have a leg to stand on.'

'Twelve shillings a week!' Fowler yelped. 'That wouldn't keep me in cigars.'

Betsy shrugged.

'Oh no, Kemp isn't that smart. I'll beat him,' her landlord said. 'What if I sell the lot to you, lock, stock and barrel. I can have it pushed through the titles office in double-quick time, and he'll look the fool.'

After worrying her way through what she could afford, Betsy finally agreed to buy the property. Fowler, thoroughly agitated now by her benign badgering, wanted the deal over and done with quickly, so his price plummeted and in the end he was pleased to offload it for a hundred pounds, only a fraction of the worth of the business.

The next morning, with the matter settled, Fowler felt regret at the loss, but he was philosophical about it. While it had lasted, it had been interesting and profitable, but now he'd do well to watch his step. And so would that Kemp fellow. By God, so would Kemp!

Chapter Four

With the women settled for the night after their long journey home, Paul went outside for his usual tour of inspection before he too called it a day. He walked quietly around the house and over to the home paddock, with his two cattle dogs padding silently behind him, pleased that their master was home and their lives could return to normal. His horse whinnied and sidled away from the others to move along the fence with him. Paul checked that the gate was secure, gave the horse a reassuring pat and turned towards the barn, hitching his rifle on to his shoulder.

He passed the dark chicken coop, did a turn around the dairy and looked out with a grin over Jeannie's vegetable garden, hoping that old Danny, their rouseabout, had looked after the precious plants – or there'd be hell to pay in the morning.

The stockmen lived in a long bungalow near the stables with the bare essentials of furniture – bunks down one end and a large pine table and chairs at the other. They were playing cards as he stuck his head in the open doorway.

'Want a game, boss?'

'No thanks, just doing the rounds. See you in the morning.' He always let them know when he was on patrol in case someone got jumpy and took a potshot at him. He only had six men working the station with him but they were reliable blokes, led by the foreman, Gus Stein, an experienced stockman, son of German immigrants.

Contrary to the usual arrangements, the MacNamaras took their meals with the men on a covered veranda at the rear of the house. At first Jeannie had objected. 'It's not done. We don't want to start off on the wrong foot with them.'

'Exactly,' Paul had said. 'I don't care what happens down south, there's a different set of rules up here. We have to stick together, work and maybe fight together. I need their confidence and respect.'

The men appreciated this gesture and the decent food prepared by Jeannie and Clara, and mealtimes had turned into pleasant meetings where Paul could discuss stock and station management with them, man to man. In time the taciturn foreman became Paul's best friend, as proud of Oberon as the owner.

As he came back to the front gate Paul looked up, to gauge the next day's weather. It was a bright moonlit night, the sky an inky blue dotted with stars, and over towards the coast a mass of pure white cloud was banked up like snow. He watched, approving, as it moved away across the mountains. In the distance he could see tiny lights that could almost be mistaken for stars, but he knew they were not. They were campfires – blacks, safe in their lofty hideouts. The mountains were mostly unexplored and they intrigued him. He wished he could go up there to see for himself the wonders of that wild country, but so far it was too dangerous. His eyes followed the uneven dark peaks silhouetted against the white cloud until they came to a break in the hills, where a steep granite bluff gleamed white in the moonlight. It would be some view from up there, he mused. A man could see right back over the valley and on out to sea. And maybe where that bluff dropped down, there would be a pass through to the coastal plains.

His land extended into the foothills; that was what he liked about Oberon, the diversity of the property. Although he was well away from the Fitzroy, a smaller river ran through the land and several other minor streams cut down from the hills in the wet season to water the pasturelands. There was plenty of scrub to shelter the cattle, and further north heavily timbered forests, while patches of the foothills were rocky summits that made good lookout points in their search for strays. In all, he was well pleased with Oberon, his herds of shorthorns were increasing and prices were high.

The dogs jumped up the steps ahead of him and settled down by the front door, familiar with the nightly routine. Paul went on through the house towards his bedroom. He found he was thinking of Laura again and made a deliberate effort to dismiss her from his mind, although he allowed himself to wonder how she was and if she had managed to shake off the would-be husband. He hoped, for her sake, that she had.

By early morning Jeannie was on the rampage. Nothing in the house, it seemed, was as it should be. There was mould in the cupboards, on their clothes, on the walls. And her best cheeses had been eaten.

'Mice I suppose,' Paul remarked mischievously as Clara served his breakfast.

'Bloody greedy men, more like it,' Jeannie snapped. 'And two of my chooks are gone, good layers they were too. And the dairy hasn't been cleaned out since I left. It stinks. I can't turn my back on this place without it falling to rack and ruin.'

All of the men got through the dawn meal in double-quick time and congregated at the stables, glad, with the boss, to escape the tongue-lashing.

'Wait till she sees the cabbages.' Gus warned. 'Danny did his best but we had a hailstorm a few days back. It was over in minutes but it didn't do them cabbages a lot of good.'

'Let's go,' Paul laughed. It was time to make a full check of the herds on this large, unfenced property, to round up bullocks for sale and calves for branding. Gus gave the men their orders and rode with Paul towards the river, which the Aborigines called Wiragulla for the hundreds of parrots that congregated there. This morning the birds were in good form, shrieking and squabbling, colours flashing brilliantly in the trees. As the men rode by a hawk appeared overhead, and the parrots took off in a body, sweeping swiftly across the blue like a multicoloured carpet.

Paul was pleased to see the river was still up – it would be well into the dry season before the levels dropped. Unable to cross at this time of the year without having to swim the horses, they made for the bridge upstream that would take them into the scrub country. But as they came over a rise, they stopped short.

'Where's the bloody bridge?' Paul exclaimed.

They cantered down the hill and examined debris along the banks. 'It was here a week ago,' Gus said. 'It couldn't have been washed away.'

'Not a chance,' Paul told him. 'There's no sign of flooding. Do you reckon it was blacks did this?'

'Wouldn't put it past them,' Gus replied. 'But they don't use saws. Look at this . . .' He shoved with his boot at a half- submerged spar. 'It's been sawn clean through.'

Paul was bewildered. 'But why? Why would anyone bother to destroy a bridge? And right out here. No one uses it but us.'

'Nuisance value. It's my guess Jack Corbett and his gang have done this. They were hanging about near the homestead while you were away. We chased them off. I told Corbett to keep his miners at their diggings or get off the property. They're not doing any good anyway, they haven't put a pick on any gold here.'

Stony-faced, Paul told Gus about his conversation with Boyd Roberts. 'The rules have changed,' he added. 'Corbett and his bullyboys scared off other prospectors and now they're going to try to scare me off. This could be just the beginning.'

They went in search of the other stockmen, and by late afternoon, with all the men assembled, they heard that stockyards out towards the boundary had been destroyed, and worse, a blacks' camp by a quiet lagoon had been raided and the people scattered.

'Anyone hurt?' Paul asked, but they were unable to say. They could tell him only that the blacks were gone and there was evidence that a group of horsemen had been through there.

As they were talking, Gus nudged Paul. 'Who's this?'

A lone Aborigine emerged from the bush. He was an elderly man with a shock of white hair and a long matted beard, but he carried his spear with dignity.

Paul dismounted and walked over to him. He held out his hand to the stranger but was ignored, so he tried again. 'What name you?'

'Gorrabah,' the man rumbled.

Paul saw that the old man was thin and shaky, and his rheumy eyes looked strained. 'You sick feller?' he asked, thinking Gorrabah had come in for help.

'Not sick,' Gorrabah said defiantly. 'You boss. That fella lagoon belonga my people. Them fella fish belonga my people.' He raised his voice angrily. 'Your fellers bust up our mob. Two blackfeller dead. We make payback! We kill you!' He wobbled on his thin legs as he pointed at the station men.

If the situation had not been so serious Paul might have laughed. For this poor old fellow to be threatening armed white men seemed futile, but it was a brave action and Paul gave him the respect he deserved. 'I'm very sorry two of your people have been killed. Very sorry.' He took off his hat, motioning to his men to do the same and hoping Gorrabah would understand the gesture. 'These are good fellers,' he told the old man. 'We'll catch the bad men.'

Gorrabah spat at his feet. 'All white men bad! You die!' He turned about and strode away into the bush.

'That does it,' Paul called to Gus. 'Let's pay a visit to Corbett and his mob.'

Gorrabah made his weary way back into the hills where his friends were waiting. It was true that he was sick. He hadn't long to live now, and he welcomed the hour that would see him into his Dreaming, for the Darambal people, his people, had fallen on hard times and evil was all about them in the form of these white invaders. He did not wish to remain for the end.

But that was not why he had volunteered to go down to that boss man. The answer was far simpler. He was the only man in the clans gathered here who could speak that new language, and even if he said so himself, he was a crafty fellow.

He knew that the white boss known as Paul was the best of a bad lot, and that his men were not dangerous, but how better to stir up action than by playing one mob off against the other? It was the digging men who had ridden mad into their camp, who had tried to grab gins. The people had run for their lives, but seeing that these devils were not just rampaging, but were after their women, they'd turned back to wrestle the women free and hurl spears at the white men. They'd saved the women, but two of their finest warriors had been killed by gunshot.

Now that the crying had begun, all the families were filled with rage. They wanted to attack, to payback for this terrible crime, but Gorrabah and other elders had insisted on patience. They couldn't afford to lose any more men. It would be better, for the time being, to set the white men against each other. And now they would find out if that boss, Paul, would keep his word and punish the murderers.

So they waited, and watched, to see if Gorrabah's play-acting had worked.

It was just on dusk when Paul MacNamara and his men, rifles loaded, galloped without warning through the miners' camp. They rounded up Corbett and the others, five in all, and roped them together in a circle.

'You killed two of the blacks, you bastard!' Paul shouted at Corbett.

'We never killed no one,' Corbett spat at him.

'It's no use lying, we've got an eyewitness. You're dead.'

'What do you mean, dead?' Corbett scoffed.

'I mean this is my property and I'm the law here. You've stirred up the blacks and put us all in danger, but there's one thing those blackfellers understand – an eye for an eye. If they see you've been punished they'll back off. We're going to hang you, Corbett, and another bloke!' He pointed at a wiry miner standing near his boss. 'You! You'll do. We'll lynch you as well.'

Gus strode over and looped a thick rope around his neck. 'You can go first,' he muttered.

The miner began to scream. 'Wasn't me, you bastards! I didn't shoot no one. I was over at the bridge. It was Corbett and Davies and Jones there.'

Tom Davies started yelling then. 'I didn't fire on anyone. I took off when the niggers got nasty. It was Corbett and Jones did the shooting.'

'Shut up, you mug,' Corbett shouted. 'They're only bluffing.'

'Don't be so sure,' Paul said, turning to the wiry man who was struggling with Gus. 'What bridge? The one that used to run over the Wiragulla River?'

'Yes. Corbett said to wreck it. We were only doing what we were told.'

The miners watched with growing apprehension as the men from Oberon systematically trampled the tents and wrecked the camp. They smashed pitheads and destroyed the winches, hurled away utensils and provisions, and collected all the weapons.

'You can't do this!' Corbett snarled. 'How are we going to get on here without our guns?'

'Where you're going you won't need them,' Paul said grimly.

Corbett began to wilt. 'Jesus! Those niggers attacked us. You think you're bloody God. We're not the only ones to cut down a couple of blacks! They're no loss!'

He screamed as Paul's stock whip slashed across his chest, ripping his shirt and raising a line of blood through the cotton. 'You wait till Mr Roberts hears about this, MacNamara,' he whined.

'What's Roberts got to do with this?' Paul asked, baiting him.

'He gives the orders,' Corbett snivelled.

'I don't believe you,' Paul said, the whip cracking dangerously near Corbett's legs.

'Then you oughta start,' Corbett said, straightening up. 'It was Roberts who told us to stir up this place, and you won't want to buck him. He gets what he wants.'

Paul called to his men. 'You all heard that?'

They nodded agreement and Paul turned to Gus. 'You'd better get back to the house and keep an eye on things there. We'll take care of this mob.'

Gus eyed Paul's stock whip nervously. 'Steady on, boss, you don't want to get too tough.'

'Don't worry,' Paul said. 'They deserve to be hanged, but we're just going to shove them on their way. It's a bloody shame, but it's all we can do.'

With rifles trained on them, the captives were ordered to saddle their horses and mount up. Then they were herded towards the outer perimeters of the station until they came to the track leading away from Oberon.

'Now get going,' Paul shouted, 'and if any of you set foot on my property again you'll be shot on sight.'

'I'll be back,' Corbett threatened.

Paul laughed. 'If I were you, mate, I'd start running. When Roberts finds out that you dobbed him in, in front of witnesses, your life won't be worth a trey. And you can rely on me to make sure he does know.'

'We'll make a deal with you,' one of the miners called. 'You give us back our weapons and we'll stay off your land.'

'No deals. You'll stay away, I'll see to it.'

'You can't send us out there without weapons,' Corbett whined. 'It's a couple of days' ride to Rockhampton. What if we get attacked by blacks?'

'You'll have the same odds as you gave them,' Paul retorted. He fired a shot into the air, and horses reared in fright. 'On your way,' Paul yelled. His men lined up beside him and they waited until the miners had disappeared down the lonely track before turning for home.

'A good night's work, boss,' one of his men commented.

'Yes,' Paul said, 'but now we have to rebuild that bloody bridge and the stockyards. And hope the blacks don't retaliate.'

Travelling back across the undulating country, Paul looked up at the dark ranges which were now studded with tiny pinpoints of light, more than he'd ever seen before. The clans were gathering, he realised, to mourn their dead. Suddenly the fires over Oberon no longer presented a starry sight; instead, to him, they seemed to glitter with menace. He had no doubt that blacks would have been watching when they confronted the miners, which was why he'd made such a show of wrecking their camp. Allowing the murderers to go free would hardly appease the blacks, but it shifted the blame from the men of Oberon Station. He should have arrested Corbett and the other fellow and waited for the police to come, but he knew it was a waste of time. They'd claim self-defence and get off. No jury in the present climate would convict them.

He still worried, though, that the blacks might decide on payback, and with so many of them gathering up there, anything could happen.

They were still miles from the homestead and he rode on silently, morosely, cursing Corbett, cursing Roberts, until eventually he tried to think of other things.

All being well, he must invite his mother and stepfather to visit; they'd never seen his station. While they were at Camelot Station, Grace Carlisle had mentioned that they had just purchased some stud bulls from Chelmsford Station in New South Wales. Since Paul had not commented, Jeannie had leapt in.'That station belongs to Paul's stepfather,' she'd said proudly.

The Carlisles had been impressed. 'It's a very famous station,' Grace had said. 'A showplace, I hear.'

Later, when they were alone, Jeannie had brought the subject up again. 'I don't need you to frown at me when I mention Chelmsford,' she complained. 'People should know who you are.'

'They know who I am,' Paul had growled.

'But they don't know about your family, and they like to hear these things. It doesn't hurt for them to find out that your stepfather is one of the wealthiest men in New South Wales.'

'What Rivadavia does has nothing to do with us.'

'Rot! He's related, whether you like it or not. You just can't forgive your mother for remarrying after your father was killed.'

'Rubbish!' he snapped. But he knew she was right and it hurt him to be confronted with this miserable situation again.

His brother, John, had accepted Dolour's announcement with pleasure, but Paul had not. It had seemed to him to be a sellout, an affront to his father's memory. He'd been young at the time, though, only about eighteen. He had attended the wedding without enthusiasm and from then on had found it difficult to change his attitude. He had seen them at family gatherings on many occasions since then, but had kept his distance, unable to unbend.

When John's baby was christened, he'd overheard him talking to Dolour. 'I'm sorry, Mother. I don't know what's got into Paul. He used to be so fond of Juan, and now he treats him like a stranger.'

Paul could still hear his mother's soft Irish voice. 'Never mind him, he's too much like your father. Finds it terrible hard to forgive. He'll come around.'

From that day Paul had realised what a fool he'd been, that there was nothing to forgive except his own stubborn streak. He couldn't bring himself to apologise to them, to tell them that he loved them both, because the subject was too emotional, but he vowed to make it up to them. Distance, though, had been against him. Distance and the hard work needed to bring the cattle station up to its full potential. He hadn't been south since he took on Oberon.

'As a matter of fact,' he'd told Jeannie, 'I was thinking of inviting Mother and Juan to Oberon now that the homestead is habitable.'

She had been climbing into the canopied double bed as he spoke, and had stopped, poised on the edge, delighted. 'That would be wonderful! When?'

'When we get settled again and the country dries out. Winter's the best time for visitors up here.'

'That's marvellous. And can I invite people to meet them?'

'I suppose so.'

He smiled as he cantered on. She'd been so excited she'd talked half the night about the parties they could have and the extras she'd need, and so forth.

Yes, he told himself, he would invite them. He'd write to them himself. Once the blacks had settled. Once he'd rebuilt the bridge and done a thousand other things. If Juan were coming, Paul wanted him to see that his station, his herds, were all in splendid order. Juan Rivadavia had emigrated from Argentinia as a young man, armed with the wealth and experience of a family of cattle barons, and he'd been very successful in Australia. It would be interesting to hear Juan's appraisal of his methods and management of Oberon.

And Jeannie could entertain, she could have her parties and the fun of impressing the locals with her guests. He was beginning to look forward to their visit himself.

The meeting of the elders of the Darambal people went on for days and the families continued to mourn the deaths of two men of the Kutabura clan. Gorrabah and his colleagues wore the feathers and white paint designated for burial ceremonies and attended to their official duties while hundreds of men gathered to witness the rituals. Then they sat cross-legged singing their ancient repetitive songs to the throaty groan of a didgeridoo, while before them, painted dancers performed slow, meticulous movements, telling the story of the tragedy.

Further across the mountain their women mourned. They were not permitted access to this particular ceremony but they had their own mourning practices. They squatted tearfully at the edge of a clearing while the immediate relatives wailed and screamed their grief, slicing at their breasts with sharp stones and smearing their faces with blood and clay.

But when the mourning time ended and families were left to continue their crying in private, the other women joined the men for serious talk. Their mood was harsh and unforgiving, and their voices were raised with those of the men in demanding fast and immediate payback.

At first Gorrabah was astonished at the number of Darambal people who attended this gathering, guessing there had to be more than six hundred, including children, assembled in the high forest. Too many to feed, he worried; the Kutabura clan scattered along the ranges had limited resources now. Once known as a proud and fierce mob they had been driven into the hills, their hunting grounds lost.

86

Gorrabah recognised members of the Kuinmerbura and Bekalbura clans who claimed they had come to pay their respects. He knew, though, that there was more to it than that. It wasn't usual for those men from the north, and the river people, to be bothered with Kutabura troubles. However, protocol allowed their elders to join Gorrabah and his colleagues in their meetings, making an unwieldy group of twenty, which irritated and worried Gorrabah. It was difficult to make wise decisions with hotheads from other clans in their midst. Too much shouting and arguing. Besides, he was not feeling well.

He called on his old friend Harrabura, man of the sky, to restore order. Harrabura in his day had been a great warrior, but more importantly, he was respected and feared as a magic man with awesome powers.

On the fourth night, Harrabura gave permission for a representative of the Kuinmerbura people to speak without interruption. This man addressed the company with old-world respect. He thanked the Kutabura for allowing them to share their grief and commiserated with them in their loss. 'A cruel crime,' he said sadly, 'and all the nations mourn, not just our Darambal nation. We are of the Bunya lands, and here our clans are united to call on the spirits for deliverance.'

As he bowed his head and stamped gravely on the moist forest floor, Gorrabah studied his tribal scars and paint markings. He hadn't seen those yellow and white designs for a long time, nor the drooping emu feathers that hung from the man's long hair, but he correctly translated them as war signs. Despite this fellow's soft and sorry words, Gorrabah knew he was building up to a call to arms, and he nudged Harrabura. But permission had been given; they had no choice but to hear him out, and he was a powerful speaker.

He moved on to the terrible losses that had been inflicted on his clan by the murdering, ravaging white men, citing specific cases where women and children had been butchered. There was no need for him to call for revenge – others, under the spell of his rhetoric, jumped to their feet screaming, not for deliverance now, but for payback.

There it was again. Gorrabah shook his head. When would they learn it was no use? There were too many whitefellers with guns and big strong horses. They should be discussing survival, not payback.

The speaker pointed at him. 'You – old man – you shake your head at me. You think we are outnumbered, and I say this is true, but we cannot cringe in caves. We have to gather the clans and fight. It is better to die in battle than to starve and watch our people starve. If we have the courage we could drive the whites out of this valley and claim it back as our own territory.' His speech was met with screams of delight.

Then it was the turn of the Bekalbura man, who, though a humbler person, wore a bone through his nose and new mourning cicatrices on his body. 'I have come,' he said with quiet dignity, 'to ask the Kutabura people to allow us to shelter in their mountains. We too have suffered mightily at the hands of the whites, whole families have been wiped out, but a worse plague is upon us. It is hard to believe, but dark men, our own people, from strange southern tribes, now work with the whites helping to kill us. And not just helping. They too have guns, and they wear white men's attire, and if it is possible they are even more vicious.'

'This is true, I have seen them,' the Kuinmerbura man shouted. 'They are devils and they show no mercy to anyone!'

His bad manners were overlooked in the shock that dazed the Kutabura elders.

'This can't be right,' Harrabura said. 'These dark men must be of another race.'

'They are not,' he was told. 'They have the same features, the same hair, skin and bone, they are of us, yet they are wanton killers of their own people.'

'We cannot fight them as well,' the Bekalbura man said, 'so we come to you for sanctuary.'

By the end of the week several decisions had been made. The Bekalbura would be given shelter as long as they scattered their people among the families on both sides of the ranges, so as not to cause more hardship to any one mob.

It was harder to deal with the Kuinmerbura elders, and the debate raged angrily. In the end, Harrabura prevailed. 'We understand your sorrow and your motives but we cannot agree to war. Too many more warriors would be killed, and who would be left to protect our children? If the Darambal nation is to survive we must protect the children.'

The last matter was debated in private. Gorrabah insisted that since the bossman, Paul, had chased away the digging men who had killed their two men, a father and son, then that was the most they could expect. 'There is nothing more we can do without bringing more pain to our people,' he said, and although the decision was met with anger and tears, the word of the Kutabura elders was law.

Jeannie was waiting with their breakfast when the men rode in. She served the beef stew and dumplings that she had prepared the night before, and joked that this was supper and breakfast all in one. The breakfast part, she said, was more dumplings, with hot golden syrup. The men ate hungrily, appreciating the solid meal, after which Paul agreed they should all take a rest.

When the men had departed, Jeannie had her say. 'Paul, I know you did your best, but was it wise to get rid of the miners?'

'I had to. We can't afford trouble. Didn't Gus tell you they killed two of the blacks?'

'Yes, but why send the lot away? I'm not blind. I saw the campfires last night, the hills are seething with blacks. We could need extra men around for our own protection.'

'Don't believe that, Jeannie. They wouldn't protect us, they were Boyd Roberts' men, hellbent on getting us off Oberon.'

'But surely you could have talked to them? Offered to let them stay if they behaved themselves.'

'It would be a waste of time.' He dragged off his boots. It was a waste of time arguing with her too, he thought wearily. The fact that the miners had killed blackfellows wouldn't cut any ice with Jeannie. 'I'm a bit worried about the mob in the hills too. Do you think you ought to take Clara and move into town for a while? Just until I see how the land lies.'

'Why should I? This is my home. And if we can't defend ourselves you should be calling in the troopers.'

'We'll stay around the homestead for the next few days to see what happens. It's a bit early to be bringing in the cavalry, they'd only make matters worse. It's my bet the blacks are having a corroboree up there to mourn the dead, that's all. After that they'll go back to their own corners.'

There was always work to do close to home base, and none of the men objected to taking on odd jobs until the coast was clear. At night they patrolled on horseback, pleased to see that fewer fires appeared in the hills, and they were all relieved that they'd overcome the problem without incident. Paul rewarded them by announcing that he'd decided to employ a full-time blacksmith and fettler, when he could find one; he realised that it was a lot of work now to keep their horses and spare mounts properly shod, not to mention the ever-present problem of repairing tools and equipment.

That news brought cheer to the men, but Paul had another motive. 'It'll mean keeping a man permanently at the homestead,' he told Gus, 'to watch out for the women.'

Gus laughed. 'Seems to me your missus'll be watching over him. She never moves an inch without that rifle of hers and she's a bloody good shot. She says you've got visitors coming soon. You ought to organise a competition when the neighbours come over.'

'Yes,' Paul said. 'That's a good idea. I'll do that.'

'And be sure you have a ladies' competition too, so that we know where to place our bets. The missus could easy earn the lads a few pounds.'

'And that's a better idea. I'd back her myself.'

He could only spare two men out on the range to check on the cattle while he worked with the others rebuilding the bridge. He borrowed a draught horse from another station to haul the logs once they'd cut the necessary timber, and even though the water level was already receding it was hard work sinking the supports and hoisting logs into place. Fortunately Gus had had some experience in bridge-building; Paul admitted he'd never have got it right otherwise, even with forty men. They toiled on, and a rough bridge began to take shape.

In the meantime, Jeannie and Clara gave themselves extra duties, making preserves and pickles, and stocking the cold room with preserved sausages, salted beef and extra cheeses. Jeannie was looking forward to the busy times with visitors, and, being a good housekeeper, she had no intention of leaving things until the last minute.

She waited for the mailman to come so that she could send him back with orders for lengths of material to make new dresses for herself, a maid's uniform for Clara, and new curtains. So much to do! Each night she and Clara pored over catalogues to choose dress patterns and study styles of hats, and to order table linen and silver. 'Whether Paul likes it or not, our visitors will be eating in our own dining room, in style,' she told Clara. 'It won't be just his parents, it will be the neighbours too, and I want them to see that we know how to entertain.'

Clara was just as excited as Jeannie was and took to each new task with enthusiasm. One day she hoped to marry a pastoralist herself, so it was good to learn all these things.

Finally the mailman came rattling along in his dray and promised to deliver Jeannie's list to the general store in Rockhampton. He handed over parcels and newspapers and letters in the canvas bag marked 'Oberon' and took delivery of her return bag which contained all their outgoing mail.

'Not much news,' he told Jeannie, 'except that the blacks have been playing merry hell again. Riders on the stations south of the river have been speared and the Kuinmer mob on the flats have gone mad, raiding homesteads. They burned one to the ground and speared a score of cattle. Almost every day there's a new attack down there. I'm glad I'm on this run, seems pretty quiet out this way.'

'But you still don't take any chances?' Jeannie remarked, indicating the double-barrelled shotgun on the floor of the dray by the driver's seat.

'Not me, missus. "Shoot first" I say.'

'So do I,' she agreed. 'There are plenty of blacks in the hills here, they had a big powwow up there recently. You ought to tell that to the troopers when you get back. It wouldn't surprise me if they hide out up there after their raids. They can cover a lot of country in a day, you know.'

'Bloody oath they can. It's worth a mention, I'll pass it on.'

Clara brought him tea, and beef and pickle sandwiches, and gave him more sandwiches wrapped in a damp teacloth to have later on his long, lonely drive.

That night Jeannie had news for Paul.

'When will you be finished with the bridge?'

'Any day now, thank God. The lads can add the trimmings. I'm stick to death of it.'

90

'That's good, because we've been invited to a party in Rockhampton.'

He was exhausted. He fetched a cold bottle of beer and two glasses and rejoined her on the veranda. 'Would you like a drink?'

'Yes please. Did you hear what I said?'

He sank down into a canvas chair beside her. 'Yes, I heard, and I don't want to go to any party in Rockhampton. I've got too much to do here.'

'Ha! But this isn't just any party.' She smiled, holding up a parchment scroll tied with gilt ribbon. 'This is an invitation from our Member of Parliament, Mr Maskey, and Mrs Maskey to attend the engagement party of their daughter! And it's to be a ball!'

Paul felt himself flush. He blessed the descending dusk for the cover of darkness and thanked his lucky stars that he had already refused to go. 'I don't care who it is,' he said, in as bored a tone as he could manage. 'We can't attend and that's that. You write them a nice letter and make our apologies.'

'I'll do no such thing. This is the first time we've been invited into real society here, and I want to go.'

'Then you go. I won't stop you. I can't afford the time.'

'Oh Paul, please.' Her voice dropped to a winsome pleading note. 'You know I couldn't possibly go on my own. And I wouldn't need a new dress. I've still got that grey satin evening dress, you know, the off-the-shoulder one I wore to our send-off. You said I looked lovely in it. I haven't worn it up here, it would be perfect.'

He felt sorry for her. If it meant that much to her, he was practically duty-bound to take her. If he were any sort of a husband. Social life was sparse for women in this isolated area, not like the busy days at Kooramin where they had finally built guest quarters to accommodate friends. But to Laura's engagement party? No. Definitely not.

'We can't go, Jeannie, and that's that.'

'You're tired, dear,' she said. 'It's weeks away yet. Once you get some rest you'll feel better about it. I'll bet all the crowd from Camelot will be there.'

He pushed his drink aside and got up.

'Where are you going?' she asked.

'The beer's a bit flat, I thought I'd get a whisky.'

'Well sit down, Paul. I'll get it for you.'

Yes, he thought. A double. A treble more like it. I need a good belt. So Laura's going to marry that bastard after all! How could she? He knew he had no right to be posing this question, even to himself. But Captain Cope? When she'd said she hated him!

Jeannie returned with the whisky bottle and a jug of cold water. 'You're right. That beer is flat. You stay there and rest. We'll talk about it tomorrow.'

They didn't talk about it the next night, they fought about it.

'Fowler Maskey is one of the most important men in the state,' she

91

cried. 'It is ridiculous to refuse his invitation. You might need his support one day, they really get things done, these people!'

'Maskey,' he laughed. 'He's an old blowhard!'

'How do you know?'

'I met him at the hotel when I was waiting for you.'

'You never told me that.'

A lot of things I haven't mentioned, he sighed. A lot of things. People change. He'd changed. He'd tried to forget about Laura but this had brought it all flooding back. If only Jeannie would stop harping on about that bloody engagement party. He'd love to go. To see her again. To confront Cope and tell him to push off and leave Laura be! Schoolboy dreams of the white knight. Who would make a bloody fool of himself. And what if she'd changed? If she were seeing Cope in a new light as a fiancé, or accepting that her parents knew what was best for their daughter? He was totally miserable and Jeannie's nagging began to annoy him. 'Once and for all, woman, I told you we are not going!'

She retaliated by refusing to speak to him; by handing the invitation about the table at supper, emphasising to him that his staff were impressed even if he were not; by talking grandly of the possibility that they might decide to accept the invitation. She infuriated and embarrassed him but he could not possibly agree to take her, and as the days passed and time ran out she raged at him for being a pig-headed fool. And he had no answer, so an angry silence developed between them.

Laura hadn't seen Amelia for days, so she rode out to visit her friend one afternoon. As she walked up the steps Amelia came to the door.

'Oh, it's you,' she said, no welcome in her voice. Laura chose not to notice; Amelia could be moody at times. 'My father and I are going out shortly,' she added.

'Oh. I won't stay long,' Laura said, taking off her hat and riding gloves. 'How have you been?'

'I am just fine, thank you. Not that you care. You never bothered to come back last Sunday. You just left me to my own devices. I never do that to my guests.'

'Yes, I am sorry about that,' Laura said, 'but I had a few problems and I had to help in the kitchen.'

Amelia plumped, pouting, into one of the well-cushioned chairs on the veranda. 'Not that it mattered. I was surrounded by beaux the minute I left the parlour. I could hardly turn round.'

'That's good, I'm glad you enjoyed yourself.'

'I always enjoy myself, otherwise I leave,' Amelia sulked. 'And since you intend to go your own way without letting me know what you are doing, I don't know why you trouble to come out here now.'

Laura frowned. 'You've heard about Bobby Cope?'

'Everyone knows you are engaged to Bobby Cope.'

'Then everyone is wrong.'

Amelia's eyes lit up. 'Wrong? He told me himself.'

'I don't care what he said. He cooked this up with my father. No one asked me, and I refused him.'

'You did?' Amelia was suspicious. 'That's not what I'm hearing.'

'Then try listening to me. You, of all people! You know I don't like him.'

'And you really have turned him down?'

Laura remained standing, staring down over the lawns. 'Yes, but my parents don't agree. They're insisting I marry him.'

'How fascinating!' Amelia was intrigued. 'Tell me more.'

'I don't want to talk about it, Amelia, if you don't mind. It's too upsetting.'

Amelia was dying to ask more questions but she knew she'd get the rest of the story in time. This had the makings of a marvellous scandal.

Just then her father joined them. He looked from one to the other, noting the rare silence between the two girls. 'Why so gloomy, you two?'

'Laura has a huge problem,' Amelia said. 'Tell him about it, Laura.'

Laura shook her head, cross with Amelia for airing her troubles to Mr Roberts, so Amelia plunged on. 'She doesn't want to marry Captain Cope and her parents say she must. You wouldn't do that to me, would you?'

'Of course not,' he laughed. 'I don't approve of arranged marriages. Which doesn't mean, my girl, I'd let you go off and marry some farmhand.'

'As if I would,' Amelia giggled. 'But if Mr Maskey insists that Laura marry the Captain, does she have to?'

'No.'

'It's not that simple,' Laura said. She knew she shouldn't be discussing her family with Boyd Roberts, but he was a man of the world, and she hoped he could give her some constructive advice. 'Father is threatening to throw me out if I don't obey him,' she whispered.

'Good God!' Roberts said. 'That does put you on the spot.'

'I know what to do,' Amelia cried. 'If he throws you out, Laura, you can come here. We'll hide you.'

Laura couldn't help laughing at Amelia's suggestion. 'And what do I do? Hide in your back room for the rest of my life?'

Boyd Roberts was very kind. 'You'll work it out,' he told her, 'but you are our friend, and if you do run into difficulty then come here by all means, and we'll talk it over.'

'There you are!' Amelia said. 'I knew Daddy would understand. We're going to a band recital in the park. Why don't you come with us?'

'Thank you, but I can't.' She smiled wanly at Mr Roberts. 'It's the political thing. I'm really sorry, but if I'm seen with you, my father would have kittens. At this stage there's no point in pouring fuel on the fire.'

'That's all right,' he said easily. 'Once the elections are over everything will be back to normal.'

'Except you'll be the Member of Parliament,' Amelia enthused, and Laura saw a trace of a frown on Roberts' face at his daughter's tactless remark.

As she rode home she wished the elections were next week, not next year, and that Boyd Roberts would defeat her father. Then there mightn't be so much fuss in the Maskey household over Fowler's place in the community. She wondered if Paul MacNamara were safe out there on his station, with all this talk about the blacks acting up again. Thoughts of him only produced curiosity about his wife, and more depression. There were occasions lately when she also wondered why she bothered to fight her parents. Since Paul wasn't free, what difference did it make whom she married? Bobby Cope really was fond of her. She could insist he leave his job and demand that her father place them managing a station. It was the life she had always wanted. Would that be so bad after all?

When Captain Cope returned from his trip he was pleased to find Laura more docile, and he courted her quietly, believing she was beginning to adjust to the idea of marriage. She even mentioned vaguely that they might manage one of the family stations. He couldn't believe his luck. He needed to get out of the army, the job was becoming too dangerous. Even if they did get rid of the blacks in this district, he'd only be sent north to take on other tribes. And there were thousands more of the bastards up there.

He became even more determined to marry Laura Maskey and went out of his way not to upset or antagonise her. He'd had to explain to Mrs Maskey that because his movements were uncertain at present, with all the unrest in the district, it would be better to postpone the engagement party until next month, and had been slightly miffed when she told him that they'd already decided to do that, to fit in with Fowler's arrangements.

'However, dear boy,' she said, 'it's best to get the invitations out nice and early because many of our guests have so far to travel. Leon is chartering a ship to bring relations and friends up from Sydney and Brisbane. So much easier, don't you think, than having them all arrive higgledy-piggledy? Really, I was just saying to Leon that it would be far more sensible to hold the wedding in Brisbane, more central for everyone, but with a politician in the family one has to take care not to offend local sensibilities . . .'

As she talked on he began to get some idea of the real wealth of these people. Chartering a ship! For God's sake! How much would that cost? Not to mention the victualling. He returned to his digs to write to Laura, a letter that took him hours to compose. He needed to put his point of view to her without her interruptions and without the stony-eyed stare she could assume.

It was a kind letter. Understanding. Generous in its warmth and affection but not flowery. She wasn't the type for that. He explained that the real basis for marriage was friendship, and that he was her friend. He was well aware by now of her reaction to Fowler's autocratic ways and he managed to place an insidious message in the letter telling her that she would be freer with him, and able to enjoy life with so many interests in common. He had courted enough women in his time to know it was important to tell them what they wanted to hear.

When Laura received the letter she thought she saw another side to Bobby Cope, a humbler, more sensible person, and she was touched. Still disturbed and depressed, knowing it was foolish to pine after Paul MacNamara, she began to believe that Bobby could release her from the iron hands of her father, and that with him she could get out into the world and have some fun for a change.

But she was not entirely convinced. She realised that the only reason she was so vulnerable at present was her lack of money, and it was up to her to make certain this didn't happen again. Not with Bobby, not with anyone.

The next time he called, she came straight to the point, turning the tables, knowing he had no choice. 'Bobby, I have decided I will marry you.'

He was delighted, and visibly relieved.

'But I have a proviso,' she continued. 'I'll make a deal with you.'

'What sort of deal?' he laughed.

'Mother says that my father is talking about a dowry, in cash, as well as offering you the position of manager of the Quilpie station.'

'Would you be happy there?' he asked. 'I believe wives should have a say in these matters.'

'Yes.'

He could hardly contain his excitement. 'Then Quilpie it will be, Laura.'

'Good, that settles your side of the deal. As for me, I want the cash.'

He was taken aback. 'My dear, what's mine is yours, we'll be partners in everything.'

'Not good enough. I haven't asked you about your financial situation and I don't want to know. The Quilpie station is a lovely property, and a money-spinner. You won't be just the manager forever – I stand to inherit that station, we'll own it, so you'll do very well out of this matter.' She smiled. 'If we're friends, Bobby, we should be open with one another, so don't look so confused. It's very simple.'

'But Laura. What if your father won't give it to you? I mean, we could lose it altogether.'

'No, we won't, you'll give it to me or you don't get the station. And if you mention this to my father the deal's off and so is the marriage.'

He was in no position to argue with her so he took the line of least resistance. 'Then I think we should seal this agreement with a kiss, don't you?'

She allowed him to kiss her and with his arms around her she tried not to think of Paul. It occurred to her then that Bobby Cope was the real loser in this situation; he was obviously very fond of her and she felt nothing. And she wondered how many other arranged marriages were as lopsided as this.

But with victory came a deadening anticlimax, as though she herself had shut the door to an empty room and now lacked the strength to wrench it open again. Her self-confidence ebbed away as she recalled her mother's angry words: 'We are doing our best for you, we have your interests at heart. Other girls understand this and obey their parents without question. I can't imagine where you get these notions. Why do you think you're so different?'

Why indeed? Laura reflected numbly.

The first person to reply to the invitation was Amelia, with a formal note stating she was unable to attend. Laura couldn't blame her – she'd have cause to be angry now, for she would think that Laura had been lying to her about Bobby Cope. When, in fact, Laura was lying only to herself.

Chapter Five

A military depot was established on Gladstone Road, south of the town, under the command of Lieutenant Gooding, who made only token patrols of inspection these days to acquaint himself with the district and its residents. He was pushing forty now, with a wife and kids down in Maryborough, and he intended to see his time out in one piece. Peter Gooding had seen enough of the backwoods fighting to last him a lifetime. He had been speared in the stomach when blacks had made a night attack on their camp out near Munduburra. He still had nightmares about the terror and the agony of that long night.

When he recovered he'd applied for administrative duties and was grateful that approval was granted, otherwise he would have resigned. This war with the blacks ran counter to all he had been taught. There were no battles, only ambushes. No lines were drawn, the blacks took no prisoners, and troopers rarely bothered either because of the language barrier and the wall of silence they encountered among the Aborigine people.

Gooding lived and worked in a small barracks that housed only twenty men, but he was satisfied. He had proved to be a very efficient administrative officer and his small office was a model of meticulous detail. The walls were covered in the latest maps of the district, as well as full particulars of the outlying stations which he had requested from the owners for their own protection.

The Lieutenant was ably backed up by Sergeant Mick O'Leary, a tough old campaigner who often joined him for a drink after supper. The two men took their duties seriously and their discussions always ranged over the immediate problems of protecting the settlers.

'The trouble is,' Gooding would say, after every outbreak of violence, 'we can't act, only react. And by the time someone gallops in with news of another attack, and we get men out there, the blacks have long gone.'

'And,' O'Leary would add, 'them amateurs get out on the job with their posses, shooting every black in sight and practically asking for bleeding paybacks.'

Finally they came to the conclusion that they were in a no-win situation with such a massive area to patrol. They were hated by the blacks and criticised by the whites for not being on hand when attacks took place.

'The only way we can succeed,' Gooding said, 'is to become more of a peacekeeping force. We need more men so that the blacks can note the presence of the military and think twice before they trot out their raiding parties.'

He sent a report to headquarters in Brisbane with a request for more troops, and was jubilant when he received a reply acceding to his request.

But the reality was an insult. One month later, Captain Robert Cope rode into the depot at the head of a troop of blackfellows. Native Mounted Police!

Gooding was furious, shocked that he should be placed in command of these renegades whom he regarded as being neither military nor police. They had a fearsome reputation for being nothing more than legalised murderers with a brief to clean out blacks from an area any way they could – and their methods were barbaric.

O'Leary, too, was shocked. 'My men will not ride with them fellers!'

The Lieutenant watched as the newcomers lined up. They wore green uniforms and peaked caps, and had cartridge bandoliers slung across their chests. They carried the latest carbines, short-barrelled, ugly-looking rifles. He turned and muttered to O'Leary, 'It beats me that black men would volunteer to fight against their black brothers.'

O'Leary seemed surprised. 'Why is that, sir? Haven't white men been fighting their white brothers for centuries? That's not what troubles me. I've seen 'em in action. All they've been taught is how to ride and shoot. Most of them are still half-wild, they know nothing of soldiering.'

Captain Cope, wearing a cavalry sabre, strode over. Gooding took the salute with a scowl. He glanced at the ten new troopers. 'I wasn't expecting anyone so soon. We don't have barrack space for your men.'

'No problem,' Cope said easily. 'They'd rather camp out anyway. Do you have officers' quarters here?'

'Not really,' Gooding was pleased to say. 'There's only my room next to the office.'

'Then I shall find lodgings in the town,' Cope said, 'if that is permissible.'

'By all means,' Gooding replied, glad to be able to distance himself from this officer, who seemed quite proud of his troops.

From then on Gooding's command became a burden. There was instant antagonism between the two officers. The Lieutenant had no choice but to deploy these reinforcements, but his men and Cope's went their separate ways.

When a complaint came in that blacks had speared several horses on a station, Cope was sent to investigate. His men swept through the nearby bush with deadly precision – they could track the blackfellows – and descended on them, guns firing, killing the innocent with the guilty and scattering families.

Some of the settlers lodged protests with Gooding as the Native Police ranged further afield and their gruesome methods became known, but mostly they cheered, delighted that at last Lieutenant Gooding was making their lands safe. So he withdrew to his office and let Cope plot his own forays and expeditions while he kept detailed records of their movements with as much truth as he could elicit from Cope's spurious reports. The rest of the time he attended to his own business and wrote long letters to his wife.

The situation now deteriorated rapidly. The Aborigines began to fight back with renewed vigour, maddened by the massacre of their families at the hands of small posses, as well as by the native troopers. The blacks were able to find refuge in the great Berserker Ranges and on the slopes of Mount Archer, from where they could fan out east and west, and race north to join up with other tribes. And they were safe in the ranges because Gooding did not have the manpower to patrol there, let alone flush them out.

Once again he wrote to headquarters, requesting that the Native Mounted Police be withdrawn, since they were only exacerbating the problem, and that he be sent sufficient trained troops to exercise some control over an area now aflame with violence.

This time there was no reply. Nor was there an answer to his subsequent requests. In desperation, Gooding made an appointment to see Fowler Maskey, Esq., MLA, to plead for his support.

Tyler Kemp was amused to see that he was travelling north on the same boat as Fowler Maskey. There was no communication between them, however, except when Maskey cast the occasional glance at him. Glances intended to wither and scorn, Tyler presumed, so this was not the time to enquire if the MP still backed Macalister's proposal for Queensland government notes. Instead, he rewarded one of the beetle-browed frowns with a wink, causing Maskey to turn his bulky back in a sudden twist, almost a pirouette in its swiftness.

Tyler laughed. If Maskey knew that this reporter had winkled out the fact of his ownership of the Spring Hill brothel, he might not be quite so shirty.

Kemp was in a merry mood. He was enjoying his first sea voyage, exhilarated by the surge and swell of the sea. Even though there had been a number of shipwrecks along this coast, Tyler was not worried – he had confidence in their sturdy ship, the steamer *Elanora*. Only last year, the SS *Star of Australia*, *en route* to Rockhampton, had gone down with the loss of seventeen lives, and Tyler had covered the story with heart-rending prose. Now he stared in awe at the crystal-blue waters, wondering about the last moments of those doomed souls.

They had fair weather all the way up the coast, and jolly company in the saloon, with singing after supper and late-night card games. Occasionally they glimpsed the mysterious green landfall to the west, and, always curious, Tyler prevailed upon the captain to allow him to study the charts so that he could learn more about this coast. It intrigued him that they were following Captain Cook's route, and that most of the landmarks had been named by Cook.

The massive coastline, so green and mysterious, seemed to loom over them as they forged north, emphasising the puny endeavours of isolated settlers in the wilderness. And that made him wonder about Rockhampton. Would this much-vaunted mining town survive?

They sailed on through idyllic tropical waters, past Cape Capricorn, now known as Curtis Island, and then across Keppel Cay and into the Fitzroy River. There was only about twenty miles to go, and Tyler was disappointed. The voyage had been too short. He wished he could travel on around the world.

He'd always had a great passion to cross the mighty oceans and visit the famous cities of the other hemisphere. This relatively short journey brought home to him the hopelessness of such dreams. Only the rich could afford such wondrous adventures. Tyler had read many books by travellers who wandered Europe, taking in the sights, staying at luxurious villas and hotels with their servants, all with infuriating disregard for the cost. The books both attracted and repelled him. On his pay he'd never be rich, no matter how hard he worked, and yet these people, obviously, had never worked in their lives.

As the *Elanora*, with shallow draught, moved steadily upstream, Tyler sat on deck studying the tropical greenery on shore and the high mountain ranges set passively in the distance against a clear blue sky. He stared curiously at the mountains; he still harboured the old mountain man's urge – when you see a hill you have to know what is on the other side.

Rockhampton was a surprise. Tyler had expected a mining village, a shanty town, but as the ship slowed he saw that the area had already been surveyed. Wide streets placed at right angles from the river disappeared inland, and along the front there were a couple of quite presentable country pubs. Grassy vacant blocks predominated, but a two-storey gentleman's residence took his eye. A prime position, he noted, with a view across the river to the hills.

'That's Mr Maskey's house,' he heard a woman say. He sneered. Of course it would be.

He watched Maskey step on to the wharf to mingle, handshaking, among the crowds and then climb into a waiting gig, driven by his son. Tyler shrugged, picked up his suitcase, planted his new boater hat firmly on his head and made for the pub across the road, dodging horsemen who seemed not to notice pedestrians.

The bar was crowded and customers spilled out into the side street. There was a motley collection of miners in red flannel shirts, uniformed troopers, and stockmen, some of whom were still wearing spurs. He shoved his way through to the counter, drank two solitary pints of beer and left his suitcase with the barman while he explored the town.

There were several stores in the next street, as well as some workers' cottages, and a post office was under construction. He passed a rickety boarding house and made a note of it – it would probably be cheaper than the hotels on the front – then peered into rough taverns that laid claim to street corners. The quality of the town deteriorated as he progressed inland. Here were the tents and shanties of itinerants scattered among tall trees. Children ran madly through the ranks of wagons and drays, washing flapped from the trees like banners and women yelled to each other as they lumped baskets about and poked at stewpots hung over campfires. Men lounged under the trees, smoking their pipes and yarning with their mates, and no one seemed to notice the smell or the clatter that seemed to Tyler incongruous in this bush setting.

Turning back along another street he was astonished to find some neater houses on large half-acre blocks, taking advantage of the brilliant trees that adorned the area. As far as he could make out, he was pleased to note, this could be quite a splendid town in time, and once he'd had the opportunity to interview some of the locals, it would make a good story to send back to the *Courier*.

There were quite a few Chinese hurrying about too, and having acquired a taste for their food in Brisbane, he pushed aside a curtain of beads and entered one of their eating houses. The dark room held only one long table, and the only customers were Chinese who, although he knew they were aware of him, seemed to ignore him. He was served soup and several other dishes and was content to be part of the cool silence, finding it very restful.

As he left, he thanked the bowing Chinaman and enquired as to the whereabouts of the local newspaper. His obliging host insisted on showing him, so they jogged for two blocks until the Chinese stopped and bowed again in front of the single-fronted timber offices of the *Capricorn Post*.

When informed of the arrival of the visitor, Cosmo Newgate himself came out to welcome Tyler. 'We're only in a small way here,' he apologised. 'I'm owner, editor and jack-of-all- trades with this paper, so you'll have to excuse us if you find our work a little amateurish.'

'Not at all,' Tyler said. 'I've just been reading a copy and you do jolly well.'

'Coming from the well-known Mr Kemp, that is a compliment,' Newgate said. 'Can I buy you a drink? Not often we are honoured by visits by fellow journalists. Nothing much happens in our little town. Are you here on a story?'

'A holiday,' Tyler said, 'and maybe a bit of work.'

The two men walked down to a hotel opposite the tiny police station and into a private bar, obviously the haunt of the better-heeled gents of the town. As Tyler had expected, their talk turned to politics.

Cosmo bewailed the state of Queensland's finances and Tyler agreed but was wary of stating his opinions. He didn't want to start off on the wrong foot, and besides, at present all he wanted to do was listen.

'You've met Mr Maskey, our local member?' Cosmo asked.

Tyler nodded. 'Yes, many times.'

'He has a big following here,' Cosmo remarked, and Tyler guessed that the newspaper proprietor was being equally noncommittal.

'I should imagine he would have,' he replied. 'I've even heard talk that he supports the separation movement up here.' He caught the quick frown on Cosmo's face and continued blandly. 'That's an interesting debating point. Good copy, it would sell plenty of papers.'

'That's true.' Cosmo smiled. 'You never get a hundred per cent agreement on these matters . . .'

They were interrupted by a tall fellow in immaculate riding clothes. The outfit of an English country squire, Tyler speculated.

'Cosmo, old chap,' the stranger said. 'Good to see you taking a break from the presses.'

'Only a short break,' Cosmo said. 'Mr Kemp, may I introduce Mr Boyd Roberts. Mr Kemp is a reporter with the *Brisbane Courier*. He just arrived this morning.'

Roberts was interested. 'Are you now?' he said to Tyler as they shook hands. 'Then you must allow me to buy you a drink. And you too, Cosmo.'

'Not me,' Cosmo said. 'I have to be running along. But I'm sure Mr Kemp will appreciate the company.'

As Roberts walked over to the bar to buy the drinks, Cosmo murmured to Tyler, 'You might find him interesting. He's standing against Fowler Maskey in the next elections.'

'More good copy?' Tyler said mischievously, and Cosmo nodded. 'My word. In this little backwater it's the clash of the titans.'

Tyler enjoyed Roberts' company. He was an amusing fellow and made no attempt to push any political barrow. In an offhand way he told of his good luck in striking gold at Canoona. Tyler was fascinated – stories of gold mines and the heady business of following those golden reefs had always held him spellbound. They talked for more than an hour before Tyler thought he might be outstaying his welcome. 'I must be off,' he said. 'I have to retrieve my suitcase from a pub on the front street.'

'That's Quay Street,' Roberts said. 'Where are you staying?'

'I spotted a lodging house not far from here. I thought I'd put up there.'

'A lodging house!' Boyd Roberts was appalled. 'We can't have our important visitors staying in those places. I have plenty of room, why don't you stay with me for a while? Since you're on holiday, I'll have to see you are taken care of.'

'I wouldn't like to intrude,' Tyler said.

Roberts laughed. 'Not a bit of it. Glad to have your company.

Consider it settled. I live a couple of miles out of town, up the hill, so I'll have to find you a horse. You wait here and I'll attend to it.'

Not only did Roberts produce a horse for him, he told Tyler not to worry about his luggage. 'I've sent a chap to collect your suitcase and bring it out to the house.'

Tyler was delighted with this demonstration of country hospitality and relieved that Roberts had insisted. As the two men cantered away from the town, Roberts glanced over at him. 'You ride well for a city lad.'

'I grew up in the bush.' Tyler smiled. 'Rode bareback for years until my dad could afford to buy me a saddle.' He was feeling very much at ease with Roberts. Even though he was quite a bit older than himself, Tyler sensed his new friend had a youthful attitude and a cheery outlook on life. What luck, he thought, to have fallen on my feet so soon. Room and board taken care of and good company to boot.

Tyler, in the course of his duties, had been inside many a Brisbane mansion but he'd never stayed in one. Although Beauview couldn't quite be classified as a mansion, it was a large, roomy place with high ceilings and was extremely well appointed. His bedroom was big enough to accommodate a family, with its double bed, chaise longue and plump armchairs that had no trouble competing for space with the mahogany dresser and wardrobe. The French windows opened on to a private veranda and Tyler walked out to look over the grounds. The room itself was a wonderful retreat, and with a twinge of envy, he thought how fortunate people were to be able to live in such pleasant surrounds.

When the maid had delivered his suitcase, he unpacked and stripped, and strolled leisurely over to the washstand to pour water from the china jug into the large basin, enjoying the luxury of space after the cramped cabin on the ship. The water was cool, the towels soft as down, which reminded him to test the high, wide bed; sure enough, it was so comfortable he wished he could take a nap there and then. But time was moving on. After giving him a short tour of the main rooms at the front of the house, Boyd had invited him to join them for drinks on the front veranda before dinner. He hadn't said who else would be present and since he had already mentioned that he was a widower, Tyler wondered who the other guests were.

Since his host had also said that they dressed for dinner, Tyler put on his dark suit, stiff shirt and black bow tie, sifting among his socks for his cuff links. The evening wear had been expensive but a good investment – it got him past many a doorman while his colleagues were left standing outside, and right now he was thankful that he'd decided to pack these clothes.

Boyd was alone. 'Come and join me,' he called as Tyler walked through the parlour. 'What's your poison?'

'A whisky, thanks.' Tyler said, watching as Boyd poured drinks from a well-laden tray set up by the railing. He estimated there must be twenty pounds' worth of grog on that tray alone.

'Your good health,' Boyd said as he handed over Tyler's glass.

The visitor took his drink and stood looking out at the magnificent view. The house was perched on the crown of the hill and the trees directly in front of it had been cleared, allowing a panoramic scene to unfold before them. Down on the flats the little town clung to the sweep of the river, insignificant in the grand landscape that surged forward to the distant blue ranges.

'It's very pleasant up here,' Tyler said, watching as dusk streaked the sky with layers of pink and a silvery mist crept over the valley.

'Indeed it is,' Boyd replied. 'And I can feel part of the town from here without being confined in it.'

'Are you a country man too?'

'No. I was born in Sydney. My old man was a schoolmaster and since I had no inclination in that direction, he shoved me into the army. I hated it. Rose to the high rank of corporal, then I gave it away. Too many bosses for my liking.'

'I can understand that. I don't think I could survive army discipline.'

Boyd laughed. 'Sit yourself down. We don't stand on ceremony here.' They settled into the comfortable chairs and Tyler luxuriated in this idyllic atmosphere, telling himself he could easily take to this life.

'What about reporting?' Boyd asked. 'That wouldn't be too hard, would it?'

'Not when you get the hang of it. When I woke up to the fact that I could write just as well, if not better than the other blokes, I stopped being ordered about and was on my way.'

'So what happens now?' Boyd asked. 'Do you have many bosses? I'm always curious about how they run big newspapers.'

'No, not really. I get along well with my editor – we have a few dust-ups occasionally, but on the whole I can handle my own job without interference.' He didn't mention that he'd just been pulled off the story about the Queensland notes; it seemed trivial now in this placid environment.

'Why did you choose Rockhampton for your holiday?' Boyd asked, but Tyler didn't have a chance to reply. A girl had hurried out on to the veranda, a pretty, dark-haired girl with the face of a cherub. She was wearing a beautiful dress, he noted, of the palest pink silk with a full skirt that rustled softly across the polished timbers. The soft *décolletage* was swathed in a sheer material that was held at a plunging cleavage by a cameo brooch. She had the creamiest skin and, he thought, as he leapt to his feet, the sort of swelling bust-line that men would die for.

'My daughter,' Boyd was saying, 'Amelia.'

He could only stare as Amelia settled herself prettily in front of the two men. 'Father has told me all about you, Mr Kemp,' she said. 'I believe you're quite famous.'

'Oh no,' he stammered. 'I'm just what they call a scribbler.'

'Don't sell yourself short,' Boyd warned, 'or she'll believe you.' He poured his daughter a sherry and she looked to Tyler as if waiting for him to speak.

'You have a lovely house here,' he said. 'It is all so beautiful.' He wished he hadn't said that – he felt he was referring to her – so he kept on. 'I mean the house, the grounds, the panoramic view . . . It is such a pleasant surprise.'

Her long eyelashes fluttered at him. 'You're very gracious, Mr Kemp,' and her reply seemed to indicate that the compliment was personal. As it was, he thought in a panic. He hoped Boyd Roberts hadn't noticed – he might not approve.

'How long are you staying, Mr Kemp?' she asked.

'Oh, only a few days,' he managed to reply.

Boyd intervened. 'A few days? Certainly not. We'd be quite put out if you don't stay longer. There isn't another ship for a fortnight, and surely you wouldn't forsake us for a lodging house.'

Amelia's voice pealed like a silver bell. 'We love having visitors, and we'll try our best to make you comfortable.'

'Oh, I am very comfortable,' he said, apology in his voice.

'Then that's settled,' she said. 'Now, Daddy, we can't have our Brisbane visitor sitting about twiddling his thumbs. We'll have to introduce him to people. I will arrange some social occasions, and perhaps a dance.'

'Whatever you think, my dear,' Boyd said, then, turning to Tyler, 'Amelia is a wonderful hostess. I think you and I are in for a good time, Tyler.'

Amelia took his arm as they went in to dinner. He was so tall she only came up to his shoulder, but she could feel his strength, and she'd already admired his looks and his physique. When her father had told her a reporter was staying with them she'd expected a wizened little man with glasses, but Tyler Kemp was something else. Brains and brawn, a rare combination. She wished she was still speaking to Laura so she could crow over this manly hunk who was actually staying in their house. Laura, that lying double-crosser, could keep Bobby Cope, he couldn't hold a candle to Tyler.

And Daddy liked him too. That was a turn-up. Otherwise he'd never have been invited to stay. Her father was very careful about things like that. The stamp of approval made Tyler even more attractive.

And he loved this house, too! Amelia saw every young man she met as a possible husband, but she soon lost interest in most of them. Not this time, though. Tyler was intelligent – that meant harmony in the house, because Boyd never suffered fools. He had a lot of men working for him out on the diggings and prospecting in the hills but he saw them in his office out by the side gate. They were never invited into his home and Amelia knew why. He didn't want them ogling his daughter. She appreciated that, she didn't need them about her either.

Amelia was already in love with Tyler, and at dinner she glowed. His clothes, she admitted to herself, were cheap and rather shabby, but that could be remedied. After all, what was a wife for?

Boyd Roberts sat in his study, his feet up on his desk, and sipped at a cognac. It had been a most fortuitous day. Kemp had gone off to bed armed with books from their small collection, and a promise to make a list for Amelia so that she could start to build a library at Beauview. He gave a snort of laughter at Amelia's sudden interest in books, meant to impress their guest. But she needn't have worried. By not mentioning his daughter Boyd had created exactly the scene that transpired. He had already ascertained that Kemp was single and unattached, and so was not at all surprised when Amelia's appearance had such an effect on their guest.

She always liked to dress up, to be stared at, so Boyd knew he could count on her to stun the male guest, no matter his age. Kemp's response didn't disappoint. The way he had gulped at Amelia, the way his eyes had fastened like limpets on Amelia's buxom bosoms, Boyd guessed that this lusty mountain lad was just about ready to ravish her on the spot. He had enjoyed Kemp's discomfort; he knew the feeling, swelling desire versus good manners.

Boyd liked younger women, but not adolescents. When he visited the East Street whorehouse, he preferred them just out of their teens, fully developed. Like Amelia's friend, Laura Maskey! Now there was a tasty one. Rounded in all the right places, a wide mouth and full lips, made for loving; little pink ears in that cascade of blonde hair. God . . . given half a chance he could ravish her. He had watched her often, sitting there gossiping with Amelia, while he stayed quietly in the background, the genteel papa, undressing her with his eyes, seeing his hands around that firm behind and on to the blonde fuzz. If only Laura knew it, he was the man for her, he could teach her what real sex was all about, teach her how to live, and shout for more as his whores did.

He laughed and poured another cognac. Not to worry, while there's life there's hope. One day he just might get his hands on the lovely Laura when she stopped bleating her kiddy stuff about that fool, Cope.

But back to Amelia, and the all-important scenario that had just fallen, heaven blessed, into his hands.

Boyd Roberts, despite his apparent ignorance, knew exactly who Tyler Kemp was. He was one of the few people in Rockhampton to receive the Brisbane newspapers. They might be weeks old but he read every word. He'd been amused by Tyler's criticism of Maskey's speeches. And then he'd read Tyler's article about the Queensland government notes, slamming Fowler for being such a fool as to support such financial chicanery. And once again he was right. Boyd agreed with him. It was madness, as was the idea of separation, of turning Queensland into two states. It was too soon. Later, he'd look into it, but Boyd's immediate aim was to unseat Fowler by fair means or foul. Fowl! Fowler! He was getting drunk and he didn't care, the situation was improving by the minute.

So he had a daughter and a top-line reporter who were raring to go, and if he knew his daughter, she'd make the next move. The important move. And if he encouraged them he could end up with a son-in-law worth his weight in gold to a man with political ambitions. The thrill of it gave him an almost physical stirring.

But Kemp was no fool. It would take a lot more than a romance with Amelia to keep him onside and blind to other activities.

To hell with MacNamara and his arrogance! He could wait. He'd wrecked expensive equipment and evicted his men, and then had tried to blame him just because some niggers got shot. But threats never bothered Boyd Roberts. Threats were a sign of weakness. He'd never threatened anyone in his life. He acted. Like at that Starlight mine at Canoona. He'd offered the old fool a good price for the mine and when he'd refused, Boyd's men had dumped him down an old shaft deep in the bush. They might find him in a hundred years. And the reef had been a beauty, it had run on and on until it had gone so deep, bad air had forced its closure. One day, when better equipment became available, Boyd intended to go back there.

And there'd been other mines. Prospecting was a waste of time. Easier to wait and watch until someone struck colour and then negotiate. The leaseholder could hand it over the easy way or the hard way, Boyd wasn't fussed. As for that bastard Corbett! He'd found a thin reef on Oberon but it had petered out within yards of the shaft. Since Boyd was now interested in joining the upper-crust cattle fraternity in this area to further his political ambitions he'd told Corbett to stay put and begin a sustained harassment of MacNamara, but he hadn't counted on that weak-kneed rat spilling the beans in front of witnesses.

One of the men had come whining to Beauview: 'We didn't have no choice! MacNamara was gonna lynch us!'

Boyd couldn't remember the miner's name. Tom Something.

'You bloody fool,' he'd shouted. 'He had to be bluffing! You should have called his bluff! Where's Corbett?'

'He took off like a whippet. Gone south, Mr Roberts. Not comin' back. I'm the only one game enough to come on in here and tell you the true story. And pick up me pay, if youse don't mind.'

Boyd had stared at him. The only one left in Rockhampton to back up MacNamara's story that Boyd's men had been acting under his orders. Well, Tom Something wouldn't be able to bear witness, if push came to shove. He was resting peacefully at the bottom of the Fitzroy River, unless the crocodiles had found him.

For the time being, Boyd decided, he'd keep his best men close to home. His miners could go on operating on established diggings, but half a dozen of his most trusted men now worked around this property as gardeners, stablehands and general maintenance hands. It suited them – they lived well in good quarters – and it suited him to have them ready if any extra duties arose.

But while we court our reporter, he mused, Beauview must stay a peaceful retreat.

He wondered how much it would take to buy out Cosmo Newgate and install his own editor at the local newspaper office. A hypothetical question at this point, but worth considering. Money talks – but newspapers have a lot more to say. If he had control of the local paper, Maskey wouldn't be in the hunt.

Boyd's thoughts trailed back to Amelia. It was time she was married, and then it would be his turn. He didn't intend to be old Grandpa, relegated to the nursery with her kids; he would have his own life. But he knew his daughter. It had given him immense pleasure to spoil her outrageously and to watch the little sod grow into this lovely young lady with pretty manners and an iron will. She was selfish and demanding and her father applauded, because she was Amelia Roberts, and proud of it. That in itself gave him a great deal of satisfaction.

He had observed the sly measures she took to spook women whom she considered might have their eyes on her father as a possible husband, and that caused him no end of amusement. She was only protecting her territory. Besides, those tittering hopefuls were not worth considering. But now that a suitor who could be useful to him was eyeing Amelia, it was time to marry her off and find a wife for himself.

Amelia seemed to think that this house was hers, but she was wrong there. Shifting her out might take a tantrum or two, but he knew his girl, she could be bribed. If need be he'd build her another place where she could roost with her husband, and God help him if he didn't toe the line.

Yes, it had been an interesting day, it had thrown up a wealth of possibilities. Congratulating himself, he snuffed out the lamps and made his way unsteadily to the master bedroom.

Even though he'd had quite a lot to drink, Tyler couldn't sleep. He lay naked on the cool sheets, allowing the small breeze flowing from the open French windows to waft over him.

He too was thinking of Amelia, looking forward to seeing much more of her in the next few days, but he was also thinking of Boyd Roberts. The genial host was excellent company and Tyler couldn't think when he'd last enjoyed an evening so much, but he had a strange feeling that all wasn't quite what it seemed.

Roberts had been entertaining – he was quite a raconteur, with yarns of his army days and the gold fields – and with his smooth dark hair, well-trimmed sideburns and moustache, and easy manner, he fitted into his elegant surroundings. But his eyes were street-smart, calculating. Tyler argued with himself over that. Roberts made no claim to a gentlemanly upbringing – apparently his parents had been quite poor, so why should he not be sharp-eyed? The man had done well for himself, so he was obviously no fool.

And look how he'd cared for his daughter, who obviously adored him! Full marks for that effort after the loss of the mother, which must have been a trying time for both of them. He'd asked Roberts why he had never remarried, and he'd looked fondly at Amelia. 'Good lord, Tyler. Amelia is the best hostess in town.'

From across the table Amelia had smiled at Tyler. 'I can look after Daddy perfectly well.'

The reply endeared her to him, but in her innocence she had not really addressed the question. Nor, though, had her father. Boyd was a fit, healthy male, as was his guest, neither of them the type to starve themselves sexually. Tyler wasn't married because he couldn't afford the girls he liked and hadn't found an alternative.

'You're aiming too high,' his mother had said, on his last visit. She wanted to see her son settled down. 'You're nearly thirty, son, don't send me to the grave without grandchildren.'

Tyler turned over restlessly. Amelia's eyes . . . green flecked with gold, so like her father's . . . But Boyd's eyes had reflected something else. As if he were laughing at her, at both of them. Not merry eyes, cold. What was the word he was looking for? He thrashed about in his mind for it, as he did so often, and came up with . . . Cruel.

But how could that be in this loving household?

Nevertheless, sleep being distant, he pursued the subject. He had long learned the art of listening, not to what people were saying, but to what they meant.

If Roberts were a candidate for the seat of Rockhampton, why had he not mentioned the fact? Good manners? Not wishing to talk shop to a guest? Maybe. But he'd be the first candidate in history with that sort of control. Especially with a reporter as captive audience.

Tyler's suspicious nature growled to the surface. A couple of times, Boyd had referred disparagingly to Fowler Maskey, and Amelia had agreed with him until a warning glance from her father had caused her to change the subject. To put them at their ease, Tyler had mentioned that he and Fowler didn't see eye to eye on a number of matters. If ever a candidate was given an opening to cash in, that was it, but Boyd had simply remarked, 'Is that so?' as if it had come as a surprise to him. He hadn't requested Tyler to enlarge.

But later, when they'd retired to the parlour, Tyler had seen the unmistakable headlines of the *Brisbane Courier* peeping out from a pile

109

of newspapers on the desk, and on his way to bed he'd checked the dates. They were current, or as new as would come to Rockhampton. Boyd would know where he stood, so why the reticence?

Tyler accepted that his host did not wish to discuss politics with him, and fair enough, that was his prerogative, but it would come. Sooner or later it would come. In the meantime he was being buttered up, and that didn't sit well with him. What else did Roberts have in mind, to waste valuable time like this?

Irritated, he got up and in the sharp moonlight didn't bother to light the lamp. He walked over to the washstand and poured himself a glass of water, his mouth now dry from the alcohol. As he stood by the open doors, drinking a second glass, his keen eyes saw movement outside. He whipped a towel about his hips and moved out on to the small veranda, edging sideways into the shadows. He saw a man carrying a gun, a rifle or shotgun, he guessed, and he was about to raise the alarm when another one, also armed, appeared. The two men conferred and then moved away in opposite directions.

Guards, he realised. But why? Were they afraid of attacks by natives? It was possible, but not likely, here, even if they were a way out of town. Highly unlikely in fact. So what were they guarding? Life or property? And from whom?

Morning was crystal-blue and the clamour of birds woke him with the dawn, disarming the troublesome imps of night. Tyler lay listening to the menagerie of sound until the birds settled and a magpie gave its solo performance, notes ringing blissfully through the trees.

That was the signal for Tyler to be up and about. He never enjoyed a sleep-in, treasured by his colleagues – morning, for him, was the best part of the day. Rather than disturb the rest of the house, he dressed and dropped lightly from the veranda to the garden, then set off to explore the grounds.

Eucalypts, mingled with palms and ancient ferns, formed a back-drop to flower gardens. The lawns were springy, touched with dew, and were certainly attractive, but as he progressed to the rear of the house he was pleased that the woods were in their natural state.

He marched on to the stables where two weary men were drinking tea with a young stablehand. 'Good morning,' he called. 'Lovely day.'

'That it is,' the stablehand replied, grabbing at his pitchfork in a belated attempt to look busy.

Tyler saw two rifles propped against the wall. 'Ah! You chaps must be tired. Night watch is a long, tiring duty.' He appeared to take it for granted that their patrol was necessary. 'Do you get to sleep now?'

'For a few hours,' one of the men replied. 'After breakfast, that is.'

'Yes, you'd need it,' he said. 'Mr Roberts must be pleased that you do such a good job. Plenty of night watchmen I know sleep on the job.'

The praise brought a grudging response. 'Not us,' the second fellow said. 'We stay on our feet, keep an eye out, like.'

'For which city people like me are grateful, I can tell you,' Tyler said. 'I hear the blacks up here are savage.'

They looked blankly at him. 'Blacks? Ain't no blacks around here.'

'Oh! That's a relief.'

He deliberately left a vacuum in the conversation, knowing that someone would feel obliged to continue, and the shorter of the two men, who looked more like bruisers than house staff, proffered a comment. 'We just keep an eye on the place for Mr Roberts. He's a rich man.'

'So I've noticed.' Tyler grinned. 'And rich men have enemies, that seems to be their lot.'

'That's a true fact,' the guard said, finishing his tea. 'Always bloody someone wanting to cause trouble, but not while we're around.'

'I'm glad to hear it. Do you mind if I have a look at the horses? This is a fine stable.'

'Go ahead. These are the toffs in here, but there's some right good nags in the paddock at the back.'

'Thank you.' Tyler went on his way, even more curious now. What enemies? And since when did rich men have a monopoly on enemies? The variety that would resort to violence.

For the next few days, Tyler's time was monopolised by Roberts, who included his daughter in all their activities – riding, picnicking by the river, where Amelia was content to watch the men fish, luncheon at the Criterion Hotel and card games in the evenings. He loved being with Amelia, looking at her and smelling her fragrance, and he longed to touch her but in the presence of her father, that joy was denied. He began to feel stifled by Roberts and frustrated by Amelia's closeness, so on the Friday morning he cried off, announcing that he had a couple of things to do in town.

'We'll come with you,' Boyd said.

'No, don't bother.' Tyler could be as firm as his host when necessary. 'I've taken up too much of your time already.'

'Will you be back for lunch?' Amelia asked.

Tyler laughed. 'Please don't wait lunch for me. I must have put on a stone since I've been here, with your delicious meals. Fasting will do me good.'

She looked a little peeved, and retaliated. 'Very well then. I have such a lot to do anyway. The dance is on Saturday night, and I have to order all the food for the supper. Daddy, you be sure to get the drawing room cleared for me so that we'll have room to dance, and make sure we have plenty of liquid refreshments.'

'Consider it done.'

Tyler's first stop was at the army barracks, where he introduced himself to Lieutenant Gooding in his official capacity as a reporter. He felt he'd wasted enough time and so far had achieved nothing.

111

The Lieutenant was an amiable chap, glad to find a sympathetic ear. 'There's a war going on up here, but the settlers don't seem to understand this. They can't grasp that we have a race of people fighting for survival.'

Tyler warmed to him. 'Let's talk off the record. I called in here because I see you have native troopers.'

'Native Mounted Police,' Gooding corrected him. 'They should be with the police but they were inflicted on me because the local sergeant of police is outranked by their command, Captain Cope. So don't go blaming their activities on me.'

'I take it you don't approve of them.'

'That's putting it mildly. I have been trying to have them withdrawn. I went to see Mr Maskey yesterday, but since Cope is to marry his daughter, he wouldn't hear a word of criticism in that direction. He did agree to request more regular troops for this area, though.'

'Oh no!' Tyler said. 'You can't be serious!'

'What else can I do? There are people being murdered on both sides.'

'More blacks than whites, though.'

'That's true. But my orders are to protect the settlers. Nothing about protecting the Aborigines. That's why those bloody native police get away with murder. I've asked for more troops to try to keep the peace and hopefully preserve life, but if you've got a better idea, believe me I'd be glad to hear it.'

It was a depressing situation so Tyler changed the subject. 'What do you know about Boyd Roberts?'

Gooding looked at him keenly. 'Why? What's your interest in him?'

'Just curious. I'm staying with him.'

The Lieutenant shrugged. 'I try not to get involved in local politics.'

'That's why I'm asking you. I don't need biased opinions. Even though I'm staying there, he hasn't mentioned that he's a candidate to oppose Maskey, and I wonder why. I find that odd.'

'He's more than odd,' Gooding warned. 'I'd say he just wants to get you full onside first. He has a big following here and he's a damn sight more popular than Maskey, but you be wary of him. My men travel about, they hear the other side of the story. Nothing you can print, mind you, but where there's smoke there's fire. I believe the man is ruthless and dangerous, behind that façade of gentlemanly charm. He considers himself above the law and employs roughhouse tactics to get what he wants.'

'For instance?'

'They say his men assaulted two miners and ran them off their claim. One of them was in town recently, threatening to kill Roberts. Is it true he's got men guarding him at Beauview now?'

'I haven't noticed,' Tyler lied. 'Next time you go out into the bush, would you mind if I joined you?'

112

'Not at all. I'm due to visit some of the stations shortly. I'll let you know.' He winked. 'You'll be safe enough with me. I try not to look for trouble.'

At the same time, Leon was reporting to his father. 'I found out where Tyler Kemp is staying.'

'Good. You keep tabs on him.'

'It won't be easy, he staying with Boyd Roberts.'

'What?'

'Yes. I wonder what the connection is?'

'It's bloody obvious, he's joined forces with Roberts to get at me. You speak to Cosmo Newgate. I don't want any of his tripe appearing in the local paper.'

'I thought you spoke to him yourself.'

'That was on another matter. I didn't know then that Kemp had palled up with Roberts.' Fowler swung about angrily in his chair. 'And where's Captain Cope? The engagement party is next week and I haven't sighted him.'

'He's out on patrol, but he'll definitely be back for the occasion. Come hell or high water I should imagine,' Leon added with a sneer, but Fowler had lost interest.

Anonymity, Tyler mused, was always a good place to sit and think. He chose a rough-hewn table at the back of one of the taverns on which to place his pint of beer and a cheese bun, settled on a bench and kept his eyes to himself. There weren't many customers about, considering it was midday, but the few burly men shouldering through to the small bar were not the types to be stared at. Quite a few wore knives or handguns slung in their belts. They fascinated him – each one would have a story to tell – but this was not the time, he had other things on his mind. Mainly Amelia.

He was shrewd enough not to be distressed by Gooding's comments about her father. He'd met many a bad lad in his day and didn't expect them to be confined to the working class. Nor did he see himself as the hero come to rescue the good citizens of Rockhampton. If Maskey and Roberts were the best they had to offer to the political scene then they deserved them. The people's choice was not always wise.

Now that he knew Roberts, it would be stupid to involve his host in the story about Fowler's brothel – he might just drop that to Cosmo himself. But he did want to meet Captain Cope and write more about the Native Mounted Police. Obviously the only way to learn of their activities was to get out into the countryside and see for himself. Go right into the battlefields, so to speak. He realised it could be dangerous, since Aborigines would see him as the enemy too, but it was time to put his money where his mouth was, instead of hiding behind a desk and writing second-hand reports.

He had asked Gooding point-blank if he could see Cope's reports

113

but had been refused. 'Not on your life,' Gooding had said. 'It wouldn't be worth my job. Besides, if you want the truth, that's not the place to look.'

Roberts and Fowler Maskey had one thing in common – neither of them disapproved of the Native Police – but where Fowler actively supported them, Roberts was not interested. 'I'm buying properties out there myself,' he'd said. 'But I won't be whining to the police to protect me every time a barn gets burned down.'

Knowing more of the man now, Tyler guessed that would be true. Roberts would have his own methods, and neither miners, blacks nor police could expect a welcome in his kingdoms.

But the sins of the parent shouldn't be visited on the daughter, so he would stay a few more days at Beauview – at least until after Amelia's dance, since she was going to so much trouble. And he would try to find a chance to court Amelia.

The thought jolted him. Was he really that keen on her? His answer was clear and decisive. Yes! This was no passing attraction, he was in love with Amelia and he already knew she was fond of him. He wanted to marry her and take her back to Brisbane . . . to what? To his digs? No, it was time for him to find a house, even buy a house and settle down. Then the real worry began to gnaw. Could he take her from that beautiful setting, her life of luxury? And more importantly, would she accept a radically lower standard of living?

'If she loves you she will,' he told himself. And then he added: 'Don't bet on it.'

Depressed now, he saw that the odds were stacked against him, that he had no right at all to offer himself as a suitor. The best thing to do, he decided, was to try to forget the whole idea. It would hurt for a while, but not as much as rejection.

Cosmo Newgate hardly looked up when Tyler walked into his office. 'What can I do for you?' he asked, his tone cold, a far cry from their first meeting.

'Not a lot,' Tyler said cheerfully. 'I've got a couple of items here you might like to look at.' He handed over an article he'd written some time back about the Native Police. One that had not been accepted by his own paper.

Cosmo's reaction was no different. 'I can't print this. I'd get run out of town.'

'Who by? Fowler Maskey? Because Cope is going to marry his daughter?'

'It's nothing to do with Fowler Maskey. But now that you come to mention it, we don't need strangers denigrating our public figures, especially when they line up with men like Roberts.'

'You introduced me to Roberts, remember?' Tyler said angrily. 'And as for your high-falutin public figures, take a look at this!' He threw down another page with a short article referring to Fowler.

'I've been expecting this from you,' Cosmo said, after a quick glance. He threw the page into his rubbish bin. 'Fowler told me that you are biased against him and that you started a rumour that he was the proprietor of a certain brothel. I found it hard to believe that a journalist of your calibre should stoop to such lies, but now I see he was right.'

'You are seeing that *I* am right,' Tyler retorted. 'You can check if you like.'

'I already have. By telegraph. And I have the reply from the titles office. Maskey does not own that property.'

'What?' Tyler was stunned. Ferret was a reliable informant but this time he must have made a mistake.

Noting Tyler's embarrassment, Cosmo smiled thinly. 'I'd say you owe Mr Maskey an apology.'

'If this is the case, I probably do,' Tyler admitted.

'Then why don't you just run along,' Cosmo said. 'Roberts is a great host, you must be living the life of Riley at Beauview.'

'Don't be sarcastic,' Tyler said. 'Roberts has made me most welcome, and he hasn't mentioned politics. And if he has a murky background, you'd have exposed him by this.'

'Expose what? Unlike you, I don't write without proof. And right now we've enough trouble in the town. If you hadn't been living up there on the hill, your head in the clouds, you'd have noticed the unrest down here on the flat. There are a lot of people out of work now since the Government has practically shut down, the townspeople are hard hit, and a food store was ransacked last night.'

'I didn't know the trouble had spread,' Tyler said. 'I'm sorry about that.'

Cosmo relented. 'Doesn't appear our Mr Maskey has noticed either,' he remarked. 'Nor, I suppose, your Mr Roberts.'

'Not *my* Mr Roberts. And no, he hasn't said a word.'

Cosmo shrugged. 'Our titans live on a higher plane. Personally I wouldn't give a bob for either of them.'

'Then help me get a first-hand story on the Native Police. I won't ask you to print it. I just want to see for myself. Give me some introductions to station people.'

'They wouldn't thank you. They have no objection to blackfellers chasing blackfellers.'

'There must be someone who could help me get the real story on them.'

'I don't know . . .' Cosmo said. Then, 'You could try MacNamara at Oberon Station, he's more lenient when it comes to the wild blacks. I've heard him say he'd rather feed them than fight them, so he might be the one to talk to.'

'Good. That's a start.'

As Tyler left he felt he at last had some purpose, a definite lead to get him on track again. And away from the impossible connection with Amelia and Boyd Roberts. He would head for Oberon Station as soon as possible.

But other events looming were to turn his plans upside down. The first of these was connected with Cosmo's remark that Fowler Maskey hadn't noticed the growing poverty in the town. At the time Tyler was too concerned with his own problems to catch the specific reference.

Boyd Roberts could have told him. He spoke to Amelia at lunch. 'I want you to scale down this dance you're having on Saturday night.'

'I'm sorry, Daddy, I can't do that. I've written out the invitations and I'm having them hand-delivered today.'

'It's clashing with Laura's engagement party.'

'I know,' she giggled. 'But quite a few people have said they'd much rather come here than go to old Fowler's shindig. He's bound to turn it into a long, boring speech-night. They'll have far more fun here.'

'They would, of course,' he agreed. 'But I want you to listen to me for once. There's a lot of criticism in the town for the money Maskey's spending on that ball, and I don't want to be accused of the same thing. Not just now, when the town is feeling the pinch. The shopkeepers are worried; if people are broke they can't pay their bills and they drift away. It wouldn't take much to topple a new town like this.'

Amelia frowned. 'Surely my party isn't going to break Rockhampton!'

'That's not the point. If I go flaunting my money in their faces now it will ruin me politically. It is much better for us to watch Maskey shooting himself in the foot.'

'So now I can't have a party?'

'Yes, you can. The table seats twelve. You can invite nine other people to dinner – that won't attract attention. I'll hire a fiddler and a piano-player so you can still have a dance afterwards. You'll enjoy yourselves.'

'And Laura wins! She has a better party than me.'

Boyd laughed. He'd guessed all along why she'd wanted to have her dance on that particular night. 'I wouldn't worry about that,' he told her. 'There might even be trouble in town that night, so you're well out of it.'

'What sort of trouble?'

'I'm not sure,' he told her. 'Sometimes people get all hot and bothered and do stupid things. But we'll be safe at home, so you have your little private dance. I think that rather an elegant idea anyway. Much nicer than a big crush.'

'You're right,' she said, thrilled. 'It will be simply superb and I'll get out all the best silver. The people who aren't invited will be green when they hear.'

Boyd Roberts assembled three of his men in his office well away from the house. It was a long sandstone building with barred windows, set among the trees. The office contained a large desk and easy chairs, and the flagstone floor merited an attractive carpet square. In one corner, bolted to the floor, was a strong safe, and in the other a tall cupboard containing innocuous files – mostly stud books, accounts, wages books, surveyors' reports and maps.

A locked and bolted door led into another room where he kept his armoury and ammunition, and a second safe for cash and gold. He was always careful when opening the safe in his office to let the men see it contained very little cash, and no one but himself was ever permitted to enter the locked room. Not under any circumstances.

'Maskey is having a big party at the Golden Nugget on Saturday night,' he told them. 'I want you to go into town today, get about the pubs and start stirring. Make sure you let the workers know that Fowler's got plenty of dough, he's not hurting! Let them know that he can spend thousands on a booze-up while families starve. Then get back in there again Saturday, shout a few drinks, I'll give you some cash . . .'

'Sounds like a bloody good time,' one of the men grinned, hitching up his pants.

'That may be, but you keep your minds on the job. Put the pressure on, dig out the screamers and give them something to yell about. By Saturday night I want them on the rampage. Get mobs stumbling out of the pubs and headed for the Golden Nugget. But ease back out of sight yourselves, I don't want any of this pinned back to me. From what I hear, the workers are already fit to fry Maskey, so all you have to do is sic them on.'

'What if they don't make a move?' a second man asked.

'Then you're out of a job too.' Their boss smiled. 'You'll be joining them on the breadline.'

As the guests assembled at the Golden Nugget Hotel to celebrate the engagement of Captain Cope and Laura Maskey, they had to run the gauntlet of an angry crowd gathered in the street shouting insults, at the ladies as well as the men, and adding coarse and ribald remarks about their fashionable clothes and demeanour.

Captain Cope and his friends tried to protect guests from this abuse by stationing themselves at the front of the hotel and ushering them in through the gates. Guests arriving in vehicles were redirected to the safety of the back yard of the hotel, where they were forced to enter through the kitchen.

Cope was bewildered. And tired. The last patrol had taken him, with six of his troopers, more than two hundred miles to the north. It was much further than he'd intended to travel this time, but there'd been an attack on the Sinclair station way up the coast and he'd been forced to respond. They'd arrived too late, as usual; the manager and two stockmen had been killed and Sinclair himself was raising hell.

117

Cope had no alternative but to go after the blacks. They'd cornered them in a ravine – cornered some of them, anyway – and had shot at least eleven bucks. But time was running out for him, he had to get back to Brisbane. He explained his predicament to old Reg Sinclair, and to mollify him left the native troopers in the district under the command of Private Charlie Penny, the most senior of the group.

Before he left, he gave instructions to Penny to stay in the area for a few more days, until the Sinclair family had settled down, and then return to Rockhampton. Penny, he said, was to divide his troop and return by separate routes on either side of the ranges. 'That way,' he told him, 'you might pick up stragglers heading for the hills. Three men each route, you got it?'

'Yes, sir.' Penny's dark face reflected his excitement. This was the first time he'd ever been put in charge.

'You keep searching all the way home,' Cope told him, 'and don't go slacking off when my back's turned.' He knew his men were next to useless without a boss, and Penny was too lazy to track a kangaroo unless he was ordered to do so, but it couldn't be helped.

As he packed his gear, he saw Penny swaggering about like a general to impress the men; the blackfellow was a nasty piece of work but that was what made him good at his job. He liked to be in at the kill, and spared no one when ordered to attack.

By the time he'd ridden into Rockhampton with a half-day to prepare for the important occasion, Captain Cope had forgotten all about his black troops.

He was affronted by the loutish behaviour of these crowds and wished Mr Maskey would come out and speak to them, but Laura's father was inside, welcoming his guests and soothing ladies upset by the abuse. 'Don't let them worry you,' he was saying. 'They'll get tired of it soon and go away. Once everyone is inside there'll be no one for them to bother. It's only a few drunken louts and rowdies, the police will send them on their way any minute.'

But there was more trouble in store. Mrs Maskey whispered to her husband, 'You'll have to come and speak to Laura. Immediately. She's in the cloakroom and won't come out.'

Since the bush hotel did not have a cloakroom, Leon had arranged to have a bedroom set aside for the ladies, and it was there that Laura sat, women swarming about her. They hurried in and hurried out, satins swirling, taffetas rustling, French laces competing with classic silks and the froth of filmy sheers. For this was not just a social event, it was the first formal ball in the river town. Proud local guests saw the occasion as living proof of the importance of their town, given that so many interstate visitors had paid them the compliment of attending. They were ashamed, however, of the battery of spoilers lined up outside, and they apologised vociferously to their visitors.

With her mother standing by her, beaming, chirping, expressing pride in her daughter, like a vicar after delivering the best sermon of his career, Laura sat numbly, as though she were not present. She felt as if she were somewhere up there in the corner above the wardrobe, where a spare chair had been stacked, observing this parade, this pretty farce in a sprawling bush inn – no matter the pretentions of the Golden Nugget – wildly at odds with the deluge of dowagers and débutantes and bemused, stiff-shirted gentlemen.

No one cared that the passageways wore coir matting instead of carpets, that the walls were not plastered or that the dining room now transformed into a ballroom was hung with hurricane lamps instead of chandeliers. No one noticed that wasps' nests adorned the rafters or that a fat tarantula the size of a hand squatted moodily over the dining-room door, because this was a night to frolic, to throw off cares and kick up heels at the expense of good old Fowler, and a night, of course, to toast his lovely daughter and her fiancé.

The cloakroom gushed with congratulations and flushed faces pressed around Laura. Girls hugged, matrons bussed, skirts were trod upon. Voices trampled each other to praise her gown with its ice-blue satin bodice, studded with seed pearls, and its lavish bouffant skirt of blue organza. They enthused about Hilda Maskey's flair for entertaining, and commiserated with her over the wretches outside the hotel. 'Making such a racket, my dear! And what for?' they asked. 'What are we supposed to do? It's not our fault times are bad.'

'They're just rabble-rousers,' Hilda soothed, defending her night of nights. 'It's such a shame their taking on so, upsetting people. Don't take any notice of them. Champagne is being served, run along and enjoy yourselves.' In her vague way, Hilda had no idea she was right, that rabble-rousers were at work inciting protesters. It was just something to say to cover her embarrassment at this public insult to her husband, the popular Member for Rockhampton. What would her interstate friends think? she worried. What would they *think*?

And while she struggled to keep her composure, despite the clamour of ugly voices outside, here was her own daughter adding to the confusion by refusing to budge from the cloakroom.

Hilda was appalled. She managed to hurry curious women out of the room, smiling them on their way, until at last she was left alone to plead with Laura. To no avail.

'I'm sorry, Mother, I really am. But I just can't go through with this.'

'Of course you can, you silly girl. It's only nerves. You always were highly strung. Now dry your eyes, you look a sight. And do be careful, the way you're sitting you're crushing your dress.'

'Why won't you listen to me?' Laura implored. This situation had been building up for days and her mother knew it. Laura rarely cried, in fact she couldn't remember the last time she'd wept before this looming engagement had overwhelmed her and she'd found herself sobbing in her sleep, or bursting into tears for no apparent reason. She blamed herself, her own weakness, not only for the weeping, which was an embarrassment in itself, but for allowing matters to go this far, and she tried to reassert herself.

'I want to see Bobby,' she said. 'Right now.'

'What for?'

'To tell him the engagement is off. Why else? I haven't been able to contact him before this. I was hoping he wouldn't be back in time.'

'You can't see him now, don't be so selfish,' her mother said angrily. 'The poor fellow is out there trying to keep those ruffians away from the guests. I don't know why those people want to upset an occasion like this, a private occasion. Mostly jealousy, of course. I wouldn't be surprised if people who were not invited are at the bottom of this offensive behaviour. But we've called the police, they'll soon chase them off. It's just too bad! I can't imagine what our friends from Brisbane and Sydney must think of such an exhibition!'

'I said the engagement is off,' Laura reminded her.

Hilda ignored her. 'It is heartbreaking to think that right up till now everything has been going so beautifully. Everyone is happy with their accommodation and they're all looking forward to a jolly time. The weather has stayed fine and the hotel decorations are quite splendid, and you should see the buffet set up in the marquee outside! I declare the cooks have excelled themselves this time. That was your father's idea, so that the dining room could be transformed into a ballroom. All the young people are so excited. You should be out there. That dress is really stunning, you'll be the belle of the ball, and rightly so, it's your night, my dear. Now come along.' Laura stood up and her mother fussed with her skirt, fluffing out the layers of blue organza to remove the creases.

'I want to go home,' Laura said.

Her mother threw up her hands in despair. 'You can't, and that's that.'

'I'm not moving from here until you go and get Bobby Cope,' Laura said, picking up a comb to tidy her hair.

'Oh very well,' Hilda said. 'I hope he can talk some sense into you.'

Relieved to be left alone, Laura stared at herself in the mirror. Her mother had done her hair for her, pinning it up into soft curls on the crown, with a cascade of long curls at the back. She had threaded silver and blue ribbons through Laura's fair hair and it did look attractive, especially with the sapphire earrings Hilda had given her. But still on the dresser, and still in its box, was the engagement ring. Laura couldn't bring herself to put it on.

The dress was beautiful, she admitted, and she wished Paul MacNamara could see her in it, but she'd been relieved that he and his wife had not accepted the invitation. Things were bad enough now, she couldn't bear him to be here and witness all this humiliation. She had a sudden urge to run away, to dash off down the passageway and run! Anywhere! But it would be better to wait and explain to Bobby. They could tell the guests that they had decided, together, not to wed, but they must all enjoy themselves just the same. They would. People did. The announcement would cause surprise, and gossip, but they'd get over it, and Fowler could go on politicking, the real reason for this shindig.

The crowd outside was still noisy but Laura didn't share her mother's anger – she welcomed the intrusion, to deflect interest from herself. The housemaids at home had told her, in their guarded way, that there was unemployment and growing poverty in Rockhampton, and apparently in Brisbane and other towns as well, and she had pretended not to notice as bundles of leftover food were taken from the house. She wished she could offer more, but her mother kept a close eye on the pantry.

'Don't you think a big function like this would be too ostentatious right now?' she'd asked her mother.

'No, I don't,' Hilda said, 'and I won't allow you to use that nonsense to put another obstacle in our path.'

Laura wondered, in a sudden return of spirit, what would happen if she went outside and spoke to people herself. And – if there were hungry women and children in the crowd – she were to invite them in? 'Chaos!' she said to the mirror. 'Utter chaos!' Amelia would enjoy that, she mused, as she waited for the Captain.

Her mother returned. Not with Bobby Cope, but with her father who slammed the door behind him. 'What's this I hear?' he shouted. 'Your mother says you're about to renege.'

'I have decided against this engagement,' Laura said. 'And that's definite. If you get Bobby Cope I'll explain to him myself.'

'You'll do more than that,' her father said, his face red with fury. 'You'll get out there and behave yourself. I won't be made a fool of like this. Your engagement will be announced at nine o'clock, as scheduled, and you will be standing on the platform with your fiancé. Do you hear me?'

'I hear you but I won't do it.'

He lashed at her with the back of his hand and his gold ring cut into her face. Laura staggered back under the blow and fell between two chairs. She put her hand to her face, feeling blood on her cheek and a weight of throbbing pain down that side of her head.

'Tidy her up and get her outside right away,' Fowler said to Hilda. 'If I have to come back for her she'll get the hiding she deserves.'

He stormed out of the door and Hilda helped Laura up. 'Come along now. Your father didn't mean that. It's your own fault, you know, you've pushed him too far.' She dabbed cold water on Laura's face and searched the dresser for some powder. 'A little powder will cover the mark, don't worry. We can say you had a fall.'

'I will not say I had a fall,' Laura said fiercely. 'I will say he struck me!' She went back to the mirror and stared at the bruise already darkening her skin.

Hilda had the power puff ready but Laura turned on her. 'Get away from me! You're as bad as he is. I wouldn't even let anyone whip my horses, but you stand there and let him do this! You'll never get me out of here now.' Her onslaught reduced Hilda to tears.

Just then the band struck up with a snappy drum roll followed by discordant brass, and then they were away with a lively tune. Until then, the street mob, quietened by threats of arrest, had begun to disperse, but the band brought them to life again. They reacted as if the gaiety of the music were a studied insult, a provocation. Men surged forward shouting abuse, others ran back to join them, waving sticks and pick handles, and the jeering crowd turned into an angry mob. They trampled the small fence and hurled rocks and stones at the hotel windows.

A stone smashed through the cloakroom window, narrowly missing Hilda, who grabbed Laura, forgetting their differences, and pulled her out into the passageway.

As missiles landed with resounding crashes on the corrugated-iron roof, guests rushed from the dining room to find out what was happening, adding to the crush in the passage.

'My God!' a woman cried. 'Look at Laura! What happened to you, dear?'

'A stone,' Hilda said swiftly. 'Those brutes smashed the window in there and one of them hit her! It's an outrage! An absolute outrage!'

Leon threaded his way through to them. 'Don't worry, everyone. It will all be over soon. Father was concerned that two policemen might not be able to handle the mob so he sent for the troopers, and just as well.'

Within minutes they heard the mounted troopers galloping down Quay Street as Lieutenant Gooding led his men into the fray, cutting a swathe between the hotel and the rioters, forcing them across the road to the river bank from where they broke up into small muttering groups then gradually drifted away rather than confront the swords of the redcoats.

Fowler's voice could be heard attempting to restore order. 'It's all over! Champagne is being served in the dining room, everyone can relax now. Come along! Come along! We won't let a few rowdies disrupt our evening.'

Bobby Cope found his way to Laura. 'My dear! They said you were hurt! And you are! Look at you! Those bastards, how dare they! I'm so sorry, forgive my language, but are you all right?' He put a protective arm around her as women stood by, dressed in their finery, clucking their sympathy.

Laura's head ached. Her face felt like a balloon from the heavy blow. She was appalled and embarrassed by her mother's convenient lie, but, surrounded by women anxious to help tend the patient, she was ushered back into the cloakroom, with Bobby at her side.

Then came the shout: 'Fire!' the dread of all, in these timber buildings. The women panicked, grabbed their skirts and ran. Leon stuck his head round the door and called to Bobby, 'It's the marquees! They've set fire to the marquees!'

Bobby Cope ran too, to do his bit. Hilda had disappeared, probably to rally the guests in the dining room, and Laura was left alone.

She stood, stunned, for a minute and then made her way to the side of the hotel where gentlemen were busy with the manly occupation of putting out small fires that had been started in a vain attempt to burn down the main marquee. She watched them for a while and then walked calmly down the steps to the stables at the rear of the hotel.

'Are the horses safe?' she asked an elderly stablehand.

'Yes, miss,' he said with a grin. 'Just a bit of a ruckus up the front there, but I thought I'd better stay put, in case. You're Miss Maskey, aren't you?'

'Yes.' Laura walked past him. 'Where's my brother's horse?'

'He's here. Smart as ever.' He accompanied Laura down the line of single boxes to where the sleek chestnut was waiting patiently. He tossed his head and whinnied recognition as Laura reached out to him. She smiled, she'd always been fond of this horse.

'You know me, don't you, boy?' she said, patting him. She felt comforted by the animal, more confident now as an idea occurred to her.

'Would you saddle him up, please?' she asked.

The old man stared. 'Does Leon want him?'

'No, I do.'

'You want to ride him now? In that pretty dress?'

'It's only a dress, and please hurry!'

He led the horse out, mumbling to himself, and went back to fetch a saddle. 'I'm borrowing you a side-saddle,' he told her, determined to adhere to some equestrian decorum. 'You can't use Leon's saddle, you'd look like a butterfly on a pumpkin.'

Finally he legged her up, shaking his head at her silver slippers.

'Thank you,' she said to him. 'If anyone asks, tell them I've gone home.'

He stood scratching his head as she rode quietly out into the dark side street and turned the horse inland, away from the hotel and away from the house. She felt better now, enjoying the cool night air, and the horse trotted amiably as if he, too, had no need to hurry. She wasn't going anywhere in particular, just riding, thinking that she'd probably go back when she'd cooled off, but the further she went the more resolute she became. Returning to the hotel would only invite trouble and going home would only postpone it. High gums hissed and whispered in the light breeze, and the occasional squeals of nocturnal animals were so familiar she wasn't nervous. A dog barked and a dingo fled across the road in front of her, reminding her that she too was running from harm. But to where? She could hardly keep riding all night, and she wished now that she hadn't been so impetuous. She should have raced home and changed her clothes before taking off on this night ride, before anyone noticed that she was gone. But what then?

In complete contrast, Amelia's dinner party was a pleasant and happy occasion. None of the guests, nor Amelia for that matter, had any idea of the dramas being enacted down in the town. They sat at the long table, dining by candlelight, with Boyd Roberts at one end and Amelia at the other, and on her right the guest of honour, Tyler Kemp.

Amelia was delighted that several of her friends, five young ladies and four gentlemen, had sent belated apologies to the Maskeys, preferring her party. That was a coup in itself!

Everyone was getting along wonderfully, and as each of the courses was served, with appropriate wines, the guests laughed and joked and congratulated the hostess on her accomplishment with such short notice. In the drawing room, the two musicians played popular songs, lending atmosphere to what Amelia felt was a perfect evening. Her father was right; a smaller party had more dignity, she told herself, and was much more intimate. With Tyler beside her it was all too romantic for words.

Amelia beamed – she glowed. The lustrous rose satin of her dress and the ruby necklace made her creamy skin even more alluring to Tyler, and noticing the effect she was having, she managed to touch him playfully and to lean forward every so often to whisper in his ear, establishing a rapport between them, and signalling to the other guests that this was her beau.

She could hardly wait for the meal to end, so that he could take her in his arms for the first dance, but as the maids were serving dessert, her own concoction of brandied fruits, marshmallows and whipped cream, one of the maids whispered to her that someone was asking for her at the front door.

'Who is it?' she asked, irritated. 'Can't you see I'm busy?'

'Miss Maskey,' the girl said. 'She wants to see you.'

'Laura? What on earth? Oh all right.' Amelia excused herself from the table and hurried out to find Laura on the veranda. 'For heaven's sake. What are you doing here? I have guests, Laura.'

'I know, I'm sorry. I didn't realise until I heard the music.'

Amelia stared at her. 'Tonight's your engagement party. Is it over already? And how did you get here? What are you doing out at this hour? And in your ball gown? Are you tipsy?'

'No. I just couldn't stand it any longer, so I took Leon's horse and rode off, and since I was out this way . . .'

The interruption didn't please Amelia at all. 'Well, I'm sure it all sounds very intriguing, and I'll have to hear about it, so why don't you come back tomorrow?'

'Yes, that would be better,' Laura said, backing away. 'I'm so sorry, I didn't mean to intrude.'

'We're still at dinner,' Amelia said, unmoved.

Her father suddenly appeared behind her. 'Laura. Is something wrong?'

'No, no. Nothing. I'm just going. I shouldn't have come here.'

Boyd stepped out on to the veranda and peered at her. 'What happened to your face? It's all bruised. I do believe you've got a black eye there.'

Amelia's curiosity got the better of her. 'She has too! Let me see. My God, what have you been up to this time?'

Laura tried to hide her face. 'Nothing. I must go. It was stupid of me to come out here.'

'No, it wasn't,' Boyd said. 'I insist you come inside.'

'I couldn't possibly. I don't want your guests to see me like this.'

'You don't have to,' Boyd said. 'You go back, Amelia, I'll take Laura in through another door.'

Amelia was only too pleased to escape and Boyd led Laura past the open French windows of the drawing room.

'I feel an absolute fool,' she said. 'I didn't stop to think you might be entertaining.'

'Never mind, you're here now,' he said, ushering her in through a side door and along to the small sitting room where she and Amelia often spent wet days playing Fish or Fiddlesticks or just talking.

Laura was pleased to be inside the quiet little haven, well away from the people in the rest of the house. 'I'll just sit here for a few minutes and then I'll go,' she said, but he wouldn't allow that.

'Definitely not,' he said. 'They won't miss me in there, they're all Amelia's friends. Just wait here a minute.'

He returned with coffee and cognac. 'I've seen you naughty girls sipping away at my cognac, so don't refuse. It'll do you good. Obviously you've had a bad night. Do you want to tell me about it?'

By the time she'd finished a second cognac, the fiery liquid had given her the courage to pour out almost the whole story to him – her refusal to go ahead with the engagement, and the riot outside the hotel.

'No one will forget your party.' He smiled. 'But you still haven't told me what happened to you.' He touched her face. 'Is it very sore? Should I get you some beefsteak?'

'Oh no, don't do that. It doesn't feel too bad now, just a bit numb.' She couldn't bring herself to admit, even to Boyd Roberts, that her father had struck her, so she fell back on Hilda's excuse. 'It was a stone. They threw stones, breaking windows, and one hit me.'

'Did it now?'

Laura had the uncomfortable impression that he didn't believe her, but he let the subject drop. 'What now? Do you want me to send you home in the carriage, or do you wish to stay here? Either way it's no trouble.'

'Right now I don't think I could face them at home. I would appreciate it, Mr Roberts, if I could stay over.'

'Call me Boyd. You make me feel old calling me Mister.'

She nodded. 'Boyd.'

'That's settled, you stay. Now, do you want to join the dance? Your dress is lovely and the face isn't that bad.'

'I'd rather not if you don't mind.'

'Fair enough. Best you have a good sleep. Everything will seem brighter in the morning.' He showed her to one of the spare bedrooms and stood back politely. 'At least you know your way about the house,' he said. 'If you want anything just ask the maids. I hope the music won't disturb you.'

'Oh heavens no, it's lovely. You're so kind. I really wouldn't have known where else to turn.'

'I told you before, we're friends.' He gave her a peck on the forehead. 'Sleep well, and don't be worrying. It's just a storm in a teacup.'

When the door had closed, Laura peeled off her dress and climbed into bed in her underwear. She was frightened. If her father had been angry with her before, how would he be now? They were probably out searching for her, and worried, she supposed. Well, let them worry! She touched her cheek gingerly. I must look a fright, and it will be worse in the morning. If Mr Roberts will let me stay, I'm not moving out of here until it clears up. She pictured her father riding up to the entrance to Beauview and demanding his daughter be handed over! 'Oh Lord,' she whispered. 'What a mess!' Then she huddled down under the covers, safe for the time being.

She awoke with a fright. Someone was shaking her.

'Laura! Wake up! I have to talk to you! I've got the most marvellous news!'

It was Amelia, in her nightdress, kneeling on the bed, whispering to her.

'What time is it?' Laura mumbled.

'I've no idea. It's the middle of the night. Are you properly awake?'

'Yes. What is it?'

'Well, let me tell you. I have to start from the beginning. It's all so delicious.' She told Laura all about Tyler Kemp, her father's guest, who was so handsome, and also single. Then she went on to describe her dinner party – who was there, what they wore, what they ate and how impressed Tyler had been. 'He's quite famous, you know, and he must have been to any amount of formal dinners, but he said mine was absolutely the best.'

Laura was battling to stay awake as the long story unfolded.

'Daddy told me what happened to you,' Amelia said, reminded then of Laura's engagement party. 'What a débâcle that must have been! I mean to say, Laura, ducking your own engagement! That's awful.' She started to laugh. 'I wonder what happened after you left?'

'I've no idea,' Laura said. 'I never wanted to be engaged to Bobby

Cope in the first place, and in the end I just couldn't go through with it. I wish I could see the funny side. I'm in the most terrible trouble now.'

'I'll say you are,' Amelia agreed cheerfully. 'Daddy said there was a riot outside the hotel too. What a night! Of course he knew that would happen. He said your father never should have taunted the poor people like that, making such a show of spending. He said he was asking for trouble.'

Laura closed her eyes, recalling all the noise and confusion. 'I suppose so,' she murmured.

Amelia moved the lamp over to get a closer look at Laura's face. 'Your cheek's gone all purple. Daddy said you were struck by a stone, but I think that's a bit far-fetched. Looks to me as if someone hit you. Who did it? Bobby Cope?'

Laura shook her head.

'Your father! I'll bet it was your father!'

When Laura wouldn't reply, Amelia nodded. 'Oh well, be that as it may. Wait till you hear the rest of my story. After dinner we all danced and Tyler danced most of the time with me and we were just perfect together. Then later, Daddy wandered off to his office. You know what he's like, he gets bored.' She giggled. 'He's a hopeless chaperon. So after that there was quite a bit of smooching going on – Nancy Leighton was outside with one of the Gordon brothers – so Tyler and I walked down into the garden. And Laura – don't you dare go to sleep on me! – he kissed me, and he said all the most wonderful things, and we kissed and kissed. It was just glorious. He's in love with me.'

Now Laura was awake. 'Did he say so?'

'No, silly, he didn't have to. And he didn't ask me to marry him, but I know he will. He's perfect. Daddy likes him, everyone likes him. Move over, I'm going to sleep here. I'm too excited to go back to my lonely old room.'

Amelia was still talking as Laura dozed off again, but it wasn't long before she too lapsed into slumber.

Tyler was up early as usual, taking his walk about the grounds. He had little curiosity about the late visitor. 'Just a girlfriend of mine,' Amelia had said. 'She had a bit of a tiff with her family, and she doesn't wish to join us.' No explanation was given to the rest of the guests, so Tyler dismissed the incident. He was suffering slight remorse for having kissed Amelia like that, but it had been impossible to resist her.

It had been her idea to take a walk in the garden in the moonlight, not that he wouldn't have suggested it, had he dared. She was so close to him, so soft and pretty, and the fragrance of her so warm and inviting, that the first kiss was inevitable. After that he was lost, and because Amelia herself was so passionate it took all his self-control to remember that he was a guest in this house. He'd had to break it up and take her back inside.

But it was selfish of him to lead her on like that when there was no future for them. And heartbreaking, because he could still feel the sweetness of her in his arms. He did love her, and wanted her all the more now.

As he strolled the grounds he felt a strangeness about him. As if everything were back to front. The natural woods at the rear of the house seemed to represent order, while the carefully landscaped area, with its lawns and garden plots and paths, spelled disorder, almost as if it all reflected Roberts himself. He recalled his anger that Fowler Maskey should welcome a son-in-law like Captain Cope and, with some trepidation, saw himself in the reverse situation. Who was he to complain? If, given the opportunity, he would not balk at having Roberts for a father-in-law.

Crunching through the bush he could almost feel the mysterious presence of the tribes who had so recently been removed from this land, and he remembered the Aborigines back in the mountains. Even though they were friendly, he had always known that their civilisation was far beyond the understanding of white man. It was too deep, too steeped in a massive past. But at least they'd been able to communicate. Obviously in this district there was little communication, only violence. The realisation made him all the more determined to go into the bush and seek some answers for himself.

Lieutenant Gooding had sent word that he was taking a patrol out on Monday as far as Camelot Station, which was on the way to Oberon, and that he could join them if he wished.

Tyler made up his mind. He would go. The politics of Rockhampton were minor compared with the life and death struggles taking place out in the bush. He couldn't help much but he might be able to contribute to sanity by writing the truth of the bush wars.

At breakfast, Boyd told him of the events in town. He yawned. 'Now you see why I prefer to live in our hilltop retreat.'

But Amelia didn't share his reticence. 'I'm dying to hear the outcome! We had our lovely peaceful evening up here and the Maskey function was an utter fiasco.'

She looked fondly at Tyler as she spoke, no doubt recalling their intimacy, and he saw that Roberts was observing them. Talk about a cat-and-mouse game, he thought, although I don't know who's the cat. I'm watching him, and now he has the parental eye on me. To take the scrutiny from himself he encouraged Amelia to continue. 'How do you know?'

'Because his daughter is here. Laura Maskey. She's my friend.'

He gulped his tea in surprise. 'Here? Maskey's daughter?'

'Yes, she was the late visitor, but she didn't want anyone to know. She had the most terrible row with her father because she has flatly refused to marry Bobby Cope.'

'Good for her,' Tyler said.

'And you know what?' Amelia said, picking daintily at small slices of toast and marmalade. 'He hit her. Her father slapped her face. It must have hurt, her face is all bruised.'

'Good God! Is she all right?'

'Yes, but she doesn't want to come out of her room just yet.'

'Pity you weren't there,' Roberts said to Tyler. 'It's quite a story. They're telling people she was hit by a stone thrown by one of the rioters, but you're in a position to write the real story. You know the truth.'

'So do you,' Tyler said, recognising the veiled challenge. 'I daresay a scandal like that would improve your chances in the elections. I hear you're planning to oppose Maskey.'

Boyd laughed. 'There's no such thing as a reporter on holiday, Amelia. Remember that. I tried to keep his mind off his trade but he's off now like a hound dog! Yes, I'll oppose Maskey and I'll beat him. You know the old saying, Tyler: "Governments don't win elections, they lose them." And Maskey is doing a great job of alienating the voters all by himself.'

'But it would be handy if I wrote an exposé on the night's events?'

'Handy, but not essential,' Boyd said coolly. 'In a small town like this, truth has a way of surfacing – a word here and word there. Riots, broken engagements, paternal brutality, the daughter fleeing the family. I would have thought your own paper, let alone the local rag, would lap it up.'

Tyler felt trapped. Roberts was right, of course, but he objected to being told what to write, being manipulated. On the other hand, Maskey was one of the state's leading political figures. Was he, a journalist, seriously considering sitting on his bum, doing nothing, with this combination of farce and scandal breaking right under his nose? And why? Just because he didn't approve of the other candidate either? It wouldn't be the first time that, knowing the candidates, he'd given both contenders the thumbs down.

He realised that, thanks to Cosmo's criticism, he'd allowed himself to go on the defensive, because he hated to be accused of bias. The story was right here and he had a job to do, otherwise he might as well give the game away. And, he consoled himself, it was still directly connected to his original aim, investigation of Cope and the Native Police. After all, the girl was or had been engaged to him.

'Would it be possible for me to interview the young lady?' he asked, at once irritated by Robert's complacent reply. 'I'm sure it would be.' To counteract that, he added his own news. 'By the way, I really do want to see some of the countryside while I'm here. Lieutenant Gooding is taking a troop out on patrol tomorrow and has invited me to join them.'

'Oh no!' Amelia was disappointed. 'What a shame! There's nothing to see out there but scrub. Do you have to go?'

'It's all new country to me,' he said gently. 'They'll take me out to Camelot Station. I'm a bushman at heart, Amelia, it will be a great experience for a city-bound chap like me.'

'If you don't get bitten by a snake or chased by blacks,' she sulked.

'I'll try to be careful,' he said, wondering if there weren't just as many dangers in town as out.

'She knows you're a newspaperman,' Amelia said, 'but you don't have to tell her you're going to write about her.'

'We'll see,' he replied.

She was sitting at the far end of the veranda and she turned nervously away as they approached.

'Don't worry about your face,' said Amelia, not the most tactful of people. 'I'll bet Tyler has seen plenty of black eyes before this. Tyler, this is Laura Maskey. She's not feeling the best, so you be kind to her.'

Laura put her book down and managed a small smile.

'I must say,' Amelia told her, 'you look most attractive in that pretty blouse.' She explained to Tyler, 'Laura could hardly wear her ballgown this morning so I had to find her something of mine to put on. She lives in shirts and riding skirts. I'm always telling her more feminine clothes suit her better.'

The girl was indeed attractive. Tyler decided Rockhampton had a lot more going for it than political upheavals, with this pair as an example. Laura, with her thick fair hair, lightly waved and tied at the back, was a beauty, despite the dark bruise. She was in direct contrast to Amelia's dark gypsy looks, and she had the elegance, he thought, with a pang of bitterness, of generations of money. The high cheekbones, full, firm mouth and well-formed teeth spoke to him of confidence even in her present adversity, and her first words added to his initial impression.

'Amelia, I wish you wouldn't talk about me as if I were not here.'

Obviously these girls knew each other very well, he noted, because Amelia didn't take offence. She laughed. 'You're not supposed to be here anyway. Tyler has offered to take Leon's horse back and tell your dad where you are. They might be dragging the river by this.'

'Would you do that?' Laura asked. 'I would appreciate it.'

'What do you intend to do?' he asked her, pulling up a chair.

'I've no idea right now,' she said miserably. 'Last night was such a débâcle.'

'Yes. It couldn't have been very pleasant for you.'

'It wasn't. Mr Kemp, I'm sorry, but I really don't wish to discuss it.'

'That's understandable. As a matter of fact, I'm more interested in Captain Cope.'

'Why?'

'A lot of people, including your brother Leon, are not impressed by

130

his activities with the Native Police.'

'Yes, I know that.'

'Is that the reason you broke the engagement?'

'No.'

'Why did you break your engagement in so public a manner, then?'

She sighed. 'You've too much of an imagination, Mr Kemp. I did not break the engagement, I simply did not become engaged. The timing was unfortunate and I shall apologise to Captain Cope.'

'Her father was forcing her to marry Bobby,' Amelia said.

Laura contradicted her, though addressing Kemp: 'As you can see, my father hasn't forced me to do anything.'

Tyler was disappointed in her noncommittal replies. He'd expected her to be critical of her father and of Cope and to give him the basis of a lead article from the point of view of the aggrieved daughter.

She seemed to read his thoughts. 'Mr Kemp, I am the daughter of a politician, so I am aware that you will quote me, in which case I have nothing further to say.'

Seeing this golden opportunity slipping away from him, he pressed her harder. 'Don't you have an opinion on the food riots? On the fact that your family's extravagance provoked hungry people?'

The question was meant to draw her out, have her blame Maskey, but she sidestepped. 'When women get the vote I'll have an opinion. Until then we might as well let you men mess things up on your own.'

'Women vote?' He was astonished. 'I can't ever see that happening!'

'I can,' she said calmly. 'And you can quote me on that if you like.'

Amelia apologised to him as they walked away. 'I'm sorry she wouldn't help you. But I did tell you Laura is quite outrageous! I think it is an absolute scream that she rode off into the night in her ballgown and left them all sitting. Now that's a true fact, so there's nothing to stop you printing it.'

Tyler nodded. It was a lively story and now he had an excuse to see Maskey and fill in the gaps.

His first stop in town was at the Golden Nugget Hotel, where he hoped to find out exactly how much Maskey had spent on the night's entertainment. Workmen were already replacing the fence and smashed windows, so there were people everywhere on what should have been a quiet Sunday morning. Among the activity in the lobby he spotted Cosmo Newgate.

'What are you doing here?' Cosmo asked. 'I thought you were leaving town.'

'I am, tomorrow. And it looks like you've got a front-page story here.'

'Yes. It was a shambles. Miss Maskey was hit by a stone and had to be taken home.'

'Is that so?' Tyler laughed. 'Well, I've got the true story, which I intend to send down to the *Brisbane Courier*. It will contradict yours, but I suppose that can't be helped because you won't print my stuff.'

131

'What have you heard?' Cosmo asked uneasily.

'Oh no! I get paid for my work. You agree to pay me and I'll give you the story.'

'As long as you can back it up.'

'I sure can.'

As he spoke, Cosmo's jaw dropped. 'Are you certain this isn't some tale concocted by Roberts?'

'Of course not. I was there when she turned up, right out of the blue. I could see they weren't expecting anyone.'

Cosmo thought about this. 'Laura and Amelia have been friends for some time. I suppose it makes sense. But I don't know about Fowler striking the girl. She's rather a madcap, you know. She could have made that part up.'

'No fear. She's got a lovely shiner. That wasn't caused by a stone.'

'And Laura told you all this – about Fowler forcing her into the engagement and then striking her while she was here?'

Tyler made a career decision. This was no time to be squeamish. 'I talked to her myself. Look outside, I'm delivering Leon's horse back to him. Fowler was bullying the girl so she took off, and the only person she could think to turn to, at that hour, was Amelia Roberts. It has nothing to do with Boyd Roberts. And it's no way for your leading citizen to behave. On top of provoking a riot.'

The deal made with Cosmo, Tyler rode down to the Maskey house, leading Leon's horse. He hitched the animals in the street and went to the door, but as he'd expected, Maskey refused to see him.

'Would you tell Mr Maskey I have a message from his daughter,' he instructed the maid, who still left him standing outside.

Maskey himself came to the door, obviously still in the rage that should have cowed his daughter. 'Yes?' he asked stiffly.

'I've brought back Leon's horse,' Tyler said.

Fowler looked past him. 'So I see.'

'Have you got any comment to make about last night, Mr Maskey?'

'No.'

'I thought you might be interested in the whereabouts of your daughter.'

'Where is she?'

'She's staying with her friend, Amelia Roberts.'

That at least brought a reaction. His eyes blazed. 'She's staying with Roberts?'

'Yes. Do you want me to give her a message from you?'

'Tell her to stay there,' Fowler snapped and slammed the door.

Tyler was pleased. Now Cosmo couldn't doubt his story. He rode back to Beauview and spent the afternoon composing a lengthy article on the real face of Fowler Maskey, with Amelia filling in the gaps.

That evening after supper Boyd had a private talk with his guest.

'Amelia is very fond of you, Tyler,' he began, 'and she is under the impression that you reciprocate. I hope you haven't been playing fast and loose with her affections, she's a delicate child.'

'No, I haven't,' Tyler said, 'but you do deserve an explanation. I am fond of Amelia, more than fond, and it was wrong of me to let her know. I couldn't possibly afford to support her like this, and it's no use pretending I could.'

'I'm glad you understand that,' Boyd said. 'She is not equipped for the role of the careworn housewife, and I would never permit her to marry below her station, because it would be disastrous. She is accustomed to the best, but – and I hope you will forgive me for saying this – you simply could not provide that, could you?'

'I'm afraid not. I'll be leaving tomorrow and I hope that I will not have caused her any distress.'

Boyd sighed. 'That's the trouble. I think you will and I'll have a very unhappy girl on my hands. Unless, of course, I try to help.'

'I don't see how,' Tyler said. 'My job is in Brisbane and I couldn't ask Amelia to come with me.'

'But you could stay here.'

'And lose my job?'

'Not necessarily. I have been thinking for quite some time of buying the local paper or starting another, but I wouldn't know how to run a paper. Now if you were to stay and be the editor, then both our problems would be solved.'

'You want me to run a paper for you?' Tyler was amazed.

'Why not?'

'I don't know. I'd have to think about it.' There was a great deal to think about, especially with Roberts as owner. Like becoming a mouthpiece for a politician with an unsavoury reputation.

'You'd be your own boss,' Roberts urged, 'and you'd earn a great deal more than you're earning now. And keep in mind that a new town like this, lacking so many things, presents any amount of possibilities for other businesses. With capital behind you, you could widen your fields of interest.'

Tyler nodded. That was certainly true, but in the first instance, to edit his own newspaper, that would be a mighty step up. The opportunity was really too good to refuse.

'If you do accept,' Roberts said, 'I will give my blessing to your courtship of Amelia. She has already indicated that she would be happy to marry you in the right circumstances.'

'You've discussed this with her?'

'Of course. Her happiness is paramount. And if it makes you feel any better, I shall give you a house here as a wedding present, so that you will not consider yourself intimidated living under the same roof as me. But it is up to you, Tyler. If you cannot accept my offer then . . .' He shrugged. 'All bets are off. You go back to Brisbane and Amelia stays with me.'

She was waiting for him, bursting with impatience at the outcome

133

of their discussions. This time he took her arm and led her down the drive to the double wrought-iron gates, buying time to collect his thoughts.

'What did Daddy say to you?' she asked breathlessly. 'I hope he wasn't too bossy, he can be like that with people sometimes. Not with me, though. I mean, what did you talk about? Oh dear . . .' She fluttered a lace handkerchief. 'I declare I'm so nervous I don't know what I'm saying.'

And Tyler wasn't sure how to answer her. This was the most important decision of his life, in fact it was several decisions wrapped up in one tight parcel, and he could either accept or reject. All or nothing.

He looked down at those cherub lips and her eager eyes, and felt resistance draining away.

'Your father has given me permission to court you,' he said at last, 'if you are amenable to the idea.'

She breathed a sigh of relief and was suddenly shy. 'Oh Tyler, you know I am. I can't pretend. I was so frightened you'd go away and I'd never see you again.' She was crying. 'I'm so happy. And isn't it wonderful that my two favourite men in the whole world are getting along so well.' She mopped her eyes. 'So silly of me to be weeping . . .'

'No, it's not.' He smiled, and kissed her eyes and her cheek and those soft enticing lips. 'I'm going away tomorrow,' he said, 'and that will give you time to think this over.'

'Don't go,' she pleaded. 'We'll look at the countryside some other time.'

'I have to go. It's more important that I go now. You've only known me a little while, I want you to be absolutely sure.'

She stood back, worried. 'You might change your mind. You might meet someone else!'

'No I won't,' he told her, knowing then that the die was cast. He felt a shiver of apprehension. Would it be possible to disassociate himself from Roberts? Despite the unsettling remarks of Cosmo and Lieutenant Gooding, Roberts had impressed him, and Tyler had noticed that he was popular in town. But then he turned on himself: wasn't he more impressed by the money than the man? And he didn't dare answer that, because his overriding consideration was to make Amelia his wife. He almost laughed aloud, because if that meant he'd have to sacrifice a poorly paid job to become editor of his own paper – and gain a fine house as well – then what was the problem?

Tyler drew Amelia into the shelter of the trees and kissed her passionately, daring now to run his hands over those lovely full breasts, unbuttoning her bodice to cup them, feeling their weight and kissing them as Amelia moaned with pleasure. He knew that in his insidious way Boyd had won, but he didn't care, he didn't care a damn that he'd taken a giant step down from his principles. Life was too short he decided, to pass up the munificence of Beauview.

So insidious indeed was Roberts' influence that Tyler had forgotten his prior, minor, it seemed, fall from grace, when he'd allowed Cosmo to believe that his information about the Maskey ball at the Golden Nugget hotel had been gleaned directly from Laura.

Since Cosmo had been present at the ball he subbed the front page himself, amalgamating his reportage of events and Tyler Kemp's subsequent information. He smiled to himself as he set Monday morning's headline: 'FIASCO'. It was one hell of a story, and no chance of libel because it was facts, facts, facts all the way.

Captain Cope was drunk. Very drunk. He'd been on a bender for days and his friends couldn't blame him. To be jilted so publicly was hard to bear, not to mention the loss of so lovely a fiancée and the splendid dowry that would have set him up for life.

At first, early in the evening, it hadn't been so bad. Everyone was shocked to hear that Laura had been struck by a stone and had been taken home. 'But by whom?' he had asked. Surely it was the right of her betrothed to have some hand in taking care of her. Leon, they said, had gone down to the Maskey house, so Bobby had dashed away after him only to find the house in darkness. She wasn't there.

'Then where the hell is she?' Bobby demanded.

'Damned if I know,' Leon had replied in that supercilious manner of his.

'You must know!' Bobby yelled furiously. 'If she's not here, where have they taken her?'

'No one has taken her anywhere. You might as well have the truth. She has run off. Bolted! I thought she might have been here, in which case I was to bring her back, but it's not on, old chap. Fact is, she changed her mind. The parents are covering. We'll go back and tell the folks she's not well enough to return.'

'But what about our engagement?' The Captain was still bewildered, he could not grasp the calamity as yet.

'For everyone's sake, it's best to keep it quiet for this evening, so we'll just carry on. There wasn't much damage done to the marquee and the mob has dispersed. Come along, we might as well go back and enjoy ourselves.'

'But shouldn't I look for her?'

'I think not. That'd be a dead giveaway. More embarrassing for you than anyone else. Just pretend she's at home nursing a sore head.'

'This is outrageous! Your sister is making an utter fool of me. I refuse to put up with it.'

'Nothing much you can do, old chap. She has made it plain she does not wish to marry you.'

'She could have spoken to me about it, not left me in the lurch like this. What am I expected to do?'

'Forget the whole idea. I daresay Fowler will compensate you since

135

he is equally irate. He can be quite generous, you know. But if you make a fuss he won't thank you. Best you come quietly and help him rescue the evening.'

The ball was a huge success. It went on until dawn, when breakfast was served in the delightful morning chill of the marquee. But Bobby Cope missed that; he'd passed out under the tree by the stables.

On Monday morning Hilda wept and Leon sat by helplessly while Fowler raged.

'That bloody girl!' he shouted. 'That bloody ingrate. Going to the press with "her side" of the story. With her lies! I'll give her more than a slap if I get my hands on her. How dare she do this with all our friends still in town? Look what it says here!' he screamed at Leon. ' "Fowler Maskey struck his daughter with such force she has a black eye and cut to her cheek!" '

He threw the paper across the room, his cheeks blazing red, and then picked it up again. 'There's more in the editorial. That bloody Cosmo. "Surely," he says, "the days are gone when daughters are forced into unappealing marriages." What the hell is unappealing? I was generosity personified. I would have given them a grand wedding and fixed them financially for life. What the hell is unappealing in that?'

After a while Leon managed to get a word in. 'This will blow over, but Captain Cope could be a problem.'

'Yes. Cope. Where is he? What did he do to her to bring this down on us?'

'Nothing. He doesn't know what's going on. He's still drunk.'

Fowler fumed, breathing heavily. 'And well he might be, she's made idiots out of us all.'

Leon agreed. 'True. But when he comes round, he could cause trouble. We want to damp this down as soon as possible. I suggest paying him off.'

His father was reading the front page again, about how the people of the town, in straightened circumstances, had been driven to protest by Maskey's insensitivity in flaunting his wealth.

'Yes, pay him off,' he said. 'Get rid of him.'

'I thought three hundred pounds,' Leon murmured. 'I believe he'd jump at that.'

'Whatever!' Fowler said impatiently. 'That damn Cosmo, that snake in the grass, accepting our hospitality and writing these lies!' He shook the paper, hurling it away from him. 'Who invited him anyway?'

Leon wisely made no reply to that question, Cosmo was always invited to Maskey socials. He was thinking of Laura. Prior to this, he'd understood and sympathised with her predicament, since he considered his sister could make a better marriage than with Cope. He'd even made a half-hearted attempt to intercede on her behalf with

Fowler, who had retorted: 'Mind your own business. There's only one suitor on the horizon now, and I want this over with. Don't be worrying about her, she'll be a match for him.'

But since Laura had chosen to retaliate by granting an interview with Tyler Kemp, thereby heaping scandal on the family name, he was almost as angry as his father.

'It's not just Cosmo,' he said. 'The article also bears Kemp's stamp and he's in cahoots with Roberts. It's apparent there's a conspiracy afoot to break your grip on the electorate.'

'Of course it's a conspiracy,' Maskey fumed. 'Any fool can see that. With my daughter helping them. Well, I'm not going to take this lying down. Go and get John Laidley. Tell him I want to see him right away. Then pay off that fellow Cope before he starts bellyaching.'

Within the hour, John Laidley, Fowler's solicitor, was at the door, his face grave. He was a young man, pleased to have Fowler's business, and having read the morning papers, he could guess why he had been summoned. He and his wife had attended the ball and they'd had a wonderful time; in fact he was still slightly hungover. The guests had accepted Fowler's explanation when the announcement of the engagement had not been made, so the morning papers had been a shock. The whole town was crackling with gossip. It was all very unfortunate, especially since he and his wife regarded Laura as a friend. They had always found her delightful company and enjoyed her rather eccentric sense of humour. He hoped, prayed, that the newspaper reports about Fowler's treatment of her were incorrect, or this interview could be awkward.

And it was. Mrs Maskey bustled in with morning tea, and with her own copy of the paper, since Fowler's copy lay mangled on the floor. That was not a good sign.

His client wanted to sue.

'Yes, I understand,' John said. 'It would be best to go over the reports one by one.'

'They've accused me of provoking a riot!' Fowler snarled.

'Not quite,' John said gently. 'They are saying that the rioters felt they had grounds.'

After some argument it was decided to pass on that subject and move on to the claim that Fowler had struck his daughter.

'Lies,' Fowler shouted, close to apoplexy, reading it again.

'Good. If this is untrue we can certainly sue for libel. It would mean, of course, that their defence could call Laura as a witness.' He shifted uncomfortably in his chair. 'Would she deny the charge? I mean, sir,' he offered, 'could she deny it, under oath?'

Fowler hedged on that. He talked about a conspiracy, he claimed that Tyler Kemp had been out to get him for ages, he even went so far as to claim that Roberts had probably arranged to incite the protestors, and John had to warn him against laying himself open to libel if he promulgated those views.

In the end, after an hour of John's mild but insistent questions, Fowler did admit that he might have given Laura 'a bit of a slap'.

'It was the heat of the moment, John,' Fowler said. 'With all that trouble outside and her playing up as well, it would have tried the patience of a saint.'

'I quite understand, sir,' John said, careful not to refer to the rest of the sad tale – wherein Laura claimed she had not wished to marry Captain Cope all along, that she had been forced into it – since that was obviously true also.

When Fowler accepted, finally, that a libel case would not succeed, he slumped back in his chair, down but not defeated. 'It seems, I gather, I'll just have to ride this out.'

'I'm afraid so, sir. These things blow over. It is most unfortunate, but there's nothing you can do.'

'That's where you're wrong. There is something I can do. I want you to draw up a new will for me. Right here and now. That girl won't get a penny. I'll leave everything to Mrs Maskey and Leon, and I want it absolutely watertight so that she gets nothing.'

'Don't you think you ought to talk to Laura first. She was upset, she probably didn't realise that this reporter, Kemp, would publish everything she said, practically verbatim. A young lady would think the conversation was private. I know Laura, sir, and I really can't see her giving statements like this to the press . . .'

'Then you don't know her at all. She understands the press perfectly well, better than Leon, even. She'd know the damage, so don't be feeling sorry for her. Now, the will. Let's get on with it.'

By the Wednesday, when the chartered ship had sailed, Fowler was glad to see the back of his interstate guests. They had all thanked him profusely, and there was no doubt they'd all had a good time, but they were careful not to refer to the newspaper reports, and Laura's absence from the wharf to see them off must have set tongues wagging again.

But political life has its ups as well as its downs, and Fowler's mail brought him good news, desperately needed at this point.

He shouted for Hilda and for Leon. 'Listen to this. It is from the Premier. Macalister agrees with me that we need more troops in north and west Queensland to counter the belligerence of wild blacks, and he has written to England, to the Home Secretary, requesting that British marines be stationed in this state.'

'That is indeed good news,' Hilda said. 'And you must make sure that Newgate publishes that information. People will be greatly relieved.'

'Ha!' Fowler crowed. 'But that's not all. In view of my support for him, and of my sustained support for the issue of government notes to relieve the financial distress of the people' – he looked up from the Premier's letter, pausing to add drama to the pronouncement – 'he offers me a seat in the Cabinet!'

138

Leon was delighted. This was truly a shot in the arm for the old man, and it also meant that more time would have to be spent in Brisbane. 'This is wonderful,' he said. 'Can we publish the Premier's letter?'

'No. You sit down and write a complete statement, emphasising the honour that has been bestowed on me, and the fact that I am doing something to help the people. That will put a stop to all their complaints. It's a bloody pity this letter didn't come last week. Get it done right away and I'll take it down to Newgate myself. Time I had a word with that skunk.'

Despite his grand news, the sight of Cosmo crouching over his desk reminded Fowler of Monday's paper – not that the hideous front page had been far from his mind since publication. He had intended to give Newgate a dignified lecture over the matter and leave it at that. Instead he ignored his lawyer's advice and roared abuse at the newspaper proprietor.

Surprisingly, Newgate took it calmly. 'I've been expecting you,' he sighed. 'I don't make the news, Fowler, I only print it. Now if you've finished shouting and have got all that off your chest, I've got work to do.'

'Work? Do you call blackening a man's character work?' Fowler yelled. 'Printing lies about a family in your filthy rag? You're the scum of the earth, Newgate! Do you hear me? The sum of the earth!'

Everyone within shouting distance heard; staff craned their necks and customers at the front counter leaned forward to get a better view of the show.

'Out!' Cosmo ordered, leaping up. 'Get out of my office. I don't have to take this from you.'

'No, you don't,' Fowler said, 'but you can take this!' He slammed down the statement Leon had prepared. 'This is news. I want it published, and if you don't publish it I'll know exactly where you stand in this community. With that blackguard Roberts!'

'I have nothing to do with Roberts,' Cosmo tried to explain.

Fowler cut him short. 'I expect to see that in print, and not a word altered.'

Cosmo picked it up and read it. He was not a strong person and he detested rows. Fowler's abuse and the attentive audience had unnerved him. 'There is no reason why I should not publish this information,' he said, with as much dignity as he could muster, but he could not bring himself to proffer congratulations to Maskey, even though they were in order.

Fowler didn't seem to notice. He strode triumphantly from the office, having said his piece and completed his mission.

Cosmo felt as if he'd been bludgeoned. He glared angrily at Fowler's statement, knowing he would have to print the news that the local member was being elevated to Cabinet. He realised that it would

139

be seen as churlish if he didn't give the item due respect. But Fowler's attitude still rankled.

That afternoon, just as he had almost finished setting up his paper a telegram from his stringer in Brisbane was delivered to his office.

Cosmo burst out laughing. Why, of course he would print Fowler's statement. In its entirety. And beside it, in a block, this piece of startling news. He immediately set about rearranging his front page.

Laura didn't see the paper on Monday morning. She was accustomed to reading it over breakfast at home, if she could get her hands on it first, but she could hardly do so at the Robertses' table.

Tyler had left very early and Amelia, bubbling with excitement at her coming betrothal, took charge of the conversation, for which Laura was grateful. Tyler had seen her father the day before, on the Sunday, and his reaction had been not unexpected. He'd said she could stay at the Robertses' house. Fair enough. She supposed he was entitled to be cranky about her disappearing act, but so was she. Best thing to do would be to wait a few days, until he'd cooled down, and then have it out with him. She wasn't afraid of her father, and now that there was no possibility of her marrying Bobby Cope, he would have to listen to her.

She did, however, write a letter of apology to Captain Cope, which reminded her of the ring. Her mother would have retrieved it from the cloakroom dresser, she was sure, and it would be returned to him.

Later in the afternoon she wandered into the kitchen for a glass of water and found the maids huddled over a newspaper.

'What's so interesting?' she asked, and they pulled away guiltily.

'Nothing, miss,' the cook said, and snatched it up.

'Let me see,' Laura said. 'I haven't read the paper today. Have you finished with it?'

Reluctantly they handed it over. One glance at the front page sent Laura rushing to her room to read it in private. She was stunned. 'Fiasco!' screamed the headline, then the article went on to describe with appalling accuracy the events of Saturday night.

She ran to find Amelia, who was washing her hair. 'Have you seen this?'

'Yes. You're quite famous.'

'Why didn't you tell me about it?'

'Daddy said not to worry you. Not that I see why you have to be worried. They've got you as the heroine of the evening.'

'The heroine? A damn fool more like it. Tyler wrote this and he gives the impression that I told him all about it, when in fact I hardly said a word to him. I said I didn't want to discuss Saturday night and look what he's written! It's terrible.'

Amelia slopped her wet hair into a towel. 'You're always so dramatic. Everyone would have heard what happened sooner or later, even if it didn't go in the silly paper.'

'You told him,' Laura accused. 'And he double-crossed me.'

Drying her hair vigorously, Amelia disagreed. 'He did not, and I won't have you talking about him like that, he'd be hurt. He is a good reporter and he just did his best. He never actually says you told him about your father striking you.'

'No, but he infers it.'

'Laura, please, do stop fussing. Comb my hair out for me and mind out for knots.'

Laura took the comb and, with Amelia complaining loudly, began to untangle the thick black curls. 'Now my father really will be furious,' she said.

'For heaven's sake! You should have thought of that before you ran off from the ball. And give me back the comb, you hurt too much.'

Laura felt too depressed to argue with Amelia any longer. She couldn't take on the whole world. Was there anyone left at all who would give her a fair go? It didn't seem so. Perhaps it would be better to write to her father first.

The letter was never delivered. Boyd Roberts offered to send someone down with it but instead he took it to his office, read her explanation and apology, and burned the letter. It was not in his scheme of things to have Laura Maskey reunited with her family. Best to leave things as they were. Silence from the Maskey household would be further proof that she was not welcome there, while he would make it clear that she was most welcome here at Beauview. The more he saw of her, the more he desired her, and she was so vulnerable. If he had his way – and he always did – Laura would stay on at Beauview.

'Amazing,' Leon said, 'how fast people turn about. I couldn't bear the stress of being a parliamentarian. Yesterday, people turned their backs or crossed the road when we walked down the street, and now, already, they're doffing their hats and angling for appointments.'

Fowler laughed. He had sent a telegram to the Premier, accepting a post in the Cabinet and suggesting that he be given the agriculture portfolio, which was of prime importance to this electorate. He'd practically have the power to make or break local pastoralists, and well they knew it. He had also drafted a letter to the Premier; the telegram had been largely for local consumption. The postmaster and his wife were notorious gossips and since they were operating from their general store until the new post office was completed, customers were already aware of the contents. And tomorrow the news would appear in the paper and travel out to all the cattle stations in his electorate.

'They know now where their bread's buttered,' he said to Leon. 'It is a great honour to have a member of Cabinet in their midst.'

'Quite so,' Leon agreed, relieved that the worries of Saturday night had abated. 'They'll forget all about the ball.'

'They will not! They'll forget the trivia and remember that it was a huge success. Which it was.'

'So what will we do about Laura?' Leon asked.

'Nothing. She has made her bed, she can lie in it.'

'You don't think, being out there with Roberts, she can cause us any more trouble?'

'No. Forget about her. I was thinking that we'd go down to Brisbane as soon as possible. Hilda can come too, and when the appointment is official we'll arrange a celebratory dinner at the Royal Exchange Hotel.' He grimaced. 'It will be my pleasure not to have to invite anyone from around here this time.'

He awoke the next morning in high spirits. From a powerful position in Cabinet he would be that much closer to his dream of a separate state in the north. Even more important, his hold on this seat had become ironclad. Roberts could never catch up now.

On this particular sunny morning, Fowler chose to take a walk and collect the paper himself. He strode in, bought a copy, not deigning to glance at it, folded it under his arm and made his way back to Quay Street. But he'd only been feigning disinterest. The pages seemed to be burning a hole in his coat; this was his moment of glory and he was dying to read about it. Casually he strolled across the road as if to take a turn along the river bank and, hidden from view by trees, unfolded the paper.

Irritated, he spotted his story reduced to a small column down in the left-hand corner. Then the headline leapt out at him: HERBERT RETURNS.

With rising horror, he read that because of the financial crisis, Sir Robert Herbert had resumed the office of premier, replacing Macalister. 'This,' the article explained, 'is a temporary measure, approved by Governor Bowen.' But nevertheless it spelled incompetence on the part of Macalister. Worse was to come. Governor Bowen had refused to permit the issue of Queensland government notes on the grounds that the move was impractical and could plunge the state into deeper debt.

Stunned, Fowler turned to the editorial, which enlarged on the matter of those notes, praising Bowen for his wisdom in preventing such a wild and ridiculous scheme. Feeling sick, Fowler turned back to his own statement; there, in black and white, was his support for that very scheme, in direct contrast to the actions of the men who were now in charge.

He staggered a few steps, realising that his hopes had come crashing down, and that this front page showed him up as an utter fool. There was no place in politics for men who'd backed the wrong horse. He hung on to the branch of a tree for support. He was having trouble focusing as he tried to make himself believe that this was all wrong. Where had Cosmo got this information from? Then he saw that the news had come through by telegram. His own letter from Macalister had been written more than a week ago.

He cried out as a sheet of pain enveloped his chest and he lost his grip on the tree. He stumbled on a few steps, trying to get home, but the pain increased and the heavy man slumped to the ground. The surge of the river, sweeping past him, seemed like a roar now, and he tried to call out for help, but his voice was choked as he fought for breath.

The wiry grasses felt cool against his face and the pain subsided. Uncaring, he watched the pages of Cosmo's paper float away in the breeze, taking small troubled flights until they were caught, flattened against bushes. He was surprised that it was becoming darker . . .

Two fishermen found Fowler Maskey's body by the Fitzroy River, too late to help him.

Hilda Maskey was distraught. She clung to her son. 'They killed him,' she wept, 'they killed him! Carping and criticising, making a fool of him in the papers all the time. Spoiling everything he tried to do.' She looked up at Leon as if to plead with him. 'Fowler was a good man, wasn't he?' There was bewilderment in her voice.

'Yes, Mother, he was.'

She was sobbing again. 'Why did they hound him so? Fowler was a fine respectable man, a pillar of this community, and they turned on him, even his own daughter. Is it any wonder he collapsed? And died out there alone.' She began to scream. 'I hope they're satisfied! He's gone now, they'll have to find someone else to hound into the grave!'

The doctor sedated her and Leon sat in the dining room trying to collect his thoughts, while the maids tiptoed by the door. He had made the funeral arrangements with the undertaker and allowed two of Hilda's friends to go up and sit with her, feeling she needed female support at this time, but he refused to receive any other callers. The Maskeys, he decided with relief, were finished with this town. Going through to the study, he wrote a short note to Laura. In it he advised her, with regret, of the death of their father. 'However,' he wrote, 'my mother is in no state to receive you at present, and because of your recent appalling behaviour, which caused our late father great distress, and no doubt contributed to his heart failure, you are not welcome in this house.' He added, 'I sincerely hope that you will not add to Mother's distress by intruding on us at this sad time.'

When he read the letter through, it reminded him of his father. That was exactly what Fowler would have written, he thought, and he felt strong now. He was stepping into his father's shoes at last. Leon Maskey was master of this house.

But she did come. As soon as the rider delivered the message Laura rode wildly into town, slamming past the maid at the front door to confront Leon, tears pouring down her cheeks. 'What happened to Father?' she demanded. 'Is this true? Where's Mother?'

He sat at Fowler's desk, his desk now, and studied her coldly.

'Lower your voice, please. Father collapsed and died this morning, over there on the river bank. If you wish any further details you can see the doctor. Mother has given strict instructions that she does not wish to see you, and if you care for her at all, you'll take pity on her and leave her alone.' He remained aloof as she sank into a chair in tears.

'When you have composed yourself I'll thank you to be on your way.'

'Leon, don't speak to me like that,' she said at length. 'I can't believe that he's gone. Poor Father, to go so suddenly like that. Mother will need my support now, I can't just walk away.'

'You don't have any choice,' he remarked, and turned his back on her.

'Of course I do. This is my home. I know you're upset, Leon, but be sensible.'

'I am being sensible,' he replied, 'and I am trying not to allow you to upset us any further.' He threw Fowler's will on to the desk. 'You can read that if you wish. You will see that this is no longer your home. Father has cut you out of his will, and you have no place here at all.' Secretly Leon was thrilled. Fowler had left the house to Hilda and a substantial trust to support her for life. The rest of his considerable estate went to his son, no longer half shares with Laura, as in the previous will. He, Leon, was to get the lot! He almost felt like thanking Laura for infuriating their father past the point of no return. Thanks to her he was a very wealthy man, beholden to no one.

Leon had already decided to persuade Hilda to sell this house and remove herself to Brisbane as soon as possible. She'd be happier back in civilised company, and a house there would give him a base for the time being. When the dust had settled he planned to be off. To fulfil his dreams of London and the Continent. It was difficult to keep a sombre countenance with all this excitement dancing within him.

His sister seemed not to have heard what he said about the will. Or maybe it hadn't sunk in. 'When is the funeral?' she whispered.

'Tomorrow afternoon,' he replied. 'Three o'clock. There will be a service beforehand at the Anglican church and the vicar is coming round to see me this evening to discuss arrangements.'

She seemed to take time to digest this information, and he wished she would just go away. Her presence made him nervous, as though she might in some way upset that precious, wonderful will, his ticket to freedom, to the high life ahead.

'May I get some clothes?' she asked meekly.

'Certainly. Where shall I send the rest of your things?'

'To the Robertses' house, I suppose,' she said.

He allowed a small sneer. 'Of course. Your friends the Robertses!'

'Leon,' she appealed, 'I don't want to stay there. I never said those things to that reporter. I didn't tell him anything at all. I wrote to Father and explained all of that to him.'

'You might have done, but he never mentioned it. Now, if you'll excuse me, I have a lot to do.'

Laura wandered out into the passageway and met one of the maids. 'Would you please tell my mother I am here and I'd like to see her.'

'Yes, miss.'

As Laura waited, she heard her mother start to scream, the familiar hysterical shouts. The girl hurried back. 'I'm sorry, Miss Laura. She won't see you, and the ladies said it would be best if you go. Mrs Maskey's bad upset over your father's death, they said they don't want you making matters worse.' She smiled wanly. 'Maybe in a few days, eh? When she's feeling better.'

The little church was packed, and mourners stared curiously at Laura, who sat between Amelia and Boyd Roberts.

At the graveside, when she ventured forward to stand by her mother, Hilda hissed at her from under the black veil, 'Get away from me. If it weren't for you and your friends, my husband would still be alive.'

Laura felt faint as she stumbled away, shocked. Cosmo Newgate took her arm. 'I'm very sorry,' he said, reciting the commiserations that had fallen leadenly on her from so many people.

She stopped and stared at him. 'You printed those lies about me, you wretched man, and my father believed you. He'll never know now,' she wept, 'that I didn't tell Tyler Kemp any of our family business. I didn't tell him anything.'

Cosmo watched her go. 'Oh God!' he said, guilt welling. Placing Fowler's elevation to Macalister's cabinet on the same page as the news that that cabinet no longer existed had seemed a joke at the time, a payback for Fowler's outburst. He had ridiculed the man publicly, but politicians were supposed to have thick skins. He already felt bad that his front page may have brought on the attack, but he'd tried to dismiss that thought. Now he knew that Kemp had lied to him about Laura and he was the cause of this further rift in the Maskey family.

He cursed himself for this grave error. He should have checked with Laura, that would have been easy enough. But Kemp was a smooth talker. As he watched Laura being assisted into Amelia Roberts' carriage he was gripped with pity for her. And with shame at his hand in her misery. Roberts, tall and elegant in black, placed an expensive wreath by the graveside. Cosmo could almost feel the evil of the man; Roberts, he was certain, was behind all this, and even though others saw the man as an upright citizen, Cosmo vowed never to be taken in again.

Cosmo, a small man in wire-rimmed glasses, with a fuzz of greying hair and an untidy grey moustache, remained standing by the grave long after most of the mourners had drifted away, clutching his cap, lost in his own thoughts. When he eventually went out through the gate and down to the hitching rail for his horse, Boyd Roberts was waiting for him.

'Cosmo, I know this isn't the best time, but I wanted to have a word with you.'

'What about?'

'I was wondering if you'd be interested in selling your paper?'

Right at that moment, with his confidence at its lowest ebb, Cosmo would have been quite happy to sell the paper and run from this guilt, but the canny newspaperman held back. 'Who wants to buy it?'

'I do, as a matter of fact.'

'It's not for sale.'

'Everything is for sale. Name your price.'

'What do you want with a paper?'

'You don't have to worry about that. You just have to name your price and I'll pay it.'

Having launched the *Capricorn Post* and built up a fairly good circulation, Cosmo had planned to sell at a profit and move on, but selling to Roberts after this tragedy? Never.

'It's not for sale.' There were many things he wanted to say to Roberts, to accuse him of, but this was not the time. Cosmo had emerged from the slums of Sydney, and by thrift and hard work he'd learned his trade and earned enough to establish this paper. He knew men harder and crueller than this dandified crook with his paid amateur henchmen would ever meet, and he now had Roberts' measure. Time to play Roberts' genteel game. 'Good God, Boyd. I couldn't sell my paper. It's my life. What would I do?'

'You could open one somewhere else.'

'Ah no. It's too much work. I'm happy where I am.'

He saw the jaw tighten, the eyes narrow, and knew he was in for trouble, but it didn't deter him. Not now. He changed the subject. 'What's happening about Jock McCann's station? I heard you bought it.'

'That's right.'

'But the stock have been sold. They say it's deserted.'

'I'll get around to it in time.'

'Nice to have that sort of money.'

'It is indeed.' Roberts smiled. 'But what about the paper? You could make a handy profit here.'

'Not the point, old chap. I'm very comfortable with it. Good day to you. I have to get back to work.'

Three times in the next two weeks Boyd approached Cosmo to buy the paper, and each time his offer was rejected.

In the meantime, Cosmo, acting on instinct, made certain that his insurance policies for the building, his equipment, his person, were all in order. He had heard that Laura Maskey had been cut off without a penny by her father and was now in the kindly, charitable hands of

Boyd Roberts. Being a bachelor, Cosmo rewrote his will, leaving all his goods and chattels to Laura.

As for Boyd, he was concentrating all his charms on his lovely guest.

In the absence of Tyler Kemp, Amelia was pleased to have Laura's company and was genuine in her concern for her friend, death being a sobering influence. But after a few days she found mourning a bore and took herself out to escape the grief that still enveloped their guest.

She was not a little put out when a wagon arrived with Laura's trunks. As they were carried into her room, Laura could only sit and stare at them while Amelia frowned. What if Laura were still here when Tyler came back? she worried. Hadn't it happened often enough, that gentlemen hardly noticed her when Laura was present? What if Tyler changed his mind and fell for Laura? The more she thought about it, the more her imagination ran riot, producing panic. And jealousy.

'How long are you staying?' she asked Laura, in a kindly way, of course.

Laura seemed to shrivel. 'Not long,' she whispered. 'You've been so kind. But I have to go soon. I just have to think what to do.' She gulped back tears. 'I mean . . . where . . .' Her voice trailed off. The reality of the bleakness of her situation was beginning to seep through her misery, but she couldn't bear to admit, even to Amelia, that she was destitute. That at present she couldn't afford to go anywhere. Even if she had somewhere to go. Perhaps she could write to Uncle William in England, but that would take months.

If she could only throw off this terrible depression and think clearly, Laura was sure she could find an answer. What did people do in these circumstances?

As was customary, details of Fowler Maskey's will were published, and Amelia fled to her father. 'Did you see this? Fowler hasn't left her a penny. That sneak Leon got Laura's share. I think that's frightful. What can Laura do now?'

'We'll have to work something out,' he said calmly.

'Like what? She can't stay here indefinitely.'

'Don't you be worrying your pretty head. Where are you off to, looking so bonny?'

Amelia preened. 'Nancy Leighton is having a musical evening at her place and she's going to no end of trouble. She's hoping her beau, Gordon, will propose.'

'Do you want me to escort you?'

'No. I'll go in the carriage and it can come back for me later.'

'Very well then, off you go, and don't be worrying about Laura.'

'You ought to talk to Leon, make him share with her.'

'We'll see.'

That evening Boyd had dinner served on the veranda, a table for two set out there on a lovely starry night. He attended to the subtleties

147

himself: lanterns set far enough apart to allow the candles in their rose shades to shed their soft light; fine white wines and glittering crystal.

Laura hardly noticed his efforts. 'I'm not very hungry,' she said.

He smiled. 'I didn't think you would be, my dear, so I've only ordered a light meal. Just some pâté and biscuits and a little cold chicken and ham. Eat what you can. And have a glass of wine. It will make you feel better.'

She picked at the meal and he didn't bother her with small talk. He wanted her to feel comfortable with him.

After several glasses of wine, she plucked up the courage to mention her father's will. 'You know what happened, I suppose?'

'Yes,' he said, 'and I'm truly sorry.'

'I don't know what to do,' she told him, a sob in her voice. 'Or where to go.'

'First things first,' he said, refilling her glass. 'Let's drink to your health and beauty. You haven't lost them.'

Laura managed a grim smile. 'For what they're worth!'

'There you are now!' He beamed. 'You smiled. You are making progress.'

The wine, on top of very little food, was having an effect. She shrugged. 'Progress to nowhere. You realise I haven't got a bean?'

'That's only temporary. Money isn't all that important. Loneliness is a worse evil.'

Laura nodded; she had never felt so lonely and bereft in her life, even here with friends. After all, she was only living on their charity. She blushed, remembering she'd inflicted herself on them, without invitation. Gratitude to this man warmed her and she listened to him fondly.

'When Amelia marries,' he was saying sorrowfully, 'things won't be the same here any more. She and Tyler will be moving into their own house and I'll be rattling about here on my own. I can't stand in their way, life goes on. I'll probably end up a lonely old man.'

'No, you won't,' she objected. 'For heaven's sake, why should you? I've often wondered why you haven't remarried.'

'Never found the right lady,' he said.

Laura rested her chin on her hands, a little more at ease now with someone else's troubles to distract her. 'If you looked about, you wouldn't have any trouble. Not a person like you with so much to offer.'

'That's good of you to say so. It has occurred to me lately that I might have found the right person, but I doubt if she'd have me.'

'Why ever not?'

'She might think I'm too old and decrepit.'

This time she did smile. 'I hardly think so.'

He sighed, toying with his glass. 'The problem is,' he confided, 'she doesn't realise how much I care for her.'

'Then you must tell her. Boyd, surely you aren't shy?'

'In this case I am.' He put the glass down. 'I couldn't consider any other ladies now, because I can't see past the lovely guest in my house.'

Laura looked down at her plate in the face of rising panic. Surely she must have misunderstood his reply. 'Who do you mean?' she stammered.

'I'm trying to tell you,' he persisted, 'that when you leave I shall miss you terribly.'

'Me?' Laura was finding it difficult to grasp.

'Don't be embarrassed,' he told her gently. 'Surely you know how beautiful you are. I didn't want to bring this up so soon, but you've been so distressed I couldn't bear to watch any longer without extending a hand to you.'

'You're feeling sorry for me,' she muttered.

He smiled. 'Oh no, my dear. I'm not that charitable. I know you're worried about your future, so to ease your mind let me first tell you that you're welcome to stay here as long as you wish. And secondly, I'm hoping that you will take the time now to see me not as Amelia's father, but as a man. And,' he added, 'a man who has become so very fond of you that I think he's making a fool of himself.'

'Oh no, you're not,' she cried. 'Really. It's just that this is a surprise. I don't know what to say.'

'You don't have to say anything. All I ask is that you think about it.' Although he'd not intended to, he could not resist going a little further. 'I am a very wealthy man, Laura, you'd never want for anything. I'd give you the moon on the plate if you'd marry me.'

There it was. Spelled out. Laura was silent for a long while. She wished the floor would swallow her up. But she had to consider his feelings; he had paid her a great compliment, and she didn't want to hurt him. 'What would Amelia say?' she asked, stalling for time.

'I'd appreciate it if you didn't mention this to Amelia for the time being,' he replied. 'She'd probably say I was being a perfect ass thinking you might be interested in me.'

'More than that, I fear,' Laura commented.

'Ah yes, but as I said, Amelia will have her own life to lead. However, let's not discuss it any more tonight. There's no hurry, I just hope you'll give the matter some serious thought. Now, on to other things. I've decided to put in a croquet lawn but I can't make up my mind where it should go . . .'

She was surprised at how easily he was able to change the subject and finish the evening without causing her discomfort. Later in her room, thoroughly confused, she did give his proposal a great deal of thought. If she married him her worries would be over, but she wished he hadn't mentioned his wealth, because it felt like a bribe. *Marry me and I'll make it worth your while.* She supposed that plenty of women would see that as an important consideration, as having made a 'good' marriage, but Laura rebelled at the thought. She had no

149

intention of being bought. Then again, maybe she was being too hard on Boyd. He'd known her for a long time, and if he wanted to marry her then at least she should appreciate his offer.

Strangely, she felt much better. Whether it was the wine, the proposal, or the temporary removal of her biggest worry – where next to lay her head – she felt more confident. She even wondered what it would be like to have Boyd Roberts make love to her, and was intrigued to find she was not repulsed as she had been thinking of Bobby Cope. The short, passionate affair with Paul had made her aware of the real obligations of marriage. She was no longer the silly virgin walking wide-eyed into the marital state.

However, she told herself as she pulled on her nightdress, she was not in love with Boyd Roberts and she must not allow herself to be enticed into marriage out of sheer desperation. He seemed to believe that now she knew of his intentions, she would see him in a different light and thus be free to fall in love with him. He was a man of experience, she thought drowsily, maybe that's how love did evolve sometimes. She really was quite fond of him, and she certainly respected him. Maybe . . .

Chapter Six

Jeannie wasn't really still angry with him, but she was not about to let him off the hook yet. The big day had come and gone, last Saturday to be exact, and the Maskey ball was over, so that was that. They'd missed the social event of the year.

She pasted the invitation in her scrap book and folded the grey satin evening gown back into the tin trunk. With it she put away her anger but it was harder to shelve the lingering spell of her dreams. It was for this reason that she was still punishing Paul, unable to stop carping at him over every little thing.

By the Tuesday he was glad to escape with the men at early dawn, to ride out with all hands over the new bridge into the northern pastures to rebuild the stockyards and start mustering the herds of cattle that had been free the last few months.

Jeannie was pleased to be rid of them. 'I swear,' she told Clara, 'if I ever got left to fend for myself I could get a job as a cook in a café any time.'

Clara agreed. Since Mr MacNamara had started to worry about the blacks, all the men had been working close to home, with the result that the two women worked overtime in the kitchen. It never occurred to the men to boil their own billies with the big black kettle so handy. Instead, they'd fronted up for morning and afternoon tea as well as the three main meals. And it wasn't just smoko, like they had out on the range; they ate their way through all the scones and cake and butter and jams the women could produce. 'I'd hate to have to feed an army,' she said, looking at the empty shelves in the pantry.

'It's a bloody nuisance,' Jeannie said. 'But I'm not doing any extra work today. We're entitled to a rest. I'll make some bread, that's all, proper bread, not damper, and this afternoon we'll go fishing. I saw some nice fat rascals in the creek the other day, just waiting for the pan.'

'Suits me,' Clara said, which meant she was delighted. She loved to fish. Often of a Sunday afternoon Mr MacNamara would come fishing with them, to their favourite river spot, a tranquil clearing shaded by weeping willows. It was the highlight of her week to be with them, just the three of them, laughing, teasing, competing. Clara had a crush on the boss, and she envied the missus her good fortune in landing a man like that.

151

Jeannie had a secret, too. She went inside to make the bed and stopped to gaze wistfully at the trunk that contained, among her other very bests, the evening dress. Because she was a physical person, and proud of it – she could ride, shoot, swim and fish as well as anyone – she would rather die than admit that she was an inveterate day-dreamer. Her fantasies were modest enough, but they were very private.

Jeannie MacNamara had seen herself at that ball, with her hand-some husband, the centre of attention. She would have her long plait of hair properly coiffured by a professional person in the township, and she would look very elegant. The Carlisles of Camelot Station, their new friends, would be there. And soon people would know that she and Paul were immediate family of the Rivadavias from the Hunter Valley. Even the Maskeys would know of them, they moved in the Governor's set. Not just here in Queensland but in Sydney, the real viceregals. And another thing, Jeannie was a good dancer, never been taught but she'd picked it up easy, and she saw herself dancing the night away. With people asking: 'Who is that?'

She sighed, the dream fading. Damn his stubborn hide! Oh well, never mind. She still had the visit of Dolour and Juan Rivadavia to look forward to. Not that they'd ever be able to organise a gathering of the size of the Maskey ball, but they could go into Rockhampton to meet the boat. And Paul could arrange a dinner party at one of the hotels. Maybe even invite the Maskeys. Why not?

It was time to get back to the chores. She was bored with damper, she'd make some real bread, high tin, and she and Clara could spoil themselves today with ham sandwiches before they went fishing.

Private Charlie Penny was having trouble with his troops. In the absence of Captain Cope they wouldn't do a thing they were told, and he was confused. He'd thought it'd be an easy job to boss them along but it wasn't going right at all.

They'd left the Sinclair station, fortunately without any trouble in front of white men – maybe because of the white men – and headed for the ranges. But once into the foothills the fights had started. Charlie had managed to pinch a bottle of rum and his mate Blackie Bob had grabbed a bottle, and they didn't mind sharing, but after they'd swigged them down they found Stan Hatbox sucking away at one on his own and getting double drunk. They punched him out and searched his packs, coming up with some real firewater, the home-made brew that Stan and his brother Billy had plundered from a cache under the stockmen's shed.

All of a sudden that seemed very funny. The stockmen wouldn't dare dob them in, for fear their homebrew would be exposed, so these bottles, found also in the packs of the young blokes, cousins Joseph and Tom Curley, were a big joke. They lit a campfire but no one could be bothered cooking as the bottles were passed around. A fight started between Tom Curley and Stan, but by that time Charlie, the boss, was too drunk to care.

Come the morning they were a weary, battered lot, staggering about with fierce headaches and tempers to match. Charlie waded fully clothed into the lagoon to sober up, and Tom Curley stood laughing at him, because to get into the deeper water he'd had to shove in among the pink water-flowers. Charlie knew he must look stupid, like a girl with a garland of flowers, but he didn't appreciate the joke. He came out and tried to make them all come to attention in a row, like Captain Cope did, but they laughed and capered about like idiots.

He picked up his waddy. It was a fearsome weapon, studded with nails, made by some enterprising wild black. Charlie had found it in a camp they'd raided. He belted Joseph across the shoulders with it, sent him staggering, so they'd know he meant business.

'You two,' he shouted, 'Joseph and Tom, stand over there. You go with them, Billy, because you're in charge of them.'

Billy obliged, doubling up with laughter, marching, knees up, across the clearing in a parody of military efficiency.

But it would do. Charlie gave his orders. 'You three go down the coast trail, like the Captain said, and we'll go down the valley.'

Joseph and Tom, standing more or less at attention, acquiesced, but Billy resisted. 'No bloody fear. I don't go nowhere without me brother.'

'I'm the boss!' Charlie yelled at him, but Billy jerked his jacket on over his bare chest and grabbed up his carbine. He strode forward, menacing Charlie, who also grabbed for his firearm.

Stan intervened. 'Ain't no difference, Charlie. You send Blackie with them fellers.'

There was no warning. They dived for cover as spears thudded around them. Joseph and Tom, standing waiting for their orders, had no chance. The first rain of spears thudded into them, and they lay sprawled, gaping up at the trees, heavy spears lodged in their bodies.

Billy and Charlie, unable to see anyone, fired into the scrub in a panic while the others, too far from their weapons to be of any use, cringed down the bank. Spears dropped about them and one found a mark in Stan's side. His screams mingled with the crack of the rifles until Charlie realised the assault was over. He swore as he waited to make certain the attackers had gone. Captain Cope would blame him for this. He wasn't so much concerned about the deaths of Tom and Joseph as about the fact that he'd forgotten to post guards. Charlie shuddered. If the tribesmen had come upon them last night, they'd all be dead by now.

Gingerly they emerged from their shelters, trying to move quietly. Stan was still screaming.

'Tell him to shut up,' Charlie said.

Blackie Bob yelled, 'Bloody spear stuck right in him!'

153

Charlie ignored them and, with Billy, went to investigate the surrounding bush. As they thought, they had fought off the tribesmen, but they were disappointed to find only one man in the scrub, shot dead. Obviously his mates hadn't had time to collect his body, but they'd be back for him. Swiftly Billy took his knife and sliced off the right ear, proof of the kill. They searched vainly for more bodies, to even up the score, until Blackie Bob joined them.

'No good, Charlie,' Bob said. 'Them lot bolted. Gone that way.' He pointed into the hills.

'How many?' Charlie asked. Blackie Bob was their best tracker.

'Five feller and the dead 'un. We go now, we catch them buggers.'

Charlie shook his head. 'Doan be stupid. If we follow we run into a trap. They have all their bloody mates waitin' for us, them wild fellers chop us to bits.'

Billy went down to see to his brother, who was lying face down in the sand, moaning with the pain of the spear which was lolling from his side. 'Get it out!' he screamed.

'Gonna hurt,' Billy warned, holding the spear steady as he studied the situation. The barb was, fortunately, made of wood, and only one side of the small, sharp wing was embedded in the flesh. He nodded sagely. 'You a lucky feller, Stan. Only half barb stuck in you. Any more and we'd have to shove it right through.'

Stan groaned.

The other men held him down as Billy wrenched out the spear, creating a jagged wound that gushed blood.

Charlie watched impassively as they staunched the blood with the rags they used to clean their rifles. He set about the business of burying the two bodies, which were already thick with flies. He was in an ugly mood, his head pounding, and he yelled at them to leave Stan and come and help him.

The graves, he knew, were too shallow, dingoes could dig the bodies out easy, but he didn't care, he just wanted to get away from this creepy place. The lagoon area was too quiet, the trees were hushed and the water birds had gone into hiding, no doubt to avoid evil spirits.

With only four of them left, and wild blacks on the attack, he ignored Cope's orders and decided not to split the party. Instead of sending only two down the coast trail they would all travel down the valley together. 'Bloody too dangerous to split up now,' he muttered to himself, somehow shifting the blame for this failure on to Cope. 'Bloody white soldiers,' he said to Blackie. 'They keep safe. Make us do the hard jobs.'

'Too right,' Blackie agreed mournfully. 'Get better tucker too.'

That reminded Charlie that he was hungry and further annoyed him. White troops got better rations; black soldiers were expected to hunt or fish for most of their tucker. Sinclair hadn't given them so much as a tin of beans when they'd left. But if the mighty Captain had been with them, they'd be carrying a swag of provisions. Nobody cared if black troopers starved, so long as they chased away the stinking tribesmen for them.

He looked at the sullen waters of the lagoon. He knew that there'd be fish aplenty under the deathly still green mantle of plants, but he was afraid to stay at this place any longer.

The others straggled to their horses in silent agreement, and they hoisted Stan on to his mount. He was in intense pain, but Billy warned him, 'You gotta ride or they'll leave us behind. So you hang on.' He turned to Charlie. 'The Captain, he said them mountains is crawling with blackfellers. Plenty hideouts up there. We ain't going there. We stick to the valley.'

Charlie knew that. They weren't expected to go up, just patrol the lowlands and catch raiding parties coming or going, but he wasn't going to let Billy give the orders. Like any little bureaucrat, he announced, as if he were contradicting Billy, that they would go across the valley. 'We head for McCann's station. Get some tucker.'

As they mounted up, Billy grabbed the spear. It was a good strong weapon, the double-edged barb well bound and gummed, still secure. Stan scowled but Billy explained, 'Catch plenty fish with this, mate.'

Then they were off. This was a Monday, but every day was the same to them. They rode down through a gorge, a mistake since they then had to slash their way through thick rain forest, which made them nervous. Blackie pointed out that this route was obviously used by blacks coming down from the heights, there were signs of their presence everywhere. 'We tell the Captain,' he said proudly.

'Bugger the Captain,' Billy replied and Charlie agreed. This was the last place they'd want to revisit. It was easy for tribesmen to travel this route but bloody hard on horseback, as well as being ideal for the enemy to jump them in the gloom.

Eventually they emerged into open forest country and followed the stream that took them in the direction of McCann's homestead. They'd ridden all day without incident and were tired and very hungry by the time they made it to the house.

It was deserted. They wandered inside to find just the shell of a house, all the furniture gone. Barn doors hung open, and there was no one about at all.

When the realisation dawned upon Charlie that the homestead had been abandoned, he flew into a rage. They searched the place, finding only scraps of food, a few tins, mildewed cheese, a half-empty bottle of gin, nothing to really fill their bellies. In retaliation they wrecked the place, smashing windows, pulling doors off their hinges, breaking down walls with their tomahawks in a frenzy of destruction. Then they set fire to the place.

Blackie caught some bush turkeys and they cooked them in the embers, along with their billies of tea, laughing now at their successful payback to the whites.

155

In the meantime Stan rested by a tree. The pain was still sharp but the bleeding had stopped. Billy doused the wound with some eucalyptus oil he'd found in a cupboard, announcing that his brother would be all right. He produced a woman's lawn petticoat, rescued from the laundry, and taking off his trousers, he capered about with it bunched over his skinny hips. They all laughed uproariously, and Charlie growled, 'No use you finding an empty dress, Billy. Why doan you find one with a woman in it?'

'I get you one, boss,' Billy grinned, 'first time back in town, you betcha.'

Charlie nodded, pleased, not because of the promise of a woman, but because Billy had called him 'boss'. Now they were waking up to who was in charge. He gazed haughtily at them from under his heavy creased eyelids. 'We ridin' on outa here first light.' He jerked a thumb at the smouldering ruins behind him. 'White feller not going to like this. We tell them we caught bad blacks here, big fight. Joseph and Tom got speared. Poor Stan over there too. We good fellers, kill plenty of them, chase 'em off. Too late to save poor house.' Charlie grinned malevolently. 'Good story, eh?'

His three troopers were enthusiastic until Blackie Bob saw a flaw. 'Captain Cope, he said three of us sojers go down the coast trail.'

Disgusted, Charlie glared at him. Blackie did have a point, though. Charlie considered the problem for a while and came up with the answer. 'We couldn't split up, well. You tracked big raiding party comin' down from them mountains, and we follow.'

'Too bloody right,' Billy cried. 'And I got the spear to prove it. And we got an ear.'

After further discussion they had their story organised. There was a small worry about the whereabouts of Joseph's and Tom's graves, since they weren't buried on the McCann property, at the scene of this nonexistent battle, until Blackie sneered, 'White men don't care about us. If it was white sojers they'd want to find the burying places. Not black sojers.'

And they knew he was right.

In the morning Stan was feeling better. 'My brother plenty tough feller,' Billy said proudly, as they mounted up and headed south for the next station, Oberon. By now they'd convinced themselves that they were the heroes of the big fight, two men lost and one wounded, and were lucky to have escaped with their lives. The boss at Oberon would be pleased, would even feel sorry for them, and so they could expect a welcome and plenty of tucker.

And they weren't all that wrong.

The two dogs were barking long before they rode up to the homestead and Jeannie was waiting, loaded rifle at her shoulder, as they rounded the bend. None of the Oberon men, she knew, would be back at this hour of the morning.

When she saw the uniforms she relaxed a little, but still questioned them. 'Where's your officer?'

Charlie reined in. 'He gone into Rockhampton, missus. Last week. Captain Cope gone to marriage party.'

Cope! At the mention of his name she relaxed. She turned back to Clara, who was standing behind her. 'That's the engagement party we were invited to.'

Nevertheless, she hadn't finished her questioning. 'What are you doing on this property?'

'Captain Cope. He got a message,' Charlie answered truthfully. 'Your boss send a message, too many bad blackfellers in them hills. He tell me to come home this way in case you got trouble.'

Jeannie was delighted. 'It wasn't Paul who sent the message,' she whispered to Clara. 'It was me.'

'Plenty trouble out here,' Charlie commented.

Jeannie stared at him. 'What trouble?' Then she noticed Stan, who was leaning heavily in his saddle, overdoing it, on Charlie's instructions, to get sympathy. 'What's the matter with him?' she asked.

'Got speared, missus. Us fellers pretty much done in. Big fight with ten . . .' He had forgotten the number they'd decided on, and looked to his mates, who nodded agreement. Whatever. 'Maybe twenty warriors,' he added. 'Two of our sojers killed in the fight. Hit by spears.' He thumped his broad chest to illustrate. 'Bang! Bang! Got stone dead.'

'Oh my God!' Jeannie said. 'Where was this?'

'At McCann house. Yesterday.'

'But there's no one there.'

'More better for them,' Charlie told her. 'Big raiding party attacked the house, burn it all down.'

Jeannie lowered the rifle and listened, horrified, as Charlie's story of the battle unfolded. His three troopers were equally fascinated, nodding agreement all the while.

'Where are the rest of the mob now?' she asked nervously.

'I dunno,' Charlie said. 'When they run off we didn't know what to do. Blackie here said we oughta keep after them but the Captain, he told me I had to come this way.'

Jeannie understood. It was typical of blacks, they were no good at making decisions. Probably they should have chased the raiders but she couldn't blame this fellow. He didn't look very bright, none of them were, but he was simply obeying orders, not knowing any better. Poor Captain Cope, she thought, it must be like having a troupe of trained monkeys on his hands.

'Maybe you give us a bit of tucker,' Charlie said, 'and we get going now. Goin' on back to Rockhampton.' He was eager to head home because Billy insisted he had meant what he said. He knew a woman, a white woman, who would drop her pants for him. She was expensive, Billy warned, three shillings against thrippence for a young gin. A

157

month's pay, Charlie knew, but it'd be worth it. He'd never got that close to a white woman. The thought of her excited him but still he haggled. 'She'd have to drop more than her pants,' he'd leered and Billy understood. 'Sure boss, she plenty fat white lady, plenty to see.'

Since his stories had gone down so well, Charlie was feeling pretty good. Water the horses, get a feed and ride like hell back to find that woman. But Jeannie upset his plans.

'No,' she said, in a strong, hard voice, as if she were their officer. 'You'll stay here. We'll give you a feed, then you go and see our boss. He'll want to hear all about this. He might decide to take a look around with you in case some of the wild blacks come this way.' She discussed this with Clara. 'Paul will want to know about this as soon as possible. He'll have to go over to McCann's to check it out. Even though it belongs to that Roberts character now.' She couldn't help feeling a mite pleased that the McCann homestead had been destroyed. If the situation weren't so dangerous and tragic, with the loss of two troopers, she'd almost cheer the wild blacks this time. Someone, at last, had hit Roberts where it hurt. Jock McCann had built a lovely big house for his wife. It would cost a fortune to replace.

Charlie, though, was not pleased. 'We gotta get back,' he told her. 'The captain said.'

'It's all right,' she told him firmly. 'My husband will explain to Captain Cope. You have to report to Mr MacNamara first. He's the boss here.'

'Where is he?' Charlie asked. It was plain to see there were no men about or they would have appeared by this.

'He's out working,' Jeannie said. 'I'll tell you how to get there. It's only a couple of hours' ride from here. You take your mate there round to the barn and let him rest. He can stay here until you get back. Are you sure he's all right?'

Stan was tiring. 'It's starting to bleed again, missus,' he called, clutching his back.

Jeannie saw the blood seeping through his uniform. 'Is the wound bandaged?'

'We ain't got no bandages,' Billy said, hanging on to his brother to prevent him from falling.

'Oh dear!' Jeannie was genuinely concerned. 'Run inside and get the disinfectant powder and bandage,' she told Clara, 'and we'll take a look at him.'

The troopers dismounted, lifting Stan down, and Clara came running back with the bandages.

'Bring him over to the barn,' Jeannie called. 'Quickly!' As the two women came out of the gate to lead the way, Jeannie sniffed the air. 'Oh my God! My bread! It's burning.'

She left Clara with the troopers and raced back to the house, propping the gun by the kitchen door. Smoke was emanating from the big oven as she threw the doors wide, cursing her forgetfulness.

Luckily, some of the bread could be saved. She grabbed oven cloths and wrenched the tins out one by one, running headlong to dump them on the table. The tops were blackened but there was still a chance, so she tipped them up, resorting to a flat knife to try to salvage the bread stuck to the tins. It took a while, but she was determined not to waste any. In the end she had to lop off half of the crusts and wrap the remainder in cloths.

'Damn!' she spluttered. 'Damn!' as she threw the charcoaled remnants into a bucket for the chooks. The tins had to be scoured while they were still hot, and the next batch of dough was ready in the cheesecloth, so she set to work to repair the damage, determined not to forget this lot.

At last, hot and flustered, the fire in the stove refuelled, Jeannie stood back. It was then that she heard Clara scream. Just one loud, piercing scream. Jeannie grabbed her rifle and flung herself past the wire door, running across the dusty track to the barn.

How it had happened, Charlie fretted fearfully afterwards, was so simple – like putting one foot after the other. All the events had been inevitable.

They were barefoot, their boots tied by their laces to saddles or packs. Captain Cope was very particular that they look after their boots, because they had to be worn when full uniform was needed. The rest of the time, though, black troopers found them restricting and uncomfortable. They led their horses down the well-worn track towards the barn, with Stan putting on a bit of an act, making out his wound was worse to win the sympathy of the white servant girl who was trudging beside them. Charlie approved; it all helped to sustain their fictional cover story of battle.

The girl had bare feet too. Not the missus, Charlie had noticed, she'd worn boots, but this one, not expecting visitors, was working without boots. He watched the little pink feet popping out from under the long black skirt, and grinned. Charlie was feeling good, very cocky now since their story had passed examination by that sharp-eyed missus. Billy caught him watching those pink feet and he winked, his broad face breaking into a leer, as if he too were pondering what else lay under the skirt.

They didn't have long to wait. As they went round a corner past the stables the girl turned to beckon them on and walked too close to a bush, catching her dress. She stopped to wrench it free, giving them a show of a white petticoat, just like the one Billy had been prancing about in. All four of them, remembering the joke, had to smother their laughter.

With the horses hitched outside, they took Stan into the barn and put him to rest on a pile of bags. The girl kneeled beside him, instructing Charlie to remove Stan's shirt and loosen the top of his trousers so that she could see the wound. This done, with Stan lying flat on his face, she took one look and pulled back, exclaiming: 'This ought to be stitched!'

'No!' Stan yelped. 'You're not stickin' needles in me.'

'Get me some water,' she told Blackie. He handed over his waterbag, and they watched as she sponged off the dried blood and, leaning down, shook white powder on the wound.

Behind her, Billy was watching the white petticoat that was now plainly visible. He glanced quickly at Charlie, who knew exactly what Billy was thinking, but his own blood was running hot too, so he didn't try to stop him.

Billy pounced, clapping his heavy hand over the girl's mouth, and rolled her with him away from Stan. Ready for action now, Charlie jerked his head at Blackie. 'You go lookout.'

Together they dragged the girl back into a dark corner, ripping away her clothes. They pushed her face into the dirt and swiftly Charlie took over, smothering her mouth while Billy produced his big knife to frighten her, to stop her fighting them. She kicked and fought, and they were amazed at her strength, but they soon had her naked, all pink and white with fat pointy breasts, and there was a great need for them to get at her.

Stan watched, spellbound, as Billy put the knife to her throat: 'You doan make a sound or I dig this in.'

She nodded, blue eyes wide with fear, and Charlie let go of her mouth to roll back and undo his belt.

All of a sudden she screamed, a terrible, piercing scream that seemed to ricochet against the walls of the barn. Billy didn't hesitate; he punched her hard on the jaw, knocking her unconscious. 'That shut her up,' he said. 'You hurry, mate, my turn next.'

Billy pulled the woman further back towards the wall, taking the opportunity to fondle her limp body, but Charlie stopped. 'Is she dead?' He was superstitious about the dead, afraid her spirit might come after him.

'No.' Billy grinned. 'She only knocked out. You feel.' He lifted her head up and Charlie reached down, his hand on the soft warm skin, to feel her heart pumping, relieved that this chance would not be denied him.

Jeannie was running. With her rifle. She dived across the track around the back of the stables and sprinted towards the rear of the barn. She didn't have to be told what had happened – the single scream and the silence that followed was enough – and she cursed herself for her stupidity. Black or white, strange men were always a danger, and these blackfellows especially. People had said they were just trained savages, but she hadn't listened, hadn't cared then. It was the uniform that had tricked her, their bloody uniforms!

She slipped in through the back door, almost catching them off guard, but Billy, facing the door, saw the woman and the rifle levelled at him and wrenched the groaning girl to her feet. She was coming round.

He grasped her in front of him, his knife at her throat. 'You put that gun down, missus,' he grated, 'or I slit her now.'

Jeannie was appalled. Poor Clara, stark naked, in the hands of these beasts. The other man, his hands up, fell back, and the sick one was on his knees now, begging. 'I never touch her, missus,' he cried. 'I never done nothing.'

Jeannie ignored him, searching the gloom for the fourth man, but Clara had first priority. She was fully awake now and aware that the pig holding her was using her for protection. The knife at her throat felt very sharp. 'Please don't shoot,' she cried. 'He'll kill me.'

To all concerned, the woman seemed to weaken, though she stood her ground, the rifle still aimed. 'Are you all right?' she called to Clara.

'Yes,' Clara managed to say, despite the agony in her jaw.

'Then duck!' Jeannie roared at her. The order struck Clara immediately. With only Billy's left arm holding her, she went down like a stone, leaving Billy defenceless. Jeannie shot him between the eyes.

But the delay had given Blackie time to size up the situation from the time of that scream. He hadn't seen the missus coming but guessed she'd be on the warpath somewhere. He circled the barn and crept in just as she shot Billy. Immediately, he whacked her across the back of her head with Charlie's waddy. The other woman was gibbering and moaning on the ground, trying to cover her nakedness.

'We gotta get out of here,' Charlie said, looking at her. It was too late to worry about Billy. The first thing now was to save their own skins. Fortunately they could expect to have plenty of time. He called to Blackie, 'Give her one too!'

Blackie obliged. He had belted gins and their kids; a white gin was no different, and this waddy was a fine weapon. He struck Clara across the head.

Now Charlie's cunning came to the fore again. 'We can blame them wild blackfellers again. We hafta clean this place up, though, and you make sure no bloody signs left, Blackie.'

They gathered up the girl's clothes and the rifle the woman had used, and carried the two limp bodies down to the river. Since the women were both still alive, Charlie felt they should take what they earned now. 'If they ever catch us we'll be sorry we didn't,' he explained to Blackie, who saw the logic in that statement. Stan, ignoring his wound, joined in. The two women were too groggy and feeble to protest, and when it was over, Blackie produced the spear that Billy had taken as a souvenir and speared the white women. He left them in the shallows, the spear still protruding from Jeannie MacNamara's body, and threw their clothes and the smashed rifle in beside them.

161

Blackie, the tracker, knew signs. He cleaned up the barn but deliberately left footprints in the dust, knowing that the large splayed prints were a clue, then dropping the waddy near the front door. He grinned. The white police would think they were real smart when they figured out what had happened here. Or thought they had.

They wrapped Billy's body in his blanket and lashed it to his horse, and remembering they needed food, they tramped through the house, smashing anything they passed, to raid the meat safe. As they rode away they could smell bread burning.

Instead of riding on to Rockhampton they returned to the burned-out McCann homestead and buried Billy deep in the bush.

After all that exertion, and the long ride, the three troopers took their rest, certain that they'd covered their tracks perfectly, as indeed they had. They agreed that the next day they'd ride back to Oberon Station, innocent men still trying to track wild blacks after the battle in which *three* of their number had been killed. Contented, Charlie slept peacefully.

The fear came on Paul MacNamara and his men as they topped the rise, just after dark in this twilightless land. As they looked towards the homestead, all they could see was a pall of black.

'No lights!' Gus said, and with that, they spurred the horses and galloped furiously across country.

Paul was in a daze. 'Where are they?' he kept shouting, racing from one outbuilding to another. 'Find them!' he screamed. 'Get more lanterns.'

They knew blackfellows had been in the house. One of the men even claimed he could smell them. White men thieve, blacks destroy. The stove was cold, and burnt bread sat hideously in the tins, so they knew the attackers were long gone.

It was no surprise when someone found the waddy, for they had already faced the dreaded conclusion that wild blacks had attacked and carried off the two women. 'Keep searching,' Paul yelled frantically. 'They could have let them go somewhere out there. You go for help,' he called to Danny. 'Get over to McCann's station.'

'No one there, boss,' Danny said miserably.

'Then ride south, to Narrabeen Station, and then across to Litchfield. I want as many men as you can rouse.' He stared up into the mountains, where pinpoints of campfires could be seen, and swore he would find the attackers if he had to scour every inch of those ranges.

The men of Oberon searched the area systematically, working far into the night, fanning out into the horse paddocks, trampling the vegetable garden, scattering the small dairy herd and crashing across the newly planted cornfield. They moved on towards the river, beating the bush beside the track until a rifle shot alerted them.

'It's Gus,' one of the men yelled, and they began to run. Only Paul held back. His mind felt as if it were closing down on him, and his legs were like lead. He clutched the lamp and stumbled forward along the

162

track that led to their fishing spot. Hope glimmered; maybe the girls were hiding down here.

Then Gus had his arm in a firm grip. 'I think you'd better come back to the house, mate.'

'Are they there?' Paul asked, his voice high-pitched, unreal.

'Yes,' Gus said softly. 'I'm sorry, it's too late to help them.'

'Dead? Are they dead? Are you sure?'

'Yes. The lads will look after them. Bring them to the house. You don't want to go down there.'

Paul wrenched free and ran wildly down the track and along the bank towards a circle of lanterns. Disbelieving, he pushed through the streaming weeping willows, and saw the naked bodies lying grotesquely in the still waters, the lanterns casting an eerie light over their faces and gently drifting hair. A spear flopping on the surface caught his eye, and he realised it was attached to Jeannie's body. He screamed in horror, 'Get it out!' and turned away, unable to face this terrible sight any more. He was cold, and yet sweat was breaking out all over him, then he felt nauseous, bile rising as if he were about to be violently ill. And then, suddenly, there was blackness.

They saw him crash down into the long grass. 'The boss!' one of the men cried. 'He's fainted!'

'Just as well,' Gus muttered. 'The brain couldn't take too much of this. I'll see to him. Get blankets quickly, we have to wrap up the ladies before we can take them up to the house.'

When he came to, Paul sat shivering nearby, weeping unashamedly as his men attended to Jeannie and Clara. He couldn't bear to watch. Gus supported him as he stumbled behind the wretched procession, two burly men carrying the small, limp bodies.

He sat alone and desolate throughout the remainder of the long, bleak night, weeping for them, tormented by their suffering, racked with guilt.

Gus brought black coffee, steaming hot, laced with whisky, and put a blanket over the shoulders of the hunched figure of his boss. His friend. But he didn't try to talk; there was time enough for that.

Through a dark mist, through the walls of this nightmare, Paul could hear the men moving about. He heard the murmur of their voices raised in prayer and he tried to pray too, but his thoughts thundered against a God who would look down on such viciousness and not raise His mighty hand. A God who condoned these awful sins against nature! No, he could never forgive that God.

Nor could he forgive himself for failing to protect his wife and the young girl in there.

Poor Jeannie. Where were the children she'd wanted? Paul was crushed, remembering how he'd laughed at her irritation. Teased her when she'd become jealous that her sister-in-law had produced a child. 'There's plenty of time,' he'd told her.

163

Plenty of time. The words came back to haunt him, rattling at him like stones in empty tins, as empty as his words. Poor Jeannie. Further thoughts of her were almost an assault on his senses, exposing him to even more agony. For the last few weeks of her life she'd been angry with him, there'd been a tense stand-off between them over that damn Maskey party. Guilt surged. His wife had died believing he hadn't cared enough about her to grant one small wish.

Then he prayed. Not to God, but to Jeannie, to forgive him, telling her that she'd been within her rights, that he had hurt her and hurt their marriage. His desolation turned to despair, for if she could hear him, knowing what was in his heart, knowing that he'd been unfaithful to her, then he was lost. It was too late now to make it up to her. She had died a frightful, terrifying death, and he dared not think any more of their pain and terror or he would go mad.

Who had done this? He swore he'd find them and kill them himself if he had to walk to the ends of the earth to do it. To the ends of the earth? he asked himself. The earth, his earth, ended in those mountains. That was where the beasts lived. She'd always hated the blacks. Was it a premonition that she too would fall victim to them one day? But he hadn't listened. Her husband, the man responsible for her safety, hadn't listened. He'd left the women here unguarded. No use now to plead that he had intended to install a blacksmith permanently on the property to watch over them. Too late again. Paul laid the blame squarely at his own feet and guilt overwhelmed him. He could never forgive himself.

He heard riders galloping up to the homestead as dawn creaked into the cluttered parlour, Jeannie's parlour, but he couldn't bring himself to move until Gus came in.

'I'm taking a posse out to see if we can find the bastards.'

Paul dragged himself up. 'I'm coming too.'

'No. You have to stay here. There are women on their way to' – he stumbled on the words – 'to see to things. They'll need you here. We've sent a message to Clara's parents. And we'll notify Jeannie's family. Come through to the kitchen and have some breakfast.'

'Just tea,' Paul said, following him out. As he stepped on to the veranda he was in a daze, accepting handshakes, expressions of sorrow from friends and strangers alike.

'We could do with some black trackers,' Gus said, loading a bandolier with bullets, 'but we'll take a sweep around the property for a start and be back by midday. We'll find them sooner or later.'

Paul's voice was stronger. 'Oh yes. We'll find them all right, we'll get every last one of them.'

Gus heard the hatred, and he shuddered, wondering if this peaceful man had been changed forever.

When he brought the men back at noon, having failed to sight any tribal blacks, three women from neighbouring stations were there. He thanked them, knowing they must have left home immediately, riding with their men through the night. They had laid out the bodies in the spare room and taken over the kitchen. They would stay on now until after the funeral, as was the custom in these parts.

A policeman, Sergeant Jim Hardcastle, who had been in the district, took charge of the posses and told Gus that he'd sent to Rockhampton for military help. Late that afternoon the two men sat with Paul, trying to offer some comfort, but he was restless, fluctuating between despair and a need to get out and do something about this crime.

When three native troopers rode up the track, the Sergeant leapt from his chair and ran down to meet them. 'I'm glad to see you blokes. Where did you spring from?'

'Bin up at Sinclairs',' Charlie said. 'Then coming back we run into a mob of blacks at McCann place. They killed three of our fellers, burn down McCann house. We bin trackin' them.'

The news had them all buzzing. Anyone could follow the path of the raiders now; they'd travelled down the eastern side of the ranges, killing and pillaging as they went. The women thought to say a prayer of thanks that the McCanns had escaped the danger. No stations to the south had been attacked, so it was obvious that after committing this terrible crime, the raiders had fled for the safety of the ranges.

Paul dispatched a messenger to Rockhampton to send telegrams to his family, advising them of the deaths of Jeannie and Clara and asking them to pray for the repose of their souls. He promised that letters would follow, but he knew he could never bring himself to write of this tragedy.

Because of the climate, the burial had to be arranged as soon as possible, and by Thursday night he was standing alone by the graves set on a small hill that looked down the valley, away from the river. As yet, he couldn't say farewell to Jeannie, but he could and did swear revenge. 'You were right,' he told her. 'I offered them peace and this is what we got in return. They'll pay,' he promised her. 'They'll all pay. I'll hound them all into the sea.'

Amelia raced inside to find Laura and tell her the news. She had just come home from a shopping expedition in Rockhampton, which wasn't very exciting, since one of the stores had closed and the other had very little of interest. As a matter of fact, while Tyler was away, she thought she might persuade her father to take her down to Brisbane to buy something decent. He didn't seem to be too busy these days. And it would serve Tyler right if he returned to find them away . . . But no, perhaps not.

Anyway, there'd been a great crowd around the police station and Amelia almost ran away, thinking it was one of the awful mobs that had stoned the Golden Nugget Hotel that night. But then she saw quite a few familiar faces, hardly people who would join a riot, so she burrowed among them and heard all the frightful stories.

'You shouldn't be here,' the vicar's wife said to her. 'These things are not fit for a young girl's ears.'

That made her all the more curious. She found a friend, Leith Gordon, and insisted he tell her exactly what had happened to make everyone so confused and angry. 'I don't know what to believe,' she complained.

Leith was only too pleased to relate what he knew to Amelia. She was shocked; two women vilely murdered, and left naked in a creek. She clapped her hands over her ears rather than be forced to contemplate why they were naked, then removed them, startling him. 'What did you say their names were?'

Leith Gordon was a bank teller. He'd known one of them. Or rather, he knew her husband, Paul MacNamara. 'A nicer man you couldn't hope to meet in a day's march,' he told Amelia. 'I saw his wife once when she came into the bank. A fine lady, she was. It's hard to believe that she is dead. Murdered by those fiends.'

People were shouting that something had to be done about the wild blacks: 'Once and for all.' They were demanding action as Amelia hurried away.

She rushed into the house, yelling for Laura. 'Where are you?'

'In here,' Laura called from the sitting room, where she'd been reading. She never seemed to do anything but read, Amelia thought, irritated. She wasn't much company any more, even if she were in mourning.

'What is it?' Laura asked her.

Amelia Roberts had her priorities. First things first. 'Did you know that the gentleman you had a crush on was married?' she demanded.

'Do you mean Paul MacNamara?' Laura asked.

'Of course I do. Did you know?'

'Yes,' Laura admitted.

'How did you know?'

'He told me.'

Amelia gasped. 'When?'

'He was at that party at our house on the Sunday afternoon,' Laura replied cautiously.

'He was there and you never told me? You never pointed him out to me?'

Laura sighed. 'He escorted Grace Carlisle. I only saw him for a few minutes.' At least that part was true. 'If you recall,' she said bitterly, 'I had problems of my own at the time.'

'Oh yes. Well, let me tell you something. Paul MacNamara isn't married any more.' She waited for that to sink in as Laura stared at her.

'How can that be?'

'Hold on to your seat,' Amelia exclaimed. 'His wife is dead. Killed.

Murdered by blacks at their station. At Oberon Station. And her servant girl too!'

'Oh my God! That's dreadful. Are you sure, Amelia?'

'Of course I'm sure.'

'Dear God. The poor woman.'

'He's all right, though,' Amelia told her. 'The blackfellows crept in while the men were out mustering and killed the two women. People are saying they're lucky they didn't have any kids or they'd have been speared too.'

'Were they speared?' Laura asked, horrified.

Amelia's voice dropped to a whisper. 'Worse, they say.'

'Oh no!'

'You ought to write to him now, a letter of condolence. It would remind him you're still here.'

Laura slammed the book down. 'How can you be so unfeeling?'

'What's unfeeling about it? You've both suffered a bereavement, surely it wouldn't be out of place for you to write him a kind note? I imagine he would appreciate hearing from you,' she said slyly.

'Not with those motives,' Laura snapped.

Amelia shrugged. 'Oh well. Whatever you think. I've got things to do.'

Laura felt sick. In normal circumstances a letter of condolence would be in order, but not now. She couldn't imagine how he must be feeling but she was sure she was the last person he'd want to hear from right now. She couldn't echo Amelia's sentiments, the cruel thought that her way was now clear. Instead, she mourned for the two women, and for him, for the suffering he'd have to take up now that theirs was, mercifully, over.

Her attitude annoyed Amelia, who discussed the tragedy with her father.

'Yes, I know,' he said testily. 'The same bastards burned down the McCann homestead. It was a fine house McCann built there, he used beautiful cedar. I doubt McCann realised its worth. A damn nuisance. I'll have to rebuild and it'll be a helluva job getting workmen out there with blacks on the rampage.'

'Just as well Laura wasn't married to Paul MacNamara,' Amelia said, following her own train of thought.

'What are you talking about?'

'She's got a big crush on him.'

'On who?'

'MacNamara. I'll bet when all this dies down we'll see a match there. Laura won't let him get away, I've never seen her so keen.'

Fuming, he let her prattle on. His first reaction was to find Laura and shake the truth out of her. Was she just using him, waiting for her lover to return? The way Amelia spoke, it sounded as if they were lovers, MacNamara and Laura. And how convenient now that the wife was dead.

167

He wondered if Fowler Maskey had uncovered an affair between the two of them? Was that why he'd struck his daughter? Was that why she'd refused to marry Cope? He'd always had a suspicion that another man might be involved, but since Amelia, who liked to know everything, who never missed much, hadn't linked her friend's name with anyone else, he'd dismissed that conjecture. Until now. And MacNamara of all people! He'd never get her. Never!

Boyd Roberts was correct. His daughter didn't miss much. And although she hadn't noticed before, blinded by the fact that her father was too old, Amelia began to notice now. He dressed for dinner in his impressive suit with the silk brocade waistcoat, he brought up their best wines, he favoured Laura in conversation, practically ignoring his daughter, and yet his questions to Laura were more demanding, more searching. He was jealous!

He wasn't the only one. Amelia sat across from them, smiling, playing her own part. The more she watched her father, the more she realised what was happening. He could hardly take his eyes off Laura, the desire shocking, but plain as day, and instinct told her that Laura knew about it. She met his eyes now as an equal, not as his daughter's friend. What a fool she'd been to allow this to happen! To allow Laura to usurp her position and probably Daddy's fortune!

She deliberately brought up the subject of the murders. Well, why not? Everyone was talking about them. But Laura had little to say beyond expressing deep sorrow.

Her father mentioned that a house he owned out there had been burned down, and that gave Amelia her opportunity. 'Laura loves stations, she really does. It's her ambition to live on a cattle station and have her own stable of horses, isn't it, Laura?'

'I grew up on a station,' Laura replied. 'I was very happy. It was a good, busy life.'

'You ought to take her to see your station, the McCann place,' Amelia suggested to Boyd.

He shook his head. 'Not right now, it's too dangerous.'

'Oh yes, I forgot. It's next door to Oberon!' She had her reward; Laura blushed and Boyd noticed. He made no comment but studied her, stroking his sideburns, a habit of his when he was in a bad mood. The next move, Amelia decided, was to get Laura out of the house, but that might not be easy. She wouldn't dare tackle Boyd – he could get very nasty if anyone interfered with his plans. Nor could she freeze Laura out, he'd be sure to notice.

She would have to think about this.

Mourning at least gave Laura the excuse to stay out of the public eye, and except for her daily rides, she made no effort to leave the grounds of Beauview. But the enforced inactivity was beginning to nettle her restless soul, made worse by her embarrassment that she was penniless. She wouldn't ask for money but she did consider approaching

Boyd for a loan, to be paid back – when? She couldn't think where else to turn. For that matter, she scolded herself, you seem to have forgotten how to think, staying here growing mould on your brain.

Amelia greeted her at lunch with her latest brilliant idea. 'The shops here are hopeless. I've asked Daddy to take me down to Brisbane to find some really smart clothes. What with my engagement coming up, I'll need lashings of things. It'll be exciting, I just adore shopping. One can go mad in Brisbane. You'll be all right here while we're away, won't you, Laura?'

Boyd came in on the end of the conversation. 'I haven't said I'd go yet, Amelia. But if we do go, Laura is welcome to come with us. A change would do you good, my dear.'

'Thank you, but really, I couldn't, she said. 'But you two go. I don't want to spoil things for you.'

That night, after Amelia had gone out with friends, Boyd strolled around the passageway with Laura. 'Why won't you come with us? We could have a good time. Dine in the best restaurants, go to the theatre, make a holiday of it.'

'I'd rather not,' Laura said.

He was insistent. 'Why not? You're not doing anything here.'

She sighed. 'I can't afford to go, don't you understand that?'

'Yes, I do, but money isn't a problem. I'll see to it that you and Amelia can shop to your hearts' content.'

'No. I can't take any more charity. I couldn't possibly.'

He moved closer to her and stroked her face. 'You know it isn't charity, Laura. You know how I feel about you. I want to spoil you, it would give me the greatest of pleasure.' He put his arms about her and kissed her on the mouth as gently as he could manage but the very feel of her, his mouth on hers at last, aroused the desire in him.

Impatiently he pushed her towards the open door of her bedroom and, once inside, closed it behind them.

'Don't, Boyd, please,' Laura said as he took her in his arms again.

He held her close to him and smiled down at her. 'The trouble with you, Laura, is that you don't know what you want.'

He lifted her easily and placed her on the bed, the weight of his body holding her as she struggled. 'Just let me kiss you for a while,' he muttered, his mouth wet on her lips, her face. 'Don't deny me this much.'

She twisted her head away, so he kissed her ear, his tongue roving, then moved down to the joy of kissing her luscious neck, sucking at the soft skin while he caressed her breasts. He began to undo her blouse, frantic for the taste of those nipples, but she stopped him, forcing his hands away.

'Why not?' he pleaded. 'I won't hurt you. Don't you know I'm made for you?' He slipped a strong arm under her and held her to him. 'You're a passionate girl, I can sense it in you. You need a man like me.'

169

'Let me up, please, Boyd.' Her voice was cold as she struggled to be free of him.

Her rejection infuriated him but he kept calm and assumed a lighter tone. 'I could take you right here and now if I wished. No one would interfere,' he teased.

'You wouldn't dare!' she snapped.

He moved lazily away from her, saving face by appearing unconcerned. 'I wouldn't want to, my dear.'

But she was right. He watched as she jumped up, straightening her clothes and her tangled hair. She was still the daughter of the late and now greatly lamented Fowler Maskey, and he had thrown in his hat as the candidate, the only candidate, for Fowler's parliamentary seat. There was a dream run ahead of him, all the way to the State House. He couldn't afford a scandal at this stage, and this little vixen would yell to the rooftops. She had her back to him now, standing stiffly at the window, waiting for him to leave. Yes, he mused, this one wouldn't shut up. From his observations she ran straight at trouble like a bolting horse heading for a too-high fence.

'I'm sorry,' he lied. 'I shouldn't have upset you like that, but you're so damned attractive, you're making it very difficult for me.'

'I thought you were a gentleman,' she replied.

He laughed. 'Never trust a gentleman, they're the worst kind. I suppose that now is a bad time to be asking you if you have considered my proposal?'

'No,' Laura said, turning to face him. 'It's exactly the right time. I am grateful to you, Boyd, but I can't marry you.'

'I see. Who are you going to marry then?'

She blinked, confused by his question. 'Why . . . no one.'

'Not ever?' He raised his eyebrows and gave Laura such a supercilious look that her anger with him returned. She'd been too embarrassed by his actions to tell him that by kissing her he'd made the decision for her. She'd felt nothing but repugnance for him, for the slobbering wetness of his mouth, and she wished now that he would go away and leave her alone.

'That's beside the point,' she answered firmly. 'But I have to ask you, what is my position here now?'

He stood up and made for the door. 'Don't worry. I may not be a gentleman like a Maskey, but I wouldn't throw a young lady out of my house. You are perfectly welcome to stay as long as you wish. Who knows?' he shrugged. 'You might change your mind.'

It was a decision time for Cosmo Newgate, too.

Solicitors representing Boyd Roberts had made further approaches on his behalf, offering to buy the newspaper, but Cosmo had insisted it was not for sale at any price. He had his own plans.

He'd hoped to see Grace Carlisle at Fowler's funeral, but she was not present. Two of her sons and their wives had attended, but it was

Grace he needed to see – she was an old friend of the Maskeys, and probably the wealthiest and most powerful woman in the district.

On two occasions he went to see Hilda Maskey. The first time, Leon agreed to see him, but Hilda would not. Cosmo pleaded with Leon, on Laura's behalf, but got a cold reception. On his next visit he found them packing. 'We can't get out of this horrible place fast enough,' Hilda told him. 'And it's just your cheek to expect me to receive you after what you did to my poor dear husband.'

'I have come about Laura,' he said. 'I hear the girl is destitute.'

'What business is it of yours?' she demanded.

'It has to be somebody's business. I explained to Leon that you people have misjudged Laura, and I hope to hear that you, Hilda, as her mother, will not forsake her.'

Hilda was packing up her silver. She slammed a bundle of spoons into a tea-chest. 'Forsake her? What fine talk coming from you! She's made her bed, let her lie in it.'

'Hilda,' he pleaded, 'I made mistakes and I'm heartily sorry, but that's another matter. She's living at the Robertses' house and she shouldn't be there.'

Hilda sniffed. 'I'm glad we agree on something. She took up with the Robertses, against her own family. She even flaunted them at the funeral.'

'That's not right. They brought her there, it would have been wrong of them not to. Please, Hilda, have a heart. If you don't take her back, where else can she go?'

'I don't care where she goes. And as for Mr Roberts, the coast is clear now; he wanted Fowler's seat and he can have it. He won't even have to wait for the Premier to call a general election, there'll be a by-election for Rockhampton shortly to replace dear Fowler. Roberts will go into Parliament and I hope the worry kills him too.'

'Roberts won't win this seat,' Cosmo said but she waved him away.

'I don't care who wins it,' she said bitterly. 'They never appreciated Fowler, they can go to hell now, for all I care.'

That night he sat down and wrote a long letter to Grace Carlisle. He outlined the political situation in Rockhampton, with Boyd Roberts the lone candidate. Hoping he wasn't offending her, he referred to Roberts as a person of low character, unfit for any public office, let alone the State Legislative Assembly. Cosmo also pointed out that in an effort to find someone to oppose Roberts he had canvassed several local gentlemen, only to find that either they could not afford the luxury of an unpaid position, however grand, or they were too busy with their own affairs.

This, he stated, was an appalling situation which could have a dire effect on a young community too naïve to see past the airs and graces of a rich and dangerous man.

Cosmo hoped that Grace would canvass the pastoralists of the huge electorate and put forward a man of worth. In the meantime, he told her, 'I intend to stand as a candidate. By doing this, I can invade the psyche of the voters so that they don't come to accept this election as a lay-down misère which does not require them to think. However, if you can come up with a candidate I shall be happy, nay relieved, to step aside. But at least I can hold the fort.'

Then, on a more personal note, Cosmo went on to explain what had become of Laura Maskey. 'I am aware that you were always very fond of this unfortunate girl and hope that somehow you might find a way to intervene.'

The next day the *Capricorn Post* ran the headline: COSMO NEWGATE TO STAND. He gave his credentials, and backed himself in the editorial, promising in the days to follow a fair outline of the statements and policies of both candidates.

Cosmo went to bed laughing. It wouldn't be an outline but an exposé of Roberts, and he'd keep it up. Even if Roberts sued him, the damage would be done. He'd pound the bastard out of the running.

Amelia had never seen her father in such a rage. He even shouted at her! 'Where's that bloody Tyler when I need him?'

She read the paper and rushed in to Laura. 'Why is he so upset? No one will vote for that silly little Newgate.'

'He owns the only newspaper,' Laura explained. 'Boyd will be lucky to get a mention from now on.'

'But does it matter? I mean Father is so well known and highly respected . . .'

In the next edition, though, the tirade against Boyd Roberts began. The two girls were shocked to read that he was implicated in claim-jumping, stand-over tactics on the diggings and the mysterious disappearance of several miners. There was also a note that more would be heard from Jock McCann, who was now safely out of the district, and many others.

'It's all lies,' Amelia screamed. 'Daddy says it's all lies. Can't he be stopped?'

'He could sue,' Laura said, but she knew that would take time. She was worried. She had always liked Cosmo, a steely little man with a staccato way of talking, but he'd let her down. And now . . . Was he telling the truth about Boyd? How far would people go in denigrating each other for political points?

Since the *Capricorn Post* came out only twice a week, they had to wait nervously for the following Monday.

Amelia accosted her father at dinner. 'Why don't you stop him? Say something!'

'I'll have some pamphlets made as soon as I can locate bloody Tyler,' he stormed. 'Newgate has the only printing press in town. I can't write them by hand. I have to find out what to buy and where to get it.'

'But people are talking,' Amelia cried. 'I was shunned in town today. People actually snubbed me. And Mr and Mrs Gordon are having a party on Saturday night for Leith's birthday, and I haven't been invited!'

'For Christ's sake, shut up!' Boyd shouted and stormed out of the room, grabbing a bottle of Scotch whisky from the sideboard as he left.

With Amelia in tears, Laura poured herself another glass of light white wine. At least this furore had taken the pressure off her for the time being. Today was her birthday, her twenty-first birthday, but she preferred not to mention the subject so as not to draw attention to herself, and, she reflected, invite gifts which would make her even more beholden to Boyd Roberts. She knew that her mother and Leon would not have forgotten, and all day she hoped for some word from them. They'd always regarded birthdays as festive occasions and Laura thought they might have taken the opportunity to make some gesture towards reconciliation, even to answer the letter she had written to them. But the day dragged on, and with the chill of evening came the cold realisation that she was not to be forgiven.

Amelia had told her that the Quay Street house was up for sale and that Hilda and Leon were preparing to quit Rockhampton. That hadn't surprised Laura – they'd both disliked living up here – but it further dampened her spirits. However, after the death of her father none of these other events, including Boyd's sudden ardour, seemed such calamities, and she refused to allow herself to become depressed. The very boldness of which she had been accused so often was now an advantage, and she began to reassert herself, to find the self-confidence that had lately deserted her and left her so numbed that she'd been unable to concentrate.

Now, she told herself, I have to stop worrying and start moving. I have plenty of friends and they're nearly all station people. And families on outback stations are always searching for governesses. Laura knew she'd have an advantage over women not accustomed to bush life, as well as being already known to these people.

She scrounged some of Amelia's notepaper and wrote off to half a dozen women, offering her services and giving her address as care of Post Office, Rockhampton. Then she borrowed ten shillings from Amelia and rode into town, wondering what had possessed her, before this, to be cringing behind the gates of Beauview.

As she walked along the street, people nodded to her, spoke to her, expressed sympathy at the death of her father, and she was touched to find that the world, after all, was normal. She handed over her letters in the post office store and told the postmaster she would be expecting replies.

'I'll send them out to you, Laura,' he said kindly.

'Thanks all the same, Mr Duncan, but I'd rather you held them, I'll come by for them.' She wanted to keep this plan to herself.

★ ★ ★

'I'm going out to Airdrie Station in the morning,' Roberts told his daughter.

'Where's Airdrie Station?'

'Oh, for God's sake, why don't you listen occasionally? It's my property and I'm sick of it being called the McCann place.' He was convinced that everyone was conspiring to annoy him. It was time he took some action; he'd been too quiet lately, letting things run on, instead of keeping a firm hand on all of his affairs. He hadn't heard from the manager of his Starlight mines for a while, either, so he'd pay him a visit too, see what was doing out on the diggings.

That cheered him. Boyd liked the excitement and constant air of expectancy that permeated the goldfields. He'd have a good look around there on the way. It would mean a detour to the east, but one never knew what might turn up, so he'd do a little exploring of his own.

But Amelia was worried. 'You said it was too dangerous to go near your station yet.'

'Too dangerous for women, but not for me. I'll have my own men with me.'

'They haven't finished the croquet lawns,' she complained.

'That can wait. I want to look at the homestead. There might be something I can salvage from the fire. They say it's been burned to the ground, but I haven't met anyone who has actually seen it – that could be just talk. For all I know, it might be only partly burned. I want to see for myself. And I'll put the men to work clearing it away so I'll have a clean site to rebuild on.'

'But what about the wild blacks? They might attack again.'

He scowled. 'I'll see to them, they won't want to come within a bull's roar of my place again.'

'And I'll be left here on my own.' She pouted.

'You've been here before on your own plenty of times. The servants will be here, and the stablehand, and you've got Laura here as well. What more do you want?'

'I thought you were going to take me to Brisbane to shop.'

'Later,' he growled. 'And when Tyler Kemp gets back – God knows where he's got to – tell him to stay in town, I've got work for him.'

'What sort of work?'

'Will you stop questioning me! I've got too much to think about as it is. Go and find something to do.'

Then there was the matter of Cosmo Newgate. The fool was pumped up with his own importance now, thinking he could win the seat of Rockhampton. That little shrimp! As a candidate, Cosmo wasn't worth a bob, but as a candidate owning that bloody paper and giving him a hard time twice a week, he was a real danger. Bad press like that could soon turn every voter in town against him, so this problem had to be resolved. Fast. And it could be done very simply.

Once out of town, with his men, Boyd planned to camp in the bush for a few days and then send two men back into town under cover of darkness to wreck those printing presses. They'd all have good alibis. He intended to buy up supplies this afternoon, letting everyone know he was heading north to inspect the burned homestead and to lend his considerable support to the search for the killers of those two women. That would go down well; feelings were still running high over that tragedy. They said Paul MacNamara was taking it hard. Boyd wondered if he might want to sell now, to get away from the reminders of his wife's tragic death. His thoughts turned to Laura. What was going on between her and MacNamara? Then he smiled. Poor MacNamara, with all the dangers out there now, the poor fellow could easily run into a spear or some other unfortunate accident.

Worth considering, he mused. Well worth considering.

After Boyd had left, Beauview was very quiet, and Laura felt more relaxed. The men who'd been working about the grounds rode out with Boyd, looking very different now. They were all heavily armed and they saddled up behind him more like a posse than workmen, leading two packhorses. She remembered her mother's words. She had called them his henchmen. Was she right after all?

With her father gone, Amelia's attitude changed. She became snappy and argumentative. Especially when Tyler's name came up, which was frequently.

'When he comes back,' she told Laura, 'Daddy insists that he stay here and wait for him because he has business to discuss with him.'

'And I'm to be the chaperone, am I?' Laura smiled but her remark did not amuse Amelia.

'I don't need a chaperon. But I also don't need you criticising Tyler. If you are to stay in our house I expect you to treat him with courtesy.'

'If?' Laura echoed. 'Do I get the impression that you'd rather I make myself scarce when Tyler returns.'

'That's up to you, of course,' Amelia replied, and Laura realised that Amelia, in her covert way, was using Boyd's absence to move her out. She was surprised to find it a relief. If she could leave now she wouldn't have to make excuses to Boyd, to face his inevitable opposition and all-too-logical arguments.

It was too soon to expect replies to her letters – they'd take weeks to reach their destinations and weeks for the return mail – nevertheless she began to haunt the post office store, and at last there was a letter for her.

'Did you hear the news?' the postmistress asked her as she was leaving the store.

'No. What news?'

'Robbers broke into the offices of the *Capricorn Post* last night,' the woman said. 'Looking for money, of course, something to steal. I don't know when all this is going to end. It'll be the banks next. You

175

mark my words. Someone stole a bag of flour from our shed yesterday, in broad daylight.'

'Did they get any money?' Laura asked.

'No. Cosmo's too smart for that. He never leaves money on the premises. That must have annoyed them. They smashed the place up, broke his presses too. Made a real mess.'

Curiosity drew her down the street and across the road to the small single-fronted building, the home of the *Capricorn Post*. The front door and windows were intact, so she guessed the robbers must have broken in at the rear. She saw Cosmo inside, talking to a police constable, and she turned quickly away, feeling suddenly guilty.

Was it robbers? The destruction of the presses was a godsend for Boyd and his ambitions. Very convenient. And timely. She tried to brush away these uncomfortable suspicions and hurried down to Quay Street, where a riverboat was preparing to depart. Not wanting to return to Beauview just yet, she wandered over to a bench to open her letter, fearing bad news, since that was all she'd come to expect lately. But the letter was from Grace Carlisle, dear Grace, inviting her to visit Camelot.

It was only a short letter, kind and to the point. Laura would be most welcome at Camelot and if she were pleased to accept the invitation she should contact Kelvin and Pamela Carlisle at the Criterion Hotel, as they would be returning to Camelot shortly . . .

Laura almost clapped her hands in relief. She'd love to go out to the Carlisle station; she could have her mail redirected to her there. She'd always been so fond of the Carlisles, a big happy family, and in truth she had thought of writing to them to ask if she could stay awhile, but her pride had held her back. Now she could go! Marvellous!

She jumped up, meaning to go across to the Criterion to find Pamela Carlisle right away, but she delayed, watching the riverboat pull away, people on the deck waving to shore. Her eye was caught by two people standing stiffly at the rails. The woman was in black and wore a large black hat with a veil. Beside her stood a young man.

Tears came flooding as Laura recognised her mother and Leon, leaving town, leaving her without a word.

Tyler Kemp was enjoying this expedition with Lieutenant Gooding and his six troopers, and considered himself fortunate that they'd allowed him to ride with them.

The countryside was beginning to dry out now and was showing signs of a long dry winter ahead, greenery fading, high grasses wilting and the sky an endless blue. They followed the great river inland but instead of fording it and heading north to Camelot Station, Gooding had been forced to detour. Bushrangers had held up a party of three men transferring gold into town, and, after killing the guard, had made off with the gold and horses, leaving an assayer and a Mines Inspector to tramp for twenty miles to raise the alarm.

176

They galloped out towards Ironstone Mountain to rendezvous with the victims at a shanty inn and commence an official search for the outlaws. With the help of a black tracker, a tribal man from a station, not a man drawn from the Native Police, they followed the trail east again, eventually coming into the tiny coastal town of Gladstone on Port Curtis, a hundred miles down the coast from the mouth of the Fitzroy River. There they discovered that one of the outlaws had already been apprehended, and that police had gone after the other one. The Government Resident, a Mr O'Connell, treated them cordially and congratulated Gooding on his diligence.

'So much for all that effort,' the Lieutenant told Tyler ruefully. 'We might as well give the horses a spell here for a day or so and head back.'

Chapter Seven

Harrabura, of the Darambal people, was shocked at the sudden turnabout of the white boss, the one whom Gorrabah had assured them was a peaceful fellow. It just showed how wrong you could be about these interlopers.

Men from the big house, led by the Paul boss, had become raiders instead of getting on with their own business of growing more and more land-trampling beasts. It had been explained to him that the cattles, having no totem and no rightful place on earth, were only for eating, and he felt pity for their joyless spirits. He had tasted the meat and it was indeed generous and life-giving, but the numbers frightened him. How many whitefellows must be out there to need such a huge supply? He had discussed this some years back with Gorrabah, who had then consulted his young friend Wodoro, a famous travelling man. The reply had filled them with awe and despair, but Wodoro had told them it was possible to survive if they retreated, kept the people calm and endeavoured to keep the peace. It was easier said than done, but Gorrabah had done his best, and sure enough in this small area, at least, families had been permitted to camp in their favourite haunts by creeks and billabongs, while others, more wary, had drifted into the ranges.

The boss man seemed to understand that the small mobs on what he now called *his* sitting-down place had lost most of their hunting grounds, so he had occasionally gifted them whole beasts to feed on. And the dark people had soon discovered that the skins of these beasts could be stripped and dried and stretched like the skins of other animals, and they were pleased to make use of them.

Then came the killing of two of their men. Hadn't the white boss, Paul, driven off the assailants? Hadn't he shown true sorrow to Gorrabah?

So why now had he turned on the dark people with such ferocity?

Admittedly, as far as Harrabura knew, no more of his people had been killed, but the men they'd rounded up were in danger. The horsemen had come charging, driving everyone, even children and old people, ahead of them like the furnace of a bush fire, roping frightened men together and yarding them like their cattles. Why?

Terrified, the women had run from them, bringing their children and the elderly into the hills, screaming hysterically, claiming that the mountains could no longer keep them safe. That the evil white devils would soon come after them too.

It had been hard to keep the mountain warriors in hand; they demanded to be allowed to take their weapons and go forth, to rescue their brothers, but Gorrabah, whose life was ebbing away, still held their respect, and he begged patience.

'You have to find out why,' he told Harrabura. 'There has to be a reason for this new war.' There were tears in his eyes. 'I thought I saw goodness in the eyes of that white boss, but perhaps I only saw what I wanted to see.'

Harrabura sat in the cave by the fragile old man and tried to comfort him. 'I'll send scouts down to see what is happening and then we'll talk again. But if they kill any of our brothers then we must act.'

The old man grasped Harrabura's arm in his bony hand. 'Use caution. A frontal attack would fail. Send for Wodoro, he speaks the language even more better than me, he will know what to do. He will speak for us.'

Harrabura smiled. Even on his deathbed Gorrabah had his pride. He could speak a little of the new language but Wodoro spoke it fluently. Everyone knew that Wodoro's father had been a white man who had despised his own people and joined forces with the great Tingum chief, Bussamarai. Together they'd waged war against the whites for years and years until Wodoro's father died a gallant death in battle. Bussamarai never succumbed, though, and he fought on until age claimed him.

Wodoro was born of a black woman, and in honour of his father, the elders appointed him as a courier, a travelling man – not a trader, far more important than that. He was carefully trained in the ancient rites, traditions and intertribal protocols and taken, as he grew into manhood, to various nations so that he could learn their languages and their ways and arrange meetings and corroborees. He was too young, being only of middle age at present, to join the elders, but from his great experiences was accepted as a wise person. On his travels he had visited the Darambal nation many times and become a great friend of Gorrabah. He would be sad to hear that Gorrabah would soon be departing.

Maybe it was too late, though. Harrabura was sad that he had forgotten about Wodoro, with all the worries they'd had lately; it would indeed be a great comfort for Gorrabah to have him by his side when parting-time came.

'I'll send for him straight away,' he said. 'We will enquire. Messengers will find him.'

He doubted whether Wodoro could help in their present difficulties. Harrabura was beginning to understand the hopelessness of their situation, and feared the end of the Darambal nation was near. Even great mountains wore away in time, or were dislodged by earthly upheavals. Perhaps their time had come. He wondered if a last great battle might not be a more fitting and prideful demise. And Wodoro was still a blackfellow – lighter-skinned and with a hook nose, but

179

every inch of the dark race. Why would the invaders care what he had to say? Why would they bother to listen? They had supreme weapons of war that spoke for them louder than the voices of any black men.

A week went by and the boss, Paul, was still on the rampage. Darambal men began climbing up from the lowlands. They had been interrogated, beaten and some even flogged, their backs ripped and bloodied by cruel whips. After their initial bewilderment they'd worked out that two women belonging to the white boss had been killed by blackfellows, hence the rage. 'They are searching for the killers,' came the report, 'and they won't stop until they find them. We are being blamed, all of us, until we bring forth the murderers.'

Another man arrived with even worse news. 'They pointed to the hills,' he said. 'They will make war on us even up here if we don't give up the killers.'

'But who did this? Who killed the women?' Harrabura demanded. No one knew.

They decided it must be the Kuinmerbura warriors who had brought this disaster upon them – they were the ones who had decided to fight on, and now look at the result, everyone was in danger.

'Have the whites killed any of our men yet?' Harrabura asked fearfully.

'No,' he was told, 'but they have the evil ones with them.'

'What evil ones?'

'The cruel dark men who wear white men's clothes and carry guns. We saw them, waiting their turn to attack, and they are just as we were warned, terrible, terrible men with gloating faces.'

Harrabura shuddered. This he would have to see for himself.

He travelled along the mountainside, through the high timbers, negotiating with ease the sudden rocky obstacles that these ancient hills threw up before him. He smiled grimly. White men with their horses would have a hard time getting in and out of the deep gullies and scaling the steep wooded slopes. He met people along the way and sat by their campfires, trying to calm distraught women, promising that the dreaded horsemen would not be permitted to harass them further.

A guide led them down at night to the camp where three black soldiers squatted, only a few paces from the main body of white men. Hidden in the scrub, Harrabura studied these renegades, his keen eyes taking in their features and watching their every move. He correctly fixed upon one with the clay pipe, the one the others called Charlie Penny, to be the boss of the trio, and with his fists he began to beat soundlessly, rhythmically on the earth. He knew what he could do, what he had to do now, but he had to prepare himself properly.

Before they disappeared back into the bush they counted nine men of their clan still held prisoner by these arrogant, ugly whites. They were bound together by their necks and waists and well guarded. There was no chance of helping them, so they had to leave, praying that their lives would be spared.

On the return journey, Harrabura made his own enquiries. He had to know who killed the white women now, because fear was upon him too. He had never seen so many horsemen gathered together as in those camps. There had to be at least twenty of them, and there would be more back at the big house. They didn't care about the killing of dark women, but apparently when their own were struck down the clans came out in force.

He met some young men who told him that the other big house further to the north had burned down. He thought that had probably been blamed on his people too, because it was a strange time for fires, too early in the dry season. Still, a house was not as important as lives, so he instructed the young men to wait until the coast was clear and then go down to take a look. If Kuinmerbura warriors had fired that empty house, it was possible that they had gone on to the other one and attacked the women. His people could not punish them, for hadn't they threatened to fight back? But they could call them to account for causing so much trouble for their innocent neighbours. No one, of course, would explain the situation to the whites – no one could find the right words anyway – because they were all Darambal people; the clans shared the homelands and it would be unthinkable to point the finger at clansmen.

That reminded him. He went on a solitary trek to the sacred places. He sat in the hidden caves and performed cleansing rituals before commencing to ask the spirits for guidance. Then he began to chant in the oldest language on earth. Over and over he sang the ancient words that had been handed down to chosen ones since the Dreaming, since the Rainbow Snake had first looked upon the empty earth, words that were unknown in the present-day language.

For two days Harrabura fasted. He spoke to the great spirits and thanked them humbly for giving him children and grandchildren, and told them that he had already chosen and was training a successor, a lad now fifteen called Malliloora, who must be preserved from danger at all costs. As he had been. Because Malliloora would inherit the magic.

He did not bother them with the present tribulations of the people, because they knew all about that, but he had to tell them of this new and abhorrent menace. Mortified, Harrabura spoke of the blackfellow renegades. He railed against them with all the disgust in his heart, explaining that they had broken all tribal laws and had long since deserted their Dreaming, if they ever had any. They may, he considered, have simply arisen from some dungheap.

And so to business. Even though it was dawn, swarms of bats fled the cave as Harrabura drew the profile of Charlie Penny in the silky red dust. He looked up at the wall paintings which could not be defiled by this face and went to the secret place where only the hands of magic men were ever registered. He placed his hand over the painting and restored it by blowing mouthfuls of white ochre over his dark and powerful fingers.

He worked then as if in a trance, with twine and bone and other ingredients as the actions were related to him. This was not a magic he could pass on to Malliloora, because it was outside his span of knowledge. His successor would have to rely on his own worthiness.

When the small, secret parcel was complete, gummed together by the sap of a tree, Harrabura sang his thanks in a long, repetitive monotone, and then went from that place.

The ceremonial redressing of his body took many hours. His face was streaked white, his long, thick hair gummed high and spiked with bones taken from the cave. Red and white ochre were mixed to adorn his body in designs that no man had ever seen, because no man could. Around his ankles, his knees, his arms and his neck were rustling bracelets of leaves, and with a sharp stone he tore a bloody gash across his stomach for dedication. Then he picked up a deadly little coloured snake and settled it about his neck, letting it nestle into the already dying leaves.

He stood tall. A terrifying figure, had anyone been able to see him.

The white men had moved camp but it was of no moment to the magic man who, like the thousands of centuries-old spirits who had heard him and loaned him their power, now possessed no name.

What mysteries hover in the millions of years of earth's habitation? This figure did not know. This figure came only from the knowledge passed down by law through thousands of centuries in an isolated continent untainted by other races.

He strode into that camp unseen and stared into their hearts. He pacified his terror-stricken clansmen and he stood before the face of the boss man, Paul, and he saw his agony, his maddened scream of revenge, and his guilt.

He walked among the other men, recognising loyalty, recognising their anxiety to assist in this revenge, and in many saw, first-hand, an irreversible hatred of his people.

But to the figure this was not important. A snake could swallow a wallaby. The earth itself could convulse and swallow a mountain. The oceans, the skies full of rain, could invade. They all had their time and place in the wondrous order of earth, as did this human face of hatred, so familiar, so futile.

He moved away to the small campfire where his quarry lay, lolling about with his two mates, chewing that clay pipe.

The figure, who was Harrabura – the man who had requested this all-important favour – and yet who was not, stood by them and listened to their whispers. He saw their shrivelled hearts and he pitied them because their souls were adrift, their Dreaming destroyed. They had only two aims, to please the white man and so survive, and to take their pleasure where they could. The figure recognised the weakness of humanity, while within him the man that was Harrabura reared up demanding his favour. The favour that he had taken pains to explain, that would fill his people with fortitude so that they would all know that they were not lost yet. They would see once and for all that after a thousand aeons they could not be defeated.

The figure sighed. The massive lean figure, gleaming black skin and iridescent white, stark human bones glinting in the moonlight on his headgear, mouth not present, not there, moved forward. The promise had been made.

A wind rose, a soft breeze at first, unsettling the horses. Dogs barked, men stirred in their blankets, a billow of clouds scudded across the night sky, night birds called, and that boss man, Paul, sat bolt upright by his fire. The figure, from out of time, wanted to go to him, to seek out and explore the mystery of this good and evil man. But the promise of Harrabura was paramount.

The figure stood by Charlie Penny, and laid the precious parcel upon his chest.

Dawn lifted a fiery light over the dark ranges, and the forests crackled into life. Currawongs, imitating other birds, lashed the air with their solitary calls, and tiny green-winged honey-eaters sallied forth, chattering, to keep contact, in voices so strong it was hard to believe that such power could emanate from their puny throats. Pairs of shrieking lorikeets shot overhead on scouting missions, and crows followed lazily, heading for the grasslands to feed on seeds in company with their families.

Below them a mob of kangaroos rose up from their sleep, stretched, sniffed the air and, smelling man, bounded away.

The camp, in the deep shadow of the ranges, was still gloomily quiet when Charlie Penny's screams rent the air.

'What the hell?'

Sleep shattered, all the men came up as one, leaping for their guns, staggering from their tents in a clatter of confusion, thinking they were under attack.

One of the night guards began to laugh. 'Nothing wrong, mates. Only silly bloody Charlie there having a nightmare.'

They growled and grumbled, but now that they were up, they might as well stay up, and so their day began.

Paul MacNamara pulled on his boots and marched over to Charlie in time to see him hurl something far into the bush. 'What's the matter with you?'

But Charlie, his dark features contorted in fear, could only gibber at him in his native tongue.

He turned to Stan and Blackie. 'What's wrong with him? What was that he threw away?'

They were mystified, too. 'A snake maybe?' Stan suggested. 'Maybe a snake got in his blanket.'

Paul nodded. 'Yes. I guess so. You pull yourself together, Charlie, we've got work to do.' He strode down to the prisoners and stood contemplating them, as if trying to decide what to do with them, ignoring their misery. They were still trussed together and were now shivering, bare-skinned, in the cold morning dew.

Gus joined him. 'We'll have to let them go,' he said. 'They don't know anything.'

Paul didn't reply. He had become cold and distant as this search went on. Unattainable.

'It's no use,' Gus persisted. 'We've covered every inch of the two stations. The trackers couldn't pick up on the men we're after, so we won't. They'd have been away in the hills before we even got back to the homestead that day. We have to let these blokes go.'

'No!'

'But Paul, they're freezing. If they'd had a hand in it' – he couldn't bring himself to mention the murders by name – 'they wouldn't be still hanging about the property. They'd have run for their lives.'

'They know something,' Paul gritted. 'Belt it out of them.'

Some of the other men joined them. They were tiring of this futile work. 'The only thing to do,' one man growled, 'is to shoot this lot. Shoot 'em all. The blacks understand payback. They'll get the message.'

'No,' Gus yelled. 'We can't do that.' He appealed to Paul. 'I left Prussia to get away from the hostage mentality. You can't kill at random.'

'Bloody oath we can,' the men muttered among themselves.

There was talk over breakfast that MacNamara was in no fit state to run this posse. That the last hostages should be shot. Get it over with so they could all go home. Gus fought to keep control.

'Listen, mister,' said one miner, 'we've done our best. We've been out here ten days now, we split up like you told us and we chased all the blacks off these two stations. The niggers we caught won't talk. Now your boss has to make his move or we'll call on someone who will.'

Gus looked about at the sullen faces. 'Like who?' he challenged.

'Boyd Roberts. We saw him yesterday at the burned-out McCann joint. That station belongs to him, remember? He's coming over to this camp today and we'll let him decide what to do. Then we're off. We can't hang about here indefinitely.'

Gus took a mug of tea over to Paul. 'Boyd Roberts is on his way. We have to break camp now. Send these blokes home before he gets here, or those poor blackfellers over there won't stand a chance.'

Paul squatted on his haunches, sipping the hot, sugary tea. 'If Roberts brings his men – and he will, he never travels alone – we'd have a big enough mob to start searching the hills. That's where they are and that's where we have to go to find them.'

'It's a waste of time, Paul. Too much territory to cover and too dangerous. These blokes are miners and station men, they won't go up there, they've got their own families to think about.'

'They have to go,' Paul insisted.

Gus gave up and returned to the others. 'Anyone who wants to, can go home now,' he told them. 'We're grateful for your help but time has beaten us.'

A miner responded. 'I reckon we'll hang about a while and see what Roberts has to say.'

With no plan for action for the day, they took their time over a breakfast of boiled eggs and grilled sliced beef, billy tea and oatmeal biscuits.

Gus remembered that the Native Police, at least, were being paid, so he put them to work. 'When you've watered the horses come back here. I want our saddles oiled and polished.'

Stan and Blackie began to move off but Charlie stayed curled up on the ground, wrapped in his blanket. 'Him a sick feller,' Blackie said.

'What's wrong with him?'

They rolled their eyes. 'Plenty sick.'

Gus jerked the blanket away and stared down at Charlie. 'He doesn't look too sick to me.' He put a hand on his forehead. 'Not hot, no fever. Where are you sick?'

Charlie sat up and grabbed for the blanket without any signs of pain. Gus kicked him. 'Get up, you lazy bastard. There's nothing wrong with you.'

Without a word, Charlie climbed to his feet and walked listlessly towards the horses.

Gus ordered the camp cook to give the food scraps to the prisoners, but instead the cook whistled to a couple of his mates and gave them the last of the meat and a loaf of damper. 'Ain't no scraps,' he spat defiantly at Gus. 'I don't cook for no niggers.'

The Oberon men were outnumbered by the other volunteers, but Gus couldn't even send them back to work. Paul was the boss, they waited patiently for his orders.

Frustrated, he took a pitcher of water to the prisoners and gave each one a drink. Even though they were still gathered and trussed in a miserable heap there seemed to be something different about them today. Their eyes were brighter, more alert, no longer downcast and beaten. It seemed to him that they didn't realise the danger they were in on this perilous morning.

He squatted by them and by a combination of signs, pidgin English and the few words he knew of their language made certain they were fully aware of the cause of the trouble. He pointed to Paul, a tall, lonely figure standing by the sluggish creek, staring down as if trying to fathom its depths, its secrets, and then he stabbed a finger at the black men. 'You talk! Give names. What fellers kill white gins?'

They shook their heads sadly and their expressions were clear. Like all the others who had been interrogated, and beaten, they did not know. Gus wished he could communicate more easily. He wanted to tell them that he'd let them go, stop this harassment of their people if they would bring in the killers themselves, but it was too difficult.

185

But if they did find out, when they returned to the tribe, who had murdered Jeannie and Clara, would they hand them over? He doubted it. What white men were ever handed over to the Darambal people for atrocities against them? Aborigines working about the stations learned by example and they learned quickly. They'd never experienced that example.

Though he found it hard to admit, as far as Gus was concerned the hunt was over. At first he'd hoped the police black trackers would help them to locate the murderers, but the trail was cold. And besides, by the time the trio had arrived, horsemen had ridden wildly over all the tracks around the homestead, on top of the initial concentrated search for the women. He couldn't blame them for the failure. But now the situation was almost out of hand, with Paul hellbent on continuing the search into the hills, and the rest baying for blood, any blood. It worried him that Paul, in this dark and brooding mood, was prepared to throw in his lot with Boyd Roberts. With the devil if necessary, by the sound of things, to find vengeance.

In the meantime, they'd abandoned the station. A generation of unbranded calves were loose out there, easy prey for dingoes. Mustering should be well under way by this, cattle should be brought in for the drovers to take them to market. With the land drier now, they'd be straying further afield in search of better grazing and becoming wilder, harder to manage. While he had no lack of sympathy for Paul, as each day passed the work-list in Gus's mind grew longer and more urgent. As foreman, he felt responsible now. Oberon should not be let slip like this. God knows, he told himself, it's tough enough as it is to get done before the wet season returns, with all hands working their guts out, without shutting down as they were doing now.

Mid-morning brought Roberts himself, leading five men like a cavalry officer, and with him the infamous Captain Cope, ready to take over his depleted native troop.

Gus dismissed Cope as harmless but immediately recognised the arrogance of Roberts, who was now their neighbour. He had never met Roberts before but he knew that he brought trouble.

Still mounted, Roberts surveyed the languid camp with a self-satisfied grin. The men were sitting about smoking, resting under trees, hats shading their faces, fires extinguished. A waiting hush hung over this meeting-place in the bush.

'What have we here?' he called. 'All on holiday, are we? Is it a private picnic or can anyone join?'

The tone of his voice, the sting of authority, had them on their feet in an instant, pulling on their boots, strapping on guns, clamping on hats, looking to him for orders.

Despairing, Gus turned to Paul, who only glanced at Roberts and withdrew into himself again.

Voices gathered force as they were drawn to the new leader, explaining that they'd come to the end of the line. The ranges loomed above them like a massive fortress, as if challenging them.

Roberts jerked his head at Paul. 'His wife and servant girl are dead,' he said. 'My house is burned to ash. And what have you heroes got to show for it?'

The replies were muttered, but a shiver of excitement rippled as the men saw real action brewing.

'What's the next move, MacNamara?' Roberts shouted.

Now Paul roused himself. 'The hills. We're going up there after them.'

Roberts caught the grumbling, negative reaction of the volunteers. 'Oh yes? Like where? North-east? South-east? Up on Mount Archer?' His arm took in the great sweep of the Berserker Ranges. 'Are there trails we can follows? Tracks, even? Where do we start? And how many months is this great search going to take?'

'I've got it worked out . . .' Paul began but Roberts gave him a pitying stare.

'I reckon you've been through enough, time you let your mates take over.'

Not recognising the patronising tone, the men murmured sympathetically, heads bowed in respect, towards Paul, and then lifting as in puppetry, in unison, to Boyd Roberts.

'Who are they?' he demanded, pointing his whip at the prisoners.

'Suspects,' he was told.

'Line them up, let's have a look at them.'

They were brought shambling forward, to stand humbly before this new boss but Gus stepped up too. 'They don't know who the raiders were. They don't know any more than we do. We're letting them go.'

'No, we ain't,' a voice in the crowd yelled, and dissension rumbled again.

Roberts caught sight of the three native policemen among the volunteers. He turned to Captain Cope. 'They're your blokes, aren't they?'

Cope nodded. It was obvious he had lost rank in Roberts' presence. 'Well, get them over here,' he was told.

The Captain obeyed, and soon Charlie Penny, Stan and Blackie Bob, correctly rigged in their uniforms and firearms, were presented to Roberts, who dismounted to inspect them. 'You talk to the prisoners,' he said to Charlie Penny.

Charlie drew back in fear. 'Can't talk to them fellers. Me sick.'

Bobby Cope was shocked at this display of insubordination in front of all these men. He was still worried that he would have to explain how three of them had been killed by blacks during his absence from duty for personal reasons. He strode forward and shoved Charlie. 'Do as you're bloody told!'

'Not me, boss,' Charlie whimpered. 'Can't go near dem.'

'True 'nuff,' Blackie remarked. 'Charlie bad sick.'

But Roberts wasn't interested. 'You go then,' he told Blackie. 'You tell them the white men want the murderers. You tell them we'll shoot

187

one of them every hour unless they hand over the killers. We want to know who they are and where they are.'

Blackie grinned. 'We can't talk to them fellers neither. We don't know their lingo.'

Roberts' riding whip slashed across his face. 'Bloody liars the lot of you! Do as you're told.'

Blackie marched over to the prisoners, and in a loud voice and his own language – the language of another nation of Aborigines who lived a world away from these people, more than a thousand miles to the south – repeated the message.

The prisoners stared blankly at him. Mystified, they looked from one to another, and then a middle-aged man with dark, beetling eyebrows and a jutting black beard decided he should reply. In his own language and in a clear voice he made his statement.

To most of the white men it appeared that they were actually conversing since the deep-throated guttural sounds were alike.

'He says he doan know nothing,' Blackie said proudly, even though he hadn't understood anything the man had said.

'He's lying,' Cope said. 'He can't understand a bloody word.'

'It doesn't matter,' Roberts said silkily. 'The object of this exercise, Captain, is to shake up the wild blacks. Let them know what happens if they kill white women. Or any whites for that matter.' He summoned Blackie Bob again. 'That bloke with the beard, he's not telling the truth, is he?'

'No, boss,' Blackie agreed happily.

'They know who killed the white women but they don't care. Isn't that the truth?'

'That'd be right, boss,' Blackie agreed.

'Then shoot him,' he whispered.

Blackie's eyes lit up and his heavy features broke into a grin. Without another word, and before anyone else realised what was happening, Blackie lifted his rifle and shot the spokesman dead.

As he fell, pulling down the others roped to him, they began to scream, cowering beside the dead man, expecting more shots. Gus raced forward, snatched the rifle from Blackie and punched him away.

Paul came running too. 'Jesus Christ! What happened here?'

'The man is dead,' Gus yelled furiously. 'It's about time you woke up and stopped standing about feeling sorry for yourself.'

'Get out of the way, MacNamara. It's not just your family at risk with these murderers on the rampage, it's all of our families.' Roberts shoved him aside.

'My wife isn't at risk,' Paul screamed. 'She's dead!'

'And it's your own fault for encouraging these animals to hang about Oberon.' He turned to the other men. 'My miners were here, right here on Oberon. They knew how to deal with the blacks, but what did he do? He chased the miners away, took the part of the blackfellers, and that was how they repaid him.'

'You get off my land,' Paul shouted but Roberts drew his revolver.

'You've missed the point, MacNamara. We know what has to be done and we'll do it. Isn't that right, mates?'

As the majority of the men raised a cheer, Gus stepped forward, his rifle trained on Roberts. 'You heard what the boss said, get out of here.'

'Whose boss?' Roberts smiled, toying with the heavy revolver and Gus was alarmed to see the hatred in his eyes as he looked back at Paul. Surely a man didn't become this obsessed just because Paul had refused to sell him Oberon? There were other stations. He tossed Blackie's rifle to Paul as the other men backed away.

'You're outnumbered,' Roberts told them, 'three to one, not counting Cope's army. Best you run along home.' He watched as the Oberon men split from the others and ranged behind Paul and Gus. 'No need for trouble, lads,' he called. 'Best you take your boss home and let him have a lie down, he doesn't look too good.'

That was true. Paul had lost weight and his face was thin and drawn from lack of sleep. But his spirit was alive and well. He yelled at his volunteers, 'Killing that man was cold-blooded murder, as was the killing of my wife and Clara. I'll have no more of it. As far as I can make out these blacks can't help us . . .'

'They'd love to help us, though,' a man jeered.

And another: 'You're piss-weak, MacNamara.'

A kinder voice offered, 'Get on home, Paul. Leave these beauties to us.'

As Gus listened he noticed that even their own men were wavering. They'd seen the women and experienced the shock too, and their hearts were eager for revenge, for blood.

Paul reloaded Blackie's carbine and appealed to Roberts. 'I don't even know what you're doing here. This is my business, I have to settle things my way.'

'That's right,' Gus said. 'For Christ's sake, he's suffered enough, he's entitled to respect, not these bloody arguments.'

Roberts spun about on his heel. 'Respect? Him? It was his poor wife who needed respect. From what I hear she wanted the blacks off the property, but would he chase them off? No fear!'

'You bastard!' Paul said, disgusted. He turned his back on Roberts to speak with Gus. 'I've had enough of him. We'll have to let these blacks go before things get worse.'

'That's right, slink off,' Boyd yelled. 'MacNamara wasn't worried about his wife. Why should he be? He's got a girlfriend in town.'

Excitement seized the startled listeners at this revelation. They surged forward, eager to catch MacNamara's reaction, which was swift. He wheeled back in a sudden fast movement which the men were later to describe with glee as a king-hit. His fist carried the force of his moving body, and the punch was so unexpected that Roberts went flying, blood pouring from his nose. He dropped the revolver as he fell, and Paul grabbed it, hurling it away. As Boyd tried to rise Paul kicked him in the ribs and sent him sprawling into the undergrowth.

'Let him up!' the men called, circling around. 'Make it a fair fight!' But Paul was in no mood to entertain them. His heavy boot crashed into Roberts' shoulder and Boyd screamed in pain, lying crumpled on the ground.

Paul retrieved his rifle and yelled to Boyd's men, 'You get him out of here now or I'll put a bullet in him.'

Lost without their leader, they needed direction. 'Where will we take him? The McCann homestead's burned down.'

'That's your problem,' Paul grated. 'Get him off Oberon or we'll come after you.'

Gus went over to talk to the other volunteers, who were all more subdued now. He thanked them for their help and told them it was time to break camp and return home. No one asked about the prisoners; they just seemed relieved it was over.

He and Paul cut the dead man loose from among the anguished prisoners, wrapped his body in a blanket and placed it to one side.

As the horsemen rode away in various directions Paul bailed up Captain Cope. 'I want that fellow, Blackie Bob, placed under arrest for murder.'

'Why?' Cope said. 'He was only acting under orders.'

'Whose orders, you idiot? Since when does Roberts give orders?'

'He's a very important man,' Cope whined. 'I can't go against him. With Fowler Maskey dead, he's all set to be our next Member of Parliament.'

'Who's dead?' Paul asked, surprised.

'Old Fowler. Didn't you know he dropped dead?'

'No, I didn't, I'm sorry to hear it.' Then he realised that this was Cope, Laura's fiancé. 'You've lost your father-in-law,' he said wearily.

'Not me.' Cope shrugged. 'I called that off. Decided not to marry the girl. She's hanging out with Boyd Roberts now. Moved in to Beauview.'

With an effort Paul tried to concentrate on the matter in hand. He was not surprised that the information didn't strike a chord within him; he was still suffering guilt over Jeannie and was finding it hard to forgive himself for being unfaithful to her. What Laura did was her affair, he thought numbly. He doubted if he could ever face her again, if he even wanted to see her again. Then anger crept over him. That remark of Roberts' about a girlfriend: Laura living at Beauview? Had she told him? He felt cold, hard, crook on the world. It was an ugly place.

'You put that bastard under arrest,' he demanded, 'or I'll have you up on charges too for dereliction of duty.'

'All right,' Cope said impatiently. 'I'll take him back into town, unless you want us to stay on here.'

'I don't need you. Where is Lieutenant Gooding? I've been expecting him with some decent troops but there's no sign of him.'

'He went south, chasing bushrangers, but they say he's due at Camelot Station any day. Overdue, they reckon.'

'Damn!' Paul said. 'I wanted to have a talk with him. I might have to get over there myself to catch up with him.'

He left Cope to pack up his men and turned his attention to the prisoners.

Gus was already cutting them loose and Paul didn't protest. Instead he walked among them. 'Gorrabah?' he asked. 'You fellers know Gorrabah?'

They nodded, repeating the name.

'You take me to Gorrabah?' he asked, pointing to himself, then to the hills. They understood but seemed wary.

'What are you thinking of?' Gus demanded. 'You can't go up there.'

'If they take me I can.'

'After we've just killed one of their men? Don't be mad. You'd get a dose of payback within the first mile.'

'I have to go,' Paul said. 'I bet that old bloke knows who killed the girls. I want to ask him.'

The problem was resolved by the prisoners themselves. No matter how much Paul argued with them, trying to tell them that he did not wish to harm Gorrabah, they flatly refused. It seemed they would prefer to remain prisoners rather than reveal the whereabouts of Gorrabah.

'All right,' Paul said at last. 'You tell him to come to me again. I want to talk to him.' He managed to get through to them that he wished to sit down with Gorrabah, and they seemed to accept this. With that he allowed them to go, and they fled into the bush, carrying the dead man.

Cope decided not to tell Blackie he was under arrest until they got back to town, so he ordered his men to mount up immediately. He became angry with Charlie, who was stumbling about like a drunk. 'Get moving, you lazy bastard,' he shouted at him.

Stan Hatbox intervened. 'Ain't no use, boss,' he said. 'Charlie dying. He be dead soon.'

'What are you talking about?'

'Charlie dying. Magic man pointed the bone at Charlie. He all finish now.'

'What magic man?'

'Doan know,' Stan said. 'But he bin here all right.'

'Bloody rubbish,' Cope said. 'Tell him to get a move on or he'll feel my whip.'

The Oberon men were the last to leave the campsite. Heading home, heading back to work.

'I want you to take over for a while,' Paul told Gus. 'I have to go over to Camelot and find Lieutenant Gooding. If Gorrabah comes down you see what you can find out. Otherwise I want Gooding and some of his men to officially escort me into the mountains. I can't give up. I thought we'd try and find some of the tribal chiefs and ask them. The uniforms might help to make them co-operate.'

'You ought to get a couple of days rest first,' Gus said. 'Let's just go home for now and think things out.'

191

Chapter Eight

The animal was soft and furry, black and white in colour. It had no pouch, and it had no interest in seeds or berries or even worms, like the other little bush animals had. This was the strangest creature they'd ever seen.

But it was a brave one, completely unafraid of humans. In fact, when stroked it gave a pretty little rumbling sound, pleased by this attention. Although in shape it was nothing like the plump furry birribis that sat in trees, their arms clinging to branches, dozing or nibbling eucalypt leaves, some claimed it was of the same family. It was as tame as a birribi but its claws were sharper and it was a swift and deadly hunter. Lazy old birribis could get angry and roar but they were not hunters, they only ate gum leaves.

Others were more wary. This oddity hissed like a snake when angry, it arched its back, too, and struck out with its claws as fast as any snake. When one of the dogs had come enquiring around it, the peculiar one had stiffened, hissed, given off the most bloodcurdling scream and with the speed of lightning had whipped a bloody scratch on the dog's nose and sent him yelping for cover. And that was one tough old dog – he'd fight a dingo or pull down a kangaroo, but this thing fixed him!

They discovered it would eat only meat, but they were shocked to find that even when fed it stalked birds and small animals, killing them, it seemed, for fun, playing with lizards until they were half-dead with fear and exhaustion and then walking away, bored with them. This waste placed the new animal in danger because people thought it was a devil spirit, another spoiler of their hunting grounds, and one that had no totem, therefore no protection under the laws.

Some wanted to kill it and throw it in the river, but that raised fears that a devil spirit could poison the water. Others, more practical, suggested they kill it and eat it, but the children wanted to keep it for a pet. They touched its pink nose and grinned in delight when the strange one licked their fingers lazily with its rough tongue.

They argued for days while the animal rolled and romped about their camp, as cheeky as you like, as if it owned the place. In the end it was decided to take it to Harrabura for advice.

It was Kamarga who had found it and brought it home in a dilly bag, and since he was a proven warrior and hunter no one disputed his

192

right to carry it over to Harrabura's camp. A dozen or so family and friends trooped off with him to hear the decision on this curiosity.

'What is it?' Harrabura asked, poking at the animal who was now sleeping soundly in the reed basket one of the girls had made for it.

'We don't know,' Kamarga said. 'We seek your opinion.'

They woke it up and let it scamper about, enjoying Harrabura's astonishment. He knew every animal in the bush, from the monster crocodiles right down to the tiny kultarr, but he'd never seen anything like this silky brute with its insidious manner.

'Where did you find it?' he asked.

'In the rain forest, down past the water-lily lagoon.'

Harrabura studied it for a while and listened to conflicting evidence of its possible kin, then he gave up. 'Wodoro is here, sitting with Gorrabah, who is beginning his flight into the Dreamtime. I will ask Wodoro. He may know.'

He asked Kamarga to stay awhile, and after the others had left turned to him, his face serious. 'When were you down at that rain forest?'

'Half a moon ago maybe,' he said proudly. 'I saw the fight too.'

'What fight?'

'Didn't they tell you? Some of the Bekalbura men were down there hunting and they came upon the camp of the hated dark soldiers who dress as whites and kill our people. They attacked and killed two of them.'

'Why did I not hear of this?' Harrabura snapped. 'Bekalbura people came up here for shelter, not to fight.'

Kamarga clapped his hand over his mouth. 'Do not say I told you then. Many of their young men disagree with the elders but they did not set out to fight. It was as I say, they just came upon them and could not let the opportunity pass.'

'But the black renegades had guns. How many men did these fellows lose?'

'Only one of the Bekalbura killed,' Kamarga said. 'They brought his body back. This I know. Maybe the families did not wish you to know in case you banished them from our mountains.'

Harrabura nodded. 'That would be correct.' Then his eyes lit up. 'They killed two of the vicious ones, did they?'

'Yes.'

'Good.' Harrabura smiled, thinking of Charlie Penny. 'That makes three disposed of.'

'Three indeed,' Kamarga told him. 'I saw the burying place of the third one.'

'What is this?' Harrabura was startled. 'What burying place?'

'Down near the burning of the house.'

Harrabura turned on him, grabbing him by the throat. 'You burned that house?'

193

Kamarga, taken by surprise, choked on his reply. 'No! No! You're hurting me!'

'Are you telling me the truth?'

'Yes. I only saw the fire from on high and I went down to see what happened. I am very careful, no one sees me. By the time I got there it was well into morning and there was no one around. The house was eaten down by fire but I did not dare approach.' He shrugged. 'There was no point.'

'Did you go on to the other house? The one on the plains, directly down from where we now sit.'

'No, I did not.' He looked at Harrabura reproachfully. 'I heard about the white women. I did not kill them if that is what you're thinking. I was up here when the valley-dwellers were rounded up.'

'Then who did? Whoever fired that house also killed the white women, that is clear. And whoever did that has caused us all great harm. The danger is not yet over.'

'I don't know,' Kamarga said. 'No one knows. It is a great mystery.'

Harrabura watched a white-bellied sea eagle drifting overhead in seemingly aimless circles and he sat, silent, for a long time. Since he had not been dismissed, Kamarga waited.

The sea eagle mesmerised Harrabura with its endless circling against the blue, and time shifted for him. He saw Charlie Penny and smiled grimly, knowing that Charlie's life was ebbing away, then he saw the white woman standing in a very dark place. She seemed a powerful woman, even though she was slight of figure, and he heard her shout. Just one word. This word he could not identify but the anger in her blazed like a fierce forest fire, full of fury. Charlie Penny was there. He was there!

As his mind returned to the present, he was confused and haunted with worry. What had he done? Did Charlie Penny have the answer to this mystery? If so, it was probably too late to ask him now.

'Tell me about the third burying place,' he said suddenly.

'I found the body of another one of the bad black men in the woods some way from the burned house.'

'Was he wounded in the fight?' Harrabura asked.

'No. The body in the uniform had been buried but dingoes dug it out. I chased them off and had a look at him. He had a bullet hole in his head. I know bullet holes.' He spat angrily. 'I've seen plenty of them.'

'A white man must have shot that one, then,' Harrabura said. 'We can leave him to the dingoes.'

'Maybe a white man killed the women too,' Kamarga said.

Harrabura shook his head miserably. 'I wish that was the truth, but I fear not.' He searched his mind for a clearer glimpse of that white woman, trying to conjure up the images again, but they faded too quickly. And Charlie Penny? He had stood before him as the leader of the three black soldiers, and in that capacity the man was doomed. He had not connected him with the white woman.

'It is reasonable that Charlie Penny, being a warrior for the whites, would have met that woman,' he said.

Kamarga stared at him. 'Who? Who is Charlie Penny?'

Harrabura could not afford to have his train of thought interrupted. He continued: 'So, seeing him in the same place as her might not have any meaning at all. A normal encounter, just as many of our own people living in the valley have met the boss man and others from the big house in peaceful circumstances.'

'Yes, even I have met them,' Kamarga said, thinking he was beginning to understand the conversation. 'The boss man, the one they call Paul, gave me a beast for our people. He gave it to me personally, telling me it was called a "bull-ok".' He licked his lips. 'That was a good feed. It is bad that he too has turned against us now. If we can no longer hunt and fish in the valley we will starve up here.'

'But she was angry,' Harrabura said, still wrestling with his own problem. 'Fighting mad.' He gave a whoop and clapped his hands. 'She had a gun,' he shouted excitedly. 'She had a gun! And bang! She fired it!' Then he stopped. Disappointed. 'But not at him. Not at Charlie Penny. Who then was she shooting at?'

Bewildered, Kamarga tried to help. 'Blackfellers I suppose. They don't shoot at their own.'

'That is true. Charlie Penny is a cowardly fellow, I saw it in his eyes. Maybe he ran off and left her, when they were attacked. That would account for him refusing to own up. If he was there.' Harrabura moaned. Instinct told him he was on the right track but he was still a long way from identifying the killers. He was almost sure that a Kuinmer mob had raided that house and killed the women, but that was not his business. His immediate problem was to convince the white men, somehow, that the Kutabura clan, who were being punished, one dead already, were innocent of this crime. If not, they were in for most severe punishments.

'What about this animal?' Kamarga asked, watching as it sharpened its claws on the bark of a tree and then rolled luxuriously in the grass. He marvelled at its colours, the black patches shining and the white as clean and unsullied as the whitest clouds.

'We'll go now,' Harrabura said.

They set off up the mountain, crunching through dim forests, then dropped down a chalky cliff and made their way up a wide stony gully, where a stream was still flowing with the last of the summer rains. Then they began the steep climb to the cave that Gorrabah had chosen as his Dreaming place.

As they approached they heard the wailing and knew he had gone from them.

Later that afternoon Harrabura walked with Wodoro right to the end of this mountain, to the lookout place where a plateau of rock jutted out over a precipice, a sheer drop. Far, far below, in the gorge, the stream was a thin silvery line and the tops of huge trees resembled a carpet of velvety green moss.

Harrabura didn't much like going too close to the edge, but Wodoro did and, he stood there now, admiring the view. He was a sturdy man, not as tall as the average Darambal man, due to the unfortunate mix of white blood in his body. Nevertheless, he was strong of limb. He bore his share of initiation scars and one front tooth was missing, a legacy of the Tingum tribe to which he belonged. They always knocked out the front tooth of a young man who had passed all the tests. Boys who failed were ostracised or deprived of their regenerative buds so as not to sully the race.

Wodoro argued strongly against this practice now, warning all tribes in his travels that they could no longer afford this waste of manhood or any other decimating rites, with their numbers dwindling so swiftly. Harrabura supposed he was right, but he worried what the great spirits would think of this interference with natural laws.

'I've always loved this place,' Wodoro said, the warm afternoon sun giving a coppery tone to his body as he turned about to take in the panorama. From there, he could see the sweep of the Fitzroy River, the great valley, and the stunted cones of once magnificent volcanoes that had thundered up from the heart of the earth. The millions of years had taken their toll and worn away the mountains, leaving only the hard cores as a reminder that they had existed.

To the east lay the green coastal plains and the wondrous blue of the ocean.

'A white man told me once,' Wodoro said, 'that that is where they come from. It takes them more than six moons to get here in their great ships from across that ocean.'

Harrabura was amazed. 'Why?' he asked. 'Are their hunting grounds so bad?'

'I don't know,' Wodoro admitted. 'They must be.'

He sat down on a rock, loosened the cord that held his thick black hair in a topknot, ran his hands through his hair and retied it. He wore no ornaments except a white stone set in his ear, a stone that shimmered milkily against his black skin.

'What is that?' Harrabura asked. 'It is very pretty.'

'White men call it a pearl. It was given to me by the Warunga people who live way to the north. They call it a Koppio stone.'

'You know many things,' Harrabura said.

Wodoro smiled. 'I learn as I go but I think you know more important things, matters of the mind.'

'That is very gracious of you. Tell me. Did the old man die in sorrow?'

'Yes. He was very worried about your people.'

'You know what has happened hereabouts?'

'His family explained that a new attack has begun, in revenge for the killing of two white women. Who was responsible?'

Harrabura looked down towards the valley, his eyes glistening as he surveyed the land he loved so much. 'I don't know. Maybe Kuinmer men, but not us. We thought we were safe enough down there. The white boss of that territory let us be. He didn't mind us.' Then he gave a snort of disgust. 'Listen to my stupid tongue! Didn't mind us! See how low I have sunk to say such a thing, grateful to be allowed to sit down on land that has belonged to us since creation. I ask you to forgive me.'

Wodoro shrugged. 'There is nothing to forgive. The old man wanted peace, you have to strive for it.'

'Should we move north? I have been thinking we ought to depart from here and find new lands, even if it means losing our spiritual homes.'

'No use. Other tribes are facing similar wars with the whites. They are everywhere in the land, moving on like plagues of locusts. You have to try to hang on here.'

'I suppose so,' Harrabura said dismally. 'In which case I have a great favour to ask of you. It may be dangerous, so I would accept your refusal.'

'What is this favour?'

'They tell me you speak the language of the white men?'

'That is so. I learned from my father.'

'And you never wished to live among his people?'

Wodoro laughed. 'Sometimes in my youth in the Tingum country to the south, I would go down and live with station blacks out of curiosity. For fun, I used to pretend I was a mute. The white men called me "The Dummy" and left me to poke about on my own. They never tried to make me work for them. So I could wander about listening to their talk as much as I liked, and I heard first-hand that many of them hate us, but not all of them. This is why you must hang on. We know from our Dreaming that goodness overcomes evil.'

'But evil must be perpetrated first to bring forth the wrath of the good spirits,' Harrabura said, turning the concept over in his mind. 'I sometimes wonder why the great spirits allow evil to function.'

'That is a difficult question. The gwardar snake that swallows a bilby is regarded by the bilby as evil, but the snake must eat. What is your favour?'

'We need someone to go down to the valley, to find the white boss, Paul, who until his women were killed treated our people with kindness. Now he is as bad as the rest. You speak his language so we want you to speak for us, tell him we are not responsible, that we want only peace.'

Wodoro nodded. 'When I received the old man's message I was warned not to go into that valley, to travel along the mountain trails. The danger you speak of lies in that valley?'

197

'Yes. They have driven all dark people out. This man could be difficult to approach.'

'And if I confront the wrong one I could get shot?' Wodoro grinned.

Harrabura could see no reason for humour. 'The man, Paul, his heart is in a rage, he might shoot you.'

'A problem,' Wodoro mused. 'Especially when I don't even know what he looks like.'

'I will send Kamarga with you. He knows some secret trails, he could get you through unseen, and he can point out the boss man.'

'And then what?'

Harrabura looked vaguely about him, unable to supply an answer.

'I'm not a warrior,' Wodoro said, 'nor especially brave.'

The other man was surprised. 'How is this? Your name is legend all along the trade routes. You killed a white man in Warunga country with a single magnificent throw of the boomerang.'

Wodoro shook his head. 'That was a long time ago. The white men were getting away after a fight with the Warunga, who were blaming me for their escape. The Warunga are fierce people, my own life would have been in danger for interfering. In the heat of the moment I grabbed a boomerang and hurled it with all my might. No one was more surprised than me when it felled that white man.'

Harrabura began to laugh. 'And of such, legends are made.'

Wodoro chuckled. 'I could hardly admit it was just a lucky shot. After that I was such a hero I was given a wife, and on my recommendation they allowed the other white man to leave. I led him out of Warunga country and sent him on his way.'

But the question remained, and in the end Wodoro agreed. 'I'll try. I can't promise anything, but if it is possible I'll talk to the white boss. What name do they give to your land now? They like to bring their own tribal names.'

'Aye. This I know. I have been told the name is "Ober-on". What does this mean?'

'It is very simple, that one. It just means over past something, maybe the great river. It does not specify.'

Harrabura grunted. 'Then what use is it?' He remembered that Kamarga was waiting to speak with Wodoro and whistled to him. 'This is the man who will take you down into the valley,' he said as Kamarga approached. 'But he has a question for you.'

Eagerly Kamarga opened the basket. 'I found this rare animal but we cannot put a name to it. What could it be?'

'It's called a cat,' Wodoro said. 'They are pretty things, much petted by the whites, who feed them daily.'

'What should I do with it?'

'Kill it. These animals are greedy creatures. They prey on our small wildlife and birds and upset nature.'

'Is it edible?' Kamarga asked.

'I wouldn't chance it,' Wodoro replied. 'White men don't eat them.'

When Kamarga had left, Wodoro requested information about his quest. 'So. If I get to see this white man and tell him your people did not kill the women, he will ask who did. What is to be my reply?'

'You say you don't know.'

Wodoro looked at him keenly. 'Does this mean *you* know?'

'It means only that I am thinking on the matter. The answer has not yet been made clear to me.'

As a courier, Wodoro was not permitted to carry weapons. His hunting spear was decorated with hawk feathers to indicate that he was a messenger, and the same feathers were arranged in his hair. His training had been long and arduous, covering several years, in which he had been handed on from tribe to tribe to learn their laws and languages, therefore facilitating communication between the various peoples along the north-east coast of this great land.

When the ceremonies to mark the passing of his old friend were over, he set off down the mountain with Kamarga to the rain forest, where they rested all day. By night they travelled swiftly across the open forests, remaining hidden during the day and pushing on again at night, until Kamarga led him to a rocky outcrop from where they could see the collection of houses which were the headquarters of these Oberon people.

They were near enough to see men riding out along the trails – some even passed below them – but Kamarga insisted the boss was not with them, that they'd have to circle around and get closer through rough scrub. This time they followed a stream, stealthily now, and lying low, inching forward until they could see the main house across the clearing.

Wodoro tried not to show it but he was nervous. Kamarga had told him that the women had been killed near here, and that was enough to give him the creeps, but there was more. Something about this area gave him a nasty feeling in the pit of his stomach, and he wished he could think of an excuse to leave.

Three men, walking down the track to the river, passed right by them, and Wodoro looked to Kamarga who shook his head.

Wodoro listened to them talking. 'The boss wants this place fenced off,' he heard a man say. 'He doesn't want this track used any more. I think for a while anyway he wants to keep the riverbank where Jeannie and Clara were killed as a sacred place.'

'Not much need to fence it,' another grumbled. 'Who'd want to come here? It's got the feel of ghosts now.'

His nerves on edge, Wodoro agreed wholeheartedly, but he remained still until they were gone.

Later, a man emerged on to the veranda of the big house and stood there alone. 'That's him!' Kamarga hissed. 'That's the boss.'

The sun was beginning its fast retreat into the western hills, and Wodoro could make out only the shadow of the man. 'From this distance I can't tell him from any of the others,' he complained.

'It's him,' Kamarga insisted. 'Often they sit out there of a night. Soon the moon will rise and you can go over to speak with him.'

'Just like that?' Wodoro said, not impressed with Kamarga's plan.

'The old man did, the one who has just died. Not long ago, when they killed two of our men, he strode down and confronted that boss with great courage.'

'You forget. This time two of his women were put to death. I will find a way to speak to him, but you must go now. I am grateful for your guidance but from here the danger is great. You go back and wait for me at the rain forest. There's no need for you to risk your life any further.'

'Are you sure?'

'Yes. You must be well away from here before I move out.'

He was relieved when Kamarga slipped silently away. It was disconcerting to have him breathing on his back, waiting for him to perform this courageous deed. Wodoro wasn't sure how to go about this, and delay would only make Kamarga impatient and maybe cause him, from sheer bravado, to do something stupid. And get his head shot off. He was already thinking that if he failed this time, he could dress like a station blackfellow, find some old clothes somewhere, and walk up in the daylight. But even that would be risky. He'd observed that this place didn't have blacks working as station hands. He was hungry now and as the moon came up he wondered what he'd let himself in for.

Two other men went up on to that veranda and stayed for ages talking to the boss. Wodoro moved as close as he dared, keeping his eyes on the light-coloured shirt, the only way he could identify the boss.

Eventually they left and it seemed the boss might then go in to sleep, but no . . . Wodoro held his breath. The boss was coming out! He strode down to the gate and Wodoro's hopes sagged. Not only was he carrying a rifle, his dogs were leaping excitedly about him.

'Damn dogs!' Wodoro cursed under his breath. He'd have no hope of approaching the white man with his dogs ready to raise the alarm, and worse, he'd never get away with those vicious dogs tracking him.

Then he saw the boss turn and shout at the dogs, ordering them back inside the fence. Disappointed, they obeyed, and the white man strode towards the river, making straight for the bush track that led on to the killing place. Wodoro, guessing where he was going, retreated quickly and took a roundabout route to the same destination. He knew he'd find it; he remembered the weeping willows that brushed the water like teardrops. He remembered it with a shudder, it still rang with the cries of the dead. And he wondered why this bereaved man should wish to go back there. He reasoned that sorrow could draw him back.

Sure enough, by the time he arrived, moving slowly through the bush, the man was sitting on the bank, staring sadly at the silvery waters, obviously just needing to be alone with his thoughts in the last living place of his women.

Wodoro was close now, behind the man. He rehearsed his role. It would be madness just to step out of the bush and startle the fellow. He'd be jumpy enough as it was. With the rifle on his knees, he might shoot in nervous reaction, especially at a blackfellow.

Wodoro could feel his skin prickle with fear, and he broke out in a sweat, the cold leaves around him chilling him to the bone. The best thing to do was to stay hidden and call to the man. He would call out: 'Sir!' in a proper white man's form of address. And then he would call: 'Sir, I come in peace,' to keep him calm. And then he would say: 'I must speak with you, sir, on a matter of importance.' By which time the white man would be placated and Wodoro could ask him not to shoot before he stepped out into the open.

But it didn't work out that way.

Wodoro was glad Kamarga wasn't there to hurry him, because it took a while for him to pluck up the courage to speak. The white man was praying. He stood and was saying the words aloud, words Wodoro had heard taught to black children. He was too superstitious to interrupt. Then he saw the sign they used to finish their prayers, a hand to the head and chest and so on, and he knew it was now or never, the man would leave. He tried to call out, but he was so nervous his voice came out as croak and, worse, a branch crackled in the undergrowth under his feet.

The boss whirled, rifle in hand. 'Who's there?'

He didn't shoot first. That was the time for Wodoro to speak, to say his next line, but he saw the man's face in the moonlight and fell back in terror, scuttling away in the blackness of the bush like a dingo disturbed from its prey. When he reached a bend in the river he dived into the silky waters and crossed cautiously to the other side, hardly making a ripple. Then he disappeared, shaking, into the bush.

For hours he crouched, trembling, hugging himself to keep warm, to fight off this panic. From the minute they'd passed by that killing place he'd known something was wrong. It wasn't just the moaning spirits of the two women, there were other ghosts and he'd seen one with his very own eyes.

When that man had turned to him, the shock had struck him like a lightning bolt. For standing before him was the man he had killed so many years ago. The man he'd brought down with his boomerang. He knew he wasn't mistaken. Hadn't he seen that head almost cleaved from the body by the force of that razor-sharp hardwood boomerang? A fighting weapon. He could still see the face, blue eyes wide, fair skin and short curling hair, soft black curling hair. He'd helped the other man bury the body, the man called Juan, who was distraught at losing his friend, and he'd seen Juan close the eyes in that fine face.

And here at this terrible place, the ghost had reared up at him, shouting at him. What had it said? Wodoro couldn't remember. I'm not a warrior, he whimpered to himself. That was the only man I have ever killed. Warriors do not suffer this awful guilt, they simply do their work. Why have I always been visited with remorse over that man? Someday, he'd always known, the spirit would reach out at him because he had broken the law. A man of his status had to renounce violence, he had been taught to reject provocation, and could only kill in self-defence. That was not self-defence.

But the Warunga warriors had been so impressed by him, they'd allowed him to take the other white man to freedom. Because Wodoro had told them it was better to let the other one go so that he could go back and warn the whites to keep out of Warunga country. But that was only a way to assuage his guilt, because he'd known the white men would keep on coming, whether they freed the man or not.

The other white man, Juan, had wept. 'Why did you have to kill him? He was a good man. He only wanted peace.' And he had said his name over and over, a fearful practice never permitted in the dark tribes, where the names of the dead were never mentioned. Juan had said his name was 'Pace', and Wodoro had tried to shut him up, knowing that was to wish evil on them.

But Pace was there now, standing at the killing place, shouting at him, Wodoro, from over the years, because everyone knew that death was timeless.

He stayed awake all night, not daring to sleep, and rather than go back to Kamarga and admit failure, he moved back to the original vantage point. Sick at heart, he circled the homestead and saw Pace saddling up his horse. He saw him strap a swag on to the saddle, the sign of a journey, and heard the other men near the stables wishing him well. Calling 'Good luck' to him and telling him to hurry back.

To Wodoro's haunted mind, this was expected. Pace had come back to haunt him, in the place of the boss man, and now, his mission over, he was leaving. Riding off alone in the direction of the big river that the whites called the Fitzroy.

By the time he caught up with Kamarga, Wodoro had shaken off the fright and was trying to pit logic against superstition, to listen to his father's voice. He hadn't known him all that well, but his mother had often said he was a cunning fellow, he could outwit the other whites any time.

What if, he asked himself, that was not Pace but his image? And the image of a man could be his son. It was possible. Juan had wept that Pace had a wife and three sons. The sons would be full-grown by now. And that raised another worry. Would he ever dare face his son? Would his guilt show like a splotch of mud? Would the father visit revenge on him through the son? All these things had to be thought through, and the worst one he tried to chase from his mind: if that was not one of his sons, or other of his kin, then he had indeed seen Pace shout at him from the grave.

'Did you talk to him?' Kamarga asked.

'No. I didn't get a chance. He rode away to the east, but he'll be back. We'll have to wait.'

Paul MacNamara headed for Camelot Station. If he'd missed Lieutenant Gooding then he'd follow him in to Rockhampton. He was determined to raise official support to search the hills for the murderers. He realised now that undisciplined posses and the brutal methods of the Native Police would only antagonise the blacks, but a troop of well-trained soldiers could, and must, persuade them to hand over the murderers, for their own good. With redcoats he could put the fear of God into them.

Gus had encouraged him to go, if only to get away from Oberon for a while, away from the anguish that tore at him from every corner of the house. As he cantered down the track, Paul wished he could keep on going, that he could head south, cross the border and ride on down to the solace of the family home at Kooramin, never to return.

That night he bunked down in a wayside tavern on the goldfields, welcoming the babble of voices from the other side of the thin wall that drowned out his own thoughts. Normally he would have joined the men at the bar for a convivial yarn, but he was feeling too low and dreaded sympathy. As he slept in fits and starts on the hessian bunk, Roberts' sneering comment flared suddenly in his mind: 'He's got a girlfriend in town!'

He could only mean Laura. Paul was too depressed to care that Laura must have confided in someone, maybe Roberts himself; it didn't matter any more. But the knife-thrust had cut deep, targeting his guilt so that he saw himself as a hypocrite, mourning the wife that he had betrayed. But he did mourn her and, knowing Jeannie, he felt she would never rest until her death had been avenged. It was the least he could do now.

A heavy body crashed against the wall, interrupting his maudlin worries, as a fight broke out in the bar. A man in the next bunk shouted at them to break it up, and Paul turned on his side, grateful for the intrusion.

The next day he felt better, riding out of the fog that was Oberon. He stopped at a lagoon to allow his horse to splash in the shallows and cool off in the heat of the day, and then he was on his way again. He wasn't looking forward to company, and Camelot, where the Carlisles loved to entertain, was the last place for a man in his mood, but it was necessary. He had heard that Grace's husband, old Justin, was back from Sydney and that thought produced a reluctant smile. The old man was known to be a bit odd, but since he was rich, he was referred to as eccentric. Childish in many ways, Justin claimed to have the sole right to bang the great brass gong at mealtimes and went at it with such gusto that it could be heard for miles. And despite his wife's objections, the surrounds of the fireplace in the parlour were studded with sovereigns, hundreds of them, Justin's pride and joy.

As he rode across country, well on to Camelot land, Paul decided that the small area on the river bank where Jeannie and Clara had died would remain fenced off. He wanted to put a small cairn there in remembrance of them, to dispel the horror, to mark the place where they'd been happy, idling away Sunday afternoons fishing, enjoying their picnics, just the three of them.

It was strange, he thought, but the other night when he'd gone down there, it had all seemed so normal again, as if the river had washed away the sight and sounds of anguish. As he'd prayed for them he couldn't help thinking about Pace. He'd seemed to dominate Paul's thoughts, as if he were trying to tell him something. He sighed. It was probably only his imagination.

Because he'd taken it easy most of the way, savouring this chance to be alone, it was well into the night, about nine o'clock, he guessed, before he turned into the tree-shaded wagon track that led to Camelot homestead. The dogs were barking at his approach but over the top of their warnings he could hear singing, joyful voices raised in hearty communion, happy people enjoying life.

In a rush of nostalgia he stopped to listen, reining his horse quietly on the moon-dappled path as tears stung his eyes. Pace had loved to sing, in his fine tenor voice, the bittersweet Irish songs, and many a night they'd spent around the piano with Dolour picking out the tune. 'By ear,' she used to boast. 'I play by ear.'

Paul wondered when the singing had gone out of his life. There was never any music on Oberon. He was too busy with that infernal work, while Jeannie had been obsessed with more and more lumps of furniture bought from that sister of hers. It occurred to him for the first time that Jeannie had been more interested in impressing her sister than in the furnishings themselves. Not that it mattered, then or now.

Two riders came galloping towards him, rifles glinting. 'Who's there?' they yelled.

'MacNamara. Oberon Station.'

'Oh. It's you, Mr MacNamara.' The voices softened. 'Bloody sorry to hear about your missus.'

Paul nodded, glad of the escort to the homestead. His confidence had suddenly deserted him, and he was a youth again, bewildered by death, by loss, needing someone else to take control. On his own, he would have turned and galloped away, taken refuge in the bush as he had done when Juan Rivadavia had come to tell them that they'd never see their beloved father again.

Dully, he went with his escort to the stables, where willing hands took his mount. He answered their questions – 'No, not yet. We haven't found them yet,' meaning the killers – and accepted their rage, their angry outbursts at such a frightful tragedy. 'Bloody terrible!' they were saying as they took his swag.

'Is Lieutenant Gooding here?' he asked them. 'I have to see him.'

'We've been waiting for the bugger for weeks,' he was told, 'or we would have sent him over to you. But he's due. Christ knows where them bloody toy soldiers have got to. Never around when you want them.'

Alerted, old Justin came down from the homestead, wearing a pink paper party hat on his flowing white hair. 'Just in time, my boy,' he said, embracing Paul. 'It's my birthday. Don't worry about a present. You can think of something tomorrow.'

Under the lamplight in the stables Paul saw the stockmen raise their eyebrows at him, and shake their heads, so he smiled at Justin Carlisle. Justin was a relief. He wished his mind could drift too so that he could learn to smile at the awful world again.

'Happy birthday, sir,' he said, returning the embrace. 'It's a joy for me to get here in time.'

'So it is,' Justin said, delighted. He peered at Paul through rheumy eyes. 'We're formal tonight, but dinner's over so you'll do. Come along with me. I can't miss the present-opening, it's better than Christmas because they're all mine.'

'I'd like to wash up first, if you don't mind,' Paul said, shoving his hat back on his head and wiping grime from his forehead. Justin allowed him to sluice down at the tank tap and grab a clean flannelette shirt from his swag. He was hurrying to button the shirt as they crossed the yard.

'How's your father?' Justin asked, but there was no need for a reply because he rattled on. 'Knew him well, you know, in the old days. The bugger bought land in the Brisbane Valley right under my nose, before it got opened up, just when I was applying to buy it. Taught me a lesson. Grab the land first, get permission later.'

'Yes,' Paul said lamely. 'I suppose so.'

'Now don't be shy,' Justin said, sensing that Paul was beginning to balk as they approached the homestead veranda lit up with Chinese lanterns. 'It's only the family. Grace is here, of course, and the boys and their wives, and a few strays. Can't remember who they are but they don't matter. You should have brought your wife.'

They marched up the back steps, through the kitchen and along the passage, past the dining room where black maids were clearing the remnants of a dinner party from the long table, and on into the parlour, which had far more 'strays' than Paul had anticipated. The room was crowded with formally dressed people, the women shining in silks and satins.

A woman standing by the piano was just finishing her solo rendition of 'Lassies of Botany Bay' when they appeared in the doorway.

There was a sudden silence, then Grace Carlisle moved swiftly. She was wearing an elegant black evening dress with a triple rope of pearls at her throat, lightened by a toy spangled tiara. Although he knew he was wrong, it seemed to Paul that she took an age to cross the room, with all those faces behind her, staring at him like the heads of dummies at a show stall, white and garish in the artificial light of crepe-wrapped lamps.

'My dear,' she said gently, putting her arms about him and kissing him on both cheeks while Justin nodded enthusiastically. 'How lovely to see you.' But he saw the tears in her eyes.

'I'm sorry,' he whispered to her. 'I didn't want to intrude. I had no idea . . .'

Visibly, she straightened up as if to give him a lead. 'Now that you're here,' she advised, in a quiet voice, 'I'd like you to stay. Do your best, dear, we'll talk later.'

She turned to her guests, 'It's a little too late for introductions; for everyone who knows him, that's fine, for the ones who don't and won't remember in the morning anyway, this is a dear friend of ours, Mr Paul MacNamara. By the looks of him he's been on the trail all day, so we'll give him a hand and a much-needed drink.'

Hands clapped, Paul managed to acknowledge them, and someone banged the piano again as Grace steered him through the throng to the adjoining dining room. Without asking, she poured him a whisky. 'Our best Scotch,' she said.

'Thank you.' He looked about him uncomfortably.

She poured herself a glass of champagne and held it up. 'To a birthday, Paul,' she said, her voice full of understanding and encouragement. 'Looks like you're stuck with this lot. Can you handle it?'

He glanced down at his clothes and shrugged. 'If they can put up with me.' He swallowed his whisky at a gulp. 'That,' he said, 'was about the best thing that has happened to me in a long while. Could I have a refill?'

'Of course.' She poured him another drink. 'I think Justin didn't realise. I'm sorry.'

'Don't be,' he said. 'It has to happen sooner or later. They say it's better to get thrown in at the deep end . . .'

Grace laughed. 'And this is the deep end?'

'It sure is.'

Drink in hand, with Grace at his side, Paul threaded his way through the gathering, acknowledging family and acquaintances, nodding to new faces, noticing their awkward sadness in a blur of introductions, knowing they'd all heard of him. Then, by the piano, he heard Grace say: 'And this is Miss Laura Maskey.'

The shock was compounded by confusion, hurt, anger – for how could he forget she was living at Beauview? – and a storm of guilt. He saw her exactly as he remembered her from not so long ago, but a lifetime away, Jeannie's lifetime. He saw the cloud of soft fair hair, topped by a silly party hat with a silver star in the centre, and her lovely eyes, so sad, and that face with her high cheekbones and the soft pink mouth that he had kissed. She was wearing blue, something in blue that was filmy and bewitching. Angel arms reaching out to him, beseeching.

'How do you do?' he said, his voice cold. He shouldered her aside, and moved on.

She made excuses for him, sitting cross-legged on her bed, trying to understand. She was wearing an eastern kimono over her underwear in case he came to her window. It was colourful and flattering, royal blue, embroidered in pink and silver, and she had a skirt and blouse handy so that she could throw them on and go out to him.

Now that the house was quiet, all he had to do was cross over from the bachelor quarters, step up on to the veranda and tap on the French windows. She had left one side open and her lamp was still lit. It would be easy enough for him to find out which one was her room. But maybe not. Perhaps he didn't like to ask.

Laura jumped down from the bed and stepped outside to stand quietly by the rail, as if taking in the cool night air. She looked over towards the bachelor quarter, but there was no movement at all.

Disappointed, she eventually gave up and came back to sit by the dressing table, brushing her hair. It had been a surprise to see him, a marvellous surprise followed by a jolt when he had ignored her except for that cold, curt nod.

He had cut her, and that hurt, but she could make allowances. He was probably equally surprised, and after all, he was in mourning; he could hardly make a fuss of her in front of everyone. But he could at least have acknowledged her. He could have said: 'We've met.' Nothing wrong with that. And he could have smiled at her, he had smiled at others he knew. Why treat her so – she hated to say it – so rudely? Then again, he probably hadn't had time to think. She'd see him tomorrow and she'd be able to tell him how sorry she was, about his wife, genuinely sorry. She couldn't ask more of him at this stage, but they were friends. Her heart went out to him, she wanted to hold his hand, to console him, to stand by him.

So why was she feeling so nervous and afraid? Their short affair. Was that all it had been? Just a fling on his part, pretending that he loved her. Then he had gone back to his wife and forgotten all about her. Laura began to blame herself. Should she have sent him a note of condolence? Written to him as his friend expressing her sincere sympathy. Had her very silence hurt him?

Never mind, she consoled herself. She still loved him. Tomorrow she'd take things slowly, just be there for him when he was ready to see her, so that they could have time alone to sort out any misunderstandings.

Two days passed and he never once looked in her direction. He went out with the men, 'Choosing,' Grace said, pleased with him, 'to keep himself busy.' All the other guests left the station after the celebrations but he remained in his quarters, waiting for the arrival of the troopers. He dined with the family and Laura of an evening, but, like the three Carlisle sons, retired early after a day's work with the cattle. He was polite to her, that was all. Not once did he address her or attempt to talk with her. She might just as well have been a hundred miles away.

Grace Carlisle was delighted that Laura had accepted her invitation, and urged her to stay on. 'I've written to your mother,' she said. 'I know Hilda. She gets all up in the air about things, but when she comes down to earth she'll miss you, and she'll be sorry she took on so.'

'I don't care any more,' Laura said dismally. 'I applied for jobs as a governess and now have two positions to choose from in New South Wales. At least I'm welcome there.'

'Laura, there's no need for that. You're welcome here too. I'll be disappointed if you run off on me so soon. Besides, I've also written to your Uncle William in London – he was my beau, you know, before I met Justin. I've explained your situation to him and I know William won't let you down. He was always very fond of you. We'll wait to hear what he has to say. He doesn't have any children, Laura, don't forget that. You have to be sensible about these things. Give him time. In the meantime just enjoy yourself and stop worrying. You look as if your world has caved in.'

As far as Laura was concerned, it had. Having Paul on the station, ignoring her, was worse than being separated from him. Far worse.

Finally she decided to take matters into her own hands.

After dinner one evening, trying to keep calm, she marched over to the bachelor quarters and knocked on the door.

Paul answered it, standing there bare-chested, looking down at her as if she were a stranger.

'Could I talk with you a minute?' she asked.

He seemed pained that she should disturb him and made no effort to invite her in.

'I wanted to tell you how terribly sorry I was to hear about your wife, Paul, and Clara too.'

'Thank you,' he said stiffly.

'Don't you believe me?'

He softened. 'Of course I do. I never expected anything less of you.'

'Is there anything I can do to help?'

'No.' A silence rose like a wall between them, but Laura refused to accept it.

'Why are you treating me like this? I thought we were friends.'

He shifted uncomfortably from one foot to the other. 'I'm sorry, I didn't mean to be unkind to you. Laura, I really would prefer it if you would leave me alone.'

'Are you hurting that bad?' she asked, trying to maintain some bond between them at the expense of her own pride, but he stepped back.

'Go to bed, Laura. It's late.'

Defeated, she stumbled away to hide in her room.

Over the past few harrowing months Laura had been sustained by thoughts of Paul MacNamara. He would listen to her, he would understand her deep sorrow at her father's death, her agony that he had died thinking she'd betrayed him when it was not true. He would understand how she'd become entangled with Boyd Roberts, and he'd probably have laughed at her. So many things had been building up inside her, so many things to tell him – because he'd said he'd be back – but now he was so immersed in his own tragedy that there was no longer any place for her. And without him she had nothing left to hold on to.

As for Paul, he lay on the bunk, his hands clasped behind his head, fighting off sentiment. There was a time just then, an exquisite second or two, when he desperately needed her to stay with him, to weep with him . . .

'What about?' an inner voice challenged him. 'The death of your wife? The death of her father who would have despised you for seducing his daughter?'

'About everything,' he replied. 'About what a bloody hell life is.'

'You hypocrite,' the voice railed. 'Staying here at Camelot, accepting all their sympathy about Jeannie, with your mistress standing watching.'

'God forgive me,' he muttered and turned his face to the wall. But he saw her in his dreams, sweet, reasonable Laura, and he clung to her, hidden from the harsh light of reality.

The next day Lieutenant Gooding rode in with six troopers and Tyler Kemp.

Grace Carlisle welcomed them, but she could be severe if she didn't like people. Gooding was billeted in the bachelor quarters with Paul, but Kemp was banned from the homestead.

'Laura Maskey is my guest,' she told the Lieutenant. 'That fellow has caused her a great deal of grief. I won't have him at my table. Put him with the troopers in one of the bunkhouses.'

Embarrassed, Gooding explained to Tyler that they'd been allotted different quarters and the reporter was furious. 'Am I to understand that I'm not wanted here?'

'Something like that. I understand you have offended Mrs Carlisle. She's a great friend of the Maskeys, and Laura is here. If you prefer not to stay you can return to Rockhampton.'

'Where are you going from here?'

'Out to Oberon Station. Paul MacNamara has been waiting for us, they tell me. I doubt he's the man you want to see now. Since his wife and the servant girl were murdered he'll hardly be in the mood for peaceful chats about the blacks.'

Tyler considered the situation. On their return journey they'd heard about the women. There was outrage everywhere, and criticism of Gooding, again, for not being on the spot. It was illogical and

209

unfair, since no one could predict where and when these attacks would take place, but Gooding wore it with patience.

'What's the point in going out to Oberon now?' Tyler asked. 'It's too late.'

'I know that. MacNamara has had posses on the job for weeks without finding the killers. I'll talk to him tonight and see what he wants us to do. Whatever it is, it's my duty to support him.'

Travelling back to Rockhampton alone on the long, lonely trail didn't appeal to Tyler so he decided to wait for the outcome of the talks.

In the morning he sought out the Lieutenant. 'What's happening?'

'Not the best news. He's scoured the valley and now wants to move into the mountains to try to find the tribal chiefs and talk them into handing over the raiders. An expedition like that is bloody dangerous for a small force. The Berserker Ranges have become the headquarters for several black clans now. God knows how many are up there. And that country is unknown, unexplored.'

The thought of venturing into those mountains excited Tyler, but meeting up with armed blacks was a worry. 'Shouldn't you wait for more troops?' he asked.

'There aren't enough in the district for a job like this. But he says he knows from the night fires where most of them camp, and he claims if we go quietly it will be possible to rustle up the chiefs. He knows one of them, an old bloke called Gorrabah. Sounds hopeless to me but I'll have to try. Now, do you want to come with us or go back to Rockhampton?'

'I'll tag along,' Tyler said, without enthusiasm.

'You can wait at Oberon Station if the expedition scares you.'

That annoyed Tyler. 'I can handle myself. I grew up on mountain ponies, it'll be interesting to see how you cope.'

'I'll manage. It's my job to escort MacNamara but not to have him think he's in control. I'll take my men just as far as I deem reasonable. We leave for Oberon first thing in the morning.'

Chapter Nine

Amelia Roberts was lonely and upset. And angry with them all. How dare they go off and leave her like this? And at such a time! When half the town looked the other way when she walked down the street and the other half stared at her as if she were wearing britches on her head. 'The world,' her father had said, 'is full of fools,' and he was certainly right. These people would have to be the stupidest on earth to believe all the lies Cosmo had written about him. And what had made Cosmo turn on Boyd Roberts? Ambition. That was all. He wanted to be the Member of Parliament himself, the squint-eyed little pest, and what better way to defeat her father than by maligning him in that newspaper?

It astonished Amelia that people actually believed Cosmo. People who had fawned over her father, falling over themselves to be invited to Beauview. Now they were staying away in droves, leaving her to twiddle her thumbs on her own.

Amelia was smart enough not to invite rejection by arranging any parties to keep herself occupied, but she plotted revenge for when this nastiness was over. She'd make them jump then. And it would be over soon, her father had said so.

Obviously he had heard that the *Capricorn Post* had been vandalised, ruined. And good riddance. That had shut Cosmo up. She wished she could show someone Boyd's letter, to prove he was a caring man. He said it was a shame that the presses had been wrecked because he had hoped to purchase the paper for Tyler, and now they'd have to start afresh. He wanted Tyler to go to Brisbane immediately and buy new presses for him so that they could start up another paper. But where was Tyler?

Only one letter had found its way in from him, to say that Lieutenant Gooding had changed his mind and they were heading south, so she had no idea where he actually was. Admittedly it was a lovely letter, and she cherished it, but he had a duty to get back here! It was irresponsible of him to be roaming the countryside when she needed him and when her father needed him.

Luckily for Tyler, she couldn't write to her father and admit that he hadn't returned yet. He'd be cross. He had his business to attend to out in the bush, but Tyler had no excuse.

Also, her father had written that he would be away a while longer because he was on the track of the blackfellows who had killed the two ladies and burned down his house. That thrilled her. If Daddy could bring in the murderers, as he expected to do, the town would think twice about criticising him. No one else had been able to find them, not even Paul MacNamara himself, so they were still at large, liable to kill more defenceless women. And rape them! Amelia shuddered. She was glad to be here in the safety of Beauview. Even though Daddy had taken his men with him she always felt secure here. Besides, the cook and two maids lived in the servants' quarters, and old Andy, the rouseabout, was always wandering around somewhere.

But it was lonely. She was furious at the way Laura Maskey had gone off. Just like that! After all she'd done for her! She'd packed her trunks and left them in the coach house to collect later. Damn cheek. Amelia had forgotten by this that she'd wanted Laura to leave, and considered her departure selfish. She could at least have waited, she fumed, until Tyler or Daddy got back.

While Amelia filled her days sleeping late, reading light romances, having the maids rearrange the furniture and taking rides in her carriage with Andy at the reins, another woman was on her way to Beauview.

Everyone on the goldfields knew her as Big Poll, and no one crossed Big Poll. She stood five feet ten in her socks and she had the build of a wrestler; her arms were massive and, it was said, she had legs like a working bullock. Poll and her husband were itinerants, picking up jobs wherever they could, but Poll did most of the work. She had at times been a drover and a station cook, then they'd found their way to the goldfields at Canoona and stayed put.

Poll like mining – there was always the chance of a big strike – and she worked harder and longer than any of the men for the sheer fun of it. Rain or shine, Poll was always on the job with her pick, or sluicing in creeks, a familiar figure in dusty clothes and a big straw hat with a net to protect her weather-beaten features from the ever-present flies and mosquitoes. When cash was short, she'd send her husband off to do a stint of station or town work, and gossips among the mining fraternity grinned, wondering why he ever came back to such a loud-mouthed, bullying harridan. There were tales galore about Poll: she'd broken a man's arm when she'd caught him stealing from her tent; she'd shot a claim-jumper in the foot; she'd belted a whore when she found out her husband was one of her customers.

But the hubby always came back. 'She's fair, my Poll,' he'd say. 'You have to give her that, and she's an honest woman.'

This time, though, he hadn't come back, and Poll was on the warpath. She'd find him, she always knew how to track her man because he couldn't pass a pub. It was just a matter of heading for Rockhampton, his stated destination, and following his trail from bar to bar.

'Can't miss him,' she'd say. 'Skinny bloke, shorter than me, carroty hair, long and scrawny, what he wears in a bit of a plait. Big nose, like a cocky's beak, and he drinks double rums, the bugger.'

And they knew him. Her best lead was a grog shop just outside Rockhampton. The proprietor poured her a tankard of his watered beer, looked at her again, and at her rifle resting on the counter, and changed his mind. He served Poll a pint of his 'right' beer. 'He's been here a few times. Once on his way into town looking for a job. Then next time I seen him he was with a gang heading north, pleased he got work. Never saw him for a good while after that, but then he turned up on his own, making for town again.'

'How long ago was this?'

'Hard to say. A month to six weeks, maybe.'

'That'd be right,' Poll said to her horse as she climbed back on. 'I give him a month or so to get hisself home as the jobs run down. I bet the bastard was on his way back then, but now another month's gone past so he's up to something. I'll wring his bloody ear when I get my hands on him.'

Three more pubs brought her into Rockhampton, where she was further enlightened. 'Yeah, I know him,' a barman told her. 'He works for Boyd Roberts. But I haven't seen him for a while.'

'Boyd Roberts?' she exclaimed. 'Stupid bugger! I told him to keep away from that crook. Where does Roberts hang out?'

Following directions, Poll rode up the hill and on through the imposing gateway. She gave a low whistle as her large horse clumped up the drive. 'We mighta known he'd be living like a bloody king,' she told her equine confidant.

'Whoa there,' a voice called and an old fellow, a gardener by the looks of things, bailed her up. 'You can't come in here!'

'I'm in here,' Poll said. 'I'm looking for my husband. Name of Tom Davies.'

'Never heard of him.'

'How long have you been working here?'

'Years.'

Poll sighed. She shook her head solemnly. Then she lifted up her rifle and aimed it at him. 'What's your name?'

His hands shot in the air as he called, 'Andy! The name's Andy! Put the gun down, you ain't got no right to come in here threatening people.'

'Shut up!' she said bluntly. 'Do some thinking instead. My husband works for Roberts and I want to know where he is.'

The boss has a lot of blokes working for him,' he whined. 'I can't remember all their names.

She pointed the gun at his foot. 'You'd better try or you'll be hopping instead of walking for a real long time.' She went on to describe Tom, his carroty hair, his beak nose, while Andy, facing the gun, his arms aching, tried to concentrate. Finally he did recall, and he let his arms drop.

'Did he have a squeaky voice?'

Poll nodded, watching closely as Andy bit his knuckles. 'Yeah, I think that'd be him. He joined up with a gang of miners. The boss sent them out prospectin'. Never seen that mob again.'

'Where did they go?'

'I couldn't tell you that. Honest.'

'Then I'd better see the boss.'

'He's not home. He's gone off north of the river someplace.'

She lowered the gun. 'When will he be back?'

'I don't know, I only work here.' He was so relieved that he was now out of danger that his mind was stimulated to try harder. 'Hang on,' he told the woman. 'Now I come to think of it, that feller did come back. I saw him myself. Yeah . . . that's right. He was on his own. Said he was just in to pick up his pay and then he was off back to Canoona. Are you *his* missus?' His tone conveyed wonderment that this bear of a woman, astride a mount parented by at least one draught horse, should be the spouse of that skinamalink.

She ignored the unspoken comment. 'Yes,' she growled. 'Sounds as if he's put his pay in a pub.'

Andy watched her leave. 'If I was married to that, I'd keep going too,' he muttered to himself, and went back to work.

Poll was confident now. 'He's blown his pay in a pub,' she figured. 'Wouldn't be bloody game to come home without it, so he'd have to find another job. I'll ferret out the bugger.'

But anger turned to concern as she stopped at first one pub and then another, until she had tried every bar in town. No one had sighted Tom Davies with cash in his pocket. She knew her Tom. He wouldn't just shoot through. After several days Poll rode back into Beauview.

This time Andy was nowhere in sight so she rode right up to the front steps of the swanky house.

A young girl with gypsy-black hair, looking pretty as a picture in pink muslin, stood angrily at the top of the steps. 'Who are you?' she demanded.

'Ada Adeline Davies, and who might you be?'

'I am Amelia Roberts. You are trespassing. I'll thank you to remove yourself!'

'You will, eh?' She dismounted, hitched up her skirts and marched up the steps. 'When'll your old man be home?'

Amelia stared at her, appalled. 'I don't know. Now go away.'

Poll took her arm in a vise-like grip and steered her along the veranda. 'You're too puny to give cheek. Now siddown! I'm looking for my husband, Tom Davies, and all trails lead to your fancy gate. I want to know if you've seen him.'

'Why would I have seen him?' Amelia stuttered, terrified of this woman, who, she was sure, had bruised her arm.

'He worked for Boyd Roberts.'

'Then I wouldn't have seen him. I don't meet the workmen.'

Poll looked at her and grinned through tobacco-stained teeth. 'No, I guess you wouldn't. But that don't alter the fact he was here. And I want to know where he's got to.'

'I wouldn't have the faintest idea.'

'He was riding a dapple-grey brumby. Have you seen that horse?'

'We have so many horses coming and going here. How would I know?'

'You can't miss Stoker,' Poll continued. 'Dapple-grey with a white blaze face on him and one of his ears got a nick in it, got winged by a bullet. The ear flops.'

The girl shrugged and looked away. 'It's ridiculous to expect me to remember their horses,' she sulked, but Poll caught a furtive expression in her eyes, a sudden dawning of recognition. She leaned over Amelia.

'You're lying,' she breathed, hoping she was right. Sometimes a bluff worked. 'I can see it in your eyes. Now, if you don't want me to brand that pretty cheek, you'd better speak up. The horse was here, wasn't it?'

Amelia began to weep. 'It might have been. I think so. It's not fair to do this to me.'

'You'll find out about fair when I'm finished with you. Now, you're coming with me around to your stables and we'll take a look.'

Petrified, Amelia clung to the chair. 'It's not there any more.'

'Good. Now we're getting somewhere. Where is it then?'

'It's been gone for weeks.'

'How long was it there?'

'I don't know. A while.'

'Then my Tom must have been here a while too, mustn't he?'

'I suppose so,' she whimpered. 'But he's gone now.'

'That's true, but if he only came here to pick up his pay, why would he leave without his horse? Can you tell me that, missy?'

'He probably took one of the other horses.'

'Oh no he didn't. He don't go no place without Stoker. You don't know my Tom, I'll grant you that, but you know the horse all right. You're a devious little brat and I wouldn't trust you any more than I'd trust your old man. Now get off your bum and come with me.'

She hauled Amelia down the steps and collected her rifle, holding it loosely in one hand while she grasped Amelia's arm in the other. 'One wrong move out of you, missy and I'll break this little pink arm. Now stand up and walk straight.'

They walked down to the stables with Poll's horse ambling along behind them. The odd trio startled the young stablehand, Teddy Wills.

'What's going on here?' he demanded.

'Nothing for you to worry about,' Poll said easily. 'We're looking for a horse. I want to buy it, don't I, miss?'

'Yes,' Amelia said in a rush.

'Which horse?' he asked suspiciously. He knew something was very wrong but the rifle warned him to be careful.

Poll described the horse. 'You know it?'

'Yeah.'

'Who owns it?'

'Mr Roberts, of course.'

'Where did it come from?' Poll asked

'It was just in the paddock. I don't know where the boss gets the horses from.'

'And where is it now?'

The stablehand looked at Amelia, as if that were a stupid question, and she blurted out the reply. 'One of the men would be riding it now and it's probably your husband. Why don't you just go away and leave us alone?'

The lad was perplexed. 'You're wrong there, miss. Don't you remember? That's the mount Mr Roberts gave to Mr Kemp.' He looked to Poll. 'But he wouldn't be for sale, missus, so you'd best look elsewhere to buy a horse. Mr Kemp fancied him.'

'My bad luck then,' Poll said, as if that settled the matter.

The stablehand scratched his head, staring as they turned away, and grinned as the woman's old nag, loaded with a swag and billy and canvas pack, wheeled about to follow his owner like a dog.

Amelia was stumbling, trying to keep up with this awful person who stank of sweat. She was too scared now even to cry, since her tears hadn't made any impact the first time.

Back at the steps Poll squeezed her arm until she yelped in pain. 'Who's Mr Kemp?'

'A guest. He's gone now.'

'With Stoker, you little bitch?'

'Yes,' Amelia screamed. 'Yes!'

'Then where is my Tom?'

'I told you I don't know.'

Poll let her go and she collapsed on to the wide steps. 'Well I want to know,' Poll snarled, 'and you tell that father of yours that until I find my Tom you lot are in big trouble. You and your dad and your fancy guest. You hear me, missy. Big bloody trouble!'

She climbed on her horse and rode back down the drive without looking back. At the gate she met Andy.

'Not you again?' He scowled.

'You never told me Tom left his horse here,' she accused him.

'What horse? I don't handle the horses. I've got enough to do here. It's bad enough getting roped in all the time to drive Miss Prissy around in her contraption.'

Poll nodded. She believed him. And she also knew something had happened to Tom. Right here.

She decided to camp out in the bush, out of reach of Roberts. He'd be bound to hear of her visit from the squalling kid. She knew his reputation, and while she intended to hang about and wait for him to get back, she wouldn't be stupid enough to make herself a target. She'd wait; sooner or later he'd be back, and then she'd have her answers.

The two maids had watched this episode from behind the curtains, giggling as the woman marched Miss Amelia about like a naughty child, but they changed their tune when their mistress came storming inside. 'How dare you leave me stuck with that old bag?' she screamed. 'She threatened me! In my own house! And all you did was stand and stare. I saw you! Never so much as lifted a finger to help me.'

'What could we do?' Dossie, the older one said. 'We'd be no match for her. And she had a gun.'

'Why didn't you run for help? She could have killed me,' Amelia raged, shoving a chair out of the way, knocking over a vase of flowers. 'You'll be sorry for this! You wait until I tell my father.'

Dossie tried to calm her. 'She's gone now. No need to get yourself in a state. What did she want anyway?'

'What did she want? It's none of your damn business what she wanted, you pair of cowards, skulking in here while I was being manhandled. When my father gets back he'll fire you, I'll see to that.'

'In that case you'd better pay us off now,' Dossie flared. 'We're paid to do the housework not mind you like you was a two-year-old.'

'Any more cheek from you and I will pay you off,' Amelia snapped. 'Now get back to work.'

'I think not,' Dossie said.

The other maid agreed. 'You can give us our pay now.'

'I haven't got any money,' Amelia stalled.

'Yes you have. In the desk drawer. You get it ready while we pack.'

Flustered, Amelia ran into her father's study, yanked open the drawer and tried to work out how much she owed them, scattering notes and coins on the table.

When they returned the cook was with them. 'If they go I go,' she declared.

'There's no need for you to leave,' Amelia said. 'I don't have any quarrel with you.'

The cook ignored her. 'Two pounds four shillings for me, and one pound seventeen shillings each for them.' She held out her hand and, shaking, Amelia counted out the money.

She watched them leave, carrying small cardboard suitcases, and then she flew into the garden searching for Andy. 'I want you to get the police up here right away.'

'What for?'

'A woman came here threatening me.'

'Who? That Mrs Davies?'

'Yes. Get the police. I want her arrested.'

'She don't mean no harm,' Andy said. 'She's only looking for her husband.' He grinned. 'He's probably bolted. You wouldn't blame him.'

'Didn't you hear what I said?' she shouted furiously. 'Go and get the police.'

Amelia considered telling off that stupid stableboy too, but he would keep. He was such a donkey he wouldn't know what she was talking about anyway. Besides, she'd had enough of staff for the time being, she felt positively ill.

It wasn't until much later that she realised she was alone in the house. She darted about, lighting lamps, and then ran down to the kitchen to find the stove stone cold and no meal prepared. Wind rattled the shutters, doors banged, timbers creaked and groaned. She hid in her bedroom, too frightened to go out into the night and search for Andy. She wasn't even sure where he slept.

Sergeant Jim Hardcastle was tired and fed up with everyone. A policeman could expect to have a busy, some would say adventurous, life, and that had suited him, until now, when everything seemed to be getting out of hand.

For a mining town, the early days of Rockhampton had been relatively peaceful, as peaceful goes. There'd been brawls and thievery and a couple of shootouts, the usual clashes with the Chinese, and a whorehouse war which resulted in a couple of the places being burned down, but nothing he couldn't handle. And that had surprised him. A big burly man of Scots-Irish descent, Jim could throw his weight around when needed, but no lawman in his right mind volunteered to take on a frontier mining town. He was a family man and when this post was offered, Jim had taken a fast step back, like all the rest.

Since no one volunteered, the authorities made their own choice, and it landed on him, because he had a good reputation and had done well in the many country towns to which he'd been assigned. Jim was angry. Surely good service shouldn't be rewarded in this manner? he had argued. These jobs should go to the rough and tough coppers like Tiger Brannigan and his mates.

To appease him, his Senior had suggested that if Jim could handle the policing of Rockhampton, they'd make it a permanent posting. Well, it was noted, for as long as the town lasted.

In the end it was his wife who had persuaded him to stop complaining and accept the assignment. She was thoroughly browned off, she said, from being shunted about from town to town. This was their chance to settle down and put their three kids to school. So the decision was made. They took up residence in a brand-new cottage beside the single-room station with the lockup round the back, and they'd come to enjoy the pleasant river town, all white and crisp now among the tropical greenery.

The gold, and new strikes, had kept the town going, but the

218

cattlemen operating the big stations in the surrounding districts had made Rockhampton their headquarters, and so its future was established. They were even building a big meatworks on the other side of the river, which would provide jobs for the unemployed; this town, like everywhere else in Queensland, was suffering from the débâcle in Brisbane.

How could a government run out of money? he kept asking himself. If he knew the answer he'd try to explain to his wife. He hadn't been paid for months and she was buying their provisions on tick, humiliating for her and exasperating for the shopkeeper, who was threatening to close the book until they paid up.

Jim had written countless polite and pleading letters to headquarters, and had received promises that all would be well soon. But when was soon? He'd even considered chucking it in and, as so many others had done, heading for the goldfields. Jim had heard a rumour that there was gold in the Ironstone Mountain not too far from the town, but it was only a rumour, nothing confirmed, so no one was taking it seriously.

The blacks were always a worry in the bush, but lately they'd gone berserk, and this on top of food riots in the town. It was ironic that he'd been called in to break up the riot outside the Golden Nugget during Maskey's party, when his own family was living on bread and dripping. Only one good thing had come out of that. After the troopers had cleared the area, Sergeant Hardcastle had been asked to remain in the hotel in case of further trouble. And what a feed he'd had that night! Not forgetting his family, and with the approval of the cooks, he'd filled up a sugarbag with leftovers – cold chickens, ham, beef, bread, and cakes for the kids. Along with the rest of the staff, he saw to it that not a scrap went to waste.

He'd gone out to Oberon Station to get a full report on the murders of the two women. He'd done his best to get the details without bothering a stunned MacNamara too much, and had stayed a couple of days with the posse to make certain the Oberon men knew they had permission to search for the killers as long as they remained within the law. Then, since there was nothing much more he could do there, he'd returned to town.

Gooding and his troop were missing, as usual, always in the wrong place at the wrong time, but he agreed with Gooding's offsider, Mick O'Leary, who had just returned from a long stint out west at Duaringa chasing mobs of blacks away from station homesteads, that his men deserved a rest. It was better that they remain on hand because the townspeople were getting jumpy, fearful of a mass attack by blacks on the township itself. Both Hardcastle and O'Leary knew that possibility was remote, but there was hysteria in the town, people driving Jim mad, demanding he do something or they'd all be murdered in their beds!

He gave a wry grin as he wrote up his daily report. O'Leary and his men, at Jim's request, kept visible, riding busily through the streets mornings and evenings to allay fears. But why they all insisted they'd be murdered in their beds, instead of getting out there and defending themselves was a mystery to him. There was a real madness in the town lately. They were all bloody mad. Too much sun, he supposed.

Mad? he thought. What about Captain Cope and his black soldiers? He'd had to pull Cope out of a pub; he'd been on a permanent binge since he'd been jilted by Laura Maskey. 'Smart girl,' Hardcastle commented to himself. Cope was showing his true colours now. No spunk at all.

'Sent Cope to take charge of his troopers,' the Sergeant wrote. 'They came south from Sinclair's station and arrived at Oberon Station several days after the attack. They had been ambushed at the McCann station.'

He crossed out 'McCann' and wrote 'Roberts', with a frown. Bloody Roberts! Darling of the would-bes in the town, throwing around money like it was going out of fashion, building up a big following, making a run for Parliament. He was one for a lowly copper to treat with care, now that Maskey was gone.

That reminded him. He hadn't written up his report on the destruction of the offices of the *Capricorn Post*. Prior to that, Cosmo Newgate had suddenly started to run articles, probably libellous, about Roberts, which the Sergeant had read with interest. Indeed, he'd filed them for reference, because suspicious though he might be about Roberts, he had nothing to go on, no proof of criminal activities. And then the *Post* was put out of action.

Newgate declared it was Roberts' work, and it probably was, but Roberts was out of town. No doubt he'd sent some men in to shut down the *Post*. Once again, though, where was the proof?

Hardcastle suddenly remembered that two days ago, Roberts' daughter had sent a fellow in, calling the police to Beauview. It hadn't sounded very important but he supposed he'd better get out there. Although why she couldn't come into town herself . . .

Anyway. Back to this written report: 'They had lost three men in a battle with tribal blacks, and the homestead there had been burned down by these blacks, who then proceeded to raid the next property, Oberon, where they killed the two women. I deployed the remaining three troopers to assist the Oberon posse until their Captain arrived.'

He wasn't sure how to write the next bit, so he closed the thick vellum book, deciding to attend to it later.

Jim had received a letter from MacNamara charging that Blackie Bob had shot dead a defenceless captive native. He'd challenged Cope about this. Cope had blamed Roberts – always Roberts when there was trouble – and said that Roberts had given the order, which Blackie had simply obeyed.

Nevertheless, Blackie was now in the lockup, complaining bitterly that he'd shot plenty black trash on orders from whitefellers, especially Cope, so what was so different now?

The difference, Jim thought, was that this time the shooting had been witnessed by men who believed in justice. Jim admired MacNamara for lodging this complaint at a time when he could be forgiven for overlooking such a shooting, but he wished someone else had written the letter. Already Cope was claiming that MacNamara was half off his head with grief and had got it all wrong. And it was MacNamara who had sent Cope and his Native Police packing, instead of keeping them there to continue the search.

Cope had brought the three of them home. Blackie was in the lockup. Stan Hatbox was lumbering around squealing about the pain in his side from the spear wound. Which had healed. And the other one, Charlie Penny, was lying out there in the grass, claiming he was dying.

Jim shook his head in disgust. He hated bookwork and this story was too much. If he wrote it he'd get certified. He'd called the doctor, who'd examined Charlie thoroughly and said there was nothing at all wrong with him. Nevertheless, Charlie was getting worse, day by day, and even a hiding hadn't made him get up on his feet.

As he passed the lockup this morning, after another attempt to shake Charlie up, Blackie had called to him, 'No hope there, boss. Magic feller point the bone at Charlie. He's a goner.'

He'd talked to Blackie and to Stan, and they were adamant. Charlie would be dead in a day or so. He'd gone back to reason with Charlie, telling him this bone business was a joke, asking who had put the spell on him, but all Charlie could do was sigh. And wait.

Jim had heard about this heathen practice but never believed it. Now he was watching it happen before his eyes. Or maybe it wouldn't. Charlie might get bored lying out there with his imaginary ills. He'd send Stan Hatbox over to him with a bottle of rum. That would wake him up.

The last straw this morning was in the post. Captain Cope's pay had arrived at last. Cope, who'd been off duty for weeks, had got his pay while Sergeant Hardcastle was still hanging out for his. Was it any wonder he was getting fed up with this job?

He decided to ride out to Beauview to see what the Roberts girl wanted.

'About time,' she snapped when she came out to answer his knock. She didn't bother to ask him in for a cup of tea, which he would dearly have loved right now.

She raved on about a woman called Ada Adeline Davies who had come to her door uninvited and threatened her.

'Why would she threaten you?'

'She was looking for her husband.' Miss Roberts sniffed. 'An awful woman she was, as big as a barn and smelled like one too. I told her I didn't know anything about her husband, a workman of some sort.

221

But she took my arm – look at it, I've still got the bruise – and dragged me around to the stables.'

'Why the stables?'

Miss Roberts began to cry. 'I'm sure I don't know. But I want her arrested. People shouldn't be allowed to march in like that and assault people.'

'Do you wish to prefer charges, miss?'

'Of course I do. I'll have her up for assault.'

'Very well. I'm sorry you were upset. You must have had a bad fright. Now you go in and take it easy. Leave things to me.'

He talked to the gardener, who was watching the conversation with interest, and then strolled around to talk to the stableboy, young Teddy Wills.

Teddy's answers enlightened him more than had the mistress of the house. She hadn't mentioned the horse.

As he made his way into town, Jim Hardcastle reckoned that Boyd Roberts might not appreciate his daughter calling the police. He had a case of a missing man, by the sounds of things, which rang a bell. Hadn't there been a fellow in town some time back who had threatened to kill Roberts for some wrong, and then had suddenly left town? And this time there was a missing horse too. Except that the horse had been found. Presented by Roberts to Tyler Kemp, that reporter fellow.

It was all very interesting. He'd have to find this Ada Adeline Davies to piece these bits together. But as for arresting her? The gardener hadn't seemed worried about her. It was just the girl being overwrought. He'd rather talk to Mrs Davies than arrest her. Maybe she'd like to lay her own charges against Roberts, if that bit about the horse would hold water.

The day had brightened up no end.

Tyler called his horse Greybeard, since no one at Beauview seemed to know or care what his name was.

'He's just a stray,' George had told him. George was, he'd discovered, Boyd's right-hand man, a lean and hungry character with an overshot jaw and a patchy moustache, which Tyler guessed was a poor effort to copy the boss's healthier bristles.

'The boss buys a few at a time,' George had explained, 'so they're on hand if they're needed. If you don't like him, pick another one. He's no youngster.'

'No. He'll do just fine, thank you,' Tyler had replied. Now, after weeks on the trail, and preparing to move out again, he was glad he had hung on to Greybeard. 'You're a good fellow,' he said, patting his horse as he mounted up with the troopers, 'even if you are a brumby. There's a good strain in your ancestors, my lad.'

Greybeard swung his head up and down as if pleased with the compliment, and Tyler laughed. The head was big and rough, not saved by the white blaze, and one ear flopped. He was a big-boned animal, with strong shoulders, but he was sure-footed as a goat and had a placid temperament. And could he move? Tyler was astonished to find that this ungainly animal could go like the wind, outrace the troopers' finer horses every time. Some good horse, this one. Tyler had offered to buy him from Boyd, who had laughed. 'No. You keep him. He's only a brumby, not worth feeding.'

After all these weeks Tyler had gained new respect for Greybeard and considered him the best deal he'd ever made. No way would he part with him now.

The other horses snorted and stamped impatiently as the troopers and Tyler waited for Lieutenant Gooding and MacNamara to take their leave of the Carlisles.

In his Brisbane days, Tyler had enjoyed being just a face in the crowd, a watcher, an intent observer, but having anonymity planted on him like a dunce's cap did not sit well with him. Astride his horse among the troopers he was just one of the obediently waiting horsemen, ignored by the station hierarchy. He tried to appear disinterested, unconcerned, as he tightened up his stirrups, checked the rifle that he'd been issued, anything to look too busy to care.

Laura Maskey was over there too. He'd had no contact with her on this short stay at Camelot but she must have known he was in Gooding's party. The thought of her reminded him of Amelia, and he was disappointed that they could not, at least, have conversed about their mutual friend, about his forthcoming marriage. Obviously that article in the *Post* had offended her and he'd been crossed off her list of acquaintances.

Tyler shrugged. That was a risk a reporter had to take. His conscience didn't bother him, it was just a nuisance that the family here had decided to take her side and punish him.

Amelia. He'd only been able to send her one letter to date, so he'd written last night and left the letter to go out with Camelot mail. He missed her terribly and told her so, and he'd promised to be back with her as soon as possible, probably only a couple of weeks now. He hadn't mentioned, though, that he'd been having the time of his life, riding away, free as a bird, no deadline to meet, no dreary articles to write, no politics to keep up with. How trivial all that seemed now. Who cared which ones were foolish, sycophantic, stupid, greedy or plain corrupt? Who cared about their policies? Now that Premier Herbert was back in control, would he be able to fix the financial bust, or would things simply right themselves according to the laws, not of the legislators, but of gravity? Tyler no longer gave a damn. He would go back to Rockhampton, marry Amelia, have his own house and his own paper which would do well because he'd fill the pages with what his local readers wanted to hear. They were interested in horses, gold and cattle, and for the women, recipes and more recipes.

They were taking their time, the lords and ladies of this homestead, and their favoured guests. There was excitement among this small group of horsemen, and trepidation. The horses seemed to feel it too, chuffing hot breaths into the cold air, sniffing at the light dawn breezes as if searching for a clue, eager to be away. At last Gooding and MacNamara were striding towards them, swinging on to their horses and, with a wave, setting off at a trot.

Not to be outdone, and feeling he was entitled to some pride of place, Tyler fell in behind them, the troopers at his rear. Unlike the others, he refused to look back. They were on a hunt now, a real adventure, no more just showing the flag. Far in the distance the great Berserker Ranges reared up and Tyler experienced a barb of fear. The ranges were unexplored, unknown, full of danger, and the writer in him suddenly felt the power and thrill of the word 'Berserker'. He'd been told that the ranges were named after a Norse God or chieftain who went berserk before or during battle. Nervously, he wondered if the name were an omen and not just an accident of time and place.

The nine men were cantering steadily across open country, Greybeard sailing along with his powerful, easy gait, the faces about the reporter calm, splendid even, in their acceptance of the dangers ahead. He cursed his imagination, a writer's gift, but, for a soldier, blessedly unnecessary.

At their first rest-stop, MacNamara came down and introduced himself. 'I didn't know you were at Camelot,' he said, obviously unaware of the undercurrents of disfavour. Probably, Tyler guessed, no one wanted to bother him with explanations, and he felt no necessity to do so now.

'I've been wanting to meet you for quite a while,' Tyler said.

MacNamara looked surprised. 'Why?'

'It's not important now, but I wanted to get a lead on the Native Police. Their activities bother me but they don't seem to bother anyone else. I was told you don't have a lot of time for them.'

'I don't.'

'Yeah, well, we might discuss them some time.'

MacNamara studied him. 'Gooding said you want to come with us when we head into the hills. Why?'

Tyler lit his pipe. 'Don't ask me. Gooding doesn't seem to think a scribbler would be any use. He can see me, feet up, at your house until you return. It's a dare I can't turn down.'

He was sorry he'd said that. MacNamara turned to him, his brown eyes full of pain, his voice quiet. 'Then you'd better stay at the house. I don't want the responsibility.'

'You don't have to. Forget that side of the story. If you can do with an extra hand I'd like to help. I mean, I'm not going to fall off my horse.'

'No,' he replied thoughtfully. 'I've noticed. But listen, we're not going up there to shoot up the blacks or even to stir them up. I just want answers.' He looked about him, frustrated with his failure to date. 'Someone knows. Someone has to tell me.' He watched the troopers watering their horses in a creek, and muttered, 'I have to find them, I won't be able to live with myself if I don't. It won't ever be over.'

A day later they were riding towards the Oberon homestead, and Tyler felt gloom settling. The day moon was a wisp of white against a sky of silky blue, the valley pastures were turning blond, and the homestead, more cottage-like than the others he had encountered, with a fading green bull-nosed roof over the long front veranda, looked deserted. They rode past the front gate, past a wretched dried-out garden edged by thirsty bushes, pushing on to a large barn, and dismounted at a clump of lank-leafed acacias that separated the house from the outbuildings.

A bald-headed man marched across the yard at the rear of the house to greet them, the only living soul, it seemed, in this beleaguered outpost, except for a rosy host of galahs seed-gathering, unconcerned, in a grassy patch behind a railed fence.

'Who are you?' Paul asked uncertainly.

'I'm the cook,' he said, folding massive arms over a dirty singlet. 'Baldy, they call me. You the boss, are you?'

'Yes. How long have you been here?'

'Gus put me on a coupla days ago. I heard you needed a cook so I just turned up, and Bob's your uncle. These blokes staying on?'

'Overnight,' Paul replied.

'Righto, boss. Don't worry about it. I know what I'm doing. Didn't expect them but I'll get them all fed.'

Tyler winced. He realised that Paul was accustomed to being met by women and was having trouble adjusting to this new order of things, this grubby knot-head only making matters worse. He should have known that returning to Oberon would be a strain for MacNamara, but until now he hadn't given it a thought. He looked to Gooding to ease the situation, and the Lieutenant nodded, moving his men into action. 'Where will they camp?' he asked Paul.

'In the bunkhouse down there,' Paul said dully. 'Gus will allot the bunks when he comes in.'

'Tyler and me?'

'The house.' Paul was standing, white-faced, looking towards the homestead, and he seemed unable to proceed. Until now, Tyler had regarded the murders as a news item, talked about, argued about, a shocking affair but distant, unrelated to his pursuits. But witnessing MacNamara's distress brought it home to him with a thud, and he didn't know what to do.

Gooding instructed his men to attend to the horses, and Tyler watched their sorrowful faces as they hurried to their tasks, young men, pathetically eager to ease things for this man, once again, or perhaps freshly, confronted with his tragedy.

Tyler considered himself hard-boiled, resilient, from the buffeting he had taken in his early days of reporting crime and vice in Brisbane. He knew that the twelve years he'd spent there since leaving the innocence of the mountains had hardened him, made him more cynical, had even – the thought lodged suddenly – laid the groundwork for him to accommodate Boyd Roberts in order to win Amelia. And consequently to aspire to the wealth that he'd disdained in others.

Watching MacNamara now, he felt a surge of pity for the man, and – God help him! – a sting of tears, as the tall, strong figure made a determined effort to walk towards his house only for his legs to buckle under him.

Tyler leapt forward and grabbed him before he fell, supporting him, with the dumb-arsed cook standing nonchalantly looking on.

'I'll be all right,' Paul gritted, pushing Tyler away, forcing himself to stand erect.

'Good!' Tyler said, resurrecting his own gruff exterior. 'I'd give a quid for a drink.'

'Me too,' his host said stiffly. Together they crossed the sun-dried yard, passing long tables under a low shingle roof, obviously an outdoor dining area. They climbed the steps into a big, untidy kitchen and went on through to a formal dining room. It was overfurnished, the mahogany table and chairs crowded by sideboards and a tallboy that lined the walls, and a heavy couch that sat lumpily under the window. It had lost the woman's touch, carrying layers of dust and a forlorn air.

MacNamara pulled out a chair and sat down. 'We never ate in here much,' he mused absently. 'I never gave her the time.'

'We never had a dining room,' Tyler responded. 'We lived and ate in the kitchen.' He spied decanters on a sideboard and sniffed at them. 'Whisky?' he asked the owner of the house.

'Yes. Glasses down below.'

Tyler poured two decent slugs of whisky, put the decanter on the table and retrieved a jug of water from the kitchen so that he could add a dash to each glass. 'We made good time,' he said, making conversation. 'Your manager will be pleased to see you back.'

'Gus? Yes . . .' Paul threw his hat on to the couch and downed half of his drink. He ran a finger along the dust on the table. 'Doesn't take long for the dust to build up,' he commented. 'We used to get terrible dust storms out west, red dust, but we're more sheltered here.'

'It's lovely country,' Tyler proffered.

Paul was tracing zigzag lines on the tabletop. He smiled. 'My mother used to say you can write your name in the dust, but not the date.'

That effort transformed the morose features, for a few seconds, into a twinkling, humorous face. Tyler felt he was seeing the real person for the first time, a cheerful man behind the mask of pain.

When Paul refilled their glasses, Tyler took his chance. This situation intrigued him. 'What if we don't find the men you want?'

226

'We'll find them.'

'But what if you don't? I can only guess at what you're going through, but you don't have any witnesses and I doubt you will find the culprits.'

'What do you care?'

Tyler sat up in his chair. 'First, I don't want any part in indiscriminate vengeance . . .'

'That won't happen.'

'I heard you've been pretty tough on your local blacks.'

'I got rid of them, that's all.'

'And one got dead. An innocent man.'

Paul stared at him over his raised glass. 'What's your second question?'

'You. You're all knotted up. You should leave this search to the proper authorities. Gooding and his men.'

'Like hell I will. What makes you such an expert?'

'Newspaper men. We see a lot. We see the aftermath that you don't read in papers, how this sort of thing can destroy families, destroy the survivors who in their turn become victims. Have you talked to anyone about this? About how you feel?'

'There's nothing to talk about, for Christ's sake! What are you? The parish priest?'

'I'm not a Catholic,' Tyler said coolly, 'but that wouldn't be a bad start.' Gooding had told him that Mrs Carlisle was very concerned about this man, who had filled in his time at Camelot with work but had hardly spoken to anyone and had refused to be drawn into any conversations. 'It's not like him at all,' she'd said. 'It mustn't go on. He has to learn how to recover.'

Paul looked moodily to the window. 'It's growing dusk. The men will be in soon. I'll show you your room.'

The meal was a gloomy occasion. Tyler soon learned that Mrs MacNamara and the servant girl had provided excellent meals, but Baldy was a disaster. Gus had sent word out that they desperately needed a capable male cook at Oberon, but in the meantime they were stuck with this one.

In deference to the boss, too loyal to complain in his presence, they all sat stolidly while Baldy dished out a greasy stew, blackened potatoes and a stodgy pudding. Eyes lowered, the stockmen watched Paul begin his stew, hoping for an eruption, hoping Baldy would meet MacNamara's Irish temper, but instead, Paul pushed his plate away, excused himself and left the table.

The aftermath was a barrage of insults, some hilarious, hurled at Baldy.

'It does no good,' Gus told Tyler. 'The bastard can't even boil water, and he thinks he's doing a great job. We never knew how spoiled we were with Jeannie and Clara doing the cooking.'

Tyler sat in on a meeting called by MacNamara with Gooding and

Gus, the foreman. They discussed the intended route into the mountains. 'You know where we're headed,' Paul said to Gus. 'We can see the main camps from here.'

'How can you tell?' Gooding asked.

'Come outside and take a look,' Gus said.

Tyler went with them, and sure enough, up in the highlands, the tiny lights of campfires dotted a definite area, so high in the blackness they were almost indistinguishable from stars.

'In the last trouble,' Gus said, without bothering to explain what that had been, 'when the clans gathered, there were so many of them that those hills looked like the Milky Way. We thought we might be attacked then, but they gradually drifted off. That's how we keep track of how many are up there.'

'How many *are* up there?' Gooding asked.

Gus shook his head. 'We only reckon it as a good few, or too many. A couple of months back there were too many, but we figure a lot of them have migrated from this valley, not to mention the local lads we've chased off, and have gone to ground in the hills.'

'Then there should be more fires.'

'Not necessarily,' Gus said. 'It's kinder country on the other side. More tropical, better tucker. They've got the sea on that side too. If they can't fish in our rivers they're better off turning to the sea.'

'Good God!' the Lieutenant exclaimed. 'And what happens to the settlers on the coastal strip?'

Tyler stared at him. 'Jesus, man! The poor buggers have to eat. Are you denying these people access to any food at all? Is this what you're about?'

'I'm about keeping the peace,' Gooding retorted.

'Doesn't sound like it to me,' Tyler growled.

Paul MacNamara intervened. 'Our immediate job is to get in there and find these killers. If they've raped and killed white women and got away with it, they'll do it again. I don't care whether we're talking about whites or blacks,' he went on. 'Men who commit these crimes will do it again if they're not caught. And you, Newspaperman, tell me I'm wrong.'

'No,' Tyler admitted. 'You're not wrong. But I object to this business of worrying about bloody settlers while you're depriving a whole tribe of their livelihood, their only sustenance.'

'Who's doing that?' Paul demanded.

'You are. I've been listening to your men tonight. They tell me that you said you're going to drive all the black bastards into the sea, and they're in total agreement. You're the one setting the fuse here, and you're using Gooding for your own purposes. You want revenge and you don't bloody care how many get mown down in the process.'

Paul MacNamara gazed at him, dark eyes thunderous. 'You don't know what you're talking about. You're not coming with us. You can stay here and teach bloody Baldy how to cook.'

In an effort to keep the peace, Gooding spoke. 'Tyler, what happens on the coastal strip is another matter. Unrelated. I do think it would be better if you remained here at Oberon.'

'Oh no you don't,' Tyler said angrily, appalled that his own temper was closing down his escape route from this perilous hunt. 'I'm the press. I still represent the *Brisbane Courier*. If you refuse to permit me to accompany you, Lieutenant, then I'm entitled to inform the public that you have reason to wish not to be observed.'

'Let him stay,' MacNamara drawled. 'Who gives a damn?'

Gus was more interested in practical matters. 'You can't leave in the morning, Paul. We just haven't got the provisions. Baldy's useless. We're flat out mustering and branding, we've got hundreds of calves out there and they're bloody beautiful. I can't wait for you to get a look at them. But if you want tucker, food you can swallow, you're going to have to stay here tomorrow and make that idiot shape up. If he puts in a day's proper cooking you'll have enough to feed your mates here for a few days at least. We haven't got any preserved meat left.'

Tyler didn't mind the delay, using it to wander about the gentle valley homestead. He observed the fenced-off area where the crimes had taken place, but from a sense of reverence, and superstition, kept well away. He stared at it from a distance, from the safety of the house, and he looked at those mountains, and a terrible fear grasped him. He had intended to write to Amelia again. Instead he wrote to his parents, telling them, for the very first time, how much he loved them, and how wonderful and carefree his childhood had been. Then he took stock of the amount of liquor he'd consumed that night and tore up the sentimental, out-of-character letter. More than a little drunk, he fell on the bed, grateful that the morrow would afford his woozy head a day of rest.

In the morning, talking to the troopers, Tyler was relieved to find that they were just as ambivalent about this expedition as he was; excited about the prospect of taking on those ranges, but apprehensive of their chances if they were attacked.

'They fight by stealth,' one man, called Rory, complained.

'This ain't the Crimea,' another fellow laughed. 'What do you expect them to do? Mark out a battleground and come at our guns?'

Corporal Sam Harvey was more positive. 'The blokes working on the station reckon MacNamara knows what he's doing. He'll catch the bastards, hang 'em and that'll be that.'

'Is that legal?' Tyler asked, confused again.

They laughed at him. 'What's legal out here?'

At Airdrie Station they'd cleared the site of McCann's burned-out homestead, managing to salvage some of the cedar, then Roberts had sent two of his men over to the goldfields with instructions to check his mines to make sure there was no thieving going on. He kept his three most trusted men with him, men, including George Petch, who had been with him for years.

To them, he seemed just to be taking it easy after the battering MacNamara had given him, but Boyd was only biding his time. MacNamara would pay and pay dearly for his actions, it was just a matter of working out how, without having the finger of blame pointed at him. There was still the bigger prize of Parliament to be considered.

Oberon cattle had wandered on to his property, so, in the guise of the good neighbour, he ordered two of the men to round them up and hand them on to Oberon stockmen. They were also told to find out what was happening on Oberon and report back. Meanwhile, he and George amused themselves on a turkey shoot.

Since Boyd always travelled with packhorses, his camp was comfortable, and he was happy to while away the days waiting for information and for a plan of action to materialise. As soon as he heard that MacNamara was back, accompanied by Lieutenant Gooding and his troops, and preparing for a peaceful expedition into the ranges, he made his decision, knowing he'd have to move quickly.

Peaceful, he grinned, was the operative work. He'd give them peaceful.

When he outlined his plan, George was raring to go, and the four men, heavily armed, rode straight for the hills. They wasted no time in the lowlands, crashing up into the forests on a search for any blacks they could find. By mid-morning, they found a trail of sorts and followed it more cautiously until they emerged at a ridge which looked over a clearing by a tumbling stream. Sure enough, a mob of blacks were camped there, serenely unaware that they were being observed.

Women were working on the banks, talking loudly, laughing, calling to each other. Children were racing about. Several men wandered among them and others dozed in the shade.

'I told you these hills were alive with them,' George muttered.

'How many?' Roberts asked, lying flat on the ridge.

'About twenty, not counting the kids.'

'Good. Can you take Baxter and get upwind of them?'

'Yes. Give us a bit of time.'

'Right. Then I'll drop down here with Freddy and we'll surprise them. Now don't forget, we've got to take three men alive. I don't care if you wing them, just get them.'

One hour later, the attack came from both sides. The gunfire was so loud and incessant it seemed that the small group of blacks were being attacked by an army. Unable to scale the ridge they raced into the stream, dragging the children, panicking and screaming as one by one their members went down, some shot dead, some wounded under the hail of indiscriminate shooting. The stream ran red with blood, there was no time to fight back, they could only think of escape.

Moving quickly forward, Boyd's men stopped two blackfellows at gunpoint, backing them against the low cliff as Boyd walked through the bodies on the beach and pointed to a black man who was lying, moaning, at the water's edge, a bullet in his shoulder.

'He'll do,' Boyd said. 'Hang on to him. There are others still alive here, a couple of gins. Finish them off.'

Once George had carried out that macabre duty, they were ready to leave. Taking their hostages, they backed away, warily now, in case of a counterattack. But all was quiet, so they edged back up to their horses, dragging the wounded man with them.

With the men roped to their saddles they began the descent, directly downhill, the horses scrambling to avoid trees and fallen logs, and the terrified prisoners, roped by the neck, choking as they ran, desperate to keep up with the pace or suffer the consequences.

Boyd led them to a narrow gully which his horse, unhindered by a prisoner, took in a leap. The others had to drop down and scale the other side. George and Baxter made it easily, with their captives pulling themselves up the steep slippery bank with more ease than the horses, but Freddy, at the rear, had the wounded native.

With blood pouring from his shoulder, he'd stumbled along, keeping clear of the hooves of the animal, and although he was in great pain he refused to make a sound, to cry out and have these white men hear his weakness. Goorari was a young, fit man, and he believed his body deserved this punishment for his humiliating failure to protect his family. As the women had fallen, he'd run forward, only to be shot in the back and, having plunged to the ground, the shock had kept him there too long. He should have jumped up and run for his spears which were nearby, but everything had happened so fast, that before he could move a gun was at his back and it was too late.

But Goorari had no intention of letting these killers drag him away. He watched for his chance and when they came to the gully he took it. Trailing the white fellow, he waited until he was above him as they descended the bank, then leapt forward, the pain a stimulant rather than a hindrance now as he landed on the white man, hurling him from his horse, strong hands tearing at that hated face, ripping and gouging.

Freddy screamed as they crashed to the ground, and to make matters worse, the horse lost its balance, lurching with the weight of the two struggling men and going down too, rolling on top of them.

'Shoot him!' Roberts roared. George obeyed, and fired at the native but he missed, and hit the horse.

There was no need to shoot Goorari. He was still tied to the knob of the saddle and the last frantic thrashings of the doomed horse had jerked him backwards and broken his neck. He was dead.

'Get him off me,' Freddy was shouting. 'Get the bloody horse off me. He's hurt me chest! And Jesus! Me bloody leg's broken.'

Immediately Baxter turned his horse about, undoing the rope that held the prisoner, handing it to George. 'You hold him. I'll go back for Freddy.'

'No you won't,' George said. 'Leave him.'

'But he's my mate!' Baxter cried. He appealed to Boyd, who shook his head.

'We haven't got time. Every nigger in the hills will be after us by this.' He spurred his horse and took off.

'We can't just leave him, they'll catch him,' Baxter yelled. George shoved the rope at him, the wild-eyed native trapped between them.

'He should have been more careful,' George said. 'You watch this one and don't let him jump you.'

Baxter was still uncertain, listening to Freddy's screams.

'He'll be dead soon anyway,' George said, 'and if you don't want to join him, you get a bloody move on.'

Baxter took one last look at the awful scene and turned away. 'Sorry, mate,' he yelled, afraid to delay any more. He jerked his prisoner into line, fastened him to his saddle again and set off after George and Roberts who were already moving out of sight.

Back at their camp at nightfall, Boyd was pleased with the raid, but he knew they were still in danger. They had a quick meal and packed up by lamplight. When the packhorses were ready he led his group, with the prisoners, west, away from Airdrie Station, avoiding Oberon, travelling slowly but steadily through the night.

He was heading for Bunya Creek, a new goldfield adjacent to the Fitzroy River. All the way along, he badgered his two prisoners, talking to them about the white gins who were killed. He even fed them, and apart from their mode of travel was generally rather kind to them. He and George smiled at them a lot, had them grinning at times, and in an insidious way gained a little of their confidence. He taught them to say 'yes'. He taught them to say 'kill' and to show him the actions of a spear. He shot a kangaroo and laid it in front of them and had them show how they could plunge a spear into it. The poor bewildered Aborigines, both in their twenties, had no idea they were being rehearsed for a suicidal play.

Baxter understood now that they were about to become heroes, bringing in murderers, and he soon forgot about Freddy, realising that it would have been nigh on impossible to bring him out of the hills without a stretcher, and that Boyd was right. To linger would have brought the wrath of the tribal blacks down on their heads. He and George joined the teaching process with gusto and soon the natives knew words like 'tucker', 'fire', 'burn', 'spear', 'woman', and quite a few more, although it was doubtful that they knew the meanings. The main object was to prove that these two could speak some English, that they had been interrogated, without injurious coercion, and had admitted to the crimes.

Boyd was in no hurry – the lessons were more important than speed – and it was four days before he rode through the diggings and the crowds of miners and their families, with two prisoners in tow – a ferocious-looking pair of coal-black naked niggers, with flaring nostrils and jaws like basalt.

Women hid their children in their skirts while they craned, fearful of these creatures, one of whom had a bone, said to be a human one, through his nose. Men spat, gathering in procession behind them.

Someone rang a bell and others came running from the heaving, littered landscape of felled trees, shafts and dusty mounds. They came from their tents at the edge of the bush and from the sluice and rattling rigs down by the creek to watch as Boyd Roberts, playing at Pontius Pilate, handed over his prisoners.

'I've done my part,' he announced. 'I believe they are guilty, but it is up to you men to decide for yourselves.'

With that, a court was assembled – a kangaroo court, some might have said. Four men, including a nervous Mines Inspector, were thrust forward to do their duty and interrogate the prisoners.

Boyd Roberts and his two men took no part in it. Nor did they bother to mention that Freddy had been killed, feeling it would confuse the now rabid mobs shouting for justice.

As Boyd had predicted, the hearing was a foregone conclusion. Questioned relentlessly before this crush of strange white people, the prisoners, not even understanding the questions, dug their own graves every time they answered in the affirmative. And so it went on, trapping them at every turn.

The verdict, eventually, was unanimous, these fellows were indeed the killers. But the punishment was not a unanimous decision. Even though guilt had been established, the Mines Inspector suggested they ought to be taken into Rockhampton. He was howled down. Fears arose that they might escape. That their tribal mates could attack the Bunya diggings to try to rescue them. Fears possible, fears preposterous, were voiced, rolling from wife to husband, from neighbour to stranger, tolling judgement. Some present had seen public hangings back home in Newgate Street and were eager to get this done, others lusted to bear witness to such an event. Their violent reactions caused the Mines Inspector to retreat.

Ropes were found, a sturdy tree was chosen, and a Christian gentleman was pushed forward to read passages from the Bible over the condemned, and therefore formalise this necessary procedure.

Understanding their fate now, the two Aborigines of the Kutabura tribe, sons of the great Darambal nation, accepted the jostling and the abuse.

Over the treetops, hundred of red-tailed black cockatoos wheeled, shrieking as if in dismay. Only the black men watched their brilliant progress. As the birds grew in number and turned about in an arc, they almost, for an instant, blotted out the sun. Then they were gone, flashing mightily across the blue, circling, screeching. Few of the whites noticed – the birds were a common sight in these parts – but the Kutabura men stood bravely erect, comforted that they would be escorted into the Dreamtime by their totem people, who had not failed them. For everything in nature, they knew had its genesis in man, and their time had come to explore the skies with these proud people.

Boyd did not wait for the hangings.

'Well, lads,' he said. 'We make fast now for Rockhampton, but keep your rifles handy. After our hard work we don't need to be gunned down by bushwhackers.'

George was disappointed at missing the hangings. 'I've never seen a hanging,' he complained.

'Then you'd better keep your mouth shut or you might see your own,' Boyd grinned. 'How are you, Baxter?'

'Goodoh, boss,' Baxter replied uncertainly.

'I'm sorry about Freddy,' Boyd said. 'He was a good hand. A bloody good hand.'

'That he was,' Baxter agreed.

'But he'd been badly hurt. All we could have done was sling him over one of our horses, and he wouldn't have thanked you for putting him through that agony, son. The horse crushed him.'

'I know that,' Baxter agreed, 'but he was always a good mate, was Freddy. When I tell his sister a bloody nigger got him killed she'll be upset, I can tell you.'

George brushed his hand across his chin and glanced at Roberts with a significant tilt of his bushy eyebrows. Boyd's deliberately kind expression froze. 'You don't have to tell her he's dead,' he offered. 'Why hurt people? Do you like his sister?'

'Oh yes,' Baxter said. 'I'm past thirty now. Time I settled down. Myra lives in Brisbane, she works in some sort of factory. I've got a few quid together now, next time down there I'm going to pop the question.'

'Then she won't want to hear you left her brother for dead,' George challenged.

'I never did!' Baxter cried. 'You know that! We didn't have any choice.' He was riding alongside George and in his distress he jerked his horse to a halt. 'Cripes! Don't lay that on me.' He took off his hat and shoved a hand through his lank fair hair. In his way Baxter was a good-looking chap, Roberts observed, not rough as bags like old George. He was sun-tanned and slim, just the type girls would go for. His facial features were even – straight nose, firm jaw and good teeth – but his eyes were pallid blue, watery, red-rimmed, they gave away his breeding. Somewhere there a brumby had got in. The eyes were as vacant, as stupid, as their owner.

'If there's an enquiry,' Boyd sighed, 'we'd have to say we went after those killers, and nothing wrong with that.' He almost laughed as Baxter nodded agreement. Having sat through that kangaroo court, Baxter, the idiot, was as convinced as the rest of the diggers, not having the brain to retain information.

234

And that was what saved Baxter, otherwise Boyd would have had to ask George to get rid of him. Sometimes stupidity was convenient, Boyd mused, then corrected himself. Nearly always stupidity was convenient, because it was from those ranks that he drew his troops. George himself wasn't all that bright, just doggedly loyal, like a cattle dog, and like the dog he knew where his bread was buttered. So Boyd used the same premise on Baxter.

'You're thinking of getting married?' he said, with a teasing smile. 'You didn't tell us this before. We've got a lover on our hands, George. I'd say she's a lucky girl.'

Baxter raised a smile. 'I'll be the lucky one,' he said shyly.

'Not if we have to tell an enquiry we deserted her brother,' George warned, picking up Boyd's train of thought.

'But we didn't,' Baxter protested. 'Not really.'

'If you think his sister will believe that, you want your head read,' George commented.

'It's a damn shame,' Boyd said. 'You'll be heading for Brisbane with your swag packed with cash, and she'll slam the door in your face.'

'What cash?' Baxter asked.

'Didn't you know?' Boyd said. 'There's a reward out for the capture of the killers of MacNamara's wife and the girl.'

'Yeah,' Baxter said. 'I did hear something about that.'

'One hundred pounds,' Boyd told him. 'A hundred pounds, and we're entitled. I've got written proof here from the Mines Inspector at the Bunya diggings. We got them, Baxter, you're a hero. But I don't need the money. I'm a fair man, I'm giving you Freddy's share, Baxter, to spend on his sister. Freddy would have liked that.'

'That's real nice of you, boss,' George said, impressed.

'Sixty-six pounds,' Boyd said to Baxter. 'Then when we get home there's your wages, plus I think both you and George are entitled to a bonus. We took a risk, we could have been killed up there in the hills. What do you say, George, if I round out the final figure to a hundred quid each?'

'A hundred quid?' George was ecstatic. 'Cripes. I wouldn't know where to spend that much money.'

'I do,' Baxter grinned, kneeing his horse. 'With a hundred quid I can buy a house in Brisbane and have more to spare, and she won't want to refuse me then.'

'She'll be mad if she does,' Boyd enthused. 'You've been a good hard worker, Baxter, I'll be sorry to see you go. But if you ever need a pound or two, you and your missus, you know where to turn.'

'Thanks, Mr Roberts,' Baxter said, gratitude racing through every pore. Then a worry dimmed his smile. 'What about Freddy? What will I say about Freddy?'

'There's a new strike up on the Cape River,' Boyd told him. 'Inland from Townsville. From what I hear, that river is laced with gold. Tell her Freddy's gone up there.' To ease Baxter's conscience, he

235

continued, aloud, with his own thoughts. 'I wouldn't mind having a look up there myself. These diggings are worked out. It's a fair way north, George, but we could go up by ship.'

'Worth a look,' George said, gold-fervour glinting. 'But what about your Parliament business?'

'Yes,' Boyd mused. 'It's a toss-up, isn't it? If the reefs up there are as rich as they say, then I ought to have a go. But I just don't like the idea of that little pipsqueak Cosmo beating me. No . . . I'll go for Parliament first. After that I can call my own tune.'

They rode on in contented silence, each with his own self-satisfied thoughts, until they reached the ferry that took them across the river and down the track to Rockhampton.

Chapter Ten

Outrage and grief swept along the ranges like a hurricane, leaving in its wake a swathe of fear and ferocity. Silent clansmen moved, brokenhearted, across the once idyllic little glade, where their families had sat down for generations, appalled at the bodies flung about on the bloodied sands. They lifted them up gently and carried them away, and brushed the desecrated bank with leafy branches, for this was not a designated fighting ground and therefore would have to be purified to placate the spirits who resided here.

People came to watch, standing high on the ridges and on the slopes, petrified with fear. 'It has begun,' they cried. 'They are coming after us now, we must flee to the other side of the mountains.'

'No!' sterner voices rang out. 'No more running. We stand and fight.'

At the hastily convened meetings there were no voices of dissent this time. The old man had gone into his Dreaming and Harrabura was away on one of his mysterious retreats. Wodoro was still with them but he never interfered in these momentous decisions. Privately, he believed they were right. It was time to fight. They couldn't allow that massacre and the capture of two of their men to go unpunished.

They'd found the bodies of Goorari and the white man by the dead horse and had deduced, correctly, that Goorari had given his life fighting for freedom. They were proud of him. His heroic actions spurred them on. Everywhere men were busy making war weapons, their women honing stones to sharp points to be attached to strong saplings with human hair soaked in beeswax and resin. Others were making the shorter spears of hardwood with vicious barbed heads.

Wodoro had to stay on. He still hadn't made good his promise to speak to the boss of Oberon. It was probably too late now, but he'd wait for Harrabura's return and discuss the matter further.

Lookouts were posted all along the hills to watch for any more incursions by white men into their territory, while preparations for war went on feverishly. It was decided that when they were ready, a full-scale attack would take place, in retaliation, against the nearest white settlement – Oberon Station. The station was to be totally destroyed and the hated cattle dispersed.

Wodoro had no sympathy for the whites. Two of their women killed, and now eight black women, plus two children and nine men, counting the two prisoners, who certainly would not survive. The white men had begun this war by driving off peaceful families and then making this cowardly attack. Now they would have to suffer the consequences.

But the war was upon them before they had time to gather their forces and go down the mountain. Scouts sent urgent messages that another group of armed white men was heading their way; this time they were redcoats.

Army men! Trained fighters! Wodoro rushed to see for himself, and the scouts pointed them out. Far in the distance he could see a small troop threading through the trees and climbing deliberately into the hills. He sat back, confused. Were they mad? As far as he could make out there were only eight or nine riders. Even though the other attack had taken place about twenty miles further north and had been carried out by only four men, did they think they could get away with it again? The last lot had gained the element of surprise, and so had succeeded, but these redcoats? They were riding straight for trouble.

It was possible, he decided, that they had no idea how many dark people were living in the mountains, and if that were so, they were about to be taught a nasty lesson. Just the same, he warned the other watchers, they must take great care. These men were warriors, the ones in the red coats, they were trained in the use of guns and would be on guard all the time.

'Perhaps you should let me speak with them first,' he suggested. 'So that I might send them away.'

'You would warn them?' a Kutabura man growled suspiciously. 'You would deprive us of our revenge?'

Angry faces loomed about him, and Wodoro remembered that other time when he'd made much the same suggestion, placing himself in the same danger he was facing now. 'It was just an idea,' he said, backing off.

'The honour of our people is at stake,' he was reminded, in reprimand. 'We will drive them away once and for all.'

Retreating, Wodoro thought sadly of 'once and for all'. That would never happen, he knew, it was a forlorn hope. But they were entitled to some hope, and some honour in retribution. They'd suffered enough, they might as well try. At least they'd make their mark and a new place in the ever-fading legends.

He wished he could find Harrabura, but no one seemed to know where he had gone.

Harrabura and three companions had travelled right to the south-east end of the Berserker Ranges, dropping down to the flat bushland that bordered the Fitzroy River. The township was across the river, but on this side was the track that led around the mountains to the north coast. They took up their positions on a lonely stretch, melting into the scrub to watch the road.

The men accompanying him were impatient, but polite. 'Why do we wait here?' they asked him, but Harrabura would not say. Indeed he could not say. He sat cross-legged, almost in a trance, chanting softly, fasting, taking only water.

He did know that Charlie Penny was dying, but as for this waiting place, he only understood that this was where he must be at this time, and he accepted his course without question.

'It has not yet been revealed to me,' he told them, and they agreed, reluctantly, to remain with him.

Had they known it, the route into the mountains taken by Roberts and his men was much easier than the climb from Oberon land. Here a mountain base curved and jutted, creating a warm, damp environment for rain forest.

Cursing, the troopers on foot slashed at vines and brutal tough greenery to clear a path for the horses, skidding on rotting leaves and tangles of bracken reeking of age. Massive drooping fig trees and ancient beeches barred their way, forcing detours. Paul was entranced. Temporarily forgetting his mission, he wished Gus were here to see this virgin forest and all its wonders. Some of these trees, he guessed, could be hundreds of years old, and here they were, right on the edge of his property.

As they moved slowly upwards, palms and bamboos creaked eerily and birds honked, cackled and screeched all about them. Overhead light filtered through a majestic canopy as if from a dome of stained glass.

'This is impossible,' Gooding complained, crouching in the saddle to avoid low clammy branches. 'We ought to turn back.'

'It'll thin out soon,' Tyler remarked, enjoying Gooding's discomfort. 'It's more exposed higher up.' He turned to Paul. 'Who owns this jungle?'

'I do,' Paul said, 'but I've never been up here before.'

'There are some magnificent stands of cedar here,' Tyler told him. 'Worth a fortune. You ought to send in some timber-getters.'

'Yes,' Paul replied, without enthusiasm.

Several hours later the way became clearer, with precarious skeletal gums stretching to the heights. They travelled along the side of the mountain until they came to a wide gully. There was a shallow stream at the base which Gooding decided would be easier to follow. Once again Tyler corrected him. 'That'd be a waste of time. It's a blind gully.'

'How do you know?' Gooding demanded.

'If you look up there,' Tyler said, pointing at the forest above them, 'you'll see a patch of bare cliff face. I'd say that's a waterfall in the wet season. If we go up there we'll run into a dead end.'

'We're not trying to cross the mountains,' Gooding argued, 'just scout out some of the blacks, and this is as good as place as any to look.'

'It's very quiet,' Paul worried. 'I thought we might have come across a few of them by now.'

'They're probably keeping well out of sight,' Tyler commented. 'If I were them I would too. We should be carrying a white flag.'

'Oh sure,' Gooding snapped. 'They'd know what that meant, wouldn't they?'

'Probably think it's our washing,' one of the troopers quipped.

Acting on Gooding's instructions, they splashed into the stream and began to follow its course inland. Fat fish plopped in the waters ahead of them as the horses stepped over the cobbled stone floor of the stream, making for sandy reaches that stretched into thick grassy borders leading on to the surrounding scrub.

In the midday hiss of the bush the atmosphere was serene, but they were all on edge. Not one Aborigine had been sighted, although they'd passed middens of shells and the blackened remains of campfires.

Some of the troopers felt they'd come far enough, and Gooding agreed. 'What now?' he asked Paul. 'It looks as if they're keeping well away.'

'Just keep it steady,' Paul urged. 'Make it obvious we're not in any hurry. They must know by now that we're only after the criminals. Every man we released was given the same message.'

'You hope,' Gooding commented.

'By gee!' one of the troopers called. 'This is a fisherman's heaven. There are so many in this creek you could net them.'

Instantly Paul was reminded of Jeannie, and his voice hardened. 'Forget the fish. Keep your weapons handy.'

Gooding nodded, relieved that MacNamara wasn't blinded to the dangers in his obsession to find these men. Gus had told him about the shooting of a captive native, and although that was an unfortunate incident, apparently it had served a purpose. The shock of seeing that sudden, cold-blooded killing has caused MacNamara to ease up, to realise that his first mad rage could have been responsible for the deaths of a lot more innocents at the hands of a posse infected by his own attitude.

But on this expedition he was still a wild card, moody and not altogether rational. Tyler was right, he had to admit, Paul shouldn't be with them, but he, Gooding, was only a public servant, at the beck and call of these cattlemen whose power went by fast track right to the top.

'We're not getting anywhere,' he said to Paul. 'Why don't we just call them? They're sure to be watching us.'

'Worth a try,' Paul said.

The troop halted and Gooding rode forward to use the bush call known to all. About the only thing they had in common with the blacks, he mused, as he cupped his hands wide to amplify the sound. 'Coo-ee! Coo-ee!' The sound echoed through the hills but there was no response, and although he tried again several times they were greeted by an ominous silence.

'Damn!' Paul said. 'Can't they see we're not trying to sneak up on them?'

'Why would they care?' Tyler asked. 'Where I come from, if the blacks wanted to talk they'd have shown themselves by now. Much as I'd love to keep going and explore this mountain, I reckon we ought to turn back.'

'No,' Paul said. 'No! We can't give up that easily. We have to communicate with them.'

'If you hadn't chased all the friendly ones into the hills, you wouldn't need to be trying to find them now,' Tyler said, ignoring Paul's obvious anger at that remark. 'If you want my advice, you'll leave them alone now. Take things quietly back on your station and let them drift back to their sitting-down places at the waterholes and their other familiar spots. Let things get back to normal, then you can talk to them.'

'That could take years,' Paul growled.

Tyler shrugged. 'That's true.'

The Lieutenant called to them from a bend in the stream. 'Come and have a look at this.'

When they caught up with him they came face to face with a tall cliff, at its base a large and very lovely waterhole, like a small lake, bordered by huge palms. The walls of the cliff were peopled with ferns of all description, ancient ferns that sprang from crevices in the rocks.

Gooding studied the area. Even though their progress was blocked by the cliff, the land either side fell away gently. Possibly the cliff had been caused by subsidence aeons back, or the land had lurched up to form the barrier. The possibility of attack hadn't left his mind for a minute and he deduced that even if it came from the rear they weren't cut off, they could easily ride to the right or the left and get themselves out of trouble.

'I was right,' Tyler crowed. 'That's the cliff face we could see from way back. The headwaters of this stream are high up there. The main fall has dried up, but that smaller fall, halfway up the cliff, is coming from an underground stream and keeping this creek alive.'

The small waterfall splashed gaily from a cave in the cliffs, dropping down to the jade-green depths below. As the sunlight sparkled on the twenty-foot fall it reflected a rainbow of colour.

'That must be some waterfall in the wet season,' Tyler said, gazing in awe at the heights. 'No wonder this watercourse is so wide, it really must tear down here when the rains come.'

Paul agreed, but he was in no mood to discuss scenery, he knew they'd have to turn back. He suspected that Gooding had known all along that this would be a dead end and had ignored Tyler's advice so that he'd have an excuse to retreat. Now his suspicions were fuelled by the Lieutenant's expertise as he deployed his men.

'We'll camp here,' Gooding said.

One of the troopers pointed to a sandy beach around the waterhole at the base of the cliff. 'There's a better spot over there, it's more sheltered.'

'Yes,' Gooding replied. 'Use your brains. It's a perfect spot for an ambush. That waterhole is bloody deep. If they come at us from downstream we can only go one way, up to the right. Think on it, you blokes, don't you realise they could work that out too and be waiting for us? We camp here. Hitch up the horses, Rory, but forget the hobbles. Two of you stay with them while they feed, and four on guard at all points. We'll light the fire and make supper.'

They ate in two shifts, with Tyler and Paul seconded to guard duty. Then, as they prepared to bed down for the night, Gooding issued new orders. 'You know the routine,' he told his men. 'Fix the dummies.'

Tyler was fascinated, but Paul's eyes narrowed. He accepted now that this officer knew his job; it was common practice in dangerous bush areas to put dummy figures wrapped in blankets about the campfires at night and for the travellers to retreat and sleep under cover of the blackness of the scrub. Paul didn't disagree with this caution, but he felt he'd been taken for a ride, that Gooding was only placating him by agreeing to make this journey, which would be over in the morning. He had misjudged Gooding, probably because he'd heard the man was known as an office-wallah.

He settled in the scrub, lying among deep ferns covered by his blanket, his rifle handy, but he couldn't sleep. The actual campsite had been abandoned and the others were close by, with two troopers on guard, hidden somewhere nearby.

The silence bothered him. He was accustomed to sleeping in the bush but – maybe he was imagining it – this place seemed too quiet. He was reassured when he heard the whisper of guards making contact, and so he began to think of the morrow.

Very well, he decided, if Gooding pulled out, he, Paul, would stay. He was not waiting years to resolve this matter. He would keep going. He knew the dangers, but he didn't care.

What sort of a life would he have after this if he let Jeannie down in the end? He could almost hear her voice urging him on, demanding he stand up and be counted on her behalf. For that matter, he reasoned, a lone man could have more success than a band of troopers. He had to find the blacks, find the elders, especially that old bloke Gorrabah, and make them listen to him. There wasn't any other way. And if he didn't make it? What the hell. He would have paid for his mistakes with his life. In those early morning hours, his life didn't seem to matter any more. Bitterly he closed his eyes, not to sleep but allow them to rest for the days ahead.

They stood and stared.

'Well, we've got our answer now,' Gooding said.

'Jesus!' Rory whispered with a shudder. 'I was on the second watch and I didn't hear a bloody thing!'

The dummies lying near the warm coals of the campfire were pinned to the ground with spears, and other spears that had missed the mark were embedded in the soft grass nearby.

They came out of the bush and examined the sandy banks but there were no footprints. 'They must have come down through the scrub,' Paul said angrily. 'The bloody fools, asking for trouble.'

'Not such fools if that had been any of us,' Gooding retorted. 'Our numbers would have been reduced by three. We're leaving. We can't hang about to get picked off through the night.'

'Good idea,' Tyler said. 'Take a look up top of the cliff.'

Above them, silhouetted against the skyline, was a wall of black men, ominous tribal figures, war-painted, ranged right along the heights, confronting them. Tall spears thumping, they began to chant, their voices rising, in the still of the dawn, into unmistakable shouts of derision and belligerence.

'There are hundreds of them,' Gooding croaked, 'Saddle up, lads. Don't panic, they might just want us to back off, and we'll be pleased to oblige.'

But around them the bush seemed to come alive with the sound of bullroarers and the rhythmic clatter of sticks on sticks, the native equivalent of drums, battering the air in a terrifying cacophony of noise.

Swiftly the horses were brought forward, and the men raced to throw on the saddles. Then, just as suddenly as it had begun, the percussion ceased, snapping off in the same mysterious way that hosts of cicadas can suddenly stop their singing, or flocks of birds take to the skies as one. The silence was a shock, frightening, as if heralding a decision.

The others were already mounted, their horses thoroughly spooked, nostrils flaring, prancing, fidgeting, but Paul grabbed the opportunity and strode forward to the shores of the waterhole.

Before Gooding could stop him he was out there in the open, shouting at the tribesmen looming above him.

'I am MacNamara,' he yelled. 'Some of you know me. I am from the big house back there.' He pointed downhill. 'I want to talk.'

'Are you mad?' Gooding cried. 'They can't understand you. Let's get out of here.'

'Someone must,' Paul insisted, looking up at the horde of blacks. None of them had moved a muscle.

'Gorrabah!' he cried desperately. 'Let me speak to Gorrabah!'

Wodoro had no influence over these events but, unable to stay away, he'd come to watch. He was up there on the precipice with the warriors, looking down on the puny little group below. From their point of view, he reckoned, this must be a magnificent sight. The Darambal men, though rather thin from a shortage of good tucker, were a strong, handsome race, with glossy skins not yet contaminated by the ugly sores inflicted on so many tribal people by contact with the dirty whites. They stood proudly now, demonstrating their power. Or some of it. Even though they were not yet ready for a full-scale attack on Oberon, they had decided that this intrusion of more whites into their territory would be a good start to the planned warfare.

Last night's attack on the camp had only been a show-off by three young men, one of them the brother of Goorari, the new hero of the Kutabura people. They claimed they had killed three white men as they slept, but in the morning, the watchers, counting numbers, had reporter that nine white men had come in and nine men were still on their feet, showing no signs of injury. Goorari's brother, Moongi, was now a laughing stock.

He was standing beside Wodoro now, furious that he'd been made a fool of, and looking forward to proving himself once again, but even though his spear was trembling in his hand he couldn't make a move without permission.

The clans had gathered swiftly, and not only was there this line of warriors on the cliff, there were many more gathering in the woods on either side of the sacred waterhole. Despite his misgivings, Wodoro was reminded of the great battles of his father's and Bussamarai's times, when they'd assembled more than six hundred warriors for battle, and he couldn't help but be thrilled.

He had already spoken to the elders. Certainly they had the numbers to wipe out this small group, but at what cost? He reminded them of the old man's warnings. Those guns could kill men faster than spears and the bullets were deadly. If they killed this mob of whites, more would come, more and more. Wouldn't it be better to frighten them off with this show of strength, to let them know who was boss in the mountains. That done, they might just stay out. They only needed the plains to graze their cattles, they didn't need the mountains.

But his arguments had again fallen on deaf ears. The cowardly attack by the mob of whites a few days back had made this fight a matter of honour.

He listened enthralled to the bullroarers doing their whirring work of creating fear in the enemy. They were working, the whites were preparing to run.

That was another reason why Moongi was so angry. Having made an idiot of himself boasting that they'd killed three men, he'd been stuck up here on the cliff where he couldn't foul up again. On the other side of Wodoro was young Malliloora. As Harrabura's protégé he was not permitted to fight either. This one had to be protected at all costs because he was being taught the ancient language of the spirits and the magic rites far beyond Wodoro's comprehension. For, while Wodoro could pass on the legends and rituals and intertribal regulations, Malliloora's education went far deeper. When Harrabura died, this lad, now fifteen, would be the keeper of the very core of Kutabura Dreaming. He was a shy boy, reticent and well mannered, but immensely strong, thanks to his rigorous training and the acceptance that, above all, he had to be kept well fed.

But what was this? Standing up there as the sun came out of the sea and cast its bright glow over the heights, Wodoro was lulled by his own contemplations into losing the drift of what was happening around him.

One of the white men had stepped forward and was shouting at them. Wodoro moved forward to the edge of the cliff, remembering with a smile that Harrabura was nervous of heights, while he, Wodoro, gloried in them.

He stared down at the man, standing out there alone, by no means out of range of spears if these men chose to use woomeras to add distance, and he saw that it was Paul, the boss man from Oberon. Not Pace. Not a ghost. He was calling to them, telling them who he was. But of course none of the others could understand him. They probably thought he was challenging them. It took great effort on Wodoro's part to shake off his fear, but the clear light of day was reassuring. He forced himself to concentrate.

'I want to talk!' the white man yelled. And so he would, Wodoro reasoned. This was the man whose women had been killed. He was still searching for the murderers. Desperately, Wodoro wished that Harrabura was here. Where was he when he was needed? This was the time to tell the boss man that these people were not responsible.

Wodoro turned about, trying to explain to the men around him. But how to balance the white man's loss against the murders of Kutabura people just two days ago? Their faces were impassive, deaf to his pleas that here was a good chance to break the present impasse between the white men and the blacks.

Then the white boss man made the greatest mistake of all. He spoke the name of the dead. Blasphemy!

'Gorrabah!' he was shouting. 'Let me speak to Gorrabah!'

Wodoro rushed forward, standing precariously on an overhang of rock, as all about him hisses of shock ricocheted into anger.

'You bloody fool whitefeller,' he shouted frantically in the white-man's language. 'Too late now. Get out quick!'

Gooding and the others needed no further telling. Yelling to Paul to come with them, they spurred their horses and took off, but to Wodoro's amazement the man, Paul, refused to budge. He remained standing by the pool and called out: 'Who are you? Talk to me. I come in peace.'

'These people did not kill your women,' Wodoro shouted. 'You must . . .'

But before he could finish the sentence Moongi lunged forward. 'Traitor!' he screamed. 'He's warning them!'

245

Down below, Gooding and his company were already racing towards the bend in the stream, rifles loaded ready to fire.

In a fury Moongi clubbed Wodoro across the back of the head. He dropped like a stone, unconscious, over the cliff, into the green depths more than a hundred feet below.

Pandemonium reigned. Triggered by the drama on the cliffs, the blacks came racing out of the scrub, hurling spears, screaming with delight as one redcoat after another went down, and roaring forward to complete the kills.

Tyler had an advantage – the redcoats seemed to be attracting the most attention, and besides, Greybeard, the brumby, was handling this race better than the classier army horses. He had his head down and was plunging on as if this were a flat track and not an uneven surface that could cost him a fetlock. Tyler blessed the horse's rough youth. On either side of him, troopers were in trouble, some mounts stumbling or the riders speared, but even though they were all firing wildly as they rode, they were managing to cut down black attackers. Tyler shot one blackfellow ahead of him just as he was poised to raise his spear, and he noticed that Gooding, with no time to reload had holstered his rifle and was using his revolver to deadly effect.

All at once, Gooding fell, or rather, his horse crashed into the stream with a spear in its side and Gooding was thrown. Ahead of Tyler, Rory was racing away from the creek bed, heading for firm ground. Tyler looked back to see that another one of the troopers, who had also lost his mount, had placed himself behind an outcrop and was covering his floundering officer with rifle fire.

On his way to safety, Tyler felt a surge of admiration for the calm efficiency of that trooper. But Gooding was exposed, and Tyler knew that bullets made little difference to enraged blacks. So, against his better judgement, he swung Greybeard around and rode right at Gooding, who, grateful for the help, flung his gun up to Tyler and grabbed his saddle as Greybeard, urged on by his rider, whisked him to safety behind the wall of rock. The trooper, by sustained fire, finally persuaded the blacks to fall back.

Gooding's horse was whinnying and floundering in mid-stream, unable to get up. 'He's broken his leg,' the Lieutenant said, and with careful aim, shot his horse. The shot, the last of the battle, lingered and echoed pathetically through the hills. After a while, a trooper's horse, uninjured, came clattering over to them. It trotted round the rocks and nudged at Greybeard as if seeking company.

'It's over,' Gooding said weakly, 'or they'd never have let the horse toddle away.'

'Just like that?' Tyler asked, his chest still heaving from exertion and fright.

'Yes. That's the way they operate. They never pursue to the bitter end. They fight, then they just get up and go away. If they didn't I wouldn't be here today. I got speared once. They had the advantage. I thought I was a goner, but they never came back. I think it's a remnant of their old ways in tribal fights. Once someone gets speared, honour is satisfied and everyone goes home. These days life is tougher.'

'I thought you said you grew up among the blacks?' the trooper asked Tyler.

'Yes. But over the years they'd had much more contact with Europeans. I had no idea there was a real war going on up here in North Queensland.'

'To the northerners,' Gooding snorted, 'this is the south. You haven't seen the half of it, mate, and I pray they'll put me out to pasture before they need more troops up there.'

The trooper interrupted them. 'Can we get out of here now, sir?'

'No, we have to wait for stragglers.'

'What if there aren't any?'

Gooding considered this. 'Well . . . Rory got away, we can bet on that. MacNamara was too exposed. He'd have to be finished. That leaves four of our men. I saw Jack and Tommy, they were speared.'

'So was Corporal Harvey, sir, he got a spear in his back.'

'That leaves young Donald. Anyone see what happened to him?'

'No.'

'We can't go back,' Gooding said. 'That would be suicide. So we'll wait.'

They delayed for what seemed to Tyler interminable hours, until they were startled by a riderless horse that fled past them, scrambling away from the creek to make its way downhill through the forest.

'That's MacNamara's horse,' Gooding said. Tyler nodded numbly, anxiety causing his heart to pound and his throat to constrict. He was still in shock, still afraid that the blacks would attack again, and appalled at the calm way Gooding had ticked off the casualties. The dead! an inner voice seemed to scream at him, correcting him, and he was gripped with such panic he was tempted to grab his horse and get the hell out of there. Let Gooding hang about if he must.

But he stayed, simply because he didn't have the strength or the will to go back alone. Crouched there with them, his legs felt weak as putty.

By noon Gooding made his decision. 'We'll have to go. Bloody MacNamara!' he said bitterly. 'Why didn't he come with us? Standing there a prime target. I swear that man had a death wish. I said all along I'd need an army to patrol these hills, but it's no consolation to the men we've lost. Donald could have got away, he might have taken to the bush, but there's nothing we can do about the others.' He turned to Tyler. 'Thanks for picking me up, I owe you. I got a whack on the head when the horse fell and for a few minutes there I didn't know where I was. Too dazed to think straight, but that horse of yours smartened me up. I was sure the bugger was going to run me down.

247

He was coming at me like a wild bull.'

Tyler managed a wan smile. 'I wasn't sure I'd be able to pull him up, but even with all his weight, he practically turned on a thrippence.' Discussing the horse settled his nerves a little, he found.

'He'd be a stock horse that one,' Gooding was saying. 'With plenty of experience. A bloody beauty. Would you mind helping me up? I'm feeling a bit giddy.'

'Can you ride?' Tyler asked.

The Lieutenant grimaced. 'To get out of here? Try me!'

As they assisted him on to the spare horse, he gazed warily about them. 'MacNamara had me convinced he'd be able to talk to the blacks. Why the hell did I believe him?'

They threaded their way into the bush, heading directly downhill, obstructed at times by deep ravines and sudden rocky outcrops that forced them to detour, all the while aware that their progress would be observed by triumphant blacks. It was with relief that they reached the foothills at dusk. They were tired and hungry but did not dare stop, even when they came to the flats. From there, without MacNamara to guide them, they dismounted and led their horses through open woodlands in what they hoped was the general direction of the Oberon homestead, cursing the brooding blackness of the night over this lonely land.

Paul MacNamara believed he had succeeded. He was not intimidated by the rows of blacks up there, nor by the bullroarers and clacking sticks. He'd heard them before. Squads of blacks had occasionally come on to Oberon, stamping and shouting and waving spears, mostly bluffing, and had been willing to accept a butchered bullock as their due. He guessed they might be preparing to attack but were not quite ready, hence this display, stalling for time. But at least he'd found them, and this was an opportunity to make someone listen to him. They must!

In the heat of the moment, in his excitement, he had lost all sense of danger. He could hear Gooding yelling at him but he couldn't leave now. He was out in the open, unarmed, his rifle in the saddle holster. The blacks could see he was no threat to them, they had to respond. In desperation he called for Gorrabah, and saw a black man stride forward to shout at him, in English! Someone up there was answering him in English! No matter that he was calling him a bloody fool, he'd made contact! He'd found an interpreter!

Then he saw that terrible thing happen, destroying his hopes. Another man, without warning, lunged forward from the ranks and clubbed the speaker, screaming abuse. Paul saw the body hurtle over the cliff and drop, as if in slow motion, a dead weight, down, down, thudding into the waterhole.

Spears were already flying as he tore off his boots and dived into the crystal-clear waters of the icy mountain pool, making straight for the spot where the man had gone down. He came up for air halfway across and dived deep again, searching frantically as if his own life depended on it. Then he saw the body, drifting limply, dredged aside by a heaving central current.

He grabbed him by the arm and yanked him to the surface, heading for the shelter of the cliff, determined not to let go. Gulping for air now, he pulled the unconscious black man towards the waterfall, grasping for support at the rough cliff face, sure he had seen a ledge along here somewhere.

From a distance this cascade had seemed gentle and velvety – in contrast to his impression of what the main falls must be like when they took their majestic leap from the heights – but it was not. The torrent crashed on to him like perpetual hail, blinding him, as he sought cover, not daring to make for the shore.

Then, at last, he found the ledge.

He pushed and shoved at the heavy, limp body, desperately trying to heave it to safety, but it was at least a four-foot gap between the water level and the slimy ledge. He could get up there without any effort but he couldn't let go of the half-drowned man, who, at least, was still alive. For how long, though? His lungs would be full of water, but Paul couldn't help him here.

Paul knew he had two choices. To let go of the black man, to let him drown and save himself; or to pull him across the waterhole to the shore in full view of the tribesmen, who obviously regarded this fellow as an enemy too. Deciding that the latter course wouldn't help either of them, he began, once again, to try to shove him up on to the ledge, knowing it was impossible.

Suddenly the weight lifted and for a second he thought his charge had regained consciousness. He saw a black face above him, and black hands hauling the limp man to the ledge. To Paul's surprise, the young blackfellow standing above him then reached down and dragged Paul up too. Startled by the strength of this native, Paul came out of the water as easily as if he'd been winched clear.

The young man heaved his comrade on to his bare shoulders and ran up the slope of the ledge, then ducked down into a cave. Given no indication of what he was to do, Paul followed. He watched as the tall native dumped the body on the ground and began shaking him to restore life. Paul pushed him aside. In their land of floods and racing rivers, Pace had taught his sons necessary first aid. He cleared the victim's mouth, turned him on his chest and pumped on his back, pressing, pushing water from his lungs, watching water and bile spew from his mouth. He worked feverishly, blowing essential air into the purpled mouth, fighting to save him, until at last, as if disgusted with their efforts, as if they were the ones preventing him from breathing, this man, with a massive lump on the back of his head, began to cough and splutter and choke and throw up more green liquid.

Paul sat back and grinned at his helper. 'He'll live,' he said, and the young man, understanding, smiled, strong white teeth gleaming in the darkness of the cave.

When Wodoro awoke and his brain unscrambled, his head felt as if it were the size of a melon. He opened his eyes and saw Pace looking down at him, and he jerked away, disorientated with terror. 'Devils!' he screamed at Malliloora in the Darambal language.

The young man soothed him. 'No. No. All is well. This man saved you from drowning.'

Wodoro's mind turned over this information, and eventually he gathered the courage to speak. In English, he asked, 'Who are you?'

'MacNamara. From Oberon Station.'

'The boss man?' Wodoro asked weakly.

'Yes.'

'You have another name?'

'Yes. I am called Paul.'

This was a relief, but Wodoro was still nervous of him.

'How do we get out of here?' Paul asked, knowing now he was far from safe.

'Ask Malliloora,' Wodoro replied, closing his eyes. He was dead tired. He remembered now that that fool Moongi had attacked him. He wished he had just shut up and let things take their course.

'He can't speak English,' Paul said. He was bursting to know more about this mysterious blackfellow who understood English so well, but obviously this was not the time. He listened to the two blacks conversing.

Finally the older one staggered to his feet. 'Us both fellers in big trouble now,' he gasped. 'You one bloody stupid white man.'

'You already told me that.' Paul remarked. 'What is your name?'

'I am Wodoro,' he said proudly. 'Very important person. But not this day. You buggered it all up. This man is Kutabura clan, he is Malliloora, most honoured. You show him respect.'

'Of course,' Paul said, nodding courteously to the young man, although he couldn't help being amused by this strange and cranky blackfellow called Wodoro. 'He fished us out of the water.'

Wodoro ignored that. 'We go with him now, bloody damn quick.'

'Where to?' Paul asked.

Wodoro shook his head in disgust. 'Bloody hell! I doan know.'

They followed the cave until it narrowed into a tunnel, forcing them to crawl and then edge along on their stomachs. As he elbowed a path behind them Paul worried about this pair. If they were so important, as Wodoro claimed, why were they worming their way through this stifling hole? Eventually, though, he felt a little cheered to see a thin shaft of light ahead of them.

Malliloora thrust himself out of their tunnel, but Wodoro didn't move on.

'Hurry up,' Paul said. 'I'm choking in here.'

'More better you choke,' Wodoro replied. 'No goin' out there. We wait.'

'What for?'

Wodoro answered him, but in a guttural burst of his own language.

Maybe he's tired, Paul thought, or he just can't be bothered speaking English any more. He felt the body ahead of him stretch out and then relax as if preparing to sleep, and decided he might as well rest too, or try to rest, lying in this rocky bolt hole like a nocturnal animal. He began to worry about Gooding and the others. He had no regrets about his own predicament but he hoped his actions hadn't caused them trouble. Still, they were already mounted when the incident with Wodoro sparked the spears, and they would have taken off very smartly. Gooding was too much of a professional soldier to hang about.

There was so much he wanted to ask Wodoro, but he dared not antagonise him. He realised he was behind enemy lines now and he'd be lucky to make it out on his own, so he'd have to learn patience, which wasn't his best suit.

Chapter Eleven

Grace Carlisle always talked things over with Justin; whether he understood or not. It lent him the dignity he so much needed these days. 'Justin, dear,' she said, 'I want to talk to you about Laura. Now put the paper away and listen to me.'

'I'm listening,' he replied, continuing to pore over a newspaper spread on the table before him.

'Laura has a problem,' she continued.

Justin looked up. 'Yes, she's run out of money. Poor girl, I'm very fond of her. Why doesn't she marry one of our lads?'

'They're already married,' she said patiently. 'I've written to her Uncle William on her behalf but it will take months to get a reply. I'm sure he'll help, but in the meantime I thought we could step in.'

'Ah, yes,' he smiled. 'William Maskey. Is he still married to that silly Freda?'

'Freda died, Justin.'

'So she did. I knew that. And Fowler Maskey's dead, too. Where's his wife, Hilda?'

'She has gone to live in Brisbane.'

Justin chuckled. 'That Hilda, she had a crush on William, didn't she? And she married Fowler on the rebound.'

'That's right,' Grace said, although it hadn't been that simple. She remembered it as if it were yesterday. They'd all grown up together and Hilda did indeed have a crush on William. Never backward in coming forward, Hilda had told William she was in love with him, but William had informed her of his intentions to marry Grace. What a time that was! In a huff, furious with Grace, Hilda had turned to Fowler, William's brother, and married him several months later. But even though she had always liked William, Grace was not in love with him. Justin Carlisle was the man for her. So handsome and witty, she'd loved him dearly. Still did for that matter. But when she and Justin announced their engagement, Hilda had been even angrier, refusing to attend the wedding. She blamed Grace for ruining her life, since William was now available. Too late for Hilda, who fretted that she'd married the wrong Maskey.

So silly of her, Grace reminisced, causing all those upsets. It was a long time ago, but Hilda had never forgiven Grace. They moved in the same circles, and their salad days were over, those matters forgotten.

Nevertheless, Hilda Maskey had always been cool to Grace, they were never real friends again. As for William, he'd married Freda but retained his affection for Grace to this day. Which was why she knew William would listen to her, rather than Laura's mother. Over the years he'd come to dislike Hilda and avoided her company as much as possible, but he was very fond of Laura, his only niece.

'I was thinking we ought to buy the Maskey house in Rockhampton,' she said to Justin.

'Do we need a house there?' he asked.'We already have one in Brisbane.'

'Laura needs a home. If we snap it up before they sell it to someone else, we could hold on to it until we hear from William.'

'Whatever you say.' Justin smiled and went back to his paper.

Grace hoped he understood. In her letter to William she had set out Laura's situation fairly. She admitted that the girl had been reckless, but all the unfortunate events surrounding her could be traced back to Fowler's insistence that she marry Captain Cope, who, in Grace's estimation, was a poor choice for his daughter. She could imagine William's reaction when he heard that a Maskey girl was not only disinherited but, thanks to her mother, destitute and homeless. William was a generous man, and proud of the family name. He wouldn't see Laura go into servitude, as she planned to do. Grace had deliberately used the word servitude to incense William, telling herself it wasn't quite a lie. Governesses were only a step above servants in the pecking order of station life.

Temporarily, the problem was solved. She would buy the Maskey house to allow Laura to go home and not feel beholden to them, and arrange a loan to support her until they heard from William. If he didn't respond as she expected, then they'd simply have to see what could be done next. In the meantime she would have to move quickly to claim that house.

She sat at her small desk to write to her Rockhampton solicitors, giving them instructions to act for her and purchase the Quay Street house. Then, having done her best for Laura, she began to compose a letter to Cosmo Newgate.

As yet, she had not been able to find anyone suitable to stand against Boyd Roberts in the forthcoming elections. It was a pity that Cosmo, in his second and rather desperate letter, was left holding the bag, as it were, since none of the townspeople of Rockhampton would volunteer. That was understandable. It was a shaky little township recently hit by unemployment, and even though the reinstated Premier Herbert was moving fast to restore confidence, they'd take time to recover. On the other hand it was rather embarrassing that no one from the station families would step forward. They were either too wealthy to care, or battling too hard to spare the time.

Grace wondered if Cosmo, in writing to her, were considering one of her sons, so she took up her pen and explained that they were all too entrenched in the Carlisle tradition of expansion and were preparing to leave Camelot to claim bigger spreads in the far north, where millions of acres of good cattle country were up for grabs. She didn't add that her sons were already arguing about who should stay on at Camelot and miss out on the big prizes. Personally, she wished they'd all go and take their wives with them, and leave her to Camelot and their perfectly competent foreman whom she would promote to manager the minute they left.

Grace sighed. That was her problem, not Cosmo's. Justin was no help – he urged them to go, claiming he could run Camelot himself, which was out of the question. Poor Justin. In his day, he could have run rings around any of them. It had been Justin who had built up the family fortunes, but now he'd been struck by these increasing bouts of senility, which doctors claimed were normal and simply caused by age. Normal? The word terrified Grace, and she vowed that if she spotted any of these signs in her own behaviour she'd march into the river until her hat floated.

'There is a possibility,' she wrote to Cosmo. 'Political personages in Brisbane are quick to note vacancies in the hallowed seats of our Parliament, and so a young man is visiting us, carrying a reference from the Governor himself. He is Captain Leslie Soames, former aide to Governor Bowen, who has relinquished his post to seek advancement, if possible in the political arena.'

It was well known that many young Britishers of excellent breeding were paid to lose themselves in the colonies to avoid embarrassing the families back home. Soames, however, was not one of these so-called remittance men, so Grace continued with delicacy:

'The gentleman is of age, I think about thirty-three, well appointed, hails from Sussex and has sufficient financial and personal attributes. Captain Soames is most interested in winning the seat of Rockhampton.'

Grace did not write that she found Soames a painful bore. He claimed he was related to aristocracy, naming several English peers who, Grace surmised, would be delighted that he had removed himself. Over the years, Grace had been hostess to several titled gentlemen, whom she had found pleasant and agreeable guests, but this chap must have been behind the door when family charm was distributed.

At first, with an enduring interest in matchmaking, she'd steered Leslie towards Laura, and he'd seemed very taken with her. But suddenly his interest flagged, and it was her daughter-in-law, Pamela, who came giggling to Grace with the latest station gossip. 'Did you notice that Captain Soames was all eyes for Laura when he first arrived?'

'Yes, I did.'

'Well, of course she wasn't the slightest bit interested. She thought he was a great yawn but he hung on her heels like a puppy, so she asked Kelvin if he could steer him away.'

Kelvin was Grace's eldest son. 'What could he do?' she asked.

Pamela doubled up laughing. 'It was easy. Kelvin told Cappy Soames that Laura was broke. Hasn't got a bean! That sent him streaking for cover!'

'That's dreadful,' Grace said. 'I will want to speak to Kelvin about this. How could he do that to Laura?'

'Don't worry,' Pamela laughed, 'Laura knows. She thinks it's hilarious. We love her, you know that, we all love her. Who gives a damn what she has or hasn't got? She'll always be our friend.'

'You young people seem to have very strange attitudes to humour,' Grace chided. 'If those sort of remarks get passed on, you won't do her a lot of good.'

'It won't do her any harm either,' Pamela argued. 'She's her own person, she doesn't need fortune-hunters.' Then Pamela started to laugh again. 'Especially when she hasn't got a fortune! I've been trying to persuade her to come north with us. I'd give the earth to have Laura for company, but she's got this mad idea about getting a job.'

That reminded Grace. As yet, Hilda had not responded to her appeal. She seemed quite determined to banish Laura from the family. 'True to form,' Grace murmured. 'You always were a mean wretch. Oh well, best of luck with Leon. He won't give a fig for you, you foolish woman.'

With an effort she returned to Cosmo's quandary.

From the day they'd met at the hotel Grace had taken a liking to Paul MacNamara. He was bright, good-looking and had a real twinkle in his eye, and he hadn't balked at escorting an old lady to Maskey's house that Sunday afternoon, strolling along with all the ease of a country gentleman. She had intended to submit his name to Cosmo as a candidate, but now she wouldn't dream of bothering him.

She sniffed away tears and reached for her handkerchief, remembering that she had once said to Paul, when discussing the blacks: 'I hope you never get put to the test.'

But there it was. Tragedy had struck. There was no point in mentioning Paul at this stage. He'd become cold and distant, intent only – as a man should be – on finding his wife's murderers. That left Soames. If he could beat Roberts, an uphill job for a new chum, then let him. Suddenly she felt too old and tired for the wearying vagaries of politics.

A week later, when her messenger returned from Rockhampton, she laughed until the tears ran. Her solicitor had made an offer for the Quay Street house and it had been accepted. But when Hilda had discovered the identity of the buyer she had tried to raise the price, dispatching caustic telegrams to both solicitors. In the end it appeared that Leon had overruled his mother. Their solicitor, John Laidley, received a curt message: 'Go ahead. Sell the place at quoted price. Leon Maskey.'

Grace studied the papers, relieved to find they'd sold the house furnished, which would save a lot of bother. She and Justin would sign them and get them back to town right away.

That evening she took Laura aside. 'We'll all be going in to Rockhampton next month for the races. Are you coming with us?'

Laura was quick to reply. Obviously she'd already given the matter thought, since all they could talk about lately on the station was the annual races. 'No,' she said. 'I'll be quite happy to stay here, thanks, Grace.'

'But we've got some of our horses entered, and there's the Carlisle Cup,' Grace teased. 'You wouldn't want to miss that.'

'It can't be helped. You know why I can't go. It's bad enough for you having to support me out here, I won't have you paying for me in town as well. You make your hotel bookings and don't worry about me.'

Grace smiled. 'My dear, finding hotel accommodation in Rockhampton during race week is like searching for hens' teeth. We booked them a year ago. But Justin and I, and you, if you'll join us, will be staying in a house.'

'Whose house?'

Grace was unable to contain the secret any longer. 'Your house!' she said excitedly. 'We bought the Quay Street house.'

'Good Lord! Why?'

'Why not? It's a good house, isn't it?'

'Yes, it's very comfortable.'

'You don't mind, do you?'

'Of course not. It's just a surprise, that's all. As a matter of fact, I'm pleased you bought it. My father built that house, it's rather sweet that it's going to friends.'

'Good. Then why don't you come to town and stay with us. You could have your old room back.' Grace took her hand. 'I hope that didn't sound crass, I didn't mean it to. What I had in mind was that if you wished you could stay on there, keep it open for us – houses get so musty in this climate if they're all shuttered down – then when any of the family go in they won't have to worry about depressing hotel rooms.'

'What have you been up to?' Laura said with a laugh. 'You're plotting again, Grace. Does my mother know you bought it?'

'She does now. But why should she mind?' Grace asked innocently.

'Well, to be truthful, you were never her favourite person. She'd be furious if she knew I was camped out here.'

'Good heavens,' Grace said serenely. 'I had no idea. But I shall be very hurt if you don't join us.'

Laura threw her arms about her. 'You're a darling. I'd love to come with you, and if you're sure it's all right, I really would like to stay on. I might be able to get a job in town.'

'You'll have a job,' Grace said, trying to sound stern. 'You can be

256

housekeeper there.' That was, she considered, an inspired reply. The girl could hardly stay there without a penny and it would be difficult to foist money on her. 'But we'll have to find a live-in cook, it wouldn't do for you to be living there alone.'

'My reputation again?' Laura grinned.

'Yes, your reputation is important. I hope you don't get into any more scrapes.' She was touched when Laura kissed her on the cheek.

'I'll try. I think I'm cured.'

Grace had three sons; her only daughter, who would have been the same age as Laura, had died of a fever at the age of two. She embraced Hilda's daughter. 'Everything is going to be all right, dear, you'll see.'

Laura wondered about that. She was pleased to be going home, if only as a guest, but her thoughts were on Paul MacNamara. A determined person, she refused to give up on him, hoping that when his grief diminished he would become his normal self again. And she would be there, in Rockhampton, waiting. She'd met a number of young 'eligibles' since she'd been at Camelot but none of them appealed to her; no one, she thought sadly, would ever replace Paul. She had no choice but to let him take his time and hope that one day . . .

And then the news came through that there had been a fight in the hills near Oberon. The expedition that had left Camelot had fought a running battle with tribal blacks. Four of the troopers had been killed. Lieutenant Gooding, Tyler Kemp and two troopers had made it back to Oberon homestead but without MacNamara himself. No one held out any hope for Paul; he had been left behind when the attack took place and then his riderless horse had found its way home.

Laura sat, white-faced, shocked, as the talk of this latest disaster raged; they could speak of nothing else, and Paul's name came up time and again. Grace Carlisle wept, and Laura wept with her. She went for long walks on her own, or retreated to her room to escape with her own anguish. Paul was dead! Laura felt her life had ended too. She couldn't wait to get away from company, to move back into the house in Quay Street, and just be left alone. She remembered with horror what Paul had said, the last time she'd seen him, the very last time . . . he'd wanted to be left alone. Just as she did now. She had intruded on his grief. And now, she'd never have a chance to ask him to forgive her.

Sergeant Hardcastle ordered Cope, and the remainder of his native troops, who included Stan Hatbox, to ford the Fitzroy and follow the river along to the coast where they were to patrol the settled areas on the flats to Emu Park and on to Yeppoon. He had come to the same conclusion as Lieutenant Gooding, that if tribal blacks were massing, in retreat, in the mountains, they'd soon move down to the coastal strip in search of food, and those dangerous raiding parties would be with them.

257

Cope argued, of course, preferring to stay in town, and attempted to pull rank, but this time Hardcastle was in no mood for Cope's complaints. 'Get out there and earn your pay!' he shouted. 'You left those numbskulls without an officer and they lost three of their men. You might be a captain but you're still with the police. They'll need a patrol on the coast and if any of your men cause any strife, stirring up the blacks needlessly, I'll hold you responsible and you'll be a bloody private come your next payday.'

'What about Blackie? He's my best tracker.'

'He stays in the lockup until the magistrate comes to town. He can decide what to do about him. And take Charlie Penny with you. I'm sick of looking at him.'

'He won't get up. I can't make him shift.'

Hardcastle grabbed his revolver and loaded it. 'The bloody loafer, pulling his tribal trick, I'll shift the bugger.' He strode out into the weedy paddock. 'On your feet, Penny,' he shouted, but Charlie, asleep under the tree, refused to move. The Sergeant fired a shot at the ground beside him but Charlie didn't even flinch.

Cope went over to take a closer look, then stood back in amazement. 'He's dead!' he said. 'Stone bloody dead!'

'Let me see.' Hardcastle pushed Cope aside and turned the body over. 'Christ! He is too.'

He stood back, staring, then he shrugged. 'That's that then. Get your men to bury him.'

Later he entered in his report book that Charlie Penny had died of an unknown cause. No suspicious circumstances.

He didn't have to search for Ada Davies, he found her squatted on a low bench outside a tavern, sucking a clay pipe, unmistakably the woman Amelia Roberts had described. He grinned as he approached the huge woman. No wonder the girl was upset, this one would give a ghost the jimmies.

'How do you do?' he said, tipping his hat. 'Are you Mrs Davies?'

'That I am.'

'I believe you are looking for your husband. Could I have his name?'

'Tom Davies,' she said firmly. 'And he's still in this here town of yours, if he ain't been set upon.'

'By whom?'

'By bloody Roberts, that's whom. And he's got Tom's horse Stoker. Never a better, gamer horse this side of the black stump and I want him back.'

'Do you want to prefer charges against Roberts?'

She spat at his feet. 'I make my own charges,' she growled. 'But if you find my Tom, you let me know, eh?'

'Yes, I'll do that,' he said, knowing he'd get more out of her in time if he took her quietly. 'Where are you camped?'

She tugged her grimy hat further down over her face, muttering,

'That's my business.' Then she looked up at him with a wink. 'I'll be around in the daytime, mister, where no one's likely to take a potshot at me.'

'Do you think you're in danger?'

Her laugh was loud and hearty. 'Not if I watch my step. And I'm bloody good at that.'

Hardcastle nodded. 'Do me a favour,' he said. 'Keep away from young Miss Roberts. You gave her a bit of a fright.'

'Why would that be?' the woman asked sarcastically. 'I found her very helpful.' She lifted her bulk from the bench and strode away down the street.

The men inside the tavern were laughing. 'You know who that is?' they asked him.

'Yes. Her name is Mrs Davies and she's looking for her husband, Tom. Any of you blokes know him?'

They didn't but they knew her. 'She's Big Poll,' they said.

'From the goldfields?' Jim asked, recognising the nickname.

'Large as life,' they replied. 'And on the bloody warpath too. You wouldn't want to be her husband when she catches up with him.'

Or Roberts, the Sergeant worried. He couldn't have this woman hanging about looking for trouble, no matter who she was. Roberts was a dangerous man to rattle. He'd have to have another talk with Big Poll; try to persuade her to let the law have a go at him.

There was cheering in the streets and the Sergeant rushed out to see what was up. Another gold strike, he guessed, always cause for celebration. That opinion wasn't changed by the sight of Roberts and two of his mates riding triumphantly towards him, surrounded by a capering, jubilant mob.

'They caught them!' men yelled to him. 'Roberts vowed he'd find them and he bloody well did!'

'Find who?'

'The killers. The ones who killed Mrs MacNamara and her maid!'

He stared in disbelief as Roberts dismounted in front of the police station, accepting the cheers of the crowd as his due. He handed the Sergeant the formal notice of the apprehension and hanging of the two murderers, leaving him to study it with growing concern while Roberts addressed the gathering.

'I am not here to collect the reward,' he called, raising murmurs of approval. 'I don't need it. George and Baxter volunteered to come with me so they're entitled. As you are all aware, I only lost the homestead that I recently purchased, but my neighbour, Paul MacNamara, was struck the worst blow that a man can experience in his lifetime. A blow that no one should have to experience. I couldn't just sit back and let those savages get away with it or none of us would be safe.'

He glanced at Jim Hardcastle as the ever-growing crowd roared in

259

agreement, knowing that this hard-nosed old policeman would try to undermine him by asking too many questions. 'Jim here,' he said patronisingly, 'has done his best. But he's got his duties back here. Our military men were off in other directions. Posses raced about as they usually do, getting no place, tripping over themselves. So I decided it was my duty, if I am to stand up and be counted as your parliamentary representative, to go after these killers myself.'

As Boyd Roberts continued with his speech, the Sergeant knew that any arguments he presented against the illegal hanging of the two prisoners would be a waste of time. He studied the report from the Mines Inspector which stated that before a chosen group of jurors, the two had admitted to the murders. And he admitted to himself, recognising a few of the names on the three-page report as those of reliable men, that Roberts had indeed caught the killers. But there was still something not quite right about all this.

'How did you locate them?' he asked, interrupting the speech.

'We had a bit of a chat to some wild niggers we cornered,' George said meanly, with a grin for the crowd, who responded eagerly. 'We just told them plain, point us at the blokes who killed the white ladies, or things are going to get bloody uncomfortable for you fellers.'

There was no doubt he meant torture and that caused even greater excitement, then laughter, as George remarked laconically, 'They're not exactly heroes! They took us straight to them.'

'And why didn't you take your prisoners to Oberon?' Jim asked. 'Why haul them across country to the goldfields?'

Roberts sighed. He flicked at his moustache and shook his head. 'Jim,' he said patiently, but in a loud enough voice for them all to hear, 'you're an officer of the law. Are you seriously suggesting that I should have marched into MacNamara's place with the men who raped and murdered his wife?' He was playing the audience like a professional actor, and the hush was awesome. 'He'd have lynched them on the spot, Jim, and you know it. We were too far from Rockhampton, so we took them to the nearest settlement, the Bunya goldfields. And if you've got any quarrel with that, you'd better say so now.'

'We did the best we could,' Baxter shouted in an aggrieved voice.

George joined in. 'Fair bloody go! We caught them, we took them in and handed them over. You ask Mr Roberts. We didn't take no part in the proceedin's from then on.'

'That's true. I won't be accused of bias,' Boyd called. 'All we did was hand them over and let true-blue justice take its course.'

'They did the right thing,' a voice called from the crowd. 'They're entitled to the reward.' Shouts echoed in sympathy.

Money, Jim thought. That's what it's come down to. Any dispute I raise will be seen as an excuse not to pay the bloody reward.

Roberts lifted a hand for quiet. 'The main thing is,' he told them piously, 'that this terrible affair is now over. I hope someone will

260

communicate my deep regrets to Paul MacNamara and let him know that his wife's death has been avenged. And to the family of that poor young girl.'

Jim Hardcastle decided he might as well make the best of it if he were to survive in this town, now so full of relief and gratitude, so he joined in, applauding Roberts and his two brave followers.

Only Cosmo Newgate, a small, wiry figure, standing silently on the sidelines, refused to join the approbation. Jim noticed, and felt sorry for him. 'There goes his chance of winning the seat,' he said to himself. 'When this gets out, Roberts can't lose. He'll be a state-wide hero. And I'd better start watching my own step or Roberts will have me out on my ear.'

Jim had arranged to have a drink with Cosmo that night when he closed the station, but he thought better of it and went home instead.

Amelia was in a panic. She hated having to stay in this empty, isolated house on her own with the servants gone. She needed more servants but she didn't know where to look. Her father had always taken care of things like that. She supposed she could go into town and ask about, but the thought of bringing strangers into the house, strangers who might be drunkards or robbers or, worse, from the wretched Rockhampton working class, terrified her.

She blamed her father for all this. Why hadn't he built a house in town like everyone else? She was beginning to hate Beauview, looking out all day at the lonely grounds that could hide creeping rogues of all descriptions. At night it was far worse, just a rustling blackness.

The grounds were patrolled when he was home but when he left he took all his men with him, leaving only Andy and that stupid Teddy, and of course those ungrateful bitches of female servants who had deserted her. Obviously he didn't care about her at all; as long as he was safe she could go jump! Well, she'd have plenty to say to him about this when he got home.

Suspicion streaked through her. Why did he need guards anyway? She recalled Cosmo Newgate's articles, those hateful pages that claimed her father used stand-over tactics, and that he was implicated in the disappearance of several people. Not that it was true, all a pack of lies, just a ploy of Cosmo's to try to wrench the parliamentary seat from her father by denigrating him. That thought reminded her. When Boyd became a Member of Parliament they'd be without equal in the social set of Rockhampton, and not just here, in Brisbane as well, where she would also act as his hostess. Tyler would be busy here running his newspaper, so she would become famous as a hostess in both towns and she'd need wardrobes of beautiful clothes.

Which didn't alter her present circumstances. She frowned. She'd been left here to die of fright by the two men whose duty it was to take care of her.

The house was an absolute mess by this and she simply didn't care.

It was all she could do to make Andy light the stove so that she could cook a chop or an egg or something, and the meat she'd ordered from the butcher when he made his weekly round was already going off. The meat she knew, vaguely, was supposed to be salted, but she had no idea how to go about that. It was the same with the groceries, which were still in their box in the pantry, attracting armies of ants. She'd tried to cook the rice but it had turned into a volcano of sludge, so she'd thrown it out and was mainly living on bread and butter and jam. This morning the butter had been rancid, for which misfortune she'd blamed her father again. Ladies in her position were not expected to cook. How dare he put her in this position? What if Tyler came home now? She would practically be ashamed to present herself. It was a complicated business washing and ironing her lovely dresses, care had to be taken so that the colours wouldn't run, and using the black iron on the stove she'd already burned a neat hole in a silk dress which had left the iron sticky with smelly silk.

It was all too much. Left to her own devices, wandering the house with nothing to do, Amelia became more like her father, suspicion raging. Brushing away the blinkers, she began to employ his own searching tactics, beginning with that horse. She'd tried to cover up but she had known that Boyd gave that horse to Tyler. That terrible woman claimed it belonged to her husband. Was it stolen? Of course not! Her father could afford to buy a dozen horses better than that.

Befuddled with all this thinking, she recalled George, her father's friend and confidant, that awful creep with the slimy eyes, about as ugly as they came. He was, she realised, Daddy's only real friend. Other men came and went, but George was always with him. They spent hours together down there in his office, not just talking business as a man might with a servant, but drinking together, because Boyd often came up to the house from there smelling of grog. But George was never invited into the house, for which she was grateful. If he was neither a servant nor a friend, what was he?

George, on the other hand, was often in that office, but she was never invited, never admitted. Amelia's dislike of George, that nobody, increased to hate. If he could go in there so could she! Damn them! Lonely and miserable, with her father out of town, Amelia decided this was as good a time as any to take a look inside her father's holy of holies, that plain-looking sandstone office down by the side gate.

She searched his desk and located a few keys that might fit, then ran down through the gardens to the office. The biggest key fitted and soon she was inside, sneering at the bare, unlovely room with its barred windows. Except for the large imported rug, it was more like a prison cell with a desk. An inner door led to the second room but it was bolted and padlocked, so she contented herself with rifling through the desk drawers, which contained only dull papers, bills, receipts and things. There was a small safe but she couldn't open that, so she turned her attention to a plain pine cupboard.

The top shelf displayed only liquor and glasses and boxes of cigars. The bottom shelf held a cash box with some change and a few hundred pounds. She considered taking the money but since she still had enough in the house, she didn't bother. The other two shelves were just as boring, with stud sheets on his good horses and some wages books. Unwilling to admit that this illicit visit had been an utter waste of her time, Amelia thumbed over the wages book, disgusted to see that George, the horrible, whose surname she now saw was Petch, was paid strange amounts ranging from two pounds to fifty pounds.

'My God!' she said angrily. 'A ridiculous wage for a servant!' If her father could throw money about like this, he was obviously even richer than she'd imagined, and despite her irritation, that was quite good news. She ran her finger down the page and a name jumped out at her:

Tom Davies. He'd been paid seventeen pounds about five weeks ago.

'Ha!' she said. 'That'll shut that stupid old woman up!' Her husband had been here, had worked for Boyd and had been paid off! So there.

Having achieved nothing that might benefit her, except for the satisfaction of a look inside the silly dull office, Amelia tramped back up to the house, only to find that monstrous woman sitting comfortably in the cane swing chair on the front veranda.

'Get out of that chair!' she ordered. 'You're too heavy for it, you'll break it.'

'I find it very comfortable,' Mrs Davies replied jauntily. 'I haven't been on a swing since I was a kid.'

'I'm not surprised.' Amelia sniffed. 'Now will you please leave or I shall have to call the police again.'

'Yes. I heard you called in the traps. But we haven't finished talking about my man Tom.'

'We have so. I told you the truth. I never met him. But,' she said, feeling imperious with her new reservoir of information, 'I have since found out that he did work for my father. He was paid off, seventeen pounds to be exact, and then he left. He is no longer in my father's employ.'

'Good girl,' Mrs Davies said. 'Give me a hand, love. Help me get out of this bloody chair. I'm sunk in it like being stuck in a dunny.'

Reluctantly, Amelia took the hand, as cold and hard as concrete, and helped to drag the woman to her feet. 'So you'd better look elsewhere for your husband,' she said sternly, 'and stop worrying me.'

'Too true,' the old woman said, launching herself down the front steps to whistle to her horse. 'You're Amelia, aren't you?'

'Yes.'

'A pretty name,' she murmured. 'Yes. A damn pretty name if ever I heard one.'

'Thank you,' Amelia said, pleased with herself that she'd finally got rid of this pest.

As she rode out through the gates once again, Big Poll scowled. Paid him off, did they? Then why did he leave Stoker behind? Never in a million years would Tom sell or leave Stoker! He loved Stoker better than he loved his wife.

She broke off the road and turned her horse into the scrub. With an unerring sense of direction, she pushed her way through ragged virgin bush for several miles until she came to her campsite a few hundred yards from a creek. To other eyes, except for those of a blackfeller, she grinned, the area was undisturbed. Poll's few belongings were well hidden and the blackened campfire patch was covered by weathered brush.

As always, she looked after the horse first, allowing it to drink, then discarding the saddle and replacing its bridle with a soft halter. She gave his worn old hide a rubdown with a currycomb. 'You like that, don't you, Matey,' she said, and the horse shuddered with pleasure as the metal teeth rippled over his ribs in Poll's firm strong hand. She called him Matey because the high-falutin name he'd been given as a colt didn't suit his personality. 'Matey' had turned out to be a wise choice, because he sure was a good and loyal friend.

'Looks like we might be on our own now,' she said. 'Tom's among the missing and Dingo's gone.' Dingo had been her dog, a red cross-cattle dog with more dingo strain than anything else – hence his name. Only recently, Dingo had fended off a death adder that had slithered into Poll's tent, but the snake had put up a fight, and even though Dingo had killed him, the snake's long fangs had done their work and within twenty minutes, Dingo, too, was dead.

Poll sighed as she put away the currycomb, and patted the horse. 'We miss Dingo, don't we, Matey?' she said. 'But never mind, we'll find a pup just like him and teach him all the tricks too.'

She settled down on a fallen log, after first testing its capacity to support her, and took a swig of rum. 'You never liked tricks much, did you?' she said to the horse. 'But by Jesus, Dingo was clever, and Stoker too. I always said the pair of them shoulda been in a circus.' The rum made her nostalgic, and she reminisced about the animals. Dingo had reacted to words, he'd known a lot of words, but Stoker had worked to a whistle. Different whistles. At a given signal he'd dance in a circle, or rear up, or drop to his knees. Like a big bloody kid he was. He had some Arab in him but, like the dog, plenty of brains that came from survival in the wilds.

She checked herself. She was thinking of Stoker as if he were dead, and of course he'd better not be, or someone would pay for him too. She remembered the name, Mr Kemp. He had Stoker now and Stoker had to be found. But first Tom.

'Are you in danger?' the police joker had asked. 'Only from snakes, with Dingo gone,' she said to the horse, that was grazing nearby. 'Not from two-legged snakes.' With that she set about lighting the fire for an early supper. There'd be no lighting fires after dark to attract attention to Poll's camp. She didn't mind the dark, that was the time to look at the stars and wonder about them, to watch the pretty little sugar-gliders swoop from tree to tree, and all the other furry animals that came out to feed. They were company, and also they were easily alerted if intruders were about.

Satisfied that he'd made a substantial impact on the voters, Boyd left George and Baxter in town and rode on home. One in the eye for Cosmo, he thought, standing there like a stunned mullet, watching them cheer me. So much for all that garbage he'd written in his now extinct newspaper; people forgot, brains like sieves most of them. The only thing a voter wanted to know was what was in it for him. And he, Boyd, had brought home the goods, he'd given them what they wanted this week. Murderers brought to justice! He laughed. He had ridden past the offices of the *Capricorn Post*, pretending not to notice the closed doors, but he'd been delighted. That had put old Cosmo out of business. Now he'd get Tyler moving to start up a new newspaper. The by-election for the now vacant seat of Rockhampton would have to be held shortly, Tyler would know exactly when. Maybe just before the election he'd stage a phoney new gold strike somewhere close. 'Boyd Roberts does it again! Bringing good fortune to the town.' That would set them cheering. After the election he could express disappointment that the new reef had gone cold. A simple matter, these things happened all the time.

As he neared the house Amelia came running down to greet him, as she always did, except now she looked like a washerwoman, her hair untidy and her clothes slovenly. He frowned, until he realised she was crying.

'What the hell's wrong with you?' he asked as he dismounted, which only caused her to start screaming hysterically. He shook her to calm her down, but unable to get any sense out of her, he took her inside to the parlour and sat her down, reaching for the bell pull to summon the maids.

'There's no one here,' she wept. 'They left, Cook too, they left me here on my own! Why did you stay away so long? It's not fair to do this to me.'

'I haven't been away that long.' He scowled. 'Pull yourself together. Where's Tyler?'

She sniffed into her handkerchief. 'He's not here either. And he should be here. He wrote to me from Camelot Station, said he was going on to Oberon.'

'When was this?' Roberts snapped.

'I don't know. I forget.' She fished in a pocket for the letter. 'Here. Read it yourself.'

Boyd passed over the endearments and the tales of Tyler's travels,

265

to where he wrote that he was heading for Oberon with Lieutenant Gooding, Paul MacNamara and some troopers to search for the killers of the women.

'Oh Christ!' he said. He hadn't heard how that expedition had fared – it was too soon – but after his own attack on the blacks he'd known, hoped, they'd get a hot reception. And that stupid Tyler was with them.

'What's wrong?' she gulped.

'Nothing's wrong, except that I expected him to be here. He's got work to do. Does he think I'll just wait around until he's bloody ready?'

'I'm sorry,' she said. 'Perhaps he didn't understand. But I do wish he'd come home. I miss him and we have to make arrangements.'

If he comes home, Boyd thought dispassionately. Bloody fool, sticking his nose in other people's business. A reporter to the end, is our Tyler, and it well might be the end, too. But that's his bad luck. I'll just have to find someone else.

He stared about him. 'Did you say the staff quit? Why?'

Amelia launched into a long, weepy tale about that terrible woman Ada Davies who had come looking for her husband, and a confused rendition of why the staff had left. 'Where is he?' she asked her father. 'That Tom Davies.'

'Never heard of him.'

'But he worked for you.'

'He didn't work for me.'

'He did,' Amelia insisted. 'I saw his name in . . .' She bit her lip. 'In a book.'

'What book?'

She looked away. 'I don't know. I can't remember.'

'What book, Amelia?' he pressed angrily.

'I had to do something,' she cried defensively. 'I looked into your wages book so that I could tell the policeman he wasn't here.'

'You got into my office? How?'

'I found the key, and there's no need for you to be so snappy. I've been through enough already. I was only trying to help.'

'What were the police doing here?'

'I called them. I had to. And I told that woman that her husband had been here but you paid him off and he left. So she needn't bother coming back here.'

Boyd had been listening to her with mounting rage. Jesus! She'd brought in the law. She'd snooped in his office and brought out that wages book, which he'd burn shortly, and she'd gone spouting information to the police and to that Tom whatsisname's wife. 'You haven't got a brain in your bloody head. Davies was never here. That was someone else.'

'It was not,' she flared. 'He left his horse here.'

Boyd jumped as if he'd been stung. 'What horse?'

'The one you gave Tyler.'

Apprehension fuelled his anger as he tried to piece this together. 'I gave him a brumby from the back paddock.'

'That's right,' she sniffed, exasperated with him. 'The woman claims it belonged to her husband.'

Immediately, Boyd recognised his mistake. He had forgotten about the bastard's horse, forgotten all about the bloody thing. They should have let it loose in the bush.

'I really don't know,' Amelia conceded, 'if it was the horse she's looking for, and who cares? She's in trouble now. I charged her with assault on my person.'

'You what?' he shouted, blood pounding in his temples. He grabbed his riding whip. 'You put her in touch with the police?'

Frightened, Amelia backed away. 'No,' she screamed. 'I set the police on to her.'

'It's the same thing!' he yelled, lashing at her with his whip, out of control now as he tried to assess the damage this witless girl had created, blaming her for uncovering his mistake. She crouched against the wall as he rained stinging blows about her shoulders and back, the taut leather whip ripping at her dress. 'I'll teach you to interfere in my business!' he shouted, ignoring her screams, flogging her until she fell into a cringing, crying heap on the floor. Then, disgusted, he threw the whip aside and stormed from the room.

Amelia was in agony. She curled herself on the carpet, wishing she could die. She could feel warm, sticky blood seeping through her cotton dress, but she was too afraid to move in case he came back. 'He's mad,' she whispered to herself through clenched teeth. 'He's gone off his head.' And that frightened her even more. She was not alone any more, she was living in a house with a madman.

Eventually he returned, standing over her. 'The kitchen stinks,' he roared. 'Get out there and clean it up. I expect my supper within the hour.'

Amelia didn't move. Her body ached from the assault and her skin felt as if it had been stung by a thousand bees, but she had stopped crying, stopped feeling sorry for herself, training her savaged emotions on him. She hated him. 'Get it yourself,' she spat at him. She didn't care if he took the whip to her again; she couldn't feel any worse. But he went to his desk, took out the keys to his office and left the house, slamming the front door.

Slowly, unsteadily, she pulled herself to her feet and staggered along the passageway to her room, using the walls for support. Once inside, she gingerly removed her torn dress, trying not to reactivate the pain as she lifted the cotton from the bloodied slashes. She was as much appalled by the brute strength he had applied to her as by the beating itself. Every blow had been like the chop of an axe.

Crying with pain and a murderous rage that equalled her father's, Amelia poured a pitcher of water into a china basin and dabbed at the whip marks, the ones she could reach, while studying the emerging ugly bruises.

'You wait,' she said, issuing threats in the silent room. 'You'll be sorry for this. Wait until Tyler gets home. Wait until he sees what's happened to me.'

Pathetically she put her faith in Tyler, praying he would hurry back and rescue her from this madman, whom she now saw as a tyrant and a liar. Not for one minute had he bothered about all the things that had happened to her. And what had put him in such a rage anyway? Using her own well-established cunning, she guessed Boyd did have something to hide, that he was afraid of the police enquiring into his affairs, and that the workman Tom Davies had something to do with this. So what had he been up to?

Cosmo Newgate had written that Boyd was a stand-over merchant, as they called people like that, and if this was what he could do to his own daughter, what would he do to his enemies? She crawled into the rumpled bed, sucking in her breath at each new stab of pain, and then she wept. She missed Laura, remembering the fuss Laura had made at the silly little slap her father had given her. How awful that had seemed at the time, but now so trivial compared with the beating she had taken.

At least Laura had had Amelia to turn to in her distress, but now, who did Amelia have? No one. And if Boyd thought an apology would make up for this, he had another think coming, she sulked. She'd never speak to him again.

The room was dark and Amelia was far from sleep when she heard a light tap on one of the French windows leading out on to the veranda. 'Who is it?' she called. If it was her father he could stay out.

'Andy, miss,' he whispered.

She dragged herself out of bed, clutching her nightdress, and opened the door carefully. 'What do you want?'

The old gardener shuffled uneasily. 'Are you all right, missy?'

'No,' she said, tears erupting again at this unexpected sympathy. 'He beat me.'

'I thought so,' Andy whispered. 'He's gone into town. What say I get you a nice cup of tea?'

'Would you?' she asked miserably.

'Yeah. You hang on. I'll be right back.'

Andy made her tea from the kettle in the workmen's shed, adding milk and sugar to be on the safe side while Teddy Wills looked at him in surprise. 'Who's that for?'

'Never you mind. And don't you budge. I want to talk to you.'

The 'cup' of tea was served in a large enamel mug, but Amelia was grateful. 'Thank you,' she said to him.

'No trouble. You get some sleep. Everything will be all right in the morning, you'll see.'

Andy returned to the shed, not sure at all that everything would be all right in the morning. He had been gardening near the house and had heard the boss roaring at his daughter. He'd picked up most of the conversation. He'd also known Roberts was giving his daughter a belting, but he didn't dare interfere.

He reminded the stablehand about the woman, Mrs Davies, who'd come looking for her husband and the horse, and Teddy laughed. Being the only two men on the premises, with the boss and his offsiders away, Teddy and Andy shared lodgings in the bunkhouse separate from the main house, and they had discussed the strange happenings, what with the woman and then the Sergeant turning up.

'If I was you,' Andy told him quietly, 'I'd get the hell out of here tonight.'

'Why? I'd lose me job.'

'You might lose more than your job,' Andy said. 'Roberts is in a helluva rage about that grey horse. There's something fishy going on. I reckon the horse was stolen. Now you was the one let the cat out of the bag, told Mrs Davies it was here when the daughter said it wasn't. You said he gave it to Mr Kemp, you told me that yourself.'

'That's right,' Teddy said, bewildered.

'Well . . . The boss has just given the girl a belting for mentioning the nag. What do you think is going to happen when he gets around to you? I hear George is back too, and Baxter.'

They were both careful to keep clear of those two heavies, and Teddy was nervous now. 'Did I do something wrong?' he asked Andy.

'No, son. You just put your foot in it, that's all. You'd better do a bolt while you can.'

'Where will I go?'

'I hear they're looking for stockmen at Gracemere Station. Get yourself moving. You'll be safe out there.'

'Safe from what?'

'How the hell do I know?' Andy said. 'Just get cracking. I'll take care of the horses in the morning and tell the boss I don't know where you got to.'

Within minutes, Teddy had packed his swag and saddled up. He rode away from Beauview down the dark back track. Andy grinned. 'You're learning,' he called to the disappearing figure. And to himself, he rehearsed, 'Me, boss? I'm just the bloody gardener. Teddy must have gone walkabout during the night.'

Chapter Twelve

Paul MacNamara's back was as stiff as a board from being stuck in this tunnel, and he groaned as he tried to rearrange him limbs.

'Malliloora come soon,' Wodoro said. 'Why you come kill these people? They doan touch your women.'

Paul jerked his head up so fast he banged it on the rocky ceiling. He was surprised that Wodoro had decided to talk after several hours of silence, and even more surprised at his statement. 'That's all we are trying to find out,' he said. 'Are you sure?'

'Damn right.'

'Then who did? I have to know.'

'They don't know neither. You damn bad feller comen here, putting blame on Kutabura people, chasemup good people, killing good people.'

'We didn't come here to kill anyone. You heard me,' he accused. 'I just wanted to talk, to ask questions.'

Wodoro gave a grunt of disbelief. 'Then why you kill the families two days aback? Take prisoners.'

'What family? We didn't kill anyone.' He listened as Wodoro told him about the sudden attack that had taken place only two days ago, of the vicious, indiscriminate shooting of a peaceful group of blacks, and that the attackers had taken prisoners. One of the prisoners had been killed as they left the hills. 'But,' Wodoro added, 'one of the white men died too. His body still there with the dead horse.' He moved about to stare down at Paul. 'Then you come in talking peace. With soldiers? You think the Kutabura people gonna smile at you and say doan matter, gibbit tucker. You mad, you blokes.'

'I don't know anything about this, I swear.'

'And the Kutabura people doan know nothing about your women neither,' Wodoro snapped, mimicking his voice. 'Then you come yelling out the name of a dead man. You bloody stupid. Set them off real proper then.'

'Isn't it permitted to say the name of dead people?' Paul asked carefully.

'Bad magic,' Wodoro muttered.

Paul considered this and chose his words with care. 'The old man of whom I spoke. Is he dead?'

'Yes. What you want of him?'

'He could speak some English, that's all. I'm sorry he's dead, he was a brave old man.'

'He was my friend,' Wodoro said. 'He didn't want no fighting. He knew his people in big trouble.'

'Are you from another tribe?'

'Yes.'

'Where?'

'Long ways,' Wodoro replied, not inclined to talk any more.

Paul tried to figure out who had attacked the blacks, not only causing death and havoc but placing Gooding's troop in danger. Probably an independent posse, trying to be helpful. But only four men? Who the hell were they? Now he was very worried. If there'd been a raid on the blacks only a day or so before he had come into the mountains with Gooding, then they'd walked into a trap. The tribal people, wanting revenge, would have been waiting for them. He hoped the others had escaped without casualties, but he felt certain now that the spears raining down on him in that pool had been only the beginning of a battle.

Who were the idiots who had caused this? he raged. Some bastards showing off? Roaring into a native camp, guns blazing, making big fellows of themselves, taking prisoners so that they could boast about how brave they were. Killing blacks as if it were a sport!

Paul groaned. He had promised Gooding that if they rode quietly into the hills, showing no signs of aggression, it would be possible to communicate with these blacks. Until the attack weeks ago by Roberts' men, they'd been a peaceful mob. That was when it had all started, and despite Gorrabah's threats he was certain they'd settled down again. Then had come the attack on Jeannie and Clara, but the signs there were clear. Only a few, maybe three or four bucks, had been involved in that horrible crime. If they'd wanted to, the Aborigines from up here could have come down in force and created havoc right across this side of the valley.

But they hadn't, and that had enabled him, after his first burst of outrage, to retain faith in his belief that they wanted peace. And so he had convinced the Lieutenant that it would be possible to talk with them, to investigate the murders without any more trouble.

He had found his answer from this strange fellow, Wodoro, that the Kutabura people had not killed Jeannie and Clara. But at what cost? He knew now that he was responsible for leading the others into a trap. Never mind who had caused the blacks to turn nasty, he was responsible, and he prayed that the others had been able to get to safety in time. If only those bloodthirsty white men had not interfered, giving them good reason to fight back. He'd find out who those blokes were and . . .

Paul stopped himself. Thoroughly depressed, he wondered when there would be an end to all this violence. He thought of the prisoner whom Blackie Bob had shot, yet another innocent casualty of this

271

escalating war, the causes becoming blurred and blame scattered about like grapeshot.

If Kemp, or Gooding, or any of the troopers had been killed by revengeful blacks then that would bring the military out in force.

'Holy Mother of God,' he whispered to himself in despair. 'Is that what you wanted?'

He nudged Worodo's foot. 'I have to get home,' he said. 'We don't want any more trouble.'

Wodoro woke with a start. He was uncomfortable in the presence of this man, grateful to him for pulling him out of the pool, but also desperately afraid of him. A true believer in the magic of the spirits, for he had seen enough of it in his day, he was scared that Pace might intervene while he was so vulnerable. That voices might call out his secret, have it echo at them from the cave, exposing his guilt to the ears of his unwanted companion. The face still haunted him and he wished he could ask this boss man Paul if he had a kinsman by the name of Pace, but he dared not say the name. Instead of replying, he tapped his fingers in the thick dust, worrying the question. If the answer were 'no' he could shake off his fears, but if 'yes', then he would probably run for his life and take his chances out there. Besides, an answer in the affirmative would only instigate more questions, ones that he was not prepared to answer.

Malliloora rescued him, whispering to him from above to come out.

'There has been a battle,' he told Wodoro. 'Many people killed on both sides. Moongi was wounded but he will be made to apologise for striking you, so you are safe. The elders are pleased you survived, they do not want the humiliation of having you killed by a Kutabura man.'

'What about this white feller?' Wodoro asked, refusing to allow Paul to budge yet, in case eyes were watching.

'I explained who he is, and his quest, and that he saved you, and opinion is divided. However, we are permitted to take him to Harrabura, who will decide.'

'Where is Harrabura?'

'It is said we will find him high on the bluff near the cave where the old man went to die.'

'That's a long way from here. Were any of the redcoats killed?'

'Yes, four of them.'

'Then more redcoats will come now.'

'The people know that, they are preparing,' Malliloora said.

'We have to stop them, send this white man home quickly. He alone knows the reason for the fight, why your people had to fight.'

Malliloora shook his head. 'You forget the white men who attacked and took prisoners.'

'But he didn't know about that,' Wodoro insisted. 'And neither did the redcoats. They only came to find who killed his women.'

Malliloora smiled serenely. 'Why do you keep talking in circles? We know *his* purpose, we do not know the purpose of the redcoats. It is only because some men spoke for this fellow, men like the powerful Kamarga, that they will let him live, for the time being anyway. But as yet, no one has the right to release him.'

Wodoro had to explain to an angry Paul MacNamara that he was not going home but further into the mountains.

'That's stupid,' Paul said. 'Let me go and I'll try to keep the peace.'

'Too late.'

Paul listened, stunned, to hear that four troopers had been killed and more than a dozen blacks shot or wounded. 'Oh my God! It's even more important now. You have to let me go.'

They had emerged from the tunnel into thick scrub on a boulder-strewn ridge. Paul looked around him as if intent on heading downhill, regardless of his instructions.

'Don't try,' Wodoro warned. 'They won't let you go.'

Paul blinked, endeavouring to focus in the dappled sunlight. For the first time, he saw painted, coal-black bodies standing almost indistinguishable among the trees. Apparently, they were to have an escort to this next important man.

Above him, in a high gum, a koala roared, and Harrabura was instantly alert. He glanced up to see a crow diving ferociously at the koala, who had climbed too close to his nest. Cross at being prodded to move off, the old-man koala growled and roared his anger. Eventually he gave in and lumbered down to climb over and scale another tree, where he settled and looked down at Harrabura with his slumberous eyes.

'We have to go further down river,' Harrabura told his companions. 'This place is no good.'

Any change suited them, so they trotted after him for several miles, still keeping that track within view, and began their vigil again.

Late that afternoon they heard the horsemen coming. Well camou-flaged with stone-grey mud to match the tree trunks, Harrabura stood among the trees to watch them pass by.

'He is there, with them,' he told his men.

'Who is?'

'The one we must take,' Harrabura whispered excitedly. 'Come quickly, we have to follow them. They will make camp soon.'

By the time they caught up, still remaining hidden, Captain Cope's native police had dismounted and were beginning their evening chores.

Harrabura pointed out Stan Hatbox among the black men in their green uniforms and caps. 'That is the one I want, so do not take your eyes from him. We have to grab him and take him to Wodoro, so I don't want him killed.'

The other three looked decidedly nervous about this operation. Stealing a man from among this group of armed soldiers would be dangerous, if not suicidal, but Harrabura insisted that the spirits

273

would be with them so there was no need to worry. 'On the other hand,' he conceded, 'it will help if you are most cautious.'

They agreed fervently.

'I believe it would be best if you take him straight away,' Harrabura added, 'while they are moving about, not expecting visitors, for later when they sit down to rest they will place guards and then it will be more difficult for you.'

His men considered the latter a grave understatement, so they crept forward without wasting any more time, all three watching that one man. They saw him remove his cap, take a drink of water from a bag at his saddle, then begin to remove the trappings from the horse. He was in no hurry, talking and laughing with the other soldiers. They were relieved to see he had left his gun with the saddle.

After a while he took three horses a short way from the camp and they moved about to keep him in sight. He was carrying irons, which, they had observed, white men used to hobble the horses to stop them from straying. Between them, the tribal blacks saw the possibility of grabbing him while he bent down to do this work. But it was risky – he was still in clear view of the other soldiers, and the horses, held in awe by these black men, might take fright at the disturbance and rear up, raising the alarm.

They nudged and signalled to each other, trying to make a decision, but Stan Hatbox made it for them. Instead of hobbling the horses right away, he dropped the irons, hitched the horses to a tree and began to walk towards his three would-be kidnappers.

Thinking they'd been spotted, they almost ran, until they saw him unbuttoning his trousers. At that, great grins spread across their faces.

Stan dropped his pants and turned his back on them as he squatted in the thick grass to empty his bowels. It was then that they pounced. A waddy knocked him senseless and he was yanked into the bush, his trousers around his knees, and spirited away without a sound.

Harrabura was delighted. 'We must hurry,' he said, as they bound Stan by his hands and feet and threw him across the shoulders of the strongest of the warriors, like a stunned kangaroo. They ran with their prey through the bush, making for the mountains.

Captain Cope was in a tearing rage. Nothing seemed to be going right for him lately. And now, when they were setting up camp, he discovered that the numbskulls had left his tent behind, and this on a winter's night when, after a hot, dusty day, the temperature would drop to forty degrees, bringing with it drenching dew. He stormed about the camp, ordering the men to strip trees and build him a 'gunyah'.

'You know what this is, don't you?' he yelled. 'Your fathers, if you had any, must have shown you. Now hop to it, you useless black bastards.'

The leafy lean-to was soon set up, the Captain's folding bunk, chair, and table installed and his lamp lit, while his rattled troops dashed about preparing his and their supper, only to find that his muslin-encased smoked leg of pork was also lost or missing. The camp environment went from bad to worse. Three horses, not properly secured, were spooked by some disturbance and bolted through the clearing, leaping over the camp fires that held billies of mutton stew over spindly flames, clipping food tins and billy tea with their hooves before they raced free to gallop off down the track.

Bobby Cope stood at the entrance to his bower, screaming instructions as chaos reigned, keeping himself warm with slugs of over-proof rum. When he was presented with a supper of charcoal-cooked potatoes and gritty stew he hurled it away. He did remember to tell his men to place guards before he lurched back to his cot, nursing the bottle, griping with self-pity at having been lumbered with a force of uniformed orang-utans.

He was curled up in his blanket with a woollen scarf wrapped about his head when one of the men woke him to tell him something else was amiss. The Captain muttered curses at him for his stupidity and told him that whatever it was, it could wait until morning.

Jack Fong, whose mother had married a Chinaman, supposed the Captain was right; there was no point in trying to look for Stan Hatbox now. He grinned as he reported back to the squad. He had no love for Stan, who took the lead among his fellow blacks in treating Jack as the lowliest of the low just because his skin was a smidgen lighter in colour. Jack had argued that his kin observed matriarchal rules and so he was just as much Aborigine as they were, but it made no difference to them or to his status in the troop. They still despised him, and Stan had given him the nickname of 'Pong', which had stuck. They made rude jokes about him and held their noses to tease him.

In the morning the Captain blamed his men for being too lazy to search for Stan Hatbox, and they wasted hours in the cold, misty light, beating the surrounding bush for the missing trooper, to no avail.

In the end Captain Cope announced that Trooper Hatbox must have gone walkabout, which sent his men into fits of suppressed laughter. 'Going walkabout', they knew, was the full extent of the knowledge of their race held by most white men, including their officer. In this instance it was very funny. These men had long since lost touch with the Dreaming, and so to them, the traditional walkabout had no meaning whatsoever. Without bothering to enlighten Cope, they figured that Stan had either been bitten by a deadly snake and was lying in the bush somewhere, or he'd just plain deserted, as many others had done.

But Cope in his wisdom, understanding that 'walkabout' meant that the miscreant would return eventually, treated them to dire threats of what would happen to Stan when he got back, then ordered them to pack up and move out.

In the meantime, Stan, having regained consciousness and retrieved his trousers, was petrified of his captors as they hustled and hounded him out of the low mists into the mountains. He was equally terrified as they forced him to climb with them up a hazardous mountain trail from a deep gorge. Higher and higher they went, through ridges in the cliffs and along narrow ledges, until he was too scared to look down. He had no idea what they wanted of him, and he couldn't enquire because they spoke what his ilk called a 'brumby' language, unintelligible to Stan, whose ancestors hailed from the once great Kamilaroi nation.

However, he was cunning enough to know that, had they wished, they could have killed him, so obviously, if he didn't break his neck, he was safe enough for now. They needed him for some reason, and when they stopped for a feed, sharing with him pretty good tucker of turkey eggs and rock wallabies, he was meticulously polite to the old man with the straggly beard and white hair on his massive chest, to make a good impression.

They climbed for days, from dawn to dusk, when they made certain their prisoner was well secured, by trussing him up with cords like a game animal. But he was so tired that sleep, even lying in this position, was a relief.

Paul MacNamara's journey with his black companions was more leisurely, taking several days, and had he not been so upset about the fate of the troopers and the turmoil that would be going on back at Oberon, he would have enjoyed the long trek. He was being led right up into the mysterious mountains and the views, looking back over the valley, were magnificent.

One of the fearsome warriors came forward and spoke to Wodoro, who turned to Paul. 'This man's name is Kamarga. He says he knows you. He says you gave his mob a bullock feed.'

Paul stared at the native, who was smiling at him. 'By God,' he said, recognising the man. 'I did too.' He stretched out his hand. 'How do you do, Kamarga?' The black man took it warmly, shaking it so hard in recognition of the white man's ways that Paul thought his arm would come loose from its socket, but he gave no sign of his discomfort.

'Would you tell him that this is an important moment,' he asked Wodoro. 'And tell him that I am very sorry that I didn't try harder before this to shake hands with his people.'

As Wodoro translated, and Kamarga listened solemnly, Paul continued, 'I am sorry too that I kept so busy and did not make the time to learn his language. I hope it is not too late for all of our peoples.'

He realised, as he spoke, that it could be too late for him anyway, depending on the attitude of the judge he was yet to meet. But right now, these men appeared reasonable and amenable, so it didn't seem to matter. He felt he was in a limbo, not of time, but between two worlds, and was calmer than he had been in a long time.

Wodoro was translating again. 'Kamarga accepts that you speak truly. And even though I have already told you, he insists that his people did not kill your women.'

Kamarga was still talking, and Wodoro looked surprised. 'He says that he thinks Harrabura knows.'

'Who is Harrabura?' Paul asked eagerly.

Wodoro looked pained. 'The man we go to meet,' he said.

Wodoro left Paul with the guards and went ahead with Malliloora to find Harrabura at the bluff. The old man was deeply distressed to hear of the attack by white men and the ensuing battle that had taken place in his absence. 'I fear it is too late for peace now,' he wailed, 'and it makes my efforts seem trivial.'

It was left to Malliloora to explain to him that he had brought a prisoner for judgement, and to relate circumstances of his capture, and his name. This was such an important matter that Harrabura did not mention his own captive just yet, he simply listened to their story. Neither Wodoro nor Malliloora would insult him by pleading for or against the life of the white man, so he questioned them closely about all the happenings. Wodoro had kept his promise, if only by accident, to speak with the man and deliver the message, so he was dismissed, leaving Harrabura to discuss this weighty matter and its consequences with his protégé.

The next day, Wodoro was recalled. 'In memory of the old man, whom this person sought, we will set the white man free on condition of honour that he strives for peace in this region,' Harrabura announced.

'He can only strive,' Wodoro commented.

'As I said,' the elder noted firmly, 'we have decided that Kamarga can escort him down the mountain as far as the white man can guarantee his safety.'

'I will inform him,' Wodoro said.

Harrabura held up his hand. 'Not yet. We have another prisoner.'

Wodoro was amazed when Harrabura, not without a smirk of pride, produced his prisoner, whom Wodoro immediately recognised by the battered uniform as a member of the hated Native Mountain Police.

Harrabura pointed at Stan Hatbox. 'The same problem repeats itself here. Although he is of the dark race, we cannot speak with him, but he speaks the English. I believe it is of the utmost importance now that Malliloora learns that language as soon as possible, otherwise when you go we can no longer communicate.'

'The white man has promised to learn from the people he will invite back into the valley,' Wodoro reminded him.

'And if his death-time comes from a snake or a fall from one of the riding beasts, what then? I wish Malliloora to learn, and we should be greatly honoured to invite you to a safe place to retire with him for as long as you can spare and give him the lessons.'

Wodoro didn't need reminding that his own life had been spared, even though he had shouted a warning, causing Moongi to attack him, so although he would have preferred to leave now, he had to agree.

'Good,' Harrabura said. He turned to Malliloora: 'Now, you listen carefully, because Wodoro is going to question this piece of dung for us.'

Stan was thrust forward and Harrabura gave the first of his commands: 'Ask him who abused and killed the white women.'

'What?' Wodoro said, stunned at this sudden turn of events, but the old man was waiting, so he put the question.

Frantically, Stan shook his head. 'I doan know. How I bloody know?'

Harrabura didn't need the reply explained to him. He nodded to two of his men, who dragged Stan to the edge of the precipice, threatening to drop him over. 'Ask him again,' he instructed Wodoro.

This time Stan responded, screaming at Wodoro to help him. 'It wasn't me,' he shouted, 'it was Charlie Penny.'

Hearing the name, Harrabura gave a sigh of relief. He was on the right track. 'That criminal is dead,' he informed Wodoro. 'Ask him who else was there.'

At first Stan claimed he knew nothing of the killings, only what he had heard, but when strong hands lifted him into space over that great gorge he screamed for mercy and was again hauled back.

'The woman shot one of them,' Harrabura said. 'Ask him which one she shot.'

When Wodoro translated this question, Stan fell to his knees in fright. 'How does he know that?' he whispered.

'He is a great magic man,' Wodoro said, 'so you'd better tell the truth to me. He knows when you lie.'

Stan understood now who had pointed the bone at Charlie, and he began to babble hysterically, but Wodoro ordered him to be quiet and repeated the question.

'She shot my brother, Billy,' Stan wept.

'Who did?'

'The missus. Mrs MacNamara.'

Wodoro gave a slow whistle of surprise, and translated.

'Ah yes,' Harrabura replied. 'I saw this in my mind but I could not interpret. Ask him more.'

Slowly the whole miserable story was revealed, from the burning of the big house to the killing of the women, with Stan leaving his part out of it, claiming he had been wounded by a spear. He was keen to lodge most of the blame with Blackie Bob, who, he told Wodoro, was in jail in Rockhampton on a different charge. He didn't want to make things worse by letting this mob know that his mate Blackie was in the lockup for shooting dead one of their people.

'Now it is all revealed,' Harrabura said, at length. 'And for all his actions much blood has been spilled. You can bring up the white man and show him the answers.'

When Paul was taken up to the plateau, Stan Hatbox was the first person he saw. 'What the hell is he doing here?' he asked.

No one replied. First Paul had to be presented to Harrabura, who sat cross-legged on the flat polished rock and motioned for the white man to join him. Paul lowered himself to the ground with far less ease than this old fellow had done.

As he waited for judgement to be passed on him, a sharp wind blew up and he could smell the sea, and he realised they'd reached the summit of the ranges. He couldn't resist a quick glance to his left and was rewarded by a glimpse of the sapphire-blue ocean.

'He still does not see the evil before him,' Harrabura commented to Wodoro, who nodded. He was watching Stan, who now seemed even more afraid. This time of the boss man, and with good reason. 'You know that man?' he asked Paul.

'Yes. He's in the Native Police.'

'He is one of the men who killed your wife,' Wodoro said quietly, and Paul's head jerked upright; he was not sure that he had heard correctly.

'They're lying, them buggers,' Stan screamed to him. 'Doan listen to them, boss. It wasn't me.'

Paul looked directly at Harrabura, into that dark, dignified face that carried the wisdom of years, and spoke only to him, knowing, somehow, that this man would understand. 'Is this true?'

Harrabura returned his gaze and nodded. Under that gaze Paul felt limp, he wanted to jump up and grab the bastard but he seemed mesmerised, unable to move.

The old man addressed Wodoro, who then spoke to Paul. 'He has asked me to tell you exactly what happened and not to spare you. He also says this man was lying, that he took part in the acts.'

As Wodoro's story unfolded, Paul covered his face with his hands, but he was forced to listen. He had always wondered how attackers could have got so close to Jeannie without a fight, and now he heard that she had shot one of them dead, defending Clara, and he wept. But when Wodoro in his fractured English came to the grisly conclusion to the scene by the willows, he leapt to his feet, charging at Stan.

Kamarga pulled him back, restraining him, as Wodoro went on to relate how the trio had covered their tracks, taking the body of Billy Hatbox to bury it near the burned house.

'You did it?' Paul shouted. 'You killed my wife!'

'It wasn't just me,' Stan yelled. 'You heard him, it was Blackie Bob too, but it doan matter now. They're gonna kill us anyway. You never get out of here alive neither!'

Paul looked over to Wodoro. 'They killed them,' he said, shocked. 'When they turned up at Oberon I never gave them a thought. Oh God,' he said. 'And to think we were pleased to see them.'

'And you went off chasing all good peoples,' Wodoro snorted. 'You bloody stupid lot.'

'Oh, for Christ's sake shut up!' Paul snapped at him. 'I want you to tell Harrabura I am very sorry for blaming his people.'

'Kutabura people and other black peoples too.'

'Just tell him,' Paul said wearily, 'and let's get on with this.'

Wodoro obeyed and Harrabura sprang lightly to his feet as he replied.

'You are free to go,' Wodoro informed Paul, adding the conditions, which Paul agreed to, expressing his thanks. 'I'll take him with me,' he added, referring to Stan Hatbox. 'The both of them will hang.'

'No,' Wodoro said, nervously. 'This is not your business. You can have the other one, Blackie Bob.'

'But I have to take him down to prove this.'

'Not possible,' Wodoro said, pointing behind Paul, who swung about as he heard Stan scream, a scream that echoed and echoed, fading to a howl as he was flung out into the gorge, his body spinning until it disappeared. Only the sound lingered.

Exhausted by that sudden horror and by Wodoro's sickening story, Paul needed time to himself. He hardly noticed that it was Kamarga who supported him as he stumbled to the far side of the plateau, and, hanging on to a tree, lowered himself to a wide ledge where he sat, staring out to sea.

He could hear, behind him, the deep, rumbling talk of all those black men, their voices reminiscent of a rushing river, words tumbling, hurrying together, confusing him. He had to hang on to that tree because his head was pounding, his mind in a turmoil.

As he sat staring, an eagle circled, carrying a snake in its beak, and then made for its huge nest in the treetops where its young squawked impatiently. He focused on them to settle his mind to some sort of normalcy, to remind him that life's machinery ground on, no matter what happened. But he was left with a terrible sadness.

His first thoughts were for Jeannie. And for Clara.

Clara had seen Jeannie come to her aid, he told himself, and Jeannie got one of the bastards. 'Right between the eyes,' Wodoro had related. Before her death she would have had that satisfaction, and that was important to Jeannie. He didn't want to think past that any more. He couldn't. It was possible to take a leap from there to the apprehension of her killers. Three of them. Two dead, one to go.

Prompted by Harrabura, his translator had said that Charlie Penny had died 'by the bone'. Wodoro, he had noticed, was a secretive man, unwilling to discuss anything outside the immediate subject, and would not offer any explanation for that information. But Paul, born on an outback station, knew that pointing the bone, in the Aborigine culture, was terrifyingly real, even for renegades like Charlie, and it didn't surprise him. So that left Blackie Bob, and Paul would find him.

'It's no consolation,' he said to Jeannie, looking out at that magnificent, uncompromising blue ocean, 'but we've got them now and I pray you rest in peace. And I won't go off and leave you, as I thought I might do. I'll stay at Oberon, and try to keep the peace with these people.' He almost added: 'So that this won't ever happen again,' until he realised what he was about to say. After all that he'd heard, that he now knew, he had almost blamed the Kutabura people again. 'Force of habit,' he groaned, recognising how difficult it would be to convince his friends and neighbours to live in peace with these people, if even he could fall into that mistake so easily. The mistake was in training uneducated, illiterate blacks to be legal killers in that Native Police troop.

There and then, Paul MacNamara made a vow to himself that he would not rest until that force was disbanded and the likes of Captain Cope given their marching orders; he knew there'd be no chance of indicting them for the murders committed by their rampaging men.

The afternoon sun was beating the last of its heat on his back and so, with a last glance at the darkening sea and the rich green of the coastlands, he climbed back up to the plateau. It was deserted except for Kamarga, standing sentinel, an ancient dark shadow against the rose flush of dusk.

'Where have they gone?' Paul asked urgently, but Kamarga just shrugged, unable to reply.

'Where is Wodoro?' Paul insisted.

Kamarga put down his spear, took a deep breath and intoned the two words that Wodoro had taught him. 'Go home,' he said, eyes searching Paul's face to see if he had got it right.

'Go home?' Paul echoed, and Kamarga grinned, delighted.

'Go home,' he repeated with more confidence.

Paul wondered where the hell Oberon was from here. Kamarga led him down a track a few notches from the plateau and took him to another lookout where he could plainly see the great Fitzroy River snaking across the valley, a ribbon of pink in this light. He recalled the first time he and his brother, John, had seen this same view from the other direction, looking across the Berserker Ranges where he now stood. On top of everything else that had happened it was too much and his emotions spilled into tears.

Kamarga tapped him on the shoulder and pointed far across the river to where the lamps of Rockhampton were beginning to twinkle into life. He realised now that he was closer to the town than to Oberon, and that that was where Kamarga would be taking him.

He nodded his understanding and acceptance of the plan but had more questions: 'Where is Wodoro? *Who* is Wodoro?'

But of course, Kamarga could not reply. Harrabura, he knew, had gone back to the clans to press for peace talks, but Wodoro, the

Tingum man? He had gone into retreat with Malliloora, after which he would go on his way to lend his knowledge and assistance to other tribes. Kamarga knew it would take at least three days to get this man down the mountain, and he intended to use the time, as Wodoro had recommended, to learn white words. The white man, Paul, seemed agitated that Wodoro had left no message of farewell, but why should he? Wodoro was only an interpreter, and although he had risked his life to warn off the boss man, the whitefeller had, in his turn, saved Wodoro's life.

It was a legendary tale that Malliloora was already preparing to preserve, and Kamarga was proud to be part of it.

On the second day, Tyler was in the lead as they tried to find their way back to Oberon, pushing on through high dry grass and endless, endless trees. Gooding, suffering from concussion, was barely able to stay on his horse, so the trooper, Hal Simmonds, was riding beside him, nursing him along.

Cattle grazed in the rough scrub, standing stolidly, almost belligerently, to watch the trio pass by, huge, wild-looking beasts that seemed to have been propped in place by a giant hand, as a lesser man might set his tin soldiers. Tyler kept his distance. Only a few miles back, an angry bull had pawed and snorted at them, his wide horns lowered, and Tyler had had visions of a couple of tons of beef and bone charging at him. Instead of taking fright, though, Tyler's big grey horse had pranced sideways, eyeing the bull, mastering the situation as if he were the aggressor, and the bull had lumbered sulkily away. These monsters were a far cry from the gentle domestic milkers back on the Kemp farm.

He knew he shouldn't be bothered by the cattle, that this was just a symptom of his frayed nerves, not helped by the fear that they were lost, unable to spot a familiar landmark in the sameness of this country. For all he knew they could be five, or thirty, miles from the homestead; heading into the afternoon sun, they could easily bypass it.

When at last a rider came towards them through the bush, Tyler thanked God help had arrived, but it was only Rory.

'Hoy there!' he called. 'Jesus, am I glad to see you. Where the hell is the house? And where are the rest of the blokes?'

The Lieutenant tried to dismount, but Hal kept him in the saddle, as Tyler gave Rory the bad news. Ashen-faced, Rory ranged his horse the other side of Gooding's mount to give his support, content to follow Tyler, whose confidence in his own ability to lead them to a speck of civilisation on this vast property was ebbing away.

They scrambled up a rise in the uneven countryside, hoping to see the homestead, but no such luck. Instead they came across roughly erected cattle yards, large, dusty enclosures, empty now but showing signs of recent habitation. Tyler decided to follow the worn tracks of the herds.

It didn't take them to Oberon, but as the sun was setting, two bemused stockmen came upon them. 'Where are you headed?' they called.

'Oberon homestead,' Tyler replied.

'You're going in the wrong direction,' he was told. 'This is a cattle trail, drovers taking a mob on to Rockhampton. We've just sent them on their way.'

One of the stockmen stared at Lieutenant Gooding. 'He don't look too good. What's the matter with him?'

'Concussion, I think,' Tyler said.

Before he could explain any further, the lanky rider realised who they were. 'Christ!' he said. 'Aren't you the blokes who went out with the boss? With MacNamara?'

'Yes,' Tyler admitted. 'We ran into trouble.'

'Where's the boss then?' the man demanded.

Tyler shook his head. 'I don't know. We were ambushed.'

'You left him there?' the stockman accused.

Tyler was too weary to bear with this. 'Just direct us to the homestead. I'll explain as we go.'

To Tyler, the lights of Oberon were a huge relief. As they headed up the track a party of horsemen, led by Gus, rode out to meet them. 'Paul's horse came home,' the foreman shouted. 'Where's the boss?'

When Tyler had explained, once again, what had happened, they were escorted back to the house, but he could feel anger all about him, as if he were entering enemy territory. The troopers were silent, and the Lieutenant was close to passing out, so the dark glances and sharp, urgent questions were reserved for him, as if he alone were responsible for this débâcle.

He wished himself a hundred miles from this place, and made up his mind that he wanted no further part in their problems. As soon as he could, he would return to Rockhampton, leaving them to deal with the blacks. The crusader in him, given a taste of reality in dealing with tribal blacks, had deserted, and he no longer cared what became of the Aborigines. Nor would he be persuaded to join in any of the posses. It wasn't his war.

A charged stillness settled on the bereft MacNamara's homestead, sounds muffled in the velvety night. Men muttered, clustered in small agitated groups about this house – now ownerless – hardly able to express their heartache at the total annihilation of the people who had lived here. The empty house had assumed the impersonal identity of an assembly hall, and they moved restlessly throughout, avoiding, in unspoken respect, the bedrooms.

They lamented the futility of Paul's death, for hadn't a rider come this very day from Rockhampton with the startling and satisfying news that the murders of the Oberon women had been apprehended and hanged.

'Bloody good job!' they'd said, agreed, repeated, relieved. 'Bloody good job.'

Gus had considered sending riders to recall the boss and the troopers, but it would have been difficult to locate them. He knew that Gooding was only making the moves under sufferance, to appease Paul, planning to spend a few days in the hills, to try to make contact with old Gorrabah and then pull out whether they found him or not. Miserably, Gus realised that even if he had sent out a rider today, it would have been too late. Another tragedy had struck, equally as devastating.

When this latest bad news burst upon the station, Gus had a hard time insisting that no immediate action be taken. Hotheads on the Oberon staff were all for a wild armed rush into the hills to exact retribution, to shoot up every nigger in sight, to wipe the bastards out once and for all. He argued that such a mission was too dangerous, that they were outnumbered, and that a mad pack-rage for revenge would cost them their own lives. In the end his authority prevailed, his stout German-accented voice shouting them down. His prowess as a horseman and his unswerving dedication, as foreman on Oberon, to the interests of the absentee boss, who needed him so badly in this traumatic time, had earned him the respect of the hard, footloose men. They relented and waited for orders.

Lieutenant Gooding had enlisted the aid of Tyler Kemp in writing a full report of the ambush and casualties. He was determined not to give in until Tyler had written every detail for him, then he had collapsed. He had a large lump on his head but there was nothing they could do for him so they let him sleep. Accidents with horses were common and the men were adept at fixing broken limbs, but head bumps had to take their chances.

Meanwhile, Tyler was questioning Gus about the capture of the two blacks, taking his own notes this time. He was surprised, and pleased, to hear that it was Boyd Roberts, operating from his own property, who had caught the murderers, but Gus wasn't taking it so well. 'I don't trust that bastard. Why didn't he bring them here? They tell me he deliberately avoided Oberon for the protection of his prisoners.'

'That's fair enough,' Tyler argued. 'Bringing the killers of Jeannie MacNamara on to MacNamara's station would have caused uproar. Even a lynching. I think it showed genuine concern for the law.'

'Since when did Roberts have genuine concern for anything but himself?' Gus snorted. 'And if he'd brought them here, with the military on the spot, there'd have been no lynching, and Paul and the troopers would still be alive. You wouldn't have needed to go into the hills at all.'

'Don't rub it in,' Tyler said miserably. 'I'm well aware of that. It was all for nothing.'

'Too bloody right it was all for nothing. And you can blame Roberts.'

'You can't blame Roberts,' Tyler snapped. 'He wasn't to know what we planned to do.'

Gus thumped his fist on the table. 'He wasn't, eh? Then you write this in your bloody book! One of our boundary riders met up with Roberts' men and he told them the troopers had arrived at Oberon. That Roberts bastard knew they were here all right. And me, I want to know how he interrogated wild blacks any better then we did.'

'I hear he used rougher persuasion,' Tyler said.

'So you say. But those blackfellers don't speak English. And if you believe that they showed him where to walk in, pick up the killers, and bring them out like little lambs, you're as bloody mad as the rest.'

'He could have,' Tyler said, uncertain now.

'And pigs fly! Look what happened to you, and you weren't trying to take prisoners. And you had the protection of mounted troopers, man. Roberts and two men taking on all those blacks? That's bullshit.'

'We haven't really heard the full story,' Tyler said, trying to defend Roberts.

'And you never will,' Gus retorted. 'In the morning I'm taking all the men to patrol the foothills in case Paul or any of the others escape and need help. You'd better stay here and rest.'

They patrolled all day but without success, nor did they sight any blacks. Gus rode with the two troopers, well armed in case of attack, but all was calm as if nothing had happened. 'I think you got payback,' he said eventually. 'Roberts captured two of their men and took them away, so the blacks punished you lot.'

'Right,' Rory said meanly. 'So the army gets the next go at them. They'll wonder what struck 'em when we come back.'

Gus shrugged, despairing. They were turning Oberon into a battleground, the last thing Paul had wanted.

Fortunately, the Lieutenant suffered no after-effects. When the search for survivors proved fruitless he decided to take his remaining troopers and return to Rockhampton for further orders, miserably aware that when a larger force was dispatched to this area he would be expected to be in the lead. So much for his quiet remaining years in the army.

He promised to send a telegram to Mrs Rivadavia, Paul's mother. 'The poor woman,' he told Gus. 'More terrible news for her. But I will have to make it formal; all I can report is that he is missing, believed killed.'

Gus nodded, emotion choking him now that the moment had come to face up to the death of his friend. 'Will you say more for me? Tell her I will stay here and keep Oberon going until the family decides what to do. And tell her I am very sorry.'

'Of course,' Gooding said.

Before they left, Gus spoke to Tyler. 'I reckon you oughta start listening with your head, not your ears, before you go writing about all this.'

A small town, Poll knew, was no different from a mining community when it came to gossip; everyone knew everyone else's business. So, sitting about with old stagers in the taverns or joining them in the shade of the grand old banyan trees to share a billy of tea, Big Poll learned a lot about the local residents. She listened to them talking about Boyd Roberts, and in answer to her questions she found out about this Mr Kemp who had Tom's horse, Stoker. She heard that he was a reporter feller, from Brisbane, a mate of Roberts, staying at his fine house. She also learned that he was out of town on a walkabout with Lieutenant Gooding and a troop of Mounted Rifles. 'Due back any day,' she was told.

Poll was there, standing impassively in the background, when Roberts and his offsiders returned to Rockhampton, riding high with all their news, which was of no interest to Poll. If her Tom were still around he'd know where to find her by this; she'd left word at the goldfields that she was on her way to 'Rocky', and every innkeeper and grog shop owner in the town was aware of her presence.

Cat and mouse, she thought, standing, hands on her wide hips, sucking on her pipe, scrutinising Roberts. Every so often, Hardcastle glanced in her direction. 'No need to worry, mate,' she said to herself. 'I'm not ready for His Eminence yet, I want to get a look at this horse first.'

By all accounts Roberts was a real ball of fire in the town, heading for the Parliament, they said, much impressed. Poll spat. She didn't know about these things and she didn't want to know, she had more important matters on her mind and plenty of time to attend to them. But she took note of the two men with Roberts. 'His trusties,' a miner told her. 'Been with him a good while.' She nodded, observing not only the trusties but their mounts, so that she could spot them if they were around.

'They'll keep,' she muttered, bored with all the talk and cheering, and stomped back for a loaf under the banyan.

Cosmo Newgate had heard that the *Brisbane Courier* was installing new presses, so he immediately arranged to purchase one of the old ones. In the meantime he tidied up his offices, preparing for the arrival by ship of his new equipment. It pleased him that he had no paper this week, because he wouldn't have to report Boyd Roberts' success in apprehending the murderers of Mrs MacNamara and the girl, but his wry amusement turned to frustration when, more than a week later, Lieutenant Gooding came back with another big story: the ambush of troopers in the Berserker Ranges by blacks, resulting in the

286

loss of four soldiers and MacNamara himself.

Distressing as this news was, especially about Paul MacNamara, Cosmo also fretted over his own losses. He could have doubled circulation printing this story and probably would have been able to put out special editions. Lord knew he needed the money now to resurrect the paper. He still claimed that Roberts was behind the destruction of his presses, but Jim Hardcastle seemed to have lost interest and Cosmo supposed that with all these other things happening, his troubles were becoming history to the busy policeman.

Nevertheless, Cosmo attended briefings at the police station and the barracks, feeling sorry for Gooding who was caught in a cleft stick, fending off complaints, blame, and demands for action by the locals while he waited for instructions from his military headquarters in Brisbane. 'They'll be slow in coming,' Cosmo commented in an aside to the Lieutenant.

'Suits me,' Gooding replied softly. 'For once I'm hoping for all talk and no action. They can chew the cud on this one down there in Brisbane for as long as they like. When I asked for more troops, they sent me Cope and his thugs. If I ride into those mountains now with every man I've got they can expect a high casualty rate.'

'Why is that?'

'Because the place is a fortress and the defenders are willing to fight. I tell you, Cosmo, when I saw that wall of blacks on the cliffs above us I nearly had a heart attack.'

'Was that when you had to leave MacNamara?'

Tyler Kemp joined them. 'We didn't have any choice. You said it yourself, Peter. The man had a death wish.'

'Someone, one of the blacks, called to him in English,' Gooding said. 'That's what delayed him.'

'He wasn't delayed,' Tyler growled. 'He was playing the great white father and nearly got us all killed. I blame him for the lives of those troopers.'

'Do you?' Cosmo asked Gooding.

'No, I don't. The responsibility rests with me. I feel bad enough without ducking it, and I'll thank you to keep your opinions to yourself, Tyler.'

'Fat chance,' Cosmo said grimly. 'We'll read his version in the *Brisbane Courier*, won't we, Kemp?'

'Why not? People are entitled to hear the facts.'

'Like the facts you wrote about Laura Maskey?' Cosmo snapped.

Tyler laughed. 'Ah, come on, Cosmo. You'd have done well out of it. I'm bloody worn out. If you don't need me any more, I'm going home.'

'To Boyd Roberts?' Cosmo retorted.

'To see my fiancée and to find some blessed rest in a comfortable bed at last. It's been a long day.'

When he left, Gooding took delight in telling Cosmo that Grace

Carlisle had lowered the boom on Tyler, because of her friend Miss Maskey, relegating him to the bunkhouse.

'Good on her,' Cosmo laughed. 'He's a bastard, that one.'

'He's not really,' Gooding replied. 'He's just hard to figure. I've listened to him. He grew up on a bootlace, crook on the moneyed class, but he's got a sharp mind and he battled himself into a good job on the *Courier*. But a taste of the high life out there at Beauview, not to mention the pretty young Amelia, has him sweating for more.'

'He's a bastard of a reporter,' the old-time journalist said. 'He doesn't let the truth get in the way of a good story.'

'Maybe that was how he was trained,' Gooding argued. 'But let us not forget that when the chips were down your bastard of a reporter came back for me.'

'Probably panic,' Cosmo sneered.

'Oh no, he's a fine horseman. I'll admit he's an argumentative bugger and a cold fish when it comes to your business, but I reckon breeding will out. And they might have been dirt-poor mountain people, but his parents, the Kemps, brought him up right.'

Cosmo's dislike of Tyler Kemp would not permit him to allow that Boyd Roberts' latest stooge had any good points. 'In that case you'd better write and thank them, because you won't get any change out of him now that he's on safe ground.'

'I intend to do just that,' the Lieutenant said, 'before I submit my resignation from the force. I was trained in artillery. I'm too old for bush warfare, let alone fighting like a mountain goat.'

In the meantime the fine horseman was riding out towards Beauview, and he was exhausted. He had almost chosen to stay in town for the night so that he could greet Amelia with the enthusiasm she deserved, not as a worn-out bushie with a scruffy ginger beard and faded, frayed clothes. But she might have heard they were back in town and would be hurt if he stayed away.

He hoped that Boyd was out somewhere, not only so that he could be alone with Amelia, but because his thoughts about her father were confused. He was not inclined to believe Gus's understandable casting about for blame at the loss of Paul MacNamara, but doubts nagged him, just as they had the first night he'd spent at Beauview.

Tyler made a determined effort to push them aside. What was done was done. When he had shaken off this awful weariness he'd write the story of the ambush, and it would be sensational. Tyler Kemp, on the spot! Better than anything else he'd written on his travels in the north, and it would earn him a packet.

The sturdy, tireless horse was cantering up the leafy track when Tyler heard another horse thudding along in the dust behind him. Instantly he halted Greybeard and wheeled about. He had no intention of being bushwhacked now, on the last lap, after all he'd been through.

'Who goes there?' he shouted. He needn't have worried. The stranger was only a bulky old woman riding astride a clumping steed. 'I'm sorry,' he said, dumping the rifle back in its sling. 'A person can't be too careful these days.'

'True enough,' she replied, the voice as rough as her appearance. 'Would you be Mr Kemp?'

'Yes.'

'Then we'd better have a talk,' she said lazily.

Tyler stared at this old bag of a woman. 'Some other time, madam. I'm beat.'

'If you like,' she said amiably. 'But first I'll have me horse back.'

'What horse?'

'The one under you, mate. He belongs to my husband, Tom.'

Tyler sighed. 'The horse belonged to Mr Roberts. It was given to me. He is mine and I do not intend to part with him.'

The woman laughed, a throaty, rumbling burst of merriment. 'You don't, eh?' She whistled, and the horse dropped to his knees so suddenly that Tyler, caught off guard, was thrown over his head.

Big Poll took Stoker's bridle, patting him on the head. 'Good lad, good lad. Ah, but it's lovely to see you again. Come on, boy.'

With Tyler running after them, shouting and cursing, Poll galloped away, Stoker pacing alongside her. She rode all the way into town and hitched the horses outside the police station.

Jim Hardcastle stared in amazement as she dumped Tyler's saddle, pack and rifle at his feet. 'I've got Tom's horse back,' she told him, 'but I'm no thief like some people we know. Them's Mr Kemp's gear. I couldn't leave his gun in case he bunged a bullet in me back.'

'I see.' Jim nodded. 'Is that the horse?'

She looked at Stoker with a smile. 'Yes, that's him.'

'Can you prove he's your horse?'

She grinned. 'Sure can. Watch this.' She gave another whistle and Stoker put his teeth to the bridle at the hitching rail, untied it and carried it over to the wooden steps. 'Do you want him to come up here on to the veranda?' she asked Jim. 'He can climb steps too.'

'No thanks,' Jim laughed. 'I doubt they'd hold his weight.' He walked down to examine the horse. 'It's the one Tyler's been riding all right,' he said, fondling the horse's head. Intelligent eyes with thick grey lashes gazed back at him and he smiled. 'Pretty smart lad, aren't you?'

Poll beamed and gave a trill of a whistle. 'Say thanks, Stoker,' she instructed, and the horse thrust out one leg and bowed his head. 'He never forgets nothing,' she said, breaking an apple to share between both horses. 'Now you tell me if anyone would sell a horse like that?'

He shook his head, worried. It was obviously her horse, but Roberts might disagree. 'I ought to impound him until we can work this out,' he said.

Poll gave a howl of dismay. 'You wouldn't be that cruel!' she cried.

289

'Poor Stoker, he must have been bloody lonely all this time. We ain't going anywhere until we find Tom, Stoker and me, so he'll be around. But listen to me, mate, I'm betting Roberts won't claim him. And if he don't, she growled, 'that oughta give you something to think about.'

Bushwhacked after all! And by a woman! A bloody woman! Tyler stormed up the remaining mile of track in a rage and trudged along the carriageway to the house, pushing against high winds that thrashed the trees and whipped across the terraces. He knocked on the front door and it was opened by a new maid.

'Yes?' she asked, looking disdainfully at him as if he were a tramp.

'Miss Roberts,' he replied.

'Who shall I say is calling?'

'Mr Kemp,' he snapped, standing impatiently, still cursing his misfortune.

Then Amelia came running. She flung herself into his arms, not caring about his appearance. 'Oh Tyler, my darling, I'm so happy to see you. It is so wonderful to have you back at last. I was beginning to think I'd never see you again.'

Boyd came out, smiling broadly, to shake his hand, pat him on the back, invite him into the parlour for a drink, with Amelia hanging lovingly on his arm. As soon as he got his breath, Tyler launched into his latest disaster. 'Here I was, coming home,' he told them, 'safe at last, and I got bushwhacked.'

'Oh no!' Amelia exclaimed. 'Were you hurt?'

'When was this?' Boyd asked.

'On the road up to the house, down the hill there. Just now.'

'Good God!' Boyd said. 'I'll get George after them. Which way did they go?'

'Not they,' Tyler said ruefully, 'her. I got held up by a bloody old woman. She conned me, came up quite pleasantly and then started talking about owning Greybeard, or some such rubbish. Spooked the damn horse. I got bucked off and she bolted with the horse, rifle, pack, everything! I was left standing there like a knot on a log. I'll report her to the police in the morning, she won't get away with it. You can't miss her. She's the size of a whale.'

Tyler became aware of a strained silence. Amelia, he could swear, looked frightened, and Boyd seemed to freeze. His jaw tightened and his eyes narrowed, and he brushed angrily at his moustache as if to wipe away this unpleasant news.

Thinking that they didn't believe him, Tyler tried again. 'I know it sounds mad, but it's true. I got done over by a grubby old woman.' To relieve the situation he managed a laugh. 'But don't worry about it. I'll see Jim Hardcastle in the morning, he'll catch up with her. It's bad enough losing all the notebooks I had in my pack, but she's not getting away with the horse.'

'Forget the horse,' Boyd said, more composed now. 'I'll give you another one. It wasn't much of a nag anyway.'

'That's very kind of you, Boyd, but I've become fond of Greybeard, he's really a great horse. I'm not going to let her take him, the bloody old witch.'

Boyd downed his whisky. 'Bugger the horse,' he said impatiently. 'We've got more important things to worry about. Robbers broke into the *Capricorn Post* and wrecked the place.'

'So I heard,' Tyler commented.

'Just when I was negotiating to buy it,' Boyd continued. 'So now we have to set up our own paper. I've been waiting for you to get back,' he snapped, 'wondering if you're serious about this business.'

'Of course I am,' Tyler said, irritated that his welcome had chilled considerably.

'Then we have to get on with it,' Boyd told him. 'I want you to get down to Brisbane and buy whatever equipment is necessary. The election is to be held in a couple of months; we have to be up and running well before then.'

'It doesn't give me much time,' Tyler worried.

'Whose fault is that?' Roberts grunted, turning his back to chose a cheroot from a silver box.

Amelia walked with Tyler to his room and kissed him fervently. 'I'll tell the maid to run a bath for you,' she whispered.

'That would be heaven,' he said. 'It is so good to see you again. Are you still going to marry me?'

'Oh yes,' she replied, clinging to him.

'You look a little tired,' he said. 'Have you been keeping well?'

'Yes, I'm just fine. I've been missing you, that's all.'

She went to her room to dress for dinner, relieved that the fading scars were well hidden by her long-sleeved dress and the high, stiff lace collar. Amelia had intended to tell him all about the whipping her father had given her, but now she knew she could not. It would be too embarrassing and it might change his attitude towards Boyd. After that last exchange between them she couldn't have Tyler and Boyd falling out; her father might forbid the marriage. The way she felt these days, she'd be happy to run off with Tyler, to elope with him, but would he? It was hard to tell. He might be just like all the rest of the men who worked for Boyd Roberts, jumping at his every command.

It occurred to Amelia that Tyler could be more embarrassed than her if she told him about the whipping. He might prefer not to know, rather than have to stand up to Boyd and ruin his chance of prosperity.

Thinking it over, she decided not to mention the incident, to let her father think it was forgotten. But standing defiantly before the mirror, she resolved not to forget. Not ever. With a smirk, she recalled Tyler's woes, having the horse stolen out from under him. Tyler wasn't hurt and he could write his old notes again, but the look on her father's face told her it had really worried him. She had been startled at the mention of the woman, thinking that somehow her father might blame her again, but – Amelia tied blue ribbons in her black hair with deft little fingers – it was nothing to do with her now. If Tyler preferred charges against the woman, Boyd couldn't stop him, he couldn't beat him up too! Not once had he let on that he knew who that woman was, and a glance from him had warned her to shut up. Amelia had seen Boyd nervous and she was delighted. What did he have to hide?

Amelia was warming to Mrs Davies by the minute. She was really stirring the pot and she wasn't afraid of Boyd Roberts.

She went down to dinner with a soft crocheted shawl wrapped around her shoulders, smiling happily, pretending to be her old self again. The new cook, employed by her father, wasn't as good as the last one, but Amelia didn't care any more. She encouraged Tyler to tell them of his travels, horrified at the tragic encounter with the blacks and his narrow escape.

'Daddy's a hero too,' she told Tyler. 'He brought in the murderers and his men won the reward.'

'Yes,' Tyler said. 'You were lucky you didn't run into the mob we met, Boyd. Where did you locate the men you captured?'

Roberts looked bored. 'Good God, Tyler, we've got better things to discuss than the bloody blacks. I'm sick of hearing about them. And as for that horse, I've no idea where it came from. We've got a new stablehand, so he's no help. Let the bloody woman have it. Wait until I show you the three Thoroughbreds I bought last week. You can take your pick.'

'That's not the point,' Tyler argued. 'I'm not going to let myself get robbed.'

Amelia smiled blankly and sliced into her roast beef, but she could have hugged him. That's right, she thought, you keep rattling him too. Any talk of that horse and Mrs Davies drives him mad. She was enjoying her father's irritation and wondering what she could do to cause him more trouble. The old bastard.

'I think I'll come with you to Brisbane,' Boyd said to Tyler.

Amelia perked up. 'Oh goody. Can I come too?'

Boyd looked at her without enthusiasm. 'I suppose so,' he said.

The next morning Tyler went straight to the police station, riding the Thoroughbred that Boyd had insisted he take. He didn't have much choice, it was a long walk into town. He was dismayed that although Hardcastle produced his gear, he was too busy to worry about the horse. 'I know all about it,' he said abruptly. 'It's her horse, without a doubt. I interviewed the stablehand while you were away. Out at Beauview they thought it was just a stray, not a breed horse by any means, so what's the worry?'

'Jesus! The bloody woman bushwhacked me.'

'Tyler, relax. Her name is Big Poll. Everyone knows her, it is just her way. You're lucky she didn't plug you. Horse-stealing rates with murder up here.'

'But I didn't steal it!'

Jim Hardcastle knew that, but he wasn't prepared to probe into Boyd Roberts' affairs. 'She wasn't to know that,' he countered. 'Fair go, Tyler, she let you off light. It's her horse and that's the end of it.'

Losing Greybeard hurt, but Tyler had to accept the decision. As he left the police station, he reflected that Beauview somehow seemed different. Boyd was edgy, a mean temper just below the surface. There was a completely new staff, with no explanation, and even Amelia had changed. She seemed brittle, nervy. But then he supposed he was to blame. He'd upset them both by staying away too long. And he could understand why Boyd was sick of relating the story about capturing the men, because he was feeling the same way about the ambush. Time to get back to business. He went to the shipping office and found that there was a ship leaving for Brisbane in two days' time. He booked three tickets. It would be fun to return to Brisbane with his fiancée. Boyd had insisted that they all stay at the Royal Exchange Hotel, which was the best in town, very posh. The trip would give Tyler a chance to pay up his landlady and collect the rest of his things. After all the excitement up here, a sojourn in luxury down in Brisbane, with Amelia on his arm, was a wonderful prospect.

With a grand future before him, Tyler decided to draw out most of his meagre savings when they arrived in Brisbane and buy Amelia an engagement ring.

That night he asked Boyd if he might announce his engagement to Amelia in Brisbane. Her father, in a much better mood, was delighted. Tyler had repeated ruefully the sad story of losing the horse, and Boyd had laughed. 'Bad luck, old crock. But it still beats me why you'd pick a brumby over a Thoroughbred.' Graciously he went off after dinner so that the lovebirds could have the parlour to themselves.

Amelia was thrilled that they were to announce their engagement in Brisbane, especially since Tyler promised to place the news in the *Brisbane Courier*. She was disappointed that all the fuss about the horse had turned into a fizzer, but she kept that to herself, and sitting there on the big couch with her famous and sophisticated lover, she allowed him to take quite naughty liberties with her, ecstatic with their lovemaking.

While the men attended to their own affairs, she spent the next afternoon shopping for absolute necessities. All the really lovely things she would buy in Brisbane, but she wanted this and that for the voyage. It was too exciting for words. Every time she made a purchase she had it delivered to her carriage, which was waiting right in the centre of town in East Street. It was a pity, she mused, that Laura wasn't here so that she could tell her the wonderful news about her engagement, quite definite now. She guessed she'd see her at the races when they returned. Everyone came to the three-day race meeting. That was why Boyd – she refused in her mind to call him Daddy any more – was in such a rush to get to Brisbane, so that he could get back for the races. Feeling so jubilant made her quite charitable about Laura who, possibly, might not even be able to afford to come to the races, she being so poor now.

It was a warm, sunny day so as she strolled along William Street, away from the shelter of shop awnings, she put up her parasol. In one of the workmen's cottages, she'd been told, there was a gypsy woman who told fortunes, and Amelia was eager to find her. Madame Rosetta was her name, and word had it that she was only 'in' to customers when a slate carrying her name was hung on the gate.

Amelia tripped along, searching for the gate behind which lurked the mysterious lady. On the way she passed one of the many ugly grog shops, and who should come lurching out but that disgusting stringy-haired fellow who worked for her father. Baxter was his name, and if he ever had a good wash he might just look presentable, but right now he was as drunk as a skunk, whatever that was.

He staggered on to the road to greet her. 'G'day, miss,' he mouthed, his eyes crossed, his mouth twisted like rubber.

Very smartly Amelia dismissed him. 'Get out of my way.' She ignored his drunken protests that he just wanted to tell her how pretty she looked, but he persisted, stumbling towards her.

'Think you're too good for me, do you?' he mumbled. 'I've got a girl of me own back home jes' as good as you.'

'Then get home and find her,' Amelia snapped.

'Miss Toffee-nose, aren't ye?' he bawled at her, grabbing her arm. 'Aren't ye? Too stuck-up to know when someone's bein' nice to youse.'

'You let go of me, you drunken lout,' she spat at him. 'My father will hear about this.'

He laughed, and croaked, 'Oh yeah. Your bloody ol' man. I don't give a shit about him. I bin paid off. I'm goin' home.' Then he looked maudlin, tears glistening in his cold, watery eyes. 'That's if I've got any cash left.'

'I said let go of me,' she cried, whacking him with her frail parasol.

Baxter laughed, enjoying the blows she was raining on him like feathers. 'You're a little tiger, aren't you?' he said, leaping about in feigned pain, and dragging her with him. 'Come and meet me mates.'

Really frightened now, as he started to drag her towards one of those houses, Amelia began to kick at him. All at once, Mrs Davies loomed up and with one backhanded swipe sent Baxter flying. She followed up with several savage kicks delivered by heavy boots into his ribs and buttocks. When Baxter managed to regain his feet, he fled.

'What are you doing down this part of town?' she demanded of Amelia.

'I was looking for a fortune-teller,' Amelia said, 'when that lout attacked me.'

Poll hooted with laughter. 'Jesus wept! Looking for a bloody fortune-teller!'

'He broke my parasol!' Amelia complained, tossing it aside.

Poll chortled. 'Bloody men. The things they do to us.'

Unaccustomed to humour, Amelia missed the point and agreed with her. 'He's a dreadful person,' she said. 'I feel quite shaky now.'

'Well, come on over and we'll have a bit of a sit-down for a minute,' Poll said. She led Amelia across the road to sit down on a couple of old sea-chests placed under the banyan tree for the convenience of her mates, who had now dispersed to their favourite watering holes.

'Thank you,' Amelia said, feeling quite weak from force of habit rather than from the state of her health. 'I'm really most grateful to you, Mrs Davies, for rescuing me.'

'Ha. You're a nice girl, you remember my name,' Poll wheezed.

'How could I forget it?' Amelia said stiffly. Her strength hadn't taken much time to return. 'I'm glad you got your horse back,' she whispered, afraid that someone might hear even though the street was deserted.

Poll caught the whiff of encouragement and went for it, playing on Amelia's nerves. 'Ah, you poor little thing. It's horrible, I say, that young girls can't walk the streets in safety, without strange men attacking them.' She knew the lout Baxter was no stranger to this girl; Poll had been shadowing him ever since he'd come into town with Roberts. She'd judged him to be the weaker of the pair, George and Baxter. The latter had been telling everyone who would listen that he was leaving town to go home and find the love of his life, but as Poll saw it, he was taking his bloody time about it. Her plan had been to grab the fool when he did leave, when no one would miss him, and starve the truth out of him.

The girl stared back across the empty road. 'He isn't a stranger,' she said eventually. 'He worked for my father.'

'Oh yes? You feeling better now, dear?'

'Thank you. Much better. Did you find your husband?'

'Not yet, love. Hey listen, I'm sorry if I gave you a bit of a bad time. But we women has to look after ourselves in this life, you know. No one else will. I wouldna hurt you.'

'You bruised me, though,' Amelia said.

Poll shrugged. 'Some people bruise easy. Me, it'd take a crowbar. That feller, the one who grabbed you. Would he know where I could find my Tom?'

'I doubt it. They wouldn't tell Baxter the time of day. He's pretty stupid.' Amelia realised what she had said, but she also grasped that somewhere here she had an ally against her father, and that became paramount in her thoughts. She forced herself to look into the plump, weather-beaten face, and was surprised to be confronted with lovely soft brown eyes, fringed by long dark lashes that she would have killed for. Somewhere back in time, she thought, a hundred years ago maybe, this poor old thing must have been a pretty girl. Amelia desperately needed someone to talk to. 'He beat me,' she whispered.

Poll stared at her, thinking that one of them had lost the drift here somewhere. 'Who beat you?'

'My father,' Amelia said, tears brimming. 'But you won't tell anyone, will you?'

'Cross my heart,' Poll replied, that heart going out to the motherless girl. 'Why would he beat you?'

'He didn't just beat me. He whipped me, because I talked to you,' she sobbed. 'I'm covered in whip marks.'

Poll nodded. 'It's as I said. Men can be bastards if you don't get their measure, then you've got nothing to grip on.'

'I'm frightened of him,' Amelia said. 'If I tell you something, will you promise never to let on I told you?'

'You can trust Big Poll, lovely,' the woman said, and Amelia, though a little confused by the nickname, knew she could.

'He's saying that he's never heard of your husband, but he has. He worked for my father. I know he did. Why would he lie?'

'Why was Tom's horse still there?' Poll replied. 'Maybe I should get hold of that feller that grabbed you and shake it out of him.'

'Who, Baxter?' Amelia asked. 'That idiot? He wouldn't know anything. It's George who knows what really happens.'

'Ah yes, George,' Poll intoned. Good and bad news. Baxter had seemed the weaker of the two, George would be a hard nut to crack. Poll had watched them both, and had chosen the wrong one.

'We're going to Brisbane tomorrow,' Amelia said. 'If you're thinking of questioning George, please wait until we leave or I should be frightened out of my wits.'

'Who is going to Brisbane?' Poll enquired.

'My father, my fiancé Mr Kemp, and I,' Amelia replied. Then she added, 'Mr Kemp was really sorry to lose the horse, he said Greybeard is a lovely animal.'

'That he is,' Poll said. 'I declare I am relieved he took good care of him. But his name is Stoker.'

'I'll tell him that,' Amelia enthused.

'If you're smart, lovely, you'll tell him nothing. Baxter over there won't remember what hit him, and you'd do as well to forget you even saw me.'

Amelia smiled. 'If you think so.'

'Righto, you take yourself back to the main street and I'll keep an eye on you as you go. You don't need no more trouble. Forget about the fortune-teller.'

'Thank you, Mrs Davies,' Amelia said politely, stepping out with the knowledge that, with an enormous amount of luck, Boyd would soon get his comeuppance for beating her. She hoped.

296

Poll made her way back to her camp, where Stoker was well hidden. She wasn't taking any chances on having him impounded, she didn't trust coppers any more than the next bastard. Now, that George . . . She poured a slug of rum into a mug of tea while she thought about him. No easy catch, that one, and if she bailed him up she'd be likely to come off second best. She'd watched him have a few drinks in the pubs and then leave. He probably did his drinking at home, and now that he and Roberts were both back, a person would have to be crazy to march in those gates cold. Come to think of it, she mused, marching in there in the first place had been a bit risky, but then she would have played her cards differently. More polite, like, just fishing about for information, doing her 'mad Alice' act which always made men feel superior – that had got her out of many a scrape.

'Keep in mind too,' she told herself, 'this George knows who you are.' They'd know who'd taken the horse, and someone would have pointed her out to him. Coming out of a pub, he'd seen her and wheeled his horse about as he mounted to get a better look, no doubt to report back to his boss.

'Mad Alice?' she muttered. 'Not a bad idea at that. But we'll wait until the family leaves tomorrow and then we'll deal with George.'

Big Poll was at the wharves to see Roberts, his daughter and her Mr Kemp board the paddle steamer, with George acting as porter, carrying their bags on board. The swells were all about in their fancy clothes, marching on board two by two like they were entering Noah's Ark, peering out from the decks at the poor creatures left behind. Poll smiled to herself. It was a real stroke of luck to have the pair of beauties, Roberts and George, separated. The last few days, she'd worried that the combination of the powerful man and his bruiser mate might be too strong for her to tackle, and she'd had to fight off her inclination to take Stoker and leave. But what about Tom? There was still no sign of him, and Poll knew in her heart that the answer lay hereabouts. 'I don't need no bloody fortune-teller,' she'd told the horses, 'nor no bloody crystal ball to tell me something's wrong.' To reassure herself, she nursed the rum bottle and sang her favourite selections of bar-room ditties.

George liked to have the place to himself. When they were away, he was boss, and he made sure all the staff knew it. He took his breakfast in the kitchen as usual, insisting that the cook set a place for him and serve him the same sort of tucker she'd prepare for the boss. He teased and ogled the two new maids and strolled through the house to make sure they were attending to their duties. There'd be no slacking with George in charge.

He spent the morning rousing on the stablehand and lazy old Andy, after which he studied the incomplete croquet lawn. Never having seen one before, it was a bit of a mystery to him, but the boss wanted it finished, so he decided to go into town and round up Chaser Barton, who was the only bloke in town who knew about these things. If Mr Roberts wanted the job finished, Chaser could just come back and get on with it.

Grudgingly, the cook gave him a three-course lunch of soup, pie and pudding, which George washed down with a bottle of plonk from the boss's cellar. Then he took a nap for an hour or so before heading into town.

As he came out of the gates, he saw that fat old pig of a woman squatting on a marker stone at the roadside a few yards away, singing her bloody head off.

'Shut up your racket,' he snarled at her, 'and get out of here.' She fell to muttering to herself and waved a rum bottle at him.

George knew who she was. Roberts had told him to keep an eye on her but to leave her be because the copper knew she was here looking for her husband, that squealer, Tom Davies. No point in drawing attention to themselves, the boss had said, so ignore her. That was all very well, George had told himself, but she'd made a fool of them, marching up and grabbing the horse. A fool of George in particular, because he'd had to cop a real telling-off from Roberts, who had been in a high old temper. He'd blamed George for leaving the grey on the property, for not getting rid of it when they got rid of Davies. 'How was I to know I was giving Kemp that bloke's horse?' he'd raged. 'A bloody dead giveaway. You'd better smarten yourself up, George, you're paid well enough. I can't afford people who make mistakes.'

Even though George knew he wouldn't be sacked – Roberts could never sack him, he knew too much – the abuse he'd copped lingered. Not that he blamed the boss, he was right, but if this fat trollop hadn't fronted, there wouldn't have been any trouble at all. She was the one who had caused it all, had brought the copper snooping about, and she deserved a bit of a lesson.

He dismounted and swaggered over to her. 'I told you to get out of here,' he rasped down at her.

'Ah, don't be like that, mate,' she mumbled, digging in her wide, thick skirts as the rum bottle slid from her hands. 'Come an' have a drink.'

He looked down at her with disgust. 'You drunken old sow.' To divert her attention, he walked into the scrub, undid his pants and pissed noisily, at the same time searching about for a stout lump of timber. He had considered using his rifle butt on her, but his new rifle had cost him a packet, and he wasn't going to wreck it on her worthless head.

He turned back to the heaving heap of lard, a rough weapon in his hand. He was looking forward to giving her a well-deserved bashing. She'd think twice about bothering Boyd Roberts again. Her face was hidden under an old hat and she was still muttering and mumbling when he came at her with the stick.

298

As he raised his arm to clout her, the bang rent the air. Birds shrieked, screaming, into the air, a dingo bolted across the road and the sky above him reeled as George went down. His horse, accustomed to gunshots, ducked, pranced and then stopped to stare at him. George, stunned, saw all this as he lay howling in the dust just a few feet from her. He saw her chuck away the rum bottle and pull a handgun out from under those skirts. She didn't seem to be in a hurry, sitting there examining the bullet holes. 'We're quits,' she remarked sourly. 'I've got a hole in me dress and you got a hole in your boot.'

Then the pain really hit him. His foot was aflame, and he could feel the blood oozing in his boot. Lying there, he tried to work his foot but there was no movement, and the agony told him that the bitch had smashed bones. He looked longingly at his rifle, still slung in the new leather pouch by his saddle, and cursed himself for not shooting her bloody dead in the first place.

Big Poll looked at it too. Then sprang up, grabbed George's new rifle and taking it by the barrel smashed it to pieces and hurled the remnants into the bush.

'I reckon you need a doctor,' she remarked, sober as a judge now.

'I'll have the law on you,' he shouted.

Unconcerned, she agreed. 'All in good time. First the doctor and then the law.'

'You're off your head,' he said, reaching down to undo his boot and inspect the damage, sweat flushing his face.

'Leave the boot,' she ordered, nudging his neck with the heavy handgun. 'It's better than a splint for the time being. You ought to know that, mister. Wait until I get you to a doctor.'

He stared at her. 'You are mad! They said you was. Everyone in town said you was as mad as a meataxe.'

'They're probably right. Now get up. You can't walk into town.'

George saw a glimmer of hope. She was going to let him ride! If he could just get on to his horse, he could get away from her. She'd have to leg him up, and if he was fast enough he could ride her down before she had time to move away. Trample the bitch, the great lumbering glob of lard. He decided to go along with her.

'All right!' he admitted, gritting his teeth through the pain of his smashed foot. George was proud of the fact that he was no whinger. So he'd been shot in the foot. He could handle it. 'I'll give you this, you're a bloody good bushwhacker.'

'Better than you,' she grinned.

Flattery. George was thinking fast. Bloody women, they fell for it every time. 'I'd have to say you're right,' he admitted, playing the good sport. 'We're quits. You win, now help me on to my horse.'

'Righto. But just hang on a minute.' Poll gave a whistle and a grey horse came trotting out of the bush. George recognised the grey, but that didn't matter now. He stumbled up, hanging on to a tree for support. She'd still have to leg him up, and then he'd get her.

But it didn't work. She made him mount the grey. 'In case you don't know,' she drawled, 'this is Stoker, and if you make a wrong move, you're mutton stew.'

George clutched the reins, one foot in the stirrup, the other hanging loose, waiting for the silly old trout to turn her back. His facial expression revealed his pain, while inside he was already feeling the glee of revenge as he clung on tight with his knees and hauled at the big horse to run her down.

Nothing happened. It was like riding a brick wall. The horse remained stock-still. Again he cursed that he wasn't wearing spurs, and pulled harder, frantically, too late, as she marched over to his horse and swung on to it as lightly as a dancer.

'Let's go,' she said, and the grey took him down the road as tame as a cat, waiting intently for her instructions. George tried to knee him into action, pounding at him, trying to make him bolt, but not a chance. It was like being stuck on a tired old bullock.

She turned off the road into the bush. 'Where are we going?' he yelled.

'Short cut,' Poll told him, holding her horse back to let them pass. 'I'll follow, Stoker knows the way.'

'There ain't no short cut down to town,' he complained.

'You don't say?' Poll replied. 'Go home, Stoker. Go home. I'm bloody hungry.'

The horse came to life, crashing down the hillside, deeper into the scrub, turning east away from the town as George clung on. Looking back, he saw she had the handgun trained on him and realised that any tricks were out of the question.

'Where are we going?' he shouted, when she came alongside him.

'Just a-ways,' she puffed, 'so we can have a talk.'

'What about?'

'Tom Davies,' Ada Adeline Davies replied.

Chapter Thirteen

'For all them fine days,' Mick O'Leary said, 'it sure can get nippy up here the minute that sun drops.'

The troopers riding with him nodded, without commenting, all of them thinking only of getting back from the bush patrol along the southern banks of the Fitzroy. They'd been right out to the coast, where the Sergeant had given them time off to swim their horses in the warm waters and roast several wild duck over campfires on the beach. The break had been welcome; it was tough going pushing through trackless scrub, and coming home always seemed to take longer.

O'Leary was satisfied with this foray into the bush. They'd met up with several small mobs of blacks who still lived along the river, but they'd been quiet, some of them even friendly. An exchange of curiosities, he mused, his blokes as curious about them and their strange ways as they were about the troopers. It was a fine thing for him to be able to report peaceful blackfellers this side of the river. And a shame it couldn't be like this all over. He knew that the lads would be drawing straws to get this patrol in the future.

Eventually they broke out of the scrub on to a narrow track, the first sign of civilisation, about eight miles from Rockhampton. It was mainly used by fishmongers who hauled their barrows out along the trail to fill them with bounty from the quieter reaches of the river, so O'Leary kept an eye out. It would finish the day off well if he could take back some fresh fish or lobster for supper.

'No sooner said than done,' he laughed, as he spied one of them tramping up ahead of them, barefoot and in battered half-mast pants like these hardy fellers always wore, never mind the chill. 'Hey there,' he yelled, as the bloke disappeared around a bend.

The fisherman turned quickly and waited for them. He was a tall man with a black beard and thick matted hair. As rough as you get, O'Leary grinned to himself, not that appearances count in this country.

'Christ! Am I glad to see you!' he said, sounding dead tired.

'At your service,' O'Leary laughed. 'How's the fishing?'

'What fishing?'

'You're not a fisherman then?'

'No, Sergeant,' he replied wearily. 'I'm Paul MacNamara. From Oberon.'

O'Leary stared and the troopers reined their horses. 'Jesus, Mary and Joseph!' he whispered. 'You're supposed to be dead! Where did you spring from?'

'I swam the river,' Paul said. All eyes, disbelieving, turned to the wide, fast-flowing river. Paul explained, 'I had a raft to help me. A native bark raft, it kept me afloat. I'd appreciate a ride into town.'

Immediately O'Leary ordered two of his men to double up and give the man a horse. Then, with MacNamara mounted beside him, he clapped him on the back. 'You'll forgive me, sir, for not recognising you, but you were given up for lost. There'll be celebrations now, our Lieutenant's been real cut up about you. Wait till he finds out you escaped!'

'I didn't escape,' Paul said as they set off. 'The blacks gave me a guide and sent me home. I came down the bluff from the ranges and across the flats.'

'The devil they did!' O'Leary exclaimed. 'Then we'd better finish the job.' They took off at the gallop, O'Leary eager to get back to town with his prize. A very satisfactory report would be a change in these times, and for a patrol, and not just any civilian, to have found MacNamara would be a real boost to morale.

MacNamara insisted on stopping at the police station first. O'Leary didn't mind. His troopers were all smiles, quick to pass on the news to bystanders. When Jim Hardcastle came out, pleased to see their man, shaking his hand, Paul had only one question for him. 'Where's Blackie Bob?'

'In the lockup,' Hardcastle replied, surprised. 'Why?'

Paul turned to O'Leary. 'Would you do me one more favour? It is a matter of urgency that you place guards immediately on the lockup to see that bastard doesn't escape.'

'Consider it done,' O'Leary replied.

Hardcastle was bewildered. 'Blackie Bob? What for? I'll get him now if you like.'

Paul's voice shook with emotion. 'No! I don't want to see him. Don't bring him out here!'

Without another word, O'Leary posted two troopers by the small lockup, which contained Blackie and two drunks. 'You'd best come with us, Jim,' he told the policeman. 'Mr MacNamara's pretty well done in, 'twill save time if you're there with Lieutenant Gooding to hear what he has to say.'

Gooding's relief was overwhelming. He threw his arms about MacNamara. 'Thank God you're safe. Thank God! Come in. Come in.' He stared at Paul's ragged clothes. 'You must be frozen. We'll get you a hot bath and some warm clobber. You'll catch your death.'

'I doubt it,' Paul said. 'If I was to catch a cold I'd have done it by this, living in those mountains. I don't even feel the cold now.'

He was devastated to have it confirmed that four of the troopers had lost their lives, and he took the time to speak to the survivors, Rory and Hal, who had come rushing up to see him. 'They're entitled to hear what happened,' Paul said to Gooding. 'What I learned concerns them too. But I'd appreciate it if I could have a bite to eat first.'

While they waited for supper to be brought over from the cookhouse, Gooding produced a bottle of his best Jamaican rum. 'We're bloody glad you're home Paul,' he said, filling glasses for all the men.

Paul nodded. 'I'm so sorry about your men. I'll have to see if there is anything I can do for their families. It's poor consolation to be offering, but I achieved what we set out to do. I found out who killed Jeannie and Clara.'

He was surprised that they took his announcement so calmly. It was Jim Hardcastle who broke the silence. 'Yes. We got them. They were hanged at Bunya Creek.'

'What are you talking about?' Paul shouted, looking from one to another. 'In God's name, who did you hang?'

'A couple of blackfellows. Wild blacks. They were brought in to the mines and admitted to the crime, in front of witnesses.'

'Oh Jesus,' Paul cried. 'Is there any end to this? You didn't catch the murderers, you bloody fools . . .'

'It wasn't us,' Jim said defensively. 'It was . . .'

Paul interrupted him. 'I'll tell you who it was,' he gritted. 'It was bloody Stan Hatbox, Blackie Bob and Charlie Penny! That bastard Cope's men. Native Mounted Police.'

'Is that why we've got the guards on Blackie?' O'Leary asked quickly.

'Yes. I heard the whole story.'

'How?' Jim Hardcastle demanded.

'One of the blacks spoke English. You must have heard him call out to me,' Paul said to Gooding.

'That's right. I thought I heard him,' Gooding replied.

'If it's true,' Hardcastle said, unwilling to admit to this, 'you won't catch Stan Hatbox. He's done a bunk.'

'No, he hasn't. He's dead. But before he died I heard the whole filthy story.'

'You killed him?' O'Leary asked, taking it for granted.

'No.'

Over supper in the crowded office, he related to his fascinated audience the events in the mountains. 'The blacks would never have attacked us,' he told Gooding. 'If some lunatics, some white men, hadn't shot up a blacks' camp only a couple of days before we went into the ranges. They killed several members of a family, including women and children, and took two prisoners. That attack was so sudden the blacks had no chance to fight back.' He shook his head. 'God knows what happened to the two poor fellows they captured.'

Depression settled on the faces of these men whose job it was to keep the peace, to administer justice. None of them spoke, not one of them looked at Paul MacNamara, they all seemed to be concentrating

303

on the thick beef sandwiches, munching quietly. Paul assumed that his length report was taking some digesting.

Rory and Hal were angry that Boyd Roberts, and it must have been Roberts, had cost their mates their lives by stirring up the blacks. O'Leary was thinking of Blackie Bob back there, the stinking murderer, and was glad he'd agreed to guards. Gooding worried about all the action he'd have to take the next morning to notify headquarters and the stations to prevent any more trouble, while Jim Hardcastle worried that he'd paid the reward money to the wrong men.

It was true! The whole town was talking. Paul MacNamara had come out of those mountains unscathed.

'A miracle!' the storekeeper's wife said. 'Praise the Lord . . . a miracle!'

A hefty grazier slammed his providoring list on the counter: 'It's no bloody miracle, it's just MacNamara the nigger-lover showing off! He knew he'd be safe up there among the Abos – he didn't give a tinker's cuss for the rest of the lads.'

'Oh, I'm sure that's not right,' she said, wilting.

'Of course it's right! Why would they kill four troopers and then let him off scot-free? I say he's in cahoots with them.'

A young woman strode up to him. 'You shut your mouth, Clem Carney! It's the likes of you that cause the trouble in the first place.'

'You'd know would you, Laura? I bet you've never met a wild black in your life!'

'I don't need to meet them to know they're human beings,' she countered.

Carney turned away from her, sneering: 'Tell that to MacNamara's wife!'

Despite this unpleasant encounter, Laura was overjoyed. He was alive and here in Rockhampton. To her it really was a miracle the way the news was affecting her. It was as if a great weight had been whisked from her shoulders. She had been certain Paul was dead and now the relief, and the suddenness of it was quite staggering. She saw Cosmo Newgate and rushed over to him, grabbing his arm, all other matters forgotten. 'It is true, isn't it?' she cried. 'Mr MacNamara is back?'

'Yes,' he smiled, 'he's home.'

'And is he well?'

'Well enough, my dear, considering he's been tramping the hills for a couple of weeks, living on blacks' tucker.'

'Where is he now?'

'At the Wexford house. Now if you'll excuse me, Laura, I'm in rather a hurry.'

She let him go and stood staring after him, smiling, she knew, quite foolishly in a euphoria of delight, and then she picked up her skirts and ran all the way home, gaiety having returned to her life once more.

Had she remained out and about, she would have heard the rest of the gossip in the town: that MacNamara claimed to have found the real murderers, news that did not augur well for Boyd Roberts. Already townspeople were making their way, on horseback and on foot, to the gates of the Wexford house where important discussions were to take place involving the police and the military.

All that mattered to Laura right now was that he was safe, and she wandered happily through the house, hugging the joyful news to herself. He was here in Rockhampton. She would see him soon. This time she wouldn't intrude, she'd wait for him to call. She'd wait for a while, anyway, for a little while, she conceded. Then if he didn't call she would find some way to see him, surely she had a right to know how things stood between them.

That thought sobered her a little and, more composed, she took her good news out to the back garden where Grace and Justin liked to take morning tea.

'Wonderful!' Grace said. 'What a relief it must be for his family, they've had enough ghastly news. We must ask him over when he has recovered.'

'Yes, of course,' Laura replied with as much dignity as she could muster.

'His wife's dead,' Justin remarked.

'That's right dear,' Grace said quietly.

Justin turned to Laura with a sweet smile on his still handsome face. 'Well then, you ought to marry him Laura. Nice fellow. Just the lad for you. I knew his dad you know . . .'

Laura blushed, made her excuses and fled, only to be met in the passageway by Leslie Soames.

'Ah Laura,' he said. 'I was hoping you'd accompany me to the race meetings.'

Still flustered, she nodded. 'I suppose so.'

Who cares about the races? she asked herself smugly. Paul is alive! And I've never felt more alive. This is the best day of my life.

Leslie shook his head as he made his way out to join the Carlisles convinced that she was quite strange, and incredibly vague. Still what could one expect in this peculiar place?

Confronting Blackie Bob was an ordeal for Paul MacNamara, but the others insisted he attend. Although Hardcastle was inclined to wait for the magistrate, who was due any day, Lieutenant Gooding demanded a preliminary hearing. 'This isn't a kangaroo court like the one they held out at Bunya Creek, Jim. We have to clarify this matter, we don't want any more mistakes.'

'You don't believe MacNamara?' Jim said hopefully, worrying about Roberts' reaction to all this and relieved that he was out of town. Jim wasn't looking forward to having to interrogate Boyd Roberts.

'Of course I believe him. But this time we go by the book.' He looked at the police sergeant curiously. 'What's your problem?'

'I don't like people interfering,' Jim said. 'This is police business. It should be left for me to handle.'

'Oh rats. The man has to be kept under heavy guard now. Are you going to stand there day and night? His superior officer, Captain Cope, will be in attendance too, so the man will have someone to speak for him. He won't be steamrollered like I suspect those other poor buggers were.'

'Cope!' Hardcastle sneered. 'If he'd kept a firm hand on his men then this wouldn't have bloody happened in the first place.'

'It's too late for recriminations,' Gooding said. 'If anyone needs a kick in the arse for interfering it's Boyd Roberts.'

'You can't charge him with nothing,' Jim retorted. 'He thought he was doing the right thing.'

'The hell he did,' Gooding said bitterly, but he knew Jim was right. No court up this way would condemn Roberts for 'cleaning out' a few blacks. Wasn't the catch-cry up here: 'The only good nigger is a dead one'? Even he had been savage about them after that attack, so a man couldn't blame people who had suffered the loss of loved ones at the hands of Aborigines. But somewhere along the line this hatred had to stop. He wondered if the majority of the white population would ever see the blacks as human beings, as normal people, as MacNamara was able to do again, thanks to his sojourn in the mountains.

He arranged for Blackie Bob's preliminary hearing to take place in the coach house at the home of William Wexford, the Lands Commissioner. It was well secluded from public notice, and Gooding told O'Leary to set troopers at the gates to keep out intruders. He then instructed an escort of troopers to collect the prisoner no earlier than ten in the morning, to give Paul time to recover.

That night, Paul lost all sense of time. O'Leary escorted him to the home of William Wexford, who was overjoyed to see him.

'Don't worry about a thing, Mr MacNamara,' O'Leary said. 'It's Rory and Hal themselves who've claimed the right to take the good news out to Oberon, and they'll be off at dawn. I fancy they'll get a right royal welcome.'

'I have to contact my family,' Paul said.

O'Leary smiled. 'The Lieutenant is attending to that. Waking up the telegraph office he is. You can do the follow-up yourself when you're up to it.'

Wexford, a courteous man, invited Sergeant O'Leary to join them in a drink, but the Irishman knew his place. 'It's terrible kind of you, sir, but I'll not be holding you up. I'll go on me way.'

Strangely, the familiar Irish expressions made Paul feel better, more alive, reminding him of his mother. 'Terrible kind' was one of her expressions. He wished he could talk to her now; until that message got through to her that he was safe, Dolour would be suffering a rerun of past tragedy. Her husband, her daughter-in-law, and now her son at the hands of blacks. 'Poor Mother,' he sighed.

'Are you all right?' William asked, ushering him into the warm parlour.

'Yes thanks, William. But I'm not fit for company.' Where, when had he said something like that recently? Or was it years ago? He couldn't recall.

'There's no company about,' William said. 'You look as if you've come through a whirlwind, son.'

'That's close,' Paul replied. 'That's about how I feel.'

'Would you like to go to bed? I won't be offended.'

'No,' Paul said thoughtfully. 'I'm glad you're here, William. I need to talk to someone who hasn't got an axe to grind.'

'Maybe I'm not the right person,' William replied gently. 'I didn't have a chance to tell you how bad I felt about your wife. I was the one who put you on to Oberon in the first place, you and your brother John. And when that happened to your wife . . . Dear boy, can you ever forgive me? I've been racked with guilt.'

'Don't be,' Paul said. 'Do you mind if I take a cigar?'

'Not at all.' The older man rushed to offer the box. 'I'll join you.' He snipped and lit their cigars.

'I know all about guilt,' Paul told him, 'and I wouldn't wish it on you, my friend. Tonight I feel old. No, ancient. I've actually been living with wild blacks and it hasn't sunk in yet.'

'Yes, I've heard part of it. Gooding sent one of his men out to ask me if I could put you up. The trooper told me what he knew of it, and I must say I'm delighted you chose to come here.'

'I didn't want to face people yet,' Paul said. 'I'm not ready. Those tribal men. It's difficult to explain. Would you think I was mad if I said I miss them? I was even a bit hurt when they left me with a guide. They went off without bothering to say goodbye.'

Interested, William gazed at him. 'Maybe they don't understand we have feelings too. We certainly haven't shown it.'

'Could be,' Paul said. 'They sure understood I was on the track of my wife's killers, that they understood.'

'Would I be asking too much of you to start from the beginning?' William asked tentatively. 'Perhaps with a glass of port.'

'I'll try. I only gave the others a bare report, but there was a lot more to it, a lot more. Have you ever heard of an English-speaking tribal black called Wodoro?'

Wexford thought for a while. 'No, can't say I have.'

'He's a half-caste,' Paul urged.

William shook his head again. 'No, I'm afraid not.'

Paul smiled. 'He was the go-between. Even though he's a half-caste, he was well marked with initiation scars, and he wore a pearl in his left ear.'

'A pearl? He must have come from up north somewhere.'

'Hard to say. He was lighter-skinned than the others, and he had a hook nose entirely different from any Abo I've seen.' Thinking of

307

Wodoro now, Paul mused. 'He was a real character. In his thirties, I'd say, and as touchy as a porcupine. One minute he'd be telling me how important he was, the next minute real cranky. Not in a vicious way, but just as if I were something sent to try him. But as it turned out, I think the younger one, Malliloora was more important.'

'Who?' William asked.

'Malliloora,' Paul said absently. 'And I met the real boss, a magic man, they told me, by the name of Harrabura.'

'Dear God!' William exclaimed.

'You should have seen this bloke,' Paul said. 'As old as the bloody hills, but what eyes! Sometimes they were all white, as if he were blind. Other times they were black, fiery black. That's what I wanted to talk to you about. After I left and was on my way home, I had a dream. I think I had a dream. He was standing beside me when I parted company with my guide, right there on the banks of the Fitzroy, and he talked to me about guilt.'

'In what language?'

'There's a point. I don't know. It must have been a dream. He said he could see guilt in my spirit and I could not take it with me to my Dreaming. Is this making sense?'

'I don't know,' William said, refilling his own glass; Paul had hardly touched his port.

They talked deep into the night, men intrigued by a civilisation they couldn't hope to comprehend but feeling privileged for the glimpse.

In the morning, Paul wore the clothes that William had so thoughtfully provided for him, and joined his host in the dining room, where he could only sip glumly at his coffee. 'I can't face this business today,' he said at length.

'I know it will be difficult,' William said, 'but Paul, the man has to be called to account. If you will forgive me for reminding you, he was part of a most hideous crime, and you are the accuser. Gooding has already been out here, early this morning. You are to have no part in it until the conclusion. You can stay here in the house.'

Cosmo Newgate demanded entry to the proceedings, wherever they were. Although he had no newspaper, he claimed he was a stringer for the *Brisbane Courier* and therefore entitled to attend. Everyone in town knew that MacNamara had made it back to Rockhampton, but as the story went, he was being kept under wraps at the barracks and would not see anyone. Even though, like everyone else, Cosmo was pleased and excited that Paul had come through that ambush unscathed, he had to know more.

He hounded Jim Hardcastle, who wouldn't talk until he saw Blackie Bob being led out in chains and placed on a horse, surrounded by mounted troopers. 'Where are they going?' Cosmo shouted. 'By God, Hardcastle, if you hang that bloke before a magistrate gets here, I'll have your hide. Even if he is guilty we have to abide by the laws here.'

'We're not going to hang him,' the police sergeant retorted, sick of this harassment. 'He's up on another charge.'

'What charge? Has this got anything to do with MacNamara?'

'Yes,' Jim said. Then he relented. 'You can come with me if you like. I'm in charge of this investigation. Not Gooding.'

So Cosmo trooped into the coach house, where a couple of garden benches had been set in place for the prisoner and the sergeant of police. The rest had to stand.

Blank-faced, bewildered, Blackie Bob was led in, accompanied by Captain Cope in full uniform, looking spruce for a change.

Jim Hardcastle hauled over an upturned tea-chest to use as a desk, dumped a notebook on it and spat on his indelible pencil. The only others present were William Wexford, who stood well to the rear, Lieutenant Gooding, who was holding a sheaf of papers, and two armed guards standing stiffly behind the prisoner. There was no sign of MacNamara. Whatever was going on here, Cosmo thought, it was definitely not legal, and he felt he ought to object, but curiosity kept him quiet.

'This is not an official court,' Hardcastle began and frowned as Cosmo intoned: 'Hear, hear.'

'Private Blackie Bob, you are hereby charged with the murders of Mrs Jean MacNamara and Miss Clara Carmody.'

Cosmo was almost as stunned as Blackie, but while he sucked in his breath and grabbed a milking stool on which to sit and take notes, Blackie rattled his chains and screamed his innocence.

'Lieutenant Gooding will put this matter to you,' Hardcastle continued. He looked over to Cope, who obviously knew what was coming, his swarthy skin now blanched with worry. 'Is that acceptable, Captain?'

Bobby Cope nodded miserably, as if his head were on the block. And well it might be, Cosmo thought, sucking his pencil. He sat spell-bound as Gooding read out the terrible indictment, move by move, of the four Native Police. The firing of Jock McCann's house, the ride on to Oberon, the attack on Clara . . .

'How do you know that?' Blackie screamed in terror, giving himself away.

Gooding looked up from his papers to ad lib. 'You stripped Clara's clothes from her,' he accused.

'That wasn't me,' Blackie screamed. 'That was the other blokes. I wasn't there, I was outside.'

And so it went on, relentlessly, to the rape and finally the murder of the women. Cosmo felt sick. No wonder MacNamara didn't want to listen to it. But who had informed? Which one?

That was the question Captain Cope asked. 'Who made these accusations. Who says this is true?'

'Stan Hatbox,' Gooding replied, looking to Blackie Bob. 'Your mate Stan Hatbox.'

309

'Then he can bloody hang too,' Blackie yelled at them. 'Just because he was crook with the spear wound, he ain't got no right to get out of it. He stuck it to them white women too.'

The pretty little coach house seemed to echo with his words and with the ramifications of this horror. Once again Captain Cope came out with what was foremost in Cosmo's mind. 'But the men who committed this crime have already been hanged.' He looked at Blackie, who was crying piteously, and tried to regain some sort of honour for his troops. 'How many blokes are you going to hang for the one crime?'

Jim Hardcastle nodded like a rubber doll, leaning towards Cope as if needing his help to restore his equilibrium. But the Lieutenant was up to the challenge. 'That is another matter,' he said sternly. 'The point of this briefing is clarification, and I believe, without any doubt, that we have come to the truth. I suggest Mr MacNamara be brought in now.'

Cosmo was tense. He saw the prisoner's guards move forward. Gooding wasn't taking any chances. MacNamara was frisked for weapons and allowed to enter from the glare outside. He was clean-shaven, a long, lonely figure walking jerkily into this impromptu court. He didn't look at Blackie.

'Paul,' Gooding said kindly, 'I have just read to the prisoner the statement of Trooper Stan Hatbox, as you gave it to me. Do you swear that it is the truth, without, at this point, the necessity of oath?'

'Yes.'

'And where is Stan Hatbox?'

'He is dead.'

'So he can't give evidence!' Cope shouted. 'It's all him. MacNamara's revenge against blacks. Any blacks.'

'How come Stan got dead?' Blackie intervened. 'You fellers tell me that.'

Paul still could not look at him. 'Harrabura took his life,' he said, his voice hollow, speaking only to Blackie. 'Harrabura of the Kutabura people, who also spoke to Charlie Penny. You're the only one left.' He made an effort to turn and look at Blackie, who slumped, defeated, on the bench, his cap slipping sideways on his head. Paul walked up to him and reached out to this poor wretch of a man, born of ignorance into a vicious world. 'Isn't that what happened?' he asked. 'What Stan said? How Stan told it?'

'Yes,' the man whispered. 'That was how it went. We didn't really mean nothin', it all just got mad, like.'

'It was a madness,' Paul said to him, feeling numb, not knowing what else to say. Blackie was doomed. He wrenched himself away and went outside to join William in the rich, life-filled green of the tropical garden. 'I am so sick of looking at death,' he muttered.

To Cosmo, it had all been rather an anticlimax. He wondered what he had expected. That MacNamara would scream and rant? That he

310

might try to kill the man with his bare hands? The other men looked disappointed too, and a pause hung over them, as if there might be a second act to this drama, as if MacNamara might reappear in the role of the vengeful husband.

'Is that it?' the police sergeant asked, and Cosmo replied: 'Looks like it.' He watched as the prisoner was led away, the journalist in him conceding Paul had shown them that decency was still alive on this racial battleground. He itched to get in there and interview him, but there was a better follow-up story looming, and Cosmo wasn't about to miss it.

He stood quietly while they decided to incarcerate Blackie Bob at the barracks rather than in the lockup so that he could not be attacked by other prisoners, or, worse, as the truth leaked out, cause a riot by his presence in the centre of town. Jim Hardcastle on his own couldn't control a lynch mob.

'Lieutenant,' Cosmo said, 'would you care to have lunch with me? At my house? I have an excellent cook.'

Gooding looked at him carefully, as if weighing up the reason for the invitation, then he asked: 'In my official capacity?'

'We might call it a business luncheon.'

'I see. Since it is now clear who killed the Oberon women, I gather you're interested in the hanging of two innocent Aborigines?'

'Yes. It leaves a large hole in Boyd Roberts' story.'

'You don't know the half of it,' Gooding said bluntly. 'I have a few things to do. What about one o'clock?'

'That'll be fine.' Then he added, 'I'm not rescinding the invitation by any means, Lieutenant, but what you have to tell me, will that be for the record? Or stuff I can't publish?'

Gooding straightened his immaculate uniform jacket and set his sword in place as he strode away. 'For the record,' he called over his shoulder. 'For the bloody record, by all means.'

'I forgot to tell you,' Cosmo said to Lieutenant Peter Gooding as he ushered him into his dining room. 'I have dinner at midday and a light meal for supper. Getting too old to go to bed on a heavy meal.'

'And I relish the opportunity to dodge army fare,' Gooding replied, 'so don't apologise.'

Over a splendid meal of mulligatawny soup, steak and kidney pudding and bread and butter custard, Gooding outlined to Cosmo the reason why his men were attacked by the blacks. All of this information, he explained, was gleaned by MacNamara in his dealings with the tribal blacks.

'We were the bunnies,' he said at length. 'We walked right into a trap set by Roberts.'

'In all fairness,' Cosmo had to say, 'though I have to agree that Roberts, in his usual roughshod manner, did run down a family of blacks and take two hostages, how was he to know that he was bringing the wrath of the blacks down on your head?'

'Gus, the foreman at Oberon – the German bloke – he claimed that Roberts would have known we were going in. I heard him talking to Tyler Kemp. He reckoned the whole scheme was a put-up job, to get rid of MacNamara, because Roberts is trying to buy Oberon to add to the McCann property, and to make a hero out of himself at the same time. I wasn't feeling too well, I didn't quite grasp it at the time.'

'I wouldn't doubt it, knowing Roberts, but it's hypothetical. There's no proof.'

'There never is with him,' Gooding said. 'Not that it makes any difference. He's clean. He can't be charged with anything, except,' he added vehemently, 'the bastard cost four of my men their lives!'

'On the record!' Cosmo complained. 'It would be different if I had my own paper, I wouldn't give a damn if he sued me, but I'm writing for the *Brisbane Courier*. They'll lap up the return of Paul MacNamara – apparently his family is well known down south – but they'll buck at this stuff on Roberts. He's being touted as the next Member of Parliament for Rockhampton. That's tough territory, they'll need facts, not supposition. You can't pin the deaths of your men on him, it won't wash.'

'You'll think of something,' Gooding urged. 'You have to. Aren't there any other starters for this election?'

'There is,' Cosmo said glumly. 'A Captain Soames, former aide to the Governor.'

'That's great! Anyone is preferable to Roberts, and this chap will have an ear where it counts.'

'Yes, but who's going to vote for him?'

'Everyone by the time we finish passing the word on about Roberts and his rotten thugs.'

After the meal, Gooding felt sleepy. This climate, especially in the summer, was made for siestas, but he shook himself and took a brisk ride out to Beauview. He didn't expect much from a conversation with George Petch, Roberts' offsider, but the fellow might drop something. In the main, he wanted to jolt this bloke with the news that they'd brought in the wrong men. Maybe not news to Petch, he pondered, but worth a mention to let him know the truth was out.

A gangly maid in an ill-fitting black dress, with a drooping lacy apron slung about her hips, answered the door. 'Yair?'

'Where can I find Mr George Petch?'

'George?' she said, flicking an interested eye at the very presentable officer. 'You tell me. I don't know where he is. He's probably off on a bender. You know,' she winked. 'When the cat's away the mice will play.'

'When do you expect him back?'

'Who cares?' she retorted. 'Is there anything I can do for you?' Her voice was arch, inviting.

The Lieutenant backed away. 'No, thank you. When do you expect Mr Roberts to return?'

'When he gets here,' she said, cold again now. 'He don't confide in us.'

Tyler's return to Brisbane was triumphant, magical. Roberts had taken three of the best rooms at the Royal Exchange Hotel, with views over the river, and they were really living it up. Amelia looked gorgeous in her new clothes and Tyler was proud to show her off, even to accompany her on shopping expeditions, while Boyd was his old self again, playing the genial host. Nothing was too good for them, and Tyler was completely captivated at how joyful life could be when money was no object. They laughed a lot, teased one another, drank champagne at breakfast to start the day, a practice Tyler would once have thought decadent but now, with this handsome pair, considered fun, marvellous fun.

He didn't even mind when Boyd took him along to his tailor and, in the process of being fitted for his own new suits, insisted that Tyler order new clothes too, including an expensive dinner suit. 'Put it all on my bill,' he said magnanimously, waving aside Tyler's weak protests. 'This gentleman will be my son-in-law shortly. One hopes you fellows will give him the same good service.' The tailors assured him they would, and to Tyler's astonishment even served them sherry and biscuits on a silver tray.

But Boyd wasn't impressed. He took all the attention as his right, and, dismissing the tailors, turned to Tyler. 'Are you sure we have everything we need?'

On the first day, Boyd hadn't wasted any time. Presses had been difficult to find but Tyler had heard of a new newspaper that had foundered within months for lack of finance and had taken Roberts down to Fortitude Valley, where they'd purchased all the equipment from the grateful owner.

'Buy the lot,' Boyd had said impatiently, when Tyler quibbled over the price of the paper. 'We take it all. Lock, stock and barrel. Tyler, you get it shipped home. And what they haven't got, you find.'

Feeling on top of the world, Tyler made a careful list of requirements, right down to pencils and notebooks, and when he was satisfied that he'd have the best money could buy, he called in at the *Brisbane Courier* to announce his resignation.

A new editor had replace his mentor, but even that didn't bother Tyler, he was walking on air.

'I was told,' the editor growled, 'that you'd be sending me some copy from up there, but I haven't seen a line.'

'Sorry about that,' Tyler replied. 'I've been too busy.' The notes of his travels had been recovered, but all that work for a few pounds hardly seemed worth the trouble now that he was preparing to open his own paper.

'We've got another stringer from Rockhampton now. A fellow called Cosmo Newgate,' the editor grumbled. 'What's he like?'

'Cosmo?' Tyler replied loftily. 'He's a good chap. Knows his business.' He could afford to be generous since Cosmo probably needed the work these days. He felt a quake of nerves for a second or two as he said: 'Newgate used to have his own paper,' but he quickly pushed the worry aside.

He marched about the office and shook hands with all his old mates. He even considered inviting them to his engagement party, which Boyd was organising at the hotel, but thought better of it. They wouldn't enjoy themselves, he decided, convincing himself that he was doing them a kindness. They'd feel out of place among all the swells. And besides, none of them had evening suits. Roberts' friends were a fast lot, many of whom Tyler had met before. This fact impressed Amelia, so he didn't bother to tell her they were only acquaintances, people he'd met at the racecourse and in the gambling saloons. In a way this gave him a edge over Boyd, because his daughter's fiancé was able to introduce him to the real society of Brisbane, gentlemen of the squatters' set, many of whom were politicians. In their turn, they were curious to meet the man who, it was touted, was in line to replace the late Fowler Maskey. Invitations were issued and accepted and the trio found themselves in a whirl of social engagements. Tyler even managed to wangle invitations to luncheon in the Governor's tent at the races. Amelia was beside herself with excitement, and even Boyd was impressed this time, Tyler noticed with no little satisfaction. He felt he was already earning his keep.

The day of the race meeting was a flawless sunny one, a perfect opportunity for the ladies to show off their finery as they strolled majestically about the reserved area, with lesser beings staring from the other side of the flag-bedecked rope fence. Amelia wore an expensive creation of ruby-red damask silk, trimmed with black satin, the tight bodice showing off her hourglass figure and the long skirt swathed across the front to meet in rich folds at the back. She topped the outfit with a high red bonnet of the same material and carried a fluffy red parasol. Tyler thought nervously that her dress might be a bit loud – the other ladies in the tent were wearing more muted tones, quite a few even in white – but Boyd didn't seem to think so. He was laughing, saying she looked very smart, and that he could have bought a racehorse for what it cost. Then again, Tyler mused, the other women were older; he supposed young ladies could be expected to bring colour and gaiety into the show. Comforted, he went off to place his bets.

He lost heavily that day and his small capital was dwindling, but he'd taken an early precaution, slipping out in the morning to purchase a ring for Amelia for fear he might hand too much to a bookmaker. It was a pretty little ruby, set in gold, and all day it had been nestling in its velvet pouch in his waistcoat pocket, reminding him that he had made an excellent choice, for it would match her dress beautifully.

In a quiet moment between races, he walked her over to the seclusion of some tall gum trees. 'I can't wait any longer,' he said. 'I simply have to give this to you today.' He took out the pouch, spilled the ring into his hand, and presented it to her.

'What is it?' she said, sounding rather tetchy.

'Some people would call it a ring, darling. An engagement ring. For Amelia from Tyler, with his love.'

'Oh,' she said. 'Thank you.'

He slid it on to her finger. 'Do you like it? It matches your dress.'

'So it does,' she remarked. As she twisted it about, he noticed she was wearing a large dark sapphire on the third finger of her right hand, and by comparison the ruby looked a poor tribute.

'It's all I could afford,' he apologised, 'but a great deal of love goes with it.'

'You shouldn't have wasted the money,' she complained. 'I had one picked out, a lovely band of diamonds.'

He smiled down at her. 'I'll buy you diamonds another time. This is our ring.'

Exasperated, she frowned. 'You're such a silly. Boyd was going to pay for the other ring, we could have got it for nothing. Now I won't get it at all.'

'I didn't want your father paying for your engagement ring.'

'Why not?' she snapped. 'It's the least he can do.'

Tyler shook his head. 'He's doing enough already, don't you think?'

'He can never do enough for me,' she retorted with an imperious toss of her head. 'Come on, we'll go back to the marquee. I'm really quite tired. I should like to sit down.'

Disappointed, Tyler followed her, aware, as the afternoon drew to a close, that Amelia did not refer to her new engagement ring. If Boyd noticed it, he made no comment either. Tyler felt his day was ruined now, and he was angry with both of them. Being an observant man, he realised that he'd just seen another chink in the armour of this fine father-daughter relationship. He remembered that Amelia had been very jumpy in the presence of her father when he'd first come in from the bush, and he wondered what was going on here. In Brisbane, though, he mused, Amelia had been as happy as a lark. Or so it seemed. Happy spending money, he corrected himself, shifting his irritation wholly to her. Roberts had his faults, that was true enough, but he was a kind and generous father, far more generous than Tyler would be as her husband. Amelia was really far too spoiled. As his wife she'd have to grow up a bit, learn that there was more to life than shopping.

The town was dark as the horse cab clattered down Eagle Street, the

315

river a wide stretch of gloom, unprepossessing and lonely at night, with all the activity removed several blocks away to the bright lights of Queen Street. Boyd was in a great mood, chatting to Tyler about the personages he'd met that day, chalking them up as being important to his career. 'The Governor, he's not a bad chap at all, is he?'

'No,' Tyler said absently, worrying about Amelia, who was withdrawn and silent in the shadows of the black leather upholstery.

'He intends to visit Rockhampton,' Boyd said. 'I'll have to plan a warm welcome for him. That'll help my cause no end, showing the Governor around. Impress the locals, eh?'

'Bowen won't turn up before the elections,' Tyler growled. 'He doesn't mix in politics.'

'Since when?'

'Not publicly anyway,' Tyler replied.

Boyd slapped his knee. 'Come on, lad, buck up. Lose your money did you?'

'A few quid,' Tyler admitted.

'Oh well, it's only money. I had a topping day! Couldn't go wrong.'

You would, Tyler thought sourly. Money makes money.

As soon as they pushed through the glass doors into the lobby of the hotel, Amelia marched straight to her room and Boyd made for the busy saloon bar, so Tyler went to find a paper.

The front page carried the story of Macalister resuming the Premiership after the easing of the bank crisis. Tyler had already heard the news, but he read the article carefully anyway, from force of habit.

Sir John Manners-Sutton, whoever he was, had been appointed Governor of Victoria, and there were warnings in the editorial that more 'bread or blood' riots could break out in Brisbane if the unemployed weren't given a fair go. It seemed to Tyler that Herbert might have quit too soon. He grinned cynically to see that they were stringing out the shipwreck stories, always good copy. The SS *Cawarra* had gone down off Newcastle with the loss of sixty lives, and only six days later the emigrant ship *Netherby* had been wrecked in Bass Strait, but this time all were saved. They'd dug up a family of emigrants who'd come on to Brisbane after their ordeal only to hear that other members of their family had been lost in the *Cawarra* disaster.

What would you call that? Tyler mused. Catholics all, by the sound of it. The Grace of God, or the Dreaded Hand of the Lord? He noticed there was no heading on the article, just a straight report of the interviews, and he didn't blame the subeditor. Too hard. Absently, he turned the page, still trying to think of a three-word heading, which was all these back columns rated. Giving up, he bypassed letters to the editor complaining about the standard of the Brisbane water supply from the new Enoggera Creek reservoir. 'Never bloody satisfied,' he grumbled, allowing them only a glance. Then his eye was caught by a small piece from Rockhampton. 'Pastoralist Saved.'

He sat bolt upright in his chair, crushing the paper in his lap as he tried to fold it into shape to better examine the article.

'Mr Paul MacNamara, a survivor of the cruel ambush by wild blacks who murdered four valiant troopers, was found to be in good health, despite his ordeal. Only recently this man suffered a tragic loss when his wife and servant girl were murdered by blacks, which makes his safe return even more poignant. Mr MacNamara is the stepson of well-known Hunter Valley grazier, Mr Juan Rivadavia.'

Tyler shook the paper. 'Is that all?' he demanded of it, ignoring the stares of passers-by in the lobby. 'Where's the rest of it? This is a front-page story, you bloody fool!' He realised that Cosmo Newgate must have telegraphed the story, and been refused permission to book the cost of enlarging to the paper. The full story would have to come down by ship. It was obvious too that Cosmo's tight report had been tampered with and the last lines added. Cosmo wouldn't have bothered about the stepfather. If anything, he would have added even more poignant lines to the effect that MacNamara's father had been killed by blacks.

He was hugely relieved that MacNamara had survived, but how? he wondered. And why was he so far off course? Frustrated, he threw the paper down, cursing this new editor. Then he recalled his own days at the paper. Would he have given the story front page? Rockhampton was only a far-off country town. There was always trouble with the blacks up north and out west. Queensland was a hotbed of tribal unrest. Had he already become parochial? It also irritated him that whoever had written up this story hadn't bothered to note that he, Tyler Kemp, until recently a long-serving journalist with the *Brisbane Courier* – with their own bloody paper! – had been on the receiving end of that ambush. Had come close to being killed by a bloody spear! He didn't even rate a mention.

Christ, he thought. When you're dead, you're dead. He remembered the many times he'd refused to use comments by politicians who had lost their seats. 'Nothing deader than a dead politician,' he'd say. Now he saw that it hadn't taken long for his comrades to bury him.

He ought to go in and tell Boyd about MacNamara, but he wasn't in the mood. He called the porter to bring him a double whisky and sat mulling over the small article, trying to decipher what Cosmo might have written, what lines had met the blue pencil. He couldn't see Cosmo's hand in any of this. Valiant troopers? All of them had run for their bloody lives, Lieutenant Gooding and Tyler Kemp too. Only MacNamara had stood there, like an idiot, asking for a spear, and yet he'd walked out unscathed. How? What a bloody great story, and here he was sitting on his backside, playing the gent in Brisbane. In the wrong place at the wrong time. If Cosmo were to write this whole story up, from go to whoa, he could get national coverage. He would get it! Tyler desperately missed his first love, journalism. He felt bereft.

It was Boyd who came for him. 'What about a game of billiards before dinner?'

'MacNamara escaped,' Tyler said.

'Yes I know. I saw it in a paper in there. Are you on for a game?'

'I was with him. Doesn't that interest you?'

'Why should it? You were all bloody fools to go in there in the first place.'

'Is that so?' Tyler replied. 'Then explain to me why we were fools and you and George were not?'

'Because I knew what I was doing,' Boyd sneered.

'What exactly did you do? You never did give me the full story.'

'You want me to explain it to you now, blow by blow?'

'Why not? Now's as good a time as any. I'd like to know how three men succeeded where nine failed.'

'Because we didn't go in with flags flying, we had more sense.'

His attitude annoyed Tyler, so he took a chance with the next remark. The comments Gus had made still bothered him. 'You weren't that smart,' he jeered, trying to take a rise out of Boyd, who was a bit drunk, swaying a little in front of him. 'You knew if you got into strife Gooding and his men weren't too far away.'

'I didn't need them,' Roberts boasted. 'A lot of good they were to you.'

Tyler followed him over to the billiard room because he couldn't think what else to do. He had a sinking feeling in the pit of his stomach that Gus had been right. Roberts hadn't contradicted him, he had known the troopers were at Oberon, in which case he'd have known why they were there. Unable to stop himself, he grabbed Boyd's arm. 'You knew we were at Oberon!' he shouted.

'I didn't know *you* were there.' Boyd shrugged. 'Anyway, so what?'

'So there goes your excuse for bypassing Oberon. Why didn't you hand your prisoners over to the military who were on the spot?'

'It's none of your bloody business,' Boyd snapped, shoving him away.

Tyler turned on his heel and stormed out, heading for the front door. As he crossed the foyer a small portly man sidled up beside him. 'Going for a stroll, Mr Kemp?' It was Ferret, his informer. 'Thought I might find you here.'

'Ah. G'day, Ferret. Why are you looking for me?'

'This and that, sir. This and that.'

'I'm not working right now. I'm not with the *Courier* any more.'

'I know,' the man said, walking outside with him. 'Just thought I'd give you a tip. No charge, like.'

'What tip?' A cold mist rising from the river brought him a shudder of apprehension.

'It's about your mate in there.'

'Who? Roberts?'

'That's the one. The papers've got a tale that he ain't the hero after all. That he hanged the wrong blokes for the murders up there.'

'Roberts didn't hang them.'

'By the sound of things he might as well have. Someone's really gunning for him.' Ferret blew his nose noisily and turned up his thin collar. 'I don't like these cold nights. Too much of a shock to the system after fine days.'

'How do they know he brought in the wrong ones?' Tyler persisted.

'Because they found the right ones, didn't they? Got confessions. It was them Native Mounted Police you kept complaining about. They did it. You were right, see. I said to my mates, "Mr Kemp, he never did have no time for them." '

'Oh Christ,' Tyler said.

'Yes, that's what I thought.' Ferret nodded. 'If your mate wants to stand for Parliament, this story won't do him a lot of good. So I figured you've still got time to scamper around to the *Courier* and try to water it down a bit. Get his side of the story into print before there's too much damage.'

Tyler stood considering this. He dug in his pocket, from habit, and gave Ferret five shillings.

'No,' Ferret said, 'I told you this one was on the house.'

'That's all right, buy yourself a drink.'

'To your health then, sir,' Ferret said and trudged away around the corner.

It was possible, Tyler thought. He should get over to the *Courier* and see what they were preparing to print. He could issue a statement on behalf of Boyd. After all, he hadn't taken part in the hanging. Who the hell were they, then? The prisoners that Boyd had brought in?

He could even threaten the editor with libel. That would damp it down. But Ferret was rarely wrong; even four lines of these facts would be disastrous. In which case why was he still standing here? This was Wednesday. They were leaving, sailing for Rockhampton, on Friday, and tomorrow night, on the eve of their departure, Boyd had arranged a dinner party with a few friends to celebrate his daughter's engagement to Tyler. Celebrate? God! With Amelia's father being held up, at the very least, to ridicule.

Then there was his comment of 'Oh Christ!' Ferret had misunderstood. Tyler wondered, miserably, what had become of his great plan to investigate the Native Police? He'd allowed himself to be sidetracked and missed the story he should have been writing.

He didn't go to the *Courier*. He walked back into the hotel. 'Why?' he asked himself. The answer was only too plain. He didn't want to become involved. His reputation as a journalist would be in shreds if he marched into the *Courier*, cap in hand, trying to find out about a story that had been right under his nose. It was all too close for comfort. Boyd would just have to ride this out on his own.

Dinner that night wasn't too difficult. Amelia had changed into a low-cut, very revealing pink satin glittering with crystal beads, but she was still sulking, flirting with every gentleman Boyd invited to their table. Boyd was at his best, ordering magnums of champagne, paying the pianist to play his favourite tunes and charming all the ladies. Sitting between this dazzling pair, who were the centre of attention in the jolly room, Tyler watched as the night dragged on and the table was extended and extended to accommodate beauties and their beaux eager to join the fun.

He got very drunk, which gave him an excuse the next morning to arrive late at the breakfast table, where Amelia and Boyd sat alone in a white damask landscape.

His first thought as he sauntered in was for Amelia, who was pathetically eager to see him, her face as white as her Indian muslin dress against the sheen of her black curls. He wished he could pick her up out of there and take her to the safety of his room, but it was not possible.

Boyd hurled the paper at him as he approached. 'Have you seen this?'

'Seen what?' He picked it up from the carpet. Boyd didn't look too good himself. For the first time, Tyler noticed, the dandy was looking his age; his hair seemed thinner, his skin yellowed from a fading suntan, his lips a hard, jagged line under the clipped moustache.

'Page three,' Boyd intoned, and Tyler unfolded noisily.

There it was. The heading, 'Innocent men hanged.' And a quarter-page allotted to the story. 'Good God,' Tyler said, feigning surprise as he pulled a chair out with one hand.

The story ran as he knew it would; halfway down, Boyd Roberts was mentioned.

'They call my father a miner,' Amelia sobbed, as Tyler read on:

'Mr Boyd Roberts, miner, with parliamentary ambitions, was credited for bringing in the murderers, but it has now been firmly established that Mr Paul MacNamara, at great risk to his own life, uncovered the truth and a Native Policeman, known only as Blackie Bob, has now been sent to trial.'

There was more, not very well written, Cosmo's facts turned into lurid prose. Another column, headed 'Husband avenges wife', back-tracked on the other events. On the next page, the story of the ambush was rerun and Lieutenant Gooding was mentioned, but not Tyler Kemp. He sighed.

Boyd roared. 'I'll sue the bastards!'

'What for?' Tyler replied, concern in his voice. 'You haven't got any grounds. They're more or less saying you made a mistake. That's not a crime.'

'I didn't make a mistake,' Boyd shouted. 'And neither did the body of men who judged them guilty. MacNamara is lying. Can't they see that? Can't you see that?'

'Why would he lie?' Tyler asked.

'Because he hates me. He's small-time and weak as piss. I made him an offer for his station so I could combine the two into a decent spread. But not him. He's a bloody dog in the manger.'

'MacNamara,' Amelia said, bewildered, apropos, it seemed, of nothing at all. 'He's the fellow Laura was keen on.'

Tyler had an instant to recall some vague station gossip – about how Boyd had accused MacNamara, in front of the posses, of having a girlfriend in town – before Boyd turned on Amelia. 'Shut up about Laura! You pushed her out, didn't you? The minute I turned my back you got rid of her, didn't you, you little brat. I've woken up to your tricks! By Jesus, you've done it once too often this time.'

Amelia ran crying from the room as Tyler, confused, tried to calm him down. 'Steady on. This is a one-day wonder. Don't take it out on Amelia.'

'Mind your own bloody business! You'll find out! She's a point-maker of the first order. Only you're such a sap you can't see it. Get me a lawyer if you can't fix this. I'll deal with this bloody paper.'

'You don't deal with anything,' Tyler said firmly. 'You ignore it. If you retaliate, Boyd, believe me, you'll give them a chance to string this story out. They'll just rewrite it, and then more people will get to read about it. Let go, don't give them the opportunity.'

'Are you sure?'

'Of course I'm sure. Stand on your dig. You don't have to answer to them.'

'That's true. And I've got all those men at Bunya Creek to back me up. They will never admit they hanged the wrong blokes.'

What was it Gus had said? Tyler worried. Listen with your head and not your ears. It was happening again. It was the inflection in Roberts' voice, as if he knew they were the wrong men.

'Oh Christ!' he muttered to himself as he rushed up the stairs to find Amelia, to console her, to tell her that she shouldn't be upset, that Boyd had only been paying out on her because she was the closest, families did that.

He hugged her, held her close. 'Don't worry,' he said softly, 'it's only a flash in the pan.'

'I hope so,' she wept, clinging to him. 'You do love me, don't you, Tyler? I am sorry about the ring, I was rude. It is beautiful.'

In the safety of her room Tyler found the Amelia he'd yearned for. No more teasing, she needed him now. In the wide, downy bed he found the voluptuous woman he'd been waiting for all this time, frantically holding him as if afraid he too might turn on her, and they became like two waifs together under the eiderdown. Tyler made love to Amelia, to that wonderful soft sweetness of her, promising he would never forsake her, and her tears mingled with their kisses and his great joy in feeling her loving, excited response.

321

Chapter Fourteen

'I don't know what you're complaining about,' Poll said. 'I fixed your foot. I didn't have to do that.'

'You didn't have to bloody shoot it either,' George snarled. 'And you haven't fixed it. I need a doctor.'

Poll sighed and poked at her campfire. 'If I hadn't taken the bullet out you'd end up with gangrene, no bloody foot at all. So pipe down.'

He was chained to a tree in the scrub, well away from her, one chain clamped on to a wrist, the other to a leg. He'd shouted a lot at first, but soon quietened down when she'd warned him that any noise would cost him his water ration. Not that anyone would hear him up here, unless by chance.

The sun glinted through the trees, dappling her camp, and the fire crackled as she put some bacon in her frying pan, grinning to herself. There was nothing like the smell of bacon cooking to stir a hungry man, and George was starving; two days without food was beginning to wear him down. She broke two eggs into the pan, facing him so that he could see what she was doing. And suffer.

When they were cooked, she set the pan aside and made some toast with bread stuck on the end of a stick.

'You have to give me something to eat,' he yelled at her. 'I'm feeling sick. I'll die here.'

'No you won't. Not for a while anyway. Horrible death, starvation, they say.'

'By Jesus, the cops'll be on to you for this.'

'Tell me about Tom Davies and I'll give you this tucker.'

'I don't know no Tom Davies.'

She squatted down and began to eat her meal, chomping noisily on the lumps of bacon. 'I hope you're wrong,' she said, between chews, 'or you'll be there until the dingoes come for you.'

Two days later he was cringing, preparing to barter. Poll was impressed; this was a real hard man. Yesterday, he'd managed to remember Tom Davies after all. 'Yeah, I remember him now,' he'd offered. 'But he's dead.'

'I figured that,' Poll replied without emotion. 'How did he get dead?'

She listened patiently to his cock-and-bull story about an accident, an accident that he hadn't reported to the police, and his claim that he couldn't remember where they'd buried his body.

'Who are they?'

'His mates. I can't remember their bloody names.'

'But they worked for Roberts too.'

'Yes. Why don't you ask him about it? I don't know why you're picking on me. Give me some of that bread.'

But today he was croaking, hanging on the ends of his chains, jerking at them like a big ape. 'You take me home and I'll tell you all about what happened.'

'I'll bet you will.'

'All right then, take me in to the coppers. I'll tell them.'

'And pigs'll fly.' She left him and went down to the creek for water, deliberately delaying, paddling in the cold, clear water and fossicking about for lobbies, little freshwater crayfish.

When she returned she gave him an ultimatum. 'I haven't got much more time, George, I'll have to leave in the morning. I'm real sorry you couldn't help me, because now I can't help you. You'll have to stay.'

He started shouting, calling her every vicious name he could lay his tongue to, but none of it was new to Poll.

In the end he gave up. 'Davies got shot.'

'Who shot him?'

'I can't remember. Roberts gave the order.'

'Why?'

'Nothing much. He got on Roberts' nerves. He talked too much.'

'You mean he knew too much?'

'Yeah, he was yapping on about something that happened out in the bush, said he wouldn't talk, wanted his pay and a bit more to keep his mouth shut.'

'He never could keep his mouth shut,' Poll recalled.

'The boss knew that, he had to put him down.'

'Like a dog.'

'Well, the boss isn't one to cross. By Christ, if he ever finds out I told you this, I'll be next.'

'Where'd you bury him?'

'What difference does it make?'

'Where'd you bury him?'

'In the river.'

'You pack of bastards,' she spat.

She went to her pack and took out the writing book and pencil she had bought for just this occasion, then sat down to transcribe his statement in a faltering, laborious hand, questioning him as she forged on. 'Who shot him?' she asked again, but he still claimed not to know. He was lying, she knew, so she wrote that Tom had been shot at the house called Beauview by George Petch on orders from Boyd Roberts. He was the obvious one to do the dirty work, she decided, so why worry about a little cribbing.

323

When her work was completed, she plodded over to him. 'Now you sign it.'

'Then you'll let me go?'

'Sure. I've got what I came for.'

'I don't trust you.'

'You have to trust me.'

She saw the light of cunning glint in his green eyes as he snatched the pencil and scrawled his name at the bottom of the page.

'Right, now let me loose,' he said, handing back the paper and the pencil.

'Not just yet,' she said. 'You must be hungry.' She cut him a thick slice of bread and some yellowing strips of smoked ham.

George ate ravenously, watching as she saddled her horse. 'Where are you going?'

'Into town.'

'You promised you'd let me go, you bitch.'

'That's right. Like you gave poor Tom his pay, had him thinking he was on his way. You lied too, didn't you?'

'You're not going to leave me here?' he shouted.

Poll refilled his water bottle and threw it to him. 'No, I'll be back. That's more of a chance than you gave Tom.'

She could hear him shouting as she rode away, leading Stoker, but she didn't care who heard him now.

When Sergeant Hardcastle returned to the police station after lunch, there was Poll, sitting on the front steps.

'Read that,' she said. 'My writing ain't too good but the truth's clear enough.'

He studied the large handwriting and then stared at the signature: 'George Petch. Did he sign this?'

She nodded. 'Now you can arrest him and that Boyd Roberts.'

Hardcastle stalled. 'I can't just arrest people on your say-so.'

'It's not my say-so. It's his. George Petch. They shot my Tom and dumped his body in the river.'

'How did you get Petch to tell you all this?'

'It wasn't hard. You arrest Roberts first and then we'll bring George in.'

'Don't tell me my job,' he snapped. 'Roberts is out of town for a start, and if this statement has been signed under duress, it's not worth the paper it's written on. But leave it with me and I'll see what I can do.'

'Oh no you don't.' She snatched it back. 'It's mine. I'll take care of it. Now you'd better pick up George Petch.'

'I'm busy now, I'll talk to him later.'

'You'll bloody talk to him now,' she shouted, causing a mild commotion in the street. 'You're the bloody law. I want him brought in now. He's waiting for you.'

'Where?'

'Get on your horse and I'll show you.'

'Listen to me, Mrs Davies, I'll come with you when I'm good and ready. I told you, I'm busy. Now come back at four o'clock.'

Poll shrugged. What was it to her if George had to wait a few extra hours. She didn't trust this copper either, so she decided to wait right there on the steps. She wasn't going to let him dodge off.

It was well after five when Poll led the angry policeman to her camp, where they found George sleeping.

'You've got him chained!' Hardcastle cried.

'Of course he's chained. Do you think I'd let him get away?'

Then, alarmed, she jumped down from her horse. 'Something's wrong with him. Oh Jesus, he's dead!'

Hardcastle came charging after her. 'You killed him!'

Poll was on her knees, examining the dead man. 'No, I didn't, mate. You did. If you'd come when I told you to, he'd still be alive. Snakebite this is. Look at his leg!' She pointed at the swollen blue skin on his calf and the tourniquet George had tried to apply using rags ripped from his shirt. 'He's still warm,' she said. 'Even an hour back you might have saved him. Bad luck, eh?'

Cosmo rubbed his hands together as his new presses were set in place by the workmen; he ducked and dived around them telling them to take care, thanking them for bringing his precious cargo straight over from the wharves, and sent his grinning clerk to find some clean rags to remove any speck of dust from his treasures. 'We'll have a paper out tomorrow,' he crowed. 'I've got so many good stories written, I hardly know where to start.'

'A feast or a famine, sir,' his clerk laughed.

'You can say that again, my boy. We'll have to work hard now; we could produce a bumper edition. But maybe not. I'll just have to look to priorities. These presses are better than my old one, more modern, so I'll have to explain their workings to you.'

'We could do with another hand,' his clerk said, putting on his apron. 'You said we'd get a proper office boy when we reopened and leave me to the printing.'

'So I did,' Cosmo said. 'I'll have to look out for someone. In the meantime, Adam, time's a-wasting. Mix up some ink.'

He put on his green eyeshade and hurried into his office to start work. First up, he decided, this bally election, and with a sigh of relief he produced the small piece wherein he withdrew his candidacy and directed his support to Captain Leslie Soames.

'Good old Grace,' he enthused.

The Carlisles were in town. Some of them staying at the Golden Nugget, but Justin and Grace, with Laura Maskey, were at the Quay Street house. He made a note that Justin Carlisle had purchased that house, an interesting bit of gossip for the locals.

Leslie Soames was anxious to see him, having deposited himself

325

temporarily at the hotel, but Cosmo couldn't spare the time today. As soon as he could, though, he would steer the gentleman through the necessary official paperwork as a candidate and round up the required number of witnesses.

More interesting, however, were his next two stories, the result of interviews with MacNamara and Gooding. He hoped Boyd Roberts was still in Brisbane to read that his hero status was crumbling. With a wealth of space at his disposal now, Cosmo chose to refer to Roberts' part in the capture and hanging of the two innocent men as irresponsible, high-handed and behaviour quite unsuitable for a man who expected the public to put their trust in him. He chuckled. This had been worth waiting for.

The story of Blackie Bob and his dead and unlamented colleagues was the real grabber, of course, but it led marvellously on to the kangaroo court and the hangings. Nothing would be done about that, he knew – the other men involved would claim they acted in good faith, and the deaths of two strange blackfellows would be forgotten – but it was a hard lesson for all concerned.

Later that afternoon, struggling with paste and rulers to fit in the new advertisements he had gained during the long weeks of forced idleness, Cosmo remembered the police report. He sent Adam off to find Jim Hardcastle and see what had been happening lately. That was a popular column.

Adam came back with several items scribbled in his notebook: cattle duffers had stolen fifty steers from Greenbank Station; there'd been a fight at the meatworks and a skinner, Joseph Leighton, had suffered severe lacerations; a bank teller had been arrested for the theft of ten shillings. He ticked off other items for inclusion, a bolting horse causing damage in the newly laid gardens, a side of beef stolen from the butcher's shop, and so on until he came to the last entry. Mr George Petch had died of a snake bite.

'George Petch?' He looked up at Adam. 'Isn't he from Beauview? Roberts' offsider.'

'I dunno. That's all Jim said. He got bit by a snake and died.'

Cosmo didn't have time to dwell on it. Snakebite was always a worry in this country. He shuddered. There were plenty of the deadly creatures about. He ought to get an expert to give him more information on snakes, their descriptions, and which ones were likely to kill. Distracted by that idea, he went ahead with the column and forgot about George Petch.

They worked late into the night, struggling with the unfamiliar equipment, but Cosmo was happy. The *Capricorn Post* was back in business, the people of Rockhampton had a paper once more, and the new edition would give them plenty to think about.

There was a knock at the back door and taking no chances now, Cosmo grabbed his rifle as Adam opened it gingerly.

'Who's there?' Cosmo called, and a very large woman loomed up from the darkness. He recognised the woman as Big Poll, who had become something of a fixture about the town lately.

'The name's Mrs Davies,' she said, deep voice rumbling in the quiet of the yard. 'I'm looking for a Mr Cosmo.'

'I'm Cosmo,' he replied politely, lowering the gun. 'What can I do for you?'

'Well,' she said, 'I ain't sure, but mates of mine told me I oughta see you.' She peered curiously over his shoulder. 'This where you write your paper, eh?'

'Yes.' He didn't want to invite her in, there wasn't much space in the workroom, and her bulk could be a hazard.

She didn't seem to expect an invitation, though, but stood blunting the stream of light in the doorway. 'Did you hear George Petch died of snake poisoning?' she asked.

'Yes, I heard that,' Cosmo replied.

She tapped a foot as if trying to decide what to do next, and then confided in Cosmo. 'I don't trust that copper, you know. But I could trust you.'

'Thank you,' Cosmo said, impatient to get back to work. 'Is there anything wrong?'

'Not for me, not any more. But I reckon someone ought to read this.' She handed him a writing book, a child's schoolbook. 'Look inside,' she prompted.

Cosmo opened the light book and took it over to the lamp. 'Who wrote this?' he asked as his eyes scrambled down the page.

'I did,' she said proudly.

'And it's fact?'

'Bloody oath it is. George put his name right there on the bottom.'

'Why would he sign an admission like this?'

'Because it's true. Tom Davies was my husband and they killed him.'

Cosmo scratched his head and adjusted his glasses. 'Did you tell Sergeant Hardcastle about this?'

'He knows all about it. Trouble is, he don't want to know, if you get my meaning. Wouldn't even charge Roberts for stealing Tom's horse.'

'This is all very interesting, Mrs Davies. If your husband has been killed, I'm very sorry to hear it, but right now I'm terribly busy. Would you mind waiting until I finish?'

'I'm not in a hurry.'

'Good, come on in. Adam, take this lady through to my office.'

He stood back, holding his breath as she progressed through the narrow aisle, without upsetting trays or tables. 'Well, well,' he said to himself. 'Another nail in your coffin, Boyd. This time we might be able to keep the lid down.'

The next day he confronted Jim Hardcastle with a copy of the statement. As he expected, the police sergeant dismissed the accusations out of hand. 'She got that out of poor George under duress.'

'I see,' Cosmo said silkily. 'Do you remember how Roberts came by those two prisoners? Think back, Jim, he boasted of duress, forcing other blacks to point them out.'

'That's nothing to do with me.'

'And the horse? The one she calls Stoker. It just happened to find its way into Beauview paddocks?'

'Yes, it was a stray. As for that statement . . . I'll have a word with Mr Roberts when he gets back.'

'I'm sure you will. Have you read the papers this morning?'

'Of course I have. Nothing new. With George dead and Baxter gone I can't get the reward back, if that's what you want.'

'You'll want to be very careful, Jim,' Cosmo warned. 'Don't go backing the wrong horse.'

'You heed your own advice, Cosmo,' Jim growled.

After his first burst of enthusiasm, and in the cold light of day, Cosmo had decided to delay publication of the confession. It was one thing to needle Roberts, challenging him to sue, but accusing him of murder was strong stuff. For maximum impact, he needed Roberts in town to face public opinion, counteracting Jim's reticence.

He'd offered Poll accommodation in the cabin at the back of his house when he discovered that she had no lodgings in town, and she'd accepted. 'No need for me to camp out now,' she said. 'But I won't be staying. I'm going home. My job's done. The rest's up to you blokes. I'd put a bullet in Roberts myself if I stuck around, but then I'd end up in the clink, and what would happen to my horses?'

He smiled, thinking what a sight they must have looked last night, trudging up the deserted road to his house. The big woman towering over him, leading her beloved horses; he'd had to travel at a trot to keep up with them.

This morning, his housekeeper had disdainfully taken Poll out her breakfast, and she'd appeared at the back door with her plates. 'Bloody lovely,' she'd said. 'The toast and tea, I mean. But I can't eat offal.'

Cosmo thought the housekeeper would choke with indignation to have her devilled kidneys returned to her untouched by this female tramp, so he'd stepped outside to say farewell to Poll.

'You take care now.'

'I always do,' she replied. 'But don't you let me down,' she added sternly, packing her rifle by her saddle and hanging a bandolier of cartridges across her chest. It almost sounded like a threat, and it could easily be, he thought, as he watched the two horses gallop up the road in a cloud of dust.

Since he'd decided that this story could keep until Roberts got back, for greater impact, he now had time to seek legal advice. In the meantime he'd leak it all over town and make life bloody uncomfortable for Jim Hardcastle.

328

There was an air of suspense in the town as everyone waited for two people to return to Rockhampton. The magistrate and Boyd Roberts. Day by day the streets became busier, with country people flooding in for the one week of the year when they all came together, far surpassing the Christmas celebrations when there was more of an exodus, with those who could travelling south to escape the heat and visit families.

Laura knew that Paul MacNamara was still in town, waiting to give evidence at the trial of Blackie Bob. He was staying with William Wexford and he must know by now that she had come home, but he'd made no attempt to contact her. There was no reason why he shouldn't call on the Carlisles, and encounter her by 'accident', she told herself, hoping to see him at the door every time the bell rang, but the days passed and her expectations turned to anger. 'He's not even a friend,' she thought angrily. 'He just used you. You're a fool to be thinking about him. And count yourself lucky you didn't get pregnant.' Initially, she'd been so much in love with him, she hadn't cared if she became pregnant – to have his child would have been living proof of their love – but later, as the reality of her situation had struck, she'd spent a few worrying days.

Looking back now at what might have happened to her, carrying the child of a man who didn't give a damn about her, Laura knew she'd had a very lucky escape. His absence caused her heart to grow harder. To hell with him, she decided.

She allowed herself to be escorted to gatherings by Leslie Soames, at the request of Grace Carlisle, to lend strength to his campaign. Laura understood the politics of that. As Fowler's daughter, she was giving Leslie the stamp of approval, even though she was sure he could beat Boyd. Laura had heard all the accusations being levelled at Roberts; she'd read a copy of the statement by George Petch and been shocked. Everyone in their immediate circle believed the confession to be true. It was flimsy evidence, but out there in the town, Roberts was spoken of with contempt, even his once-ardent supporters now claiming they never trusted the man.

They were home at last, after a miserable, rough voyage made worse not only by the knowledge that the Brisbane papers were on board, but also by the presence on the steamer of a tall, hungry-looking man with a head like a skull, who appeared to have no other clothes but a dusty black suit, more befitting a parson. This, Amelia was told, was the magistrate, Simon Cleever.

Boyd had attempted to address him, but the man had cut him dead in front of other passengers.

Amelia, with her strong constitution, had ridden out the huge battering waves, but Tyler had been sick all the way, leaving her stuck with her father, which was like accompanying a caged bear. She'd been furious with Tyler, hammering on his cabin door, telling him he'd feel better if he'd just come up on deck with her, but she'd been met with groans, and it wasn't until he stepped on to dry ground that he'd been able to throw off the nausea.

Andy was there to meet them with the carriage. His first words were: 'George is dead, boss. Snakebite.'

'What?' Boyd shouted, as if this were yet another insult he had to suffer. 'What are you talking about?'

'That's all I know,' Andy said. 'The copper came out and told us.'

'Shit!' Roberts exclaimed. As the carriage was pulling away from the wharf, a woman charged at them, shouting: 'Hey, Roberts! Where's Tom Davies?'

Amelia shrank back in her seat as if she'd been struck, and her father slammed down the blind.

'Who's Tom Davies?' Tyler asked.

'How the hell do I know?' Boyd snarled.

The small carriage spun along Quay Street, where Amelia saw a familiar figure standing on a front porch. 'There's Laura,' she cried, leaning out, waving to her. 'It's Laura. She's home. At her own place.'

She jumped up to call through the window to Andy to stop, but her father shoved her back. 'Keep going,' he shouted.

Forewarned by telegram that Mr Roberts and his daughter would be home this day, the house was in order, the pantry well stocked, and on the table in the hall was a neatly pressed copy of this week's *Capricorn Post*.

Tyler grabbed it. 'He's back in business,' he yelled. 'How did he do that?'

'Because he didn't bum around the bush like you,' Boyd roared, snatching the paper.

Amelia didn't have a chance to read it, because her father burned every page, but she didn't have to be told that whatever it contained, it was bad news. The two men shut themselves in the parlour, talking angrily, Boyd shouting at times and Tyler trying to calm him down. She wished she could go out, take a horse and ride down to Laura, just as Laura had come to her. But Tyler was here, Tyler would protect her from her father's rage.

She was glad that George was dead. Glad that God had removed his awful presence from the earth. A snakebite? That was fitting, she told herself, as she hung up all her new dresses. And with George out of the way, Boyd would now have to rely on Tyler. She placed gloves and stockings, still in their wrappings, in a long drawer and stopped for a moment to consider Boyd. 'I really think,' she said to the empty room, 'that he is going insane. Beating me for no earthly reason. Flying into rages in front of people. Probably old age.' She sniffed. 'But he'd better behave himself, or I'll have him put away.' Amelia had no idea how people were 'put away' but it was a pleasing fantasy. She hummed as she went about her unpacking, stuffing lacy handkerchiefs, bodices and unmentionables into her glory box.

They were still glum that night. No company at all. Tyler was not sure that the town could carry two newspapers. 'We might have to run at a loss for quite a while,' he told Boyd.

'So we run at a loss,' Boyd said. 'Who cares? It's my money. I want my newspaper on the streets double-quick. You get moving first thing in the morning.'

'Righto,' Tyler said. He turned to Amelia, 'We're calling the paper the *Northern Star*.'

'That sounds wonderful,' she enthused, to please them, but she was by no means thrilled. She was certain now that her father was cracked. How dare he waste money like this on a silly old paper! She decided she ought to have a look at what they were doing. 'I'll come into town with you in the morning, Tyler,' she said.

'No, you won't. You stay home,' her father snapped, and that was that.

But when she saw Sergeant Hardcastle knock at the door, she was glad Boyd had made her remain at the house. She crept around to hide in the bushes outside the open parlour window. It was always a good spot for eavesdropping, and this time she really got an earful.

She heard that George, before he died, had signed a confession, admitting to killing Tom Davies. That name again! And worse, he'd said that her father had ordered him to shoot Davies and dump his body.

Yet Boyd didn't seem to be concerned at such frightful allegations. 'Where is this so-called confession?'

'The woman took it with her.'

'You just let her march away with it?'

Hardcastle explained how Mrs Davies had come by the confession in the first place, chaining George to a tree, and Amelia almost choked with delight. 'She got the confession under duress, sir, I told her that flat, so it's no use under the law. I just thought I ought to let you know what's been happening while you were away. I don't want to upset you, but from what I hear, quite a few people have seen it. Cosmo Newgate got hold of a copy.'

'Then you might warn him that if he publishes you can arrest him. And the woman. Call it conspiracy, libel, whatever you like, but you can have him in jail before the papers come off the presses, and what's more you can confiscate every copy.'

'Can I?' Hardcastle said, bewildered.

'Without a doubt. You see, Sergeant, George Petch couldn't read or write. Everyone knows that. You said she wrote out the confession and he signed it, didn't you?'

'But if he was illiterate how could he have signed it? He didn't use a cross.'

'She had you fooled, the old crow,' Boyd laughed. 'All George could do was sign his name. I taught him that myself. Ask any of the storekeepers or the merchants. He never liked to let on that he couldn't read, so they used to tease him. When I gave him a list they'd ask him: "What's this, George?" and he'd study the list and make a guess. Always wrong. Quite hilarious, really.'

'He couldn't read at all?' Hardcastle breathed.

'Not a word, poor chap. That woman could have put a nursery rhyme under his nose and he'd have signed it. Best you run along now and break the news to Cosmo. His confession isn't worth a crumpet.'

By the time they reached the front door, Amelia was well away.

Boyd escorted his visitor down to his horse. 'Thanks, Jim, for letting me know. A man in my position has a lot of enemies willing to go to any lengths to vilify his name with their lies. This is just another political trick that hasn't worked.' He sighed. 'Fortunately, my friends and supporters aren't fooled. You must bring your wife to dinner one evening, Jim.'

'That's very kind of you, sir,' the policeman replied.

The trial of Blackie Bob coincided with the Rockhampton races, but the small courtroom and the grounds outside were still crowded. Because Magistrate Cleever insisted on hearing cases in the order that he chose, Paul was forced to hang about for days until it finally commenced. During that time he was constantly badgered by friends to nominate himself for the State seat, but he was adamant in his refusal. 'I'm not a politician,' he argued, surprised that they'd even consider him. 'I wouldn't know the rules.'

'What rules?' someone laughed.

'Ah, they'd be sure to have rules, and they'd tangle me up in no time. You need a cleverer man than me down there, lads.'

He was relieved when the hour passed and only two names remained on the nomination board: Roberts, and the Englishman, Soames.

Paul hadn't met Soames, but he was confident that the Captain, as a former aide to the Governor, would know the rules, so he sent him a hundred pounds towards campaign expenses. 'Out-shouting Roberts in the pubs will be a costly game,' he grinned, 'but a boon for the drinking fraternity.'

He had expected that the trial would be a simple matter, and that once he had given his evidence as required in the hushed atmosphere of the court, his part would be over. Instead, it was chaos from the minute the prisoner appeared. The waiting crowds erupted into a storm of hate, screaming and shouting abuse at him. They pushed and shoved their way into the already overcrowded room, knocking over chairs and benches, calling for a hanging verdict.

Since no amount of gavel-banging could restore order, the magistrate marched out, refusing to return until Hardcastle, with the assistance of troopers, had regained control. Two hours later, he returned to issue instructions that no one was permitted to stand in his court, and only those who had seats could remain. This caused arguments and further delay while several men were physically ejected.

'Now lock the doors,' he ordered Hardcastle, who shook his head nervously.

'They haven't got any locks, Your Honour.'

Peeved, the magistrate rubbed his nose and sat silently for a while before he allowed proceedings to begin. Hardcastle stood to read the charges, and to Paul's amazement several men in the room began a rumble of dissent.

'Order!' Cleever shouted. 'What's going on back there?'

'It's all lies,' a man called. 'MacNamara's story is a pack of lies.'

'Who are you?' the magistrate demanded.

'Barney Croft. I'm the Mines Inspector for this district. We caught the men who killed those women. This trial is a farce.'

Cleever leaned forward, his bald pate gleaming with sweat. He put on his glasses and peered at Croft. 'I heard about that,' he intoned ominously. 'You'll have your say another time.'

'I'll have my say now,' Croft yelled. 'This man is not guilty.'

'You mean he has to be innocent,' the magistrate countered, 'to save your necks. Let me remind you that I am the judge here and if you hanged the wrong men . . .'

'We didn't hang the wrong men!' Croft yelled.

Cleever smiled, his face smug. 'That saves me a bit of time. Arrest that man for impersonating a magistrate.'

'There's no such charge,' the Mines Inspector screamed as troopers grabbed him.

'Shows you don't know much about the law,' Cleever retorted.

As the struggling man was led away, Cleever called out to him, 'I told you you'd have your say another time.' He surveyed the room. 'It's lunchtime. Court adjourned for two hours.'

The groan in the room echoed Paul's feelings.

When the court reconvened, with everyone seated respectfully and the front doors closed, the magistrate made his entrance. He ordered that the windows to his left be closed to shut out the raucous voices of crows in a nearby paddock. It seemed to Paul that they were holding a court of their own out there, with a great deal of debate, then they were suddenly quiet.

Cleever nodded, satisfied, as if they too were acting on his instructions. 'Bring in the prisoner,' he said.

Hardcastle strode to the back door and called to a trooper, who in his turn yelled to another. 'Tell them to bring him over!'

Paul waited anxiously for them to escort Blackie Bob from the lockup. He hated having to look at him; his own emotions were in enough of a turmoil without the ordeal of witnessing the fellow's distress as well. He had asked to be excused from the court until he was needed, but Cleever had his own rules. He'd insisted Paul be present, since he'd laid the charges.

He watched a frown puckering the magistrate's brow as he tapped his desk with long yellowy fingers, impatient at being kept waiting. Feet shuffled, chairs clicked together, someone coughed and then gave a hefty sneeze. Cleever glowered at him.

Outside there was a sudden flurry of activity. Paul heard men running, heavy boots thudding across the grass, voices raised, an urgency in them, a pitch like panic. Then the police sergeant wrenched the back door open. He stumbled as he burst into the courthouse.

'He's dead!' he puffed. 'Blackie Bob's dead! In the lockup! He cut his own bloody throat!'

Amelia attended the races with her father, disappointed that Tyler was too busy to join them. 'What's the use of being engaged,' she'd fumed at him, 'if I have to go without you?'

'I'm sorry, darling,' he said. 'But I have to get the paper going as soon as possible.'

'Why don't you hire people to do that work?'

'I have, Amelia. I've hired two lads, but I have to be there to tell them what to do. As it is, I'll be lucky to be in production by next week. Everything seems to be going wrong.'

She sighed as they arrived at the course. Such as it was, she reflected. Only a rough bush track, with a couple of tin sheds for refreshments. Not a patch on the elegance of Brisbane. Nevertheless, she was wearing the red dress she'd worn in Brisbane and carrying the same parasol, and she felt quite superior to all the other girls, who looked very drab.

When she saw Laura she rushed over and threw her arms about her, her father standing by smiling. 'I'm so glad you're back,' Amelia cried. 'I've missed you. And you're back at your own house, I hear? That's wonderful.'

Boyd intervened. 'How are you, Laura? My word, you're looking very elegant. Are you feeling better now?'

'Much better, thank you, Boyd.'

'You see,' he beamed at the two girls, 'everything is back to normal now. Although I must say I was disappointed to come home and find you'd left.'

'Yes, I'm sorry about that,' Laura said, embarrassed. 'I didn't have time to explain.'

'Your things are still there,' Amelia said. 'When are you coming for them? Come tomorrow and we'll have lunch. Did you know I'm engaged? Oh, what a silly I am. I left my engagement ring at home. Oh well, never mind. Now, what have you been up to?'

A tall gentleman came to stand by Laura, and Amelia raised her eyebrows in approval, nudging at Laura for an introduction.

334

Laura's cheeks flushed pink as she was forced to introduce them to Captain Soames. Boyd carried it off well. 'How do you do, sir? My opposition, I believe? I'm delighted to meet you. Let's just say "May the best man win." Would you care to join us for a drink? I have champagne on a picnic table over by Amelia's carriage.'

Soames' response was cool. 'Good of you, sir, but not just now.'

The Englishman, though, was no match for Amelia, who took his arm. 'But you must join us! Laura and I have been friends forever. We can't be worrying about silly politics. We're here to enjoy ourselves. Now, tell me, which horses should I back?'

As she carted him away, Boyd went to take Laura's arm to follow them, but she edged free.

'Surely you can spare a few minutes with us,' he said to her.

'I'd rather not, Boyd,' she said firmly.

'Oh I see,' he sneered. 'I've outlived my usefulness, have I? Beauview was fine until you found somewhere better.'

'It's not like that at all,' she replied. 'I appreciate what you did to help me, but I have to get on with my own life.'

'Which excludes me?'

Laura looked up at him, her gaze firm as she nodded. 'I'm afraid so.'

She saw him flinch as if she'd struck him, and then his pale eyes narrowed as he leered at her. 'Clearing the decks for MacNamara, are you?'

'What?' she cried, but the barb had found its mark and a blush flooded across her face. Confused, she tried to turn away but he stepped in front of her and touched her cheek.

'Dead giveaway, darling. It makes one wonder who really did kill his wife. Was he clearing the decks too?'

'You're disgusting!' she flared and pushed him aside.

She could hear Amelia calling to her as she ran from them.

Blackie Bob had killed himself with a hunting knife, had cut his own throat in one sharp, bloody thrust. But who had given him the knife? Friend or foe? His lifeblood had pumped on to the dirt floor of the small lockup while his captors were at lunch. That was the end of another life, Paul sorrowed, the end of the court case, and the end of the official investigation into the deaths of Jeannie and Clara.

'Now we'll never know for sure,' Hardcastle had shrugged.

Paul had grabbed him by the shirt. 'You know as well as I do, you weak-kneed bastard.'

But it was over now. All over and he was going home. He would leave in the morning, he decided. It would be a relief to be away on his own, to cross the Fitzroy again, the easy way this time, and go home. He would have to come to terms with what had happened there, to fulfil his promise to the blacks. His land would be safe for all.

'Not with Roberts living next door,' he muttered to himself, as he rode back to Wexford's house. 'There'll be no peace with him around.'

Then he had an idea. A proposition he could put to Roberts. Worth a try. Roberts would have to learn he wasn't the only bully in town. Other people, like the MacNamaras for instance, could play just as rough. He'd seen Roberts riding through the town with a new pair of henchmen – miners, he was told, hired to take the place of George Petch – lording it over everyone, knowing that he could never be brought to account for the death of one of his own men. Cosmo was still wailing over that. To Paul, it was something for the town to worry about. He couldn't take on the world. His mission now was to begin the job of patching up relations between the blacks and the whites, and there could be a small beginning at Oberon. If he could make Roberts see reason.

He took out his watch. The races were over. William would be home any minute. Better to go now and confront Roberts on his own turf, without the interference of friends.

Remembering that Roberts always had his hired guns nearby, Paul took the handgun and holster that was hanging in William's cloak-room. Not that he intended to use it, he told himself, as he checked and loaded the gun. It was just a precaution in case the help were trigger-happy, a reminder that the visitor was armed.

For that reason he discarded his jacket and waistcoat – his townie clothes, he smiled – and slung the holster about his hips, buckling it into place and snapping the gun pouch closed.

Amelia was upset. As usual, she thought bitterly. What had happened to her life? Superstitiously she decided, as she wandered lonely and miserable about the grounds of Beauview, that everything had gone wrong from the day she'd parted friends with Laura. From the day Laura had left Beauview. Amelia was in tears. She wanted her friend back. She could tell Laura everything; they'd been such happy, naughty girls.

They'd only stayed at the races for a few hours while Boyd did his political showing off. Just as Amelia was starting to enjoy herself he'd told her they were leaving. All afternoon, behind his public face, she'd known he was in a foul mood again, so she hadn't dared complain. Andy had packed everything up and driven them home. While everyone else was out there enjoying themselves! There'd be parties after the races, she knew, and she'd been whisked away. It was all so unfair.

Often, though, Amelia tried to look on the good side of things, and now she invoked, in consolation, two good things that had happened today. The first one was Laura. Although she'd been a bit standoffish, Amelia had seen a genuine softness in her eyes when she'd approached Laura, and so she knew they were still friends. Although, goodness, why shouldn't they be?

The other thing was – and Amelia sneaked a glance about her as she strolled down the drive, for want of anything better to do – Captain Soames. He was divine. Far more elegant than Tyler. And so gorgeously British, with that beautiful voice, she'd almost swooned at it. At the carriage, with Andy serving the champagne, when they'd left Laura and her father behind, Amelia had asked him point-blank if he were Laura's beau. And Leslie had assured her he was not. That was interesting news. Tyler was all right, she supposed, but he was only a reporter, working for her father. Leslie had told her that he was not only a former aide to the Governor himself, but that he came from an aristocratic family. Amelia concluded he meant dukes and earls and she was thrilled.

'I'm so sorry,' she whispered to Leslie, 'that you and Daddy are on opposite sides. I wish he'd let you have the seat. He doesn't really need it. It's just a whim on his part.'

'I can assure you,' Leslie sniffed, 'that I don't need it, as you say, either. Nor do I need your father to hand me the seat, even though it is only a whim on his part. He seems to have a most peculiar attitude.'

'True,' Amelia said wistfully. 'But then you appreciate the honour. To my father, prestige is only related to money. I'm sure you have higher principles.'

'One would hope so,' Leslie replied. 'Now if you'll forgive me, I must away.'

'My father is a fool,' Amelia told the gatepost as she stared down the road. 'If he was nicer to me I might be nicer about him.'

She kicked spitefully at a bank of violets. 'I hope he doesn't win anyway. He's getting too big for his boots.'

A horseman was approaching the gate, coming out of the glare of the western sun. 'Good afternoon.' He smiled, raising his hat. 'You must be Miss Roberts.'

Amelia smiled sunnily. Two handsome men in one day! How gorgeous! 'And who might you be?'

'Paul MacNamara, miss. Is your father at home?'

MacNamara? she breathed to herself. Oh my God! It's him! No wonder Laura fell for him. Wait until she hears about this!

'Yes, he's home.' She smiled, ready to continue the conversation.

'Thank you,' he said. 'Would you excuse me.'

'Of course,' she said, standing back, and he rode away up the long drive. Amelia almost tripped over herself trying to catch up, but he'd rounded the bend in the carriageway before she'd gone even a few steps.

Boyd Roberts saw him coming.

Since they'd arrived home from the races, Boyd had been fuelling his fury with whisky, trying to work out how to get Laura back. Next to her, at the races, his own daughter had looked like a floozie. He hadn't noticed before that she dressed like a chorus girl, making a fool of him. And that stupid Tyler didn't know any better. But Laura! They'd turned her against him, all of them. Starting with MacNamara. It was true, he knew now. She'd just been using him, lodging in his house for protection until her lover came for her.

And the day at the races had been a disaster.

Backs had been turned. Drinks he'd proffered had been poured on to the grass. He'd been snubbed until he could bear it no longer. The Carlisles and their friends were out in force, with Laura by their side, looking down their long noses at him.

He'd gone down to the cheaper shed to shout jugs of liquor, but he'd seen the grins of derision on the faces of the men as they accepted free grog, and Boyd Roberts knew then that his great dream was lost. It had been the same in town, despite his brave front, despite his promises; all those people who had clamoured to support him had deserted, undermined by Newgate's vicious propaganda.

And who was to blame? Two people. Tyler for wasting all this time, for not being there to counteract Newgate. And MacNamara. Oh yes, MacNamara, with his cock-and-bull story about escaping the blacks. He'd settle with them. Tyler was a nobody, he'd kick him out on his ear.

As for MacNamara? He wouldn't get Laura. Not a chance.

Boyd poured himself another neat whisky. So what if he didn't win the election? It would be smarter to just pull out and then he couldn't lose. Claim illness. Claim pressure of business. He might sell this place and move to Brisbane. Life was a damn sight more fun down there, people weren't so picky. And the women weren't so uppity. Not like Laura. But he still yearned for her. Loved her. Hadn't he watched over her, been her friend, cared for her in her troubles? What more could she want? Until MacNamara, the bloody hypocrite, had got to her.

He knocked the bottle over as he lunged for his rifle, loading it quickly and storming out to the veranda. 'Stop right there!'

His visitor shrugged. 'Put the gun away, I just want to talk.'

'What about?'

'You don't need that property next to mine. Jock McCann's place.'

'You mean Airdrie Station. My place.'

'Right, your place. What do you want for it?'

'*You* want to buy it? Haven't you had enough punishment? I haven't started on you yet.'

Paul sat back in the saddle, taking a cautious look about for Roberts' cronies, but there was no one in sight except for the daughter, who was hurrying up the drive. 'Now you listen to me,' he warned Roberts. 'I *have* had enough punishment and I'm not taking any more. You've been trying to run me off my land, and now it's my turn. You sell to me – I'll give you a fair price – or I'll see to it that Airdrie can't operate. I'll run your men and your cattle off the minute they show their noses. I'm there, I'm established, I've got the whip

338

hand and you know it. So name your price.'

'You couldn't afford it!' Roberts sneered.

'Try me,' Paul replied, as Boyd steadied himself against the veranda post, glaring down at the man who had robbed him of happiness with Laura. 'You don't want the place, you don't need any more trouble, Roberts,' he was saying. 'Why not, for once, just give over?'

'The gall of you! What are you doing? Trying to impress Laura with a double spread out there?'

'Laura?' He sounded confused. 'What's she got to do with this?'

'Plenty,' Boyd grated, his hatred of this man overwhelming him, his jealousy causing him to boast. 'You'll never get her,' he cried. 'She's going to marry me.'

Amelia ran forward. 'What's this?' she accused her father. 'You're going to marry Laura?'

'Get inside,' her father snapped.

Amelia looked up at Paul. 'Is this true?'

'I'll believe it when I see it,' he remarked. Then he rode over to the bottom of the steps. 'It's your move. Think it over. Let me buy Airdrie Station and be done with it, man.'

He turned his horse and smiled at Amelia, lifting his hat. 'Good afternoon, miss.'

The rider crossed the terraced clearing in front of the house and was just turning into the tree-shaded drive when the shot rang out.

Two miners recently recruited to Roberts' staff had come up the back track to stable their horses when they heard the shot. They leapt back on to their horses and galloped past the coach house, on and round the house to the front. They hauled their horses to a halt when they saw the body, and the boss, rifle in hand, standing on the elegant front veranda. They looked at each other and nodded in mutual agreement. Their mates had warned them that working for Roberts might pay big money but it was a hazardous occupation. With Roberts shouting at them to come back, they spurred their horses and rode full pelt past him, away from this. They wanted no part of it.

Amelia was screaming. Paul MacNamara, shot in the back, had crashed from his horse and was sprawled beside her, blood oozing, blood everywhere. His horse shied, pranced and fled away, following the other horses.

She knelt beside him. 'You shot him!' she screamed at her father. 'He's dead! I think he's dead!' In her panic she threw herself across the body, as if to protect it from more bullets. 'Oh God! Oh God! No. Don't be dead.' Shocked, she appealed to her father. 'Help me.' But he stood there, at the top of the steps, with a smug, self-satisfied smile on his face, as if this were some sort of achievement, like bagging a fox or a dingo.

Lying across Paul, her nice dress bloodied, she screamed at her father again as he came down the steps. 'You're mad!' At the same time she was fumbling with the revolver strapped about Paul's waist, a plan formulating. 'You're mad!' she kept screaming as he descended leisurely, imperiously, the lord of his manor.

Amelia had the gun in her hand. She knew about guns. Hadn't the madman over there taught her to defend herself. She felt the weight of the handgun, her fingers searching, praying it was loaded, otherwise she'd have to wait her chance. Hurrying, rushing, shaking, she thanked the Lord that it was loaded, that Paul was wearing a handgun and not a rifle. A rifle anyway would have gone with the horse, and no one travelled with a loaded rifle, it was too dangerous, you could shoot your foot off.

He was at the bottom of the steps, undecided now. 'You haven't got George any more!' she yelled at him, stalling for time, hearing the click of the safety catch. 'Who's going to clean up for you?'

'Shut up,' he said. 'Get away from there.'

He was coming to inspect his handiwork.

Limply, Amelia raised herself then slumped back on her haunches, her skirts spreading around her. She held the gun firmly as she turned, and aiming it at the madman coming towards her, she fired. Her father was a handsome man, she didn't want to spoil his face, so she fired dead at his heart.

It had seemed like hours to her but it had only been a matter of minutes. She dropped the gun beside Paul and ran screaming into the house, into the arms of the cook, who had been hiding with the housemaid in the kitchen, too afraid to peer out.

'They've shot each other,' she wept. 'Oh my God! They've killed each other! My father and Mr MacNamara!' Then she collapsed.

They left her there, running past her, rushing outside to find the boss stone dead out there on the terrace, and the other man moaning, badly hurt, with a bullet in his back.

'You shot him, didn't you?' Tyler said.

Amelia had taken off her ruined dress and changed into the fluttery white silk she reserved for morning church, but that didn't mean she felt better and she resented Tyler's tone. In fact she felt terrible, all shaky and wobbly and distraught. Yes, distraught. Her house was full of people. The doctor was in there attending to Paul MacNamara, in her father's bedroom as a matter of fact, but she'd pretended not to notice. They'd said he might live.

The policeman, Hardcastle, was marching about as if he owned her house. Amelia had no time for him, her father had always said he was an idiot. And there were army men wandering the grounds, with the rather nice Lieutenant Gooding being very solicitous, as he should be, patting her hand, telling her she must rest. Other people were there, she had seen them with quick glimpses under her long dark eyelashes. Cosmo Newgate, for instance, and Justin Carlisle. Amelia had always wanted to meet Mr Carlisle and now she found he was the sweetest of the lot. A dear old man who kept bringing her cups of tea laced with brandy, who chatted with her as if nothing had happened. Indeed, what had happened was not her fault. Mr Carlisle talked to her about the gardens of Beauview, he found them quite beautiful, as they were. Amelia, in her weakened, shocked state, liked listening to Mr Carlisle, she really appreciated his kindness.

Everyone had been terribly kind to her. But now this. From Tyler, of all people.

'You shot him, didn't you. Your father?'

Amelia cried, 'How can you say such a thing?' She wept, clutching a wad of stiff new lace handkerchiefs. 'My father is dead. My father!' Sobs, dreadful, heart-rending sobs, shook her whole body, but Tyler persisted.

'You must have shot him. I've been going over the scene and it couldn't have happened the way you told Hardcastle. MacNamara didn't shoot your father. You did.'

Amelia turned from him and burrowed into the leather couch. She had insisted on being put to bed in the parlour under her comfy white eiderdown with the broderie trims rather than be locked away in her room, not knowing what was going on. Tyler was spoiling everything.

'Leave me alone,' she whispered. 'Don't you understand I'm an orphan now?'

'Amelia,' he said softly, pushing aside her dark curls to kiss her on the neck. 'It's all right, I love you, but just tell me what really happened.'

'I told them,' she wept. 'How many times do I have to go over it? I feel sick. Go away and leave me alone.'

The women came the next day. Laura came but she didn't go into the sickroom. She sat with Amelia but neither of them said much, because Mrs Carlisle, whom Laura called Grace, seemed to have taken over. Not that Amelia minded; looking after a house full of strangers was quite beyond her. It was easier to let it all go over her head. She sat, numbed, on the veranda, and indeed she really did feel numb now, the whole business too much to contemplate. Deep down she was terrified. Not of these people, but of her father. She had shot him and she was sure he would come back in a frightful rage and punish her. At every turn his personality, raving mad at her, permeated the house, shouting, threatening her with terrible punishments, threatening to hound her to the grave, to her own grave.

And still Tyler questioned, badgered her. 'What really happened, Amelia?' Until she began to scream and was taken to her bed in hysterics.

As the days passed, Paul MacNamara became stronger. The bullet had missed his spine but had entered his left lung, and the doctor had performed a delicate operation to remove the bullet. It was touch and go, everyone said, but he was healthy, and the other lung would just have to work harder. While he was recovering, Amelia, beset by nightmares of her father dragging her down to hell with him, screamed in terror, night after night.

The woman employed to nurse Paul was kept on her toes trying to soothe the girl. She had to constantly relight lamps, to allay Amelia's fear of the dark. 'Poor love,' she said to Paul, 'seeing her dad shot dead in front of her! Enough to send any young girl off her head. She's a nervy little thing, real high-strung you know, she may never get over it.'

She plumped Paul's pillows and tucked his sheets in so tightly he felt bandaged to the bed. 'Just as well you're not superstitious, mister, lying there in a dead man's bed, and him the one you shot.'

'It's not a comforting thought, Mrs Moloney,' Paul said. 'I didn't have any choice. They just bundled me in here, and I'd be obliged if you'd look about for another room for me, since, as you say, I'm the one did the deed.'

''Tis still no choice you've got,' she said. 'Doctor says you should stay put, and anyway, the rooms are all taken, what with me and Mr Kemp in the spares. Just say your prayers and the good Lord will take care of you. That's what I've been telling young missy there, but Protestant prayers, they don't seem to be working. Do you think we ought to baptise her?'

He tried not to laugh. It hurt. 'I don't think that'll be necessary,' he replied gently. 'Why don't you ask her to come in and see me. I haven't set eyes on her. The least I can do is thank her for having me in the house.'

Mrs Moloney shook her head doubtfully. 'I've told her you're back in the land of the living but she don't seem all that keen to be visiting. Put yourself in her place, Mr Mac. You did shoot her dad. Right or wrong. I'm not saying he didn't deserve it, what with the things a person hears about him, and the villain shooting you in the back, but still . . .' She shuffled about the room in her slippers. 'With all due respect, it's hard for the daughter to swallow.'

He watched as she opened up the French windows, clipping back the curtains to allow a warm breeze to flow into the room.

'That's the end of winter,' she remarked, 'or what they're pleased to call winter out here. They don't know they're alive do they?'

'I suppose not,' he mused. He'd been surprised, when he'd eventually sorted out a haze of confusing conversations that had come at him through a fog, that everyone took it for granted that he'd shot Roberts.

'Self-defence,' Jim Hardcastle had said, with other people in the room. Paul couldn't remember who, exactly, but William Wexford had been there. The faces looking at him had been anxious for him, hovering, talking over him. A priest had come to give him Extreme Unction, praying quietly, and Paul recalled his shocked expression when he'd muttered, 'You're wasting your time. I'm not going anywhere.'

'You did a good job,' Hardcastle had said, a calloused hand stroking his forehead like sandpaper. 'You rest, Paul. Everything's fine. Roberts met his match.'

Now Paul distinctly remembered that. They were congratulating him. What for? he wondered at the time. But he'd decided to say nothing, just to listen until he'd sorted this out.

In the first place, he didn't remember being shot. But the evidence of that was present in the pain that registered when he took a deep breath. And his visitors agreed that Roberts had shot him in the back. That would be right; he recalled that Roberts had been waving a rifle at him and raving on about Laura. What was it he'd said about Laura? Paul didn't know. Too hard to think about that now. His conversation with Roberts had ended with nothing resolved, as far as he could remember, and so he'd given up and was riding away. Leaving Beauview.

But what had happened next? He had to concentrate. He was lying face down and there was a warm sticky feeling on his back. Face into the ground. He'd heard his horse thunder away, and then someone was covering him. Perfume. He could smell perfume, a sweetness. A woman was lying over him, making an awful noise. Screeching. He could see his hands there in front of him, his left hand had been just there under his face and his right hand had looked huge, gross, at eyelevel, refusing to respond, to push him up from a pit.

He could hear her, Amelia. She was screaming, 'You're mad!' Someone was mad, but it wasn't him, he had no strength, no power left in him. And then the shot. Right by his ear, like an explosion, deafening.

And he'd shot Roberts then? Not likely. Impossible.

'Mrs Moloney,' he said. 'Can you spare a minute?'

'And what else am I here for?'

He grinned. 'I can't seem to grasp what happened. Can you tell me?'

Mrs Moloney turned, her generous bosom, encased in black bombazine, looming pridefully over, 'Ah, there's a sign we're on our way.' She beamed. 'You won't be needing me much longer.'

'Roberts shot me?' he asked.

'He did an' all, the villain, the coward. Got you in the back.'

'And then?'

'And then – Miss Amelia told us what happened, with a lot of crying and going on, mind you – you fell to the ground and pulled out your handgun, with the villain pacing towards you to finish you off, so youse grabbed your handgun and got him before it was too late. And then you passed out again.'

'I did?'

'Chip off the old block, my husband says. He knew your dad. Pace MacNamara, was it not?'

'That's true.'

'Oh, glory be! Wait till I tell him he was right. He said your dad was a crack shot back in the old country. A sniper, high up in the Movement, you know.'

'I didn't know,' Paul said, astonished at this sudden glimpse of his father, the peacemaker.

'Well, of course, nobody talks about these things out here, but you sure proved the MacNamaras haven't lost their touch. My husband, he says if Roberts wanted to live, he should have got it right first time, 'cos then it'd be too late. You got the bastard, if you'll excuse my French, and no one in town is complaining. So don't you go worrying now, I'll be getting your porridge.'

Paul lay back on the pillows, staring out at hard blue skies. He wished she'd close the drapes – the light was too strong – but he didn't have the heart to ask. One day, though, he'd ask his mother, Dolour, what that was all about. The old country? The Movement? How much family history is lost by parents who come from another land? he wondered. By parents who don't want to talk about it and sons who never ask, until it is too late. He'd had no idea his father was connected in any way with the uprisings in Ireland, and he bet that John, his twin brother, didn't know either. But that was for a later time.

Right now, it appeared that he was lying here a false hero, having been shot by Roberts, then, practically out for the count, raising the strength to pull his gun and shoot his assailant dead, from that low angle. Some shot.

'Some shot!' That's what they'd been saying. Paul knew he could handle a gun, but he was no hotshot. Jeannie had been the sharp-shooter because she'd practised, she'd had targets set up for practice, it had been her hobby. From the angle where he'd been lying, Paul doubted if he could have hit a horse, let alone a man walking towards him, right in the heart. Taking in his physical condition at the time.

But what was he thinking about? He eased the pain by moving slowly, cautiously, from his side until he was almost face-down in the pillows. That small movement tore at the incision in his back, alerting shattered ribs to send stabs of pain at him. Paul lay very still, waiting for the pain to subside, and then he said: 'Bulldust!'

He knew he hadn't shot Roberts.

So who had?

Amelia. Miss Roberts. Boyd's daughter. She had saved his life. She had thrown herself across him. The perfume. Protected him. She had grabbed his handgun and shot her father.

As long as he was very still, there was no pain, Paul understood that. But his mind was racing. Why had she lied? Why didn't she just say that she had witnessed her father shoot the visitor, and to protect the wounded man she'd had no choice but to shoot Roberts?

'Oh, Christ,' he whispered. No wonder the poor girl was having nightmares.

344

He turned his investigations in on himself. If he'd shot his father, his own father, would he be volunteering that information to the authorities? He realised that Amelia was placing her bets on the hope that he wouldn't recall what had really happened.

'Oh, Christ,' he said again, feeling sorry for the girl, and grateful to her. She was a sweet little thing and probably had no idea what her old man had been up to. Girls like her were sheltered from reality, living up here in the heights, playing at ladies. Paul dismissed the fiancé, Tyler Kemp, who had come in and out of his room, displaying concern for the patient. He had been somehow distant. Not real. Not delaying for more than a few minutes because he had business in town. His paper.

'Mrs Moloney,' he called. 'Would you please tell Miss Amelia that I want to see her. I have to thank her for her kindness.'

'I'll get her,' his nurse replied. 'I'll bring her in if I have to piggyback her.'

And there was Amelia at his door. White-faced against a mop of black curls, wearing a sober black dress.

Paul reached out his hand, and with an effort held it up to her until she came forward and took it. Her hand was cold, thin, weak.

'Are you feeling better?' he asked, not thinking that this was the question she should have been asking of him. She nodded, nervously.

'You did what you had to do,' he said, holding her hand, drawing her to him.

Then she spoke, her voice high, unreal. 'I sent Andy for the doctor and for the police. I didn't know what to do.'

'You saved my life. Do you mind if I call you Amelia?'

She shook her head. 'No. I'm glad you're recovering. Can I get you something? Mrs Moloney is making you an egg-flip. I'll get it for you.'

'No. Don't go, Amelia. Sit down.'

She sat abruptly in the chair by the bed, as if not daring to disobey. There was a silence between them. Paul deliberately left it untouched, exposing her to a vacuum.

He saw her take out a handkerchief, sniff into it, return it to her sleeve, finger the pearl buttons at her collar as if the day had become too hot to endure.

'Amelia,' he said at length, but that silence had been too much for her.

'You won't tell them, will you?' she begged.

'No,' he said decisively. 'I won't tell them. I feel a bit of a fool, but if that's what you want . . .'

She threw her arms about him, her soft skin caressing his face. 'What else could I do? He'd gone mad. He shot you. He was coming at us . . . I didn't know whether he was going to shoot you again, or me. I was so frightened.' Her tears were damp on his cheek and her hair was sweet-smelling, fresh, delicious. 'You mustn't tell them. They think you shot him. Oh please, what would become of me if they knew? What would people say? I can't sleep,' she went on frantically. 'He's there every night, pointing at me, damning me! I'll never rest again.'

'Yes, you will,' he said, smoothing the curls from her face. 'Your father was not in his right mind at the time. Remember him as he was. I've heard he was always very good to you, he loved you. We know that he was drunk, that something terrible happened and you had to shoot him. Are you listening to me? You have to stop blaming yourself. You thought I was dead. A few minutes later,' he told her, looking to the ceiling over her head for forgiveness for this necessary lie, to protect her sanity, 'I'd have defended myself, Amelia. You know I would have done that, don't you?'

She nodded, her head buried in the pillows, clinging to him.

'I beg your forgiveness,' he said, 'for the death of your father. I didn't realise that he was past reason.'

Amelia came up, blue eyes, so limpid and appealing, looking at him. 'I didn't do it, did I?'

'No,' he said, bleakly. 'Leave it be. They've all made up their minds, there's no sense in disturbing them. Now, we want no more of your bad dreams, it's a terrible, sad business but the grief will pass, believe me. You think of the good times, Amelia, and if you've a bad night, you come in here and sit in that big chair where I can see you.'

Amelia stood up and looked at him. 'You wouldn't mind?'

'No. It'd be company for me too. The nights are long when you're stuck in bed all day.'

'What's going on here?' Mrs Moloney, with her tray, was at the foot of the bed. 'You haven't been making her cry, have you, Mr Mac?'

'No,' Amelia said. 'He's been very kind.'

Outside, she said to Mrs Moloney, 'I feel just terrible. He thanked me for saving his life and apologised for shooting my father. Isn't that just the most awful thing? I don't know what to do any more.'

'Ah, you poor lass, you poor thing, it's a dreadful business. But there's some hot milk on the stove still. I'll make you an egg-flip too, with hot scones, and you have a nice little rest, there's a good girl.'

The lady of the house tripped out into the sunlight. She hated the grim smell of sickrooms, and she was sure she'd never get rid of the stink of ether from her house. But she'd soon have it all to herself, and then she'd order a spring-clean. After all, she smiled, it was spring.

She felt better now, Paul had seen to that. He wouldn't tell anyone, he was a gentleman, not inclined to ruin her reputation by admitting . . . well, that. And anyway it was quite clear, she realised now, that she had done her father a favour. They would have hanged him. She shuddered, and pulled her shawl about her. How frightful that would have been. How utterly frightful. It just didn't bear thinking about. In her shattered state, after what had happened, she'd been afraid that they might have hanged her. Scared stiff. And too frightened to talk to anyone about it.

But Boyd Roberts was dead and buried. There was no need to be afraid of him any more; she had saved him from a public hanging, and saved their name from disgrace.

She strolled across the still incomplete croquet lawn and decided to rip it up. She'd lost interest in croquet. A gazebo would look pretty here, trellised in white, surrounded by a rose-garden. There were so many things to think about now. She supposed she ought to be grateful to Paul for keeping his mouth shut, but then again, he'd come out the hero, so why worry? The only person, Amelia thought darkly, to question the official stance was Tyler. How dare he? What did it have to do with him? If the police and Paul MacNamara were satisfied, what right did he have to complicate things? He could be such a bore at times.

That evening, Amelia pinned her hair up and added diamond earrings and a necklace of pearls to her dreary black dress. She even put on her little engagement ring, to please Tyler.

She sipped sherry wine as Tyler sank into a comfortable chair in the parlour with a tankard of chilled beer. He was tired, but pleased with his day.

'How's the patient?' he asked.

'In good spirits. He'll be leaving here any day. Going back to Mr Wexford's place to recuperate. You look pleased with yourself.'

'So I should be. I've finally figured out how to make this paper work. I won't be in competition with the *Capricorn Post*. I've decided to make my paper a monthly. People here are starved of reading matter. I'll have a news section, and all the latest on cattle sales and so forth, but more features. A short story, maybe two, and space for really interesting articles. It'll be a winner, more like a magazine.' He glanced at her. 'Are you listening?'

'Of course I am. But I was wondering when we'll be married. People will talk to see an engaged couple living here unchaperoned. It was different when my dear father was alive.' She dabbed at her eyes with a lawn handkerchief.

'Oh my dear.' Tyler rushed over and took her hand, kissing her on the cheek. 'You name the day. I've been missing you so much and it's breaking my heart to hear you so upset at night. But,' he smiled wanly, 'that Mrs Moloney seems to regard you as her property too.'

'She worries about me,' Amelia said.

'And rightly so. You've been through a lot.'

Amelia waited, but at last he had given up on interrogating her. That was a relief. 'Normally,' she announced, 'one should wait after a bereavement before setting the date, but in our circumstances, once Mr MacNamara leaves here I really think we should make the arrangements.'

'By all means, darling. I suppose you'll have to order the wedding dress.'

'I had it made in Brisbane,' she giggled. 'It is absolutely divine and hidden well away from you, my love.'

'Well, that's settled. Tell me what I have to do and I'll get on to it right away. But there's one pressing matter I have to speak to you about.'

'What's that?'

'I hate to ask you, but I need money to keep the paper going. Expenses, wages, they mount up.'

Amelia nuzzled against him. 'Do we need the paper now?'

He drew back and stared at her.'Of course we do. I just explained, I can make it pay.'

'But when, Tyler? When? Will I have to keep forking out money on the off chance that people will buy it?'

'I admit it's a bit of a gamble, but worth a try.'

Amelia studied her hankie. 'You seem to forget where the money's coming from, dear. The gold mines. I can't have you pottering about with your hobby, spending my money, ignoring the mines. My father checked them himself at least once a month. He never trusted the mines managers. I mean, who would?'

Tyler was nervous. 'I don't know much about gold mining.'

'Neither did he, but he learned.'

Her fiancé stood up, drank his beer and poured another. 'Amelia, I didn't want to worry you before this with business matters, but you seem to be up to them now.'

'I'm not incapable, Tyler.'

'No, but you shouldn't have to be worried. I've been talking to a few people, assayers and the like, and I believe you can get an excellent price for those mines. You don't need them. I took the liberty of opening up your father's inner office . . .'

'You did what?' Amelia had been looking forward to her own unencumbered investigations when she had the house to herself again. When she felt better. 'Where did you find the keys?'

'In his bedroom,' Tyler said. 'Hardcastle insisted we check it out.'

'I see,' she said quietly, ominously. 'And what did you find?'

'We didn't touch anything.' He produced the keys and handed them to her. 'The heavy one is the key to the second safe. Apparently your father didn't trust banks. That little room was like a fortress. But believe me, Amelia, there were no papers. Nothing incriminating. Nothing at all that would tie him to the disappearance of the fellow Davies. That missing man.'

'I could have told you that,' she said tartly. 'My father wasn't stupid. What else will I find, now that you have already had access to my private business?'

'Don't be like that,' Tyler reasoned. 'I was only there to protect your interests.'

'So what did you find?'

'You've got the keys.' He shrugged. 'See for yourself. There's more than half a million pounds in that safe.'

Amelia nodded. It was no more than she expected. How many times did Tyler have to be told that her father was a very wealthy man? But now, the money would have to be moved. And quickly. Damn them for interfering!

'Do you recall where that money came from?' she demanded. 'From gold mines. And you want me to sell them? Those reefs are still bearing. God knows where they could lead.'

'They could also run dry.'

'Who the hell have you been talking to? Nobody buys a mine that's going to peter out. And if the reefs are bearing, my father would have staked claims on the perimeters. There's a limit to the area of a claim. You wouldn't be selling a couple of mines, you could be selling a whole damn reef.'

He was astonished. 'How do you know this?'

'Do you think I'm deaf or something? My father was a gold miner. His claim deeds are right here in his desk, all notarised, plain as day. The main Starlight mines are only part of it. To stay in business you have to keep expanding, prospecting. What do you think he talked about all these years, with no one to listen but me? Claims run out after three months if they're not worked, so he had to keep renewing to cover the area. I wouldn't sell a gold mine in a fit.'

Tyler was stunned by her vehemence and by the emergence of a woman he hardly recognised. 'Darling,' he said, to soothe her. 'What's the worry? We have more money than we could spend in a lifetime. We don't need any more.'

'You just said you do. For the paper.'

He laughed. Female reasoning. Unreasoning. 'We can afford the paper.'

'But I don't want a paper, Tyler. I want my gold mines. Now, if you're not prepared to forget the silly paper and start looking after my gold mines, then what use are you to me?'

She sipped the last of her sherry wine and handed him the crystal glass. 'Pour me another, darling, please.'

Tyler took the glass but stood over her. 'Let's start with tomorrow. What happens to my paper?'

'You shut down. We haven't time for it.'

'What if I say I don't want to shut it down?' he growled. 'I'm not accustomed to being made a fool of.'

'Nobody's making a fool of you.'

'Yes, you are, you want me to work for you. In what capacity?'

'Since you put it that way,' she said sweetly, 'I suppose I'm suggesting that you become general manager of my mines.'

'Our mines,' he reminded her. 'When we are married . . .' He didn't complete the sentence, because he realised suddenly that he was walking into new territory. Looking at her, he saw the cold, hard smile of Boyd Roberts.

'Yes, I've been thinking about that,' Amelia said. 'And I need your

349

answer. If you insist on the paper or magazine or whatever you call it, you do it yourself. I don't want a husband who isn't loyal to me.'

'But, Amelia, I love you. Can't you see that?'

Their discussion turned into an argument, which deteriorated into a blazing row. 'You can't run me,' he shouted. 'I won't let you run my life. I'm a journalist, a wordsmith, not a bloody miner.'

'Oh really? And you think I'm just going to let you potter about and spend my money until we've got nothing left? I'm accustomed to the best, I don't intend to end up broke! I'm keeping the mines.'

'And if I refuse to take them on, what are you going to do? Run them yourself? Who else can you trust?'

Tyler slammed out of the parlour, faced with the humiliation of having to shut down a magazine that had never seen the light of day.

Quietly, Amelia took off the ruby ring and placed it on the mantelpiece. 'Who else can you trust?' he'd asked. That was a good question. Until recently, she would have had to agree with him to let the precious mines go, but there was someone she could trust, someone who knew the business and who would run her mines with a first of iron. There'd be no slacking and no cheating. Compared with this one, her father's dodgy mates were chicken feed.

'It's a pity,' she sighed to herself. 'I really did want to get married, but Tyler has such a limited view of money. What suits him wouldn't do for me.'

She really must find Laura tomorrow and bring her up to see Mr MacNamara. She'd been avoiding him like the plague, and he hadn't asked for her. Something might come of it, there'd been enough hints around. What had her father shouted? That he intended to marry Laura? Well, he must have been off his head. For goodness' sake! At his age!

But more important than Laura, or Tyler, was the Captain, Leslie Soames.

Amelia dined alone in the quiet house, an empty chair beside her because Tyler had declined. But it didn't matter. She saw her rightful place in this world, with Captain Soames, the Member for Rockhampton, beside her. As the only candidate, he had to win the seat.

Yes. She really must look Laura up tomorrow.

A penitent Tyler waited for her in the morning, lingering over his coffee until the maid informed him that Miss Roberts was having breakfast in her room.

'Tell her I'd like a word with her,' he instructed. The girl returned with the message that her mistress would be out shortly, so he took himself off to the front veranda to avoid curious glances from the staff, who, he was sure, would be wondering why he was still hanging about the house when he had his 'office' to run.

Time, he knew, meant nothing to Amelia, so he dozed in a wide cane chair until she finally appeared. She had discarded mourning and looked fresh as a daisy in a billowing pale-yellow dress, her dark hair tied with a simple ribbon. He sprang up, remembering the first time he'd seen her, right here. 'My dear, you do look lovely,' he said, kissing her on the cheek. 'I'm so sorry we had that foolish argument last night. I'm sure we can work things out.'

'How?' she asked, the hard tone of her voice in sharp contrast to the pretty picture she presented, standing there in the sunlight.

'Why don't we keep the paper and the mines, for the time being. I could find someone to manage the mines.'

'Since you're not interested in them, I will attend to that, and don't think you can talk me around. I told you I don't want that newspaper. And that's the end of it.'

'In other words, you leave me no choice but to take over the mines.'

'I wouldn't dream of making you do something that displeases you, Tyler. That offer is withdrawn.'

'What do you mean, withdrawn?' he scowled.

'You were quite right. You don't know the first thing about mines. The position is no longer available.'

He was so angry he was stammering. 'How dare you speak to me like that. As if I were your servant. You're getting too high-hatted, Amelia. I think the money's gone to your head. I'll do as I please, do you hear me?'

'No need to shout, and no one's stopping you from doing exactly as you please.'

'I left a good job in Brisbane to run this paper,' he growled, 'and if I don't have that I've got nothing. I can't believe you're reneging on those arrangements.'

'Which you made with my father. Not with me. And it's quite cruel to say you've got nothing. I'm still here, and when we're married you can stay here and keep me company.'

Tyler controlled his anger with an effort. She was being ridiculous, but marriage would alter the power base. A husband was legally entitled to his wife's assets. Not that he would rush things. Before long she'd have a child, children, and they'd keep her busy. In the meantime he'd have the money in his own right to start the paper. 'Oh, very well.' He smiled, putting an arm around her. 'You're a determined little miss, aren't you? But I like that.' He kissed and fondled her. 'It will make marriage more exciting, having my fiery little lady in my bed.'

But Amelia pulled away. 'Don't do that. Not here. There are people about. I was thinking, too, that it wouldn't be a good idea for us to get married too soon, while I'm still in mourning.'

'You don't look as if you're in mourning,' he whispered slyly.

'Well, I am,' she pouted. 'When I go out I'll be expected to be wearing mourning clothes. It was horrible enough to have my father die like that without creating more talk. So I think it would be best if you move into lodgings until the wedding.'

351

Tyler was appalled. Lodgings? He hardly had a bean left. What would he live on? But he was damned if he'd ask her for cash, the little witch. 'When do you think the wedding can take place, then?' he asked stiffly.

'I really don't know how long one should remain in mourning,' she said airily. 'Six months, I think.'

He strode into the house and packed his bag, then went through the rear of the house to the stables.

Amelia was standing at the top of the steps when he rode out, and her new arrogance was so reminiscent of her father that he could barely address her. 'I'll send the horse back,' he said.

'No need,' she chirruped happily. 'You keep it.'

'I won't be riding to Brisbane,' he snapped. 'I'll be going by ship. If you want that paper shut down, do it yourself. I'll send you my Brisbane address, and when you think it is socially acceptable for us to marry, let me know. I may still be available, but don't bet on it.'

She shrugged as she watched him leave.

Then she went to find Andy. 'Take this letter into town right away and post it for me.'

Andy looked at it: 'Mrs Ada Adeline Davies? At Canoona? Why are you writing to her?'

'I've got a job for her.'

'Doing what?'

'You'll see.'

He stared at the envelope again. 'Yeah. Well . . . if you want your letter to get to her, best you write "Big Poll" on it. I'll bet no one out there ever heard of Ada Adeline.'

'Oh, very well. Give it to me.' She hurried back inside and printed 'Big Poll' over the address. She blew on the wet ink, and grinned. Mrs Davies was worth two men. She'd make the best mines manager in the district.

William Wexford came, with a big bunch of flowers for Amelia, to collect Paul and Mrs Moloney, and with all the strangers gone from her house Amelia whirled from room to room in delight. Her house! Her place! What a time she'd have now.

She dressed in black, with a diamond pin at her throat, and went into town. Her father didn't trust banks, but Amelia would have to – not one bank, but several, to be on the safe side. There were four banks in town so she had four boxes in the carriage and had the greatest of fun travelling from bank to bank to make the deposits, with the managers falling all over themselves in gratitude that she had chosen their establishment to safeguard her interests, all of them promising her the best service. She giggled. It wouldn't take them long to find out she'd chosen all four.

Then she called on the handsome young solicitor, John Laidley. 'Even though he's bound to win now, since he's the only candidate,' she told John sadly, 'I feel it is my duty to offer Captain Soames my support. I've been through a difficult time, John, but I haven't lost sight of the fact that a parliamentary career is rigorous and costly. Men like my father and Fowler could afford it but it will be hard for a young man to keep up appearances.'

'That's true, Amelia,' John said. 'What did you have in mind?'

'I believe the people of Rockhampton should get behind our representative. We mustn't let the side down.' She planted a prettily wrapped parcel on the desk. 'There's a thousand pounds. I want you to give it to Mr Soames and just tell him it is from a citizen, to welcome him to our ranks.'

'That's very generous,' he cried. 'Captain Soames will be delighted. And you want it to be anonymous?'

'Yes.' She smiled.

Climbing back into her carriage, she laughed. Anonymous? It would take even less time than the meeting of the bank managers for Leslie to discover the identity of his patroness. And then she could expect him to call.

And after that, with her looks and her money, it would be plain sailing. She wouldn't be just the daughter of the MP, she'd be the wife. Much more fun.

'Shall I close the front door?' Leslie Soames asked Laura.

'No, leave it open, thank you. I like the breeze from the river.'

'But people passing by can peer in!'

'What does it matter?'

Leslie sighed. 'Dear me, you are a strange girl.' He put his cane and hat in the hall stand and followed her into the dining room. 'Aren't you lonely living here on your own?'

'No. I wish Justin and Grace could have stayed longer, but they had to get back to Camelot, and I'm quite happy here. Now, look what I found in the shed. This is what I wanted you to see. These boxes contain copies of my father's speeches in the House and notes on various issues. I thought you might find them useful.'

'Very interesting,' Leslie said. 'Might give me some background, what?'

Laura sat on the floor and began sorting through the boxes. She was interrupted by a knock at the door. She looked up. 'See who that is, will you, Leslie?'

He bridled. 'I can hardly answer your door. Where is the maid?'

'She's out. Answer the door, Leslie.'

He stuck his head out and peered down the passageway, then ducked back again. 'Good God! It's that common girl who pasted herself on to me at the races!'

Laura jumped up. 'She's a friend of mine, Leslie, and she's had a bad time of it lately.'

'So I believe,' he sniffed. 'The father was an absolute blackguard.'

'Yoo-hoo!' Amelia called. 'Anyone home?'

'Coming,' Laura replied. And then to Leslie, 'I expect you to be polite.'

'I'm always polite,' he said as she disappeared. 'That's my trouble.'

Unable to escape, he found himself at morning tea with the two ladies, or rather with Laura acting the serving maid and this girl gushing all over him once more. A dreadful bore, but he had to sit it out until the guest left and Laura could return to sorting the boxes.

For her part, Amelia couldn't be more thrilled to find Leslie on the spot. It was two days since she'd made that splendid donation, and here was his chance to thank her.

But not a word. Obviously John Laidley hadn't told him yet. What a disappointment! Why did he have to be so correct?

She was suspicious, too, of finding Leslie with Laura again. And jealous. So she set about the business of winning him to her side. 'By the way, Laura. Did you know that Mr Kemp and I are no longer engaged?'

'No, I didn't. Why? What happened?'

'Nothing to worry about. Quite an amicable separation. I had to tell Mr Kemp that we really weren't suited. The engagement was my father's idea, not mine. You'd understand how I feel, Laura, you had to break your engagement too.' She saw Laura frown but pretended not to notice. 'It's a terrible strain being promised to someone quite unsuitable. Don't you think so, Captain?'

He coughed. 'I'm afraid I have not had the experience.'

'Lucky you.' She smiled. 'Poor Laura and I have suffered the deaths of our fathers – we don't need any more upsets. And certainly not being tied to the wrong gentleman. But we must look to the future and be happy. Now that we're fancy-free again.' She sipped her tea. 'At least I am. Have you heard from Mr MacNamara, Laura?'

Her friend froze, but Amelia kept on. It was for Laura's own good, she told herself.

'Do you mean you haven't heard from him?'

'He's very ill,' Laura said.

'Don't you believe it. He's recovering quite well. He left my home days ago under the care of Mr Wexford.'

'That's nice,' Laura replied, busily refilling Leslie's cup from the silver teapot.

'Nice? You are dreadful. You ought to go and see him.'

'Why should I? More cake, Leslie?'

'Er . . . no, thank you.' These two peculiar girls might be friends but he was aware of a tension between them, and he resented being drawn into their woman talk.

'Because Paul wasn't too happy,' Amelia continued, 'when my father announced he was going to marry you.'

'Who said that?' Laura demanded, as if she hadn't heard correctly.

'I told you, my father did.'

'I never said I'd marry him.'

Amelia nibbled on a biscuit. 'You must have given him some encouragement. Although I do declare it was a surprise to me. As well as to Paul. Did you discuss marriage with my father?'

Leslie put down his teacup and brushed a lock of fair hair from his sunburned brow. This was too much. He looked from one to the other, astonished that two such pretty girls could be . . . well, quite mad. Entirely lacking in propriety. 'I believe we should attend to those papers another time,' he said, rising from his seat. 'If you will excuse me, Laura.'

'Oh, was I interrupting something?' Amelia squealed.

'Not at all,' Leslie said, at the same time as Laura snapped: 'Yes.'

But Leslie had had enough. 'I'll be on my way,' he told Laura, almost dashing for the door.

She hurried to see him out, relieved that he was leaving so that she could go back and take Amelia to task. She knew perfectly well what Amelia was up to, she was accustomed to her tricks. Amelia was after Leslie, and her method was to make other women look stupid. This time she'd excelled herself, but she'd only confused her prey.

'I really think, my dear,' Leslie said pompously, 'that you should keep this door closed. It is not the done thing, you know. And I'd choose my friends with more care.'

Laura stared at him. They deserved one another, this pair. 'Leslie,' she said, 'you told me you had an anonymous patron.'

'That is so,' he intoned, 'and when I discover the source I shall be eternally grateful.'

'Well, the source is damn well sitting in there,' she said.

'Who? What?' He dropped his cane, floundering.

'It was Amelia, a little bird told me.'

'But how hugely kind of her,' he stuttered.

'She can afford it,' Laura said, showing him out. 'The general estimate is that what with cash, property and the gold mines, Boyd Roberts left her close to a million pounds, so she won't miss a thousand.'

He clung to his cane as if it were a lifeline. 'Good God. Do you think I ought to go back and thank her? I mean, I wouldn't want her to think I'm ungracious.'

'Some other time,' Laura said and slammed the door.

She marched back into the sitting room to find that Amelia had swiftly bypassed the morning tea and found a decanter of wine. 'There's no one to boss us around any more.' She grinned. 'Have a glass with me.'

'Your behaviour was disgraceful,' Laura said.

'No worse than yours,' Amelia laughed. 'Get the glasses.' She kicked off her shoes and curled up on the couch while Laura, feeling that she might as well, found two glasses and poured the white wine.

'Do you think he liked me?' Amelia asked.

355

'No, he hated you.'

'Why?'

'You made a bad impression with that horrible red dress.'

'So I'll burn it. You'll have to help me shop so that I'll look more dignified.'

Laura drained her glass and glared at Amelia. 'I wouldn't help you cross the road after what you did to me today.'

'What did I do? I was just trying to help. And anyway . . . you didn't answer my question about you and my father.'

'Was what you said true? I thought you were lying.'

'Why would I lie?'

'Oh God! That's a joke!'

Amelia pattered across the room in her stockinged feet to refill their glasses. 'Not that I care now, but was my father in love with you?'

Laura sensed a warning note there, a too brittle, too casual reference to her father, to Boyd. She took her time in replying, waiting for Amelia to settle down. 'You do care,' she said quietly. 'I might have had my differences with my father, but when he died I was devastated. I know how you feel, Amelia, despite the brave front.'

'You don't know at all,' Amelia said harshly. 'He beat the hell out of me. And it only started when you took my place in his life.'

Her friend sat, stunned.

'Oh, dear God,' she whispered. 'I'm so sorry. I didn't know. He was so gracious, so protective, I didn't understand myself what was happening.'

'But he wanted to marry you?' Amelia insisted.

'Yes.'

'Oh, bully for you. Did you want to be my stepmother?'

'No. Don't be so cruel. I had to leave Beauview. I couldn't tell you. What could I say? Excuse me, but your father says he loves me?'

'Did he?'

'I don't know.'

Amelia shifted in her seat and stretched out her legs. 'He probably did, you know, in his way. You'd have been another prize, a possession, like I was. And he'd have thrown you aside too, when it suited him.' She smiled and held up her glass. 'One should never speak ill of the dead. I'm glad he's dead. May he have a long and happy eternity!'

'Amelia!'

'Oh, stop being polite and pleasant, Laura. It doesn't become you. You're lying to me now. You came to his pathetic little funeral, and that was jolly nice of you, I won't forget it. You and about four other people, including the policeman. No one else would dare to be seen there, not at the funeral of a man who deserved to be hanged.' She burst into tears. 'But you came, didn't you? Because you are Laura Maskey. You always were a law unto yourself. Why is that? What makes you a cut above the rest? Why will I always be a nobody?'

Laura rushed over to Amelia and held her as she wept, until the sobs subsided. 'Shush now. That's not true. Despite his faults, your father was always kind to me. And despite my faults you saw something in me that you liked, and Amelia, I always appreciated that.'

'Did you really?' Amelia asked. 'I thought you just put up with me because you had nothing better to do.'

Laura giggled. 'No one better to do things with, you mean. You broke the boredom for me. And you still owe me for that dare. When I went out to visit the gentlemen swimmers. Did I get hell!'

Amelia dabbed at her tears. 'That's right. I remember. It seems like a hundred years ago. I told Daddy, you know. And he laughed. He absolutely went into fits laughing.' Amelia looked at Laura soberly. 'I think that was the beginning. I think that was when he began to take notice of you.'

For a while the two girls were lost in their own thoughts. Then Amelia said, 'It was the brigand in him, I think. He was a brigand, I know that now, a real live and true brigand, living out of his time, and I think he saw that in you. Talk about my behaviour! You were awful! Riding out on that engagement party. What happened to Bobby Cope?'

'Bobby who?' Laura said, and the tears turned to smiles and laughter.

'Are you feeling better?' Laura asked.

'I think so,' Amelia said. 'Why doesn't Leslie Soames like me?'

'Oh, God. I think he might now. I'm sorry. I'll put him off. He's too pompous for you.'

'No, he's not. He reminds me of your father. I like pompous people. I always wanted an important man like your father. If you put him off I'll never speak to you again. What are you going to do about Paul MacNamara?'

'That's over.'

Amelia sat up and grabbed her hand. 'So there was something? You haven't changed at all. I knew it all along. What's going on that I don't know about?'

'Nothing really.'

'You're just going to let him think you were ready to marry my father?'

'If that's what he wants to believe.'

'Huh! He didn't believe it. He just laughed and said: "I'll believe it when I see it." That's when he, my father . . . that's when . . .' She took a deep breath. 'Laura, that's why Paul got shot. He nearly died, and you wouldn't visit him.'

Laura crumpled. She put her head in her hands. 'I couldn't go in to him, Amelia. The last time I saw him he shut me out. He told me point-blank he wanted to be left alone. I made a fool of myself. I intruded on his grief.'

357

'And what about your grief? You lost your father about the same time. Didn't that count?'

'I don't know. I have no idea. Maybe it didn't seem so bad to him.'

'Like Captain Soames,' Amelia said. 'He has no sympathy for my loss. Next time I see him I really should be . . .'

'Does everything have to revolve about you?' Laura asked, but Amelia ignored her.

'What's for lunch? I'm starving.'

A week, eight days had passed. Dragged. As long as Paul was in town, Laura couldn't seem to get on with anything. She made lists of things she had to do and things she wanted to do, lost them, rewrote them, and in the end went about her daily duties of organising the household and the garden. Grace had installed a live-in cook and employed a daily maid, and Laura had found their old gardener, Wang Lu, who was delighted to return to work at the house.

With everything running smoothly now, she ought to have been able to enjoy herself, but instead she was bored. She refused to allow herself to be depressed over the attitude her mother and Leon had taken. 'If they choose not to know me,' she told herself, 'then good luck to them.' But she missed them, missed teasing them, missed her role as the *enfant terrible* of the Maskey household. She was so damned ladylike these days, with everyone up here being so kind that there were no challenges left.

Amelia had said she ought to go and visit Paul, and that she was mad not to have called on him before this. But what if he didn't want to see her? There were no messages from him, so why should she?

Then she cringed. Oh God! What must he think of her? Laura wished Amelia hadn't told her what Boyd had said. Telling Paul, of all people, that she was going to marry him! That was just great! Paul MacNamara must think she was quite mad. And even if he didn't believe it . . . She recalled one of her mother's pet phrases: 'No smoke without fire.' Why, Paul would ask himself, would Boyd Roberts make such a statement unless there was some modicum of truth in it? Even Amelia had been suspicious.

Already Amelia had stopped wearing mourning clothes. She could find an excuse for anything. 'Black reminds them of my father and I won't be held responsible for his actions.' Laura smiled. That cleared the way for Amelia to begin to entertain again, and this afternoon she was holding a garden party at Beauview to impress Leslie Soames, who, of course, was the guest of honour.

One thing, she mused, as she dressed for the occasion, Amelia knew how to go after what she wanted. Leslie had quickly overcome his distaste for Amelia's 'commonness', explaining to Laura that he'd been too hasty. 'After all, the poor girl is alone in the world. She just needs guidance.'

Laura knew that Amelia would be wearing one of her tea dresses, as would the other ladies, but Laura couldn't be bothered. If she dressed up she'd have to take the gig, and she'd much prefer to ride, so she took out a black skirt and white silk blouse. 'That will do,' she said to herself as she pulled on her short riding boots. 'I don't even want to go.'

In deference to her hostess, she pinned up her fair hair and added a burnished-straw boater to her outfit, securing it with a hatpin so that it wouldn't blow off. She'd never hear the end of it if she wore her favourite riding hat, a wide American felt.

As she rode out, storm clouds were gathering from the coast, forerunners of the ominous dark sky beyond. It didn't augur well for a garden party. Laura hoped Amelia had made alternative arrangements, or they'd all get drowned.

As the horse headed up the hill, she wondered why she was going to a dull old garden party when there were other things she'd rather do. 'Like what?' she asked herself.

The answer was already forming as she turned the horse back to take another route. Being on horseback always made her feel more alive, more alert. Even bolder. There was a challenge here. 'And why not?' she asked, as she headed for William Wexford's house. 'I'll just bowl in and say I'd like to see Mr MacNamara. I can't sit about indefinitely, wondering what that man is thinking. I'll go dotty. Better to find out and get it over with.'

All very well, but by the time she reached the gate, a sprinkling of rain had turned into a deluge, and there she was, within sight of the house, sitting her horse, drenched. She cursed herself for being so stupid, for not going on to Beauview, for not taking the gig which had a canopy, because now she had no choice but to go home.

Miserably, she turned the horse to ride away, only to meet another rider. William Wexford!

He peered at her through the pouring rain. 'Why, it's you, Laura. What are you doing out in this weather?'

'I was just riding and I got caught in it,' she said, forcing a laugh.

'You can't go back in rain like this. Come on inside.'

'I'd rather not,' she protested, but he unlatched the gate.

'Hurry up, I'm getting drowned too, you know.'

He was sitting there in the parlour, rugged up, warm, looking paler than usual, but still strong-jawed, handsome. William pushed her through the door and sent for towels. Paul made an effort to stand, and there was a big grin on his face. 'Well! Look at you! Have you been swimming?'

She knew she'd never looked worse. She was soaked to the skin, her clothes clinging to her, and the stupid hat had collapsed about her face. Flustered, she pushed wet strands of hair from her eyes and grabbed the towels that a maid rushed to hand her, using them to cover her confusion because she couldn't think of a damn thing to say.

'I'll have to change,' William said, 'if you'll excuse me. I'll send the girls in to set the fire, Laura, so that we can dry you out.'

'Damn rain,' Laura managed to say when he'd left. 'I got caught in it.'

'I thought you liked the rain,' he teased.

She took off the ruined hat and dried her hair. 'How are you?'

'Much better, thank you. I'll be on my way soon.'

'Oh, that's good.'

'Were you coming to see me?'

'No, I was just passing by.'

'Then I have the rain to thank for your company.'

A maid hurried in, carrying an armful of wood and chips. 'Oh, Miss Maskey,' she giggled, 'you do look a sight.'

'Thanks,' Laura replied, picking up hairpins from the carpet.

'I think she looks charming, Daisy,' he countered.

The maid grinned at him. 'You finished with this paper?'

'Yes, thank you.'

They watched as the girl set the fire, lit it, blew on it and sat back on her haunches until it caught. 'There you go,' she said at length. 'Just keep an eye on it for a few minutes, then it'll be all right. It's a good fireplace, this one, throws out plenty of heat. You'll dry out in no time, miss.' She stood up. 'What about a cup of tea?'

'Thank you,' Laura said.

When the girl had left, he asked her, 'Why haven't you been to see me? I'm a poor sick person.'

'You didn't give any indication that you wished to see me,' she retorted, facing the fire. 'I got short shrift last time.'

'That was a hundred years ago. It was very selfish of me. I'm sorry.' He sighed. 'I'm ashamed of the way I behaved towards you. Your father died too, I heard that somewhere along the line but it didn't register.'

'That's all right,' she said.

'No, it's not. I did intend to come to see you before I left, to find out if you were still talking to me.'

'Why didn't you send me a note?'

'Too risky.' He smiled. 'What if you'd still stayed away? I prefer to handle my problems myself.'

'Am I a problem?'

'That remains to be seen.'

Laura had to ask him. 'You didn't believe what Boyd Roberts said, about marrying me? Did you?'

'No. At least, I didn't want to.'

She shook her head. 'I stayed with them at Beauview when I fell out with my family, but he made the situation worse. I had to get out of there. You know I'm back at Quay Street now?'

'Yes, for the time being.'

'What do you mean? I'm not going anywhere.'

'That's good, because I was planning, when I got out of here, to come and see you, to talk about us. I have to go back to Oberon, but I'll make it safe in time. I couldn't ask you to live there after what happened, but if you'd consider marrying me, we'll have a home somewhere.'

Laura shivered nervously. 'This is very sudden.'

'No, it's not, you know that. As a matter of fact, this is the first patch of heavy rain we've had since last summer, so I was thinking of you today, remembering the rain, and how much I love you. And the next thing, there you were.'

'Looking charming,' she laughed.

'Of course. So do you still care enough to marry me, or will I have to begin intense courting?'

Laura kissed him. 'Both.'

She was standing by the fire, her face flushed, when William returned. 'Ha! I see you're warming up, Laura. How nice for us to have a visitor on a miserable old day like this.'

Chapter Fifteen

The doctor put away his stethoscope. 'Righto, young Mac. I think we can let you loose on the world again.'

'About time,' Paul said.

'You take it easy, just the same. Don't go galloping off into the bush right away.'

'I can't do that anyway, I have quite a few things to do in town yet.'

'His stepfather's arriving by ship tomorrow,' William said, 'so I'll have the pleasure of his company for a while longer.'

'Your stepfather?' the doctor said, packing his bag. 'Isn't that Juan Rivadavia?'

'Yes,' Paul said stiffly. He wasn't ready to face Juan yet. So much had happened this year, he hadn't kept that promise to himself, to apologise to Juan for refusing to accept him when he married Dolour. And now Juan was coming to extend a helping hand, once again. He always seemed to be beholden to the man. So much for his plan of welcoming Dolour and Juan to his own patch, his comfortable home and well-run station. Instead he'd allowed disaster to run riot. He'd failed his wife and poor Clara.

'I've met him,' the doctor was saying. 'Fine fellow. Met him once in Sydney, and then again in Brisbane when he made that incredible lone ride down the wilds. My word, that caused a sensation.'

'Why?' William asked.

'It was years ago, of course,' the doctor continued, and Paul cringed. He was an affable old bloke who loved a good yarn, and William was a good audience. Trying not to listen, Paul dressed, tucking a shirt into his trousers and sitting on the edge of the bed to pull on his boots.

'He and his mate rode north from the border to claim cattle-grazing country inland from what is now Townsville. This town wasn't even heard of in those days, so they were looking at a thousand-mile ride. They got the tip from Leichhardt himself, didn't they, Paul?'

'Yes.' Paul knew what was coming. He hated this story, just as much as he knew he would always hate hearing the other story that would go down in folklore, of the two women who were murdered at Oberon Station. Would Oberon ever live it down? He doubted it. He felt weak, a wash of perspiration on his face as if the fever had returned.

362

The doctor droned on. 'I surely would like to meet Mr Rivadavia again.'

'Then you must,' William said. 'Join us for dinner tomorrow night.'

'I was there when he made it back to Brisbane, you know,' the doctor said proudly. 'I attended him. Just skin and bone he was, but a tough man for a Spaniard.'

'Argentinian,' Paul corrected, dully.

'Is that right? Well, it seems they got up north just fine, riding fast on a couple of Rivadavia's horses, a magnificent ride. They staked their claims all right, but then they fell foul of the blacks. I mean, they're bad enough here, but the further north you go – I don't care what anyone says – the more savage the tribes get. I mean, I wouldn't want to set foot up there, not for all the gold in the world.'

'But they weren't after gold, were they?' William asked.

'No. I got off the track there. No, they were cattlemen. Real frontiersmen. They found good pastureland, blazed out the boundaries and were getting ready for the return journey when the blacks attacked. Rivadavia escaped but they got his partner. He was an Irishman, they say. I don't recall his name right now.'

'By Jove,' William said. 'Here was I looking forward to welcoming your stepfather to Queensland, Paul. I thought he was just a New South Wales squatter, when obviously he knows more about our state than I do. You should have told me, Paul.'

Paul felt weak. He'd been eager to be dressed and out of there, but now he stared at the large open wardrobe where William had hung the clothes he'd kindly purchased for him. There was a brand-new leather jacket within reach, but he didn't have the strength to take it from its hanger. He needed to be alone again to deal with ghosts.

He forced himself to stand, he had to make a move. He was only comfortable talking to his brother, John, about Pace, but if he didn't open up now, how long would it take him to handle Jeannie's death? He realised now that he'd be hearing about Jeannie – like this, from strangers – for the rest of his life. And he had to stop cringing away as he did when men spoke of that ride, of Rivadavia and his partner, as if he knew nothing of it, keeping himself remote, afraid of an emotional spill. Afraid of making a fool of himself.

Fighting back tears, he took a deep breath and waded right into that well of misery. 'William,' he called, as the two men were leaving the room, surprised at the firmness of his voice.

They both turned back.

'Rivadavia's partner. His name was Pace MacNamara.'

They stared. And then the doctor came back. 'Would that have been your father?'

'Yes, sir.'

'Well then, lad,' the old man exclaimed, 'you must be very proud. What a right fool I am not to have remembered. Forgive me. By God, what a story you'll have to tell Mr Rivadavia. You made it back from the land of the lost too.' He shook Paul's hand warmly. 'Pace MacNamara's son! Well, what do you know?'

Paul felt himself relaxing, not upset, not fighting that awful heartache, just knowing that this lover of the yarn could now expand his story for all who wanted to listen. He saw some humour in this, at least. Pace had liked a good yarn himself, and to have gone down as a folk hero would have filled him with delight. 'You made your mark all right,' Paul said to the empty room, as he struggled painfully into that leather jacket. 'But you set a cracking pace for your sons to try to follow.' He found himself laughing at the pun. Maybe it wouldn't be so bad facing Juan Rivadavia after all.

His first call was on Amelia Roberts, to thank her for having him in her house and to reassure her that their secret was safe with him. She was an astonishing person, a bit queer, he thought. When he arrived, she threw her arms about him, shoved him into a chair and dashed about to get him a drink, enquiring as to his health and reassuring him, without so much of a blink, that she didn't hold it against him for shooting her father, who, she explained, had quite lost his wits. 'I had seen it coming for a long time, Paul, so don't feel bad. He had fits of raving, and I was terrified; I didn't know what to do.'

Thunderstruck, he listened to her. 'He beat me to within an inch of my life, Paul, with his whip. My father, who had always been so kind, turned on me like an animal. But you must never tell anyone. I knew he was going mad, but who could I tell? It was terrifying! He might have killed me, but you saved me. I'll never forget you.'

'Are you all right now?' he asked, wondering which one of them was now away with the pixies.

'Oh yes, I'm quite well now, thank you. You know that Captain Soames won the election?'

Paul choked back a laugh. Being the only runner, Soames had won by default. 'Yes.'

'It's so exciting. We're to be married, you know, and we'll have a house in Brisbane as well so that we'll have somewhere presentable to live while the House is in session. You must come to the wedding.'

'I'll try,' he said vaguely. 'But I wanted to talk to you about Airdrie Station. It adjoins mine. I still want to buy it, Amelia, it is important that the blacks out there learn that white people in the valley want peace.'

'Darling,' she cried, 'you can have it. I'll give it to you.'

'No,' he said firmly. 'You mustn't do that. I'll buy it from you.'

'Done,' she said. 'You fix it up. Talk to my solicitor, John Laidley. Now, I insist you have another drink. Don't I make really nice whisky sodas? They're the latest thing.'

As if Amelia weren't confusing enough for his first day back in the world, a huge woman now lumbered past the veranda. 'Who's that?' he asked.

'Mrs Davies!' Amelia called. 'Come up here! I want you to meet a friend of mine, Mr MacNamara.'

The woman picked up her skirts and mounted the steps to take Paul's hand in a grip of iron. 'G'day,' she said.

Paul retrieved his hand and stood. 'I'm pleased to meet you, Mrs Davies.'

'This lady is my new mines manager.' Amelia smiled. 'And she's going to do a great job out there.'

'You can bet on that,' the woman rumbled, and Paul believed her.

'What do you do?' she asked him.

'Cattle,' he said quickly, as though he might get a belt in the ear from her if he didn't get it right. 'Oberon Station.'

'Ah,' she said sadly. 'Oberon.' He flinched. There it was again. The permanent reminder. 'Are you going back?' she asked.

'Yes.'

She nodded. 'You've got guts.'

'You can call it that.' He shrugged. 'I promised the blacks I'd stay, that's all.

'Don't give me that bullshit,' she spat. 'It's the players or the stayers in this country. You're a stayer if ever I saw one. I wish you luck, mate. I've got to get going, Miss Amelia. I've got to pick up some supplies in town.'

'By all means, Ada,' Amelia said graciously.

Mrs Davies gave a piercing whistle, and a saddled horse, his bridle looped loosely over his head, came trotting round to the front of the house.

'Good God!' Paul said. 'That's Greybeard, Tyler's horse!'

'The hell it is!' Mrs Davies snorted. 'That's Stoker.' She dropped back down the steps and hauled herself on to the grey horse.

'Who is Stoker?' Paul asked, bewildered.

Amelia brushed that question aside. 'We won't talk about it now. Have you seen Laura? She's very fond of you.'

'That's nice to know.'

He went from there to see Laura. 'Amelia tells me you're very fond of me.'

'Oh, that Amelia! You can't believe a word she says. Are you supposed to be out?'

'Yes, I'm cured.' He put an arm around her and winced. 'Well, almost. But I've been given leave for the day. I thought you might keep me company.'

'Have we progressed from courting to keeping company already?' she laughed.

'We haven't got a lot of time. Why don't you lock that front door?'

'Your horse is outside. People will talk.'

'We're in for a lot more talk yet. Will that upset you?'

'No. It seems to be my natural state. They'll come down harder on you, Paul.' She sighed. 'But I think you know that.'

365

He waited for her in the drawing room, where he'd stood, all that time ago, with Grace Carlisle, acting the escort. He'd found the room stuffy and unpleasant then, but now it was fresh and inviting, the tall windows open, and a soft breeze brushing the light, lacy curtains that had replaced the heavy drapes.

'The house looks better now,' he remarked. 'You've lightened it up.'

'Yes, my mother would have a fit if she knew.'

'I heard Grace bought it.'

'She's very kind. She doesn't need it, she just wanted me to have a roof.'

'And you like it here?'

'I love it.'

'Then why don't we buy if from her?'

She kissed him. 'No need to rush. Grace is betting that my Uncle William will buy it for me. He won't have his favourite niece homeless.' Then she looked at him nervously. 'You don't mind, do you?'

'Of course not, I already like Uncle William. But listen, we have a more pressing matter. My stepfather is due here tomorrow. Do you want to meet him?'

Laura perched on the edge of the couch and considered this. 'I don't think so,' she replied thoughtfully. 'Not yet. You haven't seen any of your family since Jeannie died. I think it would be better for all concerned if I were to keep out of the way.'

'I hoped you'd say that, but I didn't want you to feel pushed aside. He'll only be here a couple of days and then we're going out to Oberon.'

'Just the two of you? Are you well enough?'

'It won't be the two of us. He's bringing a few stockmen from his own station to help out at Oberon. We'll need extra hands to get all the work done and the mustering finished before the wet sets in. And then, my lady,' he took both of her hands, 'I'll be back for you.'

'What then?' she asked, looking up at him.

'You can do the planning from then on, as long as it includes marrying me.'

'I suppose I can arrange that. Come on, I'll show you the rest of the house.'

'The house can wait,' he murmured.

The arrival of the paddle steamer, slurping up the waters for its thirsty engines, was always an occasion in Rockhampton, and everyone who stepped ashore was gazed upon with interest.

This day there was the usual collection of miners and returning locals; squatters and stockmen stood back to make way for ladies in their crackling new dresses, children plunged down the gangplank to hurtle into the crowd, and Chinamen pattered silently on to the wharf, pigtails flapping in the breeze and hands hiding who knew what in those deep, covert sleeves. But one man, politely waiting his turn, required extra attention. Men nudged and grinned patronisingly at the city slicker while nearby, women rippled with interest, eyes drawn irresistibly towards him.

The men saw a swarthy Latin type in an outrageous sombrero edged with silver. To them he was just dressed in black with a dark-green velvet stock at his throat, the flashiness carrying over to a large diamond pin on the velvet and an ornate silver ring on his left hand. The women, though, saw a superbly cut fine-wool morning coat over fitted breeches and high polished boots, all accentuating his wide shoulders and splendid physique. He wasn't a young man, but they were attracted by his dark flashing eyes and his brilliant smile. The fancy hat, they admitted, whispering now, was strange, but it suited him and he wore it well.

Unperturbed by the sensation he was causing, Juan Rivadavia strode towards his stepson and embraced him, causing another wave of whispers, for men did not hug other men, not even the peculiar Chinese.

'I'm pleased to see you looking so well,' he said. 'Your mother will be greatly relieved. She did not believe you were being properly nursed.'

Paul laughed. 'I'm surprised you got away without her.'

'She wanted to come, right from that first terrible message, and I had a hard time convincing her that Oberon was no place for women. You received our letters?'

'Thank you, they were beautiful.'

Rivadavia looked at him sadly. 'I am glad, though, that you allowed me to come and express deep sorrow to you myself at the tragedy of your wife and the young lady.'

Paul nodded. The guilt again. Always the guilt.

The older man picked up a tooled-leather suitcase. 'But time has passed. I hope you don't dwell on something that was beyond your control.'

'I'm not so sure about that,' Paul admitted.

'Leave self-flagellation to the saints,' Juan replied gently. 'I had to learn that after the death of your father, which is why I have come here now. I hope you have put away your mourning.'

'Just about,' Paul said. 'So many other things have happened since then.'

'Good Lord, yes! Your mother flatly refuses to receive any more telegrams. Come. I will introduce you to my men. They are skilled cattlemen. I can only stay a couple of weeks but they'll remain until the weather breaks.'

Paul looked over at the three men standing smoking on the far side of the wharf, surveying the new town, and he was surprised to see that one of them was an Aborigine.

His stepfather noticed. 'You don't mind a blackfellow?'

'No. Not at all.'

'Good. He's an excellent horseman. He'll make a good head stockman one day.

Paul smiled. Rivadavia was a very clever man. He didn't doubt that bringing an Aborigine was Juan's way of checking his reactions now to the blacks. But all was well. This man could help to heal the breach. He extended his hand, first, to the smiling black stockman.

Mail came in on the same boat and among his bills Cosmo Newgate found a letter from Tyler Kemp. Or rather, a scribbled note, attached to an article for publication. The note informed him that Mr Kemp was now political roundsman for the prestigious *Sydney Mail*. Cosmo was impressed. Quite a step up from the Brisbane paper.

He turned to the piece Tyler had submitted. It was entitled: *What really happened at Beauview*. Lighting his pipe, Cosmo read it through. Then he nodded. 'You're probably right, old son. I guessed as much myself.'

His pipe had gone out, so Cosmo, puffing heartily, lit it again, using the same match to set fire to Tyler's pages, watching idly as they disintegrated and came to rest in his flat marble ashtray. He sighed as he prepared for the business of the day. 'And they say "A woman scorned . . .",' he commented.

The men of Oberon welcomed them with relief. They were all pleased to have the boss home at last and happy to greet the three new stockmen, who were sorely needed.

'Is that cook, Baldy, still here?' Paul asked Gus.

'No, I got threatened with mutiny if I didn't get rid of him, so I got us a Chinaman, and he can cook up a storm.'

'Thank God for that. Juan is fussy about his food, one of them would have to go.' He noticed that his men, Gus included, were barely covering their amusement at the appearance of his stepfather. Juan had been in Australia since he was a young man but he'd refused to alter his mode of dress. He came from a family of Argentinian cattle barons and to them it was unthinkable that they dress like peasants. Paul had long ago learned to take Juan's outfits for granted, and now he grinned, comparing Juan's white shirt and elegant black waistcoat, tight black breeches and the inevitable sombrero with the Oberon uniform of check shirts, baggy dungarees and battered boots. 'Pass the word along,' he said to Gus. 'Don't underestimate this chap. He knows more about cattle then we'd learn in a lifetime, and he can make the best stockmen look like amateurs.'

They hadn't seen Paul since he was 'captured' by the blacks, so everyone was anxious to hear his story first-hand. That night they had a special celebratory dinner, roasting a side of beef on the spit while Mr Chow, as the cook insisted on being called, served the trimmings.

368

Juan sat quietly at the large table, listening to Paul's story, gratified to see that Dolour's son had established such excellent camaraderie with his men. He approved, as Jeannie had not, of Paul's decision to eat the evening meal in the company of his workers. It made them feel part of the progress of the station. The peasants in his own land had their families, but these men lived lonely, isolated lives. It wasn't wise to isolate them even more from a family environment. He could picture the scene when Jeannie and the girl had been there, women at the table with their softening influence. Their deaths had been a tragedy for all.

As they ate, the men fired questions at Paul, who tried to answer them, explaining the part of the half-caste, Wodoro. Juan had heard bits and pieces of this story as they'd ridden out here, but had made no comment. Hearing it in sequence now, he listened intently, and it wasn't until he lit a cigar to have with his coffee – which, by the way, he found disgusting, making a mental note to send some of his own blends to Oberon – that he asked casually, 'This fellow Wodoro. If he didn't belong to this tribe, where did he come from?'

'I don't know. He wouldn't say. He could be quite cranky at times, as if I was a real pain in the neck. After I nearly got speared dragging him out of that damned waterhole! Which was bloody freezing, up there in the mountains.'

'But they treated him with respect?'

'Oh yes. Apparently they didn't approve of one of their men whacking him over the skull.' Paul laughed. 'He told me he was important.'

'I bet he was one of their magic men,' Gus said.

'No, I reckon the old bloke I told you about, Harrabura, was, though. His eyes looked centuries old.'

'They wouldn't make a half-caste a magic man,' Juan commented. 'That wouldn't be possible. Your fellow was probably a courier, an intertribal courier.'

'What do they need couriers for?' one of the men asked.

'Why do we have ambassadors?' Juan said. 'They train men in the various languages and they travel from place to place to organise meetings and ceremonies. So in that sense he would be important, and in the normal course of events, under their laws, protected from attack even among warring tribes.'

'And to have one who spoke English as well, that would be handy.'

'Indeed,' Rivadavia said. 'Whoever chose him knew what he was doing.'

'If I'd just got to him sooner,' Paul said, 'those troopers would still be alive.'

Gus shook his head. 'No, Paul, if we'd known that those bastards Charlie Penny and his mates were guilty of . . .' He stopped. 'That they were right under our noses, it would have all gone differently.'

The men fell silent, reminded now of Jeannie and Clara. Paul poured himself another glass of the fine port Juan had brought with him, and the chill of the night settled over them.

'If you gentlemen will forgive me,' Juan said, 'it is better to remember the ladies in happier times. You should not avoid speaking of them. They earned your respect here, and I am most proud to see this, as they would be. Pioneer women face perils from man and nature but they pave the way for other women to follow.' He smiled. 'They'll follow, to make your lives easier. We should charge our glasses and drink to the ladies.'

They looked uneasily to Paul, needing his approval.

He hesitated, and then pushed back his chair to stand. 'I want to thank you all for your support, especially Gus. Now charge your glasses, beer or port, and we'll drink to happy memories of Jeannie and Clara.' He managed to get through the toast, trembling a little inside, and he was surprised at the response. It released the tension. Already they felt free to talk.

As he and Juan left the table and walked back inside, he heard one of the stockmen say, in wonder, 'I never thought of them as pioneers.'

'Yeah,' another man replied. 'And that Jeannie, could she shoot!'

'Got one of the bastards square between the eyes,' a proud voice added.

Later that night, before they retired, Paul spoke to Juan. 'I owe you and Mother an apology. I treated you badly when you married.'

'Yes, you did,' Juan said. 'But we knew you'd recover your manners in time. I will tell her you had the grace to apologise, that will make her very happy.'

'It's not only that,' Paul said. 'I don't want to be seen as a hypocrite. I'm planning to remarry too.'

Rivadavia clapped him on the shoulder. 'Ah, I was not wrong! You have the air of a man in love, I have been telling myself, but one would not wish to intrude on such a delicate matter. Is she of good family?'

'The best.' Paul grinned. He had been expecting a lecture on propriety, forgetting this man's temperament.

'And beautiful?' Juan asked.

'Very. Fair-haired, tall, lovely.'

'I am happy for you.'

For two days Juan rode with Paul, inspecting the station in the fine clear weather, and examining the stock. He offered advice on breeds and promised to assist Paul in stocking the adjoining property with the best cattle available. 'The country is drying out fast, though, as the heat rises.'

'Yes, it can be too wet or too dry up here.'

'Then balance your herds to what the land can afford. If you overstock, they'll starve. Are you well enough to go back to work?'

'Yes, I'm all right now. I wasn't going to die from a bullet in the back! By the way, I forgot to tell you, I didn't shoot Roberts, contrary to the tale abroad.'

'You didn't?'

'No, we haven't mentioned it, but his daughter shot him. He would have finished me off if she hadn't, but she's not keen on having people know she did the deed.'

'I should think not!' Juan replied. 'It would ruin her socially. Her background is bad enough.' He looked at Paul in alarm. 'She's not your lady, is she?'

'God, no! She's set to marry a politician.'

'Foolish man,' Juan sniffed. 'I hope she has a dowry worth the sacrifice.'

'She has that,' Paul laughed.

As they rode back to the homestead Juan looked about him. 'This is indeed a fine property, I am impressed. But I can entertain myself from now on, you attend to your work.'

'I will, if you don't mind. A lot of cows are still calving.'

'Ah!' Rivadavia said. 'The prairie mothers. You take good care of them.'

He was glad to be left to his own devices. As soon as the men rode off in the early dawn, he saddled his horse, strapping on a waterbag, armed himself with a rifle and cartridges and rode towards the hills on a private mission.

It took him until noon to reach a low plateau where he arranged small stones into the sign of a boomerang, easily recognised from the heights above. Then he stood back and shouted: 'Wodoro! Wodoro!'

His voice sounded and resounded through the hills, and he added the call he'd learned in this country. 'Coo-ee! Coo-ee!' It rang out like the clear travelling sound of a whip bird, distinctive, purposeful.

Then he waited. If Wodoro were still in the area, he would hear about this, the watchers would inform him. Juan had to know if the man Paul spoke of was his man, the half-caste blackfellow who had killed Pace and then, by dint of his prowess with the boomerang, had been given permission by the savage Warunga warriors to escort the other interloper out of their territory.

This fellow might not be the Wodoro he knew, Juan reasoned. Someone might have taken his name. But it was unlikely – the name would mean nothing to the blacks, it had no connection with the land. Ever since Paul had mentioned the name Juan had been itching to ask for a description, even for his age, but caution stilled his voice. He could not afford to have Pace's son ask if he knew or had met the man, because then he would have had to say where, and that meant lies. This Wodoro intrigued Paul so much that questions Juan would not answer would have rained on him. There were things in this life that had to remain buried.

For two days he returned to the same place, receiving no response, and for two nights he sat thoughtfully with the Oberon men, becoming better acquainted with them, referring to his absence from the homestead only as 'wanderings'.

'Is he safe out there?' Gus asked Paul.

'As safe as we are,' Paul said. 'Compared to his travels, this patch is surburban.'

On the third day, Juan noticed that his stone boomerang had been rearranged. It now faced the other way, and another set of stones had been placed in a spear, pointing back towards the homestead. The message was clear. He was being told to go home. He squatted down resolutely, his back to a cliff, and lit a cigar. It was warm here, very pleasant surveying Oberon. Back home, the Hunter Valley would be in the grip of winter. When it was safe he would bring Dolour up to visit. Or better still, when Paul married this lady, he should invite all her family to Chelmsford for celebration to put all Paul's troubles behind him.

From behind him, above him, a voice said: 'I knew you was here.'

Juan rose and looked up at Wodoro. Thinner, bonier, he thought sadly, but still Wodoro, the hook nose of his forebears at odds with the flatter nose of his mother's people. 'I'm sure you did,' he replied. 'It's good to see you again.'

Wodoro dropped down to stand apart from him on the slated rock, his polished black skin glimmering in the high sunlight, wearing a pearl in his ear as Paul had described. 'What do you want?'

'It's been a long time.' Juan smiled to coax him from his truculent, defensive position.

'Time passin'.' The black man shrugged.

'I have been hearing of you. A long story. A good story. Paul MacNamara from that big house speaks well of you.'

'And what did you tell him?'

'Nothing.'

'Yet you are his friend?'

Wodoro moved about as if circling a problem, while Juan found a ledge to rest on.

'Who is he?' the black man asked nervously.

'I think you know,' Juan said. 'He is the son of Pace.' He saw Wodoro suck in his breath and hurried to explain. 'In the white man's world of which you are a part, it is respectful to speak of the dead, so don't be worrying.'

Wodoro gave a sigh of relief, not so much for the name as for the news. He grinned. 'I thought he was a ghost. I tell you, he frighten shit out of me.'

'I can well imagine. He's the spitting image of his father. And what's more, he has a twin brother.'

'This twin. Two of the same?'

'Yes.'

Wodoro threw back his head and laughed. 'By gee, say these

372

blackfellers killed him and I ran into the brudder. I be plenty spooked, eh?'

'Anyone would,' Juan agreed.

More relaxed now, Wodoro squatted across from Juan. 'I remember you have the name of Wan and you spik funny English.'

'Your English is much improved.'

'What does the son Paul say of me?'

'That he saved your life.'

'Yeah, pretty funny that.'

'No, not funny. This is the good side of life.'

'If he knew I kill his father, maybe he drown me, eh?'

'I don't know, these things are not for me to say. But I have come to thank you for helping him. A translator is an important man. He sees you as that, he is sorry that he didn't meet you earlier and many lives could have been saved. Will you be staying here?'

'No.'

'Where will you go?'

'Somewheres.'

Juan tried to reach out to him. 'Wodoro, you are Tingum. I remember that. Your families are being scattered. The same will happen up here. I want you to bring your wife, who nursed me when I was sick with fever in the hot country where Pace died, and come to live at my place. It is a valley, greener than this in the winter. You will be free there. And safe.'

'My wife died of the white man's coughing,' he replied.

'I'm very sorry to hear that. All the more reason why you must come south from these wars.'

'I am free out here. Safe is a prison.'

'No,' Juan pleaded. 'You mustn't think like that. Listen to me. I traced your father. I always hoped I'd find you again so that I could tell you.'

'My father was a Tingum warrior. He fought with the great Bussamarai against the whites.'

'That is true,' Juan admitted. 'But his white-man name was Jack Wodrow.'

'He threw away his white life.'

'Only because he was an escaped convict.'

'They put him in lockups?'

'Yes.'

Wodoro sat back and grinned. 'Serve 'em bloody right. He gave 'em plenty payback. Bloody too right he did, that Jack.'

'That is so. But he still wanted you to know who you were. That's why he gave you the name of Wodoro so that white people, if they took the time, could work it out.'

'And you took the time?'

'Yes. Do you have any children?'

'Two sons.'

'Then I beg you. Bring them to my place. They will be safe. They will be educated.'

Wodoro's mood shifted again. He scowled at Juan. 'Even if he was Jack Wodrow, a white man, my father chose the good people. My sons will stay safe because I know how to make them safe. Safe is to know that this is their country.' He tapped his head. 'That how I keep them clean, proud men. You edjicate them to be servants. I seen this. And I seen the poison grog. I edjicate my sons to mind the Dreaming.'

'Wodoro,' Juan said patiently, 'the white men are moving across this land. You know that. I'm offering them a chance to survive. Big cities are growing. In many places there is no Dreaming.'

'Why do you keep on so?' Wodoro was irritated. 'You still doan understand. The Dreaming is like the wind that howl through these mountains. It is the waves that keep comen on shores since creation. Tap. Tap. Tap. For always. You cannot destroy the wind or the waves. Or the Dreaming. It is there.' He laughed. 'You say survive. The desert people say more better you look at your own selfs. We done a better job than you.'

Juan spoke softly. 'Do you hate us so?'

'Hating time gone. Living time more better. No looking backwards. An emu can't walk backwards. A kangaroo can't neither. These things I heard from the desert magic men. The Dreamtime minds the backwards . . .'

'The past?'

'That's it. The past. I tell you, Mr Wan,' he said confidentially, 'my people bin in bad times long before the white fellers. You think they haven't? Thousands and thousands and thousands of years they bin here. You mob just a lightning strike.' He stood and stamped the earth. 'This land take care of its own fellers. Plenty trouble now, but the Dreaming people never die.'

They sat together, looking out over the valley as the afternoon shadows stretched. Finally, Juan said: 'I have to go now.'

'Me too,' Wodoro replied. 'You pretty good feller.' He grinned. 'Wodoro, son of Jack. Good, eh? Giving half a white man, I can say that without fright. And say: "Paul, son of Pace." It is over that stuff. No more ghosts.'

With that he whistled and a blackfellow emerged from the scrub carrying a tall spear. 'This is Kamarga. He will not speak of our meeting. He has been waiting for your friend Paul to return so he can take his people back into their valley. You do me a favour, mate?'

Juan grinned at this compliment.

'You take Kamarga to the house for sit-down talks?'

'I am honoured,' Juan said. 'And I wish you well, Wodoro. But if you ever need help, you ask for me in Kamilaroi country.'

Wodoro nodded sagely. 'And if you needem me,' he replied with an arrogant toss of his head, 'you ask for me in any of these nations as far west as the great desert and north to the land end. Wodoro, son of Jack.'

He held a brief conversation with Kamarga in his language and then sent them on their way.

The sun sank from a dizzying yellow into a wash of pinks as a mob of cattle trundled past and drovers stopped to stare as the boss's stepfather, in his big black hat, rode towards the homestead accompanied by a bare-arsed blackfellow. This one was huge, well over six foot, with rippling muscles and thick wiry hair that met a full, matted beard. He wore the trappings of the ages, his body carefully spotted in red and yellow ochre. He loped comfortably beside the trotting horse.

'What the hell?' Paul came out to meet them.

'This is Kamarga,' Juan said.

'I know,' Paul replied, greeting his formal guide with pleasure. 'Where did you find him?'

'Out there,' Juan said vaguely.

Kamarga put down his spear, looked squarely at Paul and burst into a torrent of words. They were English words but they came in such a rush as to be unintelligible. 'Wodoro' was all Paul could rescue from the outburst, so he held up his hand. 'Slow,' he mouthed. 'Slow.'

The black man looked to Juan for help.

'He's too excited,' Juan explained. 'I gather you taught him some English, and your friend Wodoro taught him some more. He's been practising all the way. He's trying to say something like he seeks friendship for the people.'

'That's wonderful.' Paul nodded to Kamarga.

'I believe he has a gift for you,' Juan added. He nudged Kamarga, who stepped forward, holding out his clenched left hand.

'What is it?' Paul asked, staring, until Kamarga released his fingers one by one to reveal a plump pearl resting in his palm.

'For God's sake! It's Wodoro's pearl!'

Kamarga was all smiles as Paul took the gift. 'Wodoro say gibbit,' he managed to announce, and beamed at Paul's reply.

'Thank you, Kamarga, that Wodoro is a good feller.'

Juan smiled to himself at Wodoro's farewell gift. The ghosts were laid.

Afterword

The Fitzroy River was discovered and named by Scottish explorers, the Archer brothers, in 1853. They also named the Berserker Ranges, calling up a Norse god as a reminder of their previous sojourn in Scandinavia. They returned with their herds in 1855 to open Gracemere Station in the Fitzroy Valley. Delighted with their splendid new environment, they added orchards of tropical and other fruits to the property.

In 1858, a gold rush to nearby Canoona created a town on the Fitzroy River, at a site where rocks protrude into the wide stream, preventing further upriver traffic. Hence the name, 'Rock-hampton'.

By October that year, Rockhampton was proclaimed an official port of entry, and the first land sales took place in November. All land around Rockhampton was stocked, mainly with cattle, by the year 1860. However, the previous year Queensland was proclaimed a separate state from New South Wales and these new towns struggled to survive.

Fortune was to smile on Rockhampton, though. Further gold discoveries in the area assisted the economic growth of the town, and then came the big one. That old Ironstone Mountain turned out to be a treasure chest of gold, although it took until 1882 for the populace to realise what they had on their doorstep. Renamed Mount Morgan, it was the largest single gold mine in the world – the nearest known thing to an actual mountain of gold. By 1888, eight men held one million one-pound shares in a mine of incalculable wealth, and Rockhampton prospered.

It was proclaimed a city on 26 December 1902, the same day as was Brisbane. Grazing, mining and farming became the basic industries, and the valley has lost none of its charm. The whole of Quay Street has been listed by the National Trust as a historic streetscape, unique in Australia. However, Rockhampton is probably better known as Australia's beef capital.